Lin Putnam
1399 No. Chestnut

Great Russian Short Novels

GOGOL

TURGENEV

LESKOV

DOSTOEVSKY

CHEKHOV

TOLSTOY

BUNIN

OLYESHA

A PERMANENT LIBRARY BOOK

GREAT
RUSSIAN
SHORT NOVELS

EDITED WITH AN INTRODUCTION BY PHILIP RAHV

 New York  THE DIAL PRESS

The Publishers dedicate this volume
to the Memory of
Maurice Serle Kaplan
who designed it.

Contents

Contents

T H E long short story or short novel or novella is a narrative-form which Russian writers laid hold of with immense success from the very opening of the great period of Russian fiction in the second quarter of the nineteenth century. Gogol expanded some of his finest creative energies in this form, and so did Tolstoy and Dostoevsky. The best work of Nikolay Leskov (1831-95), a fiction writer of classic rank who even at this late date is virtually unknown to American readers, is to be found precisely in his tales rather than in his full-length novels. Chekhov wrote no novels of course, having discovered early in his career that the story, long and short, provided a sufficient framework for his fictional inspiration. As for Ivan Bunin, quite a few Russian critics have maintained that *Dry Valley* is his *chef-d'oeuvre*, the one major composition in which his imaginative powers are fully mobilized and brought to consummate realization. In this anthology, to be sure, I have been able to include only eight examples of the Russian novella, and it goes without saying that the riches of this form in the Russian language are scarcely exhausted by this particular selection. Within the limits of a single volume it is plainly impossible to prepare a selection of this kind which is complete in all respects. All that the editor may claim is that, despite certain inescapable restrictions, what he has made available has unity and value within the chosen context. There are no miscellaneous items in this collection. All the narratives in it, with the probable exception of the last one, are masterpieces of prose fiction; and all eight of them, while adequately representing the tenor and import of the total work of their respective authors, stand in a significant relationship to Russian literature considered as an integral expression of the national character and history.

This volume opens with Gogol's long story *The Overcoat*, of which it can be said with complete justice that it is the one indispensable item in the canon of Russian fiction. Even if Dostoevsky's famous remark that all important Russian prose writers emerged from under Gogol's "Overcoat" is not strictly accurate, as it ignores, mainly, Tolstoy's so very different derivations and affiliations, still it is to be taken as an historic tribute, to this day resonant with truth and meaning, paying off the indebtedness of an entire literature to the genius of one writer and, more particularly, the enormous debt owed by Dostoevsky himself. *Poor Folk*, his first novel, was written under the direct impetus of *The Overcoat*. Devushkin, the hero of that first novel, could scarcely have been conceived independently of Gogol's hero, Akaky Akakyevitch, the prototype of the petty insignificant clerk who so obsessively recurs in Russian literature—the clerk, leading a mole-like existence in a government bureau, whose infinitely pitiable need for self-respect, for the discovery of the dignity of the human image in his own beaten-down ego, drives him toward the performance of some ritualistic act of self-confirmation, an act which though at once ludicrous and tortuous is none the less liberating and life-affirming.

The theme of the petty little clerk is of course inseparable in Dostoevsky from his truly comprehensive theme, partly derived from Gogol, of "the insulted and injured," to which he gave such astonishingly varied elaboration throughout his creative career. Even in so late a work as *The Eternal Husband* (included in this volume) you find a direct echo of the celebrated passage in *The Overcoat* which tells of a young man who, having once joined in poking fun at Akaky Akakyevitch, could never again be the same person, for always he is haunted by the memory of the badgered meek little clerk in whose heart-piercing words, "Leave me alone! Why do you insult me?" he catches the ringing sound of other words, such as "I am your brother!" In *The Eternal Husband* Dostoevsky echoes that passage, and by no means for the first time in his writings, while describing Velchaninov's nervous depression: "Suddenly, for instance, apropos of nothing, he remembered the forgotten, utterly forgotten, figure of a harmless, grey-headed and absurd old clerk, whom he had once, long, long ago, and with absolute impunity, insulted in public simply to gratify his own conceit, simply for the sake of an amusing and successful jest. . . ."

What transpires in *The Overcoat* is a nearly miraculous fusion of realistic and symbolic elements, with the result that in stressing one side of it the story is converted into a civic protest, in the sense that Belinsky, the great radical critic, first read it on its appearance in 1842, thus establishing the interpretation of it traditional to Russian literary history. If the other side of the story is stressed, however, it may well be read, in the manner of the aesthetes of the symbolist period in Russian literature, as an unspeakably grotesque phantasy of human inconsequence and distortion, a phantasy having nothing to do with bureaucratic oppression, the suffering of the masses, or any social circumstances whatsoever.

Still another reading suggests itself from the psychoanalytic standpoint. If we recall Freud's polar dicta that in dreams "clothes and uniforms stand for nakedness" and also that "a cloak or a hat is used as a symbol of the male organ," then Akaky Akakyevitch's prodigious effort to acquire a new overcoat becomes the equivalent of an effort on his part to recover his masculinity; the loss of the overcoat to the robbers who waylay him on the street after a gay party becomes symbolic of his renewed impotence; and, finally, after he dies crushed by the calamity that has overtaken him, his masculinity is resurrected as he makes his spectral assault on a general being driven to visit his mistress, stripping him by main force of his richly elegant overcoat. Not a few details of the

text support this reading. For example, we are told that Akaky
Akakyevitch, laboring to pay the tailor for the longed-for garment,
often falls into meditations on "the eternal idea of the new overcoat," and it seems to him that "his existence had become fuller,
as though he had married," . . . and this feminine helpmate was
none other than this very same overcoat, with "its thick wadding,
and strong durable lining." No wonder, then, that at the end of
the story we are told that the clerk, so puny in life, having made
good his fearsome need by stripping a general of his overcoat,
makes his last spectral appearance sporting a pair of enormous
moustaches and shaking a fist "such as you never see among the
living." And my point in bringing to bear a Freudian analysis
upon Gogol's story is not to dispute the more established inter-
pretations of it but rather to bring home to the reader its multiple
meanings, which far from annulling actually enhance and reinforce
each other.

Turgenev's *First Love* stands somewhat apart from the main
body of his work in that it is untouched by civic issues or by the
ferment of the *Zeitgeist*. The truth is that Turgenev was not
really at his best when writing in the civic vein, so typical of the
Russian realists of his age; his novels, with the single exception of
Fathers and Sons, no longer impress us with their idea-content.
What survives, of course, is his splendidly poetical art which
reaches its culmination, perhaps, in a tale like *First Love*, where
we are made aware of the tensions of elemental desire and extreme
states of domination and submission through the lyrical response
of the adolescent narrator, with his feelings, of youthful sorrow
and perplexity, serving as the gauge of his thwarted love. Zinaida
and the narrator's father have a toughness of fiber and a primal
vitality that notably mark the difference between them and the
characteristic figures of Turgenev's fiction—the men stricken by
a peculiar dubiety and the women unrelievedly pure in their fine
strength. There is doubtless a good deal of the author's personal
history in *First Love*, though it is difficult to determine to what
extent the literary scholars are right in habitually associating the
narrator's father with Turgenev's family experience.

The educated Russian reader is nowadays apt to place the fictional art of Leskov above that of Turgenev. That may well be an injustice; but it corresponds to a certain modern taste for a type of writing which is not too patently "literary" and which secures its effects by the incisiveness and immediacy of its verbal texture. It is probable that this latter quality chiefly accounts for the fact that Leskov is so little known among us. His grainy idiomatic language, into which numerous varieties of slang are creatively assimilated, is not so readily translatable as the more normal language of the universally known masters of Russian fiction. Another reason is that Leskov is a storyteller unperturbed by ideas and moral notions, and he is therefore likely to strike the foreign reader as quite untypical of the Russian genius. His great gift, apart from the verbal impact, is for narration enlivened by the thoroughly active movement of strong even if primitive characters; and the energy of that movement is tempered by the author's bias toward humor, his inclination to make the comical prevail, whenever possible, over the barbarous and implacable. In Prince Mirsky's *History of Russian Literature* there is a brief passage summing up the literary personality of Leskov with lively insight: "There is no haze, no atmosphere, no mellowness in Leskov's vision of the world: he chooses the most crying colors, the boldest relief, and the sharpest outlines. If Turgenev's or Chekhov's world may be compared to a landscape by Corot, Leskov's is a picture by Breughel the Elder, full of gay and bright colors and grotesque forms. Great virtue, extraordinary originality, strong vices, powerful passions, and grotesque humors are his favorite matter. He is at once a hero-worshipper and a humorist. It can almost be said that the more heroic his heroes, the more humorously he treats them." *The Amazon* perfectly illustrates Leskov's humor, though the protagonist, Domna Platonovna, with her "fat little heart" and her intact and so flawlessly unworried hypocrisy, is no heroine in a positive sense but a personification of vice so wonderfully invulnerable as to acquire the reality of a *thing* solidly planted in the objective world.

Dostoevsky is also greatly accomplished as a humorous writer, though his virtues in that respect have been obscured by his dramatic and dialectical prowess. And if I have picked *The Eternal Husband* to represent him in this volume, as against the usual choice of *Notes from Underground* in collections of this sort, it is largely because I wished to put the emphasis on that side of his fiction in which the Comic Muse appears in the guise of a super-modern psychologist. For in this novelist the gift for uncovering psychological truth—surely of all truths the most discomforting since it is nothing less than our self-love which is nearly always its target—is at times identical with his gift for comic expression. Thus *The Eternal Husband*, written after the completion of *The Idiot* and just before the planning of *The Possessed*, is essentially built around the stock-situation of a French farce reworked with the finesse and profundity of a psychologist of genius. And it seems to me that structurally this novella is the most controlled and beautifully organized of Dostoevsky's shorter fictions. Its content is thoroughly enveloped and shaped by the form. It is as if for once, given a subject lifted entire from the popular literary tradition and writing in that beneficially relaxed state which he but seldom attained under the disquieting conditions of his life, Dostoevsky was able to concentrate on the formal aspects of the work at hand, calculating the relative weights and stresses of each scene and incident, integrating the parts into a complete whole, and so demonstrating that in the matter of artistic method and economy he too could make the creative end issue strictly from the creative means.

In psychological fiction there are few things so fine as the opening pages of this narrative, given over to the description of Velchaninov's nervous depression and the onset of memories and images that disorganize his habitual equilibrium, estranging him from the world which he had always been disposed to take for granted and in which he had played his part not without some telling successes. It is a masterful account of neurotic decline toward the critical stage. But at this point there appears on the scene the incomparable figure of Pavel Pavlovitch Trusotsky, the type of the eternal husband; and that is the *coup de force* which both arrests Velchaninov's descent into the depths of neurosis and provides the narrative with its dramatic complication. Trusotsky is, of course, entirely at home in the Dostoevskyean world, being the type of the resentful buffoon split through and through by the need to gratify his vanity and simultaneously to suffer the humiliations which his psyche craves. Though conceived on a higher intellectual plane, the hero of *Notes from Underground* is none the less another such buffoon; and so is Foma Fomitch in *The Friend of the Family*, Lebedev in *The Idiot*, Captain Lebyadkin in *The Possessed*, and to a large degree even Ilusha's father and the old man Karamazov himself in *The Brothers Karamazov*.

The novelistic imagination knows no greater contrast than that enforced by a comparison between Tolstoy's *Hadji Murad* and *The Eternal Husband*. The difference between the given materials and themes of the two tales is obvious; what is important is the difference between their fictional modes, which is so radical as seemingly to eliminate any conceivable area of resemblance. But not really all. Where Tolstoy and Dostoevsky are actually as one is in the transcendent generosity of their imaginative identification with human beings. That is a form of love and this love is the secret of the energy of both novelists. Hence their superb openness to emotion, an openness with which very few literary artists of their intellectual caliber have ever been endowed. It can be said of Tolstoy the man that he was a rationalist who was usually at odds with human beings; nor did he especially love them. As a novelist, however, he was not merely exceptionally aware of them but was capable of investing them with an heroic sympathy that broke through the barriers to their inner being. In the portrait of Hadji Murad we at once sense the author's love of this warrior chieftain who is fated, by his tribal code and indeed the whole weight of the past, to be crushed like a lone thistle-flower in a ploughed field. The twin images that recur through the story—that of the nightingales' song of love and death and that of the crimson thistle-plant tenaciously clinging to its bit of soil—serve both as a musical motif drawing together the narrative parts and as a symbol, marvelous in its aptness and simplicity, of the inviolable rhythm of nature and human destiny. Nature and human destiny!—that their rhythm is eternally one is the very essence of Tolstoy's vision of life. His religious conversion forced him to modify this central idea or intuition, and it is wholly appropriate that in *Hadji Murad*, a late work written many years after his renunciation of the objective art of his great novels, he should have reverted to the vision of his major creative period. To himself Tolstoy might have explained away the lapse by claiming that this work of his old age conformed to his notion of "good universal art," which he of course placed in a category below that of religious art; still it is worth noting that he refrained from publishing *Hadji Murad* and that it appeared in print only after his death.

Chekhov did not so much love human beings as he was tormented by his inability to love them with all the fervor that his nature demanded when he observed their feeble and sloppy conduct and the misery of the conditions under which they lived. That is the burden, the theme of *Ward No. 6*, which belongs, I think, with the very finest of Chekhov's work. He wrote too much and far too rapidly, but in this long story there is scarcely a superfluous word and not a gesture that one would want to dispense with. The plot of the story, the plot, that is, understood in the Aristotelian sense as the soul of the action, is entirely at one with the meaning of it; their integration is so complete that it has the finality of an historic act never to be undone. Doctor Raghin, who is going to seed while consoling himself with ideas of rationalization and philosophic equanimity, is a surpassing creation of human staleness; but at the same time his redemption is indicated when he befriends the madman Gromov, whom he declares to be "the one intelligent person in the whole town."

Ward No. 6 is of course part and parcel of the literature of protest against the Czarist autocracy. Yet if it were no more than that we would not read it today. The images of staleness it evokes are universally viable in that they disclose some of the permanent traits of human experience. The emotion of the tale, of grief and despair, is far from passive; on the contrary, it is the emotion requisite to the moment of truth and the recognition that life

contains within it the promise of change and release. The madness of Gromov is that of a man who, in spite of his weakness, has
suffered the vertiginous experience of absorbing this truth into
his very flesh and bones. Significantly, it is Gromov who is the
irreconcilable foe of quiescence and who, while denouncing "human baseness and oppression trampling up truth," proclaims his
faith in "a splendid life which will in time prevail upon the earth."
In his talk we catch the authentic voice of his author, who was
likewise irreconcilable and likewise firm in his feeling that it is
given to men to act upon their own lives and that to stand still is
to fall back and eventually to collapse into the mire.

This irreconcilability is not the least of Chekhov's qualities that
make good his claim to a place in the line of the masters of Russian
letters. It is exactly this meaningful aspect of the Russian classic
tradition that was impassionedly recalled by the symbolist poet
Alexander Blok in his essay *The Intelligentsia and the Revolution*
(1918) when he wrote that "the great Russian artists—Pushkin,
Gogol, Dostoevsky, Tolstoy—were submerged in darkness, but it
was never their will to stay hidden in it; for they believed in the
light. They knew the light. Each one of them, like the whole
nation which carried them under its heart, ground his teeth in the
darkness, seized by despair and fury. Yet they knew that sooner or
later life will be renewed because life is beautiful." It is the
tragedy of Russian history that it is precisely the Revolution, which
promised to dispel the darkness, that has again drained the light
from Russian life. In the Soviet Union lip-service is paid to the
great writers of the national past, but one may doubt that their
truth is now legible to a generation raised in the impenetrable
darkness of Communism triumphant.

Unlike Chekhov, Ivan Bunin is no protestant or frustrated lover
of humanity; and this can be said of him in spite of the relentless
realism of "social" novels like *The Village* and his other studies of
the stagnation of peasant life in provincial Russia. For all his deep
roots in the national tradition, Bunin unmistakably reminds us
of the type of professional man of letters who has so long dominated the literary art of western Europe. Bunin is typically that,

and no more than that, in his stories on foreign themes, but in *Dry Valley* he takes hold of an indigenous subject with rare mastery, modulating his poetically evocative use of language with an astonishing command of the resources of prose composition. Consider the skill with which the "point of view," in the technical sense of that term, is managed in *Dry Valley*, I mean the manner in which the voice of the "I" is made to mingle so naturally with that of the peasant nurse Nathalia to whom the role of principal narrator is assigned, the voice of the "I" at once subdued and penetrating, serving the other voice both to vary its tonality and to amplify the elemental consciousness behind it, and you will note that in this respect Bunin's performance exemplifies a triumph of technique more considerable than anything you are likely to find in Henry James. *Dry Valley* is the story of the decline of a family and with it the decline of an historic way of life—a thematic genre much employed in the literature of all countries; and Bunin's short novel is, I think, the finest example of the genre in Russian fiction. In it the regional interest acquires an imaginative appeal, a true enchantment of the sensibility, by which its specificity is raised to a higher potential and its small local world transformed into a precious emblem of the world at large.

With Yuri Olyesha's *Envy* we come to the Soviet period in Russian writing, a period which particularly since the late 1920's and the definitive control of the regime secured by Stalin, is marked throughout by falling standards and systematic intellectual dishonesty. Olyesha belonged to that group of writers, most of whom have long since retired into silence or, worse still, suffered exile or death, who resisted as long as they could, endeavoring to redeem the time by keeping alive the high traditions of Russian literature.

Envy, published in 1927, was much discussed in the Soviet Union for a number of years; I doubt that it is still permitted to circulate. It is a novel that looks back to Dostoevsky's *Notes from Underground* and forward to such records of disillusionment with the Revolution as Koestler's *Darkness at Noon*. But the reader should be warned not to expect to come upon any overt political assertions in its pages. It is composed in the Aesopian mode, the only mode open to authors working under a dictatorship; and it is full of ambiguities, not contrived but genuine ambiguities, since on the one hand Olyesha is writing a lament for a dying age and, on the other, he is trying with might and main to reconcile himself to the new realities of "socialism." The attempted reconciliation is unconvincing; there is a marked distemper in it and the rhetoric of low policy. Babichev, Commissar of the Food Trust and a specialist in sausages and mechanized cafeterias, will not attract the sympathy of sensitive people; willy-nilly that sympathy is drawn to his brother Ivan who, even if helpless and preposterous, has the temerity to dream of leading "the last parade of the sentiments" and of organizing a conspiracy of banished feelings. Kavalerov, the chief protagonist of the novel, a resentful and shiftless young man who loves fame, poetic imagery, and the uncollectivized human personality, is represented as eaten up by envy of the rising generation. In him the perishing Russian intelligentsia is embodied with real though shamefaced fidelity and with willed scorn.

Philip Rahv

September, 1951

GOGOL *The Overcoat*

GOGOL *The Overcoat*

IN THE department of . . . but I had better not mention in what department. There is nothing in the world more readily moved to wrath than a department, a regiment, a government office, and in fact any sort of official body. Nowadays every private individual considers all society insulted in his person. I have been told that very lately a petition was handed in from a police-captain of what town I don't recollect, and that in this petition he set forth clearly that the institutions of the State were in danger and that its sacred name was being taken in vain; and, in proof thereof, he appended to his petition an enormously long volume of some work of romance in which a police-captain appeared on every tenth page, occasionally, indeed, in an intoxicated condition. And so, to avoid any unpleasantness, we had better call the department of which we are speaking a certain department.

And so, in a certain department there was a government clerk; a clerk of whom it cannot be said that he was very remarkable; he was short, somewhat pock-marked, with rather reddish hair and rather dim, bleary eyes, with a small bald patch on the top of his head, with wrinkles on both sides of his cheeks and the sort of complexion which is usually associated with hæmorrhoids . . . no help for that, it is the Petersburg climate. As for his grade in the service (for among us the grade is what must be put first), he was what is called a perpetual titular councillor, a class at which, as

3

we all know, various writers who indulge in the praiseworthy habit of attacking those who cannot defend themselves jeer and jibe to their hearts' content. This clerk's surname was Bashmatchkin. From the very name it is clear that it must have been derived from a shoe (*bashmak*); but when and under what circumstances it was derived from a shoe, it is impossible to say. Both his father and his grandfather and even his brother-in-law, and all the Bashmatchkins without exception wore boots, which they simply re-soled two or three times a year. His name was Akaky Akakyevitch. Perhaps it may strike the reader as a rather strange and far-fetched name, but I can assure him that it was not far-fetched at all, that the circumstances were such that it was quite out of the question to give him any other name. Akaky Akakyevitch was born towards nightfall, if my memory does not deceive me, on the twenty-third of March. His mother, the wife of a government clerk, a very good woman, made arrangements in due course to christen the child. She was still lying in bed, facing the door, while on her right hand stood the godfather, an excellent man called Ivan Ivanovitch Yeroshkin, one of the head clerks in the Senate, and the godmother, the wife of a police official, and a woman of rare qualities, Arina Semyonovna Byelobryushkov. Three names were offered to the happy mother for selection— Moky, Sossy, or the name of the martyr Hozdazat. "No," thought the poor lady, "they are all such names!" To satisfy her, they opened the calendar at another place, and the names which turned up were: Trifily, Dula, Varahasy. "What an infliction!" said the mother. "What names they all are! I really never heard such names. Varadat or Varuh would be bad enough, but Trifily and Varahasy!" They turned over another page and the names were: Pavsikahy and Vahtisy. "Well, I see," said the mother, "it is clear that it is his fate. Since that is how it is, he had better be called after his father, his father is Akaky, let the son be Akaky, too." This was how he came to be Akaky Akakyevitch. The baby was christened and cried and made wry faces during the ceremony, as though he foresaw that he would be a titular councillor. So that was how it all came to pass. We have recalled it here so that

the reader may see for himself that it happened quite inevitably
and that to give him any other name was out of the question. No
one has been able to remember when and how long ago he entered the department, nor who gave him the job. However many
directors and higher officials of all sorts came and went, he was
always seen in the same place, in the same position, at the very
same duty, precisely the same copying clerk, so that they used to
declare that he must have been born a copying clerk in uniform
all complete and with a bald patch on his head. No respect at all
was shown him in the department. The porters, far from getting
up from their seats when he came in, took no more notice of him
than if a simple fly had flown across the vestibule. His superiors
treated him with a sort of domineering chilliness. The head clerk's
assistant used to throw papers under his nose without even saying:
"Copy this" or "Here is an interesting, nice little case" or some
agreeable remark of the sort, as is usually done in well-behaved
offices. And he would take it, gazing only at the paper without
looking to see who had put it there and whether he had the right
to do so; he would take it and at once set to work to copy it. The
young clerks jeered and made jokes at him to the best of their
clerkly wit, and told before his face all sorts of stories of their
own invention about him; they would say of his landlady, an old
woman of seventy, that she beat him, would enquire when the
wedding was to take place, and would scatter bits of paper on his
head, calling them snow. Akaky Akakyevitch never answered a
word, however, but behaved as though there were no one there. It
had no influence on his work even; in the midst of all this teasing,
he never made a single mistake in his copying. Only when the
jokes were too unbearable, when they jolted his arm and prevented him from going on with his work, he would bring out:
"Leave me alone! Why do you insult me?" and there was something strange in the words and in the voice in which they were
uttered. There was a note in it of something that aroused compassion, so that one young man, new to the office, who, following
the example of the rest, had allowed himself to mock at him,
suddenly stopped as though cut to the heart, and from that time

forth, everything was, as it were, changed and appeared in a different light to him. Some unnatural force seemed to thrust him away from the companions with whom he had become acquainted, accepting them as well-bred, polished people. And long afterwards, at moments of the greatest gaiety, the figure of the humble little clerk with a bald patch on his head rose before him with his heart-rending words: "Leave me alone! Why do you insult me?" and in those heart-rending words he heard others: "I am your brother." And the poor young man hid his face in his hands, and many times afterwards in his life he shuddered, seeing how much inhumanity there is in man, how much savage brutality lies hidden under refined, cultured politeness, and, my God! even in a man whom the world accepts as a gentleman and a man of honor. . . .

It would be hard to find a man who lived in his work as did Akaky Akakyevitch. To say that he was zealous in his work is not enough; no, he loved his work. In it, in that copying, he found a varied and agreeable world of his own. There was a look of enjoyment on his face; certain letters were favorites with him, and when he came to them he was delighted; he chuckled to himself and winked and moved his lips, so that it seemed as though every letter his pen was forming could be read in his face. If rewards had been given according to the measure of zeal in the service, he might to his amazement have even found himself a civil councillor; but all he gained in the service, as the wits, his fellow-clerks expressed it, was a buckle in his button-hole and a pain in his back. It cannot be said, however, that no notice had ever been taken of him. One director, being a good-natured man and anxious to reward him for his long service, sent him something a little more important than his ordinary copying; he was instructed from a finished document to make some sort of report for another office; the work consisted only of altering the headings and in places changing the first person into the third. This cost him such an effort that it threw him into a regular perspiration: he mopped his brow and said at last, "No, better let me copy something."

From that time forth they left him to go on copying for ever. It seemed as though nothing in the world existed for him outside his copying. He gave no thought at all to his clothes; his uniform was—well, not green but some sort of rusty, muddy color. His collar was very short and narrow, so that, although his neck was not particularly long, yet, standing out of the collar, it looked as immensely long as those of the plaster kittens that wag their heads and are carried about on trays on the heads of dozens of foreigners living in Russia. And there were always things sticking to his uniform, either bits of hay or threads; moreover, he had a special art of passing under a window at the very moment when various rubbish was being flung out into the street, and so was continually carrying off bits of melon rind and similar litter on his hat. He had never once in his life noticed what was being done and going on in the street, all those things at which, as we all know, his colleagues, the young clerks, always stare, carrying their sharp sight so far even as to notice anyone on the other side of the pavement with a trouser strap hanging loose—a detail which always calls forth a sly grin. Whatever Akaky Akakyevitch looked at, he saw nothing anywhere but his clear, evenly written lines, and only perhaps when a horse's head suddenly appeared from nowhere just on his shoulder, and its nostrils blew a perfect gale upon his cheek, did he notice that he was not in the middle of his writing, but rather in the middle of the street.

On reaching home, he would sit down at once to the table, hurriedly sup his soup and eat a piece of beef with an onion; he did not notice the taste at all, but ate it all up together with the flies and anything else that Providence chanced to send him. When he felt that his stomach was beginning to be full, he would rise up from the table, get out a bottle of ink and set to copying the papers he had brought home with him. When he had none to do, he would make a copy expressly for his own pleasure, particularly if the document were remarkable not for the beauty of its style but for the fact of its being addressed to some new or important personage.

Even at those hours when the grey Petersburg sky is completely overcast and the whole population of clerks have dined and eaten their fill, each as best he can, according to the salary he receives and his personal tastes; when they are all resting after the scratching of pens and bustle of the office, their own necessary work and other people's, and all the tasks that an over-zealous man voluntarily sets himself even beyond what is necessary; when the clerks are hastening to devote what is left of their time to pleasure; some more enterprising are flying to the theatre, others to the street to spend their leisure, staring at women's hats, some to spend the evening paying compliments to some attractive girl, the star of a little official circle, while some—and this is the most frequent of all—go simply to a fellow-clerk's flat on the third or fourth storey, two little rooms with an entry or a kitchen, with some pretentions to style, with a lamp or some such article that has cost many sacrifices of dinners and excursions—at the time when all the clerks are scattered about the little flats of their friends, playing a tempestuous game of whist, sipping tea out of glasses to the accompaniment of farthing rusks, sucking in smoke from long pipes, telling, as the cards are dealt, some scandal that has floated down from higher circles, a pleasure which the Russian can never by any possibility deny himself, or, when there is nothing better to talk about, repeating the everlasting anecdote of the commanding officer who was told that the tail had been cut off his horse on the Falconet monument—in short, even when every one was eagerly seeking entertainment, Akaky Akakyevitch did not give himself up to any amusement. No one could say that they had ever seen him at an evening party. After working to his heart's content, he would go to bed, smiling at the thought of the next day and wondering what God would send him to copy. So flowed on the peaceful life of a man who knew how to be content with his fate on a salary of four hundred roubles, and so perhaps it would have flowed on to extreme old age, had it not been for the various calamities that bestrew the path through life, not only of titular, but even of privy, actual court and all other councillors, even those who neither give counsel to others nor accept it themselves.

There is in Petersburg a mighty foe of all who receive a salary of four hundred roubles or about that sum. That foe is none other than our northern frost, although it is said to be very good for the health. Between eight and nine in the morning, precisely at the hour when the streets are full of clerks going to their departments, the frost begins giving such sharp and stinging flips at all their noses indiscriminately that the poor fellows don't know what to do with them. At that time, when even those in the higher grade have a pain in their brows and tears in their eyes from the frost, the poor titular councillors are sometimes almost defenceless. Their only protection lies in running as fast as they can through five or six streets in a wretched, thin little overcoat and then warming their feet thoroughly in the porter's room, till all their faculties and qualifications for their various duties thaw again after being frozen on the way. Akaky Akakyevitch had for some time been feeling that his back and shoulders were particularly nipped by the cold, although he did try to run the regular distance as fast as he could. He wondered at last whether there were any defects in his overcoat. After examining it thoroughly in the privacy of his home, he discovered that in two or three places, to wit on the back and the shoulders, it had become a regular sieve; the cloth was so worn that you could see through it and the lining was coming out. I must observe that Akaky Akakyevitch's overcoat had also served as a butt for the jibes of the clerks. It had even been deprived of the honorable name of overcoat and had been referred to as the "dressing jacket." It was indeed of rather a strange make. Its collar had been growing smaller year by year as it served to patch the other parts. The patches were not good specimens of the tailor's art, and they certainly looked clumsy and ugly. On seeing what was wrong, Akaky Akakyevitch decided that he would have to take the overcoat to Petrovitch, a tailor who lived on a fourth storey up a back staircase, and, in spite of having only one eye and being pock-marked all over his face, was rather successful in repairing the trousers and coats of clerks and others—that is, when he was sober, be it understood, and had no other enterprise in his mind. Of this tailor I ought not, of course, to say much, but since it is now the rule that the character of every person in a novel must be completely drawn, well, there is no help for it, here is Petrovitch too. At first he was called simply Grigory, and was a serf belonging to some gentleman or other. He began to be called Petrovitch from the time that he got his freedom and began to drink rather heavily on every holiday, at first only on the chief holidays, but afterwards on all church holidays indiscriminately, wherever there is a cross in the calendar. On that side he was true to the customs of his forefathers, and when he quarrelled with his wife used to call her "a worldly woman and a German." Since we have now mentioned the wife, it will be necessary to say a few words about her too, but unfortunately not much is known about her, except indeed that Petrovitch had a wife and that she wore a cap and not a kerchief, but apparently she could not boast of beauty; anyway, none but soldiers of the Guards peeped under her cap when they met her, and they twitched their moustaches and gave vent to a rather peculiar sound.

As he climbed the stairs, leading to Petrovitch's—which, to do them justice, were all soaked with water and slops and saturated through and through with that smell of spirits which makes the eyes smart, and is, as we all know, inseparable from the back-stairs of Petersburg houses—Akaky Akakyevitch was already wondering how much Petrovitch would ask for the job, and inwardly resolving not to give more than two roubles. The door was open, for Petrovitch's wife was frying some fish and had so filled the kitchen with smoke that you could not even see the black-beetles. Akaky Akakyevitch crossed the kitchen unnoticed by the good woman, and walked at last into a room where he saw Petrovitch sitting on a big, wooden, unpainted table with his legs tucked under him like a Turkish Pasha. The feet, as is usual with tailors when they sit at work, were bare; and the first object that caught Akaky Akakyevitch's eye was the big toe, with which he was already familiar, with a misshapen nail as thick and strong as the shell of a tortoise. Round Petrovitch's neck hung a skein of silk and another of thread and on his knees was a rag of some sort. He had for the last three minutes been trying to thread his needle, but could not get the thread into the eye and so was very angry with the darkness and indeed with the thread itself, muttering in an undertone: "It won't go in, the savage! You wear me out, you rascal." Akaky Akakyevitch was vexed that he had come just at the minute when Petrovitch was in a bad humor; he liked to give him an order when he was a little "elevated," or, as his wife expressed it, "had fortified himself with fizz, the one-eyed devil." In such circumstances Petrovitch was as a rule very ready to give way and agree, and invariably bowed and thanked him, indeed. Afterwards, it is true, his wife would come wailing that her husband had been drunk and so had asked too little, but adding a single ten-kopeck piece would settle that. But on this occasion Petrovitch was apparently sober and consequently curt, unwilling to bargain, and the devil knows what price he would be ready to lay on. Akaky Akakyevitch perceived this, and was, as the saying is, beating a retreat, but things had gone too far, for Petrovitch was screwing up his solitary eye very attentively at him and Akaky Akakyevitch involuntarily brought out: "Good day, Petrovitch!" "I wish you a good day, sir," said Petrovitch, and squinted at Akaky Akakyevitch's hands, trying to discover what sort of goods he had brought.

"Here I have come to you, Petrovitch, do you see . . . !"

It must be noticed that Akaky Akakyevitch for the most part explained himself by apologies, vague phrases, and particles which have absolutely no significance whatever. If the subject were a very difficult one, it was his habit indeed to leave his sentences quite unfinished, so that very often after a sentence had begun with the words, "It really is, don't you know . . ." nothing at all would follow and he himself would be quite oblivious, supposing he had said all that was necessary.

"What is it?" said Petrovitch, and at the same time with his solitary eye he scrutinized his whole uniform from the collar to the sleeves, the back, the skirts, the button-holes—with all of which he was very familiar, they were all his own work. Such scrutiny is habitual with tailors, it is the first thing they do on meeting one.

"It's like this, Petrovitch . . . the overcoat, the cloth . . . you see everywhere else it is quite strong; it's a little dusty and looks as though it were old, but it is new and it is only in one place just a little . . . on the back, and just a little worn on one shoulder and on this shoulder, too, a little . . . do you see? that's all, and it's not much work. . . ."

Petrovitch took the "dressing jacket," first spread it out over the table, examined it for a long time, shook his head and put his hand out to the window for a round snuff-box with a portrait on the lid of some general—which precisely I can't say, for a finger had been thrust through the spot where a face should have been, and the hole had been pasted up with a square bit of paper. After taking a pinch of snuff, Petrovitch held the "dressing jacket" up in his hands and looked at it against the light, and again he shook his head; then he turned it with the lining upwards and once more shook his head; again he took off the lid with the general pasted up with paper and stuffed a pinch into his nose, shut the box, put it away and at last said: "No, it can't be repaired; a wretched garment!" Akaky Akakyevitch's heart sank at those words.

"Why can't it, Petrovitch?" he said, almost in the imploring voice of a child. "Why, the only thing is it is a bit worn on the shoulders; why, you have got some little pieces. . . ."

"Yes, the pieces will be found all right," said Petrovitch, "but it can't be patched, the stuff is quite rotten; if you put a needle in it, it would give way."

"Let it give way, but you just put a patch on it."

"There is nothing to put a patch on. There is nothing for it to hold on to; there is a great strain on it, it is not worth calling cloth, it would fly away at a breath of wind."

"Well, then, strengthen it with something—upon my word, really, this is . . . !"

"No," said Petrovitch resolutely, "there is nothing to be done, the thing is no good at all. You had far better, when the cold winter weather comes, make yourself leg wrappings out of it, for there is no warmth in stockings, the Germans invented them just to make money." (Petrovitch was fond of a dig at the Germans occasionally.) "And as for the overcoat, it is clear that you will have to have a new one."

At the word "new" there was a mist before Akaky Akakyevitch's eyes, and everything in the room seemed blurred. He could see nothing clearly but the general with the piece of paper over his face on the lid of Petrovitch's snuff-box.

"A new one?" he said, still feeling as though he were in a dream; "why, I haven't the money for it."

"Yes, a new one," Petrovitch repeated with barbarous composure.

"Well, and if I did have a new one, how much would it . . . ?"

"You mean what will it cost?"

"Yes."

"Well, three fifty-rouble notes or more," said Petrovitch, and he compressed his lips significantly. He was very fond of making an effect, he was fond of suddenly disconcerting a man completely and then squinting sideways to see what sort of a face he made.

"A hundred and fifty roubles for an overcoat," screamed poor Akaky Akakyevitch—it was perhaps the first time he had screamed in his life, for he was always distinguished by the softness of his voice.

"Yes," said Petrovitch, "and even then it's according to the coat. If I were to put marten on the collar, and add a hood with silk linings, it would come to two hundred."

"Petrovitch, please," said Akaky Akakyevitch in an imploring voice, not hearing and not trying to hear what Petrovitch said, and missing all his effects, "do repair it somehow, so that it will serve a little longer."

"No, that would be wasting work and spending money for nothing," said Petrovitch, and after that Akaky Akakyevitch went away completely crushed, and when he had gone Petrovitch remained standing for a long time with his lips pursed up significantly before he took up his work again, feeling pleased that he had not demeaned himself nor lowered the dignity of the tailor's art.

When he got into the street, Akaky Akakyevitch was as though in a dream. "So that is how it is," he said to himself. "I really did not think it would be so . . ." and then after a pause he added, "So there it is! so that's how it is at last! and I really could never have supposed it would have been so. And there . . ." There followed another long silence, after which he brought out: "So there it is! well, it really is so utterly unexpected . . . who would have thought . . . what a circumstance. . . ." Saying this, instead of going home he walked off in quite the opposite direction without suspecting what he was doing. On the way a clumsy sweep brushed the whole of his sooty side against him and blackened all his shoulder; a regular hatful of plaster scattered upon him from the top of a house that was being built. He noticed nothing of this, and only after he had jostled against a sentry who had set his halberd down beside him and was shaking some snuff out of his horn into his rough fist, he came to himself a little and then only because the sentry said: "Why are you poking yourself right in one's face, haven't you the pavement to yourself?" This made him look round and turn homeward; only there he began to collect his thoughts, to see his position in a clear and true light and began talking to himself no longer incoherently but reasonably and openly as with a sensible friend with whom one can discuss the most intimate and vital matters. "No, indeed," said Akaky Akakyevitch, "it is no use talking to Petrovitch now; just now he really is . . . his wife must have been giving it to him. I had better go to him on Sunday morning; after the Saturday evening he will be squinting and sleepy, so he'll want a little drink to carry it off and his wife won't give him a penny. I'll slip ten kopecks into his hand and then he will be more accommodating and maybe take the overcoat. . . ."

So reasoning with himself, Akaky Akakyevitch cheered up and waited until the next Sunday; then, seeing from a distance Petrovitch's wife leaving the house, he went straight in. Petrovitch certainly was very tipsy after the Saturday. He could hardly hold his head up and was very drowsy: but, for all that, as soon as he heard what he was speaking about, it seemed as though the devil had nudged him. "I can't," he said, "you must kindly order a new one." Akaky Akakyevitch at once slipped a ten-kopeck piece into his hand. "I thank you, sir, I will have just a drop to your health, but don't trouble yourself about the overcoat; it is not a bit of good for anything. I'll make you a fine new coat, you can trust me for that."

Akaky Akakyevitch would have said more about repairs, but Petrovitch, without listening, said: "A new one now I'll make you without fail; you can rely upon that, I'll do my best. It could even be like the fashion that has come in with the collar to button with silver claws under appliqué."

Then Akaky Akakyevitch saw that there was no escape from a new overcoat and he was utterly depressed. How indeed, for what, with what money could he get it? Of course he could to some extent rely on the bonus for the coming holiday, but that money had long ago been appropriated and its use determined beforehand. It was needed for new trousers and to pay the cobbler an old debt for putting some new tops to some old boot-legs, and he had to order three shirts from a seamstress as well as two specimens of an under-garment which it is improper to mention in print; in short, all that money absolutely must be spent, and even if the director were to be so gracious as to assign him a gratuity of forty-five or even fifty, instead of forty roubles, there would be still left a mere trifle, which would be but as a drop in the ocean beside the fortune needed for an overcoat. Though, of course, he knew that Petrovitch had a strange craze for suddenly putting on the devil knows what enormous price, so that at times his own wife could not help crying out: "Why, you are out of your wits, you idiot! Another time he'll undertake a job for nothing, and here the devil has bewitched him to ask more than he is worth himself." Though, of course, he knew that Petrovitch would undertake to make it for eighty roubles, still where would he get those eighty roubles? He might manage half of that sum; half of it could be found, perhaps even a little more; but where could he get the other half? . . . But, first of all, the reader ought to know where that first half was to be found. Akaky Akakyevitch had the habit every time he spent a rouble of putting aside two kopecks in a little locked-up box with a slit in the lid for slipping the money in. At the end of every half-year he would inspect the pile of coppers there and change them for small silver. He had done this for a long time, and in the course of many years the sum had mounted up to forty roubles and so he had half the money in his hands, but where was he to get the other half, where was he to get another forty roubles? Akaky Akakyevitch pondered and pondered and decided at last that he would have to diminish his ordinary expenses, at least for a year; give up burning candles in the evening, and if he had to do anything he must go into the landlady's room and work by her candle; that as he walked along the streets he must walk as lightly and carefully as possible, almost on tiptoe, on the cobbles and flagstones, so that his soles might last a little longer than usual; that he must send his linen to the wash less frequently, and that, to preserve it from being worn, he must take it off every day when he came home and sit in a thin cotton-shoddy dressing-gown, a very ancient garment which Time itself had spared. To tell the truth, he found it at first rather hard to get used to these privations, but after a while it became a habit and went smoothly enough—he even became quite accustomed to being hungry in the evening; on the other hand, he had spiritual nourishment, for he carried ever in his thoughts the idea of his future overcoat. His whole existence had in a sense become fuller, as though he had married, as though some other person were present with him, as though he were no longer alone, but an agreeable companion had consented to walk the path of life hand in hand with him, and that companion was no other than the new overcoat with its thick wadding and its strong, durable lining. He became, as it were, more alive, even more strong-willed, like a man who has set before himself a definite aim. Uncertainty, indecision, in fact all the hesitating and vague characteristics vanished from his face and his manners. At times there was a gleam in his eyes, indeed, the most bold and audacious ideas flashed through his mind. Why not really have marten on the collar? Meditation on the subject always made him absent-minded. On one occasion when he was copying a document, he very nearly made a mistake, so that he almost cried out "ough" aloud and crossed himself. At least once every month he went to Petrovitch to talk about the overcoat, where it would be best to buy the cloth, and what color it should be, and what price, and, though he returned home a little anxious, he was always pleased at the thought that at last the time was at hand when everything would be bought and the overcoat would be made. Things moved even faster than he had anticipated. Contrary to all expectations, the director bestowed on Akaky Akakyevitch a gratuity of no less than sixty roubles. Whether it was that he had an inkling that Akaky Akakyevitch needed a greatcoat, or whether it happened so by chance, owing to this he found he had twenty roubles extra. This circumstance hastened the course of affairs. Another two or three months of partial fasting and Akaky Akakyevitch had actually saved up nearly eighty roubles. His heart, as a rule very tranquil, began to throb. The very first day he set off in company with Petrovitch to the shops. They bought some very good cloth, and no wonder, since they had been thinking of it for more than six months before, and scarcely a month had passed without their going to the shop to compare prices; now Petrovitch himself declared that there was no better cloth to be had. For the lining they chose calico, but of a stout quality, which in Petrovitch's words was even better than silk, and actually as strong and handsome to look at. Marten they did not buy, because it certainly was dear, but instead they chose cat fur, the best to be found in the shop—cat which in the distance might almost be taken for marten. Petrovitch was busy over the coat for a whole fortnight, because there were a great many buttonholes, otherwise it would have been ready sooner. Petrovitch asked twelve roubles for the work; less than that it hardly could have been, everything was sewn with silk, with fine double seams, and Petrovitch went over every seam afterwards with his own teeth imprinting various figures with them. It was . . . it is hard to say precisely on what day, but probably on the most triumphant day of the life of Akaky Akakyevitch that Petrovich at last brought the overcoat. He brought it in the morning, just before it was time to set off for the department. The overcoat could not have arrived more in the nick of time, for rather sharp frosts were just beginning and seemed threatening to be even more severe. Petrovitch brought the greatcoat himself as a good tailor should. There was an expression of importance on his face, such as Akaky Akakyevitch had never seen there before. He seemed fully conscious of having completed a work of no little moment and of having shown in his own person the gulf that separates tailors who only put in linings and do repairs from those who make up new materials. He took the greatcoat out of the pocket-handkerchief in which he had brought it (the pocket-handkerchief had just come home from the wash), he then folded it up and put it in his pocket for future use. After taking out the overcoat, he looked at it with much pride and, holding it in both hands, threw in very deftly over Akaky Akakyevitch's shoulders, then pulled it down and smoothed it out behind with his hands; then draped it about Akaky Akakyevitch with somewhat jaunty care-lessness. The latter, as a man advanced in years, wished to try it with his arms in the sleeves. Petrovitch helped him to put it on, and it appeared that it looked splendid too with his arms in the sleeves. In fact it turned out that the overcoat was completely and entirely successful. Petrovitch did not let slip the occasion for observing that it was only because he lived in a small street and had no signboard, and because he had known Akaky Akakyevitch so long, that he had done it so cheaply, but on the Nevsky Prospect they would have asked him seventy-five roubles for the work alone. Akaky Akakyevitch had no inclination to discuss this with Petrovitch, besides he was frightened of the big sums that Petrovitch was fond of flinging airily about in conversation. He paid him, thanked him, and went off on the spot, with his new overcoat on, to the department. Petrovitch followed him out and stopped in the street, staring for a good time at the coat from a distance and then purposely turned off and, taking a short cut by a side street, came back into the street and got another view of the coat from the other side, that is, from the front.

Meanwhile Akaky Akakyevitch walked along with every emotion

in its most holiday mood. He felt every second that he had a new
overcoat on his shoulders, and several times he actually laughed
from inward satisfaction. Indeed, it had two advantages, one
that it was warm and the other that it was good. He did not notice
the way at all and found himself all at once at the department;
in the porter's room he took off the overcoat, looked it over and
put it in the porter's special care. I cannot tell how it happened,
but all at once every one in the department learned that Akaky
Akakyevitch had a new overcoat and that the "dressing jacket" no
longer existed. They all ran out at once into the porter's room to
look at Akaky Akakyevitch's new overcoat, they began welcoming
him and congratulating him so that at first he could do nothing
but smile and afterwards felt positively abashed. When, coming
up to him, they all began saying that he must "sprinkle" the new
overcoat and that he ought at least to stand them all a supper,
Akaky Akakyevitch lost his head completely and did not know
what to do, how to get out of it, nor what to answer. A few
minutes later, flushing crimson, he even began assuring them with
great simplicity that it was not a new overcoat at all, that it was
just nothing, that it was an old overcoat. At last one of the clerks,
indeed the assistant of the head clerk of the room, probably in
order to show that he was not proud and was able to get on with
those beneath him, said: "So be it, I'll give a party instead of
Akaky Akakyevitch and invite you all to tea with me this evening;
as luck would have it, it is my nameday." The clerks naturally
congratulated the assistant head clerk and eagerly accepted the
invitation. Akaky Akakyevitch was beginning to make excuses, but
they all declared that it was uncivil of him, that it was simply
a shame and a disgrace and that he could not possibly refuse.
However, he felt pleased about it afterwards when he remembered
that through this he would have the opportunity of going out in
the evening, too, in his new overcoat. That whole day was for
Akaky Akakyevitch the most triumphant and festive day in his
life. He returned home in the happiest frame of mind, took off
the overcoat and hung it carefully on the wall, admiring the cloth
and lining once more, and then pulled out his old "dressing

jacket," now completely coming to pieces, on purpose to compare them. He glanced at it and positively laughed, the difference was so immense! And long afterwards he went on laughing at dinner, as the position in which the "dressing jacket" was placed recurred to his mind. He dined in excellent spirits and after dinner wrote nothing, no papers at all, but just took his ease for a little while on his bed, till it got dark, then, without putting things off, he dressed, put on his overcoat, and went out into the street. Where precisely the clerk who had invited him lived we regret to say that we cannot tell; our memory is beginning to fail sadly, and everything there is in Petersburg, all the streets and houses, are so blurred and muddled in our head that it is a very difficult business to put anything in orderly fashion. However that may have been, there is no doubt that the clerk lived in the better part of the town and consequently a very long distance from Akaky Akakyevitch. At first the latter had to walk through deserted streets, scantily lighted, but as he approached his destination the streets became more lively, more full of people, and more brightly lighted; passers-by began to be more frequent, ladies began to appear, here and there, beautifully dressed, beaver collars were to be seen on the men. Cabmen with wooden trellis-work sledges, studded with gilt nails, were less frequently to be met; on the other hand, jaunty drivers in raspberry colored velvet caps with varnished sledges and bearskin rugs appeared, and carriages with decorated boxes dashed along the streets, their wheels crunching through the snow.

Akaky Akakyevitch looked at all this as a novelty; for several years he had not gone out into the streets in the evening. He stopped with curiosity before a lighted shop-window to look at a picture in which a beautiful woman was represented in the act of taking off her shoe and displaying as she did so the whole of a very shapely leg, while behind her back a gentleman with whiskers and a handsome imperial on his chin was putting his head in at the door. Akaky Akakyevitch shook his head and smiled and then went on his way. Why did he smile? Was it because he had come across something quite unfamiliar to him, though every man retains some instinctive feeling on the subject, or was it that he reflected, like many other clerks, as follows: "Well, upon my soul, those Frenchmen! it's beyond anything! if they try on anything of the sort, it really is . . . !" Though possibly he did not even think that; there is no creeping into a man's soul and finding out all that he thinks. At last he reached the house in which the assistant head clerk lived in fine style; there was a lamp burning on the stairs, and the flat was on the second floor. As he went into the entry Akaky Akakyevitch saw whole rows of goloshes. Amongst them in the middle of the room stood a samovar hissing and letting off clouds of steam. On the walls hung coats and cloaks, among which some actually had beaver collars or velvet revers. The other side of the wall there was noise and talk, which suddenly became clear and loud when the door opened and the footman came out with a tray full of empty glasses, a jug of cream, and a basket of biscuits. It was evident that the clerks had arrived long before and had already drunk their first glass of tea. Akaky Akakyevitch, after hanging up his coat with his own hands, went into the room, and at the same moment there flashed before his eyes a vision of candles, clerks, pipes, and card tables, together with the confused sounds of conversation rising up on all sides and the noise of moving chairs. He stopped very awkwardly in the middle of the room, looking about and trying to think what to do, but he was observed and received with a shout and they all went at once into the entry and again took a look at his overcoat. Though Akaky Akakyevitch was somewhat embarrassed, yet, being a simple-hearted man, he could not help being pleased at seeing how they all admired his coat. Then of course they all abandoned him and his coat, and turned their attention as usual to the tables set for whist. All this—the noise, the talk, and the crowd of people—was strange and wonderful to Akaky Akakyevitch. He simply did not know how to behave, what to do with his arms and legs and his whole figure; at last he sat down beside the players, looked at the cards, stared first at one and then at another of the faces, and in a little while began to yawn and felt that he was bored—especially as it was long past the time at which he usually went to bed. He tried to take leave of his hosts, but they would not let him go, saying that he absolutely must have a glass of champagne in honor of the new coat. An hour later supper was served, consisting of salad, cold veal, a pasty, pies, and tarts from the confectioner's, and champagne. They made Akaky Akakyevitch drink two glasses, after which he felt that things were much more cheerful, though he could not forget that it was twelve o'clock and that he ought to have been home long ago. That his host might not take it into his head to detain him, he slipped out of the room, hunted in the entry for his greatcoat, which he found, not without regret, lying on the floor, shook it, removed some fluff from it, put it on, and went down the stairs into the street. It was still light in the streets. Some little general shops, those perpetual clubs for house-serfs and all sorts of people, were open; others which were closed showed, however, a long streak of light at every crack of the door, proving that they were not yet deserted, and probably maids and men-servants were still finishing their conversation and discussion, driving their masters to utter perplexity as to their whereabouts. Akaky Akakyevitch walked along in a cheerful state of mind; he was even on the point of running, goodness knows why, after a lady of some sort who passed by like lightning with every part of her frame in violent motion. He checked himself at once, however, and again walked along very gently, feeling positively surprised himself at the inexplicable impulse that had seized him. Soon the deserted streets, which are not particularly cheerful by day and even less so in the evening, stretched before him. Now they were still more dead and deserted; the light of street lamps was scantier, the oil was evidently running low; then came wooden houses and fences; not a soul anywhere; only the snow gleamed on the streets and the low-pitched slumbering hovels looked black and gloomy with their closed shutters. He approached the spot where the street was intersected by an endless square, which looked like a fearful desert with its houses scarcely visible on the further side.

In the distance, goodness knows where, there was a gleam of light from some sentry-box which seemed to be standing at the end of the world. Akaky Akakyevitch's light-heartedness grew somehow sensibly less at this place. He stepped into the square, not without an involuntary uneasiness, as though his heart had a foreboding of evil. He looked behind him and to both sides—it was as though the sea were all round him. "No, better not look," he thought, and walked on, shutting his eyes, and when he opened them to see whether the end of the square were near, he suddenly saw standing before him, almost under his very nose, some men with moustaches; just what they were like he could not even distinguish. There was a mist before his eyes and a throbbing in his chest. "I say the overcoat is mine!" said one of them in a voice like a clap of thunder, seizing him by the collar. Akaky Akakyevitch was on the point of shouting "Help" when another put a fist the size of a clerk's head against his very lips, saying: "You just shout now." Akaky Akakyevitch felt only that they took the overcoat off, and gave him a kick with their knees, and he fell on his face in the snow and was conscious of nothing more. A few minutes later he came to himself and got on to his feet, but there was no one there. He felt that it was cold on the ground and that he had no overcoat, and began screaming, but it seemed as though his voice could not carry to the end of the square. Overwhelmed with despair and continuing to scream, he ran across the square straight to the sentry-box, beside which stood a sentry leaning on his halberd and, so it seemed, looking with curiosity to see who the devil the man was who was screaming and running towards him from the distance. As Akaky Akakyevitch reached him, he began breathlessly shouting that he was asleep and not looking after his duty not to see that a man was being robbed. The sentry answered that he had seen nothing, that he had only seen him stopped in the middle of the square by two men, and supposed that they were his friends, and that, instead of abusing him for nothing, he had better go the next day to the superintendent and that he would find out who had taken the overcoat. Akaky Akakyevitch ran home in a terrible state: his hair, which was still comparatively abundant on his temples and the back of his head, was completely dishevelled; his sides and chest and his trousers were

all covered with snow. When his old landlady heard a fearful
knock at the door she jumped hurriedly out of bed and, with only
one slipper on, ran to open it, modestly holding her shift across
her bosom; but when she opened it she stepped back, seeing what
a state Akaky Akakyevitch was in. When he told her what had
happened, she clasped her hands in horror and said that he must
go straight to the superintendent, that the police constable of the
quarter would deceive him, make promises and lead him a dance;
that it would be best of all to go to the superintendent, and that
she knew him indeed, because Anna the Finnish girl who was once
her cook was now in service as a nurse at the superintendent's;
and that she often saw him himself when he passed by their house,
and that he used to be every Sunday at church too, saying his
prayers and at the same time looking goodhumoredly at every
one, and that therefore by every token he must be a kind-hearted
man. After listening to this advice, Akaky Akakyevitch made his
way very gloomily to his room, and how he spent that night I
leave to the imagination of those who are in the least able to picture the position of others. Early in the morning he set off to the
police superintendent's, but was told that he was asleep. He came
at ten o'clock, he was told again that he was asleep; he came at
eleven and was told that the superintendent was not at home; he
came at dinner-time, but the clerks in the ante-room would not
let him in, and insisted on knowing what was the matter and
what business had brought him and exactly what had happened;
so that at last Akaky Akakyevitch for the first time in his life
tried to show the strength of his character and said curtly that he
must see the superintendent himself, that they dare not refuse to
admit him, that he had come from the department on government
business, and that if he made complaint of them they would see.
The clerks dared say nothing to this, and one of them went to
summon the superintendent. The latter received his story of being
robbed of his overcoat in an extremely strange way. Instead of
attending to the main point, he began asking Akaky Akakyevitch
questions, why had he been coming home so late? wasn't he going,
or hadn't he been, to some house of ill-fame? so that Akaky

Akakyevitch was overwhelmed with confusion, and went away without knowing whether or not the proper measures would be taken in regard to his overcoat. He was absent from the office all that day (the only time that it had happened in his life). Next day he appeared with a pale face, wearing his old "dressing jacket" which had become a still more pitiful sight. The tidings of the theft of the overcoat—though there were clerks who did not let even this chance slip of jeering at Akaky Akakyevitch—touched many of them. They decided on the spot to get up a subscription for him, but collected only a very trifling sum, because the clerks had already spent a good deal on subscribing to the director's portrait and on the purchase of a book, at the suggestion of the head of their department, who was a friend of the author, and so the total realized was very insignificant. One of the clerks, moved by compassion, ventured at any rate to assist Akaky Akakyevitch with good advice, telling him not to go to the district police inspector, because, though it might happen that the latter might be sufficiently zealous of gaining the approval of his superiors to succeed in finding the overcoat, it would remain in the possession of the police unless he presented legal proofs that it belonged to him; he urged that far the best thing would be to appeal to a Person of Consequence; that the Person of Consequence, by writing and getting into communication with the proper authorities, could push the matter through more successfully. There was nothing else for it. Akaky Akakyevitch made up his mind to go to the Person of Consequence. What precisely was the nature of the functions of the Person of Consequence has remained a matter of uncertainty. It must be noted that this Person of Consequence had only lately become a person of consequence, and until recently had been a person of no consequence. Though, indeed, his position even now was not reckoned of consequence in comparison with others of still greater consequence. But there is always to be found a circle of persons to whom a person of little consequence in the eyes of others is a person of consequence. It is true that he did his utmost to increase the consequence of his position in various ways, for instance by insisting that his subordinates should come out on to the stairs to meet him when he arrived at his office; that no one should venture to approach him directly but all proceedings should be by the strictest order of precedence, that a collegiate registration clerk should report the matter to the provincial secretary, and the provincial secretary to the titular councillor or whomsoever it might be, and that business should only reach him by this channel. Every one in Holy Russia has a craze for imitation, every one apes and mimics his superiors. I have actually been told that a titular councillor who was put in charge of a small separate office, immediately partitioned off a special room for himself, calling it the head office, and set special porters at the door with red collars and gold lace, who took hold of the handle of the door and opened it for every one who went in, though the "head office" was so tiny that it was with difficulty that an ordinary writing table could be put into it. The manners and habits of the Person of Consequence were dignified and majestic, but not complex. The chief foundation of his system was strictness, "strictness, strictness, and—strictness!" he used to say, and at the last word he would look very significantly at the person he was addressing, though, indeed, he had no reason to do so, for the dozen clerks who made up the whole administrative mechanism of his office stood in befitting awe of him; any clerk who saw him in the distance would leave his work and remain standing at attention till his superior had left the room. His conversation with his subordinates was usually marked by severity and almost confined to three phrases: "How dare you? Do you know to whom you are speaking? Do you understand who I am?" He was, however, at heart a good-natured man, pleasant and obliging with his colleagues; but the grade of general had completely turned his head. When he received it, he was perplexed, thrown off his balance, and quite at a loss how to behave. If he chanced to be with his equals, he was still quite a decent man, a very gentlemanly man, in fact, and in many ways even an intelligent man, but as soon as he was in company with men who were even one grade below him, there was simply no doing anything with him: he sat silent and his position excited compassion, the more so as he himself felt that he might have been spending his time to incomparably more advantage. At times there could be seen in his eyes an intense desire to join in some interesting conversation, but he was restrained by the doubt whether it would not be too much on his part, whether it would not be too great a familiarity and lowering of his dignity, and in consequence of these reflections he remained everlastingly in the same mute condition, only uttering from time to time monosyllabic sounds, and in this way he gained the reputation of being a very tiresome man.

So this was the Person of Consequence to whom our friend Akaky Akakyevitch appealed, and he appealed to him at a most unpropitious moment, very unfortunate for himself, though fortunate, indeed, for the Person of Consequence. The latter happened to be in his study, talking in the very best of spirits with an old friend of his childhood who had only just arrived and whom he had not seen for several years. It was at this moment that he was informed that a man called Bashmatchkin was asking to see him. He asked abruptly, "What sort of man is he?" and received the answer, "A government clerk." "Ah! he can wait, I haven't time now," said the Person of Consequence. Here I must observe that this was a complete lie on the part of the Person of Consequence: he had time; his friend and he had long ago said all they had to say to each other and their conversation had begun to be broken by very long pauses during which they merely slapped each other on the knee, saying, "So that's how things are, Ivan Abramovitch!" —"There it is, Stepan Varlamovitch!" but, for all that, he told the clerk to wait in order to show his friend, who had left the service years before and was living at home in the country how long clerks had to wait in his ante-room. At last after they had talked, or rather been silent to their heart's content and had smoked a cigar in very comfortable arm-chairs with sloping backs, he seemed suddenly to recollect, and said to the secretary, who was standing at the door with papers for his signature: "Oh, by the way, there is a clerk waiting, isn't there? tell him he can come in." When he saw Akaky Akakyevitch's meek appearance and old uniform, he turned to him at once and said: "What do you want?" in a firm and abrupt voice, which he had purposely practiced in his own room in solitude before the looking-glass for a week before receiving his present post and the grade of a general. Akaky Akakyevitch, who was overwhelmed with befitting awe beforehand, was somewhat confused and, as far as his tongue would allow him, explained to the best of his powers, with even more frequent "ers" than usual, that he had had a perfectly new overcoat and now he had been robbed of it in the most inhuman way, and that now he had come to beg him by his intervention either to correspond with his honor the head policemaster or anybody else, and find the overcoat. This mode of proceeding struck the general for some reason as taking a great liberty. "What next sir," he went on as abruptly, "don't you know the way to proceed? To whom are you addressing yourself? Don't you know how things are done? You ought first to have handed in a petition to the office; it would have gone to the head clerk of the room, and to the head clerk of the section, then it would have been handed to the secretary and the secretary would have brought it to me. . . ."

"But, your Excellency," said Akaky Akakyevitch, trying to collect all the small allowance of presence of mind he possessed and feeling at the same time that he was getting into a terrible perspiration, "I ventured, your Excellency, to trouble you because secretaries . . . er . . . are people you can't depend on. . . ."

"What? what? what?" said the Person of Consequence, "where did you get hold of that spirit? where did you pick up such ideas? What insubordination is spreading among young men against their superiors and betters." The Person of Consequence did not apparently observe that Akaky Akakyevitch was well over fifty, and therefore if he could have been called a young man it would only have been in comparison with a man of seventy. "Do you know to whom you are speaking? do you understand who I am? do you understand that, I ask you?" At this point he stamped, and raised his voice to such a powerful note that Akaky Akakyevitch was not the only one to be terrified. Akaky Akakyevitch was positively petrified; he staggered, trembling all over, and could not stand; if the porters had not run up to support him, he would have flopped upon the floor; he was led out almost unconscious. The Person of Consequence, pleased that the effect had surpassed his expectations and enchanted at the idea that his words could even deprive a man of consciousness, stole a sideway glance at his friend to see how he was taking it, and perceived not without satisfaction that his friend was feeling very uncertain and even beginning to be a little terrified himself.

How he got downstairs, how he went out into the street—of all that Akaky Akakyevitch remembered nothing, he had no feeling in his arms or his legs. In all his life he had never been so severely reprimanded by a general, and this was by one of another department, too. He went out into the snowstorm, that was whistling through the streets, with his mouth open, and as he went he stumbled off the pavement; the wind, as its way is in Petersburg, blew upon him from all points of the compass and from every side street. In an instant it had blown a quinsy into his throat, and when he got home he was not able to utter a word; with a swollen face and throat he went to bed. So violent is sometimes the effect of a suitable reprimand!

Next day he was in a high fever. Thanks to the gracious assistance of the Petersburg climate, the disease made more rapid progress than could have been expected, and when the doctor came, after feeling his pulse he could find nothing to do but prescribe a fomentation, and that simply that the patient might not be left without the benefit of medical assistance; however, two days later he informed him that his end was at hand, after which he turned to his landlady and said: "And you had better lose no time, my good woman, but order him now a deal coffin, for an oak one will be too dear for him." Whether Akaky Akakyevitch heard these fateful words or not, whether they produced a shattering effect upon him, and whether he regretted his pitiful life, no one can tell, for he was all the time in delirium and fever. Apparitions, each stranger than the one before, were continually haunting him: first, he saw Petrovitch and was ordering him to make a greatcoat trimmed with some sort of traps for robbers, who were, he fancied, continually under the bed, and he was calling his landlady every minute to pull out a thief who had even got under the quilt; then he kept asking why his old "dressing jacket" was hanging before him when he had a new overcoat, then he fancied he was standing before the general listening to the appropriate reprimand and saying "I am sorry, your Excellency," then finally he became abusive, uttering the most awful language, so that his old landlady positively crossed herself, having never heard anything of the kind from him before, and the more horrified because these dreadful words followed immediately upon the phrase "your Excellency." Later on, his talk was a mere medley of nonsense, so that it was quite unintelligible; all that could be seen was that his incoherent words and thoughts were concerned with nothing but the overcoat. At last poor Akaky Akakyevitch gave up the ghost. No seal was put upon his room nor upon his things, because, in the first place, he had no heirs and, in the second, the property left was very small, to wit, a bundle of goose-feathers, a quire of white government paper, three pairs of socks, two or three buttons that had come off his trousers, and the "dressing jacket" with which the reader is already familiar. Who came into all this wealth God only knows, even I who tell the tale must own that I have not troubled to enquire. And Petersburg remained without Akaky Akakyevitch, as though, indeed, he had never been in the city. A creature had vanished and departed whose cause no one had championed, who was dear to no one, of interest to no one, who never even attracted the attention of the student of natural history, though the latter does not disdain to fix a common fly upon a pin and look at him under the microscope—a creature who bore patiently the jeers of the office and for no particular reason went to his grave, though even he at the very end of his life was visited by a gleam of brightness in the form of an overcoat that for one instant brought color into his poor life—a creature on whom calamity broke as insufferably as it breaks upon the heads of the mighty ones of this world . . . !

Several days after his death, the porter from the department was sent to his lodgings with instructions that he should go at once to the office, for his chief was asking for him; but the porter was obliged to return without him, explaining that he could not come, and to the enquiry "Why?" he added, "Well, you see: the fact is he is dead, he was buried three days ago." This was how they learned at the office of the death of Akaky Akakyevitch, and the next day there was sitting in his seat a new clerk who was very much taller and who wrote not in the same upright hand but made his letters more slanting and crooked.

But who could have imagined that this was not all there was to tell about Akaky Akakyevitch, that he was destined for a few days to make a noise in the world after his death, as though to make up for his life having been unnoticed by anyone? But so it happened, and our poor story unexpectedly finishes with a fantastic ending. Rumors were suddenly floating about Petersburg that in the neighborhood of the Kalinkin Bridge and for a little distance beyond, a corpse had taken to appearing at night in the form of a clerk looking for a stolen overcoat, and stripping from the shoulders of all passers-by, regardless of grade and calling, overcoats of all descriptions—trimmed with cat fur, or beaver or wadded, lined with raccoon, fox and bear—made, in fact, of all sorts of skin which men have adapted for the covering of their own. One of the clerks of the department saw the corpse with his own eyes and at once recognized it as Akaky Akakyevitch; but it excited in him such terror, however, that he ran away as fast as his legs could carry him and so could not get a very clear view of him, and only saw him hold up his finger threateningly in the distance.

From all sides complaints were continualy coming that backs and shoulders, not of mere titular councillors, but even of upper court councillors, had been exposed to taking chills, owing to being stripped of their greatcoats. Orders were given to the police to catch the corpse regardless of trouble or expense, alive or dead, and to punish him in the cruellest way, as an example to others, and, indeed, they very nearly succeeded in doing so. The sentry of one district police station in Kiryushkin Place snatched a corpse by the collar on the spot of the crime in the very act of attempting to snatch a frieze overcoat from a retired musician, who used in his day to play the flute. Having caught him by the collar, he shouted until he had brought two other comrades, whom he charged to hold him while he felt just a minute in his boot to get out a snuff-box in order to revive his nose which had six times in his life been frost-bitten, but the snuff was probably so strong that not even a dead man could stand it. The sentry had hardly had time to put his finger over his right nostril and draw up some snuff in the left when the corpse sneezed violently right into the eyes of all three. While they were putting their fists up to wipe them, the corpse completely vanished, so that they were not even sure whether he had actually been in their hands. From that time forward, the sentries conceived such a horror of the dead that they were even afraid to seize the living and confined themselves to shouting from the distance: "Hi, you there, be off!" and the dead clerk began to appear even on the other side of the Kalinkin Bridge, rousing no little terror in all timid people.

We have, however, quite deserted the Person of Consequence, who may in reality almost be said to be the cause of the fantastic ending of this perfectly true story. To begin with, my duty requires me to do justice to the Person of Consequence by recording that soon after poor Akaky Akakyevitch had gone away crushed to powder, he felt something not unlike regret. Sympathy was a feeling not unknown to him; his heart was open to many kindly impulses, although his exalted grade very often prevented them from being shown. As soon as his friend had gone out of his study, he even began brooding over poor Akaky Akakyevich, and from that time forward, he was almost every day haunted by the image of the poor clerk who had succumbed so completely to the befitting reprimand. The thought of the man so worried him that a week later he actually decided to send a clerk to find out how he was and whether he really could help him in any way. And when they brought him word that Akaky Akakyevitch had died suddenly in delirium and fever, it made a great impression on him, his conscience reproached him and he was depressed all day. Anxious to distract his mind and to forget the unpleasant impression, he went to spend the evening with one of his friends, where he found a genteel company and, what was best of all, almost everyone was of the same grade so that he was able to be quite free from restraint. This had a wonderful effect on his spirits, he expanded, became affable and genial—in short, spent a very agreeable evening. At supper he drank a couple of glasses of champagne—a proceeding which we all know has a happy effect in inducing good humor. The champagne made him inclined to do something unusual, and he decided not to go home yet but to visit a lady of his acquaintance, one Karolina Ivanovna—a lady apparently of German extraction, for whom he entertained extremely friendly feelings. It must be noted that the Person of Consequence was a man no longer young, an excellent husband, and the respectable father of a family. He had two sons, one already serving in his office, and a nice-looking daughter of sixteen with a rather turned-up, pretty little nose, who used to come every morning to kiss his hand, saying: "*Bon jour, Papa.*" His wife, who was still blooming and decidedly good-looking, indeed, used first to give him her hand to kiss and then would kiss his hand, turning it the other side upwards. But though the Person of Consequence was perfectly satisfied with the kind amenities of his domestic life, he thought it proper to have a lady friend in another quarter of the town. This lady friend was not a bit better looking nor younger than his wife, but these mysterious facts exist in the world and it is not our business to criticize them. And so the Person of Consequence went downstairs, got into his sledge, and said to his coachman, "To Karolina Ivanovna," while luxuriously wrapped in his warm fur coat he remained in that agreeable frame of mind sweeter to a Russian than anything that could be invented, that is, when one thinks of nothing while thoughts come into the mind of themselves, one pleasanter than the other, without the labor of following them or looking for them. Full of satisfaction, he recalled all the amusing moments of the evening he had spent, all the phrases that had set the little circle laughing; many of them he repeated in an undertone and found them as amusing as before, and so, very naturally, laughed very heartily at them again. From time to time, however, he was disturbed by a gust of wind which, blowing suddenly, God knows whence and wherefore, cut him in the face,

pelting him with flakes of snow, puffing out his coat-collar like a
sack, or suddenly flinging it with unnatural force over his head and
giving him endless trouble to extricate himself from it. All at once,
the Person of Consequence felt that some one had clutched him
very tightly by the collar. Turning round he saw a short man in
a shabby old uniform, and not without horror recognized him as
Akaky Akakyevitch. The clerk's face was white as snow and looked
like that of a corpse, but the horror of the Person of Consequence
was beyond all bounds when he saw the mouth of the corpse distorted into speech and, breathing upon him the chill of the grave,
it uttered the following words: "Ah, so here you are at last! At last
I've . . . er . . . caught you by the collar. It's your overcoat I want,
you refused to help me and abused me into the bargain! So now
give me yours!" The poor Person of Consequence very nearly died.
Resolute and determined as he was in his office and before subordinates in general, and though any one looking at his manly
air and figure would have said: "Oh, what a man of character!"
yet in this plight he felt, like very many persons of athletic appearance, such terror that not without reason he began to be afraid
he would have some sort of fit. He actually flung his overcoat off
his shoulders as fast as he could and shouted to his coachman in
a voice unlike his own: "Drive home and make haste!" The coachman, hearing the tone which he had only heard in critical moments
and then accompanied by something even more rousing, hunched
his shoulders up to his ears in case of worse following, swung his
whip and flew on like an arrow. In a little over six minutes the
Person of Consequence was at the entrance of his own house.
Pale, panic-stricken, and without his overcoat, he arrived home
instead of at Karolina Ivanovna's, dragged himself to his own room
and spent the night in great perturbation, so that next morning
his daughter said to him at breakfast, "You look quite pale today,
Papa": but her papa remained mute and said not a word to anyone of what had happened to him, where he had been, and where
he had been going. The incident made a great impression upon
him. Indeed, it happened far more rarely that he said to his subordinates, "How dare you? do you understand who I am?" and he

never uttered those words at all until he had first heard all the rights of the case.

What was even more remarkable is that from that time the apparition of the dead clerk ceased entirely: apparently the general's overcoat had fitted him perfectly, anyway nothing more was heard of overcoats being snatched from anyone. Many restless and anxious people refused, however, to be pacified, and still maintained that in remote parts of the town the ghost of the dead clerk went on appearing. One sentry in Kolomna, for instance, saw with his own eyes a ghost appear from behind a house; but, being by natural constitution somewhat feeble—so much so that on one occasion an ordinary, well-grown pig, making a sudden dash out of some building, knocked him off his feet to the vast entertainment of the cabmen standing round, from whom he exacted two kopecks each for snuff for such rudeness—he did not dare to stop it, and so followed it in the dark until the ghost suddenly looked round and, stopping, asked him: "What do you want?" displaying a fist such as you never see among the living. The sentry said: "Nothing," and turned back on the spot. This ghost, however, was considerably taller and adorned with immense moustaches, and, directing its steps apparently towards Obuhov Bridge, vanished into the darkness of the night.

1842 A.D.

TURGENEV *First Love*

TURGENEV *First Love*

THE guests had long since departed. The clock had struck half-past twelve. There remained in the room only the host, Sergyei Nikolaevitch, and Vladimir Petrovitch.

The host rang and ordered the remains of the supper to be removed.—"So then, the matter is settled," he said, ensconcing himself more deeply in his arm-chair, and lighting a cigar:—"each of us is to narrate the history of his first love. 'Tis your turn, Sergyei Nikolaevitch."

Sergyei Nikolaevitch, a rather corpulent man, with a plump, fair-skinned face, first looked at the host, then raised his eyes to the ceiling.—"I had no first love,"—he began at last:—"I began straight off with the second."

"How was that?"

"Very simply. I was eighteen years of age when, for the first time, I dangled after a very charming young lady; but I courted her as though it were no new thing to me: exactly as I courted others afterward. To tell the truth, I fell in love, for the first and last time, at the age of six, with my nurse;—but that is a very long time ago. The details of our relations have been erased from my memory; but even if I remembered them, who would be interested in them?"

"Then what are we to do?"—began the host.—"There was nothing very startling about my first love either; I never fell in love

39

with anyone before Anna Ivanovna, now my wife; and everything ran as though on oil with us; our fathers made up the match, we very promptly fell in love with each other, and entered the bonds of matrimony without delay. My story can be told in two words. I must confess, gentlemen, that in raising the question of first love, I set my hopes on you, I will not say old, but yet no longer young bachelors. Will not you divert us with something, Vladimir Petrovitch?"

"My first love belongs, as a matter of fact, not altogether to the ordinary category,"—replied, with a slight hesitation, Vladimir Petrovitch, a man of forty, whose black hair was sprinkled with grey.

"Ah!"—said the host and Sergyei Nikolaevitch in one breath.— "So much the better. . . . Tell us."

"As you like . . . . or no: I will not narrate; I am no great hand at telling a story; it turns out dry and short, or long-drawn-out and artificial. But if you will permit me, I will write down all that I remember in a note-book, and will read it aloud to you."

At first the friends would not consent, but Vladimir Petrovitch insisted on having his own way. A fortnight later they came together again, and Vladimir Petrovitch kept his promise.

This is what his note-book contained.

1

I w a s sixteen years old at the time. The affair took place in the summer of 1833.

I was living in Moscow, in my parents' house. They had hired a villa near the Kaluga barrier, opposite the Neskutchny Park.[1]—I was preparing for the university, but was working very little and was not in a hurry.

---

[1] The finest of the public parks in Moscow, situated near the famous Sparrow Hills, is called "Neskutchny"—"Not Tiresome," generally rendered "Sans Souci." It contains an imperial residence, the Alexander Palace, used as an official summer home by the Governor-General of Moscow.—TRANS-LATOR.

No one restricted my freedom. I had done whatever I pleased ever since I had parted with my last French governor, who was utterly unable to reconcile himself to the thought that he had fallen "like a bomb (*comme une bombe*) into Russia, and with a stubborn expression on his face, wallowed in bed for whole days at a time. My father treated me in an indifferently affectionate way; my mother paid hardly any attention to me, although she had no children except me: other cares engrossed her. My father, still a young man and very handsome, had married her from calculation; she was ten years older than he. My mother led a melancholy life: she was incessantly in a state of agitation, jealousy, and wrath—but not in the presence of my father; she was very much afraid of him, and he maintained a stern, cold, and distant manner . . . I have never seen a man more exquisitely calm, self-confident, and self-controlled.

I shall never forget the first weeks I spent at the villa. The weather was magnificent; we had left town the ninth of May, on St. Nicholas's day. I rambled,—sometimes in the garden of our villa, sometimes in Neskutchny Park, sometimes beyond the city barriers; I took with me some book or other,—a course of Kaidanoff,—but rarely opened it, and chiefly recited aloud poems, of which I knew a great many by heart. The blood was fermenting in me, and my heart was aching—so sweetly and absurdly; I was always waiting for something, shrinking at something, and wondering at everything, and was all ready for anything at a moment's notice. My fancy was beginning to play, and hovered swiftly ever around the selfsame image, as martins hover round a belfry at sunset. But even athwart my tears and athwart the melancholy, inspired now by a melodious verse, now by the beauty of the evening, there peered forth, like grass in springtime, the joyous sensation of young, bubbling life.

I had a saddle-horse; I was in the habit of saddling it myself, and when I rode off alone as far as possible, in some direction, launching out at a gallop and fancying myself a knight at a tourney —how blithely the wind whistled in my ears!—Or, turning my face skyward, I welcomed its beaming light and azure into my open soul.

I remember, at that time, the image of woman, the phantom of woman's love, almost never entered my mind in clearly defined outlines; but in everything I thought, in everything I felt, there lay hidden the half-conscious, shamefaced presentiment of something new, inexpressibly sweet, feminine. . . .

This presentiment, this expectation permeated my whole being; I breathed it, it coursed through my veins in every drop of blood . . . . it was fated to be speedily realized.

Our villa consisted of a wooden manor-house with columns, and two tiny outlying wings; in the wing to the left a tiny factory of cheap wallpapers was installed. . . . More than once I went thither to watch how half a score of gaunt, dishevelled young fellows in dirty smocks and with tipsy faces were incessantly galloping about at the wooden levers which jammed down the square blocks of the press, and in that manner, by the weight of their puny bodies, printed the motley-hued patterns of the wallpapers. The wing on the right stood empty and was for rent. One day—three weeks after the ninth of May—the shutters on the windows of this wing were opened, and women's faces made their appearance in them; some family or other had moved into it. I remember how, that same day at dinner, my mother inquired of the butler who our new neighbors were, and on hearing the name of Princess Zasyekin, said at first, not without some respect: —"Ah! a Princess" . . . . and then she added:—"She must be some poor person!"

"They came in three hired carriages, ma'am,"—remarked the butler, as he respectfully presented a dish. "They have no carriage of their own, ma'am, and their furniture is of the very plainest sort."

"Yes,"—returned my mother,—"and nevertheless, it is better so."

My father shot a cold glance at her; she subsided into silence.

As a matter of fact, Princess Zasyekin could not be a wealthy woman: the wing she had hired was so old and tiny and low-roofed that people in the least well-to-do would not have been willing to inhabit it.—However, I let this go in at one ear and out at the other. The princely title had little effect on me: I had recently been reading Schiller's "The Brigands."

2

I HAD a habit of prowling about our garden every evening, gun in hand, and standing guard against the crows.—I had long cherished a hatred for those wary, rapacious and crafty birds. On the day of which I have been speaking, I went into the garden as usual, and, after having fruitlessly made the round of all the alleys (the crows recognized me from afar, and merely cawed spasmodically at a distance), I accidentally approached the low fence which separated *our* territory from the narrow strip of garden extending behind the right-hand wing and appertaining to it. I was walking along with drooping head. Suddenly I heard voices: I glanced over the fence—and was petrified. . . . . A strange spectacle presented itself to me.

A few paces distant from me, on a grass-plot between green raspberry-bushes, stood a tall, graceful young girl, in a striped, pink frock and with a white kerchief on her head; around her pressed four young men, and she was tapping them in turn on the brow with those small grey flowers, the name of which I do not know, but which are familiar to children; these little flowers form tiny sacs, and burst with a pop when they are struck against anything hard. The young men offered their foreheads to her so willingly, and in the girl's movements (I saw her form in profile) there was something so bewitching, caressing, mocking, and charming, that I almost cried aloud in wonder and pleasure; and I believe I would have given everything in the world if those lovely little fingers had only consented to tap me on the brow. My gun slid down on the grass, I forgot everything, I devoured with my eyes that slender waist, and the neck and the beautiful arms, and the slightly ruffled fair hair, the intelligent eyes and those lashes, and the delicate cheek beneath them. . . .

"Young man, hey there, young man!"—suddenly spoke up a voice near me:—"Is it permissible to stare like that at strange young ladies?"

I trembled all over, I was stupefied. . . . . Beside me, on the other side of the fence, stood a man with closely clipped black hair, gazing ironically at me. At that same moment, the young girl turned toward me. . . . I beheld huge grey eyes in a mobile, animated face—and this whole face suddenly began to quiver, and to laugh, and the white teeth gleamed from it, the brows elevated themselves in an amusing way. . . . I flushed, picked up my gun from the ground, and, pursued by ringing but not malicious laughter, I ran to my own room, flung myself on the bed, and covered my face with my hands. My heart was fairly leaping within me; I felt very much ashamed and very merry: I experienced an unprecedented emotion.

After I had rested awhile, I brushed my hair, made myself neat and went down-stairs to tea. The image of the young girl floated in front of me; my heart had ceased to leap, but ached in an agreeable sort of way.

"What ails thee?"—my father suddenly asked me:—"hast thou killed a crow?"

I was on the point of telling him all, but refrained and only smiled to myself. As I was preparing for bed, I whirled round thrice on one foot, I know not why, pomaded my hair, got into bed and slept all night like a dead man. Toward morning I awoke for a moment, raised my head, cast a glance of rapture around me—and fell asleep again.

3

"How am I to get acquainted with them?" was my first thought, as soon as I awoke in the morning. I went out into the garden before tea, but did not approach too close to the fence, and saw no one. After tea I walked several times up and down the street

in front of the villa, and cast a distant glance at the windows. . . .
I thought I descried *her* face behind the curtains, and retreated
with all possible despatch. "But I must get acquainted,"—I
thought, as I walked with irregular strides up and down the sandy
stretch which extends in front of the Neskutchny Park . . . . "but
how? that is the question." I recalled the most trifling incidents
of the meeting on the previous evening; for some reason, her manner of laughing at me presented itself to me with particular clearness. . . . But while I was fretting thus and constructing various
plans, Fate was already providing for me.

During my absence, my mother had received a letter from
her new neighbor on grey paper sealed with brown wax, such
as is used only on postal notices, and on the corks of cheap wine.
In this letter, written in illiterate language, and with a slovenly
chirography, the Princess requested my mother to grant her her
protection: my mother, according to the Princess's words, was
well acquainted with the prominent people on whom the fortune
of herself and her children depended, as she had some extremely
important law-suits: "I apeal tyou,"—she wrote,—"as a knoble
woman to a knoble woman, and moarover, it is agriable to me
to makeus of this oportunity." In conclusion, she asked permission
of my mother to call upon her. I found my mother in an unpleasant frame of mind: my father was not at home, and she
had no one with whom to take counsel. It was impossible not to
reply to a "knoble woman," and to a Princess into the bargain;
but how to reply perplexed my mother. It seemed to her ill-judged
to write a note in French, and my mother was not strong in Russian orthography herself—and was aware of the fact—and did
not wish to compromise herself. She was delighted at my arrival,
and immediately ordered me to go to the Princess and explain to
her verbally that my mother was always ready, to the extent of
her ability, to be of service to Her Radiance[1] and begged that she
would call upon her about one o'clock.

[1] Princes, princesses, counts, and countesses have the title of *Siyatelstvo*
(*siyam*—to shine, to be radiant); generally translated "Illustrious Highness"
or "Serenity."—TRANSLATOR.

This unexpectedly swift fulfillment of my secret wishes both delighted and frightened me; but I did not betray the emotion which held possession of me, and preliminarily betook myself to my room for the purpose of donning a new neck-cloth and coat; at home I went about in a round-jacket and turn-over collars, although I detested them greatly.

4

I N T H E cramped and dirty anteroom of the wing, which I entered with an involuntary trembling of my whole body, I was received by a grey-haired old serving-man with a face the hue of dark copper, pig-like, surly little eyes, and such deep wrinkles on his forehead as I had never seen before in my life. He was carrying on a platter the gnawed spinal bone of a herring, and, pushing to with his foot the door which led into the adjoining room, he said abruptly:—
"What do you want?"
"Is Princess Zasyekin at home?"—I inquired.
"Vonifaty!"—screamed a quavering female voice on the other side of the door.
The servant silently turned his back on me, thereby displaying the badly worn rear of his livery with its solitary, rusted, armouried button, and went away, leaving the platter on the floor.
"Hast thou been to the police-station?"—went on that same feminine voice. The servant muttered something in reply.—"Hey? . . . . Someone has come?"—was the next thing audible. . . . . .
"The young gentleman from next door?—Well, ask him in."
"Please come into the drawing-room, sir,"—said the servant, making his appearance again before me, and picking up the platter from the floor. I adjusted my attire and entered the "drawing-room."
I found myself in a tiny and not altogether clean room, with shabby furniture which seemed to have been hastily set in place. At the window, in an easy-chair with a broken arm, sat a woman

of fifty, with uncovered hair[1] and plain-featured, clad in an old green gown, and with a variegated worsted kerchief round her neck. Her small black eyes fairly bored into me.

I went up to her and made my bow.

"I have the honor of speaking to Princess Zasyekin?"

"I am Princess Zasyekin: and you are the son of Mr. B—?"

"Yes, madam. I have come to you with a message from my mother."

"Pray be seated. Vonifaty! where are my keys? Hast thou seen them?"

I communicated to Madame Zasyekin my mother's answer to her note. She listened to me, tapping the window-pane with her thick, red fingers, and when I had finished she riveted her eyes on me once more.

"Very good; I shall certainly go,"—said she at last.—"But how young you are still! How old are you, allow me to ask?"

"Sixteen,"—I replied with involuntary hesitation.

The Princess pulled out of her pocket some dirty, written documents, raised them up to her very nose and began to sort them over.

" 'Tis a good age,"—she suddenly articulated, turning and fidgeting in her chair.—"And please do not stand on ceremony. We are plain folks."

"Too plain,"—I thought, with involuntary disgust taking in with a glance the whole of her homely figure.

At that moment, the other door of the drawing-room was swiftly thrown wide open, and on the threshold appeared the young girl whom I had seen in the garden the evening before. She raised her hand and a smile flitted across her face.

"And here is my daughter,"—said the Princess, pointing at her with her elbow.—"Zinotchka, the son of our neighbor, Mr. B—. What is your name, permit me to inquire?"

"Vladimir,"—I replied, rising and lisping with agitation.

[1] The custom still prevails in Russia, to a great extent, for all elderly women to wear caps. In the peasant class it is considered as extremely indecorous to go "simple-haired," as the expression runs.—TRANSLATOR.

"And your patronymic?"

"Petrovitch."

"Yes! I once had an acquaintance, a chief of police, whose name was Vladimir Petrovich also. Vonifaty! don't hunt for the keys; the keys are in my pocket."

The young girl continued to gaze at me with the same smile as before, slightly puckering up her eyes and bending her head a little on one side.

"I have already seen M'sieu Voldemar,"—she began. (The silvery tone of her voice coursed through me like a sweet chill.)— "Will you permit me to call you so?"

"Pray do, madam,"—I lisped.

"Where was that?"—asked the Princess.

The young Princess did not answer her mother.

"Are you busy now?"—she said, without taking her eyes off me.

"Not in the least, madam."

"Then will you help me to wind some wool? Come hither, to me."

She nodded her head at me and left the drawing-room. I followed her.

In the room which we entered the furniture was a little better and was arranged with great taste.—But at that moment I was almost unable to notice anything; I moved as though in a dream and felt a sort of intense sensation of well-being verging on stupidity throughout my frame.

The young Princess sat down, produced a knot of red wool, and pointing me to a chair opposite her, she carefully unbound the skein and placed it on my hands. She did all this in silence, with a sort of diverting deliberation, and with the same brilliant and crafty smile on her slightly parted lips. She began to wind the wool upon a card doubled together, and suddenly illumined me with such a clear, swift glance, that I involuntarily dropped my eyes. When her eyes, which were generally half closed, opened to their full extent her face underwent a complete change; it was as though light had inundated it.

"What did you think of me yesterday, M'sieu Voldemar?"—

she asked, after a brief pause.—"You certainly must have condemned me?"

"I . . . . Princess . . . . I thought nothing . . . . how can I . . . ." I replied, in confusion.

"Listen,"—she returned.—"You do not know me yet; I want people always to speak the truth to me. You are sixteen, I heard, and I am twenty-one; you see that I am a great deal older than you, and therefore you must always speak the truth to me . . . and obey me,"—she added. —"Look at me; why don't you look at me?"

I became still more confused; but I raised my eyes to hers, nevertheless. She smiled, only not in her former manner, but with a different, an approving smile.—"Look at me,"—she said, caressingly lowering her voice:—"I don't like that. . . . Your face pleases me; I foresee that we shall be friends. And do you like me?"—she added slyly.

"Princess . . . ." I was beginning. . . .

"In the first place, call me Zinaida Alexandrovna; and in the second place,—what sort of a habit is it for children"—(she corrected herself)—"for young men—not to say straight out what they feel? You do like me, don't you?"

Although it was very pleasant to me to have her talk so frankly to me, still I was somewhat nettled. I wanted to show her that she was not dealing with a small boy, and, assuming as easy and serious a mien as I could, I said:—"Of course I like you very much, Zinaida Alexandrovna; I have no desire to conceal the fact."

She shook her head, pausing at intervals.—"Have you a governor?"—she suddenly inquired.

"No, I have not had a governor this long time past."

I lied: a month had not yet elapsed since I had parted with my Frenchman.

"Oh, yes, I see: you are quite grown up."

She slapped me lightly on the fingers.—"Hold your hands straight!"—And she busied herself diligently with winding her ball.

I took advantage of the fact that she did not raise her eyes, and set to scrutinizing her, first by stealth, then more and more boldly. Her face seemed to me even more charming than on the day before: everything about it was so delicate, intelligent and lovely. She was sitting with her back to the window, which was hung with a white shade; a ray of sunlight making its way through that shade inundated with a flood of light her fluffy golden hair, her innocent neck, sloping shoulders, and calm, tender bosom.—I gazed at her —and how near and dear she became to me! It seemed to me both that I had known her for a long time and that I had known nothing and had not lived before she came. . . . She wore a rather dark, already shabby gown, with an apron; I believe I would willingly have caressed every fold of that gown and of that apron. The tips of her shoes peeped out from under her gown; I would have bowed down to those little boots. . . . "And here I sit, in front of her,"—I thought.—"I have become acquainted with her . . . . what happiness, my God!" I came near bouncing out of my chair with rapture, but I merely dangled my feet to and fro a little, like a child who is enjoying dainties.

I felt as much at my ease as a fish does in water, and I would have liked never to leave that room again as long as I lived.

Her eyelids slowly rose, and again her brilliant eyes beamed caressingly before me, and again she laughed.

"How you stare at me!"—she said slowly, shaking her finger at me.

I flushed scarlet. . . . . "She understands all, she sees all,"— flashed through my head. "And how could she fail to see and understand all?"

Suddenly there was a clattering in the next room, and a sword clanked.

"Zina!"—screamed the old Princess from the drawing-room.— "Byelovzoroff has brought thee a kitten."

"A kitten!"—cried Zinaida, and springing headlong from her chair, she flung the ball on my knees and ran out.

I also rose, and, laying the skein of wool on the window-sill, went into the drawing-room, and stopped short in amazement. In the centre of the room lay a kitten with outstretched paws:

Zinaida was kneeling in front of it, and carefully raising its snout. By the side of the young Princess, taking up nearly the entire wall-space between the windows, was visible a fair-complexioned, curly-haired young man, a hussar, with a rosy face and protruding eyes.

"How ridiculous!"—Zinaida kept repeating:—"and its eyes are not grey, but green, and what big ears it has! Thank you, Viktor Egoritch! you are very kind."

The hussar, in whom I recognized one of the young men whom I had seen on the preceding evening, smiled and bowed, clicking his spurs and clanking the links of his sword as he did so.

"You were pleased to say yesterday that you wished to possess a striped kitten with large ears . . . . so I have got it, madam. Your word is my law."—And again he bowed.

The kitten mewed faintly, and began to sniff at the floor.

"He is hungry!"—cried Zinaida.—"Vonifaty! Sonya! bring some milk."

The chambermaid, in an old yellow gown and with a faded kerchief on her head, entered with a saucer of milk in her hand, and placed it in front of the kitten. The kitten quivered, blinked, and began to lap.

"What a rosy tongue it has,"—remarked Zinaida, bending her head down almost to the floor, and looking sideways at it, under its very nose.

The kitten drank its fill, and began to purr, affectedly contracting and relaxing its paws. Zinaida rose to her feet, and turning to the maid, said indifferently:—"Take it away."

"Your hand—in return for the kitten,"—said the hussar, displaying his teeth, and bending over the whole of his huge body, tightly confined in a new uniform.

"Both hands,"—replied Zinaida, offering him her hands. While he was kissing them, she gazed at me over his shoulder.

I stood motionless on one spot, and did not know whether to laugh or to say something, or to hold my peace. Suddenly, through the open door of the anteroom, the figure of our footman, Feodor, caught my eye. He was making signs to me. I mechanically went out to him.

"What dost thou want?"—I asked.

"Your mamma has sent for you,"—he said in a whisper.—"She is angry because you do not return with an answer."

"Why, have I been here long?"

"More than an hour."

"More than an hour!"—I repeated involuntarily, and returning to the drawing-room, I began to bow and scrape my foot.

"Where are you going?"—the young Princess asked me, with a glance at the hussar.

"I must go home, madam. So I am to say,"—I added, addressing the old woman,—"that you will call upon us at two o'clock."

"Say that, my dear fellow."

The old Princess hurriedly drew out her snuff-box, and took a pinch so noisily that I fairly jumped.—"Say that,"—she repeated, tearfully blinking and grunting.

I bowed once more, turned and left the room with the same sensation of awkwardness in my back which a very young man experiences when he knows that people are staring after him.

"Look here, M'sieu Voldemar, you must drop in to see us,"—called Zinaida, and again burst out laughing.

"What makes her laugh all the time?" I thought, as I wended my way home accompanied by Feodor, who said nothing to me, but moved along disapprovingly behind me. My mother reproved me, and inquired, with surprise, "What could I have been doing so long at the Princess's?" I made her no answer, and went off to my own room. I had suddenly grown very melancholy. . . . I tried not to weep. . . . I was jealous of the hussar.

5

THE Princess, according to her promise, called on my mother, and did not please her. I was not present at their meeting, but at table my mother narrated to my father that that Princess Zasyekin seemed to her a *femme très vulgaire*; that she had bored her immensely with her requests that she would intervene on her behalf with Prince Sergyei; that she was always having such law-suits and affairs,—*de vilaines affaires d'argent*,—and that she must be a great rogue. But my mother added that she had invited her with her daughter to dine on the following day (on hearing the words "with her daughter," I dropped my nose into my plate),—because, notwithstanding, she was a neighbor, and with a name. Thereupon my father informed my mother that he now recalled who the lady was: that in his youth he had known the late Prince Zasyekin, a capitally-educated but flighty and captious man; that in society he was called *"le Parisien,"* because of his long residence in Paris; that he had been very wealthy, but had gambled away all his property —and, no one knew why, though probably it had been for the sake of the money,—"although he might have made a better choice,"—added my father, with a cold smile,—he had married the daughter of some clerk in a chancellery, and after his marriage had gone into speculation, and ruined himself definitively.

" 'Tis a wonder she did not try to borrow money,"—remarked my mother.

"She is very likely to do it,"—said my father, calmly.—"Does she speak French?"

"Very badly."

"M-m-m. However, that makes no difference. I think thou saidst that thou hadst invited her daughter; some one assured me that she is a very charming and well-educated girl."

"Ah! Then she does not take after her mother."

"Nor after her father,"—returned my father.—"He was also well educated, but stupid."

My mother sighed, and became thoughtful. My father relapsed into silence. I felt very awkward during the course of that conversation.

After dinner I betook myself to the garden, but without my gun. I had pledged my word to myself that I would not go near the "Zasyekin garden"; but an irresistible force drew me thither, and not in vain. I had no sooner approached the fence than I caught sight of Zinaida. This time she was alone. She was holding a small book in her hands and strolling slowly along the path. She did not notice me. I came near letting her slip past; but suddenly caught myself up and coughed.

She turned round but did not pause, put aside with one hand the broad blue ribbon of her round straw hat, looked at me, smiled quietly, and again riveted her eyes on her book.

I pulled off my cap, and after fidgeting about a while on one spot, I went away with a heavy heart. *"Que suis-je pour elle?"*—I thought (God knows why) in French.

Familiar footsteps resounded behind me; I glanced round and beheld my father advancing toward me with swift, rapid strides.

"Is that the young Princess?"—he asked me.

"Yes."

"Dost thou know her?"

"I saw her this morning at the Princess her mother's."

My father halted and, wheeling abruptly round on his heels, retraced his steps. As he came on a level with Zinaida he bowed courteously to her. She bowed to him in return, not without some surprise on her face, and lowered her book. I saw that she followed him with her eyes. My father always dressed very elegantly, originally and simply; but his figure had never seemed to me more graceful, never had his grey hat sat more handsomely on his curls, which were barely beginning to grow thin.

I was on the point of directing my course toward Zinaida, but she did not even look at me, but raised her book once more and walked away.

6

I SPENT the whole of that evening and the following day in a sort of gloomy stupor. I remember that I made an effort to work, and took up Kaidanoff; but in vain did the large-printed lines and pages of the famous text-book flit before my eyes. Ten times in succession I read the words: "Julius Cæsar was distinguished for military daring," without understanding a word, and I flung aside my book. Before dinner I pomaded my hair again, and again donned my frock-coat and neckerchief.

"What's that for?"—inquired my mother.—"Thou art not a student yet, and God knows whether thou wilt pass thy examination. And thy round-jacket was made not very long ago. Thou must not discard it!"

"There are to be guests,"—I whispered, almost in despair.

"What nonsense! What sort of guests are they?"

I was compelled to submit. I exchanged my coat for my round-jacket, but did not remove my neckerchief. The Princess and her daughter made their appearance half an hour before dinner; the old woman had thrown a yellow shawl over her green gown, with which I was familiar, and had donned an old-fashioned mob-cap with ribbons of a fiery hue. She immediately began to talk about her notes of hand, to sigh and to bewail her poverty, and to "importune," but did not stand in the least upon ceremony; and she took snuff noisily and fidgeted and wriggled in her chair as before. It never seemed to enter her head that she was a Princess. On the other hand, Zinaida bore herself very stiffly, almost haughtily, like a real young Princess. Cold impassivity and dignity had made their appearance on her countenance, and I did not recognize her,—did not recognize her looks or her smile, although in this new aspect she seemed to me very beautiful. She wore a thin barège gown with pale-blue figures; her hair fell in long curls along her cheeks, in the English fashion: this coiffure suited the cold expression of her face.

My father sat beside her during dinner, and with the exquisite and imperturbable courtesy which was characteristic of him, showed attention to his neighbor. He glanced at her from time to time, and she glanced at him now and then, but in such a strange, almost hostile, manner. Their conversation proceeded in French;—I remember that I was surprised at the purity of Zinaida's accent. The old Princess, as before, did not restrain herself in the slightest degree during dinner, but ate a great deal and praised the food. My mother evidently found her wearisome, and answered her with a sort of sad indifference; my father contracted his brows in a slight frown from time to time. My mother did not like Zinaida either.

"She's a haughty young sprig,"—she said the next day.—"And when one comes to think of it, what is there for her to be proud of?—*avec sa mine de grisette!*"

"Evidently, thou hast not seen any grisettes,"—my father remarked to her.

"Of course I haven't, God be thanked! . . . . Only, how art thou capable of judging of them?"

Zinaida paid absolutely no attention whatever to me. Soon after dinner the old Princess began to take her leave.

"I shall rely upon your protection, Marya Nikolaevna and Piotr Vasilievitch,"—she said, in a sing-song tone, to my father and mother.—"What is to be done! I have seen prosperous days, but they are gone. Here am I a Radiance,"—she added, with an unpleasant laugh,—"but what's the good of an honor when you've nothing to eat?"—My father bowed respectfully to her and escorted her to the door of the anteroom. I was standing there in my round-jacket, and staring at the floor, as though condemned to death. Zinaida's behavior toward me had definitively annihilated me. What, then, was my amazement when, as she passed me, she whispered to me hastily, and with her former affectionate expression in her eyes:—"Come to us at eight o'clock, do you hear? without fail. . . ." I merely threw my hands apart in amazement;—but she was already retreating, having thrown a white scarf over her head.

7

PRECISELY at eight o'clock I entered the tiny wing inhabited by the Princess, clad in my coat, and with my hair brushed up into a crest on top of my head. The old servant glared surlily at me, and rose reluctantly from his bench. Merry voices resounded in the drawing-room. I opened the door and retreated a pace in aston-

ishment. In the middle of the room, on a chair, stood the young
Princess, holding a man's hat in front of her; around the chair
thronged five men. They were trying to dip their hands into the
hat, but she kept raising it on high and shaking it violently. On
catching sight of me she exclaimed:—

"Stay, stay! Here's a new guest; he must be given a ticket,"—
and springing lightly from the chair, she seized me by the lapel of
my coat.—"Come along,"—said she;—"why do you stand there?
Messieurs, allow me to make you acquainted: this is Monsieur
Voldemar, the son of our neighbor. And this,"—she added, turning to me, and pointing to the visitors in turn,—"is Count Malevsky, Doctor Lushin, the poet Maidanoff, retired Captain Nirmatzky, and Byelovzoroff the hussar, whom you have already seen.
I beg that you will love and favor each other."

I was so confused that I did not even bow to any one; in Doctor
Lushin I recognized that same swarthy gentleman who had so ruthlessly put me to shame in the garden; the others were strangers to
me.

"Count!"—pursued Zinaida,—"write a ticket for M'sieu Voldemar."

"That is unjust,"—returned the Count, with a slight accent,—a
very handsome and foppishly-attired man, with a dark complexion, expressive brown eyes, a thin, white little nose, and a
slender moustache over his tiny mouth.—"He has not been playing at forfeits with us."

" 'Tis unjust,"—repeated Byelovzoroff and the gentleman who
had been alluded to as the retired Captain,—a man of forty, horribly pock-marked, curly-haired as a negro, round-shouldered, bow-
legged, and dressed in a military coat without epaulets, worn open
on the breast.

"Write a ticket, I tell you,"—repeated the Princess.—"What
sort of a rebellion is this? M'sieu Voldemar is with us for the first
time, and to-day no law applies to him. No grumbling—write; I
will have it so."

The Count shrugged his shoulders, but submissively bowing his head, he took a pen in his white, ring-decked hand, tore off a scrap of paper and began to write on it.

"Permit me at least to explain to M'sieu Voldemar what it is all about,"—began Lushin, in a bantering tone;—"otherwise he will be utterly at a loss. You see, young man, we are playing at forfeits; the Princess must pay a fine, and the one who draws out the lucky ticket must kiss her hand. Do you understand what I have told you?"

I merely glanced at him and continued to stand as though in a fog, while the Princess again sprang upon the chair and again began to shake the hat. All reached up to her—I among the rest.

"Maidanoff,"—said the Princess to the tall young man with a gaunt face, tiny mole-like eyes and extremely long, black hair,— "you, as a poet, ought to be magnanimous and surrender your ticket to M'sieu Voldemar, so that he may have two chances instead of one."

But Maidanoff shook his head in refusal and tossed his hair. I put in my hand into the hat after all the rest, drew out and unfolded a ticket. . . . O Lord! what were my sensations when I beheld on it, "Kiss!"

"Kiss!"—I cried involuntarily.

"Bravo! He has won,"—chimed in the Princess.—"How delighted I am!"—She descended from the chair, and gazed into my eyes so clearly and sweetly that my heart fairly laughed with joy.— "And are you glad?"—she asked me.

"I?" . . . I stammered.

"Sell me your ticket,"—suddenly blurted out Byelovzoroff, right in my ear.—"I'll give you one hundred rubles for it."

I replied to the hussar by such a wrathful look that Zinaida clapped her hands, and Lushin cried:—"That's a gallant fellow!"

"But,"—he went on,—"in my capacity of master of ceremonies, I am bound to see that all the regulations are carried out. M'sieu Voldemar, get down on one knee. That is our rule."

Zinaida stood before me with her head bent a little to one side, as though the better to scrutinize me, and offered me her hand with dignity. Things grew dim before my eyes; I tried to get down on one knee, plumped down on both knees, and applied my lips to Zinaida's fingers in so awkward a manner that I scratched the tip of my nose slightly on her nails.

"Good!"—shouted Lushin, and helped me to rise.

The game of forfeits continued. Zinaida placed me beside her. What penalties they did invent! Among other things, she had to impersonate a "statue"—and she selected as a pedestal the monstrously homely Nirmatzky, ordering him to lie flat on the floor, and to tuck his face into his breast. The laughter did not cease for a single moment. All this noise and uproar, this unceremonious, almost tumultuous merriment, these unprecedented relations with strangers, fairly flew to my head; for I was a boy who had been reared soberly, and in solitude, and had grown up in a stately home of gentry. I became simply intoxicated, as though with wine. I began to shout with laughter and chatter more loudly than the rest, so that even the old Princess, who was sitting in the adjoining room with some sort of pettifogger from the Iversky Gate[1] who had been summoned for a conference, came out to take a look at me. But I felt so happy that, as the saying is, I didn't care a farthing for anybody's ridicule, or anybody's oblique glances.

Zinaida continued to display a preference for me and never let me leave her side. In one forfeit I was made to sit by her, covered up with one and the same silk kerchief: I was bound to tell her *my secret*. I remember how our two heads found themselves suddenly in choking, semitransparent, fragrant gloom; how near and softly her eyes sparkled in that gloom, and how hotly her parted lips breathed; and her teeth were visible, and the tips of her hair tickled and burned me. I maintained silence. She smiled mysteriously and slyly, and at last whispered to me: "Well, what is it?" But I merely flushed and laughed, and turned away, and could hardly draw my breath. We got tired of forfeits, and began to play "string." Good heavens! what rapture I felt when, forgetting myself with gaping, I received from her a strong, sharp rap on my fingers;

[1] The famous gate from the "White town" into the "China town," in Moscow, where there is a renowned holy picture of the Iberian Virgin, in a chapel. Evidently the lawyers' quarter was in this vicinity.—TRANSLATOR.

and how afterward I tried to pretend that I was yawning with in-
attention, but she mocked at me and did not touch my hands,
which were awaiting the blow!

But what a lot of other pranks we played that same evening!
We played on the piano, and sang, and danced, and represented
a gipsy camp. We dressed Nirmatzky up like a bear, and fed him
with water and salt. Count Malevsky showed us several card tricks,
and ended by stacking the cards and dealing himself all the trumps
at whist; upon which Lushin "had the honor of congratulating
him." Maidanoff declaimed to us fragments from his poem, "The
Murderer" (this occurred in the very thick of romanticism), which
he intended to publish in a black binding, with the title in letters
of the color of blood. We stole his hat from the knees of the pettifogger from the Iversky Gate, and made him dance the kazak
dance by way of redeeming it. We dressed old Vonifaty up in a
mob-cap, and the young Princess put on a man's hat. . . . It is impossible to recount all we did. Byelovzoroff alone remained most
of the time in a corner, angry and frowning. . . . Sometimes his
eyes became suffused with blood, he grew scarlet all over and
seemed to be on the very point of swooping down upon all of us
and scattering us on all sides, like chips; but the Princess glanced
at him, menaced him with her finger, and again he retired into
his corner.

We were completely exhausted at last. The old Princess was
equal to anything, as she put it,—no shouts disconcerted her,—but
she felt tired and wished to rest. At midnight supper was served,
consisting of a bit of old, dry cheese and a few cold patties filled
with minced ham, which seemed to us more savory than any
pasty; there was only one bottle of wine, and that was rather
queer:—dark, with a swollen neck, and the wine in it left an after-
taste of pinkish dye; however, no one drank it. Weary and happy
to exhaustion, I emerged from the wing; a thunder-storm seemed
to be brewing; the black storm-clouds grew larger and crept across
the sky, visibly altering their smoky outlines. A light breeze was uneasily quivering in the dark trees, and somewhere beyond the hori-

zon the thunder was growling angrily and dully, as though to itself.

I made my way through the back door to my room. My nurse-valet was sleeping on the floor and I was obliged to step over him; he woke up, saw me, and reported that my mother was angry with me, and had wanted to send after me again, but that my father had restrained her. I never went to bed without having bidden my mother good night and begged her blessing. There was no help for it! I told my valet that I would undress myself and go to bed unaided,—and extinguished the candle. But I did not undress and I did not go to bed.

I seated myself on a chair and sat there for a long time, as thought enchanted. That which I felt was so new and so sweet . . . . . I sat there, hardly looking around me and without moving, breathing slowly, and only laughing silently now, as I recalled, now inwardly turning cold at the thought that I was in love, that here it was, that love. Zinaida's face floated softly before me in the darkness—floated, but did not float away; her lips still smiled as mysteriously as ever, her eyes gazed somewhat askance at me, interrogatively, thoughtfully and tenderly . . . . as at the moment when I had parted from her. At last I rose on tiptoe, stepped to my bed and cautiously, without undressing, laid my head on the pillow, as though endeavoring by the sharp movement to frighten off that wherewith I was filled to overflowing. . . .

I lay down, but did not even close an eye. I speedily perceived that certain faint reflections kept constantly falling into my room. . . . . I raised myself and looked out of the window. Its frame was distinctly defined from the mysteriously and confusedly whitened panes. " 'Tis the thunder-storm,"—I thought,—and so, in fact, there was a thunder-storm; but it had passed very far away, so that even the claps of thunder were not audible; only in the sky long, indistinct, branching flashes of lightning, as it were, were uninterruptedly flashing up. They were not flashing up so much as they were quivering and twitching, like the wing of a dying bird. I rose, went to the window, and stood there until morning. . . . The lightning-flashes never ceased for a moment; it was what is called a pitch-black night. I gazed at the dumb, sandy plain, at the dark mass of the Neskutchny Park, at the yellowish façades of the distant buildings, which also seemed to be trembling at every faint flash. . . . I gazed, and could not tear myself away; those dumb lightning-flashes, those restrained gleams, seemed to be responding to the dumb and secret outbursts which were flaring up within me also. Morning began to break; the dawn started forth in scarlet patches. With the approach of the sun the lightning-flashes grew paler and paler; they quivered more and more infrequently, and vanished at last, drowned in the sobering and unequivocal light of the breaking day.

And my lightning-flashes vanished within me also. I felt great fatigue and tranquillity . . . but Zinaida's image continued to hover triumphantly over my soul. Only it, that image, seemed calm; like a flying swan from the marshy sedges, it separated itself from the other ignoble figures which surrounded it, and as I fell asleep, I bowed down before it for the last time in farewell and confiding adoration. . . .

Oh, gentle emotions, soft sounds, kindness and calming of the deeply-moved soul, melting joy of the first feelings of love,—where are ye, where are ye?

8

ON THE following morning, when I went downstairs to tea, my mother scolded me,—although less than I had anticipated,—and made me narrate how I had spent the preceding evening. I answered her in few words, omitting many particulars and endeavoring to impart to my narrative the most innocent of aspects.

"Nevertheless, they are not people *comme il faut*,"—remarked my mother;—"and I do not wish thee to run after them, instead of preparing thyself for the examination, and occupying thyself."

As I knew that my mother's anxiety was confined to these few words, I did not consider it necessary to make her any reply; but after tea my father linked his arm in mine, and betaking himself to the garden with me, made me tell him everything I had done and seen at the Zasyekins'.

My father possessed a strange influence over me, and our relations were strange. He paid hardly any attention to my education, but he never wounded me; he respected my liberty—he was even, if I may so express it, courteous to me . . . . only, he did not allow me to get close to him. I loved him, I admired him; he seemed to me a model man; and great heavens! how passionately attached to him I should have been, had I not constantly felt his hand warding me off! On the other hand, when he wished, he understood how to evoke in me, instantaneously, with one word, one movement, unbounded confidence in him. My soul opened, I chatted with him as with an intelligent friend, as with an indulgent preceptor . . . . then, with equal suddenness, he abandoned me, and again his hand repulsed me, caressingly and softly, but repulsed nevertheless.

Sometimes a fit of mirth came over him, and then he was ready to frolic and play with me like a boy (he was fond of every sort of energetic bodily exercise); once—only once—did he caress me with so much tenderness that I came near bursting into tears. . . . But his mirth and tenderness also vanished without leaving a trace, and what had taken place between us gave me no hopes for the future; it was just as though I had seen it all in a dream. I used to stand and scrutinize his clever, handsome, brilliant face . . . . and my heart would begin to quiver, and my whole being would yearn toward him, ... and he would seem to feel what was going on within me, and would pat me on the cheek in passing—and either go away, or begin to occupy himself with something, or suddenly freeze all over,—as he alone knew how to freeze,—and I would immediately shrivel up and grow frigid also. His rare fits of affection for me were never called forth by my speechless but intelligible entreaties; they always came upon him without warning. When meditating, in after years, upon my father's character, I came to the conclusion that he did not care for me or for family life; he loved something different, and enjoyed that other thing to the full. "Seize what thou canst thyself, and do not give thyself into any one's power; the whole art of life consists in belonging to one's self,"—he said to me once. On another occasion I, in my capacity of a young democrat, launched out in his presence into arguments about liberty (he was what I called "kind" that day; at such times one could say whatever one liked to him).—"Liberty,"—he repeated,—"but dost thou know what can give a man liberty?"

"What?"

"Will, his own will, and the power which it gives is better than liberty. Learn to will, and thou wilt be free, and wilt command."

My father wished, first of all and most of all, to enjoy life—and he did enjoy life. . . . . Perhaps he had a presentiment that he was not fated long to take advantage of the "art" of living: he died at the age of forty-two.

I described to my father in detail my visit to the Zasyekins. He listened to me half-attentively, half-abstractedly, as he sat on the bench and drew figures on the sand with the tip of his riding-whip. Now and then he laughed, glanced at me in a brilliant, amused sort of way, and spurred me on by brief questions and exclamations. At first I could not bring myself even to utter Zinaida's name, but I could not hold out, and began to laud her. My father still continued to laugh. Then he became thoughtful, dropped his eyes and rose to his feet.

I recalled the fact that, as he came out of the house, he had given orders that his horse should be saddled. He was a capital rider, and knew much better how to tame the wildest horses than did Mr. Rarey.

"Shall I ride with thee, papa?"—I asked him.

"No,"—he replied, and his face assumed its habitual indifferently-caressing expression.—"Go alone, if thou wishest; but tell the coachman that I shall not go."

He turned his back on me and walked swiftly away. I followed him with my eyes, until he disappeared beyond the gate. I saw his hat moving along the fence; he went into the Zasyekins' house.

He remained with them no more than an hour, but immediately thereafter went off to town and did not return home until evening.

After dinner I went to the Zasyekins' myself. I found no one in the drawing-room but the old Princess. When she saw me, she scratched her head under her cap with the end of her knitting-needle, and suddenly asked me: would I copy a petition for her?

"With pleasure,"—I replied, and sat down on the edge of a chair.

"Only look out, and see that you make the letters as large as possible,"—said the Princess, handing me a sheet of paper scrawled over in a slovenly manner:—"and couldn't you do it today, my dear fellow?"

"I will copy it this very day, madam."

The door of the adjoining room opened a mere crack and Zinaida's face showed itself in the aperture,—pale, thoughtful, with hair thrown carelessly back. She stared at me with her large, cold eyes, and softly shut the door.

"Zina,—hey there, Zina!"—said the old woman. Zinaida did not answer. I carried away the old woman's petition, and sat over it the whole evening.

9

My "PASSION" began with that day. I remember that I then felt something of that which a man must feel when he enters the service: I had already ceased to be a young lad; I was in love. I have said that my passion dated from that day; I might have added that my sufferings also dated from that day. I languished when absent from Zinaida; my mind would not work, everything fell from my hands; I thought intently of her for days together. . . . I languished . . . . but in her presence I was no more at ease. I was jealous, I recognized my insignificance, I stupidly sulked and stupidly fawned; and nevertheless, an irresistible force drew me to her, and every time I stepped across the threshold of her room, it

was with an involuntary thrill of happiness. Zinaida immediately
divined that I had fallen in love with her, and I never thought of
concealing the fact; she mocked at my passion, played tricks on
me, petted and tormented me. It is sweet to be the sole source, the
autocratic and irresponsible cause of the greatest joys and the pro-
foundest woe to another person, and I was like soft wax in Zinaida's
hands. However, I was not the only one who was in love with her;
all the men who were in the habit of visiting her house were crazy
over her, and she kept them all in a leash at her feet. It amused
her to arouse in them now hopes, now fears, to twist them about at
her caprice—(she called it, "knocking people against one another"),—and they never thought of resisting, and willingly sub-
mitted to her. In all her vivacious and beautiful being there was a
certain peculiarly bewitching mixture of guilefulness and heedless-
ness, of artificiality and simplicity, of tranquillity and playfulness;
over everything she did or said, over her every movement, hovered
a light, delicate charm, and an original, sparkling force made itself
felt in everything. And her face was incessantly changing and
sparkling also; it expressed almost simultaneously derision, pensiveness, and passion. The most varied emotions, light, fleeting as the
shadows of the clouds on a sunny, windy day, kept flitting over
her eyes and lips.

Every one of her adorers was necessary to her. Byelovzoroff,
whom she sometimes called "my wild beast," and sometimes
simply "my own," would gladly have flung himself into the fire for
her; without trusting to his mental capacities and other merits, he
kept proposing that he should marry her, and hinting that the
others were merely talking idly. Maidanoff responded to the poetical chords of her soul: a rather cold man, as nearly all writers are,
he assured her with intense force—and perhaps himself also—that
he adored her. He sang her praises in interminable verses and read
them to her with an unnatural and a genuine sort of enthusiasm.
And she was interested in him and jeered lightly at him; she did
not believe in him greatly, and after listening to his effusions she
made him read Pushkin, in order, as she said, to purify the air.
Lushin, the sneering doctor, who was cynical in speech, knew her

best of all and loved her best of all, although he abused her to her face and behind her back. She respected him, but would not let him go, and sometimes, with a peculiar, malicious pleasure, made him feel that he was in her hands. "I am a coquette, I am heartless, I have the nature of an actress," she said to him one day in my presence; "and 'tis well! So give me your hand and I will stick a pin into it, and you will feel ashamed before this young man, and it will hurt you; but nevertheless, Mr. Upright Man, you will be so good as to laugh." Lushin flushed crimson, turned away and bit his lips, but ended by putting out his hand. She pricked it, and he actually did break out laughing . . . . and she laughed also, thrusting the pin in pretty deeply and gazing into his eyes while he vainly endeavored to glance aside. . . .

I understood least of all the relations existing between Zinaida and Count Malevsky. That he was handsome, adroit, and clever even I felt, but the presence in him of some false, dubious element, was palpable even to me, a lad of sixteen, and I was amazed that Zinaida did not notice it. But perhaps she did detect that false element and it did not repel her. An irregular education, strange acquaintances, the constant presence of her mother, the poverty and disorder in the house—all this, beginning with the very freedom which the young girl enjoyed, together with the consciousness of her own superiority to the people who surrounded her, had developed in her a certain half-scornful carelessness and lack of exaction. No matter what happened—whether Vonifaty came to report that there was no sugar, or some wretched bit of gossip came to light, or the visitors got into a quarrel among themselves, she merely shook her curls, and said: "Nonsense!"—and grieved very little over it.

On the contrary, all my blood would begin to seethe when Malevsky would approach her, swaying his body cunningly like a fox, lean elegantly over the back of her chair and begin to whisper in her ear with a conceited and challenging smile, while she would fold her arms on her breast, gaze attentively at him and smile also, shaking her head the while.

"What possesses you to receive Malevsky?"—I asked her one day.

"Why, he has such handsome eyes,"—she replied.—"But that is no business of yours."

"You are not to think that I am in love with him,"—she said to me on another occasion.—"No; I cannot love people upon whom I am forced to look down. I must have some one who can subdue me. . . . And I shall not hit upon such an one, for God is merciful! I shall not spare any one who falls into my paws—no, no!"

"Do you mean to say that you will never fall in love?"

"And how about you? Don't I love you?"—she said, tapping me on the nose with the tip of her glove.

Yes, Zinaida made great fun of me. For the space of three weeks I saw her every day; and what was there that she did not do to me! She came to us rarely, but I did not regret that; in our house she was converted into a young lady, a Princess,—and I avoided her. I was afraid of betraying myself to my mother; she was not at all well disposed toward Zinaida, and kept a disagreeable watch on us. I was not so much afraid of my father; he did not appear to notice me, and talked little with her, but that little in a peculiarly clever and significant manner. I ceased to work, to read; I even ceased to stroll about the environs and to ride on horseback. Like a beetle tied by the leg, I hovered incessantly around the beloved wing; I believe I would have liked to remain there forever . . . . but that was impossible. My mother grumbled at me, and sometimes Zinaida herself drove me out. On such occasions I shut myself up in my own room, or walked off to the very end of the garden, climbed upon the sound remnant of a tall stone hothouse, and dangling my legs over the wall, I sat there for hours and stared,—stared without seeing anything. White butterflies lazily flitted among the nettles beside me; an audacious sparrow perched not far off on the half-demolished red bricks and twittered in an irritating manner, incessantly twisting his whole body about and spreading out his tail; the still distrustful crows now and then emitted a caw, as they sat high, high above me on the naked crest of a birch-tree; the sun and the wind played softly through its sparse branches; the chiming of the bells, calm and melancholy, at the Don Monastery was wafted to me now and then,—and I sat on, gazing and listening, and became filled with a certain nameless sensation which embraced everything: sadness and joy, and a presentiment of the future, and the desire and the fear of life. But I understood nothing at the time of all that which was fermenting within me, or I would have called it all by one name, the name of Zinaida.

But Zinaida continued to play with me as a cat plays with a mouse. Now she coquetted with me, and I grew agitated and melted with emotion; now she repulsed me, and I dared not approach her, dared not look at her.

I remember that she was very cold toward me for several days in succession and I thoroughly quailed, and when I timidly ran to the wing to see them, I tried to keep near the old Princess, despite the fact that she was scolding and screaming a great deal just at that time: her affairs connected with her notes of hand were going badly, and she had also had two scenes with the police-captain of the precinct.

One day I was walking through the garden, past the familiar fence, when I caught sight of Zinaida. Propped up on both arms, she was sitting motionless on the grass. I tried to withdraw cautiously, but she suddenly raised her head and made an imperious sign to me. I became petrified on the spot; I did not understand her the first time. She repeated her sign. I immediately sprang over the fence and ran joyfully to her; but she stopped me with a look and pointed to the path a couple of paces from her. In my confusion, not knowing what to do, I knelt down on the edge of the path. She was so pale, such bitter grief, such profound weariness were revealed in her every feature, that my heart contracted within me, and I involuntarily murmured: "What is the matter with you?"

Zinaida put out her hand, plucked a blade of grass, bit it, and tossed it away as far as she could.

"Do you love me very much?"—she inquired suddenly.—"Yes?"

I made no answer,—and what answer was there for me to make?

"Yes,"—she repeated, gazing at me as before.—"It is so. They are the same eyes,"—she added, becoming pensive, and covering her face with her hands.—"Everything has become repulsive to me,"—she whispered;—"I would like to go to the end of the world; I cannot endure this, I cannot reconcile myself. . . . And what is in store for me? . . . . Akh, I am heavy at heart . . . . my God, how heavy at heart!"

"Why?"—I timidly inquired.

Zinaida did not answer me and merely shrugged her shoulders. I continued to kneel and to gaze at her with profound melancholy. Every word of hers fairly cut me to the heart. At that moment, I think I would willingly have given my life to keep her from grieving. I gazed at her, and nevertheless, not understanding why she was heavy at heart, I vividly pictured to myself how, in a fit of uncontrollable sorrow, she had suddenly gone into the garden, and had fallen on the earth, as though she had been mowed down. All around was bright and green; the breeze was rustling in the foliage of the trees, now and then rocking a branch of raspberry over Zinaida's head. Doves were cooing somewhere and the bees were humming as they flew low over the scanty grass. Overhead the sky shone blue,—but I was so sad. . . . .

"Recite some poetry to me,"—said Zinaida in a low voice, leaning on her elbow.—"I like to hear you recite verses. You make them go in a sing-song, but that does not matter, it is youthful. Recite to me: 'On the Hills of Georgia.'—Only, sit down first."

I sat down and recited, "On the Hills of Georgia."

" 'That it is impossible not to love,' "—repeated Zinaida.—"That is why poetry is so nice; it says to us that which does not exist, and which is not only better than what does exist, but even more like the truth. . . . " 'That it is impossible not to love'?—I would like to, but cannot!"—Again she fell silent for a space, then suddenly started and rose to her feet.—"Come along. Maidanoff is sitting with mamma; he brought his poem to me, but I left him. He also is embittered now . . . . how can it be helped? Some day you will find out . . . . but you must not be angry with me!"

Zinaida hastily squeezed my hand, and ran on ahead. We returned to the wing. Maidanoff set to reading us his poem of "The Murderer," which had only just been printed, but I did not listen. He shrieked out his four-footed iambics in a sing-song voice; the rhymes alternated and jingled like sleigh-bells, hollow and loud; but I kept staring all the while at Zinaida, and striving to understand the meaning of her strange words.

> "Or, perchance, a secret rival
> Has unexpectedly subjugated thee?"

suddenly exclaimed Maidanoff through his nose—and my eyes and Zinaida's met. She dropped hers and blushed faintly. I saw that she was blushing, and turned cold with fright. I had been jealous before, but only at that moment did the thought that she had fallen in love flash through my mind. "My God! She is in love!"

10

My real tortures began from that moment. I cudgelled my brains, I pondered and pondered again, and watched Zinaida importunately, but secretly, as far as possible. A change had taken place in her, that was evident. She took to going off alone to walk, and walked a long while. Sometimes she did not show herself to her visitors; she sat for hours together in her chamber. This had not been her habit hitherto. Suddenly I became—or it seemed to me that I became—extremely penetrating. "Is it he? Or is it not he?"—I asked myself, as in trepidation I mentally ran from one of her admirers to another. Count Malevsky (although I felt ashamed to admit it for Zinaida's sake) privately seemed to me more dangerous than the others.

My powers of observation extended no further than the end of my own nose, and my dissimulation probably failed to deceive any one; at all events, Doctor Lushin speedily saw through me. Moreover, he also had undergone a change of late; he had grown thin, he laughed as frequently as ever, but somehow it was in a duller, more spiteful, a briefer way;—an involuntary, nervous irritability had replaced his former light irony and feigned cynicism.

"Why are you forever tagging on here, young man?"—he said to me one day, when he was left alone with me in the Zasyekins' drawing-room. (The young Princess had not yet returned from her stroll and the shrill voice of the old Princess was resounding in the upper story; she was wrangling with her maid.)—"You ought to be studying your lessons, working while you are young;—but instead of that, what are you doing?"

"You cannot tell whether I work at home,"—I retorted not without arrogance, but also not without confusion.

"Much work you do! That's not what you have in your head. Well, I will not dispute . . . at your age, that is in the natural order of things. But your choice is far from a happy one. Can't you see what sort of a house this is?"

"I do not understand you,"—I remarked.

"You don't understand me? So much the worse for you. I regard it as my duty to warn you. Fellows like me, old bachelors, may sit here: what harm will it do us? We are a hardened lot. You can't pierce our hide, but your skin is still tender; the air here is injurious for you,—believe me, you may become infected."

"How so?"

"Because you may. Are you healthy now? Are you in a normal condition? Is what you are feeling useful to you, good for you?"

"But what am I feeling?"—said I;—and in my secret soul I admitted that the doctor was right.

"Eh, young man, young man,"—pursued the doctor, with an expression as though something extremely insulting to me were contained in those two words;—"there's no use in your dissimulating, for what you have in your soul you still show in your face, thank God! But what's the use of arguing? I would not come hither myself, if . . . ." (the doctor set his teeth) . . . . "if I were not such an eccentric fellow. Only this is what amazes me—how you, with your intelligence, can fail to see what is going on around you."

"But what is going on?"—I interposed, pricking up my ears.

The doctor looked at me with a sort of sneering compassion.

"A nice person I am,"—said he, as though speaking to himself. —"What possessed me to say that to him. In a word,"—he added, raising his voice,—"I repeat to you: the atmosphere here is not good for you. You find it pleasant here, and no wonder! And the scent of a hot-house is pleasant also—but one cannot live in it! Hey! hearken to me,—set to work again on Kadianoff."

The old Princess entered and began to complain to the doctor of toothache. Then Zinaida made her appearance.

"Here,"—added the old Princess,—"scold her, doctor, do. She drinks iced water all day long; is that healthy for her, with her weak chest?"

"Why do you do that?"—inquired Lushin.

"But what result can it have?"

"What result? You may take cold and die."

"Really? Is it possible? Well, all right—that just suits me!"

"You don't say so!"—growled the doctor. The old Princess went away.

"I do say so,"—retorted Zinaida.—"Is living such a cheerful thing? Look about you . . . Well—is it nice? Or do you think that I do not understand it, do not feel it? It affords me pleasure to drink iced water, and you can seriously assure me that such a life is worth too much for me to imperil it for a moment's pleasure— I do not speak of happiness."

"Well, yes,"—remarked Lushin:—"caprice and independence. . . . Those two words sum you up completely; your whole nature lies in those two words."

Zinaida burst into a nervous laugh.

"You're too late by one mail, my dear doctor. You observe badly; you are falling behind.—Put on your spectacles.—I am in no mood for caprices now; how jolly to play pranks on you or on myself!—and as for independence. . . . M'sieu Voldemar,"— added Zinaida, suddenly stamping her foot,—"don't wear a melancholy face. I cannot endure to have people commiserating me."— She hastily withdrew.

"This atmosphere is injurious, injurious to you, young man,"— said Lushin to me once more.

ON THE evening of that same day the customary visitors assembled at the Zasyekins'; I was among the number.

The conversation turned on Maidanoff's poem; Zinaida candidly praised it.—"But do you know what?"—she said:—"If I were a poet, I would select other subjects. Perhaps this is all nonsense, but strange thoughts sometimes come into my head, especially when I am wakeful toward morning, when the sky is beginning to turn pink and grey.—I would, for example . . . You will not laugh at me?"

"No! No!"—we all exclaimed with one voice.

"I would depict,"—she went on, crossing her arms on her breast, and turning her eyes aside,—"a whole company of young girls, by night, in a big boat, on a tranquil river. The moon is shining, and they are all in white and wear garlands of white flowers, and they are singing, you know, something in the nature of a hymn."

"I understand, I understand, go on,"—said Maidanoff significantly and dreamily.

"Suddenly there is a noise—laughter, torches, tambourines on the shore. . . . It is a throng of bacchantes running with songs and outcries. It is your business to draw the picture, Mr. Poet . . . only I would like to have the torches red and very smoky, and that the eyes of the bacchantes should gleam beneath their wreaths, and that the wreaths should be dark. Don't forget also tiger-skins and cups—and gold, a great deal of gold."

"But where is the gold to be?" inquired Maidanoff, tossing back his lank hair and inflating his nostrils.

"Where? On the shoulders, the hands, the feet, everywhere. They say that in ancient times women wore golden rings on their ankles.—The bacchantes call the young girls in the boat to come to them. The girls have ceased to chant their hymn,—they cannot go on with it,—but they do not stir; the river drifts them to the shore. And now suddenly one of them rises quietly. . . . This must be well described: how she rises quietly in the moonlight, and how startled her companions are. . . . She has stepped over the edge of the boat, the bacchantes have surrounded her, they have dashed off into the night, into the gloom. . . . Present at this point smoke in clouds; and everything has become thoroughly confused. Nothing is to be heard but their whimpering, and her wreath has been left lying on the shore."

Zinaida ceased speaking. "Oh, she is in love!"—I thought again.

"Is that all?"—asked Maidanoff.

"That is all,"—she replied.

"That cannot be made the subject of an entire poem,"—he remarked pompously,—"but I will utilize your idea for some lyrical verses."

"In the romantic vein?"—asked Malevsky.

"Of course, in the romantic vein—in Byron's style."

"But in my opinion, Hugo is better than Byron,"—remarked the young Count, carelessly:—"he is more interesting."

"Hugo is a writer of the first class,"—rejoined Maidanoff, "and my friend Tonkosheeff, in his Spanish romance, 'El Trovador' . . ."

"Ah, that's the book with the question-marks turned upside down?"—interrupted Zinaida.

"Yes. That is the accepted custom among the Spaniards. I was about to say that Tonkosheeff. . . ."

"Come now! You will begin to wrangle again about classicism and romanticism,"—Zinaida interrupted him again.—"Let us rather play . . ."

"At forfeits?"—put in Lushin.

"No, forfeits is tiresome; but at comparisons." (This game had been invented by Zinaida herself; some object was named, and each person tried to compare it with something or other, and the one who matched the thing with the best comparison received a prize.) She went to the window. The sun had just set; long, crimson clouds hung high aloft in the sky.

"What are those clouds like?"—inquired Zinaida and, without

waiting for our answers, she said:—"I think that they resemble those crimson sails which were on Cleopatra's golden ship, when she went to meet Antony. You were telling me about that not long ago, do you remember, Maidanoff?"

All of us, like Polonius in "Hamlet," decided that the clouds reminded us precisely of those sails, and that none of us could find a better comparison.

"And how old was Antony at that time?"—asked Zinaida.

"He was assuredly still a young man,"—remarked Malevsky.

"Yes, he was young,"—assented Maidanoff confidently.

"Excuse me,"—exclaimed Lushin,—"he was over forty years of age."

"Over forty years of age,"—repeated Zinaida, darting a swift glance at him. . . .

I soon went home.—"She is in love," my lips whispered involuntarily. . . . "But with whom?"

12

THE days passed by. Zinaida grew more and more strange, more and more incomprehensible. One day I entered her house and found her sitting on a straw-bottomed chair, with her head pressed against the sharp edge of a table. She straightened up . . . her face was again all bathed in tears.

"Ah! It's you!"—she said, with a harsh grimace.—"Come hither."

I went up to her: she laid her hand on my head and, suddenly seizing me by the hair, began to pull it.

"It hurts" . . . I said at last.

"Ah! It hurts! And doesn't it hurt me- Doesn't it hurt me?"—she repeated.

"Ai!"—she suddenly cried, perceiving that she had pulled out a small tuft of my hair.—"What have I done? Poor M'sieu Voldemar!" She carefully straightened out the hairs she had plucked out, wound them round her finger, and twisted them into a ring.

"I will put your hair in my locket and wear it,"—she said, and tears glistened in her eyes.—"Perhaps that will comfort you a little . . . but now, good-bye."

I returned home and found an unpleasant state of things there. A scene was in progress between my father and my mother; she was upbraiding him for something or other, while he, according to his wont, was maintaining a cold, polite silence—and speedily went away. I could not hear what my mother was talking about, neither did I care to know: I remember only, that, at the conclusion of the scene, she ordered me to be called to her boudoir, and expressed herself with the great dissatisfaction about my frequent visits at the house of the old Princess, who was, according to her assertions, *une femme capable de tout.* I kissed her hand (I always did that when I wanted to put an end to the conversation), and went off to my own room. Zinaida's tears had completely discomfited me; I positively did not know what to think, and was ready to cry myself: I was still a child, in spite of my sixteen years. I thought no more of Malevsky, although Byelovzoroff became more and more menacing every day, and glared at the shifty Count like a wolf at a sheep; but I was not thinking of anything or of anybody. I lost myself in conjectures and kept seeking isolated spots. I took a special fancy to the ruins of the hothouse. I could clamber up on the high wall, seat myself, and sit there such an unhappy, lonely, and sad youth that I felt sorry for myself—and how delightful those mournful sensations were, how I gloated over them! . . .

One day, I was sitting thus on the wall, gazing off into the distance and listening to the chiming of the bells . . . when suddenly something ran over me—not a breeze exactly, not a shiver, but something resembling a breath, the consciousness of some one's proximity. . . . I dropped my eyes. Below me, in a light grey gown, with a pink parasol on her shoulder, Zinaida was walking hastily along the road. She saw me, halted, and, pushing up the brim of her straw hat, raised her velvety eyes to mine.

"What are you doing there, on such a height?"—she asked me,

with a strange sort of smile.—"There now,"—she went on,—"you are always declaring that you love me—jump down to me here on the road if you really do love me."

Before the words were well out of Zinaida's mouth I had flown down, exactly as though some one had given me a push from behind. The wall was about two fathoms high. I landed on the ground with my feet, but the shock was so violent that I could not retain my balance; I fell, and lost consciousness for a moment. When I came to myself I felt, without opening my eyes, that Zinaida was by my side.—"My dear boy,"—she was saying, as she bent over me—and tender anxiety was audible in her voice—"how couldst thou do that, how couldst thou obey? . . . I love thee . . . rise."

Her breast was heaving beside me, her hands were touching my head, and suddenly—what were my sensations then!—her soft, fresh lips began to cover my whole face with kisses . . . they touched my lips. . . . But at this point Zinaida probably divined from the expression of my face that I had already recovered consciousness, although I still did not open my eyes—and swiftly rising to her feet, she said:—"Come, get up, you rogue, you foolish fellow! Why do you lie there in the dust?"—I got up.

"Give me my parasol,"—said Zinaida.—"I have thrown it somewhere; and don't look at me like that . . . what nonsense is this? You are hurt? You have burned yourself with the nettles, I suppose. Don't look at me like that, I tell you. . . . Why, he understands nothing, he doesn't answer me,"—she added, as though speaking to herself. . . . "Go home, M'sieu Voldemar, brush yourself off, and don't dare to follow me—if you do I shall be very angry, and I shall never again . . ."

She did not finish her speech and walked briskly away, while I sat down by the roadside . . . my legs would not support me. The nettles had stung my hands, my back ached, and my head was reeling; but the sensation of beatitude which I then experienced has never since been repeated in my life. It hung like a sweet pain in all my limbs and broke out at last in rapturous leaps and exclamations. As a matter of fact, I was still a child.

13

I was so happy and proud all that day; I preserved so vividly on my visage the feeling of Zinaida's kisses; I recalled her every word with such ecstasy; I so cherished my unexpected happiness that I even became frightened; I did not even wish to see her who was the cause of those new sensations. It seemed to me that I could ask nothing more of Fate, that now I must "take and draw a deep breath for the last time, and die." On the other hand, when I set off for the wing next day, I felt a great agitation, which I vainly endeavored to conceal beneath the discreet facial ease suitable for a man who wishes to let it be understood that he knows how to keep a secret. Zinaida received me very simply, without any emotion, merely shaking her finger at me and asking: Had I any bruises? All my discreet ease of manner and mysteriousness instantly disappeared, and along with them my agitation. Of course I had not expected anything in particular, but Zinaida's composure acted on me like a dash of cold water. I understood that I was a child in her eyes—and my heart waxed very heavy! Zinaida paced to and fro in the room, smiling swiftly every time she glanced at me; but her thoughts were far away, I saw that clearly. . . . "Shall I allude to what happened yesterday myself,"—I thought;—"shall I ask her where she was going in such haste, in order to find out, definitively?" . . . but I merely waved my hand in despair and sat down in a corner.

Byelovzoroff entered; I was delighted to see him.

"I have not found you a gentle saddle-horse,"—he began in a surly tone;—"Freitag vouches to me for one—but I am not convinced. I am afraid."

"Of what are you afraid, allow me to inquire?" asked Zinaida.

"Of what? Why, you don't know how to ride. God forbid that any accident should happen! And what has put that freak into your head?"

"Come, that's my affair, M'sieu my wild beast. In that case, I will ask Piotr Vasilievitch" . . . (My father was called Piotr Vasilievitch . . . I was amazed that she should mention his name so lightly and freely, exactly as though she were convinced of his readiness to serve her.)

"You don't say so!"—retorted Byelovzoroff.—"Is it with him that you wish to ride?"

"With him or some one else,—that makes no difference to you. Only not with you."

"Not with me,"—said Byelovzoroff.—"As you like. What does it matter? I will get you the horse."

"But see to it that it is not a cow-like beast. I warn you in advance that I mean to gallop."

"Gallop, if you wish. . . . But is it with Malevsky that you are going to ride?"

"And why shouldn't I ride with him, warrior? Come, quiet down. I'll take you too. You know that for me Malevsky is now— fie!"—She shook her head.

"You say that just to console me,"—growled Byelovzoroff.

Zinaida narrowed her eyes.—"Does that console you? . . . oh . . . oh . . . oh . . . warrior!"—she said at last, as though unable to find any other word.—"And would you like to ride with us, M'sieu Voldemar?"

"I'm not fond of riding . . . in a large party," . . . I muttered, without raising my eyes.

"You prefer a *tête-à-tête*? . . . Well, everyone to his taste,"— she said, with a sigh.—"But go, Byelovzoroff, make an effort. I want the horse for tomorrow."

"Yes; but where am I to get the money?"—interposed the old Princess.

Zinaida frowned.

"I am not asking any from you; Byelovzoroff will trust me."

"He will, he will," . . . grumbled the old Princess—and suddenly screamed at the top of her voice:—"Dunyashka!"

"*Maman*, I made you a present of a bell,"—remarked the young Princess.

"Dunyashka!"—repeated the old woman.

Byelovzoroff bowed himself out; I went out with him. Zinaida did not detain me.

14

I ROSE early the next morning, cut myself a staff, and went off beyond the city barrier. "I'll have a walk and banish my grief,"— I said to myself. It was a beautiful day, brilliant but not too hot; a cheerful, fresh breeze was blowing over the earth and rustling and playing moderately, keeping in constant motion and agitating nothing. For a long time I roamed about on the hills and in the forests. I did not feel happy; I had left home with the intention of surrendering myself to melancholy;—but youth, the fine weather, the fresh air, the diversion of brisk pedestrian exercise, the delight of lying in solitude on the thick grass, produced their effect; the memory of those unforgettable words, of those kisses, again thrust themselves into my soul. It was pleasant to me to think that Zinaida could not, nevertheless, fail to do justice to my decision, to my heroism. . . . "Others are better for her than I,"—I thought: —"so be it! On the other hand, the others only say what they will do, but I have done it! And what else am I capable of doing for her?"—My imagination began to ferment. I began to picture to myself how I would save her from the hands of enemies; how, all bathed in blood, I would wrest her out of prison; how I would die at her feet. I recalled a picture which hung in our drawing-room of Malek-Adel carrying off Matilda—and thereupon became engrossed in the appearance of a big, speckled woodpecker which was busily ascending the slender trunk of a birch-tree, and uneasily peering out from behind it, now on the right, now on the left, like a musician from behind the neck of his bass-viol.

Then I began to sing: "Not the white snows,"—and ran off into the romance which was well known at that period, "I will await thee when the playful breeze"; then I began to recite aloud Ermak's invocation to the stars in Khomyakoff's tragedy; I tried to compose something in a sentimental vein; I even thought out the line wherewith the whole poem was to conclude: "Oh, Zinaida! Zinaida!"—But it came to nothing. Meanwhile, dinner-time was approaching. I descended into the valley; a narrow, sandy path wound through it and led toward the town. I strolled along that path. . . . The dull trampling of horses' hoofs resounded behind me. I glanced round, involuntarily came to a standstill and pulled off my cap. I beheld my father and Zinaida. They were riding side by side. My father was saying something to her, bending his whole body toward her, and resting his hand on the neck of her horse; he was smiling. Zinaida was listening to him in silence, with her eyes severely downcast and lips compressed. At first I saw only them; it was not until several moments later that Byelovzoroff made his appearance from round a turn in the valley, dressed in hussar uniform with pelisse, and mounted on a foam-flecked black horse. The good steed was tossing his head, snorting and cur-vetting; the rider was both reining him in and spurring him on. I stepped aside. My father gathered up his reins and moved away from Zinaida; she slowly raised her eyes to his—and both set off at a gallop. . . . Byelovzoroff dashed headlong after them with clanking sword. "He is as red as a crab,"—I thought,—"and she. . . . Why is she so pale? She has been riding the whole morning— and yet she is pale?"

I redoubled my pace and managed to reach home just before dinner. My father was already sitting, re-dressed, well-washed and fresh, beside my mother's arm-chair, and reading aloud to her in his even, sonorous voice, the feuilleton of the *Journal des Débats*; but my mother was listening to him inattentively and, on catching sight of me, inquired where I had been all day, adding, that she did not like to have me prowling about God only knew where and God only knew with whom. "But I have been walking alone,"—I was on the point of replying; but I glanced at my father and for some reason or other held my peace.

15

DURING the course of the next five or six days I hardly saw Zinaida; she gave it out that she was ill, which did not, however, prevent the habitual visitors from presenting themselves at the wing—"to take their turn in attendance,"—as they expressed it;—all except Maidanoff, who immediately became dispirited as soon as he had no opportunity to go into raptures. Byelovzoroff sat morosely in a corner, all tightly buttoned up and red in the face; on Count Malevsky's delicate visage hovered constantly a sort of evil smile; he really had fallen into disfavor with Zinaida and listened with particular pains to the old Princess, and drove with her to the Governor-General's in a hired carriage. But this trip proved unsuccessful and even resulted in an unpleasantness for Malevsky: he was reminded of some row with certain Puteisk officers, and was compelled, in self-justification, to say that he was inexperienced at the time. Lushin came twice a day, but did not remain long. I was somewhat afraid of him after our last explanation and, at the same time, I felt a sincere attachment for him. One day he went for a stroll with me in the Neskutchny Park, was very good-natured and amiable, imparted to me the names and properties of various plants and flowers, and suddenly exclaimed—without rhyme or reason, as the saying is—as he smote himself on the brow: "And I, like a fool, thought she was a coquette! Evidently, it is sweet to sacrifice one's self—for some people!"

"What do you mean to say by that?"—I asked.

"I don't mean to say anything to you,"—returned Lushin, abruptly.

Zinaida avoided me; my appearance—I could not but perceive the fact—produced an unpleasant impression on her. She involuntarily turned away from me . . . involuntarily; that was what was bitter, that was what broke my heart! But there was no help for it and I tried to keep out of her sight and only stand guard over her from a distance, in which I was not always successful. As before, something incomprehensible was taking place with her; her face had become different—she was altogether a different person. I was particularly struck by the change which had taken place in her on a certain warm, tranquil evening. I was sitting on a low bench under a wide-spreading elder-bush; I loved that little nook; the window of Zinaida's chamber was visible thence. I was sitting there; over my head, in the darkened foliage, a tiny bird was rummaging fussily about; a great cat with outstretched back had stolen into the garden, and the first beetles were booming heavily in the air, which was still transparent although no longer light. I sat there and stared at the window, and waited to see whether some one would not open it: and, in fact, it did open, and Zinaida made her appearance in it. She wore a white gown, and she herself—her face, her shoulders and her hands—was pale to whiteness. She remained for a long time motionless, and for a long time stared, without moving, straight in front of her from beneath her contracted brows. I did not recognize that look in her. Then she clasped her hands very, very tightly, raised them to her lips, to her forehead—and suddenly, unlocking her fingers, pushed her hair away from her ears, shook it back and, throwing her head downward from above with a certain decisiveness, she shut the window with a bang.

Two days later she met me in the park. I tried to step aside, but she stopped me.

"Give me your hand,"—she said to me, with her former affection.—"It is a long time since you and I have had a chat."

I looked at her; her eyes were beaming softly and her face was smiling, as though athwart a mist.

"Are you still ailing?"—I asked her.

"No, everything has passed off now,"—she replied, breaking off a small, red rose.—"I am a little tired, but that will pass off also."

"And will you be once more the same as you used to be?"—I queried.

Zinaida raised the rose to her face, and it seemed to me as though the reflection of the brilliant petals fell upon her cheeks.—"Have I changed?"—she asked me.

"Yes, you have changed,"—I replied in a low voice.

"I was cold toward you,—I know that,"—began Zinaida;—"but you must not pay any heed to that. . . . I could not do otherwise. . . . Come, what's the use of talking about that?"

"You do not want me to love you—that's what!" I exclaimed gloomily, with involuntary impetuosity.

"Yes, love me, but not as before."

"How then?"

"Let us be friends,—that is how!"—Zinaida allowed me to smell of the rose.—"Listen; I am much older than you, you know—I might be your aunt, really; well, if not your aunt, then your elder sister. While you . . ."

"I am a child to you," I interrupted her.

"Well, yes, you are a child, but a dear, good, clever child, of whom I am very fond. Do you know what? I will appoint you to the post of my page from this day forth; and you are not to forget that pages must not be separated from their mistress. Here is a token of your new dignity for you,"—she added, sticking the rose into the button-hole of my round-jacket; "a token of our favor toward you."

"I have received many favors from you in the past,"—I murmured.

"Ah!"—said Zinaida, and darting a sidelong glance at me.— "What a memory you have! Well? And I am ready now also . . ."

And bending toward me, she imprinted on my brow a pure, calm kiss.

I only stared at her—but she turned away and, saying,—"Follow me, my page,"—walked to the wing. I followed her—and was in a constant state of bewilderment.—"Is it possible,"—I thought,— "that this gentle, sensible young girl is that same Zinaida whom I used to know?"—And her very walk seemed to me more quiet, her whole figure more majestic, more graceful. . . .

And, my God! with what fresh violence did love flame up within me!

16

AFTER dinner the visitors were assembled again in the wing, and the young Princess came out to them. The whole company was present, in full force, as on that first evening, never to be forgotten by me: even Nirmatzky had dragged himself thither. Maidanoff had arrived earlier than all the rest; he had brought some new verses. The game of forfeits began again, but this time without the strange sallies, without pranks and uproar; the gipsy element had vanished. Zinaida gave a new mood to our gathering. I sat beside her, as a page should. Among other things, she proposed that the one whose forfeit was drawn should narrate his dream; but this was not a success. The dreams turned out to be either uninteresting (Byelovzoroff had dreamed that he had fed his horse on carp, and that it had a wooden head), or unnatural, fictitious. Maidanoff regaled us with a complete novel; there were sepulchres and angels with harps, and burning lights and sounds wafted from afar. Zinaida did not allow him to finish. "If it is a question of invention,"—said she,—"then let each one relate something which is positively made up."—Byelovzoroff had to speak first.

The young hussar became confused.—"I cannot invent anything!"—he exclaimed.

"What nonsense!"—interposed Zinaida.—"Come, imagine, for instance, that you are married, and tell us how you would pass the time with your wife. Would you lock her up?"

"I would."

"And would you sit with her yourself?"

"I certainly would sit with her myself."

"Very good. Well, and what if that bored her, and she betrayed you?"

"I would kill her."

"Just so. Well, now supposing that I were your wife, what would you do then?"

Byelovzoroff made no answer for a while.—"I would kill myself . . ."

Zinaida burst out laughing.—"I see that there's not much to be got out of you."

The second forfeit fell to Zinaida's share. She raised her eyes to the ceiling and meditated.—"See here,"—she began at last,—"this is what I have devised. . . . Imagine to yourselves a magnificent palace, a summer night, and a marvelous ball. This ball is given by the young Queen. Everywhere there are gold, marble, silk, lights, diamonds, flowers, the smoke of incense—all the whims of luxury."

"Do you love luxury?"—interrupted Lushin.

"Luxury is beautiful,"—she returned;—"I love everything that is beautiful."

"More than what is fine?"—he asked.

"That is difficult; somehow I don't understand. Don't bother me. So then, there is a magnificent ball. There are many guests, they are all young, very handsome, brave; all are desperately in love with the Queen."

"Are there no women among the guests?"—inquired Malevsky.

"No—or stay—yes, there are."

"Also very handsome?"

"Charming. But the men are all in love with the Queen. She is tall and slender; she wears a small gold diadem on her black hair."

I looked at Zinaida—and at that moment she seemed so far above us, her white forehead and her impassive eyebrows exhaled so much clear intelligence and such sovereignty, that I said to myself: "Thou thyself art that Queen!"

"All throng around her,"—pursued Zinaida;—"all lavish the most flattering speeches on her."

"And is she fond of flattery?"—asked Lushin.

"How intolerable! He is continually interrupting . . . Who does not like flattery?"

"One more final question,"—remarked Malevsky:—"Has the Queen a husband?"

"I have not thought about that. No, why should she have a husband?"

"Of course,"—assented Malevsky;—"why should she have a husband?"

"Silence!"—exclaimed, in English, Maidanoff, who spoke French badly.

"*Merci*,"—said Zinaida to him.—"So then, the Queen listens to those speeches, listens to the music, but does not look at a single one of the guests. Six windows are open from top to bottom, from ceiling to floor, and behind them are the dark sky with great stars and the dark garden with huge trees. The Queen gazes into the garden. There, near the trees is a fountain: it gleams white athwart the gloom—long, as long as a spectre. The Queen hears the quiet plashing of its waters in the midst of the conversation and the music. She gazes and thinks: 'All of you gentlemen are noble, clever, wealthy; you are all ready to die at my feet, I rule over you; . . . but yonder, by the side of the fountain, by the side of that plashing water, there is standing and waiting for me the man whom I love, who rules over me. He wears no rich garments, nor precious jewels; no one knows him; but he is waiting for me, and is convinced that I shall come—and I shall come, and there is no power in existence which can stop me when I wish to go to him and remain with him and lose myself with him yonder, in the gloom of the park, beneath the rustling of the trees, beneath the plashing of the fountain . . .'"

Zinaida ceased speaking.

"Is that an invention?"—asked Malevsky slyly.

Zinaida did not even glance at him.

"But what should we do, gentlemen,"—suddenly spoke up Lushin,—"if we were among the guests and knew about that lucky man by the fountain?"

"Stay, stay,"—interposed Zinaida:—"I myself will tell you what each one of you would do. You, Byelovzoroff, would challenge him to a duel; you, Maidanoff, would write an epigram on him. . . . But no—you do not know how to write epigrams; you would compose a long iambic poem on him, after the style of Barbier, and would insert your production in the *Telegraph*. You, Nirmatzky, would borrow from him . . . no, you would lend him money on interest; you, doctor . . ." She paused. . . . "I really do not know about you,—what you would do."

"In my capacity of Court-physician," replied Lushin, "I would advise the Queen not to give balls when she did not feel in the mood for guests . . ."

"Perhaps you would be in the right. And you, Count?"

"And I?"—repeated Malevsky, with an evil smile.

"And you would offer him some poisoned sugar-plums."

Malevsky's face writhed a little and assumed for a moment a Jewish expression; but he immediately burst into a guffaw.

"As for you, M'sieu Voldemar . . ." went on Zinaida,—"but enough of this; let us play at some other game."

"M'sieu Voldemar, in his capacity of page to the Queen, would hold up her train when she ran off into the park,"—remarked Malevsky viciously.

I flared up, but Zinaida swiftly laid her hand on my shoulder and rising, said in a slightly tremulous voice:—"I have never given Your Radiance the right to be insolent, and therefore I beg that you will withdraw."—She pointed him to the door.

"Have mercy, Princess,"—mumbled Malevsky, turning pale all over.

"The Princess is right,"—exclaimed Byelovzoroff, rising to his feet also.

"By God! I never in the least expected this,"—went on Malevsky:—"I think there was nothing in my words which . . . I had no intention of offending you. . . . Forgive me."

Zinaida surveyed him with a cold glance, and smiled coldly.— "Remain, if you like,"—she said, with a careless wave of her hand. —"M'sieu Voldemar and I have taken offence without cause. You find it merry to jest. . . . I wish you well."

"Forgive me,"—repeated Malevsky once more; and I, recalling Zinaida's movement, thought again that a real queen could not have ordered an insolent man out of the room with more majesty.

The game of forfeits did not continue long after this little scene; all felt somewhat awkward, not so much in consequence of the scene itself as from another, not entirely defined, but oppressive sensation. No one alluded to it, but each one was conscious of its existence within himself and in his neighbor. Maidanoff recited to us all his poems—and Malevsky lauded them with exaggerated warmth.

"How hard he is trying to appear amiable now,"—Lushin whispered to me.

We soon dispersed. Zinaida had suddenly grown pensive; the

old Princess sent word that she had a headache; Nirmatzky began to complain of his rheumatism. . . .

For a long time I could not get to sleep; Zinaida's narrative had impressed me.—"Is it possible that it contains a hint?"—I asked myself:—"and at whom was she hinting? And if there really is some one to hint about . . . what must I decide to do? No, no, it cannot be,"—I whispered, turning over from one burning cheek to the other. . . . But I called to mind the expression of Zinaida's face during her narration. . . . I called to mind the exclamation which had broken from Lushin in the Neskutchny Park, the sudden changes in her treatment of me—and lost myself in conjectures. "Who is he?" Those three words seemed to stand in front of my eyes, outlined in the darkness; a low-lying, ominous cloud seemed to be hanging over me—and I felt its pressure—and waited every moment for it to burst. I had grown used to many things of late; I had seen many things at the Zasyekins'; their disorderliness, tallow candle-ends, broken knives and forks, gloomy Vonifaty, the shabby maids, the manners of the old Princess herself,—all that strange life no longer surprised me. . . . But to that which I now dimly felt in Zinaida I could not get used . . . "An adventuress,"— my mother had one day said concerning her. An adventuress—she, my idol, my divinity! That appellation seared me; I tried to escape from it by burrowing into my pillow; I raged—and at the same time, to what would not I have agreed, what would not I have given, if only I might be that happy mortal by the fountain! . . .

My blood grew hot and seethed within me. "A garden . . . a fountain," . . . I thought. . . . "I will go into the garden." I dressed myself quickly and slipped out of the house. The night was dark, the trees were barely whispering; a quiet chill was descending from the sky, an odor of fennel was wafted from the vegetable-garden. I made the round of all the alleys; the light sound of my footsteps both disconcerted me and gave me courage; I halted, waiting and listening to hear how my heart was beating quickly and violently. At last I approached the fence and leaned against a slender post. All at once—or was it only my imagination? —a woman's figure flitted past a few paces distant from me. . . . I strained my eyes intently on the darkness; I held my breath.

What was this? Was it footsteps that I heard or was it the thumping of my heart again?—"Who is here?"—I stammered in barely audible tones. What was that again? A suppressed laugh? . . . or a rustling in the leaves? . . . or a sigh close to my very ear? I was terrified. . . . "Who is here?"—I repeated, in a still lower voice.

The breeze began to flutter for a moment; a fiery band flashed across the sky; a star shot down.—"Is it Zinaida?"—I tried to ask, but the sound died on my lips. And suddenly everything became profoundly silent all around, as often happens in the middle of the night. . . . Even the katydids ceased to shrill in the trees; only a window rattled somewhere. I stood and stood, then returned to my chamber, to my cold bed. I felt a strange agitation—exactly as though I had gone to a tryst, and had remained alone, and had passed by someone else's happiness.

17

THE next day I caught only a glimpse of Zinaida; she drove away somewhere with the old Princess in a hired carriage. On the other hand, I saw Lushin—who, however, barely deigned to bestow a greeting on me—and Malevsky. The young Count grinned and entered into conversation with me in friendly wise. Among all the visitors to the wing he alone had managed to effect an entrance to our house, and my mother had taken a fancy to him. My father did not favor him and treated him politely to the point of insult.

"Ah, *monsieur le page*,"—began Malevsky,—"I am very glad to meet you. What is your beauteous queen doing?"

His fresh, handsome face was so repulsive to me at that moment, and he looked at me with such a scornfully-playful stare, that I made him no answer whatsoever.

"Are you still in a bad humor?"—he went on.—"There is no occasion for it. It was not I, you know, who called you a page; and pages are chiefly with queens. But permit me to observe to you that you are fulfilling your duties badly."

"How so?"

"Pages ought to be inseparable from their sovereigns; pages ought to know everything that they do; they ought even to watch over them,"—he added, lowering his voice,—"day and night."

"What do you mean by that?"

"What do I mean? I think I have expressed myself plainly. Day—and night. It does not matter so much about the day; by day it is light and there are people about; but by night—that's exactly the time to expect a catastrophe. I advise you not to sleep o' nights and to watch, watch with all your might. Remember— in a garden, by night, near the fountain—that's where you must keep guard. You will thank me for this."

Malevsky laughed and turned his back on me. He did not, in all probability, attribute any special importance to what he had said to me; he bore the reputation of being a capital hand at mystification, and was renowned for his cleverness in fooling people at the masquerades, in which that almost unconscious disposition to lie, wherewith his whole being was permeated, greatly aided him. . . . He had merely wished to tease me; but every word of his trickled like poison through all my veins.—The blood flew to my head.

"Ah! so that's it!"—I said to myself:—"good! So it was not for nothing that I felt drawn to the garden! That shall not be!" I exclaimed, smiting myself on the breast with my fist; although I really did not know what it was that I was determined not to permit.—"Whether Malevsky himself comes into the garden,"— I thought (perhaps he had blurted out a secret; he was insolent enough for that),—"or someone else,"—(the fence of our vege-table-garden was very low and it cost no effort to climb over it)— "at any rate, it will be all the worse for the person whom I catch! I would not advise anyone to encounter me! I'll show the whole world and her, the traitress,"—(I actually called her a traitress) —"that I know how to avenge myself!"

I returned to my own room, took out of my writing-table a recently purchased English knife, felt of the sharp blade, and, knitting my brows, thrust it into my pocket with a cold and con-centrated decision, exactly as though it was nothing remarkable for me to do such deeds, and this was not the first occasion. My heart swelled angrily within me and grew stony; I did not unbend my brows until nightfall and did not relax my lips, and kept striding back and forth, clutching the knife which had grown warm in my pocket, and preparing myself in advance for something terrible. These new, unprecedented emotions so engrossed and even cheered me, that I thought very little about Zinaida herself. There kept constantly flitting through my head Aleko, the young gipsy:[1]— "Where art thou going, handsome youth?—Lie down . . ." and then: "Thou'rt all with blood bespattered! . . . Oh, what is't that thou hast done? . . . Nothing!" With what a harsh smile I repeated that: that "Nothing!"

My father was not at home; but my mother, who for some time past had been in a state of almost constant, dull irritation, noticed my baleful aspect at supper, and said to me:—"What art thou sulking at, like a mouse at groats?"—I merely smiled patronisingly at her by way of reply and thought to myself: "If they only knew!" —The clock struck eleven; I went to my own room but did not undress; I was waiting for midnight; at last it struck.—" 'Tis time!"—I hissed between my teeth, and buttoning my coat to the throat and even turning up my sleeves I betook myself to the garden.

I had selected a place beforehand where I meant to stand on guard. At the end of the garden, at the spot where the fence, which separated our property from the Zasyekins', abutted on the party-wall, grew a solitary spruce-tree. Standing beneath its low, thick branches, I could see well, as far as the nocturnal gloom permitted, all that went on around; there also meandered a path which always seemed to me mysterious; like a serpent it wound under the fence, which at that point bore traces of clambering feet, and led to an arbor of dense acacias. I reached the spruce-tree, leaned against its trunk and began my watch.

The night was as tranquil as the preceding one had been; but there were fewer storm-clouds in the sky, and the outlines of the bushes, even of the tall flowers, were more plainly discernible. The first moments of waiting were wearisome, almost terrible. I

[1] In Pushkin's poem, "The Gipsies."—TRANSLATOR.

had made up my mind to everything; I was merely considering how I ought to act. Ought I to thunder out: "Who goes there? Halt! Confess—or die!"—or simply smite . . . Every sound, every noise and rustling seemed to me significant, unusual . . . . I made ready . . . . I bent forward. . . . But half an hour, an hour, elapsed; my blood quieted down and turned cold; the consciousness that I was doing all this in vain, that I was even somewhat ridiculous, that Malevsky had been making fun of me, began to steal into my soul. I abandoned my ambush and made the round of the entire garden. As though expressly, not the slightest sound was to be heard anywhere; everything was at rest; even our dog was asleep, curled up in a ball at the gate. I climbed up on the ruin of the hothouse, beheld before me the distant plain, recalled my meeting with Zinaida, and became immersed in meditation. . . .

I started . . . . I thought I heard the creak of an opening door, then the light crackling of a broken twig. In two bounds I had descended from the ruin—and stood petrified on the spot. Swift, light but cautious footsteps were plainly audible in the garden. They were coming toward me. "Here he is. . . . Here he is, at last!" —darted through my heart. I convulsively jerked the knife out of my pocket, convulsively opened it—red sparks whirled before my eyes, the hair stood up on my head with fright and wrath. . . . The steps were coming straight toward me—I bent over, and went to meet them. . . . . A man made his appearance. . . . My God! It was my father!

I recognized him instantly, although he was all enveloped in a dark cloak,—and had pulled his hat down over his face. He went past me on tip-toe. He did not notice me although nothing concealed me; but I had so contracted myself and shrunk together that I think I must have been on a level with the ground. The jealous Othello, prepared to murder, had suddenly been converted into the school-boy. . . . I was so frightened by the unexpected apparition of my father that I did not even take note, at first, in what direction he was going and where he had disappeared. I merely straightened up at the moment and thought: "Why is my father walking in the garden by night?"—when everything around had relapsed into silence. In my alarm I had dropped my knife in the grass, but I did not even try to find it; I felt very much ashamed. I became sobered on the instant. But as I wended my way home, I stepped up to my little bench under the elder-bush and cast a glance at the little window of Zinaida's chamber. The small, somewhat curved panes of the little window gleamed dully blue in the faint light which fell from the night sky. Suddenly their color began to undergo a change. . . . Behind them —I saw it, saw it clearly,—a whitish shade was lowered, descended to the sill,—and there remained motionless.

"What is the meaning of that?"—I said aloud, almost involuntarily, when I again found myself in my own room.—"Was it a dream, an accident, or . . . ." The surmises which suddenly came into my head were so new and strange that I dared not even yield to them.

18

I ROSE in the morning with a headache. My agitation of the night before had vanished. It had been replaced by an oppressive perplexity and a certain, hitherto unknown sadness,—exactly as though something had died in me.

"What makes you look like a rabbit which has had half of its brain removed?"—said Lushin, who happened to meet me. At breakfast I kept casting covert glances now at my father, now at my mother; he was calm, as usual; she, as usual, was secretly irritated. I waited to see whether my father would address me in a friendly way, as he sometimes did. . . . But he did not even caress me with his cold, everyday affection.—"Shall I tell Zinaida all?"—I thought. . . . "For it makes no difference now—everything is over between us." I went to her, but I not only did not tell her anything,—I did not even get a chance to talk to her as I would have liked. The old Princess's son, a cadet aged twelve, had come from Petersburg to spend his vacation with her; Zinaida immediately confided her brother to me.—"Here, my dear Volodya,"—said she (she called me so for the first time), "is a comrade for you. His name is Volodya also. Pray, like him; he's a wild little fellow still, but he has a good heart. Show him Neskutchny Park, walk with him, take him under your protection. You will do that, will you not? You, too, are such a good fellow!"—She laid both hands affectionately on my shoulder—and I was reduced to utter confusion. The arrival of that boy turned me into a boy. I stared in silence at the cadet, who riveted his eyes in corresponding silence on me. Zinaida burst out laughing and pushed us toward each other.—"Come, embrace, children!"—We embraced.—"I'll take you into the garden if you wish,—shall I?"—I asked the cadet.

"Certainly, sir,"—he replied, in a hoarse, genuine cadet voice. Again Zinaida indulged in a burst of laughter. . . . I managed to notice that never before had she had such charming color in her face. The cadet and I went off together. In our garden stood an old swing. I seated him on the thin little board and began to swing him. He sat motionless in his new little uniform of thick cloth with broad gold galloon, and clung tightly to the ropes.

"You had better unhook your collar,"—I said to him.

"Never mind, sir,[1] we are used to it, sir"—he said, and cleared his throat.

He resembled his sister; his eyes were particularly suggestive of her. It was pleasant to me to be of service to him; and, at the same time, that aching pain kept quietly gnawing at my heart. "Now I really am a child," I thought; "but last night . . . ." I remembered where I had dropped my knife and found it. The cadet asked me to lend it to him, plucked a thick stalk of lovage, cut a whistle from it, and began to pipe. Othello piped also.

But in the evening, on the other hand, how he did weep, that same Othello, over Zinaida's hands when, having sought him out in a corner of the garden, she asked him what made him so melancholy. My tears streamed with such violence that she was frightened.—"What is the matter with you? What is the matter with you, Volodya?"—she kept repeating, and seeing that I made her

---

[1] The respectful "s," which is an abbreviation of "sir" or "madam."—
Translator.

no reply, she took it into her head to kiss my wet cheek. But I turned away from her and whispered through my sobs:—"I know everything: why have you trifled with me? .... Why did you want my love?"

"I am to blame toward you, Volodya" .... said Zinaida.—"Akh, I am very much to blame" ... she said, and clenched her hands.— "How much evil, dark, sinful, there is in me! ... But I am not trifling with you now, I love you—you do not suspect why and how. ... But what is it you know?"

What could I say to her? She stood before me and gazed at me—and I belonged to her wholly, from head to foot, as soon as she looked at me. ... A quarter of an hour later I was running a race with the cadet and Zinaida; I was not weeping; I was laughing, although my swollen eyelids dropped tears from laughing; on my neck, in place of a tie, was bound a ribbon of Zinaida's, and I shouted with joy when I succeeded in seizing her around the waist. She did with me whatsoever she would.

19

I SHOULD be hard put to it, if I were made to narrate in detail all that went on within me in the course of the week which followed my unsuccessful nocturnal expedition. It was a strange, feverish time, a sort of chaos in which the most opposite emotions, thoughts, suspicions, hopes, joys, and sufferings revolved in a whirlwind; I was afraid to look into myself, if a sixteen-year-old can look into himself; I was afraid to account to myself for anything whatsoever; I simply made haste to live through the day until the evening; on the other hand, at night I slept ... childish giddiness helped me. I did not want to know whether I was beloved, and would not admit to myself that I was not beloved; I shunned my father—but could not shun Zinaida. ... I burned as with fire in her presence, ... but what was the use of my knowing what sort of fire it was wherewith I burned and melted—

seeing that it was sweet to me to burn and melt! I surrendered myself entirely to my impressions, and dealt artfully with myself, turned away from my memories and shut my eyes to that of which I had a presentiment in the future. . . . This anguish probably would not have continued long . . . a thunder-clap put an instantaneous end to everything and hurled me into a new course.

On returning home one day to dinner from a rather long walk, I learned with surprise that I was to dine alone; that my father had gone away, while my mother was ill, did not wish to dine and had shut herself up in her bedroom. From the footmen's faces I divined that something unusual had taken place. . . . I dared not interrogate them, but I had a friend, the young butler Philipp, who was passionately fond of poetry and an artist on the guitar; I applied to him. From him I learned that a frightful scene had taken place between my father and mother (for in the maids' room everything was audible, to the last word; a great deal had been said in French, but the maid Masha had lived for five years with a dressmaker from Paris and understood it all); that my mother had accused my father of infidelity, of being intimate with the young lady our neighbor; that my father had first defended himself, then had flared up and in his turn had made some harsh remark "seemingly about her age," which had set my mother to crying; that my mother had also referred to a note of hand, which appeared to have been given to the old Princess, and expressed herself very vilely about her, and about the young lady as well; and that then my father had threatened her.—"And the whole trouble arose,"—pursued Philipp, "out of an anonymous letter; but who wrote it no one knows; otherwise there was no reason why this affair should have come out."

"But has there been anything?"—I enunciated with difficulty, while my hands and feet turned cold, and something began to quiver in the very depths of my breast.

Philipp winked significantly.—"There has. You can't conceal such doings, cautious as your papa has been in this case;—still, what possessed him, for example, to hire a carriage, or to . . . for you can't get along without people there also."

I dismissed Philipp, and flung myself down on my bed. I did not sob, I did not give myself up to despair; I did not ask myself when and how all this had taken place; I was not surprised that I had not guessed it sooner, long before—I did not even murmur against my father. . . . That which I had learned was beyond my strength; this sudden discovery had crushed me. . . . All was over. All my flowers had been plucked up at one blow and lay strewn around me, scattered and trampled under foot.

20

ON THE following day my mother announced that she was going to remove to town. My father went into her bedroom in the morning and sat there a long time alone with her. No one heard what he said to her, but my mother did not weep any more; she calmed down and asked for something to eat, but did not show herself and did not alter her intention. I remember that I wandered about all day long, but did not go into the garden and did not glance even once at the wing—and in the evening I was the witness of an amazing occurrence; my father took Count Malevsky by the arm and led him out of the hall into the anteroom and, in the presence of a lackey, said coldly to him: "Several days ago Your Radiance was shown the door in a certain house. I shall not enter into explanations with you now, but I have the honor to inform you that if you come to my house again I shall fling you through the window. I don't like your handwriting." The Count bowed, set his teeth, shrank together, and disappeared.

Preparations began for removing to town, on the Arbat,[1] where our house was situated. Probably my father himself no longer cared to remain in the villa; but it was evident that he had succeeded in persuading my mother not to make a row. Everything was done quietly, without haste; my mother even sent her compliments to the old Princess and expressed her regret that, owing to

[1] A square in MOSCOW.—TRANSLATOR.

ill-health, she would be unable to see her before her departure. I
prowled about like a crazy person, and desired but one thing,—
that everything might come to an end as speedily as possible. One
thought never quitted my head: how could she, a young girl,—
well, and a princess into the bargain,—bring herself to such a step,
knowing that my father was not a free man while she had the
possibility of marrying Byelovzoroff at least, for example? What
had she hoped for? How was it that she had not been afraid to
ruin her whole future?—"Yes,"—I thought,—"that's what love is,
—that is passion,—that is devotion," . . . and I recalled Lushin's
words to me: "Self-sacrifice is sweet—for some people." Once I
happened to catch sight of a white spot in one of the windows of
the wing. . . . "Can that be Zinaida's face?"—I thought; . . . and
it really was her face. I could not hold out. I could not part from
her without bidding her a last farewell. I seized a convenient
moment and betook myself to the wing.

In the drawing-room the old Princess received me with her
customary, slovenly-careless greeting.

"What has made your folks uneasy so early, my dear fellow?"—
she said, stuffing snuff up both her nostrils. I looked at her, and a
weight was removed from my heart. The word "note of hand"
uttered by Philipp tormented me. She suspected nothing . . . so
it seemed to me then, at least. Zinaida made her appearance from
the adjoining room in a black gown, pale, with hair out of curl;
she silently took me by the hand and led me away to her room.

"I heard your voice,"—she began,—"and came out at once. And
did you find it so easy to desert us, naughty boy?"

"I have come to take leave of you, Princess,"—I replied,—
"probably forever. You may have heard we are going away."

Zinaida gazed intently at me.

"Yes, I have heard. Thank you for coming. I was beginning to
think that I should not see you.—Think kindly of me. I have
sometimes tormented you; but nevertheless I am not the sort of
person you think I am."

She turned away and leaned against the window-casing.

"Really, I am not that sort of person. I know that you have a
bad opinion of me."

"I?"

"Yes, you . . . you."

"I?"—I repeated sorrowfully, and my heart began to quiver as of old, beneath the influence of the irresistible, inexpressible witchery.—"I? Believe me, Zinaida Alexandrovna, whatever you may have done, however you may have tormented me, I shall love and adore you until the end of my life."

She turned swiftly toward me and opening her arms widely, she clasped my head, and kissed me heartily and warmly. God knows whom that long, farewell kiss was seeking, but I eagerly tasted its sweetness. I knew that it would never more be repeated.—"Farewell, farewell!" I kept saying. . . .

She wrenched herself away and left the room. And I withdrew also. I am unable to describe the feeling with which I retired. I should not wish ever to have it repeated; but I should consider myself unhappy if I had never experienced it.

We removed to town. I did not speedily detach myself from the past, I did not speedily take up my work. My wound healed slowly; but I really had no evil feeling toward my father. On the contrary, he seemed to have gained in stature in my eyes . . . let the psychologists explain this contradiction as best they may. One day I was walking along the boulevard when, to my indescribable joy, I encountered Lushin. I liked him for his straightforward, sincere character; and, moreover, he was dear to me in virtue of the memories which he awakened in me. I rushed at him.

"Aha!"—he said, with a scowl.—"Is it you, young man? Come, let me have a look at you. You are still all sallow, and yet there is not the olden trash in your eyes. You look like a man, not like a lap-dog. That's good. Well, and how are you? Are you working?"

I heaved a sigh. I did not wish to lie, and I was ashamed to tell the truth.

"Well, never mind,"—went on Lushin,—"don't be afraid. The principal thing is to live in normal fashion and not to yield to impulses. Otherwise, where's the good? No matter whither the wave bears one—'tis bad; let a man stand on a stone if need be, but on his own feet. Here I am croaking . . . but Byelovzoroff—have you heard about him?"

"What about him? No."

"He has disappeared without leaving a trace; they say he has gone to the Caucasus. A lesson to you, young man. And the whole thing arises from not knowing how to say good-bye,—to break bonds in time. You, now, seem to have jumped out successfully. Look out, don't fall in again. Farewell."

"I shall not fall in,"—I thought. . . . "I shall see her no more." But I was fated to see Zinaida once more.

21

MY FATHER was in the habit of riding on horesback every day; he had a splendid red-roan English horse, with a long, slender neck and long legs, indefatigable and vicious. Its name was Electric. No one could ride it except my father. One day he came to me in a kindly frame of mind, which had not happened with him for a long time: he was preparing to ride, and had donned his spurs. I began to entreat him to take me with him.

"Let us, rather, play at leap-frog,"—replied my father,—"for thou wilt not be able to keep up with me on thy cob."

"Yes, I shall; I will put on spurs also."

"Well, come along."

We set out. I had a shaggy, black little horse, strong on its feet and fairly spirited; it had to gallop with all its might, it is true, when Electric was going at a full trot; but nevertheless I did not fall behind. I have never seen such a horseman as my father. His seat was so fine and so carelessly-adroit that the horse under him seemed to be conscious of it and to take pride in it. We rode the whole length of all the boulevards, reached the Maidens' Field,[1] leaped over several enclosures (at first I was afraid to leap, but my father despised timid people, and I ceased to be afraid), crossed

[1] A great plain situated on the outskirts of the town. So called because (says tradition) it was here that annually were assembled the young girls who were sent, in addition to the money tribute, to the Khan, during the Tatar period, in the thirteenth and fourteenth centuries.—TRANSLATOR.

the Moscow river twice;—and I was beginning to think that we were on our way homeward, the more so as my father remarked that my horse was tired, when suddenly he turned away from me in the direction of the Crimean Ford, and galloped along the shore.—I dashed after him. When he came on a level with a lofty pile of old beams which lay heaped together, he sprang nimbly from Electric, ordered me to alight and, handing me the bridle of his horse, told me to wait for him on that spot, near the beams; then he turned into a narrow alley and disappeared. I began to pace back and forth along the shore, leading the horses after me and scolding Electric, who as he walked kept incessantly twitching his head, shaking himself, snorting and neighing; when I stood still, he alternately pawed the earth with his hoof, and squealed and bit my cob on the neck; in a word, behaved like a spoiled darling, *pur sang*. My father did not return. A disagreeable humidity was wafted from the river; a fine rain set in and mottled the stupid, grey beams, around which I was hovering and of which I was so heartily tired, with tiny, dark spots. Anxiety took possession of me, but still my father did not come. A Finnish sentry, also all grey, with a huge, old-fashioned shako, in the form of a pot, on his head, and armed with a halberd (why should there be a sentry, I thought, on the shores of the Moscow river?), approached me, and turning his elderly, wrinkled face to me, he said:

"What are you doing here with those horses, my little gentleman? Hand them over to me; I'll hold them."

I did not answer him; he asked me for some tobacco. In order to rid myself of him (moreover, I was tortured by impatience), I advanced a few paces in the direction in which my father had retreated; then I walked through the alley to the very end, turned a corner, and came to a standstill. On the street, forty paces distant from me, in front of the open window of a small wooden house, with his back to me, stood my father; he was leaning his breast on the windowsill, while in the house, half concealed by the curtain, sat a woman in a dark gown talking with my father: the woman was Zinaida.

I stood rooted to the spot in amazement. I must confess that

I had in nowise expected this. My first impulse was to flee. "My father will glance round," I thought,—"and then I am lost." . . . But a strange feeling—a feeling more powerful than curiosity, more powerful even than jealousy, more powerful than fear,— stopped me. I began to stare, I tried to hear. My father appeared to be insisting upon something. Zinaida would not consent. I seem to see her face now—sad, serious, beautiful, and with an indescribable imprint of adoration, grief, love, and a sort of despair. She uttered monosyllabic words, did not raise her eyes, and only smiled —submissively and obstinately. From that smile alone I recognized my former Zinaida. My father shrugged his shoulders, and set his hat straight on his head—which was always a sign of impatience with him. . . . Then the words became audible: "Vous devez vous séparer de cette." . . . Zinaida drew herself up and stretched out her hand. . . . Suddenly, before my very eyes, an incredible thing came to pass:—all at once, my father raised the riding-whip, with which he had been lashing the dust from his coat-tails,—and the sound of a sharp blow on that arm, which was bare to the elbow, rang out. I could hardly keep from shrieking, but Zinaida started, gazed in silence at my father, and slowly raising her arm to her lips, kissed the mark which glowed scarlet upon it.

My father hurled his riding-whip from him, and running hastily up the steps of the porch, burst into the house. . . . Zinaida turned round, and stretching out her arms, and throwing back her head, she also quitted the window.

My heart swooning with terror, and with a sort of alarmed perplexity, I darted backward; and dashing through the alley, and almost letting go of Electric, I returned to the bank of the river . . . I could understand nothing. I knew that my cold and self-contained father was sometimes seized by fits of wild fury; and yet I could not in the least comprehend what I had seen. . . . But I immediately felt that no matter how long I might live, it would be impossible for me ever to forget that movement, Zinaida's glance and smile; that her image, that new image which had suddenly been presented to me, had forever imprinted itself on my memory. I stared stupidly at the river and did not notice that my tears were flowing. "She is being beaten,"—I thought. . . . "She is being beaten . . . beaten . . ."

"Come, what ails thee?—Give me my horse!"—rang out my father's voice behind me.

I mechanically gave him the bridle. He sprang upon Electric . . . the half-frozen horse reared on his hind legs and leaped forward half a fathom . . . but my father speedily got him under control; he dug his spurs into his flanks and beat him on the neck with his fist. . . . "Ekh, I have no whip,"—he muttered.

I remembered the recent swish through the air and the blow of that same whip, and shuddered.

"What hast thou done with it?"—I asked my father, after waiting a little.

My father did not answer me and galloped on. I dashed after him. I was determined to get a look at his face.

"Didst thou get bored in my absence?"—he said through his teeth.

"A little. But where didst thou drop thy whip?"—I asked him again.

My father shot a swift glance at me.—"I did not drop it,"—he said,—"I threw it away."—He reflected for a space and dropped his head . . . and then, for the first and probably for the last time, I saw how much tenderness and compunction his stern features were capable of expressing.

He set off again at a gallop, and this time I could not keep up with him; I reached home a quarter of an hour after him.

"That's what love is,"—I said to myself again, as I sat at night before my writing-table, on which copy-books and text-books had already begun to make their appearance,—"that is what passion is! . . . How is it possible not to revolt, how is it possible to endure a blow from any one whomsoever . . . even from the hand that is most dear? But evidently it can be done if one is in love. . . . And I . . . I imagined . . ."

The last month had aged me greatly, and my love, with all its agitations and sufferings, seemed to me like something very petty and childish and wretched in comparison with that other unknown something at which I could hardly even guess, and which frightened me like a strange, beautiful but menacing face that one strives, in vain, to get a good look at in the semi-darkness. . . .

That night I had a strange and dreadful dream. I thought I was entering a low, dark room. . . . My father was standing there, riding-whip in hand, and stamping his feet; Zinaida was crouching in one corner and had a red mark, not on her arm, but on her forehead . . . and behind the two rose up Byelovzoroff, all bathed in blood, with his pale lips open, and wrathfully menacing my father.

Two months later I entered the university, and six months afterward my father died (of an apoplectic stroke) in Petersburg, whither he had just removed with my mother and myself. A few days before his death my father had received a letter from Moscow which had agitated him extremely. . . . He went to beg something of my mother and, I was told, even wept,—he, my father! On the very morning of the day on which he had the stroke, he had begun a letter to me in the French language: "My son,"—he wrote to me,—"fear the love of women, fear that happiness, that poison . . . ." After his death my mother sent a very considerable sum of money to Moscow.

22

F o u r years passed. I had but just left the university, and did not yet quite know what to do with myself, at what door to knock; in the meanwhile, I was lounging about without occupation. One fine evening I encountered Maidanoff in the theatre. He had contrived to marry and enter the government service; but I found him unchanged. He went into unnecessary raptures, just as of old, and became low-spirited as suddenly as ever.

"You know,"—he said to me,—"by the way, that Madame Dolsky is here."

"What Madame Dolsky?"

"Is it possible that you have forgotten? The former Princess Zasyekin, with whom we were all in love, you included. At the villa, near Neskutchny Park, you remember?"

"Did she marry Dolsky?"

"Yes."

"And is she here in the theatre?"

"No, in Petersburg; she arrived here a few days ago; she is preparing to go abroad."

"What sort of a man is her husband?"—I asked.

"A very fine young fellow and wealthy. He's my comrade in the service, a Moscow man. You understand—after that scandal . . . you must be well acquainted with all that . . ." (Maidanoff smiled significantly), "it was not easy for her to find a husband; there were consequences . . . but with her brains everything is possible. Go to her; she will be delighted to see you. She is handsomer than ever."

Maidanoff gave me Zinaida's address. She was stopping in the Hotel Demuth. Old memories began to stir in me. . . . I promised myself that I would call upon my former "passion" the next day. But certain affairs turned up: a week elapsed, and when, at last, I betook myself to the Hotel Demuth and inquired for Madame Dolsky I learned that she had died four days previously, almost suddenly, in childbirth.

Something seemed to deal me a blow in the heart. The thought that I might have seen her but had not, and that I should never see her,—that bitter thought seized upon me with all the force of irresistible reproach. "Dead!" I repeated, staring dully at the door-porter, then quietly made my way to the street and walked away, without knowing whither. The whole past surged up at one blow and stood before me. And now this was the way it had ended, this was the goal of that young, fiery, brilliant life? I thought that—I pictured to myself those dear features, those eyes, those curls in the narrow box, in the damp, underground gloom, —right there, not far from me, who was still alive, and, perchance, only a few paces from my father. . . . I thought all that, I strained my imagination, and yet—

From a mouth indifferent I heard the news of death,
And with indifference did I receive it—

resounded through my soul. O youth, youth! Thou carest for nothing: thou possessest, as it were, all the treasures of the universe; even sorrow comforts thee, even melancholy becomes thee; thou are self-confident and audacious; thou sayest: "I alone live— behold!"—But the days speed on and vanish without a trace and without reckoning, and everything vanishes in thee, like wax in the sun, like snow. . . . And perchance the whole secret of thy charm consists not in the power to do everything, but in the possibility of thinking that thou wilt do everything—consists precisely in the fact that thou scatterest to the winds thy powers which thou hast not understood how to employ in any other way,—in the fact that each one of us seriously regards himself as a prodigal, seriously assumes that he has a right to say: "Oh, what could I not have done, had I not wasted my time!"

And I myself . . . what did I hope for, what did I expect, what rich future did I foresee, when I barely accompanied with a single sigh, with a single mournful emotion, the spectre of my first love which had arisen for a brief moment?

And what has come to pass of all for which I hoped? Even now, when the shades of evening are beginning to close in upon my life, what is there that has remained for me fresher, more precious than the memory of that morning spring thunder-storm which sped so swiftly past?

But I calumniate myself without cause. Even then, at that frivolous, youthful epoch, I did not remain deaf to the sorrowful voice which responded within me to the triumphant sound which was wafted to me from beyond the grave. I remember that a few days after I learned of Zinaida's death I was present, by my own irresistible longing, at the death-bed of a poor old woman who lived in the same house with us. Covered with rags, with a sack under her head, she died heavily and with difficulty. Her whole life had been passed in a bitter struggle with daily want; she had seen no joy, she had not tasted the honey of happiness—it seemed

as though she could not have failed to rejoice at death, at her
release, her repose. But nevertheless, as long as her decrepit body
held out, as long as her breast heaved under the icy hand which
was laid upon it, until her last strength deserted her, the old
woman kept crossing herself and whispering:—"O Lord, forgive
my sins,"—and only with the last spark of consciousness did there
vanish from her eyes the expression of fear and horror at her
approaching end. And I remember that there, by the bedside of
that poor old woman, I felt terrified for Zinaida, and felt like praying for her, for my father—and for myself.

1860 A.D.

LESKOV *The Amazon*

1

"Now, now, don't start an argument with me, there's a dear!"

"Come, come, my dear Domna Platonovna, why shouldn't I have an argument with you? Why indeed should you think that nobody ought to breathe a word against you?"

"It isn't me, dear, it's you, all of you, who think yourselves so clever that you're ready to start an argument about everything under the sun! You'd better wait a bit longer, dear. When you're as old as I am, then it'll be time for you to argue. People who haven't had any experience don't appreciate the way things are done in Petersburg, and my advice to them is to sit still and listen to what older people, who know all the circumstances here, have to say."

It was thus that Domna Platonovna, a great friend of mine who sold lace for a living, used to stop me every time I happened to disagree with her about the world and people in general. It was thus that she used to stop any of her friends who were so bold as to express an opinion which was contrary to Domna Platonovna's own convictions. The circle of Domna Platonovna's friends was very large; indeed, as she used to say herself, it was "vast" and very varied, including as it did shop-assistants, counts, princes, liveried flunkeys, inn-keepers, actors and rich merchants. In a word, Domna Platonovna's friends belonged to every class and breed. As for her women friends, she had thousands of them, but having rather a

113

low opinion of the fair sex, she was not particularly proud of them.

"Women," she used to remark whenever the occasion arose, "why, I know them inside out! It's as if I had them all here!" Domna Platonovna would clench her fist and show it to me. "That's where I've got them," she'd repeat, "right in there!"

So great and heterogeneous was the circle of Domna Platonovna's friends in so populous a city as St. Petersburg that to many people it was a matter of real wonder, and some of them could not help asking her with a gasp of unconcealed admiration, "My dear Domna Platonovna, how do you do it?"

"Do what?"

"I mean how do you manage to know them all?"

"Know them all? Of course, I know them all, dear. I know almost everybody who's anybody here."

"But how did you get to know them? There must, surely, be some explanation of it."

"It's all because I'm so simple-hearted, dear."

"Oh? Are you quite sure it's only because of that?"

"Why, yes, dear. You see, they all love me because I'm such a simple soul, and it's just because of my simplicity and the goodness of my heart that I've had to put up with so much sorrow in the world, swallow so many insults, have so many people slander and traduce me and, I don't mind telling you, dear, even beat me, yes, beat me many a time! But for all that, people can't help loving me."

"I suppose that's why you know the world and its ways so well, isn't it?"

"Yes, dear, I know this rotten world well enough, that I do. Know every rogue in it, just as if I had him here in the palm of my hand. And there's something else I'd like to tell you, but on second thoughts perhaps I'd better not. . . ." Domna Platonovna would add, looking a little embarrassed and falling into a muse.

"Why, what is it?"

"Well, dear," she'd reply with a sigh, "if you want to know, it's like this: today, you see, they're always thinking out some new trick and everyone seems to be getting more and more clever."

"How do you mean they're getting more clever, Domna Platonovna?"

"I mean, dear, that nowadays while you think you're getting to
know a man by looking at his face, he, as like as not, will trip you
up with his foot. Why, it's a real wonder to me, it is, that there
should be so many people about whose only business in the world
is to cheat you and tell you lies: one man thinks he's got a clever
idea into his head, but another one gets one that is even cleverer."

"But really, Domna Platonovna, isn't there anything else but
cheating in the world?"

"Now, don't you start arguing with me, dear! Better tell me
what's your opinion of the world today? Can you find anything
else in it but deceit and cunning?"

"But surely, Domna Platonovna, there are good men in the
world, too?"

"Yes, dear, I daresay you'll find them in the cemeteries among
our parents, but they're not much good to us, are they? As for them
who're still alive, they're all villains, black-hearted villains, all of
'em: it's just one abomination of desolation, it is, dear."

"So according to you, Domna Platonovna, everybody you meet
is either a rogue or a liar and you can't trust any of them, is
that it?"

"I didn't say anything about not trusting them, dear. Trust them
by all means, if you must. Look at me: I trusted a general's wife,
that Shemelfenig woman, trusted her with twenty-seven yards of
lace, I did, but when I went to see her the other day and said to
her, 'Would you mind settling that old account of mine, madam?'
she, if you please, said to me, 'But I've paid you already!' I says to
her, I says, 'You have not paid me, madam! I've never got a penny
from you!' but she screamed at me, 'How dare you speak to me
like that, you low creature? Get out!' and her footman, of course,
at once seized me by the arms and put me out into the street. I
left my piece of lace there, but, thank goodness, it wasn't an expensive one. That's how much you can trust them!"

"But," said I, "there's only one here and there like that."

"One? No, dear, not one. Their name's legion. Mind you, in the

old days when our gentry still owned their peasants, it may have
been true to say that it was only among the lower orders that you
were likely to come across a thief, but nowadays when they have
no more peasants, they don't mind doing a bit of thieving of their
own. Why, doesn't everybody know who stole the diamond necklace at that ball the other evening? Yes, dear, nowadays nobody
minds getting something that doesn't belong to him. Take, for
instance, that Mrs. Karaulova, Avdotya Petrovna. To look at her
you'd say she was a real lady, but she pinched a lace collar under
my very nose at that country house of hers!"

"How do you mean she pinched it? Just think what you're saying, my dear Domna Platonovna! Would a lady steal a lace collar?"

"To be sure, she stole it, dear, just like anybody else. I wonder
what you'd say if I told you that directly I noticed that one of my
lace collars was missing, I said to her, speaking very politely and
diplomatically, of course, 'Pardon me, madam,' I said, 'I think
I've dropped a lace collar here. You didn't see it by any chance,
did you? For,' I said, 'I'm sure one of my lace collars is missing.'
What do you think she did? She slapped my face, that's what she
did, dear, and said to her footman, 'Show her out!' So, of course,
I was turned out immediately. I says to the footman, I says, 'My
dear sir, you're in service here and you ought to know that I can't
afford to lose my property.' And he says to me, 'Of course, you
can't afford it,' he says, 'but that's the way she always acts.' That's
all there is to it, dear. She can afford to act as she likes, seeing
what her position in the world is, but I, being poor, have to hold
my tongue."

"So what do you think that shows, Domna Platonovna?"

"What does that show, dear? Well, it's hardly my business to
think what that shows, since it's they who do the showing out.
But that everybody's a rogue nowadays, that, dear, is something
you'd better not try arguing with me about, because, thank God,
I've only to look at a man's face to tell what he's like inside."

So how is one to argue with Domna Platonovna after that? No.
However clever a dialectician you may be, Domna Platonovna is
quite certain to get the better of you in an argument, for you won't

be able to convince her whatever you say. The only thing you can do is show her the door, but that, of course, is a different matter. Otherwise you may be sure that she will always have the last word.

2

I FEEL I must describe Domna Platonovna to my readers at greater length.

Domna Platonovna is not a tall woman; in fact, she is rather short, but she looks big. This optical illusion is caused by the fact that Domna Platonovna is, as they say, broad in the beam, and what she lacks in height, she makes up for in breadth. Her health is not particularly good, although no one seems to remember her ever being ill, and to look at her you would never suspect that there was anything the matter with her. Her bosom alone is so immense that you cannot but be overcome at the sight of it. But she herself, Domna Platonovna, I mean, is always complaining about her poor health.

"To look at me," she'd say, "you would think I was robust, but there isn't any real strength in me as in other women of my size, and as for my sleep, it is just dreadful! Heavy is not the word for it. The minute my head touches the pillow, off I go and for all I care you can put me in the garden to scare away the birds. Until I've had my fill of sleep, I'm as good as dead. Yes, that's what I am, as good as dead!"

Domna Platonovna regarded her mighty sleep, too, as one of the ailments of her corpulent body and, as we shall see later, it had, in fact, given her a lot of trouble and caused her much unhappiness.

Domna Platonovna enjoyed nothing better than to pester people about the state of her health and ask them for medical advice. She would describe her ailments to them at great length, but she refused to take any medicines and believed only in "Haarlem" drops, which she called "Harem" drops, and a phial of which she always carried in the right-hand pocket of her capacious silk *capote*. According to her own account, she was always somewhere about forty-five years of age, but to judge by her fresh complexion and her cheerful mien, no one would give her more than forty. At the time of my first acquaintance with her, Domna Platonovna's hair was of a dark brown color, and there was not a single grey hair to be seen on her head. Her skin was quite unusually white and her red cheeks glowed with health, which, however, never satisfied her, for she used to buy some French *papier poudré* in the upper gallery of the Arcade, which greatly deepened the natural color of her cheeks, a color which steadfastly refused to be affected by any of her troubles or by the Finnish winds and fogs. Domna Platonovna's eyebrows looked as if they had been made of black satin: they were as black as jet and they shone with an unnatural glitter, for Domna Platonovna used to smear them thickly with a kind of black preparation and draw them into a thin line with her fingers. Her eyes were just like two black plums besprinkled with fresh morning dew. A mutual friend of ours, a Turkish prisoner of war by the name of Ispulat, who had been brought to St. Petersburg during the Crimean war, could never gaze calmly at Domna Platonova's eyes. So potent was their influence on him that the poor fellow would completely lose his head and begin to give voice to his admiration in loud, ecstatic tones.

"Oh, what beautiful eyes! What lovely Greek eyes!"

Any other woman would, of course, be flattered by so sincere a compliment, but Domna Platonovna was never taken in by these Turkish blandishments and she always insisted on her pure Russian origin.

"Don't talk such rubbish, you damned infidel!" she'd reply with a merry twinkle in those "Greek" eyes of hers. "Don't you dare tell me such a thing again, you big-bellied toad! I come of a well-known and respectable family, I do, and there aren't any Greeks in the factory in our town and never have been!"

Domna Platonovna's nose was hardly what you might call a nose, so small, slender and straight was it. A nose like that you never

come across on the Oka or the Zusha and, if you do, it is by mere
accident. Her mouth, though, was rather big: you could tell at
once that she'd been fed with a large spoon as a baby, but it was a
pleasant mouth none the less and it looked so fresh, of a regular
shape, with scarlet lips and teeth that might have been cut out of
a young turnip. In a word, not only on an uninhabited island, but
even in so big and populous a city as St. Petersburg any man who
regarded the kissing of a pretty girl as a kind of duty would not
by any means consider it a hardship to kiss Domna Platonovna.
But there could be no doubt that the greatest attractions of
Domna Platonovna's face were her chin, a chin that was a real
peach, and the general expression of her features, which was so
soft and child-like that if the thought ever crossed your mind
how a woman whose face bespoke such bottomless good-nature
could talk of nothing else but human treachery and malice, you
could not help saying to yourself, "Oh, curse you a hundred times,
Domna Platonovna, for, damn it! one look at your face is enough
to conjure up such a multitude of the most dreadful problems in
my head!"

Domna Platonovna was of a very sociable disposition; she was
a really cheerful soul, good-hearted, not given to taking offence
easily, rather simple-minded, perhaps, and a bit superstitious, too,
but, on the whole, honest and straightforward, although, to be
sure, as in every Russian, there was a streak of cunning in her.
Work and worry were Domna Platonovna's usual lot and she did
not seem to be able to live without either. She was always busy,
always rushing about, always worrying about something, devising
some new scheme or other, or carrying it out.

"I live a lonely life," she used to say, "have no one except myself to look after in the whole world and yet to earn my bare living I have to lead a most aggravating sort of existence, running
about the market like a scalded cat, and if it isn't one, then it is
another who's always trying to catch me by the tail."

"But," you'd sometimes say to her, "you can't possibly do everything at once, can you?"

"Well, perhaps not everything," she'd reply, "but all the same let me tell you that it's very trying. Well, so long at present, good-bye, dear: there are people waiting for me in a dozen different places!" and she'd actually rush off in a devil of a hurry.

Domna Platonovna quite often realized herself that she did not labor for her bread alone and that her hard work and aggravating existence could be made considerably less hard and aggravating without any harm to her own personal interests; but she just could not restrain herself from bustling about.

"I can't bear the thought of losing any business," she used to say. "I'm jealous, you see, of anyone else getting it. To see something coming my way is enough to make my heart leap with joy."

But, as a matter of fact, what Domna Platonovna was jealous of was not that anybody should derive any profit from some business she might lose. No. That side often left her strangely cold. What did matter to her was that she might miss the worry and bustle involved in bringing the business to a successful issue.

"He's deceived me, the villain!" or "She's deceived me, the beast!" she'd go on complaining all day long, but next time you met her, she was again rushing about and worrying herself to death for the same villain or beast and telling herself beforehand that they would quite certainly deceive her again.

Domna Platonovna's business which gave her so much trouble was of a most diverse character. Officially, to be sure, she was just a seller of lace, that is to say, women of the artisan class and wives of poor merchants and priests used to send her from "their own parts" all kinds of lace collars, strips of lace material and cuffs which she hawked around Petersburg, or, in summer, around the different holiday resorts in the vicinity of the capital, sending back to "their own parts" the money she received after the deduction of her commission and expenses. But, besides her lace business, Domna Platonovna engaged in a most complicated business of a private character, in the carrying out of which the lace and the collars merely played the part of a pass to places where she would not otherwise have been admitted. Thus she found husbands and wives for all sorts of people, found purchasers for furniture and second-hand ladies' garments, raised loans for people with and

without security, ran a kind of domestic agency of her own, finding jobs for governesses, caretakers and footmen, took confidential
messages to the most famous *salons* and *boudoirs* in town of the
sort that could not possibly be entrusted to the post and brought
replies from the ladies in question, ladies surrounded by an atmosphere of frigid piety and devotion to good works.

But in spite of all her enthusiasm and connections, Domna
Platonovna never got rich or even made a comfortable living. She
had enough for her own needs, dressed, in her own words, "decently" and never begrudged herself anything; but she never had
any spare money, either because she was too preoccupied with her
different business worries or because her customers often deceived
her, and, besides, all sorts of curious accidents always happened to
her with her money.

Her chief trouble was that she was an artist: she got too much
carried away by her own handiwork. Although she would invariably
tell you that she had to work so hard for the sake of her daily
bread, that claim of hers was scarcely just. Domna Platonovna
loved her work as an artist loves his art: to contrive something, to
collect something, to concoct something and then to admire her
own handiwork—that was the main thing, that was what she really
cared about, that was what she spent her money on and sacrificed
any profit she might have obtained from the business in question
which a more practical business woman would never have sacrificed.

Domna Platonovna found her vocation by sheer chance. At first
she was quite satisfied with hawking her lace and it never entered
her head to combine her trade with any other occupation; but the
magic of our capital transformed this rather absurd Mtsensk
woman into the accomplished factotum whom I knew as the in-
imitable Domna Platonovna, a woman who applied her native wit
to any kind of business and who secured an entrée everywhere.
Soon she had established herself so firmly that it was quite impossible for her not to get in wherever she wanted. She always carried a large embroidered bag on her arm, she was always dressed
in a brand-new silk *capote,* round her neck she always wore a lace

collar with large, tapering points, and round her shoulders a blue French shawl with a white border, in her free hand a snow-white linen handkerchief, and on her head either a violet or a mauve gros-de-Naples band, in a word, a perfect lady! And her face? Why, it was meekness and piety itself! Indeed, Domna Platonovna possessed the invaluable gift of being able to control the expression of her face at will.

"Without it," she used to say, "I shouldn't be able to do anything in my line of business: you must never show whether you're an Ananias or just a common or garden rascal."

In addition, Domna Platonovna had a very polite form of address. For instance, she'd never say in a drawing room, as others would in her place, that she'd been to "the public baths," but she would say, "I had the great pleasure, sir, of visiting a bathing establishment yesterday," and she'd never say, as others would, of a pregnant woman that she was pregnant, but she'd always say "she's in the family way," or something of the kind.

She was, generally speaking, a lady of the most impeccable manners and, if necessary, she was quite able to impress people by her education. But in spite of all that, Domna Platonovna was never known to show off, and she was what one might call a highly patriotic woman besides. Since her political horizon, however, was rather narrow, her patriotism, too, was of the narrowest kind, that is to say, she thought it her duty to speak highly of her own Orel province and to do her utmost for any man or woman who hailed from "her own parts."

"I'd like to know what you make of it," she used to say to me. "I know quite well that our Orel people are the worst scoundrels and the biggest thieves in the world and yet even if you were the blackest villain in your own town, even if you were worse than that cross-eyed Turk, Ispulat, I should never let you down and I wouldn't change you for the most honest and upright man from another province."

I'm afraid I could offer her no explanation of it. Both of us, in fact, were greatly puzzled, and all we could do was to ask each other:

"Now, why's that really?"

3

I GOT acquainted with Domna Platonovna by sheer chance. At
the time when I first met her I had a room in the flat of a Polish
lady, the wife of a colonel, who spoke six European languages, not
counting Polish, and who invariably ended up her conversation in
any of those languages in her native tongue. Domna Platonovna
knew hundreds of such colonels' wives in St. Petersburg and she
carried out different commissions for almost every one of them:
affairs of the heart or affairs of business or, again, both business
and heart affairs. My own landlady was, as a matter of fact, a
highly educated lady who knew the world, carried herself with the
utmost decorum, used to pretend with some success that what
she liked most about people was their sincerity and humanity, read
a lot, was thrown into unfeigned raptures by the poets and liked
to recite the lines from the Polish poet Maczewski's "Maria":

> *Everything in this world will death destroy,*
> *There's a canker in the loveliest of roses.*

It was in my landlady's flat that I met Domna Platonovna for
the first time. I was sitting at the table and drinking tea while the
colonel's wife recited to me:

> *Everything in this world will death destroy,*
> *There's a canker in the loveliest of roses.*

Domna Platonovna came in, uttered a prayer, stopped at the
door and bowed in every direction, although there was no one
else in the room except my landlady and myself, placed her volu-
minous bag on the table and said:
"Well, here I am!"
At that time Domna Platonovna wore a brown silk *capote*, a
blue French shawl, a lace collar with tapering points and a mauve
gros-de-Naples head-band, in short, she was dressed in her uniform, in which I would beg my readers to picture her to themselves
in their imaginations.

My landlady was very glad to see her, although she seemed perhaps to have blushed slightly at her entrance. She welcomed her in a friendly way, though with a certain reserve.

"Why haven't you been to see me for such a long time, my dear Domna Platonovna?" the colonel's wife asked her.

"I was very busy, ma'am," answered Domna Platonovna, sitting down and observing me closely.

"What were you so busy with?"

"Well, there's you, ma'am, and there's somebody else and somebody else again and I'm always trying to do my best for all of you and that's why I'm so busy," replied Domna Platonovna, and, after sipping her tea in silence for a while, she said, "That business you asked me about, ma'am . . . You remember, don't you? Well, I went there the other day and I spoke to . . ."

Here I got up and took my leave.

That was absolutely all that happened at my first meeting with Domna Platonovna, and it looked as if our acquaintance would hardly thrive, but thrive it did.

A few days after that meeting I was sitting in my room when there was a knock at my door.

"Come in," I said without looking round.

I could hear that something very large had crept into the room and was moving about in it. I looked round and saw Domna Platonovna.

"Where, my dear sir," she asked, "is your icon?"

"There," I said, "over the curtain in the corner."

"Is it a Polish icon or one of ours, a Christian one?" she asked again, raising her hand slowly to cross herself.

"I believe it's a Russian one," I replied.

Domna Platonovna shielded her eyes with her hand, gazed at the icon for some time and then just dismissed it with a wave of the hand, "Makes no difference," so to speak, and uttered a prayer.

"Where can I put my bag?" she asked, looking round the room.

"Put it where you like," I said.

"If you don't mind," she said, "I shall put it on the divan for the time being," and, putting down her bag, she sat down herself.

"What a nice visitor!" I said to myself. "Doesn't stand on ceremony, does she?"

"Fancy, how small icons are nowadays, you can hardly see them," Domna Platonovna began. "It's a new fashion, I suppose. All the aristocratic families in town have these small icons, but I must say I don't like it."

"Why don't you like it?"

"Why should I? It means that they're anxious to hide God away so that you can't find Him, doesn't it?"

I said nothing.

"But really," Domna Platonovna went on, "an icon ought to be of a proper size, oughtn't it?"

"What size would you suggest?" I asked. "Is there a proper size for an icon, Domna Platonovna?" and having said that, I somehow, you know, began to look on her as an old friend.

"Of course there is!" Domna Platonovna said with conviction. "Just look at our merchants, my dear friend! They always have an icon of the right size: you couldn't miss it even if you wanted to, and with a lamp that sheds its radiance all round, everything as it should be. But these tiny icons, why, what else do they signify but that our gentry are trying to run away from God and that God Himself is far from them. The other day, it was during Holy Week, I went to see a general's wife and while I was there a footman came in and announced the arrival of the clergy. 'Tell them I'm busy,' she said. 'Why should you tell them that, ma'am?' I asked. 'Isn't it a great sin not to admit them?' But she said, 'I hate priests!' Well, of course, it's her business," continued Domna Platonovna. "If she doesn't want to have 'em in her home, she needn't have 'em, but what I say is, if you don't like the men sent to your house, He who sent them won't like you."

"Oh," I said, "what a shrewd woman you are, Domna Platonovna!"

"Well, my friend," replied Domna Platonovna, "you must have your wits about you nowadays, you know. How much do you pay for your room?"

"Twenty-five roubles."

"That's a lot of money, dear."

"Well, as a matter of fact, I, too, think it's rather a lot to pay."

"Why don't you move?"

"Oh," I said, "it's too much bother."

"Your landlady is pretty, isn't she?"

"Now, please," I said, "leave my landlady out of it."

"Tut-tut," she said, "tell that to someone else, not to me. I know the kind of scoundrels you men are!"

"Well," I said to myself, "you certainly put a nice construction on everything, my dear lady."

"They're clever, though, the Polish women, I mean," said Domna Platonovna, yawning and crossing her mouth. "They don't do anything for nothing."

"You shouldn't say such things about my landlady, Domna Platonovna," I said. "She's an honest woman."

"Who said she wasn't an honest woman, dear? There's no question here of her being honest or not: she's still a young woman."

"I'm sure you know what you're talking about," I said, "but whatever it is I assure you I have nothing to do with it."

"Well," said Domna Platonovna, "I daresay you haven't, dear, but you may have, you know, you may. I know the Petersburg circumstances all right and I needn't waste any words on them."

"I can see, my dear lady," I said to myself, "that I shan't be able to convince you."

"But remember," said Domna Platonovna, bending over me and giving me a soft tap on the shoulder, "never take any advantage of the poor soul: pay her for your room!"

"But I do pay her for my room!" I protested.

"That's right, dear, because the first thing a man who makes an impression on a poor woman does, is to live at her expense."

"Now, really, Domna Platonovna," I tried to stop her, "what are you talking about?"

"Ah, my friend, a woman, and especially a Russian woman, is so very stupid about love. 'Take it, darling, take everything I have!'

Poor creature, she's ready to cut off her right arm for him and he, the low cad, is only too pleased to make use of her."

"That is very reprehensible, I'm sure," I said, "but you're not by any chance suggesting that I'm her lover, are you?"

"No, but you should take pity on her all the same, dear. For, say what you will, a woman is a poor helpless creature, ever such a helpless creature she is! They all ought to be thrashed within an inch of their lives to keep them away as far as possible from you, villains that you all are. And really, dear, why is it that the world seems to be so full of wicked men? What are they good for? And then again, look at it another way and the world would be a dull place without them, for sometimes you do seem to miss them. Oh, the devil take 'em!" Domna Platonovna exclaimed angrily, spat, and went on, "The other day I went to see Mrs. Domuk-hovskaya, another colonel's wife . . . Do you know her?"

"No," I said, "I don't know her."

"A real beauty!"

"Is she?"

"Yes, a Polish lady."

"Well, what about it?" I asked. "You don't expect me to know every Polish woman in town, do you?"

"But she isn't a real Polish lady, she's a convert, one of our faith."

"I'm afraid," I said, "that doesn't help me much. Even if Mrs. Domukhovskaya isn't really a Polish lady, but one of our faith, I still don't know who she is. I don't know her, I tell you!"

"Her husband's a doctor."

"I thought you said she was the wife of a colonel."

"Well, and so she is. What's that got to do with it?"

"Oh, never mind," I said. "What about her?"

"Well, you see, dear, she fell out with her husband."

"Oh?"

"Yes, dear, they seem to have disagreed about something and they decided to go their own ways. Anyway, that's what that Lekanida woman did. 'Can't stand his high moral tone, Domna Platonovna,' she says to me."

I just nodded.

"'Can't stand his antics,' she says to me. 'My nerves,' she says, 'can't put up with his tantrums any more.'"

I again nodded silently.

"Nerves, indeed, I thought to myself," Domna Platonovna went on, "why don't I suffer from nerves? A month passes and her ladyship, I see, has rented a flat. 'Am going to get lodgers,' she said. Well, I thought to myself, got sick of your husband, have you? Let's see the sort of trouble you're letting yourself in for now! Couldn't live decently while your husband was looking after you, so now, my dear girl, try to live by your own wits and may the Lord help you. For pride goes before a fall, it does, and when you have had enough of it, you'll be glad to go back to him, but he, my pretty one, may not be so glad to have you back! After another month I went to see her again and, as I expected, she had a lodger all right, a fine-looking fellow, except that he was maybe a bit on the thin side and a bit pockmarked, too, poor soul. 'Oh, my dear Domna Platonovna,' she says to me, 'I've such a nice lodger,' she says, 'such perfect manners, so well educated and so kind-hearted. Does everything for me, the dear man does, looks after all my affairs, he does!'"

So I said to her, "They've all got perfect manners nowadays, my dear," I said, "but since he looks after all your affairs for you, I suppose nothing could be more legal than that, could it now?"

I was just joking, you understand, but I could see that she'd taken offence, in fact, she got red in the face and looked daggers at me and we didn't part on the best of terms, I can tell you. Well, as I look at it, dear, everybody knows best what's good for him and, I thought, if that lodger of hers is really a good man, no one in his right mind would condemn her and God Himself would probably forgive her. I saw her twice afterwards and every time I found her in her little room crying her eyes out.

"What's the matter, my dear?" I asked her. "A bit too early for tears, isn't it?"

"Oh, my dear Domna Platonovna," she said, "I'm so unhappy!" and not another word would she say.

"What are you so unhappy about?" I asked. "Not in trouble, are you?"

"Oh, no," she said, "thank God it's not that."

"Well," I said, "if it isn't that then there's nothing to worry about."

"I haven't got a penny, Domna Platonovna," she said.

"So that's it," I thought to myself. "That certainly is bad."

But I know, of course, that when people find themselves penniless it is only right to cheer them up a bit. "What does money matter, my dear?" I said to her. "If you haven't got any money today, you'll get some tomorrow. What about your lodgers?"

"One has paid me," she said, "but I'm afraid two of my rooms are empty."

"I'm sorry to hear that, my dear," I said, "for in your business there can be nothing worse than empty rooms. But what about that sweetheart of yours?"

I asked her right out, without ceremony. However, she did not reply, but went on crying. Poor thing, I felt so sorry for her, for I could see that she was just a weak, silly woman.

"Well," I said, "if he really is such a rotter, then why not get rid of him?"

That made her burst out sobbing bitterly and biting the ends of her wet handkerchief.

"They're none of them worth crying over or breaking your heart for, the dirty rotters," I said. "And if you don't want to have anything to do with him any more, then it's good riddance to bad rubbish! I shall find you another one who'll not only cherish you, but will be a real help to you and never give you any occasion to cry, let alone break your heart."

But she began to wave her hands at me frantically.

"Don't, don't, don't!" she cried, flinging herself on her bed and burying her face in the pillows, her body shaking so violently that it was a wonder her dress did not split at the back.

As it happened I knew a merchant (his father owned a shop in Surovskaya Lane) who was very anxious that I should introduce him to a young lady. "Please, Domna Platonovna," he said to me, "introduce me to a nice girl or even to a married woman, I don't mind which, so long as she's highly educated. I'm fed up with uneducated women!" I could well believe it, for his father and the other menfolk in his family were all married to fools, and he himself was also married to a real nitwit of a woman. Every time I went there, she was sitting about sucking boiled sweets.

Now, I thought to myself, what could be nicer than to bring him and Lekanida together? But I could see that she hadn't learnt her lesson yet, so I left her: let her, I said to myself, ripen in the sun a little longer!

For about two months I didn't go near her. Mind you, I was very sorry for her, but I thought if the fool had no sense and did not appreciate what was good for her, then nobody could do anything for her. Anyway, about Lent I happened to be in the same house where she had her flat, sold some lace there, and I suddenly took a fancy for some coffee, simply dying for a cup of coffee I was. So I said to myself, "Why not go and see Mrs. Domukhovskaya? Surely, Lekanida Petrovna won't mind treating me to a cup of coffee!" I went up the back stairs and opened the kitchen door, but there was nobody there. "Keeping open house, it seems," I said to myself. "Take anything you like!" for there was the *samovar* and the pots and pans and everything on the shelves.

No sooner did the thought cross my mind (I was walking along the passage just then) than I heard something going bang, bang, bang. Good gracious, I thought, what could that be? I opened the door of her room and there was that sweetheart of hers—he was an actor, and not what you might call a good actor, either, although he liked to call himself an artist—well, there he was, standing over Lekanida with a riding whip in his hand.

"Oh, you brute! You brute!" I shouted at him. "What are you doing to this poor, helpless woman, you brute?" and I rushed between them, shielded myself with my bag and just rushed between them!

Domna Platonovna paused and addressed herself to me.

"So you see," she said, "what bullies like you do to a poor woman!"

I held my peace.

Well (Domna Platonovna went on with her story), so I separated them. He stopped horsewhipping her in my presence and she—why, she began to apologize for him!

"Don't take it so seriously," she said to me. "He was only joking!"

"Well, my dear," I said to her, "if he was only joking, then of course it's all right, but all the same you'd better make sure you haven't split your dress open from laughing at his jokes!"

However, they seemed to make it up: he went on living at her flat, but he didn't pay her a penny, the villain didn't.

"Is that all?" I asked.

"Certainly not!" replied Domna Platonovna.

After a little time the rows started again. He began knocking her about almost every day, and just at the time she took in a woman lodger, one of those young provincial ladies, a merchant's wife. Well, everybody knows what our merchants' wives are like: the minute they leave their homes, they're ready for any mischief. So, as I said, that artist fellow carried on as before and, in addition, he began making up to the woman lodger. Well, there were such goings on there that I even stopped visiting Lekanida Petrovna.

"This is no business of mine," I thought to myself. "You've made your bed, so now lie on it."

Only on the thirteenth of September, on the eve of the raising of the Holy and Life-Giving Cross, I went to the Znamenye Cathedral for evening mass. Walking out of the church after the service, I saw Lekanida Petrovna kneeling on the top of the steps by the entrance. Poor soul, she looked so miserable, kneeling there in an old, threadbare coat and crying as if her heart was about to burst. Well, I couldn't help feeling sorry for her again.

"How are you, Lekanida Petrovna?" I said, going up to her.

"Oh, my dear Domna Platonovna," she said with tears streaming down her cheeks, "I'm so glad to see you! I'm sure it must have been God Himself Who sent you here!"

"Well, my dear," I said to her, "I shouldn't think it was God who sent me, for God only sends disembodied angels as His messengers and I'm as great a sinner as anybody else. There, there," I said to her, "stop crying, my dear, and let's go somewhere where we can sit down under a roof and where you can tell me what your trouble is. Perhaps I could think of something to help you."

So we went.

"Has that brute been knocking you about again?" I asked.

"I haven't got anyone any more," she said, "brute or no brute."

"But where are you going?" I asked her, for her flat was in Seshtilavochnaya Street and she was turning into Gryaznaya Street.

It seemed that she had no flat any more, either. Little by little everything came out: the little furniture she had, had been taken away by her landlord for arrears of rent, her sweetheart had disappeared, and a good thing, too, if you ask me! and she was living in a little room which she rented from Avdotya Ivanovna Dislen. Now Avdotya Ivanovna is one of the meanest women in town, proud though she is of her gentility and of being a major's daughter. As mean as they make 'em, that's her! I was nearly dragged off to a police station on account of that mean cat, silly old fool that I am!

"I know that Dislen woman very well," I said to Lekanida. "My dear," I said, "she's a real harpy, she is!"

"But what can I do?" she wailed. "Dear Domna Platonovna, what can I do?"

And she wrung her hands, poor soul, so that my heart bled to look at her.

"Won't you come to my place?" she asked.

"No, my dear," I said. "My heart bleeds for you, poor thing, but I shall not go to that Dislen woman's flat. I nearly got locked up by the police once on account of that worthless creature, I did. Why not come to my place instead, my dear, if you want to talk to me?"

So she went with me to my place. I gave her tea, did my best to make her warm and comfortable, shared whatever the good Lord had sent me for supper and even put her to bed with me.

"Does that satisfy you?" Domna Platonovna interrupted her story and turned to me.

I nodded silently.

That night, I can tell you, she scared me good and proper. She'd lie quietly for a while, then she'd give a start, sit down on the bed and begin to wail.

"Dear Domna Platonovna," she'd say, "what am I going to do with myself?"

I could see that it was getting very late, so I said, "Stop worrying, my dear, and go to sleep. We'll think of something tomorrow."

I could hardly keep awake, for I'm such a sound sleeper. At last I managed to fall asleep and I slept like a log until it was time for me to get up. When I woke up I saw that Lekanida was sitting on a chair in her chemise with her legs crossed under her and smoking a cigarette. She looked such a picture, so lovely, so white —just like soft down in white satin!

"Would you mind putting on the *samovar*, my dear?" I asked.

"I'll try," she said.

She slipped on her cheap cotton skirt and went into my little kitchen. I stayed in bed, feeling a little lazy that morning. She brought in the *samovar* and we had tea.

"Do you know what I've been thinking of, Domna Platonovna?" she asked.

"I'm afraid I don't, my dear," I replied. "No use trying to guess somebody else's thoughts, is it?"

"I was thinking of going back to my husband," she said.

"Well," I said, "what could be better than being an honest woman again! But are you sure, my dear, that he will take you back?"

"Oh, he's such a good man!" she said. "I realize now that he's a much better man than any of them."

"I'm very glad he's such a good man, my dear," I said, "but how long is it since you left him?"

"I left him almost a year ago."

"Oh, so it's almost a year since you left him, is it? That," I said, "is quite a long time, my dear lady."

"What do you mean by that, Domna Platonovna?" she said.

"Oh, nothing, my dear," I said, "except that I'm just wondering if he hasn't got somebody in your place, some pretty miss who can cook a nice meal for him or bake some fine pastries."

"I hadn't even thought of it," she said.

"That's the trouble, my dear, that you hadn't even thought of it," I said. "None of you ever do, none of you ever think of it! But you should have thought of it, my dear, for if you had, you wouldn't have been in such a mess now!"

That fairly floored her, that did. I could see that she was eating her heart out, the poor creature. She bit her lips and said so softly that I could only just catch her words, "I'm sure he isn't like that at all!"

"Oh, you little fools!" I thought to myself. "You think nothing of jumping like goats into a row of peas, but when it comes to your husband, then it's a different matter! 'My husband may be an awful bore, but he mustn't even glance at a whore!' It fair makes my blood boil every time I hear some silly woman talk like that!

"I hope you don't mind my saying so," I told her, "but, as I see it, you have no right to talk like that. What kind of a man is your husband, what special kind of a man, I mean, is he that you should say he's not 'like that?' I shall never believe it. I can't help thinking that he's just like the rest of them: flesh and blood! And as for you, my dear," I said, "you'd better consider that as a woman you didn't observe your marriage vows very strictly, so why should he be blamed if he did the same as you, particularly, my dear angel, as a man is just like a hawk: he swoops down, ruffles up his feathers, shakes himself and off he flies where his fancy takes him, while all a poor woman knows is the way from the door to the kitchen stove!"

And addressing herself to me, Domna Platonovna said, "To one of you fellows a poor woman is just what a bagpipe is to a fool: he plays a few tunes on it and throws it away. Isn't it so?"

I made no reply and Domna Platonovna, I'm glad to say, did not wait for my reply, but went on:

Well, so this grand lady of mine, this Lekanida Petrovna, said to me after I had finished talking to her, "I shan't hide anything from my husband," she said, "I shall tell him everything. I shall confess and let him do what he likes with me."

"If you don't mind my saying so, my dear," I said, "that doesn't sound good sense to me, either, for however much you've sinned, what is the good of telling your husband about it? What's done, is done. He won't thank you for telling him about it, will he? So take my advice, my dear, and don't say a word to him about it."

"No, no," she said, "I don't want to lie to him."

"It doesn't matter whether you want to or not," I said. "People say it's a sin to steal, but you must have your meal!"

"No, no, no!" she went on. "I shan't tell him a lie, I shan't! Deceit is such an awful thing!"

She went on like that and I could do nothing to change her mind.

"First of all," she said, "I shall write and tell him everything, and if he forgives me, I'll go back to him immediately I receive his letter."

"All right, my dear," I said, "do as you think best. I can see that you won't listen to sense. One thing about you women, though," I said, "does seem funny to me. For you seem to be acting according to quite new rules: when you make up your minds to be unfaithful to your husbands, you don't tell them anything about it, but when it comes to going back to them, you consider it a point of honor to tell them all about your iniquities. Be warned in time, my sweet," I said, "or you'll be sorry for the rest of your life!"

Well, I was right, of course. She wrote her letter and goodness only knows what she did say to her husband in it, probably explained everything. However, there was no reply. She'd come to see me and cry and cry, but . . . there was no reply!

"I shall go back to him whether he replies or not," she said. "I don't mind slaving for him for the rest of my life."

I thought it over and . . . well, I couldn't help thinking that there might be something in what she said. After all, she was very pretty and even if her husband should get nasty, things might turn out right in the end if he saw her every day and at night . . . well, flesh is weak! The cuckoo that calls at night, they say, always sings longer than the one who only calls in the daytime.

"Very well," I said, "go back to him, for after all a husband isn't a lover: a man's more likely to take pity on a poor erring woman if she's his wife."

"But, my dear Domna Platonovna," she said, "where am I to get the money for my fares?"

"Why," said I, "haven't you got any money of your own at all?"

"Not a penny," she said, "I even owe my landlady for my rent."

"Well, my dear," I said, "money is not so easily come by these days and least of all here."

"But aren't you sorry for me?" she cried. "Can't you see my tears?"

"What about your tears, my dear?" I said. "Tears are one thing and money's another. I'm very sorry for you, as you know, but Moscow doesn't believe in tears, the proverb says. Nobody will give you any money for your tears, my dear."

She just went on crying and I sat beside her and, as we were talking to each other, there was a knock at the front door and in walked that colonel . . . now, what's his name?

Domna Platonovna paused and looked at me.

"What are you asking me for?" I said. "I'm sure I don't know his name."

"A Uhlan . . . now what do they call 'em? . . . engineer?"

"What does it matter, Domna Platonovna?" I asked.

"Larkin I think his name was, or was it? Anyway, it was a bird-like name and it began either with an L or a K . . ."

"Never mind his name!"

"You see, dear, I know so many people and I can always tell you where they live, but blest if I can remember their names!"

However (Domna Platonovna continued with her tale), in walks that colonel and, catching sight of Lekanida through the half-open door, starts teasing me about her and whispers in my ear:

"Who is the young lady?"

She's quite a grown-up woman, you know, but he called her a young lady: looked much younger than her age, she did.

I told him who she was.

"Does she come from the provinces?"

"You guessed it the first time," I said. "She does come from the provinces."

Not being a young scamp to whom every pretty face is fair game, but a man of some position and rank, he liked a woman, for a short time, at any rate, to be modest and to observe certain rules, not like our Petersburg ladies who have neither modesty, nor shame and, as for principles, a girl with a shaven head has more hair than *they* have principles! That was why he was so glad to hear that Lekanida was from the provinces.

"Do me a favor, Domna Pantaloonovna," he said (all army men, it seems have such a habit: they won't call me Domna Platonovna, but Domna Pantaloonovna!) "I don't mind what it costs me, Domna Pantaloonovna," he said, "but arrange this matter for me, will you?"

I said nothing at all to him, but just raised my eyebrows and motioned in the direction of Lekanida, giving him to understand that it was, so to speak, "difficult."

"It isn't out of the question, is it?" he asked.

"That, my dear general," I said, "I can't possibly say, because everything depends entirely on what she decides to do and although," I said, "I'm not very hopeful, I shall do my best for you."

He immediately said to me, "Don't let's waste any words, Domna Pantaloonovna. Here's fifty roubles—let her have them at once!"

"Did you give her the money?" I asked Domna Platonovna.

"Don't be in such a hurry, dear," Domna Platonovna replied. "If
you want to hear my story, you mustn't interrupt me."

I accepted the money, for, I thought to myself, although, to be
sure, I had never discussed a matter of the sort with her and
hardly knew under what pretext to give her the money, yet knowing the Petersburg circumstances as well as I do, I could not help
concluding that the poor thing would probably be too glad to take
the money. So, leaving the colonel in the other room, I went back
to Lekanida and said, "I can see, Lekanida Petrovna, that you've
been born with a silver spoon in your mouth, for we've just been
talking about money and here it is!"

She began asking me excitedly, "Who gave you the money?
How did it happen? Where did you get it from?"

I said in a loud voice, "God has sent it to you," and, bending
over, I whispered in her ear, "The gentleman in the other room
has asked me to give it to you because he wants you to be friends
with him . . . Go on," I said, "take it!"

I looked at her, and there were big tears in her eyes and they
began rolling down her cheeks on to the table just like large peas.
I couldn't tell whether she was pleased or not, but what was there
to cry about?

"Come on," I said, "don't be silly, take the money and just go
to the other room for a minute, while I stay here and pretend to be
busy! . . ."

"Well," Domna Platonovna addressed me, "what do you say?
Done her a good turn, hadn't I? And so quickly, too!"

I looked at Domna Platonovna: there was not a glimmer of
subterfuge in her eyes, not a trace of cunning about her lips, her
speech was sincere and frank, her whole face expressed her keen
desire to do the poor, penniless girl a really good turn and her fear
lest something should happen to destroy the unexpected piece of
good fortune which seemed to have dropped out of the blue, fear
not for what she, but the luckless Lekanida, might lose.

"Well, what do you say?" Domna Platonovna exclaimed, jumping up from her seat and striking the table a resounding blow with

her hand, her face flushing angrily. "Did I or did I not do all I could for her? But she, the mean creature, what did she do? Why, she rushed out of the room without saying a word to me and ran down the back stairs, howling at the top of her voice! Disgraced me, she did! I went quickly back to my little room and he, too, snatched up his hat and made off. I looked round and there was her old, worn out merino-wool coat. She must have forgotten it. You wait, my pet, I thought to myself, I shan't let you off so easily when you come back, that I shan't, you hussy, you!"

In a day or two (Domna Platonovna resumed her story after having calmed down), I came back home and lo and behold! her ladyship had honored me with a visit! Although I was not particularly angry with her, being very quick-tempered but never nursing a grudge against people, I pretended to be furious with her.

"Good evening, Domna Platonovna," she said.

"Good evening, my dear," I said. "Have you come for your coat? Here it is."

"I'm sorry, Domna Platonovna," she said, "but I got so frightened the other day."

"Well," I said, "thank you very much, my dear. I must say you repaid me for my kindness, that you did. If I'd been your worst enemy, you could hardly have done it better."

"I was so frightened, Domna Platonovna," she said. "Please, forgive me."

"I've nothing to forgive you for," I said, "but I don't like people to kick up a row in the house where I live, run down the stairs and scream the place down. You must remember," I said, "that the tenants here are respectable people and the landlord, too, is a moneylender, people come to him at all hours of the day and he does not want to hear any screams in his house."

"I'm sorry, Domna Platonovna, but—don't you see?—I never expected such a proposal."

"Are you so different from anybody else," I said, "that such a proposal should have offended you? Why, there's no law against anybody making you any offer he likes, for you're a woman who's in need of money. Besides, no one was trying to force you to do anything, so there was no reason at all why you should have made such a row, was there?"

Well, she kept on imploring me to forgive her, and, of course, I forgave her, began talking to her as if nothing had happened, and even offered her a cup of tea.

"I've come to ask you to help me, Domna Platonovna," she said. "Can you tell me how I can earn enough money to pay for my fares to my husband?"

"How do you expect to earn it, madam?" I asked. "You've had your chance, and you missed it, now you'd better think of something yourself. I'm sure I don't know how you can earn any money."

"I can sew," she said, "and I can make hats."

"Well, my dear," I said, "I know all about that. I know the Petersburg circumstances better than you. Such work, even if you were lucky enough to get it, is done by professional seamstresses and even they would walk about in rags, if they did not get their clothes by selling their favors."

"So what shall I do?" she asked, and started wringing her hands again.

"What you should have done," I said, "was not to have been so particular, for then you could have gone back to your husband the next day."

Oh, how she flared up at that! Her cheeks flamed and her eyes blazed. "What are you saying, Domna Platonovna?" she cried. "Do you really think I'd do a thing like that?"

"Didn't you do it, my dear, without asking me?"

She reddened even more. "That," she said, "was different. It was my fault, no doubt, but I couldn't help myself because I was in love, but to do such a vile thing now that I have repented and made up my mind to go back to my husband—no, never!"

"I don't know what you're talking about, my dear," I said. "I can't see anything vile about it. If you ask me, a woman who's made up her mind to turn over a new leaf should not snap her fingers at such an opportunity."

"Well," she said, "I do snap my fingers at that proposal of yours!"

"A great lady, aren't you? You didn't mind living in sin for months with that ruffian of yours, but when it's a question of business, when your own peace of mind depends on it, when your only chance of living a decent life in the future is at stake, you won't take the one step necessary to give you all you want, you can't spare a minute, can you?"

I looked again at Domna Platonovna. No, there was nothing at all about her that distinguishes those who specialize in the training of victims of the "social malady"; on the contrary, there sat before me a very good-natured woman and she talked her abominations with an air of imperturbable conviction in her own goodness and the inexcusable stupidity of Mrs. Lekanida Domukhovskaya.

"You're in the capital now," I said (Domna Platonovna continued), "and here nobody will give you anything for nothing, nobody will lift a finger to help you, let alone give you money."

So we had our talk and she went away. Off she went and I don't think I saw her again for the next fortnight. At last the poor thing showed up again, and again she was in tears, moaning and groaning.

"Sigh as much as you like, my dear," I said to her, "you may sigh until there's no more breath left in your body, but knowing the Petersburg circumstances as well as I do, I can tell you that your tears won't improve your position a bit."

"Oh dear," she moaned, "I've cried my eyes out, my head aches, and I've got such an awful pain in my chest. I've even applied for help to charitable institutions, been everywhere, but got nothing."

"Well," I said, "it's your own fault, isn't it? You should have asked me first about those charitable institutions and you'd have saved yourself a lot of unnecessary trouble. People go there only to wear out their last pair of boots."

"Just look at me," she said. "What an awful sight I am!"

"I can see, my dear, I can see," I replied, "and I'm not in the least surprised, either, for sorrow, they say, only improves a crab's complexion. I'm sorry, my dear, but I can't do anything for you."

She spent about an hour in my place, crying all the time and, to tell the truth, I was beginning to get a bit fed up with her.

"What's the use of crying?" I said to her at last. "Crying won't help you, will it? Wouldn't it be much better to swallow your pride and give in?"

I could see that though she never stopped crying, she listened to me and was no longer angry with me.

"I'm afraid, my dear," I said, "there's nothing else you can do. Remember," I said, "you're not the first and you won't be the last."

"Oh, if only I could borrow fifty roubles from somewhere, Domna Platonovna," she said.

"Nobody will lend you fifty kopecks, let alone fifty roubles," I said. "This isn't just any town, it's a capital city. You had fifty roubles in your hands but you weren't clever enough to keep them, so what can I do for you?"

So she cried and cried and went away. A little later, on the eve of St. John of Rhyl I think it was, two days before the holy day of the Icons of the Kazan Virgin, I felt a little indisposed. The night before I'd been to see a merchant's wife in Okhta and I suppose I must have caught a cold coming back on that terrible ferry. I stayed at home and didn't even go to morning mass. Put some grease on my nose and stayed in bed. It was on that day that Lekanida Petrovna did me the honor of paying me another visit. She came in without her cloak, just covered with a kerchief.

"Good afternoon, Domna Platonovna," she said.

"Good afternoon, my dear," I replied. "Why aren't you dressed properly?"

"Oh," she said, "I've only come out for a minute," but I could see that she was greatly upset, for her face kept on changing color, red one minute and white as a sheet another. She didn't cry any more, though, I must say that gave me a nasty shock, that did, for I could not help thinking that the Dislen creature must have thrown her out into the street.

"You haven't had any unpleasantness with that Dislen woman, have you?" I asked.

Her lips twitched and I could see that she wanted to tell me something, but couldn't bring herself to.

"What's the matter, my dear? Do tell me, please."

"I've come to you, Domna Platonovna," she said.

I was silent.

"How are you, Domna Platonovna?" she said.

"Nothing to grumble about," I said. "One's day's just like another with me."

"Well," she said, "I . . . I'm dead beat."

"I expect," I said, "there's been no change in your position, either."

"I'm afraid not," she said. "I've been everywhere, I really don't think I know the meaning of shame any more: been to all sorts of rich people for help. I was told there was a rich man in Kuznechy Lane who helps poor people. I went to see him and I went to see another in Znamensky Square."

"And how much, my dear, did they give you?"

"Three roubles each."

"You're lucky," I said. "I know a merchant at Five Corners who changes a rouble into kopecks and distributes a kopeck each to the poor on Sundays. 'In the eyes of God,' he says, 'it's like doing a hundred good deeds.' But as for getting your fifty roubles," I said, "I don't think you'll find a rich man in the whole of Petersburg who'd give them to you for nothing."

"I think you're wrong," she said. "I'm told there is one man who'd give me the money."

"Is there now? Who told you that? Whoever met a man like that?"

"A woman told me about it. We waited together to see that rich merchant in Kuznechy Lane. There's a Greek on the Nevsky, she told me, and he helps people a lot."

"Why does he help people?" I asked. "Just because he likes the look of them?"

"He just helps people, Domna Platonovna, that's all."

"Fiddlesticks!" I said. "Don't make me laugh!"

"But why shouldn't you believe it? That lady told me he had helped her. She's been separated from her husband for six years, and every time she goes there, she gets fifty roubles."

"She was pulling your leg, that lady of yours," I said.

"She was not," she said, "I'm sure she wasn't."

"She's lying, my dear," I said. "I shall never believe it. Who ever heard of a man giving a woman fifty roubles for nothing?"

"But I'm telling you it's true!"

"Why?" I asked, "Have you been there yourself?"

She flushed crimson, poor thing, didn't know where to hide her face.

"Really, Domna Platonovna, what are you trying to suggest? You don't think there's anything wrong, do you? Why, he's eighty years old! Many well-educated women go to him and he demands nothing from them."

"Is it only your beauty he likes to admire?" I said.

"*My* beauty? Why do you insist that I've been there?" she asked, reddening to the roots of her hair.

"Why shouldn't I? Can't I see that you've been there?"

"Well, what if I have? All right, I have been there."

"Well," I said, "I'm glad you were so fortunate as to visit such a fine house."

"I didn't notice anything particularly fine about it," she said. "I just went to see the lady who knows him and I told her about my circumstances. At first, she, too, suggested that I should do what the others had been telling me to do, but as I wouldn't hear of it, she said to me, 'Wouldn't you like to go and see a rich Greek who doesn't ask anything and helps many pretty women?' She gave me his address and she told me that he had a daughter who was studying to play the piano. She advised me to go there and say that I was a music teacher, but insist on seeing him personally. She assured me that he'd do nothing to annoy me and that he'd give me the money. You see, Domna Platonovna, he's such a very old man!"

"I don't see anything," I said.

I noticed that she was getting angry with me for being so dense, not that I was so stupid, either, for I could see very well what she was driving at, but I wanted to make her properly ashamed of herself so that her conscience should prick her just a little.

"But why don't you see it?" she asked.

"Because," I said, "I just can't make out what it is all about, and, what's more, I don't want to know what it's all about, either."

"Why don't you?"

"Because," I said, "it's an abomination! It's disgusting!" I said. "Fie, for shame!" I said.

I made her feel ashamed all right that time. She blinked at me a few times, then she flung herself into my arms and burst out crying, asking me again and again where she could get the money for her fares.

"But haven't you got your fares?" I asked. "Didn't he give you the money for your fares?"

"No," she said, "he only gave me ten roubles."

"Why only ten? He gives fifty to everybody, doesn't he? Why did he give you only ten?"

"Goodness knows," she exclaimed angrily, and even stopped crying for sheer vexation.

"So that's it! It seems you didn't quite please him, did you? Oh," I said, "you fine ladies! Didn't I, an ordinary woman, give you much more sensible advice than that fine lady of yours?"

"Yes," she said, "I realize it myself now."

"You should have realized it before," I said.

"Well, Domna Platonovna," she said, "I've now . . . I've made up my mind," and she looked down on the ground.

"What have you made up your mind about?" I asked.

"What else can I do?" she said. "I'm afraid, Domna Platonovna, I just must do as you said. I can see there's nothing else left for me to do. If only he were a decent man . . ."

"Very well," I said, trying not to embarrass her by my words, "I'll do my best for you. I'll look around. Only remember, my dear, be sensible and don't go changing your mind!"

"Of course not," she said, "I understand . . ."

I could see that the words were almost choking her, but she said in a firm voice, "See what you can do, Domna Platonovna, I'll try to be sensible."

I found out from her that the Dislen woman had given her notice to clear out of her room, and not only that, but she'd taken the ten roubles the poor thing had brought from that Greek and had, in fact, already thrown her out, taking her things, the few rags she still had, in payment of the rent she owed her.

"Well," I said, "I'd expect that from that cat."

"I think," she said, "she just wanted to sell me."

"You could hardly have expected anything else from her," I replied.

"I helped her out many a time when I had money," she said, "but now she treats me just as if I were a street walker."

"Well, my dear," I said, "you needn't look for gratitude from people today. The more you help them, the more eager they are to do you a bad turn. When they're drowning, they'll promise you the keys of heaven, but when they're safe again, they won't offer you even an ordinary doorkey."

I talked to her like that and it never occurred to me that she herself, the hussy, would show her gratitude to me in just the same way.

Domna Platonovna fetched a deep sigh.

I saw that she wanted to ask me something (Domna Platonovna went on), so I said to her, "What is it, my dear? Do you want to ask me something? Speak up, there's a dear, I shan't bite you."

"When will it be?" she asked.

"Well, my dear," I said, "you must have patience. You can't do such things just like that."

"But I have nowhere to go to, Domna Platonovna."

I have a little room (if you come up to see me one day, dear, I'll show it to you), where I keep my things, the few things I have, and if a young lady should be looking for a job or just waiting for something to turn up, I usually rent it to her. Just then the little room was free, so I told Lekanida to move in and stay there for the time being.

Her moving in just meant that she stayed there in what she came: that mean Dislen creature had taken all she had for the money Lekanida owed her.

Seeing how poor she was, I gave her a dress a merchant had given me as a present, a lovely dress it was, too, crêpe-de-chine or whatever the material is called. I couldn't wear it myself because it was too narrow in the waist. The dressmaker, the silly woman, had made a proper mess of it and, as a matter of fact, I am not very fond myself of fashionable dresses, too tight round the bosom they are, if you ask me, and that's why I always walk about in a *capote*.

Anyway, I gave her that dress and some lace, too. She altered the dress, sewed on a bit of lace here and there and made herself a lovely garment. I myself went and got her a pair of shoes with little tassels and high heels, and I gave her a few lace collars and cuffs, in short, got her up like a princess, so that not only was she pleased, but she need not have been ashamed to show herself in it to anybody. I couldn't help saying to her, "You're a really smart woman now, my dear! You certainly know how to dress!"

So one week went by and then another and we seemed to be getting on very nicely together: I was out all day on business and she stayed at home. Then suddenly I was asked by a woman, and not just an ordinary woman, either, but a real lady, though not in her first bloom—an ugly-looking Jezebel she was, as a matter of fact—if I could get her a young student as a tutor for her son. I knew, of course, the kind of student she wanted.

"He must be clean," she said to me, "not one of those what-d'you-call-'ems—Socialists, for they, I expect, don't even know where to buy soap!"

"No, of course not, ma'am," I said, "we certainly don't want any of them. They are no good for anything."

"And," she said, "he must be a grown-up man. I don't want anyone looking like a baby or the children won't pay any attention to him."

"I see what you mean, ma'am," I said.

So I found her a student: a youngish fellow, but well grown

and very clean, too, understands everything without having to be told. I went to see the lady about that business, gave her the student's address, told her when to expect a call from him and the rest of it and explained to her that if she didn't fancy him, I could find her another. So that was settled and I left. As I was walking down the stairs, I saw in the hall a general I knew who had just come in. This general (he wasn't a real general, but a high civil servant) was a highly-educated man, lived in a sumptuously furnished house with large mirrors, chandeliers, gold everywhere, carpets, footmen in white gloves, a smell of expensive scent in every room. In short, the house belonged to him and he lived on two floors, like a real lord. As you entered the house, his own suite was on the ground floor on the left, eight rooms occupied by himself, and on the right there was another suite in which his son, who was married, had lived for the past two years. The son, too, had married a very rich woman, and everybody in the house could not praise her enough, everybody agreeing that she was a very kind-hearted young lady. The only trouble was that she was suspected to be suffering from consumption, looked very thin, she did. On the first floor, just on top of that fine staircase—such a wide staircase it was with flowerpots on either side—the old lady herself lived—the general's wife, just like a blackgrouse on her feeding ground, with her children and their tutors. Lived in great state, they did!

The general saw me and said, "How are you, Domna Platonovna?" A very civil gentleman!

"How are you, sir?" I replied.

"Been to see my wife?" he asked.

"Yes, sir," I said. "I've been to see her ladyship your wife, brought her some lace, I have."

"Got anything else besides your lace? Something pretty?"

"Yes, indeed, sir," I said. "I've always got something nice for nice people."

"Well, let's go for a stroll," he said. "The weather's so lovely," he said.

"Yes, sir," I said, "the weather's certainly very lovely, we seldom get such a fine day."

He walked out of the house and I followed him and his carriage followed behind us. So we walked along Mokhovaya Street together, the general and I, such a nice gentleman he was and so unaffected, ever so simple and kind.

"Well," he said, "what nice thing have you got for me today, Domna Platonovna?"

"I've got something for you, sir," I replied, "which I know you will appreciate."

"Are you quite sure you're telling me the truth?" he asked.

He did not believe me because he was a man of great experience, always went to all the circuses and ballets, knew his way about everywhere, especially where pretty girls were concerned.

"Well, sir," I said, "I don't want to boast, for I believe you know me well enough, sir, to realize that I never talk at random; but if you feel like it, you can come up to my place any time you please. It's always better," I said, "to see a thing for yourself than to hear it praised."

"So you're telling me the truth, are you? Something worth while, eh?"

"I don't want to waste any more words, sir," I replied. "It isn't the sort of merchandise that needs advertising."

"All right," he said, "we shall see."

"You're welcome, sir," I said. "When are we to expect you, sir?"

"I shall probably come up one day this week," he said.

"I'm afraid that won't suit me, sir," I said. "You'd better tell me on what day to expect you for certain and we shall be waiting for you, for, you see, sir," I said, "I'm not always in myself. A wolf is fed by his feet, as the saying is."

"All right," he said, "in that case I'll come straight from the office the day after tomorrow, on Friday."

"Very good, sir," I said. "I'll tell her to expect you."

"And," he asked me, "haven't you got something nice in this bag of yours?"

"Yes, sir," I said, "I have a piece of lovely black lace here. Your wife took half of it," I lied to him, "and the other half I've still got. Worth twenty roubles, it is, sir."

"Give her that from me," he said. "Tell her *her good genius* is sending it to to her," he said it as a joke, but he gave me twenty-five roubles and, "Keep the change," he said, "and buy yourself something with it!"

Well, you could have knocked me down with a feather! Without as much as having cast an eye on her, he was already giving me such a present!

He got into his carriage at Semyonovsky Bridge and I walked home along the Fontanka embankment.

"Well, Lekanida Petrovna," I said, "you're a very lucky woman!"

"Why? What happened?"

So I told her everything just as it happened. I praised him without, however, concealing the truth. He was not very young, I told her, but he was a very important-looking gentleman, stoutish, wore fine linen, a pair of gold spectacles . . .

But she just sat there all of a tremble.

"There's nothing to be afraid of, my dear," I said. "He may look terrifying to some of the officials of his department, but your business with him is of quite a different kind. You see if he won't be kissing your hands and feet one day. One Polish lady I introduced him to," I said, "did anything she liked with him, and she even managed to have her own lovers besides and he got them excellent jobs. She used to tell him they were her brothers. You can take my word for it, my dear, and have no fear of him, for I know him very well. That Polish lady, for instance, used to beat him! She'd make a scene and knock his spectacles off so that the glass would go tinkling all over the place, and you're as well educated as she. In the meantime," I said, "here's a present for you from him," and I took out the lace and put it in front of her.

When I came back home again in the evening, I found her sitting at the table darning a stocking, her eyes red with weeping. The lace, I noticed, was still lying where I had left it.

"Why don't you put the lace away?" I asked her. "You should have put it in the chest of drawers. It cost a lot of money, you know."

"What do I want it for?" she said.

"Well, if you don't want it, my dear," I said, "I'll give you back the ten roubles I got for it."

"Just as you like," she said.

I picked up the lace, made sure that it was all there, rolled it up and, without measuring it, put it back in my bag.

"You owe me for my dress," I said, "but I shan't charge you too much for it. What do you say if I sell it to you for seven roubles? Your shoes cost me another three roubles, so that we are quits now. As for the rest, we'll settle it later."

"All right," she said and burst into tears again.

"I can't for the life of me see what you're crying about now," I said.

"Don't begrudge me my last tears," she said. "You needn't worry about my looks. He'll like me all right."

"Well," I said, "I've done all I could for you, my dear, so you needn't be so high and mighty with me. Look at her! The airs she's giving herself!"

So I just stopped talking to her. Thursday came and went and I still did not talk to her. On Friday I had my tea and, before leaving, I said to her, "You'd better get yourself ready, my lady. He'll be coming today."

"Today?" she exclaimed, jumping up from her chair. "Are you sure it is today?"

"Didn't I tell you that he promised to call on Friday? And it was Thursday yesterday, wasn't it?"

"Oh, my dear Domna Platonovna," she said, biting her fingers, "please, please . . ." and down she flopped at my feet.

"What's the matter?" I said. "Have you lost your senses?"

"Save me!"

"What shall I save you from?"

"Have pity on me! Protect me!"

"What are you talking about?" I said. "Didn't you ask me to arrange it for you yourself?"

She just buried her face in her hands and sobbed and sobbed, "Please, Domna Platonovna, tell him to come tomorrow, tell him to come the day after tomorrow!"

Well, I could see that it was a waste of time listening to her, so I slammed the door and went away. Let him come, I said to myself, and they'll soon reach some understanding. It wasn't the first time I'd seen women act like that: they're all a bit silly at first.

And turning to me, Domna Platonovna said, "What are you looking at me like that for? I'm telling you the truth: all of them act as if their hearts would break."

"Go on, Domna Platonovna," I said.

"Well, what do you think that hussy did?"

"How should I know what the devil made her do?" I could not help exclaiming in a sudden fit of fury.

"Aye, dear, it was the devil all right who made her do a thing like that!" Domna Platonovna said, as if complimenting me on my insight.

Such a man (she went on), such an important gentleman and she didn't even let him into the house! He knocked and knocked, rang the bell, but she just sat there without answering the door. The cunning she-devil! I never thought she'd have the sauce to do a thing like that. Sitting there behind a locked door, as if she wasn't in at all!

I went to see him the same evening without knowing what had happened. They let me in at once and I asked him, "Well, sir, did I deceive you?" But he looked daggers at me. Told me everything that had happened and how he went away with nothing.

"That's not the way to treat decent people, Domna Platonovna," he said.

"I've never heard of such a thing, sir," I said. "I suppose, she must have gone out a minute for something and she didn't hear you," but to myself I thought, "Oh, you little beast, you rattlesnake, you shameless hussy!"

"Come again tomorrow, sir," I said to him. "I give you my word that everything will be all right."

I left him and ran all the way home and when I came in I shouted at her, "Oh, you little beast, what have you done to me now? You've probably ruined me with such a man. Why, not only you, but all your relations and the whole of your province aren't worth his little finger! A word from him and all of you, aye, and the officials of your province, too, will vanish from the face of the earth! What are you playing the grand lady for, you good for nothing idler? What do you think I'm feeding you for? A poor woman like me, you can see yourself how I'm running about day and night trying to earn a few pence here and a few pence there! Can't you see for yourself what an aggravating life I live? And now I've got to feed you, too, have I?"

What names did I not call her! Oh, I was so mad at her that I called her every name under the sun. I felt like scratching her eyes out, I did.

Domna Platonovna brushed away a tear from one of her eyes and added in parenthesis: "I can't help feeling sorry for her even now when I remember how I abused her then!"

"You pauper, you! Call yourself a gentlewoman, do you?" I said to her. "Get out of my house! I don't want to see you again! I hate to breathe the same air as you!" and I even pulled her by the sleeve towards the door.

I was so furious that I didn't know what I was doing. And, really, I seemed to have completely forgotten that I had invited such an important gentleman to come to see her next morning!

No sooner did I tell her to clear out than she got up and made for the door. I was beginning to feel sorry for her, but when she turned away without speaking a word and made for the door, I got furious with her again.

"Where are you off to, you so and so?" I shouted at her.

I can't even remember the names I called her.

"Don't you dare to leave!" I said. "You're to stay here!"

"No," she said, "I'm not going to stay here another minute. I'm going," she said.

"You'll do nothing of the kind!" I said. "Don't you dare to go!"

"But if you're so angry with me, Domna Platonovna," she said, "I'd better go."

"Angry?" I said. "Why, I'm not only angry with you, but I shall beat you black and blue in a minute."

She uttered a little scream and rushed straight to the door, but I caught her by the hand and pulled her back and, furious as I was, I slapped her face six times as hard as I could.

"You're a thief!" I shouted at her. "A thief and not a lady!"

She remained standing in the corner where I had struck her, trembling like a jelly, but even then, mind you, she did not forget she was a lady.

"What have I stolen from you?" she asked.

"You'd better tidy your hair," I said, for I had made a proper mess of her coiffure. "So you want to know what you have stolen from me, do you?" I went on. "Why, you slut, haven't I fed you for two weeks? Haven't I dressed and shod you? I'm running about all day long," I said, "trying to earn an honest living, leading such an aggravating life and now must I be robbed of my last crust of bread because you've got me into trouble with such an important man?"

While I was talking, she quietly did up her plaits into a coil, filled a jug with cold water and washed her face. Then she brushed her hair and sat down at the window without saying a word, only from time to time putting the back of the metal hand-mirror to her burning cheeks. I pretended not to look at her, put out my lace on the table and tried to busy myself, but I could see that her cheeks were burning.

"Oh," I thought to myself, "I shouldn't have insulted her like that, brute that I am!"

The longer I stood at the table, the sorrier I felt for her, and the more I thought of what I had done, the more I pitied her.

"It's that kind-hearted I am!" Domna Platonovna addressed me. "Can't get the better of that good nature of mine. I felt angry with myself for having struck her. Although I knew that it was all

her own doing and that she deserved what she got, I was still sorry
for her."

So (Domna Platonovna went on with her story) I rushed out
for a moment to the pastrycook's in the basement of our house
and bought a few pastries for her. As soon as I came back, I put
the *samovar* on the table, poured her out a cup of tea and offered
it to her with the pastries. She took the tea and pastry from my
hands, bit off a piece of the pastry and just kept it there between
her teeth and . . . smiled, yes, smiled a gay kind of smile, while
tears were rolling down her cheeks. The tears didn't just flow out
of her eyes, they gushed out in a flood, just as if you took a cut
lemon and squeezed the juice out of it.

"Now, now," I said, "don't take it to heart so, there's a dear!"

"Never mind," she said, "never mind, never mind . . ." and she
went on repeating that "never mind" of hers without stopping.

"Good Lord," I thought, "she hasn't gone out of her mind, has
she?"

I splashed some cold water on her face and after a while she
calmed down and seemed to have completely recovered. She sat
down on the edge of the bed and there she remained sitting for a
long time. My conscience was still pricking me for the way I had
treated her, so I said a prayer a priest had taught me while I was
still in Mtsensk, a special prayer against madness, beginning with
the words, "O merciful Mother of the most merciful God, holy
and pure Virgin," and afterwards I took off my gown and, going
up to her in my petticoat only, I said, "Listen to me, Lekanida
Petrovna, it is written in the Scriptures, 'Let not the sun go down
upon your wrath' so please forgive me for forgetting myself. Come,
my dear, let's be friends!" Then I bowed to the ground before her
and I took her hand and kissed it. Yes, I kissed her hand, and she
bent over me and touched my shoulder with her lips and, then, she
also kissed my hand, and we embraced and kissed each other.

"My dear friend," I said, "believe me, I didn't do it out of spite
or out of greed, but for your own good!"

I went on talking to her like that, stroking her head, and she said breathlessly:

"I know, I know . . . Thank you, Domna Platonovna, thank you."

"You realize, my dear," I said, "that he'll be here tomorrow, don't you?"

"Yes," she said, "I realize that. Let him come. Yes, let him come."

I went on stroking her head and smoothing her hair round her ears, and she sat there without taking her eyes off the icon. The lamp burnt so gently before the icon and its radiance fell upon her face and I could see that she was moving her lips, but no sound came from them.

"What are you doing, my dear?" I asked. "Are you praying?"

"No, Domna Platonovna," she said, "I just can't help it."

"I thought you were saying your prayers, my dear," I said, "but you mustn't go on talking to yourself like that. It's only lunatics who talk to themselves."

"Oh, Domna Platonovna," she said, "I think I must be mad. What am I doing? What am I doing?" she went on repeating, smiting her breast with all her strength.

"It can't be helped, my dear," I said. "I suppose this is the hard heritage that has been appointed to you."

"How do you mean this heritage has been appointed to me? I was an honest woman! O God, O God, where are you? Where are you, O God?"

"It is written," I said, "that no man has ever seen God and that He is nowhere to be seen."

"But where are the good, merciful Christians? Where are they? Where?"

"The Christians, my dear, are here."

"Where?"

"What do you mean where? They are here, the whole of Russia is Christian, we're all Christians, you and I are Christians."

"Yes, yes, of course," she said, "I know that we're Christians . . ."

I glanced at her and I saw a strange look come into her face as she said those words, just as if she was talking to someone who was invisible.

"Good gracious, my dear," I said, "you haven't really lost your reason, have you? What are you trying to frighten me for? What are you murmuring against your Creator for?"

She calmed down again, but soon she burst into tears once more and started talking softly to herself.

"Why have I done it?" she said. "Why have I been my own worst enemy? Why did I listen to those people? It is they who made me quarrel with my husband, it is they who told me over and over again that he was a tyrant and a brute, but it wasn't true! It was I, stupid and pampered fool that I was, who poisoned his life instead of making him happy. Oh, you wicked people, you've misled me, you promised me untold riches, but forgot to mention the rivers of burning brimstone. My husband doesn't want to know me any more, he doesn't want to look at me again, he doesn't even read my letters, and tomorrow, tomorrow . . ." she shuddered violently. "Mother," she cried, "oh, mother, if you could only see me now, my darling! If you, my pure angel, could only look at me now from your grave! Oh, Domna Platonovna, you can't imagine the care she lavished on us! What a fine life we had, always dressed in spotlessly clean clothes . . . Oh, everything was so lovely in our house, mother adored flowers . . . She'd sometimes take me by the hand and we'd go for long walks in the country together . . . across fields and meadows . . ."

That night I had a most extraordinary dream. I fell asleep on her bed listening to the story of her childhood, just as I was in my petticoat, so I fell into a heavy sleep. Now, I usually sleep like a log and I never have any dreams, except perhaps sometimes I dream about somebody trying to burgle my flat, but that night I kept on dreaming of woods and meadows and gardens and about her, too, about Lekanida Petrovna, I mean. I saw her in my dream as a little girl, such a pretty little girl, too, with fair, curly hair, carrying a bunch of flowers in one hand and followed by a little dog, a little white dog, which was barking all the time, bow-wow, bow-wow, bow-wow! as if he was angry and wanted to bite me.

I bent down to pick up a stick to drive the dog away and just at that moment a dead hand was suddenly thrust out of the ground and it caught me here by the wrist. I woke up and I found that I had been asleep there the whole night and that it was time for me to get up. I must have lain on my hand with all my weight, for it had gone dead.

I got up, said my prayers and had my tea, but she was still asleep.

"Get up, Lekanida Petrovna," I said, "it's late. Your tea is on the table. I'm going out now, my dear."

I kissed her on the forehead as she lay on the bed. I was sorry for her just as if she was my own daughter, but as I went out of the front door, I took out the key quietly, locked the door on the outside and put it in my pocket.

"That," I thought to myself, "should make things a lot easier all round!"

Then I went straight to the general and said, "Well, sir, now everything depends on you. I did my best for you, but you'd better hurry!" and I gave him the key.

"Surely, my dear Domna Platonovna," I said, "that's not the end of your story, is it?"

Domna Platonovna laughed and shook her head, as if wishing to say, "Oh, how funny people are!"

I came home late on purpose that day (Domna Platonovna went on) and I was surprised to see that no lamp was lit in any of the rooms.

"Lekanida Petrovna!" I called.

I heard her moving about on my bed.

"Are you asleep?" I asked, hardly able to restrain my laughter.

"No, I'm not asleep," she replied.

"Why don't you light a candle?" I asked.

"What do I want a light for?" she replied.

I lit a candle, blew on the charcoal in the *samovar* and then called to her to get up and join me in a cup of tea.

"Don't want to," she said, turning her face to the wall.

"Well, why don't you get up and go to your own bed? I have to make my bed."

She got up, glowering like a wolf, looked frowningly at the lighted candle and shielded her eyes from the light.

"What are you covering your eyes for?" I asked.

"It hurts me to look at the light," she replied.

So she went off to her cubby-hole and I could hear her fling herself on her bed without undressing.

I undressed and said my prayers as usual, but all the time I was dying to know how they had fared, the two of them, while I was out. I was afraid to pay the general another visit, for, I thought to myself, I might get into hot water again. I ought, of course, to have asked Lekanida about it, but she did not seem in the mood for exchanging intimacies with me. Let's try a bit of cunning, I thought, and going into her room, I said, "Has anyone called while I was out?"

She was silent.

"Why don't you answer my question, my dear?" I asked.

She turned on me furiously and said, "What do you want to ask me questions for?"

"What do you mean?" I said. "I'm the landlady here, aren't I?"

"You know everything perfectly well without asking me about it," she said, and, mind, she was speaking in quite a different tone to me now.

But, of course, I knew all I wanted to now. I went back to my room and I heard her sighing all the time, and while I was undressing and until I fell asleep, she was still sighing.

"So that's the end of your story, Domna Platonovna?" I asked.

"No, dear," she replied, "that is only the end of the first act."

"And what happened in the second act?"

"In the second act that hussy declared war to the death on me, that's what happened in the second act, dear."

"How did that happen?" I asked. "That seems to be interesting, Domna Platonovna!"

"Well, dear, it happened just as things usually happen in life.

As soon as a man feels his power, he begins to behave like a swine!"

"How long did it take for her attitude towards you to change?"

"How long? Why, the very next day she showed herself in her true colors!" Domna Platonovna replied and resumed her tale:

I got up early as usual and got the *samovar* going. Having made tea, I went to her little room and sat down beside her bed with my cup of tea.

"Get up, Lekanida Petrovna," I said, "have a wash and say your prayers, it's time for a cup of tea."

Without saying a word, she jumped out of her bed all dressed as she was, and I noticed that a piece of paper fell out of her pocket. I bent down to pick it up, but she swooped down on it like a hawk.

"Don't touch it," she said, grasping it in her hand.

I saw that it was a hundred rouble note. "What are you growling at me like that for, my dear?" I said.

"I shall growl at you if I like," she said.

"Calm yourself, my dear," I said, "I'm not that Dislen landlady of yours! Nobody will take away what belongs to you in my house."

Not a word did she say in reply. Drinking my tea, she was, but too proud even to look at me! Who would not feel hurt at being treated like that? However, I let that pass too, thinking that she was still feeling upset and, indeed, I could see how every now and then a shiver would pass across her bare chest (her chemise was cut very low). She had, as I mentioned before, a lovely body, pink and white, just like soft down in satin, but that morning her skin seemed to have gone dark and her bare shoulders, poor thing! were covered with goose-pimples, as if from cold. "A pampered miss finds the first cold blast a bit disconcerting," I thought, and I even pitied her in my heart, little dreaming that she could be so spiteful!

When I came home in the evening, I found her sitting before a candle sewing herself a new chemise, and on the table in front of her lay three or four more already cut out for sewing.

"How much did you pay for the linen?" I asked.

"I'd thank you not to bother me in future with any of your conversation, Domna Platonovna," she replied in an unnaturally quiet voice.

I shot a glance at her: she looked entirely self-composed, as if she wasn't a bit angry with me. All right, my dear, I thought to myself, if you're so high and mighty, then I too will be quite different with you!

"In my own house, Lekanida Petrovna," I said to her, "I am the mistress and I can say whatever I like, and if," I said, "you don't like my conversation, then you can go where you like."

"Don't worry," she said, "I'm going."

"But before you go," I said, "you'd better settle your account. Honest people don't leave without paying what they owe."

"You needn't worry about that, either," she said.

"I'm not worrying," I said, and I went on to tell her what she owed me for board and lodging for the six weeks she had been at my place: ten roubles for her room, fifteen roubles for her food and, I said, "Let's say another three roubles for tea and three more roubles for your laundry, making altogether," I said, "thirty-one roubles." I forgot to charge her for the candles, and it quite slipped my mind that I had also taken her with me twice to the baths.

"Very well," she said, "you'll be paid all that."

When I returned home in the evening of the following day, I found her again sitting at the table and sewing herself a chemise and on the wall, just opposite her, there hung on a nail a lovely new cloak of black satin with a gros-de-Naples lining and padded with down. It made my blood boil to think that it was through me, through my zeal for her, that she had got it all and that she should be buying everything now without me and even in an underhand way.

"If I was you, my dear," I said, "I should not have been in such a hurry to buy myself cloaks, but would first have paid my debts."

She at once put that dainty hand of hers into her pocket and, taking out a wrapped-up piece of paper, handed it to me. I unwrapped the paper and found exactly thirty-one roubles there.

I took the money and "Thank you very much, madam," I said, calling her "madam" on purpose.

"Don't mention it," she said without even deigning to look up at me from her work.

She kept on sewing and sewing, the needle simply flying between her fingers. "You just wait, you green serpent, you!" I thought to myself. "Don't you give yourself such airs, my girl, just because you paid what you owed me!" And I said aloud, "You've paid me for my expenses, Lekanida Petrovna, but what do you propose to give me for the services I've rendered you?"

"What sort of services?" she asked.

"Do you want me to explain it to you?" I asked. "Can't you understand yourself?"

She went on sewing, pressing the hem down with her thimble. "Let him who wanted your services," she said without looking up, "pay you for them."

"Wasn't it you who wanted them most?" I said.

"No," she replied, "I didn't want them at all, and," she added, "I'd be greatly obliged if you left me alone!"

How do you like that? The impudence of the woman! However, I ignored it, left her alone and didn't talk to her again.

The following morning, it was just about breakfast time, she put on the chemise she'd been sewing, wrapped up the others which weren't ready yet in a kerchief, dressed and, bending down and taking out a cardboard box from under her bed, got a new hat out of it . . . It was a lovely hat! and it suited her perfectly . . . She put it on and said, "Good-bye, Domna Platonovna!"

Again I felt sorry for her as if she was my own child. "Won't you wait and have a cup of tea with me, my dear?"

"No, thank you," she said, "I shall have tea at my own place."

At her own place, if you please! Well, heaven forgive her, I ignored that, too. "Where are you going to live?" I asked.

"In Vladimirskaya Street," she said, "in Tarkhov's house."

"Oh, I know it very well," I said. "It's a nice house except that the house-porters there like to run after girls."

"I assure you," she said, "I'm not interested in house-porters."

"Of course not, my dear, of course not!" I said. "Have you rented a room there?"

"No," she replied, "I've taken a flat. I'm going to live there with my cook."

"So that's the way things are with you now!" I thought to myself and said aloud, "You're a real one, aren't you?" and I shook a finger at her, joking like. "Why did you deceive me then? Why did you tell me you wanted to go back to your husband?"

"So you think I deceived you, do you?" she said.

"What did you expect me to think?" I said. "If you really wanted to go back to your husband, you wouldn't have rented a flat, would you?"

"I'm sorry for you, Domna Platonovna," she said, "you don't seem to understand anything."

"Don't try to be too clever with me, my dear," I said. "I can see that you've managed everything beautifully!"

"What are you talking about?" she exclaimed. "Do you think sluts like me go back to their husbands?"

"Oh, my dear," I said, "what are *you* talking about? Slut, indeed! I know women who're ten times worse than you and who still live with their husbands!"

She was standing at the door just then and was about to open it and go out, when she suddenly smiled and, turning to me, said, "Forgive me, Domna Platonovna, for having been angry with you. I can see now that one ought never to be angry with you, for you are such a stupid woman!"

That was her way of saying good-bye to me! Nice, wasn't it? "Well," I thought, after she had gone, "stupid or not, I seem to be cleverer than you, anyway, for I did exactly what I liked with you, clever and educated lady that you are!"

So that was how we parted. We had not exactly quarrelled, but we had not been particularly nice to each other, either. I did not see her after that day for I should think almost a year. I happened to have been particularly busy at the time, married off four merchants, found a husband for a colonel's daughter, got a wife for a State Councillor, the widow of a merchant, and in between there were lots of other things to be seen to and, of course, there was also my lace to sell—I was sent yards and yards of it at the time from the provinces, so what with one thing and another the time passed. Well, one fine day it so happened that I had to visit the house of the general to whom I had introduced my Lekanida, to see his daughter-in-law. His son I had known a long time: a chip of the old block he was, like father, like son! Anyway, so I went to see the general's daughter-in-law, who wanted to sell me a white silk cloak, but she wasn't at home: gone to Voronezh, I was told, to pray at the tomb of St. Mitrofany. Well, I said to myself, why not go and see her husband for old times' sake?

I went in through the back door, but found no one there. I peeped into one room, then into another and suddenly I heard Lekanida's voice. "Darling," she was saying, "I love you. You're the only treasure I have in the whole world!"

"Well, well," I said to myself, "so my dear Lekanida Petrovna is having a fine time, it seems, making love to father and son!" and off I went, without making a sound, the same way I came in. I started making enquiries, for I was curious to find out how she had got to know the son. Well, it seemed that it was the son's wife who took pity on her and began visiting her surreptitiously, all because, you see, she was so sorry for her, because of her being such a nice, educated young lady, Lekanida, that is. Well, so my dear Lekanida had paid her back in the same coin as she had me. All right, it was none of my business, so I said nothing about it and, in a manner of speaking, I even became an accomplice in her treachery, for even where I ought to have spoken out, I never showed by a look that I knew what was going on.

Nearly another year passed. At the time, Lekanida lived in Kirpichny Lane. It was the fourth week of Lent and I was getting ready to go to confession when, walking through Kirpichny Lane one day, I looked up at the house where she lived and I said to myself, "What an awful shame I haven't made it up with Lekanida Petrovna! I'm now getting ready to partake of the holy Eucharist and what could be more seemly than being friends with her

again?" So I went in. She lived in such style that you couldn't ask
for anything better, even the parlor maid looked a real lady.

"Tell your mistress, my pretty one," I said to her, "that Domna
Platonovna, the lace woman, would like to see her."

She went in, and returning almost at once, said, "Please
come in."

I went into the drawing room where everything was in very fine
style, too, and there on a divan sat Lekanida Petrovna and the
general's daughter-in-law: they were both of them having coffee.
Lekanida met me just as if nothing had happened between us,
just as if we had seen each other only the night before.

I, simple-hearted that I am, began to congratulate her on her
nice flat, saying, "What a lovely flat you have, my dear! I hope
the Lord will shower even greater blessings upon you!"

She began talking quickly in French to the other one, and I
couldn't understand a word they were saying to each other. I just
sat there like a fool, staring at the walls until I began to yawn.

"Oh, I'm so sorry, Domna Platonovna," Lekanida suddenly said
to me, "would you like some coffee?"

"Thank you, my dear," I said, "I shouldn't mind a cup."

She at once rang a silver hand-bell and said to her maid,
"Dasha," she said, "see that Domna Platonovna has some coffee,
will you?"

Fool that I am, I did not at the time realize what she meant
by her "see that she has some coffee!" But in a minute or two the
same Dasha came in and announced, "The coffee's ready, ma'am."

"Thank you," said Lekanida to her and, turning to me, she said,
"Won't you go with her to the kitchen, Domna Platonovna? She'll
see that you have some coffee!"

Well, that was the last straw! I was ready to burst with anger.
"I shall expose her!" I thought to myself, still controlling myself,
though.

I got up and said, "Thank you very much, Lekanida Petrovna,
you're very kind I'm sure, but poor as I am," I said, "I can afford
my own coffee."

"Why are you so angry with me?" she asked.

"Why?" I said, looking straight into her eyes. "Because, my dear, you did not mind eating my food at my table with me and now you want me to have coffee with your maid. No wonder I'm feeling hurt."

"But Dasha's an honest girl," she said, "and her company cannot possibly be an affront to you," and it seemed to me that, as she said it, she was smiling to herself.

"Oh, you viper," I thought to myself, "I've nourished you in my bosom and now you're turning on me, are you?" and I said aloud, "I haven't said a word against the young lady's morals, but I didn't expect you, Lekanida Petrovna, to put me at a table with your servants!"

"And why shouldn't I, Domna Platonovna?" she asked.

"Because, my dear," I said, "you ought to remember what you were and you should take a look at yourself now and consider to whom you owe it all."

"I remember very well," she said, "that I was an honest woman and that now I'm trash and that I owe it all to your kindness, Domna Platonovna."

"Quite right, my dear," I said, "you are nothing but trash! I'm telling you that straight to your face and I don't care who hears me: you're trash! You were trash and trash you are and it was certainly not I who made you trash!" And picking up my bag, I said, "Good-bye, your ladyship!" and was about to leave them, when the general's daughter-in-law, the sickly one, jumped up from her seat looking all flustered and shouted at me:

"How dare you speak like that to Lekanida Petrovna?"

"Why shouldn't I, pray, speak to her like that?" I asked.

"Lekanida Petrovna," she said, "has been very kind to you, but I shan't allow her to be insulted in my presence: she's my friend!"

"Some friend!" I said.

But here Lekanida, too, jumped to her feet and screamed at me, "Get out of here, you abominable creature!"

"Oh," said I, "so I'm an abominable creature, am I? Well, I may be abominable, but I've never made love to other women's husbands. However bad I may be, I never tried to seduce a father and his son by flaunting my charms before them. That's what you friend has done, madam," I said, addressing the general's daughter-in-law, "this dear friend of yours?"

"You lie," she said. "I shall never believe you. You're saying that about Lekanida Petrovna out of spite!"

"Well," I said, "if it is out of spite I'm saying that, then you'll have to excuse me, Lekanida Petrovna, if I expose you now!" And I laid it all on the table before them, told them everything I had heard Lekanida saying to the other woman's husband, and went away.

"Well, and what happened then, Domna Platonovna?" I asked.

"The old gentleman would have nothing to do with her after that scandal."

"And the young one?"

"The young one did not keep her, did he? With the young one everything was, as they say, *pour amour*, he was in love with her and she with him! A worthless baggage like that, but she, if you please, could not live without love. Yes, she had to have a real love affair same's a police officer has to have a pair of trousers. But now she makes do without love, she does!"

"How do you know that?" I asked.

"How do I know it, dear? Why, the poor thing has to make do without love living the life she does now. One day it's a prince, another—a count, then an Englishman, and the day after an Italian, and the day after that some Spaniard. That is no longer love, dear, but filthy lucre. Goes out shopping like a countess and you should have seen the carriage in which she goes driving on Nevsky Avenue, the horses alone must have cost her thousands . . ."

"So since then you haven't been meeting her, have you?"

"No, dear. Not that I bear her any grudge, but I've never been to see her again. To tell you the truth, I don't care what happens to her now! The other day I went to see a lady in Morskaya Street and, as I came out, I met her coming up the front steps of the house. I let her pass and said to her, 'Good morning, Lekanida Petrovna!' She went green in the face, bent over to me from the top step and, smiling sweetly, said, "Good morning, you beast!"

Here I could no longer contain myself and burst out laughing.

"Yes dear," Domna Platonovna assured me, "that's what she said to me: 'Good morning, you beast!' I wanted to say to her, "Don't you beast me, my dear, you're a proper beast yourself now,' but her servant was coming up the steps, carrying a large umbrella, so I thought to myself, 'Go in peace, my French marquise!' "

4

F I V E years have passed since the day when Domna Platonovna told me the story of Lekanida Petrovna. During those years I left St. Petersburg several times, coming back again to hear the city's ceaseless din, to look at the pale, worried, crushed faces of its inhabitants, to breathe the stench of its exhalations and to give way to fits of the blackest melancholy during its consumptive "white nights." Domna Platonovna was still the same. She used to come across me accidentally in whatever part of the city I happened to live, welcomed me always with open arms and friendly kisses, and never tired of complaining about the treacherous machinations of man who seemed to have picked her out as his favorite victim and perpetual plaything.

Innumerable were the stories Domna Platonovna told me during those five years and in all of them she was always trampled upon, insulted and humiliated, a sacrifice to her own virtues and a martyr to her own eternal solicitude for the happiness of other people.

These diverting and ingenuous tales of my dear, simple-hearted Domna Platonovna abounded in all sorts of strange and wonderful adventures. It was from her that I learnt about different kinds of weddings, deaths and inheritances; it was she who told me of the latest thefts, burglaries and confidence tricks; it was entirely due to her that my eyes were opened to every instance of open and covert immorality in the capital; it was she who initiated me into the various Petersburg mysteries, and it was she, finally, who gave me the latest news about you, my friends, who hail from the same parts as Lekanida Petrovna, and about your edifying adventures—yes, about you who bring to us from the wide Volga, the limitless Saratov steppes, the gentle Oka and the golden, thrice-blessed Ukraine, your fresh, healthy bodies, your ardent, but far from wicked hearts, your quite insanely audacious faith in fate or chance or in your own strength and your dreams which are of no use whatever to anybody here.

But let us return to our friend Domna Platonovna. You must not be offended, dear reader, whoever you may be, if I speak of Domna Platonovna as our mutual friend. Since I am assuming that every reader of mine possesses at least a nodding acquaintance with Shakespeare, I should like him to remember Hamlet's words: "Use every man after his desert, and who should 'scape whipping." It is indeed difficult to penetrate into the secret places of a man's heart!

So Domna Platonovna and I kept up our meetings and friendship; she went on looking me up and, although she was always hurrying off somewhere on some important business errand, she used to stay with me hours at a time. I, too, visited Domna Platonovna at her flat, not far from the cathedral, and I saw the cubby-hole where Lekanida Petrovna took refuge until her act of renunciation, and the pastrycook's shop where Domna Platonovna had bought the pastries with which to please and comfort her and, finally, I had the good fortune to see two freshly arrived "young ladies" who had come to St. Petersburg in search of happiness and found themselves in Domna Platonovna's flat "in Lekanida's place." But what I could never discover from Domna Platonovna was how she had reached her present position, or how she came to hold her highly original views about her own absolute uprightness and the insatiable craving for every kind of evil-doing on the part of the rest of mankind. I wanted very much to know what happened to Domna Platonovna before she got into the habit of meeting all objections with, "Now, now, don't you start an argument with me, there's a dear, for I know everything much better than you." I wanted to know what that blessed merchant's family on the Zusha was like in which this plump Domna Platonovna had grown up, this woman in whom prayers and fasts

and her own chastity, of which she was inordinately proud, and
her pity for the unfortunate were combined with barefaced lying
in her professional capacity as matchmaker and an artistic flair
for bringing about short-lived marriages, not for love, but for
money, etc., etc. How, I wondered, could all that be accommo-
dated in one fat little heart where such an amazing harmony
reigned that one moment Domna Platonovna was driven by her
feelings to slap the weeping Lekanida Petrovna's face time after
time and the next moment to rush downstairs to buy her some
pastries; the same heart which contracted painfully when she
dreamt about Lekanida Petrovna as a little girl in her Sunday
clothes going for a walk with her mother, but which beat calmly
when she invited some fat hog to defile the same Lekanida
Petrovna who could not even protect her body any more by locking the door!

I realized very well that Domna Platonovna did not engage in
that kind of business as a profession, but looked upon it *in the
St. Petersburg way*, and accepted it as a kind of law that no
woman could possibly extricate herself from any trouble except
through her own moral downfall. But all the same, what exactly
are you, Domna Platonovna? Who first gave you the idea of following this path? But Domna Platonovna, for all her talkativeness,
could not be induced to talk about her past.

One day, however, it so happened that Domna Platonovna,
quite accidentally and of her own accord, told me how *simple*
she had been and how "they" had *taught* her so that at last she
no longer believed anybody or took anything on trust. Do not
expect, dear reader, to find anything coherent in this story of
Domna Platonovna, which will hardly help anyone to understand
the mental process of this Petersburg business woman. I am telling
you what happened to her later just to entertain you a little and,
perhaps, to give you a chance to reflect upon that blind, but
terrible force of "the Petersburg circumstances," which not only
produce a Domna Platonovna, but also deliver into her hands
those who rush across a river without troubling to look for a ford,

the numberless Lekanidas over whom Domna tyrannized here, while everywhere else she would have realized herself that in their company she was nothing but a pariah or, at best, a clown.

5

I WAS ill at the time. I lived in Kolomna in a flat which was, to quote Domna Platonovna's description of it, "a bit peculiar." It consisted of two spacious rooms in an ancient wooden house owned by a little, wooden-faced old woman. Her husband, a merchant of great piety, having only recently died, my landlady, as behoved her widowed state, engaged in money-lending and let out her former bedroom with its huge double-bed and the adjacent sitting room with its enormous icon-case before which her late husband used to offer up his daily prayers.

In my so-called "parlor" I had a divàn upholstered in real Russian hide, a round table covered with a cloth of faded violet plush with an entirely colorless silk border, a table-clock with a copper negro, a stove with a figure in high relief in a cavity where home-made liqueurs were usually placed to mature, a long mirror of excellent quality with a bronze harp on the top ledge of its tall frame. On the walls hung an oil-painting of the late Emperor Alexander I, and beside it, behind the glass of a heavy, gilt frame, a huge lithograph depicting four scenes from the life of Queen Guinevere, a portrait of the Emperor Napoleon in infantry uniform and another in cavalry uniform, a mountain landscape, a dog swimming in its own kennel, and a portrait of a Russian merchant with a medal on an Anne ribbon. In a far corner stood a tall, three-tiered icon-shrine with three large icons with dark visages which gazed sternly out of their shining, gilt garments; in front of the shrine was a lamp which was always carefully lit by my pious landlady and below, under the icons, was a little cupboard with semi-circular doors with a bronze ridge instead of a handle. All this gave me the feeling that I was not

living in St. Petersburg, but in Zamoskvoryechye, the old merchants' quarter of Moscow, or even in the provincial town of
Mtsensk itself.

My bedroom was even more Mtsensk-like: it sometimes seemed
to me that the enormous double bed in whose featherbeds I sank
as in a sea, was not a bed at all, but the town of Mtsensk itself,
which was carrying on an incognito existence in St. Petersburg.
No sooner did I sink in those featherbed waves than a kind of
narcotic, poppy-like substance descended like a veil on my eyes
and hid from them the whole of St. Petersburg with its cheerful
boredom and its boring cheerfulness. It was there, in that becalm-
ing Mtsensk atmosphere, that I was again destined to have long
heart-to-heart talks with Domna Platonovna.

I caught a cold and the doctor ordered me to stay in bed for a
few days.

On one of those days, about twelve o'clock on a greyish March
morning, I was lying in bed, already convalescing from my illness,
and, having read as much as I fancied, I was thinking that it
would not be a bad idea if someone came to see me. No sooner
did that thought cross my mind than the door of my parlor opened
with a creaking noise and I heard Domna Platonovna's cheerful
voice exclaiming, "Oh, how lovely everything is here, dear. What
fine icons and how gloriously they shine! Yes, dear, you have got
a lovely place!"

"Is it you, my dear Domna Platonovna?" I asked.

"Of course, it's me," she replied. "Who else would it be
but me?"

We exchanged greetings.

"Sit down, please," I urged Domna Platonovna.

She sat down in an armchair opposite my bed and put her little
hands, in one of which she grasped her snow-white linen handkerchief, on her knees.

"What's wrong with you?" she asked.

"Caught a cold," I replied.

"Lots of people are suffering from stomach complaints at present," she said.

"There's nothing wrong with my stomach," I said.

"Well," she said, "if there's nothing wrong with your stomach, you'll soon be better. You've got a lovely flat, dear."

"Not bad, Domna Platonovna," I said.

"An excellent flat. I've known your landlady, Lyubov Petrovna, a long time. She's a fine woman. She was a bit touched in the head one time and she used to scream in different voices, but I expect that must have passed off now."

"I don't know," I said. "I've never heard anything. She doesn't appear to be screaming any more."

"Oh, dear, I'm in proper trouble just now," said Domna Platonovna in a most pitiful voice.

"Why, what's the matter, Domna Platonovna?"

"Oh, such awful trouble, dear, such awful trouble that . . . it's something terrible, really, trouble and bad luck all together. Can't you see what I'm carrying my lace in now?"

Leaning over I had a look and I saw that Domna Platonovna's lace was lying on the little table, tied in a black silk kerchief with a white border.

"Are you in mourning?" I asked.

"Yes, in mourning indeed and *what* mourning!"

"I'm sorry to hear that," I said, "but where's your bag?"

"Why, dear, it's my bag I'm in mourning for. It's gone, yes . . . my bag's gone!"

"How do you mean it's gone?"

"Well, dear, it's just gone, and for the last two days every time I think of it I cannot help saying, 'O Lord, am I really such a miserable sinner that Thou shouldst try me like that?' You see, it all happened in such a funny way: it all began with a dream. I dreamt that an unknown priest came to see me and he brought me a loaf, the kind of loaf they bake in our town out of wheat porridge. 'Here,' he said, 'take this loaf, woman.' 'Father,' I said, 'whatever do I want this loaf for?' But you can see now what he brought me that loaf for, can't you?—to warn me that I was going to lose something!"

"How did it all happen, Domna Platonovna?"

"Oh, it happened in the queerest way, dear. You know the merchant's wife, Mrs. Kosheverova, don't you?"

"No," I said, "I don't know her."

"Oh, well, if you don't know her, then it doesn't matter. I'm an old friend of hers, or, perhaps, I shouldn't say, dear, that I'm a friend of hers, for she's a most spiteful woman and as mean as they make 'em! I just happen to know her, just as I do you, dear. The other evening I went to see her and, to my misfortune, I stayed a bit late. She kept on saying to me, 'What's your hurry, Domna Platonovna? Please, stay a little longer!' Drat the woman, has nothing to do, so she's worrying herself to death because her husband isn't jealous, although heaven knows why he should be jealous, seeing that she's as ugly as sin and that her tongue is as long as a parrot's. She told me she had toothache once and the doctor told her to apply a medicinal leech to her tooth, but the district nurse's boy applied it to her tongue instead and ever since her tongue has been swollen. I had some other business to see to that evening, had to visit a house at Five Corners to see a merchant who wants me to find him a wife, but that Kosheverova woman wouldn't let me. 'Wait,' she said, 'let's have a glass of Kiev brandy and, besides,' she said, 'Fadey Semyonovich will be coming from evening mass soon and then we'll have a cup of tea. What are you in such a hurry for?' 'But I *am* in a hurry, dear!' I said, but to my misfortune I did stay and drank so much of that vodka, or brandy, or whatever it was, that my head began to spin. 'You'll have to excuse me, Varvara Petrovna,' I said, 'it's very kind of you, I'm sure, but I can't drink another drop.' But she wouldn't leave me alone, kept on begging me to have a little more, but I said, 'No, dear, you'd better not ask me to have a drop more. I know how much is good for me and I can't possibly have another drop, dear, not another drop!' She says to me, 'But you'll wait for my husband, won't you?' I said, 'No, my dear, I shan't wait for your husband, either.' So I put my foot down and insisted on going, for, you see, my head was going round and round. So, my dear sir, out of the gates I went, then turned into Razyezhaya Street, thinking, I'd better take a cab, and there

was a cab, just waiting for me at the corner of the street. I says
to the cabby, 'What will you charge me, my fine fellow, to the
Znamenye Cathedral of the Holy Virgin?' and he says, 'Fifteen
kopecks, lady!' 'Oh, no,' I said, 'five kopecks!' Well, he wouldn't
agree, so I walked along Razyezhaya Street. It was very light, the
street lamps were burning, gaslight in the shop-windows . . . I
said to myself, 'I'll get home on foot rather than pay fifteen
kopecks to that hooligan for taking me a few yards in his cab.'
Then all of a sudden, dear, there sprang out of the ground a
funny kind of man—goodness only knows where he'd come from
—in an overcoat, a hat and goloshes, in a word, a real gentleman!
I tell you, dear, I couldn't for the life of me make out where he
had sprung from so sudden like. 'Excuse me, madam,' he said
(called me 'madam,' the rascal did), 'could you tell me where
Vladimirskaya Street is?' 'Yes, sir,' I said, 'go straight ahead till
you come to the first turning on the right . . .' But no sooner did
I say that, raised my hand, you know, to show him, than he
gave a pull at my bag, 'Thanks very much, lady,' he said, 'greatly
obliged I'm sure!' and off he ran in the opposite direction. 'Oh,
you hooligan,' I said, 'you rogue!' thinking that he'd just been
playing a silly trick on me, but then, looking for my bag, I saw
that it was gone! 'Help, help!' I shouted. 'Stop thief, stop thief!'
and I started running after him, knocking against people, catching hold of people's hands, dragging them after me, shouting,
'Help! A man's run off with my bag!' So I ran and ran until I
was tired out, but there was no trace of the thief. And indeed
how could a person of my size hope to catch a fast-running rogue
like him? I turned to the people in the street: 'Oh, you rogues,'
I shouted, 'what are you staring at me for? Are you Christians at
all? Can't you help a poor woman that's been robbed?' Anyway,
I ran and ran and then I stopped and began to howl at the top
of my voice like a fool. Sat down on a curbstone and howled. A
whole crowd gathered round me and I could hear them saying
to each other, 'Must be drunk!' But I said to them, 'You're drunk
yourselves, you rogues. I've had my bag snatched from my hand
just this minute.' Here a policeman came up. 'You'd better come

to the police-station with me, lady,' he said. So we went to the police-station and there I started another row. Then an inspector came out of a door and said, 'What are you making such an infernal noise for, woman?' 'Oh, sir,' I said, 'I've just had my bag snatched out of my hands in the street!' So he said, 'We'll have to have a written report about it.' So they wrote the report and then he said to me, 'You can go now.' So I went. Next day I came back. 'What about my bag?' I asked. 'You can go home now,' they said. 'Your report has been sent off. You'll have to wait.' So I waited and waited until I got a summons to call at the police-station. When I came there, they took me to a big room where there were hundreds of bags. A police captain, a very civil gentleman, good-looking, too, said to me, 'Can you identify your bag?' I looked and looked, but mine was not among them. 'No, sir,' I said, 'my bag isn't here.' So he said, 'Give her a paper!' 'What's this paper for, sir?' I asked. 'It is an official notice that you've been robbed,' he said. 'But how will that paper help me, sir?' I asked. 'Well, madam,' he said, 'what else do you want me to do for you?' So they gave me the paper which said that I had been robbed and said, 'Go to the lost property office now.' So off I went to the lost property office and showed them the paper and out came an official in a colonel's uniform and he took me to a room where there were thousands of bags and he told me to look for mine among them. I looked, but mine was not there. 'Wait,' he said, 'the general must sign your paper first.' So I waited hours till the general arrived and he was given my paper and signed it. 'What has the general signed on my paper?' I asked an official. 'He signed that you've been robbed,' he replied. So now I always carry this paper about with me," Domna Platonovna finished the story about the loss of her bag.

"Yes, by all means, carry it about, Domna Platonovna," I said.

"Who knows, dear, it may turn up one day."

"Well," I said, "the most unlikely things do happen sometimes."

"Yes, indeed," she said. "If I had known I'd have stayed the night at Mrs. Kosheverova's."

"If only," I said, "you'd agreed to pay the cabby what he had asked you!"

"Oh, don't speak to me of the cabby, dear," she said. "He, too, was a rogue. They're all birds of a feather, the blackguards."

"Now, really, Domna Platonovna," I said, "how can you say such a thing? Why, there are so many of them for one thing!"

"Don't you start arguing with me, dear! I know how little the rogues can be trusted, believe me. I know all their rogueries like that!" Here Domna Platonovna clenched her fist, and, raising it, regarded it with a certain pride. "When I was still new here, one cabby did something to me which, I can tell you, was much worse than bag-snatching," she said, putting down her hand. "Gave me a nasty fall, he did, and picked me clean into the bargain."

"A fall?" I said. "How on earth did he do that?"

"Just pitched me out, that's how. It happened in winter. I had to go to the other end of the town to deliver a cloak to a lady in the cadet corps barracks. A little woman she was and so delicate-looking you'd think she couldn't hurt a fly, but when she started bargaining, she'd scream the place down, the prima-donna! When I came out of there, it was already getting dark. It gets dark very early in winter, you know. I was hurrying along, for I was anxious to get back to Nevsky Avenue as soon as possible, when suddenly a cabby appeared from behind a street corner, one of those hairy little peasants, you know. 'I don't charge much, lady,' he said. I offered him fifteen kopecks to the Znamenye Cathedral . . .'"

"But, my dear Domna Platonovna," I interrupted her, "How could you have the heart to offer him so little?"

"Well, dear, as you see, I could. 'Take you the quick way,' he said. 'Oh, all right,' I said, sitting down in the sledge. I had no bag at the time and I used to carry everything about wrapped up in a kerchief, just as I'm doing now. So that devil of a cabman took me the quick way, somewhere behind the fortress and across the Neva and as he came to the bank of the frozen river, opposite the Liteynaya embankment, he tumbled me out into a hole in the ice, just as if, you know, somebody gave the bottom of the sledge a big blow and I . . . well, I just tumbled out. I was pitched out one way and my bundle flew out goodness knows where. I got up, soaked to the skin, for the holes in the ice were full of water. 'Oh, you rogue,' I shouted at my cabby, 'what have you done to me, you rogue, you!' But he said, 'This is the quickest way, lady. Sorry I pitched you out, but it ain't my fault.' 'How do you mean, it isn't your fault, you brute? Is that the way to treat your fare?' But he, the blackguard, went on saying, 'This way, ma'am, people always get chucked out. That's why I only took fifteen kopecks from you because you didn't mind coming the quick way!' Well, what was one to say to such a ruffian? I wiped my clothes and started looking round for the bundle, for as I told you, I was pitched out one way and my bundle another. All of a sudden an officer appeared at my side, or perhaps he wasn't an officer, but a civil servant, he wore some kind of uniform, anyway, and he had a moustache, that's about all I can remember of him, and he began abusing my driver, calling him all sorts of names.

"'Why weren't you more careful, you rogue,' he said, 'and with so fat a lady as your fare, too?' Oh, he was so angry with the cabby that he nearly knocked his teeth out. 'Sit down, madam,' he said, 'please, sit down in the sledge and let me put the cover over you.' 'But I've dropped my bundle, sir,' I said. 'It fell out of the sledge when that monster tipped me out.' 'Here's your bundle, madam,' he said, handing it to me. 'Go on, you rogue,' he shouted to the driver, 'and look sharp! And you, madam,' he said to me, 'don't hesitate for a moment to box his ears, if he tips you out again!' 'Thank you very much, sir,' I said, 'but I'm afraid we women are quite helpless against such villians!' So off we drove. When we came to my house, I got out and said, 'I have half a mind to punish you, you villain, and take at least five kopecks off your fare, but I don't want any more trouble with you, so,' I said, 'here's your fifteen kopeck bit!' But he said, 'It wasn't my fault, ma'am. You can't help tipping your fare out if you takes the quick way. It didn't do you no harm, ma'am,' he said. 'It'll make you grow,' he said. 'Oh, you scoundrel,' I said, 'what a pity your former master didn't thrash you enough.' But he cried to me, 'Look out, madam, don't drop what he put in your bundle!' and 'Gee-up!' he shouted at his horse and off he drove. I came home put the samovar on the table and picked up my bundle to make sure that it hadn't got wet. I undid it and nearly dropped dead, I tell you. Wanted to scream, but no sound would come from my throat, wanted to rush out of the house, but my feet wouldn't move! . . ."

"What was in that parcel?"

"What was in it? Why, I'm ashamed to tell you. Just some rubbish."

"What kind of rubbish?"

"Well, you know what kind of rubbish—a pair of torn, dirty pants, that's what was in it."

"But how did they get there?"

"That I don't know myself, dear. You see, I couldn't see how he managed to take 'em off on the Neva and put 'em in my bundle. It seemed uncanny to me. I looked and looked and couldn't believe my eyes. I rushed off to the police station, 'This isn't my bundle!' I shouted. 'All right,' the policeman said, 'it isn't your bundle. What about it?' So I told him and he took me straight to the criminal department, where I told them my story again, but the detective just laughed. 'Must have been coming from the public baths, the scoundrel,' he said. Well, I don't know where he was coming from, but how could he have palmed off such a bundle on me?"

"In the dark," I said, "that wouldn't be so difficult, Domna Platonovna."

"But what about the cabby? You remember I told you he said to me, 'Don't drop what's been put into it!' What did he mean by that?"

"You should have examined your bundle when you sat down in the sledge," I said.

"However sharp you look, dear," she said, "if they want to cheat you, they'll cheat you."

"Well," I said, "there you're a bit . . . er . . ."

"Now, now," she interrupted me, "please don't talk about things you don't know anything about, dear. They'll cheat you under your very nose, make out you are something you aren't.

I can tell you of a case where I myself was cheated under my very nose. I was walking along the street one day—it was shortly after my arrival here—and I had to cross over Apraxin bridge. It used to be very crowded there, not like now since the fires, now it's a pleasure to walk there, but then it was just too awful. All right, so I was walking along when suddenly, out of nowhere it seemed, a young fellow accosted me, a handsome-looking chap: 'Want to buy a chemise, madam? A lovely chemise!' I had a look at it and it was a brand-new chemise of excellent quality, a cotton one it was, but, as I said, of first-class quality, you could not have got such cotton material anywhere for less than sixty kopecks a yard. 'How much do you want for it?' I asked. 'Two and a half roubles,' he said. 'What about letting me have it for a little less than half the price?' I asked. 'Which half?' he asked. 'Any you like,' I said, for I'd been long enough here to have learnt that if you are offered anything for sale, you must always give half the price they ask you. 'No, madam,' he said, 'I can see it's no use offering you anything decent,' and he was about to pull the thing out of my hand, but I said, 'Give it to me,' for I could see that it was worth at least three roubles even to someone who didn't need it. 'Will you take a rouble for it?' I asked. 'Let's have it back,' he said and, pulling it out of my hand, he wrapped it under his coat, looking round to make sure that nobody had seen him. Well, I thought, it must have been stolen, and I was walking away when he jumped suddenly out of the line of hawkers and said to me, 'All right, madam,' he said, 'here you are and let's have the money quick,' he said, 'you ain't half lucky today, madam!' he said. I gave him a rouble note and he gave me the same crumpled up chemise. I put my purse back into my pocket and as I unwrapped my purchase, something fell out of it at my feet. What was it? Why, some old shavings you find inside furniture. Not knowing all the Petersburg circumstances at the time, I looked and looked at it wondering what it could mean, but when I glanced at my other hand in which I thought I was holding the chemise, I saw that it was not a chemise at all, but just a worthless rag. A rag, just a rag, dear, half a yard long. And the hawkers and shop-assistants in the street raised an awful clamor, 'Come on, ma'am, look at our stuff: lovely linen for silly women!' And one of 'em rushed up to me and said, 'We've a lovely second-hand winding sheet for you, ma'am, beautiful material!' But I took no notice. Get away with you, I thought to myself. The fact is, dear, I was flabbergasted, aye, and scared, too, for I couldn't for the life of me think where that rag had come from. I tell you I saw the chemise with my own eyes and suddenly it turned into a rag! Aye, dear, they're capable of any villainy. Do whatever they like with you, they do. Do you know Colonel Yegoopov?"

"No, I don't know him."

"How do you mean you don't know him? A fine figure of a man with a big paunch: a very handsome man. Nine horses killed under him during the war and he escaped untouched: they wrote about it in the papers."

"Afraid I still don't know him," I said.

"Well, what do you think one villain did to him and me? It's something they ought to put into a novel and not just any novel, either, but one of the best, or, better still, they ought to put it on the stage . . ."

"Don't keep me in suspense, Domna Platonovna," I said. "Do go on with your story."

"Yes, dear, it's a story worth telling all right. What's his name now? . . . There's a surveyor here . . . Kumoveyev or Maka-veyev, served in the seventh company of the Izmaylovsky regiment . . ."

"Never mind!"

"Never mind? Why, he's the real villain of the piece, he is!"

"I mean, never mind his name!"

"Oh, his name? Well, yes, there's nothing wrong with his name, just an ordinary name, but the man himself's a villain, one of the worst villains in town. Kept pestering me, he did, 'Find me a wife, Domna Platonovna.' I said to him, 'With pleasure,' I said, 'I'd be delighted to find you a wife! Give me a little time and I will find you a wife.' Looked quite handsome, the creature did, good complexion and nice moustache, well waxed and pointed upwards. So I began looking for a wife for him, rushed about here, there, everywhere, and found one at last, a girl from a merchant's family, her father owns a house on the Sands, good-looking, too, she was, red cheeks, plump . . . There was something wrong with her nose, it's true, a sort of blemish on the bridge, but it wasn't much, really, a mark left by scrofula, poor dear! So I brought the two of them together, her and that villain, I mean, and everything seemed to be getting on as well as could be! I kept an eye on him, of course, for I had heard a rumor that he had got himself engaged to a girl, a merchant's daughter she was, too, and wormed two hundred roubles out of her to get himself clothes, giving them a kind of receipt, but, as it turned out, the receipt wasn't worth the paper it was written on and they couldn't do anything to him, either. Now, of course, knowing the sort of man he was, I kept an eye on him and went to see him from time to time to make sure he hadn't run off. Well, so one day, my dear sir, I went to see him and, perhaps, I should have told you before that he lived in two rooms: one was his bedroom and the other a kind of sitting room. I went in and I found that his bedroom door was locked and in his sitting room an important-looking gentleman was sitting in an armchair and smoking a pipe, a gentleman of some importance he was because he wore a kind of sash over his shoulder. That was the Colonel Yegoopov I mentioned, dear.

"Well," Domna Platonovna went on, "I turned to him and asked him, 'Is Stepan Matveyevich at home, sir?' He just shook his head sternly, but said nothing, so that I couldn't really be sure whether the surveyor was at home or not. Perhaps, I thought, he had a young lady with him in the bedroom, for although he was about to get married, *that* doesn't make much difference, does it? So I sat down and waited. But you can hardly sit in a room with a person without speaking, for if you don't say anything, people may think that you're too silly to open your mouth. So I said to him, 'What lovely weather we're having just now, sir.' He glared at me and boomed out as though speaking from the bottom of an empty barrel, 'What did you say?' So I said again, 'We're having such nice weather, sir,' but he boomed back, 'Fiddlesticks, ma'am, nothing but damned dust!' Now, of course, it was quite true that there was rather a lot of dust about, but all the same I couldn't help thinking, 'And who might you be, my dear sir, to growl at me so angrily?' So I said to him, 'Are you by any chance a relative of Stepan Matveyevich or just a friend of his?' 'A friend,' he said. 'What an excellent man Stepan Matveyevich is, sir!' I said. 'A rotter,' he said, 'a first-class rotter!' So I said to myself, 'That means that Stepan Matveyevich isn't at home,' and aloud I said, 'Have you known him for some time, sir?' 'Yes,' he said, 'I've known him when the woman was still a maid.' 'Why, sir,' I said, 'I, too, have known him as long as that, for many a maid has grown into a woman since, but I haven't noticed anything wrong about that.' Well, he says very scornfully, 'What have you got in your attic—straw?' 'Excuse me, sir,' I said, 'thank God I haven't an attic but a head on my shoulders and there isn't any straw in it, but what the Lord has appointed to be there for every man.' 'Talking through your hat,' he said. 'A country yokel,' I thought to myself, 'that's what you are—a country yokel!' Suddenly he began questioning me. 'Do you know his brother Maxim Matveyevich?' 'No, sir,' I replied, 'I don't know him, and if I don't know a man I never pretend to know him.' 'This one here,' he said, 'is a rogue, but the other one is an even bigger rogue. Deaf!' 'Beg your pardon, sir,' I said, 'did you say he was deaf?' 'Yes,' he said, 'when I say deaf, I mean deaf. Born deaf in one ear and grown deaf in the other. Can't hear a thing with either.' 'Dear, dear,' I said, 'how extraordinary!' 'Nothing extraordinary about it,' he said. 'What I mean, sir,' I said, 'is that it is very extraordinary that one brother should be such a handsome man and the other should be deaf.' 'Exactly,' he said, 'that's what I mean, too: there's nothing extraordinary about it. I have two sisters and each of them has a huge red birthmark on her cheek, just like a big toad, not that it makes any difference to me!' 'I expect,' I said, 'your mother must have got frightened when she was in the family way.' 'A maid,' he said, 'upset the *samovar* on her belly.' I said very politely that I was sorry to hear that. 'Maids are the limit, sir,' I said, 'never look what they're doing.' He said to me then, 'I take it, madam,' he said, 'that you're not altogether a born fool and I'd therefore like to ask you your opinion about a certain matter. That deaf brother of his, you see, is very keen on exchanging horses.' 'Yes, sir,' I said. 'So wishing to get him out of that bad habit of his,' he said, 'I gave him a blind horse in exchange for one which wasn't blind, one, you know, which always rushes into a fence with its head.' 'Yes, sir,' I said. 'Well,' he said, 'the other day I wanted to get a bull from his farm. I paid him for a bull, but when the animal arrived I found that it wasn't a bull at all, but a steer.' 'Goodness gracious,' I said, 'what a shame! I don't suppose a steer's any good to you, is it?' 'Well, of course,' he said, 'if it's a steer, then it's no damn good to me. Well, so now I'm going to play a trick on him, the deaf one, I mean. I've got an I.O.U. from his brother Stepan Matveyevich for one hundred roubles and I know that neither of them has any money, so I'm going to show them the sort of fellow I am.' 'That's right, sir,' I said, 'I don't suppose there's anything to stop you from showing them that.' 'Well, so I just want to warn you, madam,' he said, 'that Maxim Matveyevich is a scoundrel, and as for his brother, I'm just waiting for him to come home before I put him in the debtors' jail.' 'I don't know either of them very well, sir,' I said, 'but seeing that I'm getting a wife for Stepan Matveyevich, I oughtn't to say anything against him.' 'Getting a wife for him?' he roared at me. 'Yes, sir.' 'Oh, you fool!' he said, 'Don't you know he's married?' 'You must be mistaken, sir,' I said. 'Mistaken?' he roared. 'Why, he's got three children.' 'Dear me,' I said and I thought to myself, 'Well, Stepan Matveyevich, what a joke you've played on me to be sure!' And I said aloud, 'I can see, sir, he's a swindler all right.' But the colonel said to me that if I wanted to find a husband for some likely girl, he'd be only too glad to oblige, for, as a matter of fact, he was himself looking for a girl to marry. 'With pleasure, sir,' I said. 'I'm not joking, madam,' he said, 'I mean it.' 'Very well, sir,' I said, 'I'll do it with pleasure.' 'Don't you believe me?' he asked. 'Why, of course, I believe you, sir,' I said, 'for if a man feels an inclination to settle down and give up his state of bachelorhood, he can't do anything better than marry a nice girl.' 'I don't mind if she's a widow,' he said, 'so long as she has capital.' 'Of course,' I said, 'there's nothing wrong about a widow.'

"So we discussed the whole matter then and there and he gave me his address and I began to visit him. You can't imagine the trouble that wretch caused me! A big man he was and quite mad, talked to people just as the spirit moved him. Of course, people have different dispositions, but I pity any woman who married a man like Yegoopov! He'd suddenly get up, for instance, glare at you with bulging eyes, his face purple like a bed-bug that's had a good feed on you, and roar at you, 'I'll turn you inside out, I'll flay you alive!' To look at him in one of his mad fits, you'd think somebody must have hurt his feelings badly, but usually it was some trifle or other. Well, I found him a wife, a merchant's widow, just a match for him, as if made to order, a carcase as big as his. Well, my dear sir, I introduced them to each other and everything went off well and an engagement party was arranged.

"I arrived at the party with him, the colonel, I mean. There were crowds of people there, relatives and friends of the fiancée, all of them well-to-do people, but among the guests I also noticed that surveyor, Stepan Matveyevich. I said nothing, although to tell the truth, I didn't like his being there a bit. 'I suppose,' I said to myself, 'he must have been released from the debtors' jail and he's here by invitation from the colonel.'

"However, everything seemed to be going on all right. The engagement had been officially announced, the betrothed had been blessed with the icon, and nothing untoward had happened. The fiancée's uncle, the merchant Semyon Ivanych Kolobov, to be sure, arrived at the party drunk and began telling everybody that Yegoopov wasn't a colonel at all, but the son of Fyodorovna, the bath-house attendant. 'Let someone lick him behind the ear,' he said, 'and he'll immediately start a fight: he always does. I know him very well,' he went on shouting, 'he's just put on his epaulettes to show off. I'll tear his epaulettes off, I will!' But the people wouldn't let him do that and, to prevent any mischief, Semyon Ivanych was locked up in an empty room. But all of a sudden, just as the father of the fiancée raised the icon to bless the betrothed couple, an awful, blood-curdling howl was heard in the room and then a voice said very clearly, 'Do not sing of Isaiah when Emmanuel is in the womb.' Dear me, how everybody in the room got scared! The poor fiancée was terribly embarrassed and Yegoopov glared angrily at me with his bulging eyes. 'What are you glaring at me for?' I thought. 'Eyeing me like the devil a priest!' In the meantime, somebody in the room again began to moan and again a voice said very clearly, 'Dust covereth the face of heaven when a bride to a married man is given. Pray to God, poor, deceived woman, cry your eyes out.' They tried to discover the owner of that terrifying voice, but all in vain, and, my goodness, what a to-do there was! The father of the fiancée put down the icon and rushed at me, vowing to thrash me within an inch of my life, and I, seeing how black things looked for me, lifted up my skirt as high as I could and just ran as fast as my feet would carry me. Yegoopov swore that he had never been married, asked them to make enquiries, if they wished, but the mysterious voice went on proclaiming so loudly that all in the room could hear it, 'Do not be deceived, brethren, do not heap dust and ashes upon the head of the maid!' The party broke up in terrible confusion and who do you think was to blame for it all? Well, after a week, Yegoopov came to see me and said, 'It was that blackguard of a surveyor,' he said, 'it was he who was speaking through his navel!' "

"Through his navel, Domna Platonovna?" I asked.

"Yes, dear, his navel or his belly, or the devil knows through what he proclaimed those slanderous lies of his," Domna Platonovna said. "As I told you before, dear," she went on, looking at me gravely, "they're all trying to outwit each other, everybody is trying to trick and deceive everybody else and, take my word for it, in the end they'll embroil the whole State in their knaveries and throw it to the dogs!"

I must confess that Domna Platonovna's sombre view of the future of the Russian State rather confounded me, for I myself hardly expected such an awful fate to be in store for us all. Domna

Platonovna, naturally, noticed the confusion into which her proph-
ecy had thrown me and she wished to enjoy to the full the political
sensation she had created.

"I mean every word of it, dear," she said, raising her voice
one note higher. "Just think, dear, of all the new tricks they're
now inventing. One starts flying, which only birds have been
given to do, another starts swimming like a fish and thinks nothing
of going down to the bottom of the sea, a third, like the man on
Admiralty Square, is swallowing sulphurous fire, a fourth talks
through his belly, a fifth does something else no human being
should do . . . Why, I should not be at all surprised if Satan
himself was not today at their beck and call, for whatever they
do, is certainly not to man's advantage, but to his eternal undoing.
I don't mind telling you, dear, that I was once thrown to the
devil myself and suffered ignominiously at his hands!"

"Dear me," I said, "did that really happen to you?"

"It did!"

"Please don't keep me in suspense, dear Domna Platonovna!
Tell me about it."

It happened a long time ago (Domna Platonovna said), about
twelve years ago. I was young then and inexperienced and, having
just lost my husband, I decided to engage in some business. But
what kind of business? I made up my mind that the best thing I
could do in the ladies' line of business was to sell cloth, for a
woman understands more about that kind of trade than any other.
So I decided to buy some cloth in the market and then sit down on
a bench by some gates in our town and try to sell it. I went to the
market, bought the cloth and was about to return home with it,
but the question arose how I was to take it home with me? While
I was thinking about it, a cart driven by a team of three horses rode
into the yard of the inn where I was stranded.

"We were bringing a load of nuts from Kiev on seven carts,
each cart driven by a team of three horses," the driver told me,
"but the nuts got wet on the way and the merchants deducted

their losses from our pay and now we're returning home without any money at all."

"Where are your mates?" I asked.

"My mates," he replied, "have all gone back to their own villages, but I'm trying to find some fares to take back with me."

"Where are you from?" I asked him.

"I'm from the village of Kurakina," he said.

As it happened it was just my way and, "Here," I said, "is your first fare."

We talked it over and he agreed to take me home for one rouble. He said he'd go round the inns to pick up more passengers and that we'd leave the next day after breakfast.

Next morning, one, two, five, eight people came to the yard of the inn, all of them men and every one of them big and handsome. One of them carried a sack, another a satchel, a third a trunk, and one even had a shotgun.

"How will you squeeze us all in?" I asked the driver.

"Never you mind," he said, "you'll get in all right, it's a big cart, carried three and a half ton, it has."

I was in half a mind to stay behind, but I had already given him a rouble and there was no other driver about to take me back to town.

With a heavy heart I clambered into the cart and off we drove. No sooner had we passed the toll-gate than one of our fares shouted, "Stop at the next pub!" So we stopped at the pub and they all got off and had many drinks there and stood the driver drinks, too. Then off we drove again. We had only gone about a mile when another of our passengers shouted, "Stop! Ivan Ivanych Yelkin lives here and I must see him!" and so they kept on stopping about a dozen times, each one at his own particular Ivan Ivanych Yelkin's. It was getting dark and our driver was as drunk as a lord by then.

"Don't you dare to have another drop," I said to him.

"Why shouldn't I dare?" he replied. "I ain't a daring one, anyway. I'm acting like that just because I don't dare to refuse, see?"

"You're a yokel," I said, "just a stupid country yokel."

"What if I am a yokel?" he said. "So long as I can get a drink I don't mind what I am."

"Oh, you fool," I said, "you fool! you'd better look after your horses!"

"I'm looking after my horses, ain't I?" he replied and, raising his whip, he began flogging them.

The cart was jolting terribly and I was afraid that we might be tipped out any minute and killed. The men were all drunk and raising a awful din. One of them produced an accordion, another was bawling a song, a third one was firing his gun, while I was just praying, "Holy Mother of God, save us, I beseech thee!"

Our horses careered along until they got tired, and we were again crawling at a snail's pace. It got dark in the meantime and, although it was not raining, it seemed as if a cold, wet mist was enveloping us as with a blanket. My hands went numb with holding on to the sides of the cart, but I was so glad that we were no longer going at breakneck speed that I sat there quietly, without uttering a sound. The men, I could hear, had begun talking to each other, one of them saying that he had heard that there were robbers on the road who had recently held up and robbed many people, another declaring that he was not afraid of any robbers because he could fire twice from his gun, and a third starting to tell a story about dead bodies. "I'm always carrying about a bone from a corpse," he said, "and if I wave this bone over a man, he straightway falls asleep, just as if he was dead, and he'll never waken again." Another one boasted that he had a candle made from the fat of a dead man . . . I just listened to their talk when of a sudden I had an odd feeling as if somebody was pulling me by the nose and I felt so sleepy that in another minute I dropped off.

But I couldn't sleep soundly because all the time we were shaken up as if we were nuts roasted on a grill, and in my sleep I seemed to hear someone saying, "I wish we could throw that damned woman out! Can't stretch my legs, I can't." But I went on sleeping until I suddenly heard a shout and a scream, followed by a general hubbub, and I woke up. What was the matter? I looked round. It was pitch dark, our cart had stopped and everybody was running about and shouting, but what they were shouting I couldn't for the life of me make out.

"Shire-mirl, shire-mire," one of them shouted.

Our passenger with the gun pulled the trigger once and it went snap, but there was no report, he fired again, and again the trigger went snap and there was no sound. Then the one who was shouting screamed at the top of his voice again and, seizing me under the arms, swung me off the cart and began whirling me round and round. Goodness, I thought, what's going on here? I peered into the pitch darkness round me, but all I could see were some hideous, black faces and all of them were turning round and round and whirling me round with them, shouting "Shire-mire!" and, lifting me by my feet, they began to swing me to and fro.

"O Lord," I began to pray fervently, "St. Nicholas of Amchen, defender of the three virgins, protector of purity, do not, I beseech thee, let them behold my nakedness!"

No sooner did I utter that prayer in my heart than, suddenly, I became aware of a great stillness all around me and it seemed to me that I was lying in the middle of a field, on green, lush grass, and near me, just at my feet, was a small lake with wonderfully clear, transparent water and round it, just like a fringe of thick silk, the rushes were waving gently.

I forgot all about my prayer and began staring at those reeds, as though I'd never seen any before in my life.

Then, suddenly, what was that? A mist, a light blue mist rose from the other side of the lake and spread all over the field like a shroud, and under the mist, in the middle of the lake, a little ripple arose, just as if a fish had splashed its tail there, and from the ripple a little man, not bigger than a cockerel, appeared. He had a tiny face and was dressed in a long blue coat and wore a green cap on his head.

"What a funny little man," I thought, "just like a beautiful doll," and I kept looking at him, couldn't tear my eyes away from him. I was not a bit afraid of him, as if he really was a pretty little doll. But as I looked at him, he began to rise and rise out of the water and he came nearer and nearer to me until at last he just hopped on to my bosom. He was not really standing on my bosom though, but over it, hovering in the air and bowing. Raised his cap with such an important air and greeted me gravely.

I felt like screaming with laughter. "Where could you have sprung from, you funny little man?" I thought to myself.

But he doffed his cap again and said, well . . . the things that little mite did say, I declare!

"Let's have a little love frolic together, my dearest Domna," he said.

I couldn't help bursting out laughing.

"Oh, you naughty little thing," I cried. "What kind of love frolic could I have with you?"

Then he suddenly turned his back on me and crowed like a young cockerel: cock-a-doodle-doo!

Everything then burst into loud music: there was the sound of drums, fiddles, flutes and hundreds of musical instruments: my ears rang with the din! Goodness, I thought to myself, what's all this? The frogs, the carp, the bream, the crayfish—every creature in the lake began to scrape, pluck and beat fiddles, guitars, drums, while some danced and others just skipped about and others leapt into the air!

"Oh dear," I thought, "that's bad, that's very bad! Let me say a prayer to protect myself from the evil one!" and I was about to say aloud, "In the name of the Holy Resurrection," but instead I said, "Higher and still higher soar aloft . . ." and at the same time I could distinctly hear a weird sort of drumming inside my belly: tum-tara-tum, tum-tara-tum!

"What's that?" I thought. "Am I a drum or a double-bass?" and as I looked at myself, I saw that I was a double-bass and that the little man was standing over me and sawing away for all he was worth.

"Oh dear," I said to myself, "holy saints!" but he went on sawing away with his bow and what didn't he play on me? Waltzes and quadrilles and everything, while the others were standing round and egging him on, "Scrape away harder," they shouted, "scrape away harder!"

I had a terrible pain in my belly, but there I was droning like anything, and so they scraped away on me the whole night. Yes, the whole night I, a baptized Christian woman, was just a double-bass to them, kept them merry, those damned devils!

"That's terrible!" I said.

"Yes, indeed, it was terrible, but it was even more terrible when I woke up in the morning after they had had their fun with me. I looked round and I saw that I was lying in a strange field and a few yards away from me was a large pool, like a small lake with reeds and everything, just as I had seen it in the night, and the sun was roasting me, streaming down on me from the sky. My bundle with the cloth I had purchased and my small bag were lying beside me. Everything was quite safe, and only a few hundred yards away was a little village. I got up, dragged myself to the village, hired a peasant's cart and arrived home in the evening."

"But are you quite sure, Domna Platonovna, that all that had really happened to you?"

"Why, you don't think I'd be telling you lies about myself, do you?"

"I mean are you quite sure that everything had happened just as you told me?"

"Yes, dear, it happened just as I told you. Now, if there's anything you ought to be surprised at, it is that I shouldn't have uncovered my nakedness to them."

I looked duly surprised.

"Yes, dear, I prevailed with the devil, but I was not so lucky with one fiend of a man!"

"Oh? How did that happen?"

"Listen. I bought some furniture from a merchant's wife: second-hand furniture it was, chests-of-drawers, tables, bed and a child's cot with a kind of braided bottom. I paid thirteen roubles for the lot, put everything out in the passage and went out to

fetch a cart. I found a driver with a cart and he agreed to take the
furniture for a rouble and forty kopecks to St. Nicholas-the-
Seafarer's. We put the furniture in the cart and in the meantime
the people I had bought it from had gone out and locked their
flat. Suddenly, the caretakers of that block of flats—Tartars they
were—swooped down on us, shouting, "What right have you to
take the furniture?" I tried to explain to them that I had bought
it, but they wouldn't listen to me. Meanwhile, it started to rain
and the carter did not want to wait any longer. I didn't know what
to do! At last I thought of something. 'Take me to the police
station,' I said, 'I'm the wife of the police officer!' But no sooner
did I say that than the people from whom I had bought the furniture came back and, of course, they said at once, 'We've sold the
furniture,' they said, 'we've sold it to her.' Well, so that was that,
and the carter, he said to me, 'Get on the cart,' and I thought to
myself, 'Why, indeed, waste money on a cab when I can sit in
the cot and be taken home for nothing?' They had put the cot
very high up in the cart, on top of a chest-of-drawers, but I managed to climb up and sat down in it. Well, what do you think
happened? Why, directly we left the courtyard, the bottom of the
cot began to give under me. 'Heavens,' I thought, 'I'm falling
through!' and I was just about to scramble out when, crash! I did
fall through. Lord, the disgrace of it! There I was, sitting astride
a piece of webbing like a mounted policeman on his horse. My
dress, of course, shot up and my bare legs were left dangling over
the chest-of-drawers. The people in the street stared at me and
the caretakers shouted, 'Cover yourself up, police officer's wife!'
What a scoundrel!"

"Who do you mean?" I asked.

"The carter, of course! Too busy looking at his horse, if you
please! Didn't care a fig for his passenger, nearly drove through
the whole of Gorokhovaya Street like that, but for a kindly policeman who stopped us. 'What's all this?' he said. 'You can't travel
like that,' he said. 'It ain't allowed to show what you're showing!'
So that was how I showed my nakedness to the whole world . . ."

6

"I should like to ask you a question I've wanted to ask for a long time, Domna Platonovna," I said. "How old were you when your husband died? You were still quite a young woman, weren't you? Well, haven't you had any love affairs at all since then?"

"Love affairs?"

"Yes, I mean haven't you been in love with anyone?"

"Me in love? Good heavens, the nonsense you do sometimes talk, dear!"

"But why nonsense?"

"Because," she said, "it's only women who have nothing to do who have love-affairs. I'm much too busy rushing about day and night, leading so aggravating a life as I do, never a minute to my-self . . . Why, such a thought never crosses my mind!"

"Doesn't it even cross your mind, Domna Platonovna?"

"No, dear, not as much as that even!" Domna Platonovna struck one finger-nail against another and added, "Besides, dear, let me tell you this love business is just a kind of craze: 'Oh, I can't live without him or her! Oh, I shall die!' That's all you hear from them. Now, if you ask me, dear, a man who's really in love with a woman should be always ready to help her, never let her down, that, I grant you, is real love. And as for the woman, she should never give way to temptation and should always behave decently."

"So I can take it, Domna Platonovna," I said, "that you've never been guilty of any such transgression and that in the eyes of God you're as pure as driven snow. Am I right?"

"Mind your own business, dear," she replied, "and don't you go meddling with my sins. For even if I did commit a sin, it's my sin, isn't it? Anyway, it's not yours and you're not a priest to whom I ought to confess my sins, are you?"

"I merely mentioned it, Domna Platonovna," I put in propitiatingly, "Because you were so young when you lost your husband and I can see that you must have been very beautiful."

"Whether I was beautiful or not, I can't say," she replied, "but I was never considered a plain woman."

"That's it!" I said, "Anybody can see it even now."

Domna Platonovna passed a finger over an eyebrow and fell into thought.

"I've often wondered," she began slowly, "whether or not I had been guilty of a particular sin. Tell me, O Lord, was I guilty of that sin or not? That was how I'd ask for the Lord's guidance, but I never received a proper answer to that question from anyone. One nun once persuaded me to let her write down my story so that I could give it to the priest at confession. I let her write it down, but on my way to the church I dropped the paper and couldn't find it."

"What story are you referring to, Domna Platonovna?"

"I don't rightly know to this day whether it was a sin or whether I imagined it all."

"Well, even if you did imagine it all, Domna Platonovna, I should very much like to hear it."

"It all happened a very long time ago when I was still living with my husband."

"What kind of life did you have with your husband, dear Domna Platonovna?"

"Not a bad kind of life. Our house was a little too small perhaps, but it occupied a very good position, for it stood on the market place, and we had many market days in our town, mostly for household goods and provisions of one sort or another, only there was precious little of either, that was the trouble. We were not particularly well off, but we were not exactly poor, either. We sold fish, lard, liver and anything else we could. My husband, Fyodor Ilyich, was a young man, but a queer one, aye, a queer one, very haggard he was, but he had a pair of the most extraordinary lips. I never met a man with such lips in my life. He had, God forgive me, a terrible temper, very quarrelsome he was and quick to take offence, but I, too, was a real Amazon, dearly loved a fight as a girl, I did.

Having married, I was at first as meek as a lamb, but that didn't please him at all, so that every morning before breakfast we used to have a grand old fight together. I was not very much in love with him, nor did we often agree, for we both were rare fighters, and, besides, you couldn't help fighting with him, for however nice you tried to be to him, he'd always look glum and glower at you. However, we carried on for eight whole years and did not separate. Now and again, of course, we'd have a row, but it was very rarely that we had a real fight. Once, it is true, he hit me over the head, but I was not altogether blameless myself, for I had been trimming his hair at the time and I cut off a bit of his ear with the scissors. We had no children, but we had friends at Nizhny to whose children I stood godmother. They weren't well off. He called himself a tailor and even had a diploma from a society, but he didn't earn his living by his needle, but by singing psalms for the dead and being a member of the Cathedral choir. As for earning a living, getting something for their home, it was his wife, Praskovya Ivanovna, who had to worry about it. She was a woman in a thousand, brought up all her children and made ends meet somehow.

"Well, once—it was in the same year that my husband died (everything was going topsy-turvy with us just then)—Praskovya Ivanovna invited us to her place to celebrate her birthday. We went and no sooner did we arrive than it began to pour and, as I had an awful headache at the time (I had had three glasses of punch and some Caucasian brandy and there's nothing worse than that Caucasian brandy for your head), I lay down for a bit on a couch in another room. 'Stay with your guests, dear,' I said to Praskovya Ivanovna, 'and I'll just go and lie down for a rest on the couch here.' But she wouldn't let me lie down on the couch, because, she said, it was too hard, so I went and lay down on their bed and dropped off to sleep immediately. Did I do anything wrong?" Domna Platonovna asked me.

"Why, no," I said, "you didn't do anything wrong."

"Very well, now listen to what happened. I felt in my sleep that somebody was embracing me and, you see, not just embracing me, either. I thought it was my husband, Fyodor Ilyich, and yet it didn't seem to be Fyodor Ilyich, for he was rather delicate, you know and shy, but I couldn't wake up, and when at last I did wake up, it was morning. I found myself in my friend's bed and beside me lay my friend's husband. I sort of scampered over him quickly, trembling all over, and there on the floor, on a feather bed, lay my friend and beside her was my husband, Fyodor Ilyich . . . I nudged her and then she, too, realized what had happened and began crossing herself. 'How did it all happen?' I asked her. 'Oh, dear,' she said, 'it's all my fault, for after everybody went away your husband and mine sat down to finish up the drinks and I didn't want to waken you in the darkness, so I lay down where I had made a bed for you and your husband, well, I just spat, so vexed was I.' 'What shall we do now?' I asked. But she said there was nothing we could do and that we'd better keep quiet about it. Yes, dear," Domna Platonovna said, "you're the first I ever told this story to after so many years, but it has been worrying me terribly all the time and whenever I think of it, I'm ready to curse that heavy sleep of mine."

"Don't distress yourself so much, Domna Platonovna," I said, "for whatever happened was against your will."

"Of course it happened against my will! I should think so! Still, it did worry me, I can tell you, and after that I was overtaken by one trouble after another. Fyodor Ilyich soon died, and not a natural death, either. Was crushed to death, he was, under a load of logs which collapsed on top of him on the bank of a river. I had no notion of the Petersburg circumstances then and I didn't know what to do to distract myself, but sometimes of an evening when I'd remember what had happened to me at that birthday party, I'd sit down at the window, all alone in the house, and sing, 'Take away my gold, take away my honors all,' and I'd burst out crying, tears gushing in a flood out of my eyes, so that it was a real wonder my heart didn't burst with sorrow. Oh, I felt so terrible when I'd remember the words of that song, 'My dear love in the dank ground lies sleeping,' that many a time I thought of putting a noose round my neck and ending it all. So I sold everything, gave up my business and left our town, for I decided that it was best to make a clean break with my past life."

"I can believe that, Domna Platonovna," I said, "for there's nothing worse than being depressed."

"Thank you, dear, for your kind words," said Domna Platonovna. "Indeed, there's nothing worse than that and may the Holy Virgin bless you and comfort you for your pity and understanding. But you can hardly be expected to know what I have been through, if I don't tell you how scurvily I was treated once and how shamelessly I was insulted. That my bag was stolen or that Lekanida Petrovna was so ungrateful to me, all that is nothing compared with what happened to me on another occasion. For there was such a day in my life, dear, when I prayed to God to send a serpent or a scorpion to suck my eyes out and devour my heart. And who do you think it was who did that wrong to me? I'll tell you: Ispulat, the Turk, that's who it was, that infidel Turk, in league with my own friends, Christians, baptized and annointed with myrrh!"

Poor Domna Platonovna burst into a flood of tears.

"A friend of mine, the wife of a government messenger," she went on, wiping her tears, "used to live in Lopatin's house on Nevsky Avenue and that Turkish war prisoner began to worry her about getting him a job. She asked me to see if I couldn't find some work for him. 'Find some situation for that devil, Domna Platonovna,' she said to me. But what sort of a job could I find for a Turk? A footman's job was all I could think of. Well, I found him such a place and I told him about it. 'Go there,' I said, 'and you can start work at once.' So they decided to give a party to celebrate the occasion and they got a lot of drinks, for that damned Turk had renounced his religion and could now drink spirits. 'I don't want anything to drink,' I told them, but I did have a glass or two. That's the kind of silly character I have, dear. I always say 'no' at first, and drink afterwards. So it was there, too. I had a couple of drinks and got quite befuddled and lay down in the same bed with that woman friend of mine."

"And?"

"And . . . well . . . that's all there is to it and that's why now I always sew myself up before going to bed."

"Sew yourself up, Domna Platonovna?"

"Yes, dear. You see, dear, if I happen to be spending the night somewhere, I just get my feet into a kind of a sack and sew myself up, and, let me tell you, even when I am at home, I can no longer trust myself, seeing the kind of heavy sleeper I am, so I just sew myself up every night."

Domna Platonovna heaved a deep sigh and let fall her mournful head over her ample bosom.

"There you are, dear," she said after a long pause, "knowing the Petersburg circumstances as well as I do and yet I let such a thing happen to me!"

She got up, bid me good-bye and went back to her flat in Znamenskaya Street.

7

A FEW years later I had to take a poor fellow to an emergency hospital for typhus cases. Having seen him put to bed in one of the wards, I tried to find someone who could be relied on to look after him properly.

"You'd better see Sister," I was told.

"Won't you ask Sister if she will see me?" I asked.

A woman with a faded face and sagging cheeks entered the room.

"What can I do for you, sir?" she asked.

"Good heavens," I exclaimed, "Domna Platonovna!"

"Yes, sir," she said quietly, "it's me."

"How did you get here?"

"It was God's will, I suppose."

"Please, look after my friend," I said.

"I'll look after him as if he was my own son," she assured me.

"What about your business?"

"This is my business now: I gave everything up to serve the Lord. Yes, my friend, I've given up my business. Come along to my room, dear," she whispered.

I went to her room. It was a very little room, very damp and with no furniture or curtains, just an iron bedstead and a little table with a *samovar* and a little painted chest.

"Won't you have tea with me?" she asked.

"No, thank you," I said. "I'm in an awful hurry."

"Come to see me again," she said. "I'm all broken up, dear, done for, finished."

"Why, what's happened?"

"I can't tell you, dear, my heart's aching and I'd rather you didn't ask me."

"But are you sure there isn't anything the matter with you, Domna Platonovna? Why do you look so haggard?"

"Haggard? Good gracious, what are you saying? I'm sure I don't look a bit worse than I did when you saw me last!"

Domna Platonovna quickly produced a small, folding mirror, looked at her faded cheeks and said hurriedly, "I haven't changed a bit. True, I look a little tired, but that's because it's almost bedtime and I've had a tiring day. In the morning I shall be as fresh as a daisy!"

I looked at Domna Platonovna and I couldn't understand what had happened to her. It seemed to me that her face was not only faded and baggy, but also a little made up. And why all that alarm when I told her that she looked haggard? "Can't make it out at all," I thought to myself.

About a month later a soldier from the hospital came to see me and insisted that I should go immediately to Domna Platonovna. I took a cab and at the gates of the hospital I was met by Domna Platonovna, who fell on my neck, crying and sobbing.

"Please, go at once to the police station," she implored me.

"But whatever for?" I asked.

"Try to find out about a man there, see what you can do for him, dear. I'll repay you for it one day, I will."

"All right," I said, "only please stop crying and shivering like that."

"I can't help shivering," she said, "for it comes from inside, my whole inside is shivering, but I shall always be grateful to you for this service, for, you see, everybody has abandoned me now."

"All right," I said again, "but who shall I ask for?"

The old woman looked embarrassed for a moment and her faded cheeks began to twitch.

"A piano-maker's assistant was taken there yesterday, Valerian Ivanov his name is. Try to find out what you can about it, dear, and please, please put in a good word for him."

I drove to the police station. There I was told that it was quite true that a young man by the name of Valerian Ivanov had been arrested. He was an apprentice of a piano-maker, had stolen some money from his employer and had been caught redhanded. It was very probable, I was finally told, that he'd be sent away for a long stretch.

"How old is he?" I asked.

"Twenty-one," they told me.

What was it all about, I wondered, and what was that young man to Domna Platonovna?

I went back to the hospital and found Domna Platonovna in her little room, sitting on the edge of the bed with her hands crossed and looking more dead than alive.

"I know everything," she said, "don't bother to tell me any more. I sent one of our male nurses to find out and he told me everything. Oh, even before my death this soul of mine is burning in hellfire!"

I could see that my Amazon had completely gone to pieces; in less than an hour she seemed to have drooped and withered.

"Dear Lord," she said, gazing at the small hospital icon, "let my prayer go up straight to Thee in heaven, take my soul out of this body of mine and bring peace to my wicked heart."

"What is the matter with you, Domna Platonovna?" I asked.

"What's the matter with me, dear? Why, I love him, that's what's the matter with me. I love him to distraction, I love him hopelessly, desperately, old fool that I am! I clothed him and I fed him and I cherished him. He was so fond of a show, poor boy, hated to stay at home with me, always wanting to run off to

the theatre or the circus . . . I gave him all I had. I used to implore
him on my bended knees, 'Valerian, my dear, my angel, what do
you want to run off to the circus for? What good can a circus do
you?' But he'd begin stamping his feet, shouting at me and throwing his arms about! A real circus turn that was, I can tell you. He
forbade me to speak to him, so I just looked at him and then I'd
beseech him from a distance, 'Darling Valerian, my dear life, my
precious treasure, don't make friends with any man you meet!
Don't drink so much!' But he wouldn't listen to me. If I hadn't
paid the houseporter to find out what had happened, I shouldn't
have heard of this last trouble of his. Oh, Lord, sweet Lord, why
has this happened and what's going to become of him?" she
exclaimed and fell on her knees before the icon, crying more
bitterly than ever and shaking her grey head.

"I gave him all I had," she repeated, rising from her knees
after a few minutes and looking round her dreary little room
with dead eyes. "I gave him everything till I had nothing more to
give. If only I could see him just for one minute . . ."

"Why not go and see him?" I said.

"He told me never to see him again. I daren't go to him!" she
said, shaking feverishly.

I was silent and just to sober her down a bit I said:

"How old are you now, Domna Platonovna?"

"What did you say, dear?"

"How old are you?"

"I don't know really . . . I was forty-seven last January, I think."

"Where did you meet that Valerian of yours?" I asked. "Where
did you dig him up to your own undoing?"

"He's from the same town as I," she said, wiping her tears.
"A nephew of that friend of mine to whose children I stood
godmother. Sent him to me, she did, asked me to find a job for
him. Tell me," my Amazon turned to me, crying again, "are you
at least sorry for me, silly fool that I am?"

"Yes, Domna Platonovna," I said, "I'm very sorry for you."

"I daresay nobody else will be even sorry for me," she said.
"People will only laugh at me. Anybody who heard my story

would just laugh. Yes, of course, they laugh, for why should they be sorry for me? But I can't help loving him, however little joy or happiness that love has brought me. Never mind what the world thinks. People will never understand what a terrible misfortune it is for such a thing to happen to a woman at my time of life. I went to one of those old believers and he said to me. 'It's Satan who's tormenting your flesh. Do not let your soul do aught presumptuously.' I went to a priest. 'Father,' I said, 'tell me what's wrong with me?' and I told him everything. 'Read the hymn, "O Lord, alleviate my sorrow," ' he said to me. So I read that hymn and I got myself this job so that I shouldn't get into greater temptation, but . . . oh, my darling, Valerian, my dearest, my precious one, what have you done to me?"

Domna Platonovna pressed her head against the window frame and began to bang her forehead against the sill.

In that state of utter prostration and grief I left my Amazon. In another month I received news from the hospital that Domna Platonovna had ended her aggravating life. She had suffered a sudden and complete collapse and died. She lay in a black coffin, looking so small and shrivelled that it seemed as if indeed nothing was left of her but skin and bone. Her end was painless, quiet and peaceful. Domna Platonovna received extreme unction and she kept saying her prayers to the very end, and with her last breath she asked that a little chest, her pillows and a pot of jam she had been given, should be sent to me, so that I, if possible, should give it "to the man I know of," that is to say, to Valerian.

1866 A.D.

DOSTOEVSKY *The Eternal Husband*

1 VELCHANINOV

THE summer had come and, contrary to expectations, Velchaninov remained in Petersburg. The trip he had planned to the south of Russia had fallen through, and the end of his case was not in sight. This case—a lawsuit concerning an estate—had taken a very unfortunate turn. Three months earlier it had appeared to be quite straightforward, almost impossible to contest; but suddenly everything was changed. "And, in fact, everything has changed for the worse!" Velchaninov began frequently and resentfully repeating that phrase to himself. He was employing an adroit, expensive, and distinguished lawyer, and was not sparing money; but through impatience and lack of confidence he had been tempted to meddle in the case himself too. He read documents and wrote statements which the lawyer rejected point-blank, ran from one court to another, collected evidence, and probably hindered everything; the lawyer complained, at any rate, and tried to pack him off to a summer villa. But Velchaninov could not even make up his mind to go away. The dust, the stifling heat, the white nights of Petersburg, that always fret the nerves were what he was enjoying in town. His flat was near the Grand Theatre; he had only recently taken it, and it, too, was a failure. "Everything is a failure!" he thought. His nervousness increased every day; but he had for a long time past been subject to nervousness and hypochondria.

He was a man whose life had been full and varied, he was by no means young, thirty-eight or even thirty-nine, and his "old age," as he expressed it himself, had come upon him "quite unexpectedly"; but he realized himself that he had grown older less by the number than by the quality, so to say, of his years, and that if he had begun to be aware of waning powers, the change was rather from within than from without. In appearance he was still strong and hearty. He was a tall, sturdily-built fellow, with thick flaxen hair without a sign of greyness and a long fair beard almost half-way down his chest; at first sight he seemed somewhat slack and clumsy, but if you looked more attentively, you would detect at once that he was a man of excellent breeding, who had at some time received the education of an aristocrat. Velchaninov's manners were still free, assured and even gracious, in spite of his acquired grumpiness and slackness. And he was still, even now, full of the most unhesitating, the most snobbishly insolent self-confidence, the depth of which he did not himself suspect, although he was a man not merely intelligent, but even sometimes sensible, almost cultured and unmistakably gifted. His open and ruddy face had been in old days marked by a feminine softness of complexion which attracted the notice of women; and even now some people, looking at him, would say: "What a picture of health! What a complexion!" And yet this picture of health was cruelly subject to nervous depression. His eyes were large and blue, ten years earlier they had possessed great fascination; they were so bright, so gay, so careless that they could not but attract everyone who came in contact with him. Now that he was verging on the forties, the brightness and good-humor were almost extinguished. Those eyes, which were already surrounded by tiny wrinkles, had begun to betray the cynicism of a worn-out man of doubtful morals, a duplicity, an ever-increasing irony and another shade of feeling, which was new: a shade of sadness and of pain —a sort of absent-minded sadness as though about nothing in particular and yet acute. This sadness was especially marked when he was alone. And, strange to say, this man who had been only a couple of years before fond of noisy gaiety, careless and good-humored, who had been so capital a teller of funny stories, liked

nothing now so well as being absolutely alone. He purposely gave
up a great number of acquaintances whom he need not have given
up even now, in spite of his financial difficulties. It is true that
his vanity counted for something in this. With his vanity and
mistrustfulness he could not have endured the society of his old
acquaintances. But, by degrees, in solitude even his vanity began
to change its character. It grew no less, quite the contrary, indeed;
but it began to develop into a special sort of vanity which was
new in him; it began at times to suffer from different causes—
from unexpected causes which would have formerly been quite
inconceivable, from causes of a "higher order" than ever before—
"if one may use such an expression, if there really are higher or
lower causes. . . ." This he added on his own account.

Yes, he had even come to that; he was worrying about some
sort of *higher* ideas of which he would never have thought twice
in earlier days. In his own mind and in his conscience he called
"higher" all "ideas" at which (he found to his surprise) he could
not laugh in his heart—there had never been such hitherto—in his
secret heart only, of course; oh, in company it was a different matter! He knew very well, indeed, that—if only the occasion were
to arise—he would the very next day, in spite of all the mysterious
and reverent resolutions of his conscience, with perfect composure
disavow all these "higher ideas" and be the first to turn them into
ridicule, without, of course, admitting anything. And this was
really the case, in spite of a certain and, indeed, considerable independence of thought, which he had of late gained at the expense
of the "lower ideas" that had mastered him till then. And how
often, when he got up in the morning, he began to be ashamed
of the thoughts and feelings he had passed through during a sleepless night! And he had suffered continually of late from sleeplessness. He had noticed for some time past that he had become ex-
cessively sensitive about everything, trifles as well as matters of
importance, and so he made up his mind to trust his feelings as
little as possible. But he could not overlook some facts, the reality
of which he was forced to admit. Of late his thoughts and sensations were sometimes at night completely transformed, and for

the most part utterly unlike those which came to him in the early part of the day. This struck him—and he even consulted a distinguished doctor who was, however, an acquaintance; he spoke to him about it jocosely, of course. The answer he received was that the transformation of ideas and sensations, and even the possession of two distinct sets of thoughts and sensations, was a universal fact among persons "who think and feel," that the convictions of a whole lifetime were sometimes transformed under the melancholy influences of night and sleeplessness; without rhyme or reason most momentous decisions were taken; but all this, of course, was only true up to a certain point—and, in fact, if the subject were too conscious of the double nature of his feelings, so that it began to be a source of suffering to him, it was certainly a symptom of approaching illness; and then steps must be taken at once. The best thing of all was to make a radical change in the mode of life, to alter one's diet, or even to travel. Relaxing medicine was beneficial, of course.

Velchaninov did not care to hear more; but to his mind it was conclusively shown to be illness.

"And so all this is only illness, all these 'higher ideas' are mere illness and nothing more!" he sometimes exclaimed to himself resentfully. He was very loth to admit this.

Soon, however, what had happened exclusively in the hours of the night began to be repeated in the morning, only with more bitterness than at night, with anger instead of remorse, with irony instead of emotion. What really happened was that certain incidents in his past, even in his distant past, began suddenly, and God knows why, to come more and more frequently back to his mind, but they came back in quite a peculiar way. Velchaninov had, for instance, complained for a long time past of loss of memory: he would forget the faces of acquaintances, who were offended by his cutting them when they met; he sometimes completely forgot a book he had read months before; and yet in spite of this loss of memory, evident every day (and a source of great uneasiness to him), everything concerning the remote past, things that had been quite forgotten for ten or fifteen years, would sometimes

come suddenly into his mind now with such amazing exactitude
of details and impressions that he felt as though he were living
through them again. Some of the facts he remembered had been
so completely forgotten that it seemed to him a miracle that they
could be recalled. But this was not all, and, indeed, what man of
wide experience has not some memory of a peculiar sort? But the
point was that all that was recalled came back now with a quite
fresh, surprising and, till then, inconceivable point of view, and
seemed as though some one were leading up to it on purpose.
Why did some things he remembered strike him now as positive
crimes? And it was not a question of the judgment of his mind
only: he would have put little faith in his gloomy, solitary and
sick mind; but it reached the point of curses and almost of tears,
of inward tears. Why, two years before, he would not have believed
it if he had been told that he would ever shed tears! At first, however, what he remembered was rather of a mortifying than of a
sentimental character: he recalled certain failures and humiliations
in society; he remembered, for instance, how he had been slandered by an intriguing fellow, and in consequence refused admittance to a certain house; how, for instance, and not so long ago.
he had been publicly and unmistakably insulted, and had not challenged the offender to a duel; how in a circle of very pretty
women he had been made the subject of an extremely witty
epigram and had found no suitable answer. He even recollected
one or two unpaid debts—trifling ones, it is true, but debts of
honor—owing to people whom he had given up visiting and
even spoke ill of. He was also worried (but only in his worst moments) by the thought of the two fortunes, both considerable
ones, which he had squandered in the stupidest way possible.
But soon he began to remember things of a "higher order."

Suddenly, for instance, apropos of nothing, he remembered the
forgotten, utterly forgotten, figure of a harmless, grey-headed and
absurd old clerk, whom he had once, long, long ago, and with
absolute impunity, insulted in public simply to gratify his own
conceit, simply for the sake of an amusing and successful jest,
which was repeated and increased his prestige. The incident had

been so completely forgotten that he could not even recall the old man's surname, though all the surroundings of the incident rose before his mind with incredible clearness. He distinctly remembered that the old man was defending his daughter, who was unmarried, though no longer quite young, and had become the subject of gossip in the town. The old man had begun to answer angrily, but he suddenly burst out crying before the whole company, which made some sensation. They had ended by making him drunk with champagne as a joke and getting a hearty laugh out of it. And now when, apropos of nothing, Velchaninov remembered how the poor old man had sobbed and hidden his face in his hands like a child, it suddenly seemed to him as though he had never forgotten it. And, strange to say, it had all seemed to him very amusing at the time, especially some of the details, such as the way he had covered his face with his hands; but now it was quite the contrary.

Later, he recalled how, simply as a joke, he had slandered the very pretty wife of a schoolmaster, and how the slander had reached the husband's ears. Velchaninov had left the town soon after and never knew what the final consequences of his slander had been, but now he began to imagine how all might have ended —and there is no knowing to what lengths his imagination might not have gone if this memory had not suddenly been succeeded by a much more recent reminiscence of a young girl of the working-class, to whom he had not even felt attracted, and of whom, it must be admitted, he was actually ashamed. Yet, though he could not have said what had induced him, he had got her into trouble and had simply abandoned her and his child without even saying good-bye (it was true, he had no time to spare), when he left Petersburg. He had tried to find that girl for a whole year afterwards, but he had not succeeded in tracing her. He had, it seemed, hundreds of such reminiscences—and each one of them seemed to bring dozens of others in its train. By degrees his vanity, too, began to suffer.

We have said already that his vanity had degenerated into something peculiar. That was true. At moments (rare moments, however), he even forgot himself to such a degree that he ceased to be ashamed of not keeping his own carriage, that he trudged on foot from one court to another, that he began to be somewhat negligent in his dress. And if someone of his own acquaintance had scanned him with a sarcastic stare in the street or had simply refused to recognize him, he might really have had pride enough to pass him by without a frown. His indifference would have been genuine, not assumed for effect. Of course, this was only at times: these were only the moments of forgetfulness and nervous irritation, yet his vanity had by degrees grown less concerned with the subjects that had once affected it, and was becoming concentrated on one question, which haunted him continually.

"Why, one would think," he began reflecting satirically sometimes (and he almost always began by being satirical when he thought about himself), "why, one would think someone up aloft were anxious for the reformation of my morals, and were sending me these cursed reminiscences and 'tears of repentance'! So be it, but it's all useless! It is all shooting with blank cartridge! As though I did not know for certain, more certainly than certainty, that in spite of these fits of tearful remorse and self-reproach, I haven't a grain of independence for all my foolish middle age! Why, if the same temptation were to turn up tomorrow, if circumstances, for instance, were to make it to my interest to spread a rumor that the schoolmaster's wife had taken presents from me, I should certainly spread it, I shouldn't hesitate—and it would be even worse, more loathsome than the first time, just because it would be the second time and not the first time. Yes, if I were insulted again this minute by that little prince whose leg I shot off eleven years ago, though he was the only son of his mother, I should challenge him at once and condemn him to crutches again. So they are no better than blank cartridges, and there's no sense in them! And what's the good of remembering the past when I've not the slightest power of escaping from myself?"

And though the adventure with the schoolmaster's wife was not repeated, though he did not condemn anyone else to crutches, the very idea that it inevitably would be the same, if the same circumstances arose, almost killed him . . . at times. One cannot, in reality, suffer from memories all the time; one can rest and enjoy oneself in the intervals.

So, indeed, Velchaninov did: he was ready to enjoy himself in the intervals; yet his sojourn in Petersburg grew more and more unpleasant as time went on. July was approaching. Intermittently he had flashes of determination to give up everything, the lawsuit and all, and to go away somewhere without looking back, to go suddenly, on the spur of the moment, to the Crimea, for instance. But, as a rule, an hour later he had scorned the idea and had laughed at it: "These hateful thoughts won't stop short at sending me to the south, if once they've begun and if I've any sense of decency, and so it's useless to run away from them, and, indeed, there's no reason to.

"And what's the object of running away?" he went on brooding in his despondency; "it's so dusty here, so stifling, everything in the house is so messy. In those law-courts where I hang about among those busy people, there is such a scurrying to and fro like mice, such a mass of sordid cares! All the people left in town, all the faces that flit by from morning till night so naïvely and openly betray their self-love, their guileless insolence, the cowardice of their little souls, the chicken-heartedness of their little natures— why, it's a paradise for a melancholy man, seriously speaking! Everything is open, everything is clear, no one thinks it necessary to hide anything as they do among our gentry in our summer villas or at water-places abroad—and so it's more deserving of respect, if only for its openness and simplicity! . . . I won't go away! I'll stay here if I burst!"

2 THE GENTLEMAN WITH CRAPE ON HIS HAT

IT WAS the third of July. The heat and stuffiness were insufferable. The day had been a very busy one for Velchaninov; he had had to spend the whole morning in walking and driving from place to place, and he had before him the prospect of an unavoidable visit that evening to a gentleman—a lawyer and a civil councillor —whom he hoped to catch unawares at his villa out of town. At six o'clock Velchaninov went at last into a restaurant (the fare was not beyond criticism, though the cooking was French) on the Nevsky Prospect, near the Police Bridge. He sat down at the little table in his usual corner and asked for the dinner of the day.

He used to eat the dinner that was provided for a rouble and paid extra for the wine, and he regarded this as a sacrifice to the unsettled state of his finances and an act of prudence on his part. Though he wondered how he could possibly eat such stuff, he nevertheless used to devour it to the last crumb—and every time with as much appetite as though he had not eaten for three days before. "There's something morbid about it," he would mutter to himself sometimes, noticing his appetite. But on this occasion he took his seat at his little table in a very bad humor, tossed his hat down angrily, put his elbows on the table, and sank into thought.

Though he could be so polite and, on occasion, so loftily imperturbable, he would probably now, if some one dining near him had been noisy, or the boy waiting on him had failed to understand at the first word, have been as blustering as a *junker* and would perhaps have made a scene.

The soup was put before him. He took up the ladle, but before he had time to help himself, he dropped it, and almost jumped up from the table. A surprising idea suddenly dawned upon him: at that instant—and God knows by what process—he suddenly realized the cause of his depression, of the special extra depression which had tormented him of late for several days together, had for some unknown reason fastened upon him and for some unknown cause refused to be shaken off; now he suddenly saw it all and it was as plain as a pikestaff.

"It's all that hat," he muttered as though inspired. "It's nothing but that cursed bowler hat with that beastly mourning crape that is the cause of it all!"

He began pondering—and the more he pondered the more morose he grew, and the more extraordinary "the whole adventure" seemed to him.

"But . . . it is not an adventure, though," he protested, distrustful of himself. "As though there were anything in the least like an adventure about it!"

All that had happened was this. Nearly a fortnight before (he did not really remember, but he fancied it was about a fortnight), he had first met somewhere in the street, near the corner of Podyatchesky Street and Myestchansky Street, a gentleman with crape on his hat. The gentleman was like anyone else, there was nothing peculiar about him, he passed quickly, but he stared somewhat too fixedly at Velchaninov, and for some reason at once attracted his attention in a marked degree. His countenance struck Velchaninov as familiar. He had certainly at some time met it somewhere. "But I must have seen thousands of faces in my life, I can't remember them all!"

Before he had gone twenty paces further he seemed to have forgotten the encounter, in spite of the impression made at first. But the impression persisted the whole day—and it was somewhat singular, it took the form of a peculiar undefined annoyance. Now, a fortnight later, he remembered all that distinctly; he remembered, too, what he had failed to grasp at the time—that is, what his annoyance was due to; and he had so utterly failed to grasp it that he had not even connected his ill-humor all that evening with the meeting that morning.

But the gentleman had lost no time in recalling himself to Velchaninov's mind, and next day had come across the latter in the Nevsky Prospect again, and again stared at him rather strangely. Velchaninov dismissed him with a curse and immediately afterwards wondered why he cursed. It is true that there are faces that at once arouse an undefined and aimless aversion.

"Yes, I certainly have met him somewhere," he muttered thoughtfully, an hour after the meeting. And he remained in a very bad humor the whole evening afterwards; he even had a bad dream at night, and yet it never entered his head that the whole cause of this new fit of despondency was nothing but that gentleman in mourning, although he did not once think of him that evening! He had even been wrathful at the moment that such a "wretched object" could occupy his attention as long at it did and would certainly have thought it degrading to ascribe his agitation to him, if it had ever occurred to his mind to do so. Two days later they met again in a crowd coming off one of the Nevsky steamers. On this third occasion Velchaninov was ready to swear that the gentleman with the crape on his hat recognized him and made a dash for him, but was borne away in the crush; he fancied he had even had the "effrontery" to hold out his hand to him; perhaps he had even cried out and shouted his name. That, however, Velchaninov had not heard distinctly, but . . . "Who is the low fellow, though, and why does he not come up to me, if he really does know me, and if he is so anxious to?" he thought angrily, as he got into a cab and drove towards Smolny monastery. Half an hour later he was noisily arguing with his lawyer, but in the evening and the night he was suffering again from the most abominable and most fantastic attack of acute depression. "Am I in for a bilious attack?" he wondered uneasily, looking at himself in the looking-glass.

This was the third meeting. Afterwards, for five days in succession, he met "no one," and not a sign was seen of the low fellow. And yet the gentleman with the crape on his hat was continually in his mind. With some surprise Velchaninov caught himself wondering: "What's the matter with me—am I sick on his account, or what? H'm! . . . and he must have a lot to do in Petersburg, too—and for whom is he wearing crape? He evidently recognized me, but I don't recognize him. And why do these people put on crape? It's out of keeping with him somehow. . . . I fancy if I look at him closer, I shall recognize him. . . ."

And something seemed faintly stirring in his memory, like some familiar but momentarily forgotten word, which one tries with all one's might to recall; one knows it very well and knows that one knows it; one knows exactly what it means, one is close upon it and yet it refuses to be remembered, in spite of one's efforts.

"It was . . . It was long ago . . . and it was somewhere . . . There was . . . there was . . . but, damn the fellow, whatever there was or wasn't . . ." he cried angrily all at once; "it is not worth while to demean and degrade myself over that wretched fellow. . . ."

He grew horribly angry, but in the evening, when he suddenly remembered that he had been angry that morning, and "horribly" angry, it was extremely disagreeable to him; he felt as though some one had caught him in something shameful. He was bewildered and surprised.

"Then there must be reasons for my being so angry . . . apropos of nothing . . . at a mere reminiscence . . ." He left the thought unfinished.

And next day he felt angrier than ever, but this time he fancied he had grounds for it, and that he was quite right in feeling so; "It was unheard-of insolence," he thought. What had happened was the fourth meeting. The gentleman with crape on his hat had suddenly made his appearance again, as though he had sprung out of the earth. Velchaninov had just caught in the street the indispensable civil councillor before mentioned, of whom he was still in pursuit, meaning to pounce on him unawares at his summer villa, for the gentleman, whom Velchaninov scarcely knew, thought it was so necessary to see him about his business, on that occasion as on this eluded him, and was evidently keeping out of sight and extremely reluctant to meet him. Delighted at coming across him at last, Velchaninov walked hurriedly beside him, glancing into his face and straining every effort to bring the wily old fellow to the discussion of a certain subject, in which the latter might be indiscreet enough to let slip the facts of which he had so long been on the track; but the crafty old man had his own views, and kept putting him off with laughter or silence—and it was just at this extremely absorbing moment that Velchaninov descried on the opposite pavement the gentleman with crape on his hat. He was standing staring at them both—he was watching them, that was evident, and seemed to be jeering at them.

"Damnation!" cried Velchaninov in a fury, as he left the civil councillor at his destination and ascribed his failure with him to the sudden appearance of that "impudent fellow." "Damnation! is he spying on me? He's evidently following me. Hired by some one, perhaps, and . . . and . . . and, by Jove! he was jeering at me! By Jove! I'll thrash him. . . . I'm sorry I've no stick with me! I'll buy a stick! I won't let it pass. Who is he? I insist on knowing who he is."

It was three days after this fourth meeting that Velchaninov was at his restaurant, as we have described him, agitated in earnest and even somewhat overwhelmed. He could not help being conscious of it himself, in spite of his pride. He was forced at last, putting all the circumstances together, to suspect that all his depression—all this *peculiar* despondency and the agitation that had persisted for the last fortnight—was caused by no other than this gentleman in mourning, "nonentity as he was."

"I may be a hypochondriac," thought Velchaninov, "and so I am ready to make a mountain out of a mole-hill, but does it make it any better for me that all this is *perhaps* only fancy! Why, if every rogue like that is going to be able to upset one in this way, why . . . it's . . . why? . . ."

Certainly in the meeting of that day (the fifth), which had so agitated Velchaninov, the mountain had proved to be little more than a mole-hill: the gentleman had as before darted by him, but this time without scrutinizing Velchaninov, and without, as before, betraying that he recognized him; on the contrary, he dropped his eyes and seemed to be very anxious to escape being noticed. Velchaninov turned round and shouted at the top of his voice—

"Hi! you with the crape on your hat! Hiding now! Stop! Who are you?"

The question (and his shouting altogether) was very irrational, but Velchaninov only realized that after he had uttered it. The gentleman turned round at the shout, stood still for a minute disconcerted, smiled, seemed on the point of doing or saying something, was obviously for a minute in a state of the utmost indecision, then he suddenly turned and rushed away without looking back. Velchaninov looked after him with astonishment.

"And what if it's a case of my forcing myself on him, not his forcing himself on me?" he thought. "And that's all it amounts to?"

When he had finished dinner he made haste to set off to the summer villa to see the civil councillor. He did not find him; he was informed that "his honor had not returned that day, and probably would not come back till three or four o'clock in the morning, as he was staying in town to a birthday party." This was so mortifying that, in his first fury, Velchaninov decided himself to go to the birthday party, and even set off to do so; but reflecting on the road that it was a long way to go, he dismissed the cab and trudged home on foot to his flat near the Grand Theatre. He felt that he wanted exercise. He must, at all costs, overcome his usual sleeplessness, and sleep sound that night, to soothe his excited nerves; and in order to sleep he must anyway be tired. And, as it was a long walk, it was half-past ten before he reached home, and he certainly was very tired.

Though he so criticized the flat that he had taken the previous March, and abused it so malignantly—excusing himself to himself on the plea that he was only "camping there temporarily," and stranded in Petersburg through that "damned lawsuit"—the flat was by no means so bad and so unsuitable as he made out. The approach was certainly rather dark and "grubby" under the gateway, but the flat itself, on the second story, consisted of two big, lofty and bright rooms, separated from one another by a dark entry, and looking one into the street, the other into the courtyard. Adjoining the room the windows of which looked into the courtyard was a small study, which had been designed for a bedroom; but Velchaninov kept it littered with books and papers; he slept in one of the larger rooms, the one that looked into the street. He had a bed made up on the sofa. The furniture was quite decent, though second-hand, and he had besides a few articles of value— the relics of his former prosperity: bronze and china, and big, genuine Bokhara rugs; even two good pictures had been preserved; but everything had been unmistakably untidy and even dusty and nothing had been put in its place ever since his servant, Pelagea, had gone home to Novgorod for a holiday and left him alone. The oddity of having a solitary female servant for a bachelor and man of the world who was still anxious to keep up the style of a gentleman almost made Velchaninov blush, though he was very well satisfied with his Pelagea. The girl had come to him when he was taking the flat in the spring, from a family of his acquaintance who were going abroad, and she had put the flat to rights. But when she went away he could not bring himself to engage another woman; to engage a manservant was not worth while for a short time; besides, he did not like menservants. And so it was arranged that the sister of the porter's wife should come in every morning to clear up and that Velchaninov should leave the key at the porter's lodge when he went out. She did absolutely nothing, merely pocketed her wages; and he suspected her of pilfering. Yet he dismissed everything with a shrug and was positively glad that he was left quite alone in the flat. But there are limits to everything; and at some jaundiced moments the "filth" was absolutely insufferable to his nerves, and he almost always went into his rooms with a feeling of repugnance on returning home.

But this time he barely gave himself time to undress; flinging himself on the bed, he irritably resolved to think of nothing, but to go to sleep "this minute," whatever might happen; and, strange to say, he did fall asleep as soon as his head touched the pillow; such a thing had not happened to him for almost a month.

He slept for nearly three hours, but his sleep was uneasy, and he had strange dreams such as one has in fever. He dreamed of some crime which he had committed and concealed and of which he was accused by people who kept coming up to him. An immense crowd collected, but more people still came, so that the door was not shut but remained open. But his whole interest was centered on a strange person, once an intimate friend of his, who was dead, but now somehow suddenly came to see him. What made it most worrying was that Velchaninov did not know the man, had forgotten his name and could not recall it. All he knew was that he had once liked him very much. All the other people who had come up seemed expecting from this man a final word that would decide Velchaninov's guilt or innocence, and all were waiting impatiently. But he sat at the table without moving, was mute and would not speak. The noise did not cease for a moment, the general irritation grew more intense, and suddenly in a fury Velchaninov struck the man for refusing to speak, and felt a strange enjoyment in doing it. His heart thrilled with horror and misery at what he had done, but there was enjoyment in that thrill. Utterly exasperated, he struck him a second time and a third, and, drunk with rage and terror, which reached the pitch of madness, but in which there was an intense enjoyment, he lost count of his blows, and went on beating him without stopping. He wanted to demolish *it* all, all. Suddenly something happened: they all shrieked horribly and turned round to the door, as though expecting something, and at that instant there came the sound of a ring at the bell, repeated three times, with violence enough to pull the bell off. Velchaninov woke up and was wide-awake in an instant. He leapt headlong out of bed and rushed to the door; he was absolutely convinced that the ring at the bell was not a dream and that someone really had rung at his bell that moment. "It would be too unnatural for such a distinct, such a real, palpable ring to be only a dream!"

But to his surprise the ring at the bell turned out to be a dream, too. He opened the door, went out on the landing, even peeped down the stairs—there was absolutely no one there. The bell hung motionless. Surprised, but relieved, he went back into his room. When he had lighted a candle he remembered that he had left the door closed but not locked or bolted. He had sometimes in the past forgotten when he came home to lock the door for the night, not thinking it of much importance.

Pelagea had often given him a talking-to about it. He went back into the passage, shut the door, opened it once more and looked out on the landing, but only fastened the door on the inside with the hook, without taking the trouble to turn the key. The clock struck half-past two; so he must have slept three hours.

His dream had so disturbed him that he did not want to go to bed again at once, and made up his mind to walk up and down his room for half an hour or—"Time enough to smoke a cigar"—he thought. Hastily dressing, he went to the window and lifted the thick stuff curtain and the white blind behind it. It was already daylight in the street. The light summer nights of Petersburg always worked on his nerves and of late had intensified his insomnia, so that it was expressly on this account that he had, a fortnight previously, put up thick stuff curtains which completely excluded the light when they were fully drawn. Letting in the daylight and forgetting the lighted candle on the table, he fell to pacing up and down the room, still oppressed by a sort of sick and heavy feeling. The impression of the dream was still upon him. A real feeling of distress that he should have been capable of raising his hand against that man and beating him still persisted.

"That man doesn't exist, and never has existed; it's all a dream. Why am I worrying about it?"

He began thinking with exasperation, as though all his troubles were concentrated on this, that he was certainly beginning to be ill —"a sick man."

It was always painful to him to think that he was getting old and growing feebler, and in his bad moments he exaggerated his age and failing powers on purpose to irritate himself.

"Old age," he muttered; "I'm getting quite old, I'm losing my memory, I see apparitions, I dream dreams, bells ring. . . . Damn it all, I know from experience that such dreams are always a sign of fever with me. . . . I am convinced that all this business with the crape gentleman is a dream too. I was certainly right yesterday: it's I, I, who am pestering him, not he me. I've woven a romance about him, and I am hiding under the table in my fright at it. And why do I call him a low fellow? He may be a very decent person. His face is not attractive, certainly, though there is nothing particularly ugly about it; he's dressed like anyone else. Only in his eyes there's something. . . . Here I'm at it again! I'm thinking about him again!! What the devil does the look in his eyes matter to me? Can't I get on without that? . . ."

Among the thoughts that kept starting up in his mind, one rankled painfully: he felt suddenly convinced that this gentleman with the crape on his hat had once been an acquaintance on friendly terms with him, and now sneered at him when he met him because he knew some great secret about him in the past and saw him now in such a humiliating position. He went mechanically to the window, meaning to open it and get a breath of the night air, and—and he suddenly shuddered all over: it seemed to him that something incredible and unheard-of was suddenly happening before his eyes.

He had not yet opened the window but he made haste to slip behind the corner of the window and hide himself: on the deserted pavement opposite he had suddenly seen directly facing the house the man with the crape on his hat. The gentleman was standing on the pavement looking towards his windows, but evidently not noticing him, stared inquisitively at the house as though considering something. He seemed to be deliberating and unable to decide: he lifted his hand and seemed to put his finger to his forehead. At last he made up his mind: he took a cursory glance round, and began stealthily on tiptoe crossing the street. Yes: he had gone in at the gateway by the little gate (which sometimes in summer was left unbolted till three o'clock).

"He's coming to me," flashed on Velchaninov's mind, and, also on tiptoe, he ran headlong to the door and stood before it silent and numb with suspense, softly laying his trembling right hand on the hook of the door he had just fastened, listening intently for the sound of footsteps on the stairs.

His heart beat so violently that he was afraid he might not hear the stranger come up on tiptoe. He did not understand what it meant, but he felt it all with tenfold intensity. His dream seemed to have melted into reality. Velchaninov was by temperament bold. He sometimes liked to display fearlessness in the face of danger even if he were only admiring himself with no one else to look at him. But now there was something else as well. The man who had so lately been given up to hypochondria and nervous depression was completely transformed; he was not the same man. A nervous, noiseless laugh broke from him. From behind the closed door he divined every movement of the stranger.

"Ah! now he's coming in, he has come in, he's looking about him; he's listening downstairs; he's holding his breath, stealing up . . . ah! He has taken hold of the handle, he's pulling it, trying it! He reckoned on its not being locked! So he knows I sometimes forget to lock it! He's pulling at the handle again; why, does he imagine that the hook will come out? It's a pity to part! Isn't it a pity to let him go like this?"

And indeed everything must have happened just as he pictured it; someone really was standing on the other side of the door, and was softly and noiselessly trying the lock, and was pulling at the handle and—"Of course, he had his object in doing so." But by now Velchaninov had resolved to settle the question, and with a sort of glee got ready for the moment. He had an irresistible longing to unfasten the hook, suddenly to fling open the door, and to confront the "bugbear" face to face. "What may you be doing here, pray, honored sir?"

And so he did: seizing the moment, he suddenly lifted the hook, pushed the door and—almost fell over the gentleman with crape on his hat.

3 PAVEL PAVLOVITCH TRUSOTSKY

THE latter stood speechless, rooted to the spot. They stood facing one another in the doorway, and stared fixedly into each other's faces. Some moments passed and suddenly—Velchaninov recognized his visitor!

At the same time the visitor evidently realized that Velchaninov recognized him fully. There was a gleam in his eye that betrayed it. In one instant his whole face melted into a sugary smile.

"I have the pleasure, I believe, of addressing Alexey Ivanovitch?" he almost chanted in a voice of deep feeling, ludicrously incongruous with the circumstances.

"Surely you are not Pavel Pavlovitch Trusotsky?" Velchaninov brought out with an air of perplexity.

"We were acquainted nine years ago at T——, and if you will allow me to remind you—we were intimately acquainted."

"Yes . . . to be sure, but now it's three o'clock, and for the last ten minutes you've been trying whether my door was locked or not."

"Three o'clock!" cried the visitor, taking out his watch and seeming positively grieved and surprised; "why, so it is. Three! I beg your pardon, Alexey Ivanovitch, I ought to have considered before coming up: I'm quite ashamed. I'll come again and explain, in a day or two, but now . . ."

"No! If there's to be an explanation will you kindly give it me this minute!" Velchaninov caught him up. "Please walk inside, into this room—no doubt you intended to come into the room yourself, and have not turned up in the middle of the night simply to try the lock."

He was excited and at the same time disconcerted, and felt that he could not grasp the position. He was even somewhat ashamed —there proved to be neither mystery nor danger. The whole phantasmagoria had proved to be nothing; all that had turned up was the foolish figure of some Pavel Pavlovitch. And yet he did not believe that it was all so simple; he had a vague presentiment and dread of something. Making his visitor sit down in an arm-chair, he seated himself impatiently on his bed, not a yard away, bent forward with his hands on his knees and waited irritably for him to speak. He scanned him greedily and remembered him. But, strange to say, the man was silent, quite silent, and seemed not to realize that he was "in duty bound" to speak at once; on the contrary, he, too, gazed at Velchaninov with a look of expectation. It was possible that he was simply timid, feeling at first a certain awkwardness like a mouse in a trap; but Velchaninov flew into a rage.

"What do you mean by it!" he cried; "you are not a phantom or a dream, I suppose! You've not come to play at being dead, surely? Explain yourself, my good man!"

The visitor fidgeted, smiled, and began warily—

"So far as I see, what strikes you most of all is my coming at such an hour and under such peculiar circumstances. . . . So that, remembering all the past, and how we parted—it's really strange to me now. . . . Though, indeed, I had no intention of calling, and it has only happened by accident. . . ."

"How by accident? Why, I saw you through the window run across the street on tiptoe!"

"Ah, you saw me! So perhaps you know more about it all than I do! But I'm only irritating you. . . . You see, I arrived here three weeks ago on business of my own. . . . I am Pavel Pavlovitch Trusotsky, you know; you recognized me yourself. I am here to try to get transferred to another province, and to a post in another department considerably superior. . . . But all that's neither here nor there, though . . . The point is, if you must know, that I have been hanging about here for the last three weeks, and I seem to be spinning out my business on purpose—that is, the business of my transfer—and really, if it comes off I do believe I shan't notice that it has come off and shall stay on in your Petersburg, feeling as I do now. I hang about as though I had lost sight of my object and, as it were, pleased to have lost sight of it—feeling as I do! . . ."

"Feeling how?" Velchaninov asked, frowning.

The visitor raised his eyes to him, lifted his hat and pointed to the crape on it.

"Why, look; that's how I'm feeling."

Velchaninov gazed blankly first at the crape and then at the countenance of his visitor. Suddenly the color rushed into his cheeks and he grew terribly agitated.

"Surely not Natalya Vassilyevna?"

"Yes! Natalya Vassilyevna! Last March . . . consumption, and almost suddenly, after two or three months' illness! And I am left —as you see!"

As he said this the visitor, in deep emotion, put out his hands on each side, the hat with the crape on it flapping in his left one, while he made a low bow that displayed his bald head for ten seconds at least.

His air and his gesture seemed to revive Velchaninov; an ironical and even provocative smile hovered on his lips—but only for a moment: the news of the death of this lady (whom he had known so long ago and had long ago succeeded in forgetting) gave him a shock which was a complete surprise to him.

"Is it possible?"—he muttered the first words that came to his tongue—"and why didn't you come straight and tell me?"

"I thank you for your sympathy. I see it and appreciate it, in spite of . . ."

"In spite of?"

"In spite of so many years of separation, you have just shown such sympathy for my sorrow and even for me that I am, of course, sensible of gratitude. That was all I wanted to express. It's not that I had doubts of my friends: I can find here the truest friends at once—Stepan Mihalovitch Bagautov, for instance. But you know, Alexey Ivanovitch, our acquaintance with you—friendship rather, as I gratefully recall it—was over nine years ago, you never came back to us; there was no interchange of letters. . . ."

The visitor chanted his phrases as though to music, but all the while that he was holding forth he looked at the floor, though, no doubt, all the time he saw everything. But Velchaninov had by now regained his composure.

With a very strange impression, which grew stronger and stronger, he listened to Pavel Pavlovitch and watched him, and when the latter suddenly paused, the most incongruous and surprising ideas rushed in a sudden flash into his mind.

"But how was it I didn't recognize you till now?" he cried, growing more animated. "Why, we've stumbled across each other five times in the street!"

"Yes; I remember that, too; you were constantly crossing my path—twice, or perhaps three times. . . ."

"That is, you were constantly coming upon me, not I upon you."

Velchaninov stood up and suddenly, quite unexpectedly, he began laughing. Pavel Pavlovitch paused, looked at him attentively, but at once continued—

"And as for your not recognizing me, you might well have forgotten me, and, besides, I've had smallpox and it has left some traces on my face."

"Smallpox? To be sure, he has had smallpox! However did you——"

"Manage that? Anything may happen. One never can tell, Alexey Ivanovitch; one does have such misfortunes."

"Only it's awfully funny all the same. But continue, continue, my dear friend!"

"Though I met you, too . . ."

"Stay! Why did you say 'manage that' just now? I meant to use a much more polite expression. But go on, go on!"

For some reason he felt more and more good-humored. The feeling of shock was completely effaced by other emotions. He walked up and down the room with rapid steps.

"Even though I met you, and though when I set out for Petersburg I intended to seek you out, yet now, I repeat, I have been feeling so broken in spirit . . . and mentally shattered ever since March . . ."

"Oh, yes! shattered since March. . . . Stop a minute. Don't you smoke?"

"As you know, in old days when Natalya Vassilyevna was living I . . ."

"To be sure, to be sure; and since March?"

"Just a cigarette, perhaps."

"Here is a cigarette. Light it—and go on! Go on, it's awfully——"

And, lighting a cigar, Velchaninov quickly settled himself on the bed again.

Pavel Pavlovitch paused.

"But how excited you are yourself. Are you quite in good health?"

"Oh, damn my health!" Velchaninov was suddenly exasperated. "Continue!"

The visitor, for his part, looking at his companion's agitation, seemed better pleased and grew more self-confident.

"But what is there to continue?" he began again. "Imagine, Alexey Ivanovitch, in the first place, a man destroyed—that is, not simply destroyed, but fundamentally, so to say; a man whose existence is transformed after twenty years of married life, wandering about the streets with no consistent object, as though in a wilderness, almost in a state of oblivion, and finding a certain fascination in that oblivion. It is natural that sometimes when I meet an acquaintance, even a real friend, I purposely go out of my way to avoid approaching him, at such a moment of oblivion, I mean. And at another moment one remembers everything so, and so longs to see anyone who has witnessed that recent past, gone now never to return, and has taken part in it, and one's heart beats so violently that one is ready to risk throwing oneself upon a friend by night as well as by day, even though one might have to wake him up at four o'clock in the morning on purpose. . . . I have made a mistake about the time only, not about our friendship; for this moment more than makes up for it. And as for the time, I really thought it was only twelve, feeling as I do. One drinks the cup of one's sorrow till one is drunk with it. And it's not sorrow, indeed, but the novelty of my state that crushes me. . . ."

"How strangely you express yourself!" Velchaninov observed gloomily, becoming extremely grave again.

"Yes, I do express myself strangely. . . ."

"And you're . . . not joking?"

"Joking!" exclaimed Pavel Pavlovitch in pained surprise, "and at the moment when I am announcing the sad . . ."

"Ach, don't speak of that, I entreat you!"

Velchaninov got up and began pacing the room again.

So passed five minutes. The visitor seemed about to get up too, but Velchaninov shouted: "Sit still, sit still!" and Pavel Pavlovitch obediently sank back into his arm-chair at once.

"But, how you have changed though," Velchaninov began again, suddenly stopping before him as though all at once struck by the thought. "You're dreadfully changed! Extraordinarily! Quite a different person."

"That's not strange: nine years."

"No, no, no, it's not a question of years! It's incredible how you've changed in appearance; you've become a different man!"

"That, too, may well be, in nine years."

"Or is it since March!"

"He—he!" Pavel Pavlovitch sniggered slily. "That's a funny idea of yours. . . . But if I may venture—what is the change exactly?"

"You ask what! The Pavel Pavlovitch I used to know was such

a solid, decorous person, that Pavel Pavlovitch was such a clever chap, and now—this Pavel Pavlovitch is a regular *vaurien!*"

He was at that stage of irritability in which even reserved people say more than they ought.

"*Vaurien!* You think so? And not a clever chap now—not clever?" Pavel Pavlovitch chuckled with relish.

"Clever chap be damned! Now I daresay you really are too clever."

"I'm insolent, but this low fellow's more so and . . . and what is his object?" Velchaninov was thinking all the while.

"Ach, dearest, most precious friend!" cried the visitor suddenly, growing extremely agitated and turning round in his chair. "What are we saying? We are not in the world now, we're not in the society of the great and the worldly! We're two old friends, very old friends! And we've come together in the fullest sincerity to recall to one another the priceless bond of friendship of which the dear departed was the precious link!"

And he was so carried away by the ecstasy of his feeling that he bowed his head as before, hiding his face in his hat. Velchaninov watched him with aversion and uneasiness.

"What if he's simply a buffoon," flashed through his mind; "but n-no, n-no! I don't think he's drunk—he may be drunk, though: his face is red. Even if he were drunk—it comes to the same thing. What's he driving at? What does the low fellow want?"

"Do you remember, do you remember," cried Pavel Pavlovitch, removing the hat a little and seeming more and more carried away by his reminiscences, "do you remember our expeditions into the country, our evenings and little parties with dancing and innocent games at the house of His Excellency, our most hospitable Semyon Semyonovitch? And how we used to read together, the three of us, in the evening! And our first acquaintance with you, when you called on me that morning to make inquiries about your business, and even began to speak rather warmly, and suddenly Natalya Vassilyevna came in, and within ten minutes you had become a real friend of the family and so you were for a whole year, exactly as in Turgenev's play 'A Provincial Lady.'"

Velchaninov paced slowly up and down, looked at the floor, listened with impatience and repulsion, but—listened intently.

"The thought of 'A Provincial Lady' never entered my head," he interrupted, somewhat confused, "and you never used to talk in such a shrill voice and such . . . unnatural language. What is that for?"

"I certainly used to be more silent—that is, I was more reserved," Pavel Pavlovitch interposed hurriedly. "You know I used to prefer listening while the dear departed talked. You remember how she used to talk, how wittily. . . . And in regard to 'A Provincial Lady' and Stupendyev particularly, you are quite right, for I remember it was we ourselves, the precious departed and I, used to speak of that at quiet moments after you'd gone away—comparing our first meeting with that drama, for there really was a resemblance. About Stupendyev especially."

"What Stupendyev? Damn him!" cried Velchaninov, and he actually stamped, utterly disconcerted at the mention of "Stupendyev," owing to a disturbing recollection that was evoked by the name.

"Stupendyev is a character, a character in a play, the husband in 'A Provincial Lady,' " Pavel Pavlovitch piped in a voice of honeyed sweetness; "but it belonged to a different series of our precious and happy memories, when after your departure Stepan Mihalovitch Bagautov bestowed his friendship on us, exactly as you did, for five whole years."

"Bagautov? What do you mean? What Bagautov?" Velchaninov stood still as though petrified.

"Bagautov, Stepan Mihalovitch, who bestowed his friendship on us, a year after you and . . . and exactly as you did."

"Good heavens, yes! I know that!" cried Velchaninov, recovering himself at last. "Bagautov! Why, of course, he had a berth in your town. . . ."

"He had, he had! At the Governor's! From Petersburg. A very elegant young man, belonging to the best society!" Pavel Pavlovitch exclaimed in a positive ecstasy.

"Yes, yes, yes! What was I thinking of? Why, he, too . . ."

"He too, he too," Pavel Pavlovitch repeated in the same ecstasy, catching up the word his companion had incautiously dropped. "He too! Well, we acted 'A Provincial Lady' at His Excellency's, our most hospitable Semyon Semyonovitch's private theatre—Stepan Mihalovitch was the 'count,' I was the 'husband,' and the dear departed was 'The Provincial Lady'—only they took away the 'husband's' part from me, Natalya Vassilyevna insisted on it, so that I did not act the 'husband' because I was not fitted for the part. . . ."

"How the devil could you be Stupendyev? You're pre-eminently Pavel Pavlovitch Trusotsky and not Stupendyev," said Velchaninov, speaking with coarse rudeness and almost trembling with irritation. "Only, excuse me; Bagautov's in Petersburg, I saw him myself in the spring! Why don't you go and see him too?"

"I have been every blessed day, for the last fortnight. I'm not admitted! He's ill, he can't see me! And, only fancy, I've found out from first-hand sources that he really is very dangerously ill! The friend of six years. Ach, Alexey Ivanovitch, I tell you and I repeat it, that sometimes one's feelings are such that one longs to sink into the earth; yes, really; at another moment one feels as though one could embrace any one of those who have been, so to say, witnesses and participators of the past and simply that one may weep, absolutely for nothing else but that one may weep. . . ."

"Well, anyway, I've had enough of you for today, haven't I?" Velchaninov brought out abruptly.

"More than enough, more!" Pavel Pavlovitch got up from his seat at once. "It's four o'clock, and, what's worse, I have so selfishly upset you. . . ."

"Listen, I will be sure to come and see you myself, and then, I hope . . . Tell me straight out, tell me frankly, you are not drunk to-day?"

"Drunk! Not a bit of it. . . ."

"Hadn't you been drinking just before you came, or earlier?"

"Do you know, Alexey Ivanovitch, you're in a regular fever."

"I'll come and see you to-morrow morning before one o'clock."

"And I've been noticing for a long time that you seem, as it were, delirious," Pavel Pavlovitch interrupted with zest, still harping on the same subject. "I feel conscience-stricken, really, that by my awkwardness . . . but I'm going, I'm going! And you lie down and get some sleep!"

"Why, you haven't told me where you're living," Velchaninov called hastily after him.

"Didn't I tell you? At the Pokrovsky Hotel."

"What Pokrovsky Hotel?"

"Why, close to the Pokrovsky Church, close by, in the side street. I've forgotten the name of the street and I've forgotten the number, only it's close by the Pokrovsky Church."

"I shall find it!"

"You'll be very welcome."

He was by now on his way downstairs.

"Stay," Velchaninov shouted after him again; "you are not going to give me the slip?"

"How do you mean, give you the slip?" cried Pavel Pavlovitch, staring at him open-eyed and turning round to smile on the third step.

Instead of answering, Velchaninov shut the door with a loud slam, carefully locked it and fastened the hook. Returning to the room, he spat as though he had been in contact with something unclean.

After standing for some five minutes in the middle of the room, he flung himself on the bed without undressing and in one minute fell asleep. The forgotten candle burnt itself out on the table.

4 THE WIFE, THE HUSBAND AND THE LOVER

HE SLEPT very soundly and woke up at half-past nine; he remembered everything instantly, sat down on his bed and began at once thinking of "that woman's death." The shock of the sudden news of that death the night before had left a certain agitation and even pain. That pain and agitation had only for a time been smothered by a strange idea while Pavel Pavlovitch was with him.

But now, on waking up, all that had happened nine years before rose before his mind with extraordinary vividness.

This woman, this Natalya Vassilyevna, the wife of "that Trusotsky," he had once loved, and he had been her lover for the whole year that he had spent at T——, ostensibly on business of his own (that, too, was a lawsuit over a disputed inheritance), although his presence had not really been necessary for so long. The real cause of his remaining was this intrigue. The *liaison* and his love had such complete possession of him that it was as though he were in bondage to Natalya Vassilyevna, and he would probably have been ready on the spot to do anything, however monstrous and senseless, to satisfy that woman's slightest caprice.

He had never felt anything of the sort before. At the end of the year, when separation was inevitable, although it was expected to be only a brief one, Velchaninov was in such despair, as the fatal time drew near, that he proposed to Natalya Vassilyevna that she should elope with him, that he should carry her off from her husband, that they should throw up everything and that she should come abroad with him for ever. Nothing but the jibes and firm determination of the lady (who had, probably from boredom, or to amuse herself, quite approved of the project at first) could have dissuaded him and forced him to go alone. And actually, before two months had passed, he was asking himself in Petersburg the question which had always remained unanswered. Had he really loved that woman or had it been nothing but an "infatuation"? And it was not levity or the influence of some new passion that had given rise to this question: for those first two months in Petersburg he had been plunged in a sort of stupefaction and had scarcely noticed any woman, although he had at once mixed with his former acquaintances again and had seen a hundred women. At the same time he knew that if he were transported that moment to T—— he would promptly fall under the yoke of that woman's fascination again, in spite of any questions. Even five years later his conviction was unchanged. But five yars later he used to admit this to himself with indignation and he even thought of "that woman" herself with hatred. He was ashamed of that year at T——; he could not even understand how such a "stupid" passion could have been possible for him, Velchaninov. All his memories of that passion had become absurd to him; and he blushed to the point of tears and was tormented by conscience-pricks at the thought of it. It is true that a few years later he had become somewhat calmer; he tried to forget it all—and almost succeeded. And now, all at once, nine years afterwards, all this had so suddenly and strangely risen up before him again, after hearing that night of the death of Natalya Vassilyevna.

Now, sitting on his bed, with confused thoughts crowding in disorder on his mind, he felt and realized clearly one thing only— that in spite of the "shock" he had felt at the news, he was nevertheless quite undisturbed by the fact of her death. "Can it be that I have no feeling for her?" he asked himself. It is true that he had now no feeling of hatred for her, and that he could criticize her more impartially, more fairly. In the course of those nine years of separation he had long since formulated the view that Natalya Vassilyevna belonged to the class of absolutely ordinary provincial ladies moving in good provincial society "and, who knows? perhaps she really was such, perhaps it was only I who idealized her so fantastically." He had always suspected, however, that there might be an error in that view; and he felt it even now. And, indeed, the facts were opposed to it; this Bagautov, too, had for several years been connected with her and apparently he, too, had been "under the yoke of her fascination." Bagautov certainly was a young man belonging to the best Petersburg society and, as he was a most "empty-headed fellow," he could only have had a successful career in Petersburg (Velchaninov used to say of him). Yet he had neglected Petersburg—that is, sacrificed his most important interests—and remained for five years in T—— solely on account of that woman! Yes, and he had finally returned to Petersburg, perhaps only because he, too, had been cast off like "an old, worn-out shoe." So there must have been in that woman something exceptional—a power of attracting, of enslaving, of dominating.

And yet one would have thought that she had not the gifts with which to attract and to enslave. She was not exactly pretty; per-

haps she was actually plain. She was twenty-eight when Velchaninov first knew her. Though not altogether beautiful, her face was
sometimes charmingly animated, but her eyes were not pretty:
there was something like an excess of determination in them. She
was very thin. On the intellectual side she had not been well
educated; her keen intelligence was unmistakable, though she was
one-sided in her ideas. Her manners were those of a provincial
lady and at the same time, it is true, she had a great deal of tact;
she had artistic taste, but showed it principally in knowing how
to dress. In character she was resolute and domineering; she could
never make up her mind to compromise in anything: it was all or
nothing. In difficult positions her firmness and stoicism were
amazing. She was capable of generosity and at the same time
would be utterly unjust. To argue with that lady was impossible:
"twice two makes four" meant nothing to her. She never thought
herself wrong or to blame in anything. Her continual deception of
her husband and the perfidies beyond number which she practised
upon him did not weigh on her in the least. But, to quote Velchaninov's own comparison, she was like the "Madonna of the
Flagellants," who believes implicitly herself that she is the mother
of God—so Natalya Vassilyevna believed implicitly in everything
she did.

She was faithful to her lover, but only as long as he did not bore
her. She was fond of tormenting her lover, but she liked making
up for it too. She was of a passionate, cruel and sensual type. She
hated depravity and condemned it with exaggerated severity and—
was herself depraved. No sort of fact could have made her recognize her own depravity. "Most likely she *genuinely* does not know
it," Velchaninov thought about her even before he left T——.
(We may remark, by the way, that he was the accomplice of her
depravity.) "She is one of those women who are born to be unfaithful wives. Such women never become old maids; it's a law
of their nature to be married to that end. The husband is the first
lover, but never till after the wedding. No one gets married more
adroitly and easily than this type of woman. For her first infidelity
the husband is always to blame. And it is all accompanied by the

most perfect sincerity: to the end they feel themselves absolutely right and, of course, entirely innocent."

Velchaninov was convinced that there really was such a type of woman; but, on the other hand, he was also convinced that there was a type of husband corresponding to that woman, whose sole vocation was to correspond with that feminine type. To his mind, the essence of such a husband lay in his being, so to say, "the eternal husband," or rather in being, all his life, a husband and nothing more. "Such a man is born and grows up only to be a husband, and, having married, is promptly transformed into a supplement of his wife, even when he happens to have unmistakable character of his own. The chief sign of such a husband is a certain decoration. He can no more escape wearing horns than the sun can help shining; he is not only unaware of the fact, but is bound by the very laws of his nature to be unaware of it." Velchaninov firmly believed in the existence of these two types and in Pavel Pavlovitch Trusotsky's being a perfect representative of one of them. The Pavel Pavlovitch of the previous night was, of course, very different from the Pavel Pavlovitch he had known at T——. He found him incredibly changed, but Velchaninov knew that he was bound to have changed and that all that was perfectly natural; Trusotsky could only as long as his wife was alive have remained all that he used to be, but, as it was, he was only a fraction of a whole, suddenly cut off and set free; that is, something wonderful and unique.

As for the Pavel Pavlovitch of the past at T——, this is how Velchaninov remembered him and recalled him now.

"Of course, at T——, Pavel Pavlovitch had been simply a husband," and nothing more. If he were, for instance, an official in the service as well, it was solely because such a position was one of the obligations of his married life; he was in the service for the sake of his wife and her social position in T——, though he was in himself zealous in his duties. He was thirty-five then and was possessed of some little fortune. He showed no special ability in his department and showed no special lack of it either. He used to mix with all the best people in the province and was said to be on an excellent footing with them. Natalya Vassilyevna was deeply respected in T——; she did not, however, greatly appreciate that, accepting it as simply her due, but in her own house she was superb at entertaining guests, and Pavel Pavlovitch had been so well trained by her that he was able to behave with dignity even when entertaining the highest magnates of the province. Perhaps (it seemed to Velchaninov) he had intelligence too, but as Natalya Vassilyevna did not like her spouse to talk too much, his intelligence was not very noticeable. Perhaps he had many natural good qualities, as well as bad ones. But his good qualities were kept under a shade, as it were, and his evil propensities were almost completely stifled.

Velchaninov remembered, for instance, that Pavel Pavlovitch sometimes betrayed a disposition to laugh at his neighbors, but this was sternly forbidden him. He was fond, too, at times of telling anecdotes; but a watch was kept on that weakness too, and he was only allowed to tell such as were brief and of little importance. He had a weakness for a festive glass outside the house and was even capable of drinking too much with a friend; but this failing had been severely nipped in the bud. And it is noteworthy that no outside observer would have said that Pavel Pavlovitch was a henpecked husband; Natalya Vassilyevna seemed an absolutely obedient wife, and most likely believed herself to be one. It was possible that Pavel Pavlovitch loved Natalya Vassilyevna passionately; but no one noticed it, and, indeed, it was impossible to notice it, and this reserve was probably due to her domestic discipline. Several times during his life at T—— Velchaninov had asked himself whether the husband had any suspicion at all of his wife's intrigue. Several times he questioned Natalya Vassilyevna seriously about it, and always received the answer, uttered with a certain annoyance, that her husband knew nothing and never could know anything about it and that "it was no concern of his." Another characteristic of hers was that she never laughed at Pavel Pavlovich and did not consider him absurd or very plain and would, indeed, have taken his part very warmly if any one had dared to show him incivility. Having no children, she was naturally bound to become a society woman, but her home life, too, was essential to her.

Social pleasures never had complete sway of her, and at home she was very fond of needlework and looking after the house. Pavel Pavlovitch had recalled, that night, the evenings they had spent in reading; it happened that sometimes Velchaninov read aloud and sometimes Pavel Pavlovitch: to Velchaninov's surprise he read aloud excellently. Meanwhile, Natalya Vassilyevna did sewing as she listened, always calmly and serenely. They read a novel of Dickens, something from a Russian magazine, sometimes even something "serious." Natalya Vassilyevna highly appreciated Velchaninov's culture, but appreciated it in silence, as something final and established, of which there was no need to talk. Altogether, her attitude to everything intellectual and literary was rather one of indifference, as to something irrelevant though perhaps useful. Pavel Pavlovitch sometimes showed considerable warmth on the subject.

The *liaison* at T—— was broken suddenly when on Velchaninov's side it had reached its zenith—that is, almost the point of madness. In reality he was abruptly dismissed, though it was all so arranged that he went away without grasping that he had been cast off "like a worthless old shoe."

Six weeks before his departure, a young artillery officer who had just finished at the training college arrived in T—— and took to visiting the Trusotskys. Instead of three, they were now a party of four. Natalya Vassilyevna welcomed the boy graciously but treated him as a boy. No suspicion crossed Velchaninov's mind and indeed he had no thought to spare for it, for he had just been told that separation was inevitable. One of the hundreds of reasons urged by Natalya Vassilyevna for his leaving her as soon as possible was that she believed herself to be with child: and therefore, naturally, he must disappear at once for three or four months at least, so that it would not be so easy for her husband to feel any doubt if there were any kind of gossip afterwards. It was rather a far-fetched argument. After a stormy proposition on the part of Velchaninov that she should fly with him to Paris or America, he departed alone to Petersburg, "only for a brief moment, of course," that is, for no more than three months, or nothing would have induced him to go, in spite of any reason or argument. Exactly two months later he received in Petersburg a letter from Natalya Vassilyevna asking him never to return, as she already loved another; she informed him that she had been mistaken about her condition. This information was superfluous. It was all clear to him now: he remembered the young officer. With that it was all over for good. He chanced to hear afterwards, some years later, that Bagautov had appeared on the scene and spent five whole years there. He explained the disproportionate duration of that affair partly by the fact that Natalya Vassilyevna, by now, was a good deal older, and so more constant in her attachments.

He remained sitting on his bed for nearly an hour; at last he roused himself, rang for Mavra to bring his coffee, drank it hastily, and at eleven o'clock set out to look for the Pokrovsky Hotel. In going there he had a special idea which had only come to him in the morning. He felt somewhat ashamed of his behavior to Pavel Pavlovitch the night before and now he wanted to efface the impression.

The whole fantastic business with the door handle, the night before, he now put down to chance, to the tipsy condition of Pavel Pavlovitch and perhaps to something else, but he did not really know, exactly, why he was going now to form new relations with the former husband, when everything had so naturally and of its own accord ended between them. Something attracted him. He had received a peculiar impression and he was attracted in consequence of it.

5 LIZA

PAVEL PAVLOVITCH had no idea of "giving him the slip," and goodness knows why Velchaninov had asked him the question the night before; he was, indeed, at a loss to explain it himself. At his first inquiry at a little shop near the Pokrovsky Church, he was directed to the hotel in the side street a couple of paces away. At the hotel, it was explained that M. Trusotsky was staying in the lodge close by in the courtyard, in furnished rooms at Marya Sysoevna's. Going up the narrow, wet and very dirty stone stairs to the second story, where these rooms were, he suddenly heard the sound of crying. It seemed like the crying of a child of seven or eight; the sound was distressing; he heard smothered sobs which would break out and with them the stamping of feet and shouts of fury, which were smothered, too, in a hoarse falsetto voice, evidently that of a grown-up man. This man seemed to be trying to suppress the child and to be very anxious that her crying should not be heard, but was making more noise than she was. The shouts sounded pitiless, and the child seemed to be begging forgiveness. In a small passage at the top, with doors on both sides of it, Velchaninov met a tall, stout, slovenly-looking peasant woman of forty and asked for Pavel Pavlovitch. She pointed towards the door from which the sounds were coming. There was a look of some indignation on the fat, purple face of this woman.

"You see how he amuses himself!" she said gruffly and went downstairs.

Velchaninov was just about to knock at the door, but on second thoughts he walked straight in. In a small room, roughly though amply furnished with common painted furniture, stood Pavel Pavlovitch without his coat and waistcoat. With a flushed and exasperated face he was trying, by means of shouts, gesticulations and even (Velchaninov fancied) kicks, to silence a little girl of eight, shabbily dressed in a short, black, woollen frock. She seemed to be actually in hysterics, she gasped hysterically and held out her hands to Pavel Pavlovitch as though she wanted to clutch at him, to hug him, to beseech and implore him about something. In one instant the whole scene was transformed: seeing the visitor, the child cried out and dashed away into a tiny room adjoining, and Pavel Pavlovitch, for a moment disconcerted, instantly melted into smiles, exactly as he had done the night before when Velchaninov flung open the door upon him on the stairs.

"Alexey Ivanovitch!" he cried, in genuine surprise. "I could never have expected . . . but come in, come in! Here, on the sofa, or here in the arm-chair, while I . . ."

And he rushed to put on his coat, forgetting to put on his waistcoat.

"Stay as you are, don't stand on ceremony."

Velchaninov sat down in the chair.

"No, allow me to stand on ceremony; here, now I am more respectable. But why are you sitting in the corner? Sit here in the arm-chair, by the table. . . . Well, I didn't expect you, I didn't expect you!"

He, too, sat down on the edge of a rush-bottomed chair, not beside his "unexpected" visitor, but setting his chair at an angle so as to sit more nearly facing him.

"Why didn't you expect me? Why, I told you last night that I would come at this time."

"I thought you wouldn't come; and when I reflected on all that happened yesterday, on waking this morning, I despaired of ever seeing you again."

Meanwhile Velchaninov was looking about him. The room was in disorder, the bed was not made, clothes were lying about, on the table were glasses with dregs of coffee in them, crumbs and a bottle of champagne, half full, with the cork out and a glass beside it. He stole a glance towards the next room, but there all was quiet; the child was in hiding and perfectly still.

"Surely you are not drinking that now?" said Velchaninov, indicating the champagne.

"The remains . . ." said Pavel Pavlovitch in confusion.

"Well, you have changed!"

"It's a bad habit, come upon me all at once; yes, really, since that date. I'm not lying! I can't restrain myself. Don't be uneasy, Alexey Ivanovitch. I'm not drunk now, and I'm not going to play the fool now as I did at your flat yesterday; but I'm telling the truth, it's all since then. And if any one had told me six months ago that I should break down like this, if I'd been shown myself in the looking-glass—I shouldn't have believed it."

"You were drunk last night, then?"

"I was," Pavel Pavlovitch admitted in a low voice, looking down in embarrassment. "And you see I wasn't exactly drunk then, but I had been a little before. I want to explain, because I'm always worse a little while after. If I get ever so little tipsy, it is followed by a sort of violence and foolishness, and I feel my grief more intensely too. It's because of my grief, perhaps, I drink. Then I'm capable of playing all sorts of pranks and I push myself forward quite stupidly and insult people for nothing. I must have presented myself very strangely to you yesterday?"

"Do you mean to say you don't remember?"

"Not remember! I remember it all. . . ."

"You see, Pavel Pavlovitch, that's just what I thought," Velchaninov said in a conciliatory voice. "What's more, I was myself rather irritable with you last night and . . . too impatient, I readily admit it. I don't feel quite well at times, and then your unexpected arrival last night . . ."

"Yes, at night, at night!" Pavel Pavlovitch shook his head, as though surprised and disapproving. "And what possessed me! Nothing would have induced me to come in to you if you had not opened the door yourself; I should have gone away from the door. I came to you a week ago, Alexey Ivanovitch, and you were not at home, but perhaps I should never have come again. I have some pride, too, Alexey Ivanovitch, although I do recognize the position I am in. We met in the street, too, and I kept thinking: 'Why, he must recognize me and yet he turns away; nine years are no joke,' and I couldn't make up my mind to come. And last night I had wandered from the Petersburg Side and I forgot the time. It all came from that" (he pointed to the bottle), "and from my feelings. It was stupid! Very! And if it had been any one but you—for you've come to see me even after what happened yesterday, for the sake of old times—I should have given up all hope of renewing our acquaintance!"

Velchaninov listened attentively. The man seemed to him to be speaking sincerely and even with a certain dignity; and yet he did not believe one word he had heard since he came into the room.

"Tell me, Pavel Pavlovitch, you are not alone here, then? Whose little girl is that I found with you just now?"

Pavel Pavlovitch was positively amazed and raised his eyebrows, but he looked frankly and pleasantly at Velchaninov.

"Whose little girl? Why, it's Liza!" he said, with an affable smile.

"What Liza?" muttered Velchaninov, with a sort of inward tremor. The shock was too sudden. When he came in and saw Liza, just before, he was surprised, but had absolutely no presentiment of the truth, and thought nothing particular about her.

"Yes, our Liza, our daughter Liza!" Pavel Pavlovitch smiled.

"Your daughter? Do you mean that you and Natalya . . . Natalya Vassilyevna had children?" Velchaninov asked timidly and mistrustfully, in a very low voice.

"Why, of course! But there, upon my word, how should you have heard of it? What am I thinking about! It was after you went away, God blessed us with her!"

Pavel Pavlovitch positively jumped up from his chair in some agitation, though it seemed agreeable too.

"I heard nothing about it," said Velchaninov, and he turned pale.

"To be sure, to be sure; from whom could you have heard it?" said Pavel Pavlovitch, in a voice weak with emotion. "My poor wife and I had lost all hope, as no doubt you remember, and suddenly God sent us this blessing, and what it meant to me—He only knows! Just a year after you went away, I believe. No, not a year, not nearly a year. Wait a bit; why, you left us, if my memory does not deceive me, in October or November, I believe."

"I left T—— at the beginning of September, the twelfth of September; I remember it very well."

"In September, was it? H'm! . . . what was I thinking about?" cried Pavel Pavlovitch, much surprised. "Well, if that's so, let me see: you went away on the twelfth of September, and Liza was born on the eighth of May, so—September—October—November—December—January—February—March—April—a little over eight months! And if you only knew how my poor wife . . ."

"Show me . . . call her . . ." Velchaninov faltered in a breaking voice.

"Certainly!" said Pavel Pavlovitch fussily, at once breaking off what he was saying, as though it were of no consequence. "Directly, directly, I'll introduce her!"

And he went hurriedly into the other room to Liza.

Fully three or perhaps four minutes passed; there was a hurried, rapid whispering in the room, and he just caught the sound of Liza's voice. "She's begging not to be brought in," thought Velchaninov. At last they came out.

"You see, she's all confusion," said Pavel Pavlovitch; "she's so shy, and so proud . . . the image of my poor wife!"

Liza came in, looking down and no longer tearful; her father was holding her hand. She was a tall, slim, very pretty little girl. She raised her big blue eyes to glance with curiosity at the visitor, looked at him sullenly, and dropped them again at once. Her eyes were full of that gravity one sees in children when they are left alone with a stranger and, retreating into a corner, look out solemnly and mistrustfully at the unfamiliar visitor; but she had, perhaps, some other thought, by no means childish, in her mind —so Velchaninov fancied.

Her father led her straight up to him.

"This is an uncle Mother used to know long ago; he was our friend. Don't be shy, hold out your hand."

The child bent forward a little, and timidly held out her hand.

"Natalya Vassilyevna would not have her trained to curtsey, but taught her to make a little bow, and hold out her hand in the English fashion," he added by way of explanation to Velchaninov, watching him intently.

Velchaninov knew that he was being watched, but had quite ceased to trouble himself to conceal his emotion; he sat perfectly still in his chair, held Liza's hand in his and gazed at the child. But Liza was in great anxiety about something, and, forgetting her hand in the visitor's hand, she kept her eyes fixed on her father. She listened apprehensively to all that he said. Velchaninov recognized those big blue eyes at once, but what struck him most of all was the wonderful soft whiteness of her face and the color of her hair; these characteristics were so marked and so significant. Her features and the lines of the lips reminded him vividly of Natalya Vassilyevna. Meanwhile, Pavel Pavlovitch had for some time been telling him something, speaking, it seemed, with very great warmth and feeling, but Velchaninov did not hear him. He only caught the last sentence—

". . . so that you can't imagine our joy at this gift from the Lord, Alexey Ivanovitch! She became everything to me as soon as she came to us, so that I used to think that even if my tranquil happiness should, by God's will, be at an end, Liza would always be left me; that I reckoned upon for certain!"

"And Natalya Vassilyevna?" Velchaninov queried.

"Natalya Vassilyevna?" said Pavel Pavlovitch affectedly. "You know her way, you remember that she never cared to say a great deal, but the way she said good-bye to her on her death-bed . . . everything came out then! I said just now 'on her death-bed,' but yet only a day before her death she was upset and angry, said that they were trying to cure her with drugs, that there was nothing wrong with her but an ordinary fever, and that neither of our doctors understood it, and that as soon as Koch came back (do you remember our old friend the army doctor?) she would be up again in a fortnight! But there! five hours before her decease she remembered that in three weeks' time we must visit her aunt, Liza's godmother, on her name day . . ."

Velchaninov suddenly got up from his chair, still holding the child's hand. Among other things it struck him that there was something reproachful in the intense look the child kept fixed upon her father.

"She's not ill?" he asked hurriedly and somewhat strangely.

"I don't think so, but . . . our circumstances are here so . . ." said Pavel Pavlovitch, with mournful solicitude. "She's a strange child and nervous at all times; after her mother's death she was ill for a fortnight, hysterical. Why, what a weeping and wailing we had just before you came in . . . do you hear, Liza, do you

hear? And what was it all about? All because I go out and leave
her; she says it shows I don't love her any more as I used to when
mother was alive—that's her complaint against me. And a child
like that who ought to be playing with her toys, instead of fretting
over a fantastic notion like that. Though here she has no one to
play with."

"Why, how . . . you're surely not alone here?"

"Quite alone; the servant only comes in once a day."

"And you go out and leave her like this alone?"

"What else could I do? And when I went out yesterday I locked
her in, into that little room there, that's what the tears have been
about to-day. But what else could I do? Judge for yourself: the
day before yesterday she went down when I was out, and a boy
threw a stone at her in the yard and hit her on the head. Or else
she begins crying and runs round to all the lodgers in the yard,
asking where I've gone. And that's not nice, you know. And I'm
a nice one, too; I go out for an hour and come back next morning;
that's what happened yesterday. It was a nice thing, too, that
while I was away the landlady let her out, sent for a locksmith
to break the lock—such a disgrace—I literally feel myself a
monster. All mental aberration, all mental aberration. . . ."

"Father!" the child said timidly and uneasily.

"There you are, at it again! You're at the same thing again.
What did I tell you just now?"

"I won't, I won't!" Liza repeated in terror, hurriedly clasping
her hands before him.

"You can't go on like this in these surroundings," Velchaninov
said impatiently, in a voice of authority. "Why, you . . . why,
you're a man of property; how is it you're living like this—in this
lodge and in such surroundings?"

"In the lodge? But, you see, we may be going away in a week's
time, and we've wasted a great deal of money already, even though
I have property. . . ."

"Come, that's enough, that's enough." Velchaninov cut him
short with increasing impatience, as it were expressing plainly:

"There's no need to talk. I know all that you have to say, and I know with what feelings you are speaking."

"Listen, I'll make a suggestion. You said just now that you'll be staying a week, maybe possibly even a fortnight. I know a household here, that is, a family where I'm quite at home—have known them twenty years. The father, Alexander Pavlovitch Pogoryeltsev, is a Privy Councillor; he might be of use to you in your business. They are at their summer villa now. They've got a splendid villa. Klavdia Petrovna is like a sister to me or a mother. They have eight children. Let me take Liza to them at once . . . that we may lose no time. They will be delighted to take her in for the whole time you are here, and will treat her like their own child, their own child!"

He was terribly impatient and did not disguise it.

"That's scarcely possible," said Pavel Pavlovitch, with a grimace, looking, so Velchaninov fancied, slily in his face.

"Why, why impossible?"

"Why, how can I let the child go so suddenly—with such a real friend as you, of course—I don't mean, but into a house of strangers, and of such high rank, where I don't know how she'd be received either?"

"But I've told you that I'm like one of the family!" cried Velchaninov, almost wrathfully. "Klavdia Petrovna will be delighted to take her at a word from me—as though it were my child. Damn it all! Why, you know yourself that you only say all this for the sake of saying something . . . there's nothing to discuss!"

He positively stamped his foot.

"I only mean, won't it seem strange? I should have to go and see her once or twice anyway, or she would be left without a father! He—he! . . . and in such a grand household."

"But it's the simplest household, not 'grand' at all!" shouted Velchaninov. "I tell you there are a lot of children. She'll revive there, that's the whole object. . . . And I'll introduce you myself to-morrow, if you like. And of course you would have to go to thank them; we'll drive over every day, if you like."

"It's all so . . ."

"Nonsense! And, what's more, you know that yourself! Listen. Come to me this evening, and stay the night, perhaps, and we'll set off early in the morning so as to get there at twelve."

"My benefactor! And even to stay the night with you . . ." Pavel Pavlovitch agreed suddenly in a tone of fervent feeling. "You are doing me a charity literally. . . . Where is their villa?"

"Their villa is in Lyesnoe."

"Only, I say, what about her dress? For, you know, in such a distinguished household and in their summer villa, too, you know yourself . . . a father's heart . . ."

"What about her dress? She's in mourning. She couldn't be dressed differently, could she? It's the most suitable one could possibly imagine! The only thing is she ought to have clean linen . . . a clean tucker . . ."

Her tucker and what showed of her underlinen were, in fact, very dirty.

"She must change her things at once," said Pavel Pavlovitch fussily, "and we'll get together the rest of what she needs in the way of underclothes; Marya Sysoevna has got them in the wash."

"Then you should tell them to fetch a carriage," Velchaninov interposed; "and make haste if you can."

But a difficulty presented itself: Liza resolutely opposed it; she had been listening all the time in terror, and, if Velchaninov had had time to look at her attentively while he was persuading Pavel Pavlovitch, he would have seen a look of utter despair upon her little face.

"I am not going," she said firmly, in a low voice.

"There, there! You see, she's her mother over again."

"I'm not my mother over again, I'm not my mother over again!" cried Liza in despair, wringing her little hands, and as it were trying to defend herself before her father from the awful reproach of being like her mother. "Father, Father, if you leave me . . ."

She suddenly turned on Velchaninov, who was in dismay.

"If you take me I'll . . ."

But before she had time to say more, Pavel Pavlovitch clutched her by the arm and with undisguised exasperation dragged her almost by the collar into the little room. Whispering followed for some minutes; there was the sound of suppressed crying. Velchaninov was on the point of going in himself, but Pavel Pavlovitch came out and with a wry smile announced that she was coming directly. Velchaninov tried not to look at him and kept his eyes turned away.

Marya Sysoevna appeared. She was the same peasant woman that he had met just before in the passage; she began packing the linen she had brought with her in a pretty little bag belonging to Liza.

"Are you taking the little girl away then, sir?" she asked, addressing Velchaninov. "Have you a family, then? It's a good deed, sir: she's a quiet child; you are taking her from a perfect Bedlam."

"Come, come, Marya Sysoevna!" muttered Pavel Pavlovitch.

"Marya Sysoevna, indeed! That's my name, right enough. It is a Bedlam here, isn't it? Is it the proper thing for a child that can understand to see such disgraceful goings-on? They've fetched you a carriage, sir—to Lyesnoe, is it?"

"Yes, yes."

"Well, it's a blessing you came!"

Liza came out pale and, looking down, took her bag. Not one glance in Velchaninov's direction; she restrained herself and did not, as before, rush to embrace her father, even at parting; evidently she was unwilling to look at him either. Her father kissed her decorously on the head and patted it; her lips twitched as he did so and her little chin quivered, but still she did not raise her eyes to her father. Pavel Pavlovitch looked pale, and his hands were trembling—Velchaninov noticed that distinctly, though he was doing his utmost not to look at him. The one thing he longed for was to get away as quickly as possible.

"After all, it's not my fault," he thought. "It was bound to be so."

They went downstairs; there Marya Sysoevna kissed Liza good-bye, and only when she was sitting in the carriage Liza lifted her eyes to her father, flung up her hands and screamed; another minute and she would have flung herself out of the carriage to him, but the horses had started.

6 A NEW FANCY OF AN IDLE MAN

ARE you feeling ill?" asked Velchaninov in alarm. "I will tell them to stop, I'll tell them to bring water. . . ."

She turned her eyes upon him and looked at him passionately, reproachfully.

"Where are you taking me?" she asked sharply and abruptly.

"It's a very nice family, Liza. They're in a delightful summer villa now; there are a lot of children; they'll love you; they are kind. Don't be angry with me, Liza; I only wish for your good."

How strange it would have seemed to all who knew him if anyone could have seen him at that moment.

"How . . . how . . . how . . . how horrid you are!" said Liza, choking with stifled tears, glaring at him with her beautiful eyes full of anger.

"Liza, I . . ."

"You are wicked, wicked, wicked, wicked!"

She wrung her hands. Velchaninov was completely at a loss.

"Liza, darling, if you knew how despairing you make me!"

"Is it true that he will come to-morrow? Is it true?" she asked peremptorily.

"Yes, yes, I'll bring him myself; I'll take him with me and bring him."

"He'll deceive me," she whispered, looking down.

"Doesn't he love you, Liza?"

"He doesn't love me."

"Does he ill-treat you? Does he?"

Liza looked at him gloomily and was mute. She turned away from him again and sat with her eyes obstinately cast down. He began trying to coax her; he talked to her warmly, he was in a perfect fever. Liza listened with mistrust and hostility, but she did listen. Her attention delighted him extremely; he even began explaining to her what was meant by a man's drinking. He told her that he loved her himself and would look after her father. Liza lifted her eyes at last and looked at him intently. He began telling her how he used to know her mother and he saw that what he told her interested her. Little by little she began answering his questions, though cautiously and in monosyllables. She still stubbornly refused to answer his leading questions; she remained obstinately silent about everything to do with her relations with her father in the past. As he talked to her, Velchaninov took her hand in his as before and held it; she did not pull it away. The child was not silent all the time, however; she let out in her confused answers that she loved her father more than her mother, because he had always been fonder of her, and her mother had not cared so much for her, but that when her mother was dying she had kissed her and cried a great deal when everyone had gone out of the room and they were left alone . . . and that now she loved her more than anyone, more than anyone, more than anyone in the world, and every night she loved her more than anyone. But the child was certainly proud. Realizing that she had spoken too freely, she suddenly shrank into herself again and glanced with positive hatred at Velchaninov, who had led her into saying so much. Towards the end of the journey her hysterical agitation almost passed off, but she sank into brooding and had the look of a wild creature, sullen and gloomily, resolutely stubborn. The fact that she was being taken to a strange family, in which she had never been before, seemed for the time being not to trouble her much. What tormented her was something else.

Velchaninov saw that; he guessed that she was ashamed before *him*, that she was ashamed of her father's having so easily let her go with him, of his having, as it were, flung her into his keeping.

"She is ill," he thought, "perhaps very ill; she's been worried to death. . . . Oh, the drunken, abject beast! I understand him now!"

He urged on the driver; he rested his hopes on the country, the fresh air, the garden, the children, and the new, unfamiliar life, and then, later on . . . But of what would come afterwards he had no doubts at all; of the future he had the fullest, brightest hopes. One thing only he knew for certain: that he had never before felt what he was experiencing now and that it would never leave him all his life.

"Here was an object, here was life!" he thought triumphantly.

A great many thoughts flashed upon his mind, but he did not dwell upon them and obstinately put away details; so long as he avoided details it all seemed clear and unassailable. His plan of action was self-evident.

"It will be possible to work upon that wretch," he mused, "by our united forces, and he will leave Liza in Petersburg at the Pogoryeltsevs', though at first only temporarily, for a certain time, and will go away alone, and Liza will be left to me; that's the whole thing. What more do I want? And . . . of course, he wants that himself; or else why does he torment her?"

At last they arrived. The Pogoryeltsevs' country home really was a charming place; they were met first of all by a noisy crowd of children, flocking out into the porch. Velchaninov had not been there for a long time, and the children were in a frenzy of delight; they were fond of him. The elder ones shouted to him at once, before he got out of the carriage—

"And how about the case, how is your case getting on?"

The cry was caught up even by the smallest, and they shrieked it mirthfully in imitation of their elders. They used to tease him about the lawsuit. But, seeing Liza, they surrounded her at once and began scrutinizing her with intent, dumb, childish curiosity. Klavdia Petrovna came out, followed by her husband. She and her husband, too, began with a laughing question about the lawsuit.

Klavdia Petrovna was a lady about thirty-seven, a plump and still good-looking brunette, with a fresh, rosy face. Her husband was fifty-five, a shrewd and clever man, but above everything good-natured. Their house was in the fullest sense of the word "a home" to Velchaninov, as he had said himself. But underlying this was the special circumstance that, twenty years before, Klavdia

Petrovna had been on the point of marrying Velchaninov, then a
student, hardly more than a boy. It was a case of first love, ardent,
ridiculous and splendid. It had ended, however, in her marrying
Pogoryeltsev. Five years later they had met again, and it had all
ended in a quiet, serene friendship. A certain warmth, a peculiar
glow suffusing their relations, had remained for ever. All was pure
and irreproachable in Velchaninov's memories of this friendship,
and it was the dearer to him for being perhaps the solitary case
in which this was so. Here in this family he was simple, unaffected
and kind; he used to fondle the children, he admitted all his failings, confessed his shortcomings, and never gave himself airs. He
swore more than once to the Pogoryeltsevs that he should before
long give up the world, come and live with them and never leave
them again. In his heart he thought of this project seriously.

He told them all that was necessary about Liza in some detail;
but a mere request from him was enough, without any special explanations. Klavdia Petrovna kissed the "orphan" and promised for
her part to do everything. The children took possession of Liza
and carried her off to play in the garden.

After half an hour of lively conversation Velchaninov got up
and began saying good-bye. He was so impatient that everyone
noticed it. They were all astonished; he had not been to see them
for three weeks and now he was going in half an hour. He laughed
and pledged himself to come next day. They remarked that he
seemed to be in a state of great excitement; he suddenly took
Klavdia Petrovna's hand and, on the pretext of having forgotten
to tell her something important, drew her aside into another room.

"Do you remember what I told you—you alone—what even
your husband does not know—of my year at T——?"

"I remember perfectly; you often talked of it."

"It was not talking, it was a confession, to you alone, to you
alone! I never told you the surname of that woman; she was the
wife of this man Trusotsky. She is dead, and Liza is her daughter—
my daughter!"

"Is it certain? You are not mistaken?" Klavdia Petrovna asked
with some excitement.

"It's perfectly certain, perfectly certain; I am not mistaken!" Velchaninov pronounced ecstatically.

And as briefly as he could, in haste and great excitement, he told her everything. Klavdia Petrovna already knew the whole story, but not the lady's name.

Velchaninov had always been so alarmed at the very idea that any one who knew him might ever meet Madame Trusotsky and think that *he* could *so* have loved that woman, that he had not till that day dared to reveal "that woman's" name even to Klavdia Petrovna, his one friend.

"And the father knows nothing?" asked Klavdia Petrovna, when she had heard his story.

"Y-yes, he does know. . . . It worries me that I've not got to the bottom of it yet!" Velchaninov went on eagerly. "He knows, he knows; I noticed it to-day and yesterday. But I must know how much he knows. That's why I'm in a hurry now. He is coming to me this evening. I can't imagine, though, how he can have found out—found out *everything*, I mean. He knows about Bagautov, there's no doubt of that. But about me? You know how clever women are in reassuring their husbands in such cases! If an angel came down from heaven—the husband would not believe him, but he would believe his wife! Don't shake your head and don't blame me; I blame myself and have blamed myself, for the whole affair, long ago, long ago! . . . You see, I was so certain he knew when I was there this morning that I compromised myself before him. Would you believe it, I felt so wretched and ashamed at having met him so rudely yesterday (I will tell you all about it fully afterwards). He came to me yesterday from an irresistible, malicious desire to let me know that he knew of the wrong done him, and knew who had done it; that was the whole reason of his stupid visit when he was drunk. But that was so natural on his part! He simply came to work off his resentment! I was altogether too hasty with him this morning and yesterday! Careless—stupid! I betrayed myself to him. Why did he turn up at a moment when I was upset? I tell you he's even been tormenting Liza, tormenting the child, and probably that, too, was to work off his resentment—

to vent his malice if only on the child! Yes, he is spiteful—insignificant as he is, yet he is spiteful; very much so, indeed. In himself he is no more than a buffoon, though, God knows, in old days he seemed to be a very decent fellow within his limits—it's so natural that he should be going to the dogs! One must look at it from a Christian point of view! And you know, my dear, my best of friends, I want to be utterly different to him; I want to be kind to him. That would be really a 'good deed' on my part. For, you know, after all, I have wronged him! Listen, you know there's something else I must tell you. On one occasion in T—— I was in want of four thousand roubles, and he lent me the money on the spot, with no security, and showed genuine pleasure at being of use to me; and, do you know, I took it then, I took it from his hands. I borrowed money from him, do you understand, as a friend!"

"Only be more careful," Klavdia Petrovna anxiously observed, in response to all this. "And what a state of ecstasy you're in; I feel uneasy about you! Of course, Liza will be like a child of my own now. But there's so much, so much still to be settled! The great thing is that you must be more circumspect; you absolutely must be more circumspect when you are happy or so ecstatic; you're too generous when you are happy," she added, with a smile.

They all came out to see Velchaninov off. The children, who had been playing with Liza in the garden, brought her with them. They seemed to look at her with more amazement now than at first. Liza was overcome with shyness when, at parting, Velchaninov kissed her before them all, and warmly repeated his promise to come next day with her father. To the last minute she was silent and did not look at him, but then suddenly she clutched at his arm and drew him aside, fixing an imploring look on him; she wanted to tell him something. He promptly took her away into another room.

"What is it, Liza?" he asked her tenderly and reassuringly; but she, still looking about her apprehensively, drew him into the furthest corner; she wanted to be hidden from them all.

"What is it, Liza? What's the matter?"

She was dumb, she could not bring herself to speak; she gazed fixedly with her blue eyes into his face, and every feature of her little face expressed nothing but frantic terror.

"He'll . . . hang himself!" she whispered, as though in delirium.

"Who will hang himself?" asked Velchaninov in dismay.

"He, he! He tried to hang himself with a cord in the night!" the child said breathlessly. "I saw him! He tried to hang himself with a cord, he told me so, he told me so! He meant to before, he always meant to . . . I saw him in the night. . . ."

"Impossible," whispered Velchaninov in amazement.

She suddenly fell to kissing his hands; she cried, almost choking with sobs, begged and besought him, but he could make nothing of her hysterical whisperings. And the tortured face of that terror-stricken child who looked to him as her last hope remained printed on his memory for ever, haunting him awake and visiting his dreams.

"And can she, can she really love him so much?" he thought, jealously and enviously, as with feverish impatience he returned to town. "She had told me herself that morning that she loved her mother more . . . perhaps she hated him and did not love him at all! . . . And what did that mean: he will hang himself? What did she mean by that? Would the fool hang himself?" . . . He must find out, he must certainly find out! He must get to the bottom of it as soon as possible—once and for all.

7 THE HUSBAND AND THE LOVER
KISS EACH OTHER

HE WAS in terrible haste "to find out."

"This morning I was so overwhelmed. This morning I hadn't the time to realize the position," he thought, recalling his first sight of Liza, "but now I must find out." To find out more quickly he was on the point of telling the driver to take him to Trusotsky's lodging, but on second thoughts decided: "No, better let him come to me, and meanwhile I'll make haste and get this accursed legal business off my hands."

He set to work feverishly; but this time he was conscious himself that he was very absent-minded and that he was hardly capable that day of attending to business. At five o'clock, when he went out to dinner, he was struck for the first time by an absurd idea: that perhaps he really was only hindering the progress of his case, by meddling in the lawsuit himself, fussing about in the law-courts and hunting up his lawyer, who was already beginning to hide from him. He laughed gaily at his supposition. "If this idea had occurred to me yesterday, I should have been dreadfully distressed," he added, even more gaily. In spite of his gaiety, he grew more and more preoccupied and more and more impatient. He fell to musing at last; and though his restless thought clutched at one thing after another, he could arrive at nothing that would satisfy him.

"I must have that man!" he decided finally. "I must solve the riddle of that man, and then make up my mind. It's—a duel!"

Returning home at seven o'clock, he did not find Pavel Pavlovitch and was extremely surprised, then extremely wrathful, and later still extremely depressed; finally he began to be actually frightened.

"God knows, God knows how it will end!" he repeated, as he walked about the room or stretched himself on the sofa, continually looking at his watch. At last, about nine o'clock, Pavel Pavlovitch appeared. "If the fellow were trying to dupe me, he couldn't have caught me at a more favorable time—I feel so unhinged at this moment," he thought, his confidence completely restored and his spirits rising again.

To his brisk and cheerful inquiry why he was so late coming, Pavel Pavlovitch gave a wry smile, seated himself with a free and easy air, very different from his manner the night before, and carelessly threw his hat with the crape on it on another chair close by. Velchaninov at once noticed this free and easy manner and made a note of it.

Calmly, without wasting words, with none of the excitement he had shown in the morning, he told him, as though giving a report, how he had taken Liza, how kindly she had been received, how good it would be for her, and little by little, as though forgetting Liza, he imperceptibly turned the conversation entirely on the Pogoryeltsevs—what charming people they were, how long he had known them, what a splendid and influential man Pogoryeltsev was, and so on. Pavel Pavlovitch listened inattentively and from time to time glanced up from under his brows at the speaker with an ill-humored and crafty sneer.

"You're an impulsive person," he muttered, with a particularly disagreeable smile.

"You're rather ill-humored to-day, though," Velchaninov observed with vexation.

"And why shouldn't I be ill-humored, like everyone else!" Pavel Pavlovitch cried out suddenly, just as though he had only been waiting for that to bounce out.

"You're at liberty to please yourself," laughed Velchaninov. "I wondered if anything had happened to you."

"So it has!" the other exclaimed, as though boasting that something had happened.

"What is it?"

Pavel Pavlovitch delayed answering for a little.

"Why, our Stepan Mihalovitch has played me a trick . . . Bagautov, that elegant young Petersburg gentleman of the best society."

"Was he not at home again?"

"No, this time he was at home. For the first time I was admitted, and I gazed upon his face . . . only he was dead!"

"Wha-at! Bagautov is dead?" Velchaninov was awfully surprised, though there was no apparent reason for his being so surprised.

"Yes. For six years our true and constant friend! Only yesterday, almost at midday, he died, and I knew nothing of it! I was going maybe that very minute to inquire after his health. To-morrow there will be the service and the funeral, he's already in his coffin. The coffin is lined with crimson-colored velvet trimmed with gold . . . he died of brain fever. I was admitted—I was admitted to gaze upon his face! I told them at the door that I was an intimate friend, that was why I was admitted. What's one to think of the way he's treated me now, my true and constant friend for six long years—I ask you that? Perhaps it was only on his account I came to Petersburg!"

"But what are you angry with him for?" laughed Velchaninov. "Why, he did not die on purpose!"

"But I speak with my heart full of regret; he was a precious friend; this was what he meant to me."

And all at once, quite unexpectedly, Pavel Pavlovitch put up his two fingers like two horns on his bald forehead and went off into a low, prolonged chuckle. He sat like that, chuckling, for a full half-minute, staring into Velchaninov's face in a frenzy of malignant insolence. The latter was petrified as though at the sight of some ghost. But his stupefaction lasted but one brief instant; a sarcastic and insolently composed smile came slowly upon his lips.

"What's the meaning of that?" he asked, carelessly drawling the words.

"The meaning of it is—horns!" Pavel Pavlovitch rapped out, taking away his fingers from his forehead at last.

"That is . . . your horns?"

"My own, generously bestowed!" Pavel Pavlovitch said with a very nasty grimace. Both were silent.

"You're a plucky fellow, I must say!" Velchaninov pronounced.

"Because I showed you my decorations? Do you know, Alexey Ivanovitch, you'd better offer me something! You know I entertained you every blessed day for a whole year at T——. Send for just one bottle, my throat is dry."

"With pleasure; you should have said so before. What will you have?"

"Why *you*? Say *we*; we'll drink together, won't we?" said Pavel Pavlovitch, gazing into his face with a challenging but at the same time strangely uneasy look.

"Champagne?"

"What else? It's not the time for vodka yet. . . ."

Velchaninov got up deliberately, rang for Mavra and gave instructions.

"To the joy of our delightful meeting after nine years' absence," said Pavel Pavlovitch, with a quite superfluous and inappropriate snigger. "Now you, and you only, are the one friend left me! Stepan Mihalovitch Bagautov is no more! As the poet says—

> " 'Great Patrocus is no more,
> Vile Thersites still lives on!' "

And at the word "Thersites" he poked himself in the chest.

"You'd better hurry up and speak out, you swine; I don't like hints," Velchaninov thought to himself. His anger was rising and for a long time he had hardly been able to restrain himself.

"Tell me," he said in a tone of vexation, "since you accuse Stepan Mihalovitch," (he could not call him simply Bagautov now) "I should have thought you would have been glad that the man who has wronged you is dead; why are you angry about it?"

"Glad? Why glad?"

"I imagine those must be your feelings."

"He—he! You are quite mistaken about my feelings on that subject; as some wise man has said, 'A dead enemy is good, but a living one is better,' he—he!"

"But you saw him living every day for five years, I believe; you had time to get tired of the sight of him," Velchaninov observed, with spiteful impertinence.

"But you don't suppose I knew then . . . you don't suppose I knew?" Pavel Pavlovitch blurted out suddenly, just as though he had bounced out from behind a corner again, and as though he were delighted to be asked a question he had long been waiting for.

"What do you take me for, then, Alexey Ivanovitch?"

And there was a gleam in his face of something quite new and unexpected, which seemed to transform his countenance, till then full of spite and abjectly grimacing.

"Is it possible you didn't know, then?" said Velchaninov, disconcerted and completely taken by surprise.

"Is it possible I knew? Is it possible I knew? Oh, you race of Jupiters! For you a man's no more than a dog, and you judge all according to your own petty nature. I tell you that! You can swallow that!" And he banged frantically on the table with his fist, but was at once dismayed at the bang and began to look apprehensive.

Velchaninov assumed an air of dignity.

"Listen, Pavel Pavlovitch. It's absolutely nothing to me, as you can see for yourself, whether you knew, or whether you didn't. If you didn't know, it's to your credit in any case, though . . . I can't understand, however, why you've chosen to make this confidence to me?" . . .

"I didn't mean you . . . don't be angry. I didn't mean you . . ." muttered Pavel Pavlovitch, looking down.

Mavra came in with the champagne.

"Here it is!" cried Pavel Pavlovitch, evidently relieved at her entrance. "Glasses, my good girl, glasses; splendid! We ask for nothing more, my dear. And uncorked already! Honor and glory to you, charming creature! Come, you can go!"

And with renewed courage he looked impudently at Velchaninov again.

"Confess," he chuckled suddenly, "that all this is very interesting and by no means 'absolutely nothing to you,' as you were pleased to declare; so much so that you would be disappointed if I were to get up this minute and go away without explaining myself."

"I really shouldn't be disappointed."

"Oh, that's a lie!" was what Pavel Pavlovitch's smile expressed.

"Well, let's come to business!" And he filled his glass.

"Let's drink," he pronounced, taking up the glass, "to the health of our friend departed in God, Stepan Mihalovitch."

He raised his glass, and drank it.

"I'm not going to drink such a health," said Velchaninov, putting down his glass.

"Why not? It's a pleasant toast."

"I say, weren't you drunk when you came in just now?"

"I had had a little. But why?"

"Nothing particular, but I thought last night, and this morning still more, that you were genuinely grieved at the loss of Natalya Vassilyevna."

"And who told you that I'm not genuinely grieved at the loss of her now?" Pavel Pavlovitch bounced out again, exactly as though he were worked by springs.

"And I didn't mean that; but you must admit that you may be mistaken about Stepan Mihalovitch, and it is—a grave matter."

Pavel Pavlovitch smiled craftily and winked.

"And wouldn't you like to know how I found out about Stepan Mihalovitch?"

Velchaninov flushed.

"I tell you again that it's nothing to me." . . . "Hadn't I better chuck him out this minute, bottle and all?" he thought furiously, and he flushed a deeper crimson.

"That's all right!" said Pavel Pavlovitch, as though trying to encourage him, and he poured himself out another glass.

"I will explain at once how I found out all about it, and so gratify your ardent desire . . . for you are an ardent man, Alexey Ivanovitch, a terribly ardent man! He—he! Only give me a cigarette, for ever since March . . . !"

"Here's a cigarette for you."

"I have gone to the dogs since March, Alexey Ivanovitch, and I'll tell you how it's all happened—listen. Consumption, as you know yourself, my best of friends," he grew more and more familiar, "is a curious disease. Consumptives have scarcely a suspicion they may be dying tomorrow and then all in a minute they're dead. I tell you that only five hours before, Natalya Vassilyevna was planning a visit a fortnight later to her aunt, thirty miles away. You are aware, too, probably, of the practice, or rather bad habit—common in many ladies and very likely in their admirers as well—of preserving all sorts of rubbish in the way of love-letters. . . . It would be much safer to put them in the stove, wouldn't it? No, every scrap of paper is carefully stored away in a box or a *nécessaire*; even docketed in years, and in months, and in series. Whether it's a comfort to them—I don't know; but, no doubt, it's for the sake of agreeable memories. Since only five hours before her end she was arranging to go to visit her aunt, Natalya Vassilyevna naturally had no thought of death to the very last hour. She was still expecting Koch. So it happened that Natalya Vassilyevna died, and an ebony box inlaid with mother-of-pearl and silver was left standing on her bureau. And it was a charming box, with a lock and key, an heirloom that had come to her from her grandmother. In that box everything lay revealed, absolutely everything; all, without exception, with the year and the day, everything for the last twenty years. And as Stepan Mihalovitch had a distinct literary bent (he actually sent a passionate love story to a journal), his contributions ran into the hundreds—to be sure they were spread out over five years. Some specimens had been annotated in Natalya Vassilyevna's own handwriting. A pleasant surprise for a husband. What do you think of it?"

Velchaninov reflected hurriedly and felt sure that he had never sent Natalya Vassilyevna a single letter, not a note of any kind. Though he had written twice from Petersburg, his letters, in accordance with a compact between them, had been addressed to the husband as well as the wife. To Natalya Vassilyevna's last letter, in which she had decreed his banishment, he had never answered.

When he had ended his story, Pavel Pavlovitch paused for a full minute with an importunate and expectant smile.

"Why do you give me no answer to my little question?" he brought out at last, with evident anxiety.

"What little question?"

"Why, the pleasant surprise for a husband on opening that box."

"Oh! what is it to do with me!" exclaimed Velchaninov, with a gesture of disgust, and he got up and walked about the room.

"And I bet you're thinking now, you're a swine to have shown me your shame. He—he! You're a very fastidious man . . . you are."

"I think nothing about it. On the contrary, you are so much exasperated by the death of the man who wronged you and you've drunk so much wine, too. I see nothing extraordinary in all this; I quite understand why you wanted Bagautov alive, and I am ready to respect your annoyance: but . . ."

"And what did I want Bagautov for, do you suppose?"

"That's your affair."

"I bet that you were thinking of a duel!"

"Damn it all!" cried Velchaninov, growing more and more unable to control himself. "I imagine that a decent man . . . in such cases does not stoop to ridiculous babble, to stupid antics, to ludicrous complaints and disgusting insinuations, by which he only degrades himself more, but acts openly, directly, straightforwardly —like a decent man!"

"He—he! but perhaps I'm not a decent man!"

"That's your affair again . . . but in that case, what the devil did you want Bagautov alive for?"

"Why, if only to see a friend. We'd have had a bottle and drunk together."

"He wouldn't have drunk with you."

"Why not? *Noblesse oblige!* Here, you're drinking with me; in what way is he better than you?"

"I haven't drunk with you."

"Why such pride all of a sudden?"

Velchaninov suddenly broke into a nervous and irritable laugh.

"Damnation! Why, you are really a 'predatory type'! I thought you were only 'the eternal husband,' and nothing more!"

"What do you mean by 'the eternal husband,' what's that?" Pavel Pavlovitch suddenly pricked up his ears.

"Oh, it's one type of husband . . . it would be a long story. You'd better clear out, it's time you were gone; I'm sick of you."

"And predatory? You said 'predatory'!"

"I said you were a 'predatory type'; I said it ironically."

"What do you mean by a 'predatory type'? Tell me, please, Alexey Ivanovitch, for God's sake, or for Christ's sake!"

"Come, that's enough, that's enough!" cried Velchaninov, suddenly growing horribly angry. "It's time you were off. Get along."

"No, it's not enough!" Pavel Pavlovitch flared up; "even though you are sick of me it's not enough, for we must drink together and clink glasses! Let us drink together, and then I'll go, but as it is it's not enough!"

"Pavel Pavlovitch! Will you go to the devil today or will you not?"

"I can go to the devil, but first we'll drink! You said that you would not drink *with me*; but I *want* you to drink with me!"

There was no grimacing, no sniggering about him now. He seemed all at once entirely transformed, and to have become in his whole tone and appearance so completely the opposite of the Pavel Pavlovitch of the moment before that Velchaninov was quite taken aback.

"Do let us drink, Alexey Ivanovitch! Don't refuse me," Pavel Pavlovitch persisted, gripping his hand tightly and looking strangely into his eyes.

Clearly there was more at stake than merely drinking.

"Yes, if you like," muttered Velchaninov; "but how can we? . . . There's nothing left but the dregs. . . ."

"There are just two glasses left, it's thick, but we'll drink it and clink glasses! Here, take your glass."

They clinked their glasses and emptied them.

"Since that's so—since that's so . . . Ach!"

Pavel Pavlovitch clutched his forehead in his hand and remained for some moments in that position. Velchaninov had a feeling every moment that he would speak out and utter the very *final* word. But Pavel Pavlovitch uttered nothing; he simply gazed at him and smiled again the same sly, knowing smile.

"What do you want of me, you drunken fellow! You're playing the fool with me!" Velchaninov shouted furiously, stamping.

"Don't shout, don't shout; what is there to shout for?" cried Pavel Pavlovitch, gesticulating hurriedly. "I'm not playing the fool, I'm not playing the fool! Do you know what you are to me now?"

And he suddenly seized his hand and kissed it. Velchaninov was utterly taken aback.

"That's what you mean to me now! And now—and now I'll go to the devil as soon as you please!"

"Wait a minute, stay!" cried Velchaninov, recovering himself. "I forgot to tell you. . . ."

Pavel Pavlovitch turned back from the door.

"You see," muttered Velchaninov, very quickly, flushing crimson and looking away, "you must be at the Pogoryeltsevs' to-morrow . . . to make their acquaintance and thank them; you must . . ."

"Certainly, I must. I understand that, of course!" Pavel Pavlovitch acquiesced with the utmost readiness, waving his hand quickly as though to protest that there was no need to remind him.

"And besides, Liza is very anxious to see you. I promised her . . ."

"Liza!" Pavel Pavlovitch turned back. "Liza? Do you know what Liza has meant to me and means? Has meant and still means!" he cried all at once, almost frantically. "But . . . But of that later, all that can be later. . . . But now it's not enough that we've drunk together, Alexey Ivanovitch, I must have something else to be satisfied. . . ."

He laid his hat on a chair and gazed at him, gasping for breath a little as he had done just before.

"Kiss me, Alexey Ivanovitch!" he suggested suddenly.

"You're drunk!" Velchaninov declared, stepping back.

"Yes, but kiss me all the same, Alexey Ivanovitch. Oh, kiss me! Why, I kissed your hand just now."

For some minutes Velchaninov was silent, as though stunned by a blow on the head. But suddenly he bent down to Pavel Pavlovitch, whose face was on a level with his shoulder, and kissed him on the lips, which smelt very strongly of spirits. He was not, however, perfectly certain that he had kissed him.

"Well, now, now. . . ." Pavel Pavlovitch cried again in a drunken frenzy, his drunken eyes flashing; "now I'll tell you; I thought then, What if he too? What if that one, I thought, what if he too . . . whom can I trust after that!"

Pavel Pavlovitch suddenly burst into tears.

"So you understand, you're the one friend left me now!"

And he ran with his hat out of the room. Velchaninov again stood still for some minutes in the same place, just as he had done after Pavel Pavlovitch's first visit.

"Ah! a drunken fool and nothing more!" He waved his hand, dismissing the subject.

"Absolutely nothing more," he repeated energetically as he undressed and got into bed.

8 LIZA ILL

NEXT morning Velchaninov walked about his room expecting Pavel Pavlovitch, who had promised to arrive in good time to go to the Pogoryeltsevs. As he smoked and sipped his coffee he was conscious at every moment that he was like a man who on waking up in the morning cannot forget for one instant that he has received a slap in the face overnight. "H'm! . . . he quite understands the position and will take his revenge on me through Liza!" he thought with horror.

The charming figure of the poor child rose mournfully before him for a moment. His heart beat faster at the thought that he would soon, within two hours, see *his* Liza again. "Ah! it's no use talking about it!" he decided hotly—"It's my whole life and my whole object now! what do slaps in the face or memories of the past matter? What has my life been till now? Muddle and sadness . . . but now . . . it's all different, everything's changed!"

But in spite of his enthusiasm, he grew more and more doubtful.

"He is tormenting me by means of Liza—that's clear! And he is tormenting Liza too. It's in that way he will devour me utterly in revenge for everything. H'm! . . . Of course, I can't allow him to go on as he did yesterday"—he flushed crimson all at once—"and . . . here it's twelve o'clock, though, he doesn't come."

He waited a long time, till half-past twelve, and his depression grew more and more acute. Pavel Pavlovitch did not appear. At last the thought that had long been stirring in his mind, that Pavel Pavlovitch had not come on purpose, simply in order to get up another scene like that of the night before, put the finishing touch to his irritation. "He knows that I depend on him, and what a state Liza will be in now. And how can I appear before her without him?"

At last he could stand it no longer, and at one o'clock he rushed off to the Pokrovsky Hotel alone. At the lodging he was told that Pavel Pavlovitch had not slept at home, but had only turned up at nine o'clock in the morning, had stayed no more than a quarter of an hour, and then gone out again. Velchaninov stood at the door of Pavel Pavlovitch's room, listening to what the servant said, and mechanically turned the handle of the locked door and pulled it backwards and forwards. Realizing what he was doing, he uttered a curse and asked the servant to take him to Marya Sysoevna. But the landlady, hearing he was there, came out readily.

She was a good-natured woman. "A woman with generous feelings," as Velchaninov said of her when he was reporting his conversation afterwards to Klavdia Petrovna. Inquiring briefly about his journey with the child the day before, Marya Sysoevna launched out into accounts of Pavel Pavlovitch's doings. In her words: "If it had not been for the child, she would have sent him about his business long ago. He was turned out of the hotel because of his disorderly behavior. Wasn't it wicked to bring home a wench with him when there was a child here old enough to understand? He was shouting: 'She will be your mother, if I choose!' And, would you believe it? what that street wench did, she even spat in his face. 'You're not my daughter, but he's a ——!' she cried."

"Really!" Velchaninov was horrified.

"I heard it myself. Though the man was drunk till he was almost senseless, yet it was very wrong before the child; though she is but young, she broods over everything in her mind! The child cries. I can see she is worried to death. And the other day there was a terrible thing done in our building: a clerk, so folks say, took a room in the hotel overnight, and in the morning hanged himself. They say he had squandered all his money. People flocked to see. Pavel Pavlovitch was not at home, and the child was running about with no one to look after her; I looked, and there she was in the passage among the people, and peeping in behind the others: she was looking so strangely at the body. I brought her away as quickly as I could. And what do you think—she was all of a tremble, she looked quite black in the face, and as soon as I brought her in she flopped on the floor in a faint. She struggled and writhed, and it was all I could do to bring her round. It was a fit, and she's been poorly ever since that hour. He heard of it, came home, and pinched her all over—for he's not one for beating, he's more given to pinching her, and afterwards, when he came home after having a drop, he'd frighten her: 'I'll hang myself too,' he'd say; 'you'll make me hang myself; on this blind-cord here,' he'd say; and he'd make a noose before her eyes. And she'd be beside herself—she'd scream and throw her little arms round him: 'I won't!' she'd cry, 'I never will again.' It was pitiful."

Though Velchaninov had expected something strange, this story amazed him so much that he could not believe it.

Marya Sysoevna told him a great deal more; on one occasion, for instance, had it not been for Marya Sysoevna Liza might have thrown herself out of the window.

Velchaninov went out of the house reeling as though he were drunk.

"I'll knock him on the head like a dog!" was the thought that floated before his mind. And for a long time he kept repeating it to himself.

He took a cab and drove to the Pogoryeltsevs. On the way the carriage was obliged to stop at the cross-roads, near the bridge on the canal, over which a long funeral procession was passing. And on both sides of the bridge there were several carriages waiting in a block; people on foot were stopped too. It was a grand funeral and there was a very long string of carriages following it, and lo and behold! in the windows of one of these carriages Velchaninov caught a passing glimpse of the face of Pavel Pavlovitch. He would not have believed his eyes if Pavel Pavlovitch had not thrust his head out and nodded to him with a smile. Evidently he was delighted at recognizing Velchaninov; he even began beckoning to him from the carriage. Velchaninov jumped out of his cab and, in spite of the crush, in spite of the police, and in spite of the fact that Pavel Pavlovitch's carriage was driving on to the bridge, he ran right up to the window. Pavel Pavlovitch was alone.

"What's the matter with you?" cried Velchaninov; "why didn't you come? How is it you are here?"

"I'm repaying a debt. Don't shout, don't shout, I am repaying a debt," sniggered Pavel Pavlovitch, screwing up his eyes, jocosely. "I'm following the mortal remains of my faithful friend, Stepan Mihalovitch."

"That's all nonsense, you drunken, senseless man," Velchaninov shouted louder than ever, though he was taken aback for an instant. "Get out this minute and come into the cab with me."

"I can't, it's a duty. . . ."

"I'll drag you out!" Velchaninov yelled.

"And I'll scream! I'll scream!" said Pavel Pavlovitch, sniggering as jocosely as before, as though it were a game, though he did huddle into the furthest corner of the carriage. . . .

"Look out, look out! you'll be run over!" shouted a policeman.

At the further end of the bridge a carriage cutting across the procession did, in fact, cause a commotion. Velchaninov was forced to skip back; the stream of carriages and the crowd of people immediately carried him further away. With a curse he made his way back of the cab.

"No matter, I couldn't have taken a fellow like that with me, at any rate!" he thought, with a feeling of bewildered anxiety that persisted.

When he told Klavdia Petrovna Marya Sysoevna's story and described the strange meeting in the funeral procession, she grew very thoughtful.

"I feel afraid for you," she said. "You ought to break off all relations with him, and the sooner the better."

"He's a drunken fool and nothing more!" Velchaninov cried passionately; "as though I could be afraid of him! And how can I break off relations with him when there's Liza to be considered. Think of Liza!"

Liza meanwhile was lying ill; she had begun to be feverish the evening before and they were expecting a celebrated doctor, for whom they had sent an express messenger to the town in the morning. This completed Velchaninov's distress.

Klavdia Petrovna took him to the invalid.

"I watched her very carefully yesterday," she observed, stopping outside Liza's room. "She's a proud and reserved child; she is ashamed that she is here, and that her father has cast her off; that's the whole cause of her illness, to my thinking."

"How cast her off? Why do you say he's cast her off?"

"The very fact that he let her come here, among complete strangers and with a man . . . who's almost a stranger, too, or on such terms . . ."

"But it was I took her, I took her by force; I don't perceive . . ."

"Oh, my God, and even Liza, a child, perceives it! Its my belief that he simply won't come at all."

Liza was not astonished when she saw Velchaninov alone; she only smiled mournfully and turned her feverishly hot little head to the wall. She made no response to Velchaninov's timid efforts to comfort her and his fervent promises to bring her father next day without fail. On coming away from her, he suddenly burst into tears.

It was evening before the doctor came. After examining the patient, he alarmed them all from the first word, by observing that they had done wrong not to have sent for him before. When it was explained to him that the child had been taken ill only the evening before, he was at first incredulous.

"It all depends how things go on tonight," he said in conclusion. After giving various instructions, he went away, promising to come again next day as early as possible. Velchaninov would have insisted on staying the night, but Klavdia Petrovna begged him once more "to try and bring that monster."

"Try once more," Velchaninov retorted in a frenzy. "Why, this time I'll tie him hand and foot and carry him here in my arms!" The idea of tying Pavel Pavlovitch hand and foot and carrying him there took possession of him and made him violently impatient to carry it out. "I don't feel in the least guilty towards him now, not in the least!" he said to Klavdia Petrovna, as he said good-bye. "I take back all the abject, snivelling things I said here yesterday," he added indignantly.

Liza was lying with her eyes shut, apparently asleep; she seemed to be better. When Velchaninov cautiously bent over her head, to say good-bye and to kiss, if only the edge of her garment, she suddenly opened her eyes, as though she had been expecting him, and whispered to him—

"Take me away!"

It was a gentle, pitiful prayer, without a shade in it of the irritability of the previous day, but at the same time he could hear in it the conviction that he would not do what she asked. Velchaninov, in complete despair, began trying to persuade her that this was impossible.

In silence she closed her eyes and did not utter another word, as though she did not see or hear him.

On getting into Petersburg he told the driver to take him straight to Pokrovsky Hotel. It was ten o'clock; Pavel Pavlovitch was not in his lodging. Velchaninov spent a full half-hour in waiting for him and walking up and down the passage in sickening suspense. Marya Sysoevna assured him at last that Pavel Pavlovitch would not be back till early next morning. "Then I will come early in the morning," Velchaninov decided, and, beside himself, he set off for home.

But what was his astonishment when, at the door of his flat, he learned from Mavra that his yesterday's visitor had been waiting for him since ten o'clock.

"And has been pleased to drink tea here, and has sent out for wine again, and has given me a blue note to get it."

9 AN APPARITION

PAVEL PAVLOVITCH had made himself exceedingly comfortable. He was sitting in the same chair as the day before, smoking a cigarette, and had just poured himself out the fourth and last glass from a bottle of wine. The teapot and an unfinished glass of tea were standing on a table close by. His flushed face was beaming with bliss. He had even taken off his coat, as it was warm, and was sitting in his waistcoat.

"Excuse me, most faithful of friends!" he cried, seeing Velchaninov and jumping up to put on his coat. "I took it off for the greater enjoyment of the moment. . . ."

Velchaninov went up to him menacingly.

"Are you not quite drunk yet? Is it still possible to talk to you?"

Pavel Pavlovitch was a little flustered.

"No, not quite. . . . I've been commemorating the deceased, but . . . not quite. . . ."

"Will you understand me too?"

"That's what I've come for, to understand you."

"Well, then; I begin by telling you straight out that you are a worthless scoundrel!" cried Velchaninov.

"If you begin like that, how will you end?" Pavel Pavlovitch protested, evidently cowed, but Velchaninov went on shouting without heeding him.

"Your daughter is dying, she is ill; have you abandoned her or not?"

"Can she really be dying?"

"She is ill, ill, exceedingly, dangerously ill!"

"Possibly some little fit . . ."

"Don't talk nonsense! She is ex—ceed—ing—ly, dangerously ill! You ought to have gone if only to . . ."

"To express my gratitude, my gratitude for their hospitality! I quite understand that! Alexey Ivanovitch, my precious, perfect friend"—he suddenly clutched Velchaninov's hand in both of his, and with drunken sentimentality, almost with tears, as though imploring forgiveness, he kept crying out: "Alexey Ivanovitch, don't shout, don't shout! Whether I die or fall drunk into the Neva— what does it matter in the real significance of things? We have plenty of time to go to Mr. Pogoryeltsev. . . ."

Velchaninov pulled himself together and restrained himself a little.

"You're drunk, and so I don't understand the sense of what you are saying," he observed sternly. "I am always ready to have things

out with you, shall be glad to, in fact, as soon as possible. . . . I've
come indeed. . . . But first of all I warn you that I shall take steps:
you must stay the night here! To-morrow morning I'll take you and
we'll go together. I won't let you go," he yelled again. "I'll tie you
up and carry you there in my arms! . . . Would you like this sofa?"
he said breathlessly, pointing to a wide, soft sofa, which stood opposite the one against the other wall, where he used to sleep himself.

"By all means, I can sleep anywhere. . . ."

"Not anywhere, but on that sofa! Here, take your sheets, your
quilt, your pillow." All these Velchaninov took out of the cupboard
and hurriedly flung them to Pavel Pavlovitch, who held out his
arms submissively. "Make the bed at once, make it at once!"

Pavel Pavlovitch, loaded with his burden, stood in the middle
of the room as though hesitating, with a broad drunken grin on
his drunken face. But at a second menacing shout from Velchaninov he suddenly began bustling about at full speed; he pushed
back the table and began, sighing and groaning, to unfold the
sheets and make the bed. Velchaninov went to assist him; he was,
to some extent, appeased by the alarm and submissiveness of his
visitor.

"Finish your glass and go to bed," he ordered him again; he
felt as though he could not help giving orders. "You sent for that
wine yourself, didn't you?"

"Yes. . . . I knew you wouldn't send for any more, Alexey
Ivanovitch."

"It was well you knew it, and there is something more you must
know too. I tell you once more I've taken measures, I won't put up
with any more of your antics, I won't put up with your drunken
kisses as I did yesterday."

"I understand myself, Alexey Ivanovitch, that that was only possible once," sniggered Pavel Pavlovitch.

Hearing his answer, Velchaninov, who had been striding up and
down the room, stopped almost solemnly before Pavel Pavlovitch.

"Pavel Pavlovitch, tell me frankly! You're a sensible man, I've
recognized that again, but I assure you, you are on the wrong tack!

Speak straightforwardly, act straightforwardly and I give you my word of honor I will answer any question you like."

Pavel Pavlovitch grinned his broad grin again, which was enough in itself to drive Velchaninov to fury.

"Stop!" Velchaninov shouted again. "Don't sham, I see through you! I repeat: I give you my word of honor, that I am ready to answer *anything* and you shall receive every satisfaction possible, that is every sort, even the impossible! Oh, how I wish you could understand me! . . ."

"Since you are so good"—Pavel Pavlovitch moved cautiously towards him—"I was much interested in what you said last night about a 'predatory type'! . . ."

Velchaninov, with a curse, fell to pacing about the room more rapidly than ever.

"No, Alexey Ivanovitch, don't curse, because I'm so much interested, and have come on purpose to make sure. . . . I'm not very ready with my tongue, but you must forgive me. You know of that 'predatory type,' and of that 'peaceable type' I read in a magazine, in the literary criticism. I remembered it this morning . . . only I had forgotten it, and to tell the truth I did not understand it at the time. This is what I wanted you to explain: the deceased, Stepan Mihalovitch Bagautov—was he 'predatory' or 'peaceable'? How do you classify him?"

Velchaninov still remained silent, and did not cease his pacing up and down.

"The predatory type," he began, stopping suddenly in exasperation, "is the man who would sooner have put poison in Bagautov's glass when drinking champagne with him in honor of their delightful meeting, as you drank with me yesterday, than have followed his coffin to the cemetery as you have to-day, the devil only knows from what secret, underground, loathsome impulse and distorted feeling that only degrades you! Yes, degrades you!"

"It's true that I shouldn't have gone," Pavel Pavlovitch assented; "but you do pitch into me. . . ."

"It's not the man," Velchaninov, getting hotter, went on shouting, without heeding him; "it's not the man who poses to himself as goodness knows what, who reckons up his score of right and wrong, goes over and over his grievance as though it were a lesson, frets, goes in for all sorts of antics and apishness, hangs on people's necks—and most likely he has been spending all his time at it too! Is it true that you tried to hang yourself—is it?"

"When I was drunk, I did talk wildly—I don't remember. It isn't quite seemly, Alexey Ivanovitch, to put poison in wine. Apart from the fact that I am a civil servant of good repute, you know I have money of my own, and, what's more, I may want to get married again."

"Besides, you'll be sent to the gallows."

"To be sure, that unpleasantness also, though nowadays they admit many extenuating circumstances in the law-courts. I'll tell you a killing little anecdote, Alexey Ivanovitch. I thought of it this morning in the carriage. I wanted to tell you of it then. You said just now 'hangs on people's necks.' You remember, perhaps, Semyon Petrovitch Livtsov, he used to come and see us when you were in T——; well, his younger brother, who was also a young Petersburg swell, was in attendance on the governor at V——, and he, too, was distinguished for various qualities. He had a quarrel with Golubenko, a colonel, in the presence of ladies and the lady of his heart, and considered himself insulted, but he swallowed the affront and concealed it; and, meanwhile, Golubenko cut him out with the lady of his heart and made her an offer. And what do you think? This Livtsov formed a genuine friendship with Golubenko, he quite made it up with him, and, what's more, insisted on being his best man, he held the wedding crown, and when they came from under the wedding crown, he went up to kiss and congratulate Golubenko; and in the presence of the governor and all the honorable company, with his swallow-tail coat, and his hair in curl, he sticks the bridegroom in the stomach with a knife—so that he rolled over! His own best man! What a disgrace! And, what's more, when he'd stabbed him like that, he rushed about crying: 'Ach! what have I done! Oh, what is it I've done!' with floods of tears, trembling all over, flinging himself on people's necks, even ladies. 'Ach, what have I done!' he kept saying. 'What have I done now!' He—he—he! he was killing. Though one feels sorry for Golubenko, perhaps, but after all he recovered."

"I don't see why you told me the story," observed Velchaninov, frowning sternly.

"Why, all because he stuck the knife in him, you know," Pavel Pavlovitch tittered; "you can see he was not the type, but a snivelling fellow, since he forgot all good manners in his horror and flung himself on the ladies' necks in the presence of the governor —but you see he stabbed him, he got his own back! That was all I meant."

"Go to hell!" Velchaninov yelled suddenly, in a voice not his own, as though something had exploded in him. "Go to hell with your underground vileness; you are nothing but underground vileness. You thought you'd scare me—you base man, torturing a child; you scoundrel, you scoundrel, you scoundrel!" he shouted, beside himself, gasping for breath at every word.

A complete revulsion came over Pavel Pavlovitch which actually seemed to sober him; his lips quivered.

"It is you, Alexey Ivanovitch, call me a scoundrel, *you* call *me?*"

But Velchaninov had already realized what he had done.

"I am ready to apologize," he answered, after a pause of gloomy hesitation; "but only if you will act straightforwardly at once yourself."

"In your place I would apologize without any ifs, Alexey Ivanovitch."

"Very good, so be it," said Velchaninov, after another slight pause. "I apologize to you; but you'll admit yourself, Pavel Pavlovitch, that, after all this, I need not consider that I owe you anything. I'm speaking with reference to the *whole* matter and not only to the present incident."

"That's all right, why consider?" Pavel Pavlovitch sniggered, though he kept his eyes on the ground.

"So much the better, then, so much the better! Finish your wine and go to bed, for I won't let you go, anyway. . . ."

"Oh, the wine. . . ." Pavel Pavlovitch seemed, as it were, a little disconcerted. He went to the table, however, and finished the last glass of wine he had poured out so long before.

Perhaps he had drunk a great deal before, for his hand trembled and he spilt part of the wine on the floor, and on his shirt and waistcoat. He finished it all, however, as though he could not bear to leave a drop, and respectfully replacing the empty glass on the table, he went submissively to his bed to undress.

"But wouldn't it be better for me not to stay the night?" he brought out for some reason, though he had taken off one boot and was holding it in his hand.

"No, it wouldn't," Velchaninov answered wrathfully, still pacing up and down the room without looking at him.

Pavel Pavlovitch undressed and got into bed. A quarter of an hour later Velchaninov went to bed too, and put out the candle.

He fell asleep uneasily. The new element that had turned up unexpected and complicated the whole business more than ever worried him now, and at the same time he felt that he was for some reason ashamed of his uneasiness. He was just dozing off, but he was waked up all at once by a rustling sound. He looked round at once towards Pavel Pavlovitch's bed. The room was dark (the curtains were drawn), but Velchaninov fancied that Pavel Pavlovitch was not lying down, but was sitting on the bed.

"What's the matter?" Velchaninov called to him.

"A ghost," Pavel Pavlovitch said, scarcely audibly, after a brief pause.

"What do you mean, what sort of ghost?"

"There in that room, I seem to see a ghost in the doorway."

"Whose ghost?" Velchaninov asked again, after a pause.

"Natalya Vassilyevna's."

Velchaninov stood up on the rug, and looked across the passage, into the other room, the door of which always stood open. There were only blinds instead of curtains on the window, and so it was much lighter there.

"There's nothing in that room and you are drunk. Go to bed!" said Velchaninov. He got into bed and wrapped himself in the quilt.

Pavel Pavlovitch got into bed, too, without uttering a word.

"And have you ever seen ghosts before?" Velchaninov asked suddenly, ten minutes afterwards.

Pavel Pavlovitch, too, was silent for a while.

"I thought I saw one once," he responded faintly.

Silence followed again.

Velchaninov could not have said for certain whether he had been asleep or not, but about an hour had passed when he suddenly turned round again: whether he was roused again by a rustle, he was not sure, but felt as though in the pitch-dark something white was standing over him, not quite close, but in the middle of the room. He sat up in bed and for a full minute gazed into the darkness.

"Is that you, Pavel Pavlovitch?" he said, in a failing voice.

His own voice ringing out suddenly in the stillness and the dark seemed to him somehow strange.

No answer followed, but there could be no doubt that someone was standing there.

"Is that you . . . Pavel Pavlovitch?" he repeated, more loudly— so loudly, in fact, that if Pavel Pavlovitch had been quietly asleep in his bed he would certainly have waked up and answered.

But again no answer came, yet he fancied that the white, hardly distinguishable figure moved nearer to him. Then something strange followed: something seemed to explode within him, exactly as it had that evening, and he shouted at the top of his voice, in a most hideous, frantic voice, gasping for breath at each word:

"If you . . . drunken fool . . . dare to imagine . . . that you can . . . frighten me, I'll turn over to the wall, I'll put the bedclothes over my head, and won't turn round again all night . . . to show you how much I care . . . if you were to stand there till morning . . . like a fool . . . and I spit upon you . . ."

And he spat furiously in the direction, as he supposed, of Pavel Pavlovitch, turned over to the wall, drew the bedclothes over his head as he had said and grew numb in that position, not stirring a muscle. A deathlike silence followed. Whether the phantom was moving nearer or standing still he could not tell, but his heart was beating, beating, beating violently. Fully five minutes passed, and suddenly, two steps from him, he heard the meek and plaintive voice of Pavel Pavlovitch.

"I got up, Alexey Ivanovitch, to look for the . . ." (and he mentioned a quite indispensable domestic article). "I didn't find one there. . . . I meant to look quietly under your bed."

"Why didn't you speak when I shouted?" Velchaninov asked in a breaking voice, after an interval of half a minute.

"I was frightened, you shouted so. . . . I was frightened."

"There in the corner on the left, in the little cupboard. Light the candle. . . ."

"I can do without the candle," Pavel Pavlovitch brought out meekly, making for the corner. "Forgive me, Alexey Ivanovitch, for disturbing you so. . . . I was so bewildered . . ."

But Velchaninov made no reply. He still lay with his face to the wall, and lay so all night, without once turning over. Whether it was that he wanted to do as he had said and so show his contempt—he did not know himself what he was feeling; his nervous irritability passed at last almost into delirium, and it was a long time before he went to sleep. Waking next morning between nine and ten, he jumped up and sat up in bed, as though some one had given him a shove—but Pavel Pavlovitch was not in the room—the unmade bed stood there empty; he had crept away at dawn.

"I knew it would be so," cried Velchaninov, slapping himself on the forehead.

10 IN THE CEMETERY

THE doctor's fears turned out to be justified; Liza was suddenly worse—worse than Velchaninov and Klavdia Petrovna had imagined possible the evening before. Velchaninov found the invalid conscious in the morning, though she was in a high fever; afterwards he declared that she had smiled and even held out her feverish little hand to him. Whether this was really so, or whether he had imagined it, in an unconscious effort to comfort himself, he had no time to make sure; by nightfall the sick child was unconscious, and she remained so till the end. Ten days after her coming to the Pogoryeltsevs she died.

It was a sorrowful time for Velchaninov; the Pogoryeltsevs were very anxious about him. He spent those bitter days for the most part with them. During the last days of Liza's illness he would sit for whole hours together in a corner apparently thinking of nothing; Klavdia Petrovna attempted to distract his mind, but he made little response, and seemed to find it a burden even to talk to her. Klavdia Petrovna had not expected that "all this would have such an effect upon him." The children succeeded best in rousing him; in their company he sometimes even laughed, but almost every hour he would get up from his chair and go on tiptoe to look at the invalid. He sometimes fancied that she recognized him. He had no hope of her recovery, nor had anyone, but he could not tear himself away from the room in which she lay dying, and usually sat in the next room.

On two occasions in the course of those days, however, he showed great activity: he roused himself and rushed off to Petersburg to the doctors, called on all the most distinguished of them, and arranged for a consultation. The second and last consultation took place the evening before Liza's death. Three days before that Klavdia Petrovna urged upon Velchaninov the necessity of seeking out M. Trusotsky: pointing out that "if the worst happened, the funeral would be impossible without him." Velchaninov mumbled in reply that he would write to him. Pogoryeltsev thereupon declared that he would undertake to find him through the police. Velchaninov did finally write a note of two lines and took it to the Pokrovsky Hotel. Pavel Pavlovitch, as usual, was not at home, and he left the letter for him with Marya Sysoevna.

At last Liza died, on a beautiful summer evening at sunset, and only then Velchaninov seemed to wake up. When they dressed the dead child in a white frock that belonged to one of Klavdia

Petrovna's daughters and was kept for festivals, and laid her on the table in the drawing-room with flowers in her folded hands, he went up to Klavdia Petrovna with glittering eyes, and told her that he would bring the "murderer" at once. Refusing to listen to their advice to put off going till next day, he set off for Petersburg at once.

He knew where to find Pavel Pavlovitch; he had not only been to fetch the doctors when he went to Petersburg before. He had sometimes fancied during those days that if he brought her father to Liza, and she heard his voice, she might come to herself; so he had fallen to hunting for him like one possessed. Pavel Pavlovitch was in the same lodging as before, but it was useless for him to inquire there: "He hasn't slept here for the last three nights or been near the place," Marya Sysoevna reported; "and if he does come he's bound to be drunk, and before he's been here an hour he's off again: he's going to rack and ruin." The waiter at the Pokrovsky Hotel told Velchaninov, among other things, that Pavel Pavlovitch used to visit some young women in Voznesensky Prospect. Velchaninov promptly looked up these young women. When he had treated them and made them presents these persons readily remembered their visitor, chiefly from the crape on his hat, after which, of course, they abused him roundly for not having been to see them again. One of them, Katya, undertook "to find Pavel Pavlovitch any time, because nowadays he was always with Mashka Prostakov, and he had no end of money, and she ought to have been Mashka Prohvostov (*i. e.* scoundrelly) instead of Prostakov (*i. e.* simple), and she'd been in the hospital, and if she (the speaker) liked she could pack the wench off to Siberia—she had only to say the word." Katya did not, however, look up Pavel Pavlovitch on that occasion, but she promised faithfully to do so another time. It was on her help that Velchaninov was reckoning now.

On reaching Petersburg at ten o'clock, he went at once to ask for her, paid the keeper to let her go, and set off to search with her. He did not know himself what he was going to do with Pavel Pavlovitch: whether he would kill him, or whether he was looking for him simply to tell him of his daughter's death and the necessity of his presence at the funeral. At first they were unsuccessful. It turned out that this Mashka had had a fight with Pavel Pavlovitch two days before, and that a cashier "had broken his head with a stool." In fact, for a long time the search was in vain, and it was only at two o'clock in the afternoon that Velchaninov, coming out of an "establishment," to which he had been sent as a likely place, unexpectedly hit up against him.

Pavel Pavlovitch, hopelessly drunk, was being conducted to this "establishment" by two ladies, one of whom was holding his arm and supporting him. They were followed by a tall, sturdy fellow, who was shouting at the top of his voice and threatening Pavel Pavlovitch with all sorts of horrors. He bawled among other things that "Pavel Pavlovitch was exploiting him and poisoning his existence." There seemed to have been some dispute about money; the women were much frightened and flustered. Seeing Velchaninov, Pavel Pavlovitch rushed to him with outstretched hands and screamed as though he were being murdered:

"Brother, defend me!"

At the sight of Velchaninov's athletic figure the bully promptly disappeared; Pavel Pavlovitch in triumph shook his fist after him with a yell of victory; at that point Velchaninov seized him by the shoulder in a fury, and, without knowing why he did it, shook him until his teeth chattered. Pavel Pavlovitch instantly ceased yelling and stared at his tormentor in stupid, drunken terror. Probably not knowing what to do with him next, Velchaninov folded him up and sat him on the curbstone.

"Liza is dead!" he said to him.

Pavel Pavlovitch, still staring at Velchaninov, sat on the curbstone supported by one of the ladies. He understood at last, and his face suddenly looked pinched.

"Dead . . ." he whispered strangely. Whether his face wore his loathsome, drunken grin, or whether it was contorted by some feeling, Velchaninov could not distinguish, but a moment later Pavel Pavlovitch, with an effort, lifted his trembling hand to make the sign of the cross; his trembling hand dropped again without completing it. A little while after he slowly got up from the curbstone, clutched at his lady and, leaning upon her, went on his way, as though oblivious—as though Velchaninov had not been present. But the latter seized him by the shoulder again.

"Do you understand, you drunken monster, that without you she can't be buried?" he shouted breathlessly.

Pavel Pavlovitch turned his head towards him.

"The artillery . . . the lieutenant . . . do you remember him?" he stammered.

"Wha—at!" yelled Velchaninov, with a sickening pang.

"There's her father for you! Find him—for the burial."

"You're lying," Velchaninov yelled like one distraught. "You say that from spite. . . . I knew you were preparing that for me."

Beside himself, he raised his terrible fist to strike Pavel Pavlovitch. In another minute he might have killed him at one blow; the ladies squealed and were beating a retreat, but Pavel Pavlovitch did not turn a hair. His face was contorted by a frenzy of ferocious hatred.

"Do you know," he said, much more steadily, almost as though he were sober, "our Russian . . . ?" (and he uttered an absolutely unprintable term of abuse). "Well, you go to it, then!"

Then with a violent effort he tore himself out of Velchaninov's hands, stumbled and almost fell down. The ladies caught him and this time ran away, squealing and almost dragging Pavel Pavlovitch after them. Velchaninov did not follow them.

On the afternoon of the next day a very presentable-looking, middle-aged government clerk in uniform arrived at the Pogoryeltsevs' villa and politely handed Klavdia Petrovna an envelope addressed to her by Pavel Pavlovitch Trusotsky. In it was a letter enclosing three hundred roubles and the legal papers necessary for the burial. Pavel Pavlovitch wrote briefly, respectfully, and most properly. He warmly thanked Her Excellency for the kind sympathy she had shown for the little motherless girl, for which God alone could repay her. He wrote vaguely that extreme ill-health would prevent him from coming to arrange the funeral of his beloved and unhappy daughter, and he could only appeal to the angelic kindness of Her Excellency's heart. The three hundred roubles were, as he explained later in the letter, to pay for the funeral, and the expenses caused by the child's illness. If any of this money were left over he must humbly and respectfully beg that it might be spent on "a perpetual mass for the rest of the soul of the departed." The clerk who brought the letter could add nothing in explanation; it appeared, indeed, from what he said that it was only at Pavel Pavlovitch's earnest entreaty that he had undertaken to deliver the letter to Her Excellency. Pogoryeltsev was almost offended at the expression "the expenses caused by the child's illness," and after setting aside fifty roubles for the funeral —since it was impossible to prevent the father from paying for his child's burial—he proposed to send the remaining two hundred and fifty roubles back to M. Trusotsky at once. Klavdia Petrovna finally decided not to send back the two hundred and fifty roubles, but only a receipt from the cemetery church for that sum in payment for a perpetual mass for the repose of the soul of the deceased maiden Elizaveta. This receipt was afterwards given to Velchaninov to be despatched to Pavel Pavlovitch. Velchaninov posted it to his lodging.

After the funeral he left the villa. For a whole fortnight he wandered about the town aimless and alone, so lost in thought that he stumbled against people in the street. Sometimes he would lie stretched out on his sofa for days together, forgetting the commonest things of everyday life. Several times the Pogoryeltsevs went to ask him to go to them; he promised to go, but immediately forgot. Klavdia Petrovna even went herself to see him, but did not find him at home. The same thing happened to his lawyer; the lawyer had, indeed, something to tell him: his lawsuit had been very adroitly settled and his opponents had come to an amicable arrangement, agreeing to accept an insignificant fraction of the disputed inheritance. All that remained was to obtain Velchaninov's own consent. When at last he did find him at home, the lawyer was surprised at the apathy and indifference with which Velchaninov, once such a troublesome client, listened to his explanation.

The very hottest days of July had come, but Velchaninov was oblivious of time. His grief ached in his heart like a growing abscess, and he was distinctly conscious of it and every moment with agonizing acuteness. His chief suffering was the thought that, before Liza had had time to know him, she had died, not understanding with what anguish he loved her! The object in life of which he had had such a joyful glimpse had suddenly vanished into everlasting darkness. That object—he thought of it every moment now—was that Liza should be conscious of his love every day, every hour, all her life. "No one has a higher object and no one could have," he thought sometimes, with gloomy fervor. "If there are other objects none can be holier than that!" "By my love for Liza," he mused, "all my old putrid and useless life would be purified and expiated; to make up for my own idle, vicious and wasted life I would cherish and bring up that pure and exquisite creature, and for her sake everything would be forgiven me and I could forgive myself everything."

All these *conscious* thoughts always rose before his mind, together with the vivid, ever-present and ever-poignant memory of the dead child. He re-created for himself her little pale face, remembered every expression on it: he thought of her in the coffin decked with flowers, and as she had lain unconscious in fever, with fixed and open eyes. He suddenly remembered that when she was lying on the table he had noticed one of her fingers, which had somehow turned black during her illness; this had struck him so much at the time, and he had felt so sorry for that poor little finger, that for the first time he thought of seeking out Pavel Pavlovitch and killing him; until that time he had been "as though insensible." Was it wounded pride that had tortured her wounded heart, or was it those three months of suffering at the hands of her father, whose love had suddenly changed to hatred, who had insulted her with shameful words, laughing at her terror, and had abandoned her at last to strangers? All this he dwelt upon incessantly in a thousand variations. "Do you know what Liza has been to me?"—he suddenly recalled the drunkard's exclamation and felt that that exclamation was sincere, not a pose, and that there was love in it. "How could that monster be so cruel to a child whom he had loved so much, and is it credible?" But every time he made haste to dismiss that question and, as it were, brush it aside; there was something awful in that question, something he could not bear and could not solve.

One day, scarcely conscious where he was going, he wandered into the cemetery where Liza was buried and found her little grave. He had not been to the cemetery since the funeral; he had always fancied it would be too great an agony, and had been afraid to go. But, strange to say, when he had found her little grave and kissed it, his heart felt easier. It was a fine evening, the sun was setting; all round the graves the lush green grass was growing; the bees were humming in a wild rose close by; the flowers and wreaths left by the children and Klavdia Petrovna on Liza's grave were lying there with the petals half dropping. There was a gleam of something like hope in his heart after many days.

"How serene!" he thought, feeling the stillness of the cemetery, and looking at the clear, peaceful sky.

A rush of pure, calm faith flooded his soul.

"Liza has sent me this, it's Liza speaking to me," he thought.

It was quite dark when he left the cemetery and went home. Not far from the cemetery gates, in a low-pitched wooden house on the road, there was some sort of eating-house or tavern; through the windows he could see people sitting at the tables. It suddenly seemed to him that one of them close to the window was Pavel Pavlovitch, and that he saw him, too, and was staring at him inquisitively. He walked on, and soon heard some one pursuing him; Pavel Pavlovitch was, in fact, running after him; probably he had been attracted and encouraged by Velchaninov's conciliatory expression as he watched him from the window. On overtaking him he smiled timidly, but it was not his old drunken smile; he was actually not drunk.

"Good-evening," he said.

"Good-evening," answered Velchaninov.

11 PAVEL PAVLOVITCH MEANS TO MARRY

As he responded with this "Good-evening," he was surprised at himself. It struck him as extremely strange that he met this man now without a trace of anger, and that in his feeling for him at that moment there was something quite different, and actually, indeed, a sort of impulse towards something new.

"What an agreeable evening," observed Pavel Pavlovitch, looking into his face.

"You've not gone away yet," Velchaninov observed, not by way of a question, but simply making that reflection aloud as he walked on.

"Things have dragged on, but—I've obtained a post with an increase of salary. I shall be going away the day after tomorrow for certain."

"You've got a post?" he said this time, asking a question.

"Why shouldn't I?" Pavel Pavlovitch screwed up his face.

"Oh, I only asked . . ." Velchaninov said, disclaiming the insinuation, and, with a frown, he looked askance at Pavel Pavlovitch.

To his surprise, the attire, the hat with the crape band and the whole appearance of M. Trusotsky were incomparably more presentable than they had been a fortnight before.

"What was he sitting in that tavern for?" he kept wondering.

"I was intending, Alexey Ivanovitch, to communicate with you on a subject for rejoicing," Pavel Pavlovitch began again.

"Rejoicing?"

"I'm going to get married."

"What?"

"After sorrow comes rejoicing, so it is always in life; I should be so gratified, Alexey Ivanovitch, if . . . but—I don't know, perhaps you're in a hurry now, for you appear to be . . ."

"Yes, I am in a hurry . . . and I'm unwell too."

He felt a sudden and intense desire to get rid of him; his readiness for some new feeling had vanished in a flash.

"I should have liked . . ."

Pavel Pavlovitch did not say what he would have liked; Velchaninov was silent.

"In that case it must be later on, if only we meet again . . ."

"Yes, yes, later on," Velchaninov muttered rapidly, without stopping or looking at him.

They were both silent again for a minute; Pavel Pavlovitch went on walking beside him.

"In that case, good-bye till we meet again," Pavel Pavlovitch brought out at last.

"Good-bye; I hope . . ."

Velchaninov returned home thoroughly upset again. Contact with "that man" was too much for him. As he got into bed he asked himself again: "Why was he at the cemetery?"

Next morning he made up his mind to go to the Pogoryeltsevs. He made up his mind to go reluctantly; sympathy from any one, even from the Pogoryeltsevs, was too irksome for him now. But they were so anxious about him that he felt absolutely obliged to go. He suddenly had a foreboding that he would feel horribly ashamed at their first meeting again.

Should he go or not, he thought, as he made haste to finish his breakfast; when, to his intense amazement, Pavel Pavlovitch walked in.

In spite of their meeting the day before Velchaninov could never have conceived that the man would come to see him again, and was so taken aback that he stared at him and did not know what to say. But Pavel Pavlovitch was equal to the occasion. He greeted him, and sat down on the very same chair on which he had sat on his last visit. Velchaninov had a sudden and peculiarly vivid memory of that visit, and gazed uneasily and with repulsion at his visitor.

"You're surprised?" began Pavel Pavlovitch, interpreting Velchaninov's expression.

He seemed altogether much more free and easy than on the

previous day, and at the same time it could be detected that he was more nervous than he had been then. His appearance was particularly curious. M. Trusotsky was not only presentably but quite foppishly dressed—in a light summer jacket, light-colored trousers of a smart, close-fitting cut, a light waistcoat; gloves, a gold lorgnette, which he had suddenly adopted for some reason. His linen was irreproachable; he even smelt of scent. About his whole get-up there was something ridiculous, and at the same time strangely and unpleasantly suggestive.

"Of course, Alexey Ivanovitch," he went on, wriggling, "I'm surprising you by coming, and I'm sensible of it. But there is always, so I imagine, preserved between people, and to my mind there should be preserved, something higher, shouldn't there? Higher, I mean, than all the conditions and even unpleasantnesses that may come to pass. . . . Shouldn't there?"

"Pavel Pavlovitch, say what you have to say quickly, and without ceremony," said Velchaninov, frowning.

"In a couple of words," Pavel Pavlovitch began hastily, "I'm going to get married and I am just setting off to see my future bride. They are in a summer villa too. I should like to have the great honor to make bold to introduce you to the family, and have come to ask an unusual favor," (Pavel Pavlovitch bent his head humbly) "to beg you to accompany me. . . ."

"Accompany you, where?" Velchaninov stared with open eyes.

"To them, that is, to their villa. Forgive me, I am talking as though in a fever, and perhaps I've not been clear; but I'm so afraid of your declining."

And he looked plaintively at Velchaninov.

"Do you want me to go with you now to see your future bride?" Velchaninov repeated, scrutinizing him rapidly, unable to believe his eyes or ears.

"Yes," said Pavel Pavlovitch, extremely abashed. "Don't be angry, Alexey Ivanovitch. It's not impudence; I only beg you most humbly as a great favor. I had dreamed that you might not like, that being so, to refuse. . . ."

"To begin with, it's utterly out of the question." Velchaninov turned round uneasily.

"It is merely an intense desire on my part and nothing more," Pavel Pavlovitch went on, imploring him. "I will not conceal, either, that there are reasons for it, but I should have preferred not to have revealed them till later, and for the present to confine myself to the very earnest request. . . ."

And he positively got up from his seat to show his deference.

"But in any case it is quite impossible, you must admit that yourself. . . ."

Velchaninov, too, stood up.

"It is quite possible, Alexey Ivanovitch. I was proposing to present you as a friend; and besides, you are an acquaintance of theirs already; you see, it's to Zahlebinin's, to his villa. The civil councillor, Zahlebinin."

"What?" cried Velchaninov.

It was the civil councillor for whom he had been constantly looking for a month before, and had never found at home. He had, as it turned out, been acting in the interests of the other side.

"Yes, yes; yes, yes," said Pavel Pavlovitch, smiling and seeming to be greatly encouraged by Velchaninov's great astonishment; "the very man, you remember, whom you were walking beside, and talking to, while I stood opposite watching you; I was waiting to go up to him when you had finished. Twenty years ago we were in the same office, and that day, when I meant to go up to him after you had finished, I had no idea of the sort. It occurred to me suddenly, only a week ago."

"But, upon my word, they are quite a decent family," said Velchaninov, in naïve surprise.

"Well, what then, if they are?" Pavel Pavlovitch grimaced.

"No, of course, I didn't mean . . . only as far as I've observed when I was there . . ."

"They remember, they remember your being there," Pavel Pavlovitch put in joyfully; "only you couldn't have seen the family then; but he remembers you and has a great esteem for you. We talked of you with great respect."

"But when you've only been a widower three months?"

"But you see the wedding will not be at once; the wedding will be in nine or ten months, so that the year of mourning will be over. I assure you that everything is all right. To begin with, Fedosey Petrovitch has known me from a boy; he knew my late wife; he knows my style of living, and what people think of me, and what's more, I have property, and I'm receiving a post with increase of salary—so all that has weight."

"Why, is it his daughter?"

"I will tell you all about it." Pavel Pavlovitch wriggled ingratiatingly. "Allow me to light a cigarette. And you'll see her yourself today too. To begin with, such capable men as Fedosey Petrovitch are sometimes very highly thought of here in Petersburg, if they succeed in attracting notice. But you know, apart from his salary and the additional and supplementary fees, bonuses, hotel expenses, and moneys given in relief, he has nothing—that is, nothing substantial that could be called a capital. They are comfortably off, but there is no possibility of saving where there's a family. Only imagine: Fedosey Petrovitch has eight girls, and only one son, still a child. If he were to die tomorrow there would be nothing left but a niggardly pension. And eight girls! just imagine —only imagine—what it must run into simply for their shoes! Of these eight girls five are grown up, the eldest is four-and-twenty (a most charming young lady, as you will see) and the sixth, a girl of fifteen, is still at the high school. Of course, husbands must be found for the five elder ones, and that ought to be done in good time, as far as possible, so their father ought to bring them out, and what do you suppose that will cost? And then I turn up, the first suitor they have had in the house, and one they know all about, that I really have property, I mean. Well, that's all."

Pavel Pavlovitch explained with fervor.

"You're engaged to the eldest?"

"N-no, I . . . no, not to the eldest; you see, I'm proposing for the sixth, the one who is still at the high school."

"What?" said Velchaninov, with an involuntary smile. "Why, you say she's only fifteen!"

"Fifteen now; but in nine months she'll be sixteen, she'll be sixteen and three months, so what of it? But as it would be improper at present, there will be no open engagement but only an understanding with the parents. . . . I assure you that everything is all right!"

"Then it's not settled yet?"

"Yes, it is settled, it's all settled. I assure you, all is as it should be."

"And does she know?"

"Well, it's only in appearance, for the sake of propriety, that they are not telling her; of course she knows." Pavel Pavlovitch screwed up his eyes insinuatingly. "Well, do you congratulate me, Alexey Ivanovitch?" Pavel Pavlovitch concluded very timidly.

"But what should I go there for? However," he added hurriedly, "since I'm not going in any case, don't trouble to find a reason."

"Alexey Ivanovitch . . ."

"But do you expect me to go in beside you and drive off there with you? Think of it!"

The feeling of disgust and aversion came back after the momentary distraction of Pavel Pavlovitch's chatter about his future bride. In another minute he would have turned him out. He even felt angry with himself for some reason.

"Do, Alexey Ivanovitch, do, and you won't regret it!" Pavel Pavlovitch implored him in a voice fraught with feeling. "No, no, no!"—he waved his hands, catching an impatient and determined gesture from Velchaninov. "Alexey Ivanovitch, Alexey Ivanovitch, wait a bit before you decide! I see that you have perhaps misunderstood me. Of course, I know only too well that you cannot be to me, nor I to you . . . that we're not comrades; I am not so absurd as not to understand that. And that the favor I'm asking of you will not pledge you to anything in the future. And, indeed, I'm going away after tomorrow altogether, absolutely; just as though nothing had happened. Let this day be a solitary exception. I have come to you resting my hopes on the generosity of the special feelings of your heart, Alexey Ivanovitch

—those feelings which might of late have been awakened . . . I think I'm speaking clearly, am I not?"

Pavel Pavlovitch's agitation reached an extreme point. Velchaninov looked at him strangely.

"You ask for some service from me?" he questioned, hesitatingly, "and are very insistent about it. That strikes me as suspicious; I should like to know more about it."

"The only service is that you should come with me. And afterwards, on our way back, I will unfold all to you as though at confession. Alexey Ivanovitch, believe me!"

But Velchaninov still refused, and the more stubbornly because he was conscious of an oppressive and malignant impulse. This evil impulse had been faintly stirring within him from the very beginning, ever since Pavel Pavlovitch had talked of his future bride: whether it was simply curiosity, or some other quite obscure prompting, he felt tempted to consent. And the more he felt tempted, the more he resisted. He sat with his elbow on one hand, and hesitated.

Pavel Pavlovitch beside him kept coaxing and persuading.

"Very good, I'll come," he consented all at once, uneasily and almost apprehensively, getting up from his seat.

Pavel Pavlovitch was extremely delighted.

"But, Alexey Ivanovitch, you must change your clothes now," Pavel Pavlovitch cajoled him, hanging gleefully about him; "put on your best suit."

"And why must he meddle in this, too, strange fellow?" Velchaninov thought to himself.

"This is not the only service I'm expecting of you, Alexey Ivanovitch. Since you have given your consent, please be my adviser."

"In what, for example?"

"The great question, for instance, of crape. Which would be more proper, to remove the crape, or keep it on?"

"As you prefer."

"No, I want you to decide; what would you do yourself in my place, that is, if you had crape on your hat? My own idea is that, if I retain it, it points to the constancy of my feelings, and so is a flattering recommendation."

"Take it off, of course."

"Do you really think it's a matter of course?" Pavel Pavlovitch hesitated. "No, I think I had better keep it. . . ."

"As you like."

"He doesn't trust me, that's a good thing," thought Velchaninov.

They went out; Pavel Pavlovitch gazed with satisfaction at Velchaninov's smartened appearance; his countenance seemed to betray an even greater degree of deference and of dignity! Velchaninov wondered at him and even more at himself. A very good carriage stood waiting for them at the gate.

"So you had a carriage all ready too? So you felt sure I should come?"

"I engaged the carriage for myself, but I did feel confident that you would consent to accompany me," Pavel Pavlovitch replied, with the air of a perfectly happy man.

"Ah, Pavel Pavlovitch," Velchaninov said, laughing as it were irritably when they were in the carriage and had set off, "weren't you too sure of me?"

"But it's not for you, Alexey Ivanovitch, it's not for you to tell me that I'm a fool for it," Pavel Pavlovitch responded, in a voice full of feeling.

"And Liza," thought Velchaninov, and at once hastened to dismiss the thought of her as though afraid of sacrilege. And it suddenly seemed to him that he was so petty, so insignificant at that moment; it struck him that the thought that had tempted him was a thought so small and nasty . . . and he longed again, at all costs, to fling it all up, and to get out of the carriage at once, even if he had to thrash Pavel Pavlovitch. But the latter began talking and the temptation mastered his heart again.

"Alexey Ivanovitch, do you know anything about jewels?"

"What sort of jewels?"

"Diamonds."

"Yes."

"I should like to take a little present. Advise me, should I or not?"

"I think you shouldn't."

"But I feel I should so like to," returned Pavel Pavlovitch, "only, what am I to buy? A whole set, that is, a brooch, earrings, bracelets, or simply one article?"

"How much do you want to spend?"

"About four hundred or five hundred roubles?"

"Ough!"

"Is it too much, or what?" asked Pavel Pavlovitch in a flutter.

"Buy a single bracelet for a hundred roubles."

Pavel Pavlovitch was positively mortified; he was so eager to spend more and buy a "whole set" of jewels. He persisted. They drove to a shop. It ended, however, in his only buying a bracelet, and not the one that he wanted to, but the one that Velchaninov fixed upon. Pavel Pavlovitch wanted to take both. When the jeweller, who had asked a hundred and seventy-five roubles for the bracelet, consented to take a hundred and fifty for it, Pavel Pavlovitch was positively vexed; he would have paid two hundred if that sum had been asked, he was so eager to spend more.

"It doesn't matter, does it, my being in a hurry with presents?" he gushed blissfully, when they had set off again. "They're not grand people, they are very simple. The innocent creatures are fond of little presents," he said, with a sly and good-humored grin. "You smiled just now, Alexey Ivanovitch, when you heard she was fifteen; but that's just what bowled me over; that she was still going to school with the satchel on her arm full of copy books and pens, he—he! That satchel fascinated me! It's innocence that charms me, Alexey Ivanovitch; it's not so much beauty of face, it's that. She giggles in the corner with her school friend, and how she laughs, my goodness! And what at? It's all because the kitten jumped off the chest of drawers on to the bed and was curled up like a little ball. . . . And then there's that scent of fresh apples! Shall I take off the crape?"

"As you please."

"I will take it off."

He took off his hat, tore off the crape and flung it in the road. Velchaninov saw that his face was beaming with the brightest hopes, as he replaced his hat upon his bald head.

"Can it be that he is really like this?" he thought, feeling genuinely angry; "can it be there isn't some trick in his inviting me? Can he be really reckoning on my generosity?" he went on, almost offended at the last supposition. "What is he—a buffoon, a fool, or the 'eternal husband'—but it's impossible!"

12 AT THE ZAHLEBININS'

T H E Zahlebinins were really a "very decent family," as Velchaninov had expressed it, and Zahlebinin himself had an assured position in a government office and was well thought of by his superiors. All that Pavel Pavlovitch had said about their income was true too: "They live very comfortably, but if he dies there'll be nothing left."

Old Zahlebinin gave Velchaninov a warm and affable welcome, and his former "foe" seemed quite like a friend.

"I congratulate you, it was better so," he began at the first word, with a pleasant and dignified air. "I was in favor of settling it out of court myself and Pyotr Karlovitch (Velchaninov's lawyer) is priceless in such cases. Well, you get sixty thousand without any bother, without delay and dispute! And the case might have dragged on for three years!"

Velchaninov was at once presented to Madame Zahlebinin, an elderly lady of redundant figure, with a very simple and tired-looking face. The young ladies, too, began to sail in one after the other or in couples. But a very great many young ladies made their appearance; by degrees they gathered to the number of ten or twelve—Velchaninov lost count of them; some came in, others went out. But among them several were girl friends from the neighboring villas. The Zahlebinins' villa, a large wooden house, built in quaint and whimsical style, with parts added at different periods, had the advantage of a big garden; but three or four other villas looked into the garden on different sides, and it was common property, an arrangement which naturally led to friendly

relations among the girls of the different households. From the
first words of conversation Velchaninov observed that he was
expected, and that his arrival in the character of a friend of Pavel
Pavlovitch, anxious to make their acquaintance, was hailed almost
triumphantly.

His keen and experienced eye quickly detected something
special; from the over-cordial welcome of the parents, from a
certain peculiar look about the girls and their get-up (though, indeed, it was a holiday), from all that, the suspicion dawned upon
him that Pavel Pavlovitch had been scheming and, very possibly,
without, of course, saying it in so many words, had been suggesting a conception of him as a bachelor of property and of the "best
society," who was suffering from ennui and very, very likely to
make up his mind to "change his state and settle down," especially as he had just come into a fortune. The manner and the appearance of the eldest Mademoiselle Zahlebinin, Katerina Fedosyevna, the one who was twenty-four and who had been described
by Pavel Pavlovitch as a charming person, struck him as being in
keeping with that idea. She was distinguished from her sisters
by her dress and the original way in which her luxuriant hair was
done. Her sisters and the other girls all looked as though they
were firmly convinced that Velchaninov was making their acquaintance "on Katya's account" and had come "to have a look
at her." Their glances and even some words, dropped in the course
of the day, confirmed him in this surmise. Katerina Fedosyevna
was a tall blonde of generous proportions, with an exceedingly
sweet face, of a gentle, unenterprising, even torpid character.
"Strange that a girl like that should still be on hand," Velchaninov
could not help thinking, watching her with pleasure. "Of course,
she has no dowry and she'll soon grow too fat, but meantime lots
of men would admire her. . . ." All the other sisters, too, were nice-
looking, and among their friends there were several amusing and
even pretty faces. It began to divert him; he had come, moreover,
with special ideas.

Nadyezhda Fedosyevna, the sixth, the schoolgirl and Pavel
Pavlovitch's bride-elect, did not appear till later. Velchaninov

awaited her coming with an impatience which surprised him and made him laugh at himself. At last she made her entrance, and not without effect, accompanied by a lively, keen-witted girl friend, a brunette with a comical face whose name was Marie Nikititchna, and of whom, as was at once apparent, Pavel Pavlovitch stood in great dread. This Marie Nikititchna, a girl of twenty-three, with a mocking tongue and really clever, was a nursery governess in a friend's family. She had long been accepted by the Zahlebinins as one of themselves and was thought a great deal of by the girls. It was evident that Nadya found her indispensable now. Velchaninov discerned at once that all the girls were antagonistic to Pavel Pavlovitch, even the friends, and two minutes after Nadya's arrival he had made up his mind that she *detested* him. He observed, too, that Pavel Pavlovitch either failed to notice this or refused to.

Nadya was unquestionably the handsomest of the lot—a little brunette with a wild, untamed look and the boldness of a nihilist; a roguish imp with blazing eyes, with a charming but often malicious smile; with wonderful lips and teeth, slender and graceful, her face still child-like but glowing with the dawn of thought. Her age was evident in every step she took, in every word she uttered. It appeared afterwards that Pavel Pavlovitch did see her for the first time with an American leather satchel on her arm, but this time she had not got it.

The presentation of the bracelet was a complete failure, and, indeed, made an unpleasant impression. As soon as Pavel Pavlovitch saw his "future bride" come into the room he went up to her with a smirk. He presented it as a testimony "of the agreeable gratification he had experienced on his previous visit on the occasion of the charming song sung by Nadyezhda Fedosyevna at the piano. . . ." He stammered, could not finish, and stood helpless, holding out the case with the bracelet and thrusting it into the hand of Nadyezhda Fedosyevna, who did not want to take it, and, crimson with shame and anger, drew back her hands. She turned rudely to her mother, whose face betrayed embarrassment, and said aloud:

"I don't want to take it, *maman!*"

"Take it and say thank you," said her father, with calm severity: but he, too, was displeased. "Unnecessary, quite unnecessary!" he muttered reprovingly to Pavel Pavlovitch.

Nadya, seeing there was no help for it, took the case and, dropping her eyes, curtsied, as tiny children curtsey—that is, suddenly bobbed down, and popped up again as though on springs. One of her sisters went up to look at it and Nadya handed her the case unopened, showing, for her part, that she did not care to look at it. The bracelet was taken out and passed from one to the other; but they all looked at it in silence, and some even sarcastically. Only the mother murmured that the bracelet was very charming. Pavel Pavlovitch was ready to sink into the earth.

Velchaninov came to the rescue.

He began talking, loudly and eagerly, about the first thing that occurred to him, and before five minutes were over he had gained the attention of every one in the drawing-room. He was a brilliant master of the art of small talk—that is, the art of seeming perfectly frank and at the same time appearing to consider his listeners as frank as himself. He could, with perfect naturalness, appear when necessary to be the most light-hearted and happy of men. He was very clever, too, in slipping in a witty remark, a jibe, a gay insinuation or an amusing pun, always as it were accidentally and as though unconscious of doing it—though the epigram or pun and the whole conversation, perhaps, had been prepared and rehearsed long, long before and even used on more than one previous occasion. But at the present moment nature and art were at one, he felt that he was in the mood and that something was drawing him on; he felt the most absolute confidence in himself and knew that in a few minutes all these eyes would be turned upon him, all these people would be listening only to him, talking to no one but him, and laughing only at what he said. And, in fact, the laughter soon came, by degrees the others joined in the conversation—and he was exceedingly clever in making other people talk —three or four voices could be heard at once. The bored and weary face of Madame Zahlebinin was lighted up almost with joy; it was the same with Katerina Fedosyevna, who gazed and listened as though enchanted. Nadya watched him keenly from under her brows; it was evident that she was prejudiced against him. This spurred him on the more. The "mischievous" Marie Nikititchna succeeded in getting in rather a good thrust at him; she asserted quite fictitiously that Pavel Pavlovitch had introduced him as the friend of his boyhood, so putting with obvious intent at least seven years on to his age. But even the malicious Marie Nikititchna liked him. Pavel Pavlovitch was completely nonplussed. He had, of course, some idea of his friend's abilities and at first was delighted at his success; he tittered himself and joined in the conversation; but by degrees he seemed to sink into thoughtfulness, and finally into positive dejection, which was clearly apparent in his troubled countenance.

"Well, you're a visitor who doesn't need entertaining," old Zahlebinin commented gaily, as he got up to go upstairs to his own room, where, in spite of the holiday, he had some business papers awaiting his revision; "and, only fancy, I thought of you as the most gloomy, hypochondriacal of young men. What mistakes one makes!"

They had a piano; Velchaninov asked who played, and suddenly turned to Nadya:

"I believe you sing?"

"Who told you?" Nadya snapped out.

"Pavel Pavlovitch told me just now."

"It's not true. I only sing for fun. I've no voice."

"And I've no voice either, but I sing."

"Then you'll sing to us? Well, then, I'll sing to you," said Nadya, her eyes gleaming; "only not now, but after dinner. I can't endure music," she added. "I'm sick of the piano: they're all singing and playing from morning to night here—Katya's the only one worth hearing."

Velchaninov at once took this up, and it appeared that Katerina Fedosyevna was the only one who played the piano seriously. He at once begged her to play. Everyone was evidently pleased at his addressing Katya, and the mamma positively flushed crimson with gratification. Katerina Fedosyevna got up, smiling, and went to the piano, and suddenly, to her own surprise, she flushed crimson and was horribly abashed that she, such a big girl, four-and-twenty and so stout, should be blushing like a child—and all this was written clearly on her face as she sat down to play. She played something from Haydn and played it carefully though without expression, but she was shy. When she had finished Velchaninov began warmly praising to her, not her playing but Haydn, and especially the little thing which she had played, and she was evidently so pleased and listened so gratefully and happily to his praises, not of herself but of Haydn, that he could not help looking at her with more friendliness and attention: "Ah, but you are a dear!" was reflected in the gleam of his eye—and everyone seemed instantly to understand that look, especially Katerina Fedosyevna herself.

"You have a delightful garden," he said, suddenly addressing the company and looking towards the glass door that led on to the balcony. "What do you say to our all going into the garden?"

"Let us, let us!" they shrieked joyfully, as though he had guessed the general wish.

They walked in the garden till dinner-time. Madame Zahlebinin, though she had been longing to have a nap, could not resist going out with them, but wisely sat down to rest on the verandah, where she at once began to doze. In the garden Velchaninov and the girls got on to still more friendly terms. He noticed that several very young men from the villas joined them; one was a student and another simply a high school boy. They promptly made a dash each for *his* girl, and it was evident that they had come on their account; the third, a very morose and dishevelled-looking youth of twenty, in huge blue spectacles, began, with a frown, whispering hurriedly with Marie Nikititchna and Nadya. He scanned Velchaninov sternly, and seemed to consider it incumbent upon himself to treat him with extraordinary contempt. Some of the girls suggested that they should play games. To Velchaninov's question, what games they played, they said all sorts of games, and catch-catch, but in the evening they would play proverbs—that is, all would sit down and one would go out, the others choose a proverb—for instance: "More haste, less speed," and when the one outside is called in, each in turn has to say one sentence to him. One, for instance, must say a sentence in which there is the word "more," the second, one in which there is the word "haste," and so on. And from their sentences he must guess the proverb.

"That must be very amusing," said Velchaninov.

"Oh, no, it's awfully boring," cried two or three voices at once.

"Or else we play at acting," Nadya observed, suddenly addressing him. "Do you see that thick tree, round which there's a seat: behind that tree is behind the scenes, and there the actors sit, say a king, a queen, a princess, a young man—just as anyone likes; each one enters when he chooses and says anything that comes into his head, and that's the game."

"But that's delightful!" Velchaninov repeated again.

"Oh, no, it's awfully dull! At first it did turn out amusing, but lately it's always been senseless, for no one knows how to end it; perhaps with you, though, it will be more interesting. We did think you were a friend of Pavel Pavlovitch's, though, but it seems he was only bragging. I'm very glad you have come . . . for one thing. . . ."

She looked very earnestly and impressively at Velchaninov and at once walked away to Marie Nikititchna.

"We're going to play proverbs this evening," one of the girl friends whom Velchaninov had scarcely noticed before, and with whom he had not exchanged a word, whispered to him confidentially. "They're all going to make fun of Pavel Pavlovitch, and you will too, of course."

"Ah, how nice it is that you've come, we were all so dull," observed another girl in a friendly way. She was a red-haired girl with freckles, and a face absurdly flushed from walking and the heat. Goodness knows where she had sprung from; Velchaninov had not noticed her till then.

Pavel Pavlovitch's uneasiness grew more and more marked. In the garden Velchaninov made great friends with Nadya. She no longer looked at him from under her brows as she had at first; she seemed to have laid aside her critical attitude towards him, and laughed, skipped about, shrieked, and twice even seized him by the hand; she was extremely happy, she continued to take not the slightest notice of Pavel Pavlovitch, and behaved as though she were not aware of his existence. Velchaninov felt certain that there was an actual plot against Pavel Pavlovitch; Nadya and the crowd of girls drew Velchaninov aside, while some of the other girl friends lured Pavel Pavlovitch on various pretexts in another direction; but the latter broke away from them, and ran full speed straight to them—that is, to Velchaninov and Nadya, and suddenly thrust his bald head in between them with uneasy curiosity. He hardly attempted to restrain himself; the naïveté of his gestures and actions was sometimes amazing. He could not resist trying once more to turn Velchaninov's attention to Katerina Fedosyevna; it was clear to her now that he had not come on her account, but was much more interested in Nadya; but her expression was just as sweet and good-humored as ever. She seemed to be happy simply at being beside them and listening to what their new visitor was saying; she, poor thing, could never keep up her share in a conversation cleverly.

"What a darling your sister Katerina Fedosyevna is!" Velchaninov said aside to Nadya.

"Katya! No one could have a kinder heart than she has. She's an angel to all of us. I adore her," the girl responded enthusiastically.

At last dinner came at five o'clock; and it was evident that the dinner, too, was not an ordinary meal, but had been prepared expressly for visitors. There were two or three very elaborate dishes, which evidently were not part of their ordinary fare, one of them so strange that no one could find a name for it. In addition to the everyday wine there was a bottle of Tokay, obviously for the benefit of the visitors; at the end of dinner champagne was brought in for some reason. Old Zahlebinin took an extra glass, became extraordinarily good-humored and ready to laugh at anything Velchaninov said.

In the end Pavel Pavlovitch could not restrain himself. Carried away by the spirit of rivalry he suddenly attempted to make a pun too; at the end of the table, where he was sitting by Madame Zahlebinin, there was a sudden roar of loud laughter from the delighted girls.

"Papa, Papa! Pavel Pavlovitch has made a pun too," the fourth and fifth Zahlebinin girls shouted in unison. "He says we're 'damsels who dazzle all. . . .'"

"Ah, so he's punning too! Well, what was his pun?" the old man responded sedately, turning patronizingly to Pavel Pavlovitch and smiling in readiness for the expected pun.

"Why, he says we're 'damsels who dazzle all.'"

"Y-yes, well, and what then?" The old man did not understand and smiled more good-humoredly in expectation.

"Oh, Papa, how tiresome you are; you don't understand. Why, 'damsels' and then 'dazzle'; 'damsel' is like 'dazzle,' 'damsels who dazzle all. . . .'"

"A-a-ah," the old man drawled in a puzzled voice. "H'm, well, he'll make a better one next time!"

And the old man laughed good-humoredly.

"Pavel Pavlovitch, you can't have all the perfections at once," Marie Nikititchna jerked aloud. "Oh, my goodness! he's got a bone in his throat," she exclaimed, jumping up from her chair.

There was a positive hubbub, but that was just what Marie Nikititchna wanted. Pavel Pavlovitch had simply choked over the wine which he was sipping to cover his confusion, but Marie Nikititchna vowed and declared that it was a "fish bone," that she had seen it herself and that people sometimes died of it.

"Slap him on the nape of the neck," some one shouted.

"Yes, really that's the best thing to do!" the old man approved aloud.

Eager volunteers were already at him; Marie Nikititchna and the red-haired girl (who had also been invited to dinner), and, finally, the mamma herself, greatly alarmed; every one wanted to slap Pavel Pavlovitch on the back. Jumping up from the table, Pavel Pavlovitch wriggled away and was for a full minute asseverating that he had swallowed his wine too quickly and that the cough would soon be over, while the others realized that it was all a trick of Marie Nikititchna's.

"But, really, you tease . . . !" Madame Zahlebinin tried to say sternly to Marie Nikititchna: but she broke down and laughed as she very rarely did, and that made quite a sensation of a sort.

After dinner they all went out on the verandah to drink coffee.

"And what lovely days we're having!" said the old man, looking with pleasure into the garden, and serenely admiring the beauties of nature. "If only we could have some rain. Enjoy yourselves and God bless you! And you enjoy yourself too," he added, patting Pavel Pavlovitch on the shoulder as he went out.

When they had all gone out into the garden again, Pavel Pavlovitch suddenly ran up to Velchaninov and pulled him by the sleeve.

"Just one minute," he whispered impatiently.

They turned into a lonely side path.

"No, in this case, excuse me, no, I won't give up . . ." he stuttered in a furious whisper, clutching Velchaninov's arm.

"What? what?" Velchaninov asked, opening his eyes in amazement.

Pavel Pavlovitch stared at him mutely, his lips moved, and he smiled furiously.

"Where are you going? Where are you? Everything's ready," they heard the ringing, impatient voices of the girls.

Velchaninov shrugged his shoulders and returned to the rest of the party.

Pavel Pavlovitch, too, ran after him.

"I'll bet he asked you for a handkerchief," said Marie Nikititchna; "he forgot one last time too."

"He'll always forget it!" the fifth Zahlebinin girl put in.

"He's forgotten his handkerchief, Pavel Pavlovitch has forgotten his handkerchief, Mamma, Pavel Pavlovitch has forgotten his pocket-handkerchief, Mamma, Pavel Pavlovitch has a cold in his head again!" cried voices.

"Then why doesn't he say so! You do stand on ceremony, Pavel Pavlovitch!" Madame Zahlebinin drawled in a sing-song voice.

"It's dangerous to trifle with a cold; I'll send you a handkerchief directly. And why has he always got a cold in his head?" she added, as she moved away, glad of an excuse for returning home.

"I have two pocket-handkerchiefs and I haven't a cold in my head!" Pavel Pavlovitch called after her, but the lady apparently did not grasp what he said, and a minute later, when Pavel Pavlovitch was ambling after the others, keeping near Velchaninov and Nadya, a breathless maidservant overtook him and brought him a handkerchief.

"Proverbs, a game of proverbs," the girls shouted on all sides, as though they expected something wonderful from "a game of proverbs."

They fixed on a place and sat down on a seat; it fell to Marie Nikititchna's lot to guess; they insisted that she should go as far away as possible and not listen; in her absence they chose a proverb and distributed the words. Marie Nikititchna returned and guessed the proverb at once. The proverb was: "It's no use meeting troubles halfway."

Marie Nikititchna was followed by the young man with dishevelled hair and blue spectacles. They insisted on even greater precautions with him—he had to stand in the arbor and keep his face to the fence. The gloomy young man did what was required of him contemptuously, and seemed to feel morally degraded by it. When he was called he could guess nothing, he went the round of all of them and listened to what they said twice over, spent a long time in gloomy meditation, but nothing came of it. They put him to shame. The proverb was: "To pray to God and serve the Czar ne'er fail of their reward."

"And the proverb's disgusting!" the exasperated young man exclaimed indignantly, as he retreated to his place.

"Oh, how dull it is!" cried voices.

Velchaninov went out; he was hidden even further off; he, too, failed to guess.

"Oh, how dull it is!" more voices cried.

"Well, now, I'll go out," said Nadya.

"No, no, let Pavel Pavlovitch go out now, it's Pavel Pavlovitch's turn," they all shouted, growing more animated.

Pavel Pavlovitch was led away, right up to the fence in the very corner, and made to stand facing it, and that he might not look round, the red-haired girl was sent to keep watch on him. Pavel Pavlovitch, who had regained his confidence and almost his cheerfulness, was determined to do his duty properly and stood stock-still, gazing at the fence and not daring to turn round. The red-haired girl stood on guard twenty paces behind him nearer to the party in the arbor, and she exchanged signals with the girls in some excitement; it was evident that all were expecting something with trepidation; something was on foot. Suddenly the red-haired girl waved her arms as a signal to the arbor. Instantly they all jumped up and ran off at breakneck speed.

"Run, you run, too," a dozen voices whispered to Velchaninov, almost with horror at his not running.

"What's the matter? What has happened?" he asked, hurrying after them.

"Hush, don't shout! Let him stand there staring at the fence while we all run away. See, Nastya is running."

The red-haired girl (Nastya) was running at breakneck speed, waving her hands as though something extraordinary had happened. They all ran at last to the other side of the pond, the very opposite corner of the garden. When Velchaninov had got there he saw that Katerina Fedosyevna was hotly disputing with the others, especially with Nadya and Marie Nikititchna.

"Katya, darling, don't be angry!" said Nadya, kissing her.

"Very well, I won't tell Mamma, but I shall go away myself, for it's very horrid. What must he be feeling at the fence there, poor man!"

She went away—from pity—but all the others were merciless and as ruthless as before. They all insisted sternly that when Pavel Pavlovitch came back, Velchaninov should take no notice of him, as though nothing had happened.

"And let us all play catch-catch!" cried the red-haired girl ecstatically.

It was at least a quarter of an hour before Pavel Pavlovitch rejoined the party. For two-thirds of that time he had certainly been standing at the fence. The game was in full swing, and was a great success—everybody was shouting and merry. Frantic with rage, Pavel Pavlovitch went straight up to Velchaninov and pulled at his sleeve again.

"Just half a minute!"

"Good gracious, what does he want with his half-minutes!"

"He's borrowing a handkerchief again," was shouted after him once more.

"Well, this time it was you; now it's all your doing. . . ."

Pavel Pavlovitch's teeth chattered as he said this.

Velchaninov interrupted him, and mildly advised him to be livelier, or they would go on teasing him. "They tease you because you are cross when all the rest are enjoying themselves." To his surprise, these words of advice made a great impression on Pavel Pavlovitch; he subsided at once—so much so, in fact, that he went back to the party with a penitent air and submissively took his place in the game; after which they left him alone and treated him like the rest—and before half an hour had passed he had almost regained his spirits. In all the games when he had to choose a partner he picked out by preference the red-haired traitress, or one of the Zahlebinin sisters. But to his still greater surprise Velchaninov noticed that Pavel Pavlovitch did not dare try to speak to Nadya, although he continually hovered about her. At any rate he accepted his position, as an object of scorn and neglect to her, as though it were a fitting and natural thing. But towards the end they played a prank upon him again.

The game was "hide-and-seek." The one who hid, however, was allowed to run anywhere in the part of the garden allotted him. Pavel Pavlovitch, who had succeeded in concealing himself completely in some thick bushes, conceived the idea of running out and making a bolt for the house. He was seen and shouts were raised; he crept hurriedly upstairs to the first floor, knowing of a place behind a chest of drawers where he could hide. But the red-haired girl flew up after him, crept on tiptoe to the door and turned the key on him. All left off playing and ran just as they had done before to the other side of the pond, at the further end of the garden. Ten minutes later, Pavel Pavlovitch, becoming aware that no one was looking for him, peeped out of the window. There was no one to be seen. He did not dare to call out for fear of waking the parents; the maids had been sternly forbidden to answer Pavel Pavlovitch's call or go to him. Katerina Fedosyevna might have unlocked him, but, returning to her room and sitting down to dream a little, she had unexpectedly fallen asleep too. And so he stayed there about an hour. At last the girls came, as it were by chance, in twos or threes.

"Pavel Pavlovitch, why don't you come out to us? Oh, it has been fun! We've been playing at acting. Alexey Ivanovitch has been acting 'a young man.' "

"Pavel Pavlovitch, why don't you come, we want to admire you!" others observed as they passed.

"Admire what now?" they suddenly heard the voice of Madame Zahlebinin, who had only just woken up and made up her mind to come out into the garden and watch the "children's" games while waiting for tea.

"But here's Pavel Pavlovitch," they told her, pointing to the window where Pavel Pavlovitch's face, pale with anger, looked out with a wry smile.

"It's an odd fancy for a man to sit alone, when you're all enjoying yourselves!" said the mamma, shaking her head.

Meanwhile, Nadya had deigned to give Velchaninov an explanation of her words that she "was glad he had come for one reason."

The explanation took place in a secluded avenue. Marie Nikititchna purposely summoned Velchaninov, who was taking part in some game and was horribly bored, and left him alone in the avenue with Nadya.

"I am absolutely convinced," she said boldly, in a rapid patter, "that you are not such a great friend of Pavel Pavlovitch's as he boasted you were. I am reckoning on you as the one person who can do me a very great service." She took the case out of her pocket. "I humbly beg you to give this back to him at once, as I shall never speak to him again in my life. You can say so from

me, and tell him not to dare to force his company and his presents on me. I'll let him know the rest through other people. Will
you be so kind as to do what I want?"

"Oh, for mercy's sake, spare me!" Velchaninov almost cried
out, waving his hand.

"What? Spare you?" Nadya was extraordinarily surprised at his
refusal, and she gazed at him round-eyed.

The tone she had assumed for the occasion broke down immediately, and she was almost in tears.

Velchaninov laughed.

"I don't mean that. . . . I should be very glad . . . but I have my
own account to settle with him. . . ."

"I knew that you were not his friend and that he was telling
lies!" Nadya interrupted quickly and passionately. "I'll never
marry him, I tell you! Never! I can't understand how he could
presume . . . Only you must give him back his disgusting present
or else what shall I do? I particularly, particularly want him to
have it back to-day, the same day, so that his hopes may be
crushed, and if he sneaks about it to Papa he shall see what he
gets by it."

And from behind the bushes there suddenly emerged the young
man in the blue spectacles.

"It's your duty to return the bracelet," he blurted out furiously,
pouncing on Velchaninov. "If only from respect for the rights of
women, that is—if you are capable of rising to the full significance
of the question."

But before he had time to finish Nadya tugged at his sleeve with
all her might, and drew him away from Velchaninov.

"My goodness, how silly you are, Predposylov!" she cried. "Go
away, go away, go away, and don't dare to listen; I told you to
stand a long way off!" . . . She stamped her little foot at him, and
when he had crept back into the bushes she still walked up and
down across the path, with her eyes flashing and her arms folded
before her, as though she were beside herself with anger.

"You wouldn't believe how silly they are!" She stopped suddenly before Velchaninov. "It amuses you, but think what it means to me."

"That's not *he*, it's not *he*, is it?" laughed Velchaninov.

"Of course it isn't, and how could you imagine it!" cried Nadya, smiling and blushing. "That's only his friend. But I can't understand the friends he chooses; they all say that he's a 'future leader,' but I don't understand it. . . . Alexey Ivanovitch, I've no one I can appeal to; I ask you for the last time, will you give it back?"

"Oh, very well, I will; give it me."

"Ah, you are kind, you are good!" she cried, delighted, handing him the case. "I'll sing to you the whole evening for that, for I sing beautifully, do you know. I told you a fib when I said I didn't like music. Oh, you must come again—once at any rate; how glad I should be. I would tell you everything, everything, everything, and a great deal more besides, because you're so kind—as kind, as kind, as—as Katya!"

And when they went in to tea she did sing him two songs, in an utterly untrained and hardly mature, but pleasant and powerful voice. When they came in from the garden Pavel Pavlovitch was stolidly sitting with the parents at the tea-table, on which the big family samovar was already boiling, surrounded by cups of Sèvres china. He was probably discussing very grave matters with the old people, as two days later he was going away for nine whole months. He did not glance at the party as they came in from the garden, and particularly avoided looking at Velchaninov. It was evident, too, that he had not been sneaking and that all was serene so far.

But when Nadya began singing he put himself forward at once. Nadya purposely ignored one direct question he addressed her, but this did not disconcert Pavel Pavlovitch, or make him hesitate. He stood behind her chair and his whole manner showed that this was his place and he was not going to give it up to anyone.

"Alexey Ivanovitch sings, Mamma; Alexey Ivanovitch wants to sing, Mamma!" almost all the girls shouted at once, crowding round the piano at which Velchaninov confidently installed himself, intending to play his own accompaniment. The old people came in, and with them Katerina Fedosyevna, who had been sitting with them, pouring out the tea.

Velchaninov chose a song of Glinka's, now familiar to almost everyone—

> *"In the glad hour when from thy lips*
> *Come murmurs tender as a dove's."*

He sang it, addressing himself entirely to Nadya, who was standing at his elbow nearer to him than anyone. His voice had passed its prime, but what was left of it showed that it had once been a fine one. Velchaninov had, twenty years before, when he was a student, the luck to hear that song for the first time sung by Glinka himself, at the house of a friend of the composer's. It was at a literary and artistic bachelor gathering, and Glinka, growing expansive, played and sang his own favorite compositions, among them this song. He, too, had little voice left then, but Velchaninov remembered the great impression made by that song. A drawing-room singer, however skilful, would never have produced such an effect. In that song the intensity of passion rises, mounting higher and higher at every line, at every word; and, from this very intensity, the least trace of falsity, of exaggeration or unreality, such as passes muster so easily at an opera, would distort and destroy the whole value of it. To sing that slight but exceptional song it was essential to have truth, essential to have real inspiration, real passion, or a complete poetical comprehension of it. Otherwise the song would not only be a failure but might even appear unseemly and almost shameless: without them it would be impossible to express such intensity of passion without arousing repulsion, but truth and simplicity saved it. Velchaninov remembered that he had made a success with this song on some occasion. He had almost reproduced Glinka's manner of singing, but now, from the first note, from the first line, there was a gleam of inspiration in his singing which quivered in his voice.

At every word the torrent of feeling was more fervent and more boldly displayed; in the last lines the cry of passion is heard, and

when, with blazing eyes, Velchaninov addressed the last words of
the song to Nadya—

> *"Grown bolder, in thine eyes I gaze;*
> *Draw close my lips, can hear no more,*
> *I long to kiss thee, kiss thee, kiss thee!*
> *I long to kiss thee, kiss thee, kiss thee!"*—

she trembled almost with alarm, and even stepped back; the color
rushed into her cheeks, and at the same time Velchaninov seemed
to catch a glimpse of something responsive in her abashed and
almost dismayed little face. The faces of all the audience betrayed
their enchantment and also their amazement: all seemed to feel
that it was disgraceful and impossible to sing like that, and yet at
the same time all their faces were flushed and all their eyes glowed
and seemed to be expecting something more. Among those faces
Velchaninov had a vision especially of the face of Katerina Fedosyevna, which looked almost beautiful.

"What a song," old Zahlebinin muttered, a little flabbergasted;
"but . . . isn't it too strong? charming, but strong. . . ."

"Yes . . ." Madame Zahlebinin chimed in, but Pavel Pavlovitch
would not let her go on; he dashed forward suddenly like one possessed, so far forgetting himself as to seize Nadya by the arm and
pull her away from Velchaninov; he skipped up to him, gazed at
him with a desperate face and quivering lips that moved without
uttering a sound.

"Half a minute," he uttered faintly at last.

Velchaninov saw that in another minute the man might be
guilty of something ten times as absurd; he made haste to take his
arm and, regardless of the general amazement, drew him out into
the verandah, and even took some steps into the garden with him,
where it was now almost dark.

"Do you understand that you must go away with me this minute?" said Pavel Pavlovitch.

"No, I don't understand. . . ."

"Do you remember," Pavel Pavlovitch went on, in his frenzied whisper, "do you remember that you insisted that I should tell you everything, *everything* openly, 'the very last word . . .' do you remember? Well, the time has come to say that word . . . let us go!"

Velchaninov thought a minute, looked at Pavel Pavlovitch and agreed to go.

The sudden announcement of their departure upset the parents, and made all the girls horribly indignant.

"At least have another cup of tea," said Madame Zahlebinin plaintively.

"Come, what's upset you?" old Zahlebinin said in a tone of severity and displeasure, addressing Pavel Pavlovitch, who stood simpering and silent.

"Pavel Pavlovitch, why are you taking Alexey Ivanovitch away?" the girls began plaintively, looking at him with exasperation.

Nadya gazed at him so wrathfully that he positively squirmed, but he did not give way.

"You see, Pavel Pavlovitch has reminded me—many thanks to him for it—of a very important engagement which I might have missed," Velchaninov said, smiling, as he shook hands with Zahlebinin, and bowed to the mamma and the girls, especially distinguishing Katerina Fedosyevna in a manner apparent to all.

"We are very grateful for your visit and shall always be glad to see you," Zahlebinin said ponderously, in conclusion.

"Ah, we shall be so delighted . . ." the mamma chimed in with feeling.

"Come again, Alexey Ivanovitch, come again!" numerous voices were heard calling from the verandah, when he had already got into the carriage with Pavel Pavlovitch; there was perhaps one voice that called more softly than the others, "Come again, dear, dear Alexey Ivanovitch."

"That's the red-haired girl," thought Velchaninov.

13 ON WHOSE SIDE MOST?

HE MIGHT think about the red-haired girl, and yet his soul was in agonies of vexation and remorse. And, indeed, during the whole of that day, which seemed on the surface so amusingly spent, a feeling of acute depression had scarcely left him. Before singing the song he did not know how to get away from it; perhaps that was why he had sung it with such fervor.

"And I could demean myself like that . . . tear myself away from everything," he began reproaching himself, but he hurriedly cut short his thoughts. Indeed, it seemed to him humiliating to lament; it was a great deal more pleasant to be angry with some-one.

"Fool!" he whispered wrathfully, with a side glance at the silent figure of Pavel Pavlovitch sitting beside him in the carriage.

Pavel Pavlovitch remained obstinately silent, perhaps concentrated on preparing what he had got to say. With an impatient gesture he sometimes took off his hat and wiped his brow with his handkerchief.

"Perspiring!" Velchaninov thought spitefully.

On one occasion only Pavel Pavlovitch addressed a question to the coachman. "Is there going to be a storm?" he asked.

"Storm, indeed! Not a doubt of it; it's been brewing up all day."

The sky was indeed growing dark and there were flashes of lightning in the distance.

They reached the town about half-past ten.

"I am coming in with you, of course," Pavel Pavlovitch warned him, not far from the house.

"I understand, but I must tell you that I feel seriously unwell."

"I won't stay, I won't stay long."

When they went in at the gate, Pavel Pavlovitch ran in at the porter's lodge to find Mavra.

"What were you running off there for?" Velchaninov said

sternly, as the latter overtook him and they went into the room.

"Oh . . . nothing . . . the driver . . ."

"I won't have you drink!"

No answer followed. Velchaninov lighted the candle, and Pavel Pavlovitch at once sat down on the chair. Velchaninov remained standing before him, with a frown on his face.

"I, too, promised to say my 'last' word," he began, with an inward, still suppressed irritation. "Here it is—that word: I consider on my conscience that everything between us is over, so that, in fact, there is nothing for us to talk about—do you hear?—nothing; and so wouldn't it be better for you to go away at once, and I'll close the door after you?"

"Let us settle our account, Alexey Ivanovitch," said Pavel Pavlovitch, looking in his face, however, with peculiar mildness.

"Set-tle our ac-count!" repeated Velchaninov, greatly surprised. "That's a strange thing to say! Settle what account? Bah! Isn't that perhaps that 'last word' you promised . . . to reveal to me?"

"It is."

"We've no account to settle; we settled our account long ago!" Velchaninov pronounced proudly.

"Can you really think so?" Pavel Pavlovitch brought out in a voice full of feeling, clasping his hands strangely and holding them before his breast.

Velchaninov made him no answer, but continued pacing up and down the room. "Liza! Liza!" he was moaning in his heart.

"What did you want to settle, though?" he asked him, frowning, after a rather prolonged silence.

Pavel Pavlovitch had been following him about the room with his eyes all this time, still holding his hands clasped before him.

"Don't go there again," he almost whispered in a voice of entreaty, and he suddenly got up from his chair.

"What! So that's all you are thinking about?" Velchaninov laughed spitefully. "You've surprised me all day, though!" he was beginning malignantly, but suddenly his whole face changed. "Listen," he said mournfully, with deep and sincere feeling; "I consider that I have never lowered myself as I have today—to begin with, by consenting to go with you, and then—by what happened there. . . . It was so paltry, so pitiful. . . . I've defiled and debased myself by mixing myself up in it . . . and forgetting . . . But there!" he cried hastily. "Listen, you attacked me to-day in an unguarded moment when I was nervous and ill . . . but there's no need to justify myself! I'm not going there again, and I assure you I take no interest in them whatever," he concluded resolutely.

"Really, really?" cried Pavel Pavlovitch, not disguising his relief and excitement.

Velchaninov looked at him contemptuously, and began pacing up and down the room again.

"You seem to have made up your mind to be happy?" he could not refrain from observing.

"Yes," Pavel Pavlovitch repeated naïvely, in a low voice.

"What is it to me," Velchaninov reflected, "that he's a buffoon and only spiteful through stupidity? I can't help hating him, though he isn't worth it!"

"I am 'the eternal husband'!" said Pavel Pavlovitch, with an abjectly submissive smile at his own expense. "I heard that expression from you, Alexey Ivanovitch, long ago, when you were staying with us in those days. I remember a great many of your sayings in that year. Last time, when you said here, 'the eternal husband,' I reflected."

Mavra came in with a bottle of champagne and two glasses.

"Forgive me, Alexey Ivanovitch; you know that I can't get on without it! Don't think it's impudence; look upon me as an outsider not on your level."

"Yes . . ." Velchaninov muttered with repugnance, "but I assure you I feel unwell. . . ."

"Directly . . . directly . . . in one minute," said Pavel Pavlovitch fussily; "just one little glass because my throat . . ."

He greedily tossed off a glassful at a gulp and sat down, looking almost tenderly at Velchaninov.

Mavra went out.

"How beastly!" Velchaninov murmured.

"It's only those girl friends," Pavel Pavlovitch said confidently, all of a sudden completely revived.

"What? Ah, yes, you are still at that. . . ."

"It's only those girl friends! And then she's so young; we have our little airs and graces! They're charming, in fact. But then— then, you know, I shall be her slave; when she's treated with defer- ence, when she sees something of society . . . she'll be trans- formed."

"I shall have to give him back that bracelet, though," thought Velchaninov, scowling, as he felt the case in his pocket.

"You say that I'm resolved to be happy? I must get married, Alexey Ivanovitch," Pavel Pavlovitch went on confidentially and almost touchingly, "or what will become of me? You see for your- self!" He pointed to the bottle. "And that's only one-hundredth of my vices. I can't get on at all without marriage and—without new faith; I shall have faith and shall rise up again."

"But why on earth do you tell me this?" Velchaninov asked, almost bursting with laughter. It all struck him as wild. "But tell me," he cried, "what was your object in dragging me out there? What did you want me there for?"

"As a test . . ." Pavel Pavlovitch seemed suddenly embarrassed.

"A test of what?"

"The effect. . . . You see, Alexey Ivanovitch, it's only a week altogether . . . I've been looking round there." (Pavel Pavlovitch grew more and more confused.) "Yesterday I met you and thought: 'I've never yet seen her in outside, so to say, society, that is, in men's, except my own. . . .' A stupid idea; I feel that myself now; unnecessary. I expected too much . . . it's my horrible char- acter. . . ."

He suddenly raised his head and flushed crimson.

"Can he be telling the whole truth?" Velchaninov was petrified with surprise.

"Well, and what then?" he asked.

Pavel Pavlovitch gave a sugary and, as it were, crafty smile.

"It's only charming childishness! It's all those girl friends! Only forgive me for my stupid behavior before you today, Alexey

Ivanovitch; I never will again; and indeed it will never happen again."

"And I shan't be there again," said Velchaninov, with a smile.

"That's partly what I mean."

Velchaninov felt a little piqued.

"But I'm not the only man in the world, you know," he observed irritably.

Pavel Pavlovitch flushed again.

"It's sad for me to hear that, Alexey Ivanovitch, and, believe me, I've such a respect for Nadyezhda Fedosyevna . . ."

"Excuse me, excuse me, I didn't mean anything; it only seems a little strange to me that you have such an exaggerated idea of my attractions . . . and . . . such genuine confidence in me."

"I had such confidence just because it was after all . . . that happened in the past."

"Then if so, you look upon me even now as a most honorable man?" said Velchaninov, suddenly halting.

At another time he would have been horrified at the naïveté of his own question.

"I always thought you so," said Pavel Pavlovitch, dropping his eyes.

"Why, of course. . . . I didn't mean that; that is, not in that sense. I only meant to say that, in spite of any . . . preconceptions . . ."

"Yes, in spite of preconceptions."

"When you came to Petersburg?" Velchaninov could not resist asking, though he felt how utterly monstrous was his curiosity.

"When I came to Petersburg, too, I looked upon you as the most honorable of men. I always respected you, Alexey Ivanovitch."

Pavel Pavlovitch raised his eyes and looked candidly, without a trace of embarrassment, at his opponent. Velchaninov was suddenly panic-stricken; he was not at all anxious that anything should happen, or that anything should overstep a certain line, especially as he had provoked it.

"I loved you, Alexey Ivanovitch," Pavel Pavlovitch articulated, as though he had suddenly made up his mind to speak, "and all that year at T—— I loved you. You did not notice it," he went on, in a voice that quivered, to Velchaninov's positive horror; "I was too insignificant, compared with you, to let you see it. And there was no need, indeed, perhaps. And I've thought of you all these nine years, because there has never been another year in my life like that one." (Pavel Pavlovitch's eyes began to glisten.) "I remembered many of your phrases and sayings, your thoughts. I always thought of you as a man with a passion for every noble feeling, a man of education, of the highest education and of ideas: 'Great ideas spring not so much from noble intelligence as from noble feeling.' You said that yourself; perhaps you've forgotten it, but I remembered it. I always looked on you, therefore, as a man of noble feeling . . . and therefore believed in you—in spite of anything . . ."

His chin suddenly began quivering. Velchaninov was in absolute terror; this unexpected tone must be cut short at all costs.

"That's enough, Pavel Pavlovitch, please," he muttered, flushing and irritably impatient. "And why," he screamed suddenly, "why do you fasten upon a man when he is nervous and ill, when he is almost delirious, and drag him into this darkness . . . when it's . . . when it's—nothing but delusion, mirage, and falsity, and shameful, and unnatural, and—exaggerated—and that's what's worst, that's what's most shameful—that it is so exaggerated! And it's all nonsense; we are both vicious, underground, loathsome people. . . . And if you like I'll prove that you don't like me at all, but hate me with all your might, and that you're lying, though you don't know it; you insisted on taking me there, not with the absurd object of testing your future bride (what an idea!); you saw me yesterday and felt *vindictive*, and took me there to show me and say to me, 'See what a prize! She will be mine; do your worst now!' You challenged me, perhaps you didn't know it yourself; that's how it was, for that's what you were feeling . . . and without hating me you couldn't have challenged me like that; and so you hate me!"

He rushed about the room as he shouted this. What harassed

and mortified him most of all was the humiliating consciousness that he was demeaning himself so far to Pavel Pavlovitch.

"I wanted to be reconciled with you, Alexey Ivanovitch!" the other articulated suddenly, in a rapid whisper, and his chin began twitching again.

Velchaninov was overcome by furious rage, as though no one had ever insulted him so much.

"I tell you again," he yelled, "that you're fastening upon a man who's nervous and ill . . . that you're fastening upon him to extort something monstrous from him in delirium! We . . . we are men of different worlds, understand that, and . . . and . . . between us lies a grave!" he added in a furious whisper, and suddenly realized what he had done. . . .

"And how do you know"— Pavel Pavlovitch's face was suddenly pale and distorted—"how do you know what that little grave here means . . . for me!" he cried, stepping up to Velchaninov with a ridiculous but horrible gesture, pressed his fist against his heart. "I know that little grave here, and we both stand at the side of that little grave, but on my side there is more than on yours, more . . ." he whispered as though in delirium, still thumping at his heart with his fist, "more, more, more . . ."

Suddenly an extraordinarily loud ring at the door brought both of them to their senses. The bell rang so violently that it seemed as though some one had vowed to break it at the first pull.

"People don't ring like that to see me," said Velchaninov in perplexity.

"Nor to see me either," Pavel Pavlovitch whispered timidly, recovering himself too, and at once turning into the old Pavel Pavlovitch again.

Velchaninov scowled and went to open the door.

"M. Velchaninov, if I'm not mistaken?" they heard in a ringing, youthful, and exceptionally self-confident voice in the passage.

"What is it?"

"I have trustworthy information," continued the ringing voice, "that a certain Trusotsky is with you at this moment. I must see him instantly."

It would certainly have pleased Velchaninov at that moment to have given the self-confident young gentleman a vigorous kick and to have sent him flying out on the stairs; but he thought a moment, moved aside and let him in.

"Here is M. Trusotsky; come in. . . ."

14 SASHENKA AND NADENKA

THERE walked into the room a very young man, of about nine-teen, perhaps even less—to judge from the youthfulness of his handsome, self-confident, upturned face. He was fairly well dressed, or at any rate his clothes looked well on him; in height he was a little above the average; the black hair that hung in thick locks about his head, and the big, bold, dark eyes were particularly con-spicuous in his face. Except that his nose was rather broad and turned up, he was a handsome fellow. He walked in solemnly.

"I believe I have the opportunity of conversing with M. Trusotsky," he pronounced in a measured tone, emphasizing with peculiar relish the word "opportunity"—giving him to understand thereby that he did not consider it either an "honor" or a "pleas-ure" to converse with M. Trusotsky.

Velchaninov began to grasp the position; something seemed to be dawning on Pavel Pavlovitch too. There was a look of uneasiness in his face; but he stood his ground.

"Not having the honor of your acquaintance," he answered majestically, "I imagine that you cannot have business of any sort with me."

"You had better hear me first and then give your opinion," the young man admonished him self-confidently, and, taking out a tor-toiseshell lorgnette hanging on a cord, he examined through it the bottle of champagne standing on the table. When he had calmly completed his scrutiny of the bottle, he folded up the lorgnette and turned to Pavel Pavlovitch again.

"Alexandr Lobov."

"What do you mean by Alexandr Lobov?"

"That's me. Haven't you heard of me?"

"No."

"How should you, though? I've come on important business that chiefly concerns you. Allow me to sit down; I'm tired."

"Sit down," Velchaninov urged him; but the young man succeeded in sitting down before being invited to do so.

In spite of the increasing pain in his chest Velchaninov was interested in this impudent youth. In his pretty, childlike and rosy face, he fancied a remote resemblance to Nadya.

"You sit down too," the lad suggested to Pavel Pavlovitch, motioning him with a careless nod of the head to a seat opposite.

"Don't trouble; I'll stand."

"You'll be tired. You needn't go away, M. Velchaninov, if you like to stay."

"I've nowhere to go; I'm at home."

"As you please. I must confess I should prefer you to be present while I have an explanation with this gentleman. Nadyezhda Fedosyevna gave me rather a flattering account of you."

"Bah! When had she time to do that?"

"Why, just now after you left; I've just come from there, too. I've something to tell you, M. Trusotsky." He turned round to Pavel Pavlovitch, who was standing. "We—that is, Nadyezhda Fedosyevna and I," he went on, letting his words drop one by one as he lolled carelessly in the arm-chair; "we've cared for each other for ever so long, and have given each other our promise. You are in our way now; I've come to suggest that you should clear out. Will it suit you to act on my suggestion?"

Pavel Pavlovitch positively reeled; he turned pale, but a diabolical smile came on to his lips at once.

"No, it won't suit me at all," he rapped out laconically.

"You don't say so!" The young man turned round in the arm-chair and crossed one leg over the other.

"I don't know who it is I'm speaking to," added Pavel Pavlovitch. "I believe, indeed, that there's no object in continuing our conversation."

Uttering this, he too thought fit to sit down.

"I told you you would be tired," the youth observed casually. "I told you just now that my name is Alexandr Lobov, and that Nadyezhda and I are pledged to one another; consequently you can't say, as you did just now, that you don't know who it is you have to deal with; you can't imagine, either, that I have nothing more to say to you; putting myself aside, it concerns Nadyezhda Fedosyevna, whom you persist in pestering so insolently. And that alone is sufficient reason for an explanation."

All this he let drop, word by word, through his closed lips, with the air of a coxcomb who did not deign to articulate his words; he even drew out his lorgnette again and turned it upon something while he was talking.

"Excuse me, young man!" Pavel Pavlovitch exclaimed irritably; but the young man instantly snubbed him.

"At any other time I should certainly forbid your calling me 'young man,' but now you will admit that my youth is my chief advantage over you, and that you would have been jolly glad, this morning, for instance, when you presented your bracelet, to be a tiny bit younger."

"Ah, you sprat!" murmured Velchaninov.

"In any case, sir," Pavel Pavlovitch corrected himself with dignity, "I do not consider the reasons you have advanced—most unseemly and dubious reasons—sufficient to continue discussing them. I see that this is all a foolish and childish business. Tomorrow I'll make inquiries of my highly respected friend, Fedosey Semyonovitch; and now I beg you to retire."

"Do you see the sort of man he is?" the youth cried at once, unable to sustain his previous tone, and turning hotly to Velchaninov. "It's not enough for him that they've put out their tongues at him today and kicked him out—he'll go tomorrow to tell tales of us to the old man! Won't you prove by that, you obstinate man, that you want to take the girl by force, that you want to buy her of people in their dotage who in our barbarous state of society retain authority over her? I should have thought it would have been enough for you that she's shown you how she despises you; why, she gave you back your indecent present today, your bracelet. What more do you want?"

"No one has returned me a bracelet, and it's utterly out of the question!" Pavel Pavlovitch said, startled.

"Out of the question? Do you mean to say M. Velchaninov has not given it you?"

"Damnation take you!" thought Velchaninov. "Nadyezhda Fedosyevna did commission me," he said, frowning, "to give you this case, Pavel Pavlovitch. I refused to take it, but she begged me . . . here it is . . . I'm annoyed. . . ."

He took out the case and, much embarrassed, laid it before Pavel Pavlovitch, who was struck dumb.

"Why didn't you give to it him before?" said the young gentleman, addressing Velchaninov severely.

"As you see, I hadn't managed to do so yet," the latter replied, frowning.

"That's queer."

"Wha-a-at?"

"You must admit it's queer, anyway. Though I am ready to allow there may be a misunderstanding."

Velchaninov felt a great inclination to get up at once and pull the saucy urchin's ears, but he could not refrain from bursting out laughing in his face; the boy promptly laughed too. It was very different with Pavel Pavlovitch; if Velchaninov could have observed the terrible look he turned upon him when Velchaninov was laughing at Lobov, he would have realized that at that instant the man was passing through a momentous crisis. . . . But though Velchaninov did not see that glance, he felt that he must stand by Pavel Pavlovitch.

"Listen, M. Lobov," he began in a friendly tone; "without entering into discussion of other reasons upon which I don't care to touch, I would only point out to you that, in paying his addresses to Nadyezhda Fedosyevna, Pavel Pavlovitch can in any case boast of certain qualifications: in the first place, the fact that everything about him is known to that estimable family; in the second place, his excellent and highly respectable position; finally, his fortune, and consequently he must naturally be surprised at the sight of a rival like you—a man, perhaps, of great merit, but so exceedingly young that he can hardly take you for a serious suitor . . . and so he is justified in asking you to retire."

"What do you mean by 'exceedingly young'? I was nineteen last month. By law I could have been married long ago. That's all I can say."

"But what father could bring himself to give you his daughter now—even if you were to be a millionaire in the future or some benefactor of mankind? At nineteen a man cannot even answer for himself, and you are ready to take the responsibility of another person's future, that is, the future of another child like yourself! Why, do you think it's quite honorable? I have ventured to speak frankly to you because you appealed to me just now as an intermediary between you and Pavel Pavlovitch."

"Ah, to be sure, his name's Pavel Pavlovitch!" observed the boy; "how is it I kept fancying that he was Vassily Petrovitch? Well," he went on, addressing Velchaninov, "you haven't surprised me in the least; I knew you were all like that! It's odd, though, that they talked of you as a man rather new in a way. But that's all nonsense, though; far from there being anything dishonorable on my part, as you so freely expressed it, it's the very opposite, as I hope to make you see: to begin with, we've pledged our word to each other, and, what's more, I've promised her, before two witnesses, that if she ever falls in love with some one else, or simply regrets having married me and wants to separate, I will at once give her a formal declaration of my infidelity —and so will support her petition for divorce. What's more, in case I should later on go back upon my word and refuse to give her that declaration, I will give her as security on our wedding-day an I O U for a hundred thousand roubles, so that if I should be perverse about the declaration she can at once change my I O U and me into the bargain! In that way everything will be secured and I shouldn't be risking anybody's future. That's the first point."

"I bet that fellow— What's-his-name?—Predposylov invented that for you!" cried Velchaninov.

"He, he, he!" chuckled Pavel Pavlovitch viciously.

"What's that gentleman sniggering about? You guessed right, it was Predposylov's idea; and you must admit it was a shrewd one. The absurd law is completely paralyzed by it. Of course, I intend to love her for ever, and she laughs tremendously; at the same time it's ingenious, and you must admit that it's honorable, and that it's not every man who would consent to do it."

"To my thinking, so far from being honorable, it's positively disgusting."

The young man shrugged his shoulders.

"Again you don't surprise me," he observed, after a brief silence. "I have given up being surprised at that sort of thing long ago. Predposylov would tell you flatly that your lack of comprehension of the most natural things is due to the corruption of your most ordinary feelings and ideas by a long life spent idly and absurdly. But possibly we don't understand one another; they spoke well of you anyway . . . you're fifty, I suppose, aren't you?"

"Kindly keep to the point."

"Excuse my indiscretion and don't be annoyed, I didn't mean anything. I will continue: I'm by no means a future millionaire, as you expressed it (and what an idea!); I have nothing but what I stand up in, but I have complete confidence in my future. I shan't be a hero or a benefactor of mankind either, but I shall keep myself and my wife. Of course, I've nothing now; I was brought up in their house, you see, from childhood. . . ."

"How was that?"

"Well, you see, I'm the son of a distant relation of Zahlebinin's wife, and when all my people died and left me at eight years old, the old man took me in and afterwards sent me to the high school. He's really a good-natured man, if you care to know. . . ."

"I know that."

"Yes; a bit antiquated in his ideas, but kind-hearted. It's a long time now, of course, since I was under his guardianship; I want to earn my own living, and to owe no one anything."

"How long have you been independent?" Velchaninov inquired.

"Why, four months."

"Oh, well, one can understand it then: you've been friends from childhood! Well, have you a situation, then?"

"Yes, a private situation, in a notary's office, for twenty-five roubles a month. Of course, only for the time, but when I made my offer I hadn't even that. I was serving on the railway then for ten roubles a month, but only for the time."

"Do you mean to say you've made an offer of marriage?"

"Yes, a formal offer, and ever so long ago—over three weeks."

"Well, and what happened?"

"The old man laughed awfully at first, and then was awfully angry, and locked her up upstairs. But Nadya held out heroically. But that was all because he was a bit crusty with me before, for throwing up the berth in his department which he had got me into four months ago, before I went to the railway. He's a capital old chap, I tell you again, simple and jolly at home, but you can't fancy what he's like as soon as he's in his office! He's like a Jove enthroned! I naturally let him know that I was not attracted by his manners there, but the chief trouble was through the head clerk's assistant: that gentleman took it into his head that I had been 'rude' to him, and all that I said to him was that he was undeveloped. I threw them all up, and now I'm at a notary's."

"And did you get much in the department?"

"Oh, I was not on the regular staff! The old man used to give me an allowance too; I tell you he's a good sort, but we shan't give in, all the same. Of course, twenty-five roubles is not enough to support a wife, but I hope soon to have a share in the management of Count Zavileysky's neglected estates, and then to rise to three thousand straight off, or else I shall become a lawyer. People are always going to law nowadays. . . . Bah! What a clap of thunder! There'll be a storm; it's a good thing I managed to get here before it; I came on foot, I ran almost all the way."

"But, excuse me, if so, when did you manage to talk things over with Nadyezhda Fedosyevna, especially if they refuse you admittance?"

"Why, one can talk over the fence! Did you notice that red-haired girl?" he laughed. "She's very active on our side, and Marie

Nikititchna too; ah, she's a serpent, that Marie Nikititchna! . . .
Why do you wince? Are you afraid of the thunder?"

"No, I'm unwell, very unwell. . . ."

Velchaninov, in positive agony from the pain in his chest, got
up and tried to walk about the room.

"Oh, then, of course, I'm in your way. . . . Don't be uneasy, I'm
just going!"

And the youth jumped up from his seat.

"You're not in the way; it's no matter," said Velchaninov courteously.

"How can it be no matter? 'When Kobylnikov had a stomach-
ache' . . . do you remember in Shtchedrin? Are you fond of
Shtchedrin?"

"Yes."

"So am I. Well, Vassily . . . oh, hang it, Pavel Pavlovitch, let's
finish!" He turned, almost laughing, to Pavel Pavlovitch. "I will
once more for your comprehension formulate the question: do
you consent to make a formal withdrawal of all pretensions in
regard to Nadyezhda Fedosyevna to the old people to-morrow,
in my presence?"

"I certainly do not." Pavel Pavlovitch, too, got up from his seat
with an impatient and exasperated air. "And I beg you once more
to spare me . . . for all this is childish and silly."

"You had better look out." The youth held up a warning finger
with a supercilious smile. "Don't make a mistake in your calcu-
lations! Do you know what such a mistake leads to? I warn you
that in nine months' time, when you have had all your expense
and trouble, and you come back here, you'll be forced to give up
Nadyezhda Fedosyevna, or if you don't give her up it will be the
worse for you; that's what will be the end of it! I must warn you
that you're like the dog in the manger—excuse me, it's only a
comparison—getting nothing yourself and preventing others. From
motives of humanity I tell you again: reflect upon it, force yourself for once in your life to reflect rationally."

"I beg you to spare me your sermonizing!" cried Pavel Pavlovitch furiously; "and as for your nasty insinuations, I shall take measures to-morrow, severe measures!"

"Nasty insinuations? What do you mean by that? You're nasty yourself, if that's what you've got in your head. However, I agree to wait till to-morrow, but if . . . Ah, thunder again! Good-bye; very glad to make your acquaintance"—he nodded to Velchaninov and ran off, apparently in haste to get back before the storm and not to get caught in the rain.

15 THE ACCOUNT IS SETTLED

"Y o u see? You see?" Pavel Pavlovitch skipped up to Velchaninov as soon as the youth had departed.

"Yes; you've no luck!" said Velchaninov carelessly.

He would not have said those words had he not been tortured and exasperated by the pain in his chest, which was growing more and more acute.

"It was because you felt for me, you didn't give me back the bracelet, wasn't it?"

"I hadn't time. . . ."

"You felt for me from your heart, like a true friend?"

"Oh yes, I felt for you," said Velchaninov, in exasperation.

He told him briefly, however, how the bracelet had been returned to him, and how Nadyezhda Fedosyevna had almost forced him to assist in returning it. . . .

"You understand that nothing else would have induced me to take it; I've had unpleasantness enough apart from that!"

"You were fascinated and took it?" sniggered Pavel Pavlovitch.

"That's stupid on your part; however, I must excuse you. You saw for yourself just now that I'm not the leading person, that there are others in this affair."

"At the same time you were fascinated."

Pavel Pavlovitch sat down and filled up his glass.

"Do you imagine I'd give way to that wretched boy? I'll make mincemeat of him, so there! I'll go over tomorrow and polish him off. We'll smoke out that spirit from the nursery."

He emptied his glass almost at a gulp and filled it again; he began, in fact, to behave in an unusually free and easy way.

"Ah, Nadenka and Sashenka, the sweet little darlings, he-he-he!"

He was beside himself with anger. There came another louder clap of thunder, followed by a blinding flash of lightning, and the rain began streaming in bucketfuls. Pavel Pavlovitch got up and closed the open window.

"He asked you whether you were afraid of the thunder, he-he. Velchaninov afraid of thunder! Kobylnikov—what was it— Kobylnikov . . . and what about being fifty too—eh? Do you remember?" Pavel Pavlovitch sneered diabolically.

"You've established yourself here, it seems!" observed Velchaninov, hardly able to articulate the words for the pain in his chest. "I'll lie down, you can do what you like."

"Why, you couldn't turn a dog out in weather like this!" Pavel Pavlovitch retorted in an aggrieved tone, seeming almost pleased, however, at having an excuse for feeling aggrieved.

"All right, sit down, drink . . . stay the night, if you like!" muttered Velchaninov. He stretched himself on the sofa and uttered a faint groan.

"Stay the night? And you won't be afraid?"

"What of?" said Velchaninov, suddenly raising his head.

"Oh, nothing. Last time you were so frightened, or was it my fancy?"

"You're stupid!" Velchaninov could not help saying. He turned his head to the wall angrily.

"All right," responded Pavel Pavlovitch.

The sick man fell asleep suddenly, a minute after lying down. The unnatural strain upon him that day in the shattered state of his health had brought on a sudden crisis, and he was as weak as a child. But the pain asserted itself again and got the upper hand of sleep and weariness; an hour later he woke up and painfully got up from the sofa. The storm had subsided; the room was full of tobacco smoke, on the table stood an empty bottle, and Pavel Pavlovitch was asleep on another sofa. He was lying on his back,

with his head on the sofa cushion, fully dressed and with his boots
on. His lorgnette had slipped out of his pocket and was hanging
down almost to the floor. His hat was lying on the ground beside
it. Velchaninov looked at him morosely and did not attempt to
wake him. Writhing with pain and pacing about the room, for he
could no longer bear to lie down, he moaned and brooded over
his agonies.

He was afraid of that pain in his chest, and not without reason.
He had been liable to these attacks for a very long time, but they
had only occurred at intervals of a year or two. He knew that they
came from the liver. At first a dull, not acute, but irritating feeling of oppression, was, as it were, concentrated at some point in
the chest, under the shoulder-blade or higher up. Continually increasing, sometimes for ten hours at a stretch, the pain at last
would reach such a pitch, the oppression would become so insup-
portable, that the sufferer began to have visions of dying. On his
last attack, a year before, he was, when the pain ceased after ten
hours of suffering, so weak that he could scarcely move his hands
as he lay in bed, and the doctor had allowed him to take nothing
for the whole day but a few teaspoonfuls of weak tea and of bread
soaked in broth, like a tiny baby. The attacks were brought on by
different things, but never occurred except when his nerves were
out of order. It was strange, too, how the attack passed off; sometimes it was possible to arrest it at the very beginning, during the
first half-hour, by simple compresses, and it would pass away completely at once; sometimes, as on his last attack, nothing was of
any use, and the pain only subsided after numerous and continually recurring paroxysms of vomiting. The doctor confessed
afterwards that he believed it to be a case of poisoning. It was a
long time to wait till morning, and he didn't want to send for the
doctor at night; besides, he didn't like doctors. At last he could
not control himself and began moaning aloud. His groans waked
Pavel Pavlovitch; he sat up on the sofa, and for some time listened
with alarm and bewilderment, watching Velchaninov, who was
almost running backwards and forwards through the two rooms.
The bottle of champagne had had a great effect upon him, evidently more than usual, and it was some time before he could

collect himself. At last he grasped the position and rushed to Velchaninov, who mumbled something in reply to him.

"It's the liver, I know it!" cried Pavel Pavlovitch, becoming extremely animated all at once. "Pyotr Kuzmitch Polosuhin used to suffer just the same from liver. You ought to have compresses. Pyotr Kuzmitch always had compresses. . . . One may die of it! Shall I run for Mavra?"

"No need, no need!" Velchaninov waved him off irritably. "I want nothing."

But Pavel Pavlovitch, goodness knows why, seemed beside himself, as though it were a question of saving his own son. Without heeding Velchaninov's protests, he insisted on the necessity of compresses and also of two or three cups of weak tea to be drunk on the spot, "and not simply hot, but boiling!" He ran to Mavra, without waiting for permission, with her laid a fire in the kitchen, which always stood empty, and blew up the samovar; at the same time he succeeded in getting the sick man to bed, took off his clothes, wrapped him up in a quilt, and within twenty minutes had prepared tea and compresses.

"This is a hot plate, scalding hot!" he said, almost ecstatically, applying the heated plate, wrapped up in a napkin, on Velchaninov's aching chest. "There are no other compresses, and plates, I swear on my honor, will be even better: they were laid on Pyotr Kuzmitch, I saw it with my own eyes, and did it with my own hands. One may die of it, you know. Drink your tea, swallow it; never mind about scalding yourself; life is too precious . . . for one to be squeamish."

He quite flustered Mavra, who was half asleep; the plates were changed every three or four minutes. After the third plate and the second cup of tea, swallowed at a gulp, Velchaninov felt a sudden relief.

"If once they've shifted the pain, thank God, it's a good sign!" cried Pavel Pavlovitch, and he ran joyfully to fetch a fresh plate and a fresh cup of tea.

"If only we can ease the pain. If only we can keep it under!" he kept repeating.

Half an hour later the pain was much less, but the sick man was so exhausted that in spite of Pavel Pavlovitch's entreaties he refused to "put up with just one more nice little plate." He was so weak that everything was dark before his eyes.

"Sleep, sleep," he repeated in a faint voice.

"To be sure," Pavel Pavlovitch assented.

"You'll stay the night. . . . What time is it?"

"It's nearly two o'clock, it's a quarter to."

"You'll stay the night."

"I will, I will."

A minute later the sick man called Pavel Pavlovitch again.

"You, you," he muttered, when the latter had run up and was bending over him; "you are better than I am! I understand it all, all. . . . Thank you."

"Sleep, sleep," whispered Pavel Pavlovitch, and he hastened on tiptoe to his sofa.

As he fell asleep the invalid heard Pavel Pavlovitch noiselessly making up a bed for himself and taking off his clothes. Finally, putting out the candle, and almost holding his breath for fear of waking the patient, he stretched himself on his sofa.

There is no doubt that Velchaninov did sleep and that he fell asleep very soon after the candle was put out; he remembered this clearly afterwards. But all the time he was asleep, up to the very moment that he woke up, he dreamed that he was not asleep, and that in spite of his exhaustion he could not get to sleep. At last he began to dream that he was in a sort of waking delirium, and that he could not drive away the phantoms that crowded about him, although he was fully conscious that it was only delirium and not reality. The phantoms were all familiar figures; his room seemed to be full of people; and the door into the passage stood open; people were coming in in crowds and thronging the stairs. At the table, which was set in the middle of the room, there was sitting one man—exactly as in the similar dream he had had a month before. Just as in that dream, this man sat with his elbows on the table and would not speak; but this time he was wearing a round hat with crape on it. "What! could it have been Pavel

Pavlovitch that time too?" Velchaninov thought, but, glancing at the face of the silent man, he convinced himself that it was someone quite different. "Why has he got crape on?" Velchaninov wondered. The noise, the talking and the shouting of the people crowding round the table, was awful. These people seemed to be even more intensely exasperated against Velchaninov than in the previous dream; they shook their fists at him, and shouted something to him with all their might, but what it was exactly he could not make out. "But it's delirium, of course, I know it's delirium!" he thought; "I know I couldn't get to sleep and that I've got up now, because it made me too wretched to go on lying down. . . ." But the shouts, the people, their gestures were so lifelike, so real, that sometimes he was seized by doubt: "Can this be really delirium? Good heavens! What do these people want of me? But . . . if it were not an hallucination, would it be possible that such a clamor should not have waked Pavel Pavlovitch all this time? There he is asleep on the sofa!" At last something suddenly happened again, just as in that other dream; all of them made a rush for the stairs and they were closely packed in the doorway, for there was another crowd forcing its way into the room. These people were bringing something in with them, something big and heavy; he could hear how heavily the steps of those carrying it sounded on the stairs and how hurriedly their panting voices called to one another. All the people in the room shouted: "They're bringing it, they're bringing it"—all eyes were flashing and fixed on Velchaninov; all of them pointed towards the stairs, menacing and triumphant. Feeling no further doubt that it was reality and not hallucination, he stood on tiptoe so as to peep over the people's heads and find out as soon as possible what they were bringing up the stairs. His heart was beating, beating, beating, and suddenly, exactly as in that first dream, he heard three violent rings at the bell. And again it was so distinct, so real, so unmistakable a ring at the bell, that it could not be only a dream. . . .

But he did not rush to the door as he had done on awaking then. What idea guided his first movement and whether he had any idea at the moment it is impossible to say, but someone seemed to prompt him what he must do: he leapt out of bed and, with his hands stretched out before him as though to defend himself and ward off an attack, rushed straight towards the place where Pavel Pavlovitch was asleep. His hands instantly came into contact with other hands, stretched out above him, and he clutched them tight; so, someone already stood bending over him. The curtains were drawn, but it was not quite dark, for a faint light came from the other room where there were no such curtains. Suddenly, with an acute pain, something cut the palm and fingers of his left hand, and he instantly realized that he had clutched the blade of a knife or razor and was grasping it tight in his hand. . . . And at the same moment something fell heavily on the floor with a thud.

Velchaninov was perhaps three times as strong as Pavel Pavlovitch, yet the struggle between them lasted a long while, fully three minutes. He soon got him down on the floor and bent his arms back behind him, but for some reason he felt he must tie his hands behind him. Holding the murderer with his wounded left hand, he began with his right fumbling for the cord of the window curtain and for a long time could not find it, but at last got hold of it and tore it from the window. He wondered himself afterwards at the immense effort required to do this. During those three minutes neither of them uttered a word; nothing was audible but their heavy breathing and the muffled sounds of their struggling. Having at last twisted Pavel Pavlovitch's arms behind him and tied them together, Velchaninov left him on the floor, got up, drew the curtain from the window and pulled up the blind. It was already light in the deserted street. Opening the window, he stood for some moments drawing in deep breaths of fresh air. It was a little past four. Shutting the window, he went hurriedly to the cupboard, took out a clean towel and bound it tightly round his left hand to stop the bleeding. At his feet an open razor was lying on the carpet; he picked it up, shut it, put it in the razor-case, which had been left forgotten since the morning on the little table beside Pavel Pavlovitch's sofa, and locked it up in his bureau. And, only when he had done all that, he went up to Pavel Pavlovitch and began to examine him.

Meantime, the latter had with an effort got up from the floor, and seated himself in an arm-chair. He had nothing on but his shirt, not even his boots. The back and the sleeves of his shirt were soaked with blood; but the blood was not his own, it came from Velchaninov's wounded hand. Of course it was Pavel Pavlovitch, but anyone meeting him by chance might almost have failed to recognize him at the minute, so changed was his whole appearance. He was sitting awkwardly upright in the arm-chair, owing to his hands being tied behind his back, his face looked distorted, exhausted and greenish, and he quivered all over from time to time. He looked at Velchaninov fixedly, but with lustre-less, unseeing eyes. All at once he smiled vacantly, and, nodding towards a bottle of water that stood on the table, he said in a meek half-whisper—

"Water, I should like some water."

Velchaninov filled a glass and began holding it for him to drink. Pavel Pavlovitch bent down greedily to the water; after three gulps he raised his head and looked intently into the face of Velchaninov, who was standing beside him with the glass in his hand, but without uttering a word he fell to drinking again. When he had finished he sighed deeply. Velchaninov took his pillow, seized his outer garments and went into the other room, locking Pavel Pavlovitch into the first room.

The pain had passed off completely, but he was conscious of extreme weakness again after the momentary effort in which he had displayed an unaccountable strength. He tried to reflect upon what had happened, but his thoughts were hardly coherent, the shock had been too great. Sometimes there was a dimness before his eyes lasting for ten minutes or so, then he would start, wake up, recollect everything, remember his smarting hand bound up in a blood-stained towel, and would fall to thinking greedily, fever-ishly. He came to one distinct conclusion—that is, that Pavel Pavlovitch certainly had meant to cut his throat, but that perhaps only a quarter of an hour before had not known that he would do it. The razor-case had perhaps merely caught his eye the evening before, and, without arousing any thought of it at the time, had remained in his memory. (The razors were always locked up in

the bureau, and only the morning before, Velchaninov had taken
them out to shave round his moustache and whiskers, as he sometimes did.)

"If he had long been intending to murder me he would have got
a knife or pistol ready; he would not have reckoned on my razor,
which he had never seen till yesterday evening," was one reflection he made among others.

It struck six o'clock at last; Velchaninov roused himself, dressed,
and went in to Pavel Pavlovitch. Opening the door, he could not
understand why he had locked Pavel Pavlovitch in, instead of
turning him out of the house. To his surprise, the criminal was
fully dressed; most likely he had found some way of untying his
hands. He was sitting in the arm-chair, but got up at once when
Velchaninov went in. His hat was already in his hand. His uneasy
eyes seemed in haste to say—

"Don't begin talking; it's no use beginning; there's no need to
talk."

"Go," said Velchaninov. "Take your bracelet," he added, calling
after him.

Pavel Pavlovitch turned back from the door, took the case with
the bracelet from the table, put it in his pocket and went out on
the stairs. Velchaninov stood at the door to lock it behind him.
Their eyes met for the last time; Pavel Pavlovitch stopped suddenly, for five seconds the two looked into each other's eyes—as
though hesitating; finally Velchaninov waved his hand faintly.

"Well, go!" he said in a low voice, and locked the door.

16 ANALYSIS

A FEELING of immense, extraordinary relief took possession of
him; something was over, was settled; an awful weight of depression had vanished and was dissipated for ever. So it seemed to
him. It had lasted for five weeks. He raised his hand, looked at the
towel soaked with blood and muttered to himself: "Yes, now

everything is absolutely at an end!" And all that morning, for the first time in three weeks, he scarcely thought of Liza—as though that blood from his cut fingers could "settle his account" even with that misery.

He recognized clearly that he had escaped a terrible danger. "These people," he thought, "just these people who don't know a minute beforehand whether they'll murder a man or not—as soon as they take a knife in their trembling hands and feel the hot spurt of blood on their fingers don't stick at cutting your throat, but cut off your head, 'clean off,' as convicts express it. That is so."

He could not remain at home and went out into the street, feeling convinced that he must do something, or something would happen to him at once; he walked about the streets and waited. He had an intense longing to meet someone, to talk to someone, even to a stranger, and it was only that which led him at last to think of a doctor and of the necessity of binding up his hand properly. The doctor, an old acquaintance of his, examined the wound, and inquired with interest how it could have happened. Velchaninov laughed and was on the point of telling him all about it, but restrained himself. The doctor was obliged to feel his pulse and, hearing of his attack the night before, persuaded him to take some soothing medicine he had at hand. He was reassuring about the cuts: "They could have no particularly disagreeable results." Velchaninov laughed and began to assure him that they had already had the most agreeable results. An almost irresistible desire to tell the whole story came over him twice again during that day, on one occasion to a total stranger with whom he entered into conversation at a tea-shop. He had never been able to endure entering into conversation with strangers in public places before.

He went into a shop to buy a newspaper; he went to his tailor's and ordered a suit. The idea of visiting the Pogoryeltsevs was still distasteful to him, and he did not think of them, and indeed he could not have gone to their villa: he kept expecting something here in the town. He dined with enjoyment, he talked to the waiter and to his fellow-diners, and drank half a bottle of wine. The possibility of the return of his illness of the day before did not occur to him; he was convinced that the illness had passed off completely at the moment when, after falling asleep so exhausted, he had, an hour and a half later, sprung out of bed and thrown his assailant on the floor with such strength. Towards evening he began to feel giddy, and at moments was overcome by something like the delirium he had had in his sleep. It was dusk when he returned home, and he was almost afraid of his room when he went into it. It seemed dreadful and uncanny in his flat. He walked up and down it several times, and even went into his kitchen, where he had scarcely ever been before. "Here they were heating plates yesterday," he thought. He locked the door securely and lighted the candles earlier than usual. As he locked the door he remembered, half an hour before, passing the porter's lodge, he had called Mavra and asked her whether Pavel Pavlovitch had come in his absence, as though he could possibly have come.

After locking himself in carefully, he opened the bureau, took out the razor-case and opened the razor to look at it again. On the white bone handle there were still faint traces of blood. He put the razor back in the case and locked it up in the bureau again. He felt sleepy; he felt that he must go to bed at once—or "he would not be fit for tomorrow." He pictured the next day for some reason as a momentous and "decisive" day.

But the same thoughts that had haunted him all day in the street kept incessantly and persistently crowding and jostling in his sick brain, and he kept thinking, thinking, thinking, and for a long time could not get to sleep. . . .

"If it is settled that he tried to murder me *accidentally*," he went on pondering, "had the idea ever entered his head before, if only as a dream in a vindictive moment?"

He decided that question strangely—that "Pavel Pavlovitch did want to kill him, but the thought of the murder had never entered his head." In short: "Pavel Pavlovitch wanted to kill him, but didn't know he wanted to kill him. It's senseless, but that's the truth," thought Velchaninov. "It was not to get a post and it was not on Bagautov's account he came here, though he did try to get a post here, and did run to see Bagautov and was furious when he died; he thought no more of him than a chip. He came here on my account and he came here with Liza . . .

"And did I expect that he . . . would murder me?" He decided that he did, that he had expected it from the moment when he saw him in the carriage following Bagautov's funeral. "I began, as it were, to expect something . . . but, of course, not that; but, of course, not that he would murder me! . . .

"And can it be that all that was true?" he exclaimed again, suddenly raising his head from the pillow and opening his eyes. "All that that . . . madman told me yesterday about his love for me, when his chin quivered and he thumped himself on the breast with his fist?

"It was the absolute truth," he decided, still pondering and analyzing, "that Quasimodo from T—— was quite sufficiently stupid and noble to fall in love with the lover of his wife, about whom he noticed nothing suspicious in twenty years! He had been thinking of me with respect, cherishing my memory and brooding over my utterances for nine years. Good heavens! and I had no notion of it! He could not have been lying yesterday! But did he love me yesterday when he declared his feeling and said 'Let us settle our account'? Yes, it was from hatred that he loved me; that's the strongest of all loves . . .

"Of course it may have happened, of course it must have happened that I made a tremendous impression on him at T——. Tremendous and 'gratifying' is just what it was, and it's just with a Schiller like that, in the outer form of a Quasimodo, that such a thing could happen! He magnified me a hundredfold because I impressed him too much in his philosophic solitude. . . . It would be interesting to know by what I impressed him. Perhaps by my clean gloves and my knowing how to put them on. Quasimodos are fond of all that is aesthetic. Ough! aren't they fond of it! A glove is often quite enough for a noble heart, and especially one of these 'eternal husbands.' The rest they supply themselves a thousand times, and are ready to fight for you, to satisfy your slightest wish. What an opinion he had of my powers of fascination! Perhaps it was just my powers of fascination that made the most impression on him. And his cry then, 'If that one, too . . . whom can one trust!' After that cry one may well become a wild beast! . . .

"H'm! He comes here 'to embrace me and to weep,' as he expressed it in the most abject way—that is, he came here to murder me and thought he came 'to embrace me and to weep.' . . . He brought Liza too. But, who knows? if I had wept with him, perhaps, really, he would have forgiven me, for he had a terrible longing to forgive me! . . . At the first shock all that was changed into drunken antics and caricature, and into loathsome, womanish whining over his wrongs. (Those horns! those horns he made on his forehead!) He came drunk on purpose to speak out, though he was playing the fool; if he had not been drunk, even he could not have done it. . . . And how he liked playing the fool, didn't he like it! Ough! wasn't he pleased, too, when he made me kiss him! Only he didn't know then whether he would end by embracing me or murdering me. Of course, it's turned out that the best thing was to do both. A most natural solution! Yes indeed, nature dislikes monstrosities and destroys them with natural solutions. The most monstrous monster is the monster with noble feelings; I know that by personal experience, Pavel Pavlovitch! Nature is not a tender mother, but a stepmother to the monster. Nature gives birth to the deformed, but instead of pitying him she punishes him, and with good reason. Even decent people have to pay for embraces and tears of forgiveness nowadays, to say nothing of men like you and me, Pavel Pavlovitch!

"Yes, he was stupid enough to take me to see his future bride. Good heavens! His future bride! Only a Quasimodo like that could have conceived the notion of 'rising again to a new life' by means of the innocence of Mademoiselle Zahlebinin! But it was not your fault, Pavel Pavlovitch, it was not your fault: you're a monster, so everything about you is bound to be monstrous, your dreams and your hopes. But, though he was a monster, he had doubts of his dream, and that was why he needed the high sanction of

Velchaninov whom he so revered. He wanted Velchaninov to approve, he wanted him to reassure him that the dream was not a dream, but something real. He took me there from a devout respect for me and faith in the nobility of my feelings, believing, perhaps, that there, under a bush, we should embrace and shed tears near all that youthful innocence. Yes! That 'eternal husband' was obliged, sooner or later, to punish himself for everything, and to punish himself he snatched up the razor—by accident, it is true, still he did snatch it up! 'And yet he struck him with a knife, and yet he ended by stabbing him in the presence of the Governor.' And, by the way, had he any idea of that sort in his mind when he told me that anecdote about the best man? And was there really anything that night when he got out of bed and stood in the middle of the room? H'm! . . . No, he stood there then *as a joke*. He got up for other reasons, and when he saw that I was frightened of him he did not answer me for ten minutes because he was very much pleased that I was frightened of him. . . . It was at that moment, perhaps, when he stood there in the dark, that some idea of this sort first dawned upon him. . . .

"Yet if I had not forgotten that razor on the table yesterday—maybe nothing would have happened. Is that so? Is that so? To be sure he had been avoiding me before—why, he had not been to see me for a fortnight; he had been hiding from me to *spare* me! Of course, he picked out Bagautov first, not me! Why, he rushed to heat plates for me in the night, thinking to create a diversion—from the knife to pity and tenderness! . . . He wanted to save himself and me, too—with his hot plates! . . ."

And for a long time the sick brain of this "man of the world" went on working in this way, going round and round in a circle, till he grew calmer. He woke up next morning with the same headache, but with a quite *new* and quite unexpected terror in his heart.

This new terror came from the positive conviction, which suddenly grew strong within him, that he, Velchaninov (a man of the world), would end it all that day by going of his own free will to Pavel Pavlovitch. Why? What for? He had no idea and, with repugnance, refused to know; all that he knew was that, for some reason, he would go to him.

This madness, however—he could give it no other name—did, as it developed, take a rational form and fasten upon a fairly legitimate pretext: he had even, the day before, been haunted by the idea that Pavel Pavlovitch would go back to his lodging and hang himself, like the clerk about whom Marya Sysoevna had told him. This notion of the day before had passed by degrees into an unreasoning but persistent conviction. "Why should the fool hang himself?" he kept protesting to himself every half-minute. He remembered Liza's words . . . "Yet in his place, perhaps, I should hang myself" . . . he reflected once.

It ended by his turning towards Pavel Pavlovitch instead of going to dinner. "I shall simply inquire of Marya Sysoevna," he decided. But before he had come out into the street he stopped short in the gateway. "Can it be, can it be?" he cried, turning crimson with shame. "Can it be that I'm crawling there, to 'embrace and shed tears'? That senseless abjectness was all that was needed to complete the ignominy!"

But from that "senseless abjectness" he was saved by the providence that watches over all decent and well-bred people. He had no sooner stepped into the street when he stumbled upon Alexandr Lobov. The young man was in breathless haste and excitement.

"I was coming to see you! What do you think of our friend Pavel Pavlovitch, now?"

"He's hanged himself!" Velchaninov muttered wildly.

"Who's hanged himself? What for?" cried Lobov, with wide-open eyes.

"Never mind . . . I didn't mean anything; go on."

"Tfoo! damn it all! what funny ideas you have, though. He's not hanged himself at all (why should he hang himself?). On the contrary—he's gone away. I've only just put him into the train and seen him off. Tfoo! how he drinks, I tell you! We drank three bottles, Predposylov with us—but how he drinks, how he drinks! He was singing songs in the train. He remembered you, blew kisses, sent you his greetings. But he is a scoundrel, don't you think so?"

The young man certainly was a little tipsy; his flushed face, his shining eyes and faltering tongue betrayed it unmistakably.

Velchaninov laughed loudly.

"So in the end they finished up with Bruderschaft; Ha-ha! They embraced and shed tears! Ah, you Schilleresque poets!"

"Don't call me names, please. Do you know he's given it all up over *there*? He was there yesterday, and he's been there today. He sneaked horribly. They locked Nadya up—she's sitting in a room upstairs. There were tears and lamentations, but we stood firm! But how he does drink, I say, doesn't he drink! And, I say, isn't he *mauvais ton*, at least not *mauvais ton* exactly, what shall I call it? . . . He kept talking of you, but there's no comparison between you! You're a gentleman anyway, and really did move in decent society at one time and have only been forced to come down now through poverty or something. . . . Goodness knows what, I couldn't quite understand him."

"Ah, so he spoke to you of me in those terms?"

"He did, he did; don't be angry. To be a good citizen is better than being in aristocratic society. I say that because in Russia nowadays one doesn't know whom to respect. You'll agree that it's a serious malady of the age, when people don't know whom to respect, isn't it?"

"It is, it is; what did he say?"

"He? Who? Ah, to be sure! Why did he keep saying 'Velchaninov fifty, but a rake,' why *but* a rake and not *and* a rake; he laughed and repeated it a thousand times over. He got into the train, sang a song and burst out crying—it was simply revolting, pitiful, in fact—from drunkenness. Oh! I don't like fools! He fell to throwing money to the beggars for the peace of the soul of Lizaveta—his wife, is that?"

"His daughter."

"What's the matter with your hand?"

"I cut it."

"Never mind, it will get better. Damn him, you know, it's a

good thing he's gone, but I bet anything that he'll get married directly he arrives—he will—won't he?"

"Why, but you want to get married, too, don't you?"

"Me? That's a different matter. What a man you are, really! If you are fifty, he must be sixty: you must look at it logically, my dear sir! And do you know I used, long ago, to be a pure Slavophil by conviction, but now we look for dawn from the West. . . . But, good-bye; I'm glad I met you without going in; I won't come in, don't ask me, I've no time to spare! . . ."

And he was just running off.

"Oh, by the way," he cried, turning back; "why, he sent me to you with a letter! Here is the letter. Why didn't you come to see him off?"

Velchaninov returned home and opened the envelope addressed to him.

There was not one line from Pavel Pavlovitch in it, but there was a different letter Velchaninov recognized the handwriting. It was an old letter, written on paper yellow with age, with ink that had changed color. It had been written to him ten years before, two months after he had left T—— and returned to Petersburg. But the letter had never reached him; he had received a different one instead of it; this was clear from the contents of this old yellow letter. In this letter Natalya Vassilyevna took leave of him for ever, and confessed that she loved someone else, just as in the letter he had actually received; but she also did not conceal from him that she was going to have a child. On the contrary, to comfort him, she held out hopes that she might find a possibility of handing over the future child to him, declared henceforth that they had other duties—in short, there was little logic, but the object was clear: that he should no longer trouble her with his love. She even sanctioned his coming to T—— in a year's time to have a look at the child. God knows why she changed her mind and sent the other letter instead.

Velchaninov was pale as he read it, but he pictured to himself Pavel Pavlovitch finding that letter and reading it for the first time, before the opened ebony box inlaid with mother-of-pearl which was an heirloom in the family.

"He, too, must have turned pale as a corpse," he thought, catching a glimpse of his own face in the looking-glass. "He must have read it and closed his eyes, and opened them again hoping that the letter would have changed into plain white paper. . . . Most likely he had done that a second time and a third! . . ."

17 THE ETERNAL HUSBAND

ALMOST exactly two years had passed since the incidents we have described. We meet Velchaninov again on a beautiful summer day, in the train on one of our newly opened railways. He was going to Odessa for his own pleasure, to see one of his friends, and also with a view to something else of an agreeable nature. He hoped through that friend to arrange a meeting with an extremely interesting woman whose acquaintance he had long been eager to make. Without going into details we will confine ourselves to observing that he had become entirely transformed, or rather reformed, during those two years. Of his old hypochondria scarcely a trace remained. Of the various "reminiscences" and anxiety—the result of illness which had beset him two years before in Petersburg at the time of his successful lawsuit—nothing remained but a certain secret shame at the consciousness of his faint-heartedness. What partly made up for it was the conviction that it would never happen again, and that no one would ever know of it. It was true that at that time he had given up all society, had even begun to be slovenly in his dress, had crept away out of sight of everyone—and that, of course, must have been noticed by all. But he so readily acknowledged his transgressions, and at the same time with such a self-confident air of new life and vigor, that "everyone" immediately forgave his momentary falling away; in fact, those whom he had given up greeting were the first to recognize him and hold out their hands, and without any tiresome questions—just as though he had been absent on his own personal affairs, which were no business of theirs, and had only just come back from a distance. The cause of all these salutary changes for the better was, of course, the winning of his lawsuit. Velchaninov gained in all sixty thousand roubles—no great sum, of course, but of extreme importance to him; to begin with, he felt himself on firm ground again, and so he felt satisfied at heart; he knew for certain now that he would not, "like a fool," squander this money, as he had squandered his first two fortunes, and that he had enough for his whole life. "However the social edifice may totter, whatever trumpet call they're sounding," he thought sometimes, as he watched and heard all the marvellous and incredible things that were being done around him and all over Russia; "whatever shape people and ideas may take, I shall always have just such a delicate, dainty dinner as I am sitting down to now, and so I'm ready to face anything." This voluptuous, comfortable thought by degrees gained complete possession of him and produced a transformation in his physical, to say nothing of his moral, nature. He looked quite a different man from the "sluggard" whom we have described two years before and to whom such unseemly incidents had befallen—he looked cheerful, serene and dignified. Even the ill-humored wrinkles that had begun to appear under his eyes and on his forehead had almost been smoothed away; the very tint of his face had changed, his skin was whiter and ruddier.

At the moment he was sitting comfortably in a first-class carriage and a charming idea was suggesting itself to his mind. The next station was a junction and there was a new branch line going off to the right. He asked himself, "How would it be to give up the direct way for the moment and turn off to the right?" There, only two stations away, he could visit another lady of his acquaintance who had only just returned from abroad, and was now living in a provincial isolation, very tedious for her, but favorable for him; and so it would be possible to spend his time no less agreeably than at Odessa, especially as he would not miss his visit there either. But he was still hesitating and could not quite make up his mind; he was waiting for something to decide him. Meanwhile, the station was approaching and that something was not far off.

At this station the train stopped forty minutes, and the passengers had the chance of having dinner. At the entrance to the dining-room for the passengers of the first and second class there was, as there usually is, a crowd of impatient and hurried people, and as is also usual, perhaps, a scandalous scene took place. A lady from a second-class carriage, who was remarkably pretty but somewhat too gorgeously dressed for travelling, was dragging after her an Uhlan, a very young and handsome officer, who was trying to tear himself out of her hands. The youthful officer was extremely drunk, and the lady, to all appearance some elder relative, would not let him go, probably apprehending that he would make a dash for the refreshment bar. Meanwhile, in the crush, the Uhlan was jostled by a young merchant who was also disgracefully intoxicated. He had been hanging about the station for the last two days, drinking and scattering his money among the companions who surrounded him, without succeeding in getting into the train to continue his journey. A scuffle followed; the officer shouted; the merchant swore; the lady was in despair, and, trying to draw the Uhlan away from the conflict, kept exclaiming in an imploring voice, "Mitenka! Mitenka!" This seemed to strike the young merchant as too scandalous; every one laughed, indeed, but the merchant was more offended than ever at the outrage, as he conceived it, on propriety.

"Oh, I say: Mitenka!" he pronounced reproachfully, mimicking the shrill voice of the lady. "And not ashamed before folks!"

He went staggering up to the lady, who had rushed to the first chair and succeeded in making the Uhlan sit down beside her, stared at them both contemptuously and drawled in a sing-song voice—

"You're a trollop, you are, dragging your tail in the dirt!"

The lady uttered a shriek and looked about her piteously for some means of escape. She was both ashamed and frightened, and, to put the finishing touch, the officer sprang up from the chair and, with a yell, made a dash at the merchant, but, slipping, fell back into the chair with a flop. The laughter grew louder around them, and no one dreamed of helping her; but Velchaninov came to the rescue; he seized the merchant by the collar and, turning him round, thrust him five paces away from the frightened lady. And with that the scene ended; the merchant was overwhelmed by the shock and by Velchaninov's impressive figure; his companions led him away. The dignified countenance of the elegantly dressed gentleman produced a strong effect on the jeering crowd: the laughter subsided. The lady flushed and, almost in tears, was overflowing with expressions of gratitude. The Uhlan mumbled: "Fanks, fanks!" and made as though to hold out his hand to Velchaninov, but instead of doing so suddenly took it into his head to recline at full length with his feet on the chairs.

"Mitenka!" the lady moaned reproachfully, clasping her hands in horror.

Velchaninov was pleased with the adventure and with the whole situation. The lady attracted him; she was evidently a wealthy provincial, gorgeously but tastelessly dressed, and with rather ridiculous manners—in fact, she combined all the characteristics that guarantee success to a Petersburg gallant with designs on the fair sex. A conversation sprang up; the lady bitterly complained of her husband, who "had disappeared as soon as he had got out of the carriage and so was the cause of it all, for whenever he is wanted he runs off somewhere."

"Naturally," the Uhlan muttered.

"Ah, Mitenka!" She clasped her hand again.

"Well, the husband will catch it," thought Velchaninov.

"What is his name? I will go and look for him," he suggested.

"Pal Palitch," responded the Uhlan.

"Your husband's name is Pavel Pavlovitch?" Velchaninov asked, with curiosity, and suddenly a familiar bald head was thrust between him and the lady. In a flash he had a vision of the Zahlebinins' garden, the innocent games and a tiresome bald head being incessantly thrust between him and Nadyezhda Fedosyevna.

"Here you are at last!" cried his wife hysterically.

It was Pavel Pavlovitch himself; he gazed in wonder and alarm at Velchaninov, as panic-stricken at the sight of him as though he had been a ghost. His stupefaction was such that he evidently could not for some minutes take in what his offended spouse was explaining in a rapid and irritable flow of words. At last, with a start, he grasped all the horror of his position: his own guilt, and Mitenka's behavior, "and that this monsieur" (this was how the lady for some reason described Velchaninov) "has been a savior and guardian angel to us, while you—you are always out of the way when you are wanted. . . ."

Velchaninov suddenly burst out laughing.

"Why, we are friends, we've been friends since childhood!" he exclaimed to the astonished lady. Putting his right arm with patronizing familiarity round the shoulders of Pavel Pavlovitch, who smiled a pale smile, "Hasn't he talked to you of Velchaninov?"

"No, he never has," the lady responded, somewhat disconcerted.

"You might introduce me to your wife, you faithless friend!"

"Lipotchka . . . it really is M. Velchaninov," Pavel Pavlovitch was beginning, but he broke off abashed.

His wife turned crimson and flashed an angry look at him, probably for the "Lipotchka."

"And, only fancy, he never let me know he was married, and never invited me to the wedding, but you, Olimpiada . . ."

"Semyonovna," Pavel Pavlovitch prompted.

"Semyonovna," the Uhlan, who had dropped asleep, echoed suddenly.

"You must forgive him, Olimpiada Semyonovna, for my sake, in honor of our meeting . . . he's a good husband."

And Velchaninov gave Pavel Pavlovitch a friendly slap on the shoulder.

"I was . . . I was only away for a minute, my love," Pavel Pavlovitch was beginning to say.

"And let your wife to be insulted," Lipotchka put in at once. "When you're wanted there's no finding you, when you're not wanted you're always at hand . . ."

"Where you're not wanted, where you're not wanted . . . where you're not wanted . . ." the Uhlan chimed in.

Lipotchka was almost breathless with excitement; she knew it was not seemly before Velchaninov, and flushed but could not restrain herself.

"Where you shouldn't be you are too attentive, too attentive!" she burst out.

"Under the bed . . . he looks for a lover under the bed—where he shouldn't . . . where he shouldn't . . ." muttered Mitenka, suddenly growing extremely excited.

But there was no doing anything with Mitenka by now. It all ended pleasantly, however, and they got upon quite friendly terms. Pavel Pavlovitch was sent to fetch coffee and soup. Olimpiada Semyonovna explained to Velchaninov that they were on their way from O——, where her husband had a post in the service, to spend two months at their country place, that it was not far off, only thirty miles from the station, that they had a lovely house and garden there, that they always had the house full of visitors, that they had neighbors too, and if Alexey Ivanovitch would be so good as to come and stay with them "in their rustic solitude" she would welcome him "as their guardian angel," for she could not recall without horror what would have happened, if . . . and so on, and so on—in fact, he was "her guardian angel. . . ."

"And savior, and savior," the Uhlan insisted, with heat.

Velchaninov thanked her politely, and replied that he was always at her service, that he was an absolutely idle man with no duties of any sort, and that Olimpiada Semyonovna's invitation was most flattering. He followed this at once with sprightly conversation, successfully introducing two or three compliments. Lipotchka blushed with pleasure, and as soon as Pavel Pavlovitch returned she told him enthusiastically that Alexey Ivanovitch had been so kind as to accept her invitation to spend a whole month with them in the country, and had promised to come in a week. Pavel Pavlovitch smiled in mute despair. Olimpiada Semyonovna shrugged her shoulders at him, and turned her eyes up to the ceiling. At last they got up; again a gush of gratitude, again the "guardian angel," again "Mitenka," and Pavel Pavlovitch at last escorted his wife and the Uhlan to their compartment. Velchaninov lighted a cigar and began pacing to and fro on the balcony in front of the station; he knew that Pavel Pavlovitch would run out again at once to talk to him till the bell rang. And so it happened. Pavel Pavlovitch promptly appeared before him with an uneasy expression in his face and whole figure. Velchaninov laughed, took him by the elbow in a friendly way, led him to the nearest bench, sat down himself, and made him sit down beside him. He remained silent; he wanted Pavel Pavlovitch to be the first to speak.

"So you are coming to us?" faltered the latter, going straight to the point.

"I knew that would be it! You haven't changed in the least!" laughed Velchaninov. "Why, do you mean to say"—he slapped him again on the shoulder—"do you mean to say you could seriously imagine for a moment that I could actually come and stay with you, and for a whole month too—ha-ha?"

Pavel Pavlovitch was all of a twitter.

"So you—are not coming!" he cried, not in the least disguising his relief.

"I'm not coming, I'm not coming!" Velchaninov laughed complacently.

He could not have said himself, however, why he felt so particularly amused, but he was more and more amused as time went on.

"Do you really . . . do you really mean it?"

And saying this, Pavel Pavlovitch actually jumped up from his seat in a flutter of suspense.

"Yes, I've told you already that I'm not coming, you queer fellow."

"If that's so, what am I to say to Olimpiada Semyonovna a week hence, when she will be expecting you and you don't come?"

"What a difficulty! Tell her I've broken my leg or something of that sort."

"She won't believe it," Pavel Pavlovitch drawled plaintively.

"And you'll catch it?" Velchaninov went on laughing. "But I observe, my poor friend, that you tremble before your delightful wife—don't you?"

Pavel Pavlovitch tried to smile, but it did not come off. That Velchaninov had refused to visit them was a good thing, of course, but that he should be over-familiar to him about his wife was disagreeable. Pavel Pavlovitch winced; Velchaninov noticed it. Meanwhile the second bell rang; they heard a shrill voice from the train anxiously calling Pavel Pavlovitch. The latter moved, fidgeted in his chair, but did not rise at the first summons, evidently expecting something more from Velchaninov, no doubt another assurance that he would not come and stay with them.

"What was your wife's maiden name?" Velchaninov inquired, as though unaware of Pavel Pavlovitch's anxiety.

"She is our priest's daughter," replied the latter in uneasy trepidation, listening and looking towards the train.

"Ah, I understand, you married her for her beauty."

Pavel Pavlovitch winced again.

"And who's this Mitenka with you?"

"Oh, he's a distant relation of ours—that is, of mine; the son of my deceased cousin. His name's Golubtchikov, he was degraded for disorderly behavior in the army, but now he has been promoted again and we have been getting his equipment. . . . He's an unfortunate young man. . . ."

"To be sure, the regular thing; the party's complete," thought Velchaninov.

"Pavel Pavlovitch!" the call came again from the train, and by now with a marked tone of irritation in the voice.

"Pal Palitch!" they heard in another thick voice.

Pavel Pavlovitch fidgeted and moved restlessly again, but Velchaninov took him by the elbow and detained him.

"How would you like me to go this minute and tell your wife how you tried to cut my throat?"

"What, what!" Pavel Pavlovitch was terribly alarmed. "God forbid!"

"Pavel Pavlovitch! Pavel Pavlovitch!" voices were heard calling again.

"Well, be off now!" said Velchaninov, letting him go at last, and still laughing genially.

"So you won't come?" Pavel Pavlovitch whispered for the last time, almost in despair, and even put his hands before him with the palms together in his old style.

"Why, I swear I won't come! Run, there'll be trouble, you know."

And with a flourish he held out his hand to him—and was startled at the result: Pavel Pavlovitch did not take his hand, he even drew his own hand back.

The third bell rang.

In one instant something strange happened to both of them: both seemed transformed. Something, as it were, quivered and burst out in Velchaninov, who had been laughing only just before. He clutched Pavel Pavlovitch by the shoulder and held him in a tight and furious grip.

"If I—I hold out this hand to you," showing the palm of his left hand, where a big scar from the cut was still distinct, "you certainly might take it!" he whispered, with pale and trembling lips.

Pavel Pavlovitch, too, turned pale, and his lips trembled too; a convulsive quiver ran over his face.

"And Liza?" he murmured in a rapid whisper, and suddenly his lips, his cheeks and his chin began to twitch and tears gushed from his eyes.

Velchaninov stood before him stupefied.

"Pavel Pavlovitch! Pavel Pavlovitch!" they heard a scream from the train as though someone were being murdered—and suddenly the whistle sounded.

Pavel Pavlovitch roused himself, flung up his hands and ran full speed to the train; the train was already in motion, but he managed to hang on somehow, and went flying to his compartment. Velchaninov remained at the station and only in the evening set off on his original route in another train. He did not turn off to the right to see his fair friend—he felt too much out of humor. And how he regretted it afterwards!

1870 A.D.

CHEKHOV *Ward No. 6*

1

In the hospital yard there stands a small lodge surrounded by a perfect forest of burdocks, nettles, and wild hemp. Its roof is rusty, the chimney is tumbling down, the steps at the front-door are rotting away and overgrown with grass, and there are only traces left of the stucco. The front of the lodge faces the hospital; at the back it looks out into the open country, from which it is separated by the grey hospital fence with nails on it. These nails, with their points upwards, and the fence, and the lodge itself, have that peculiar, desolate, God-for-saken look which is only found in our hospital and prison buildings.

If you are not afraid of being stung by the nettles, come by the narrow footpath that leads to the lodge, and let us see what is going on inside. Opening the first door, we walk into the entry. Here along the walls and by the stove every sort of hospital rubbish lies littered about. Mattresses, old tattered dressing-gowns, trousers, blue striped shirts, boots and shoes no good for anything—all these remnants are piled up in heaps, mixed up and crumpled, moldering and giving out a sickly smell.

The porter, Nikita, an old soldier wearing rusty good-conduct stripes, is always lying on the litter with a pipe between his teeth. He has a grim, surly, battered-looking face, overhanging eyebrows which give him the expression of a sheep-dog of the steppes, and a red nose; he is short and looks thin and scraggy, but he is of imposing deportment and his fists are vigorous. He belongs to the class of simple-hearted, practical, and dull-witted people, prompt in carrying out orders, who like discipline better than anything in the world, and so are convinced that it is their duty to beat people. He showers blows on the face, on the chest, on the back, on whatever comes first, and is convinced that there would be no order in the place if he did not.

Next you come into a big, spacious room which fills up the whole lodge except for the entry. Here the walls are painted a dirty blue, the ceiling is as sooty as in a hut without a chimney—it is evident that in the winter the stove smokes and the room is full of fumes. The windows are disfigured by iron gratings on the inside. The wooden floor is grey and full of splinters. There is a stench of sour cabbage, of smoldering wicks, of bugs, and of ammonia, and for the first minute this stench gives you the impression of having walked into a menagerie. . . .

There are bedsteads screwed to the floor. Men in blue hospital dressing-gowns, and wearing nightcaps in the old style, are sitting and lying on them. These are the lunatics.

There are five of them in all here. Only one is of the upper class, the rest are all artisans. The one nearest the door—a tall, lean workman with shining red whiskers and tear-stained eyes—sits with his head propped on his hand, staring at the same point. Day and night he grieves, shaking his head, sighing and smiling bitterly. He rarely takes a part in conversation and usually makes no answer to questions; he eats and drinks mechanically when food is offered him. From his agonizing, throbbing cough, his thinness, and the flush on his cheeks, one may judge that he is in the first stage of consumption. Next him is a little, alert, very lively old man, with a pointed beard and curly black hair like a negro's. By day he walks up and down the ward from window to window, or sits on his bed, cross-legged like a Turk, and, ceaselessly as a bullfinch whistles, softly sings and titters. He shows his childish gaiety and lively character at night also when he gets up to say his prayers—that is, to beat himself on the chest with his fists, and to scratch with his fingers at the door. This is the Jew Moiseika, an imbecile, who went crazy twenty years ago when his hat factory was burnt down.

And of all the inhabitants of Ward No. 6, he is the only one who is allowed to go out of the lodge, and even out of the yard into the street. He has enjoyed this privilege for years, probably because he is an old inhabitant of the hospital—a quiet, harmless imbecile, the buffoon of the town, where people are used to seeing him surrounded by boys and dogs. In his wretched gown, in his absurd nightcap, and in slippers, sometimes with bare legs and even without trousers, he walks about the streets, stopping at the gates and little shops, and begging for a copper. In one place they will give him some kvass, in another some bread, in another a copper, so that he generally goes back to the ward feeling rich and well fed. Everything that he brings back Nikita takes from him for his own benefit. The soldier does this roughly, angrily, turning the Jew's pockets inside out, and calling God to witness that he will not let him go into the street again, and that breach of the regulations is worse to him than anything in the world.

Moiseika likes to make himself useful. He gives his companions water, and covers them up when they are asleep; he promises each of them to bring him back a kopeck, and to make him a new cap; he feeds with a spoon his neighbor on the left, who is paralyzed. He acts in this way, not from compassion nor from any considerations of a humane kind, but through imitation, unconsciously dominated by Gromov, his neighbor on the right hand.

Ivan Dmitritch Gromov, a man of thirty-three, who is a gentleman by birth, and has been a court usher and provincial secretary, suffers from the mania of persecution. He either lies curled up in bed, or walks from corner to corner as though for exercise; he very rarely sits down. He is always excited, agitated, and overwrought by a sort of vague, undefined expectation. The faintest rustle in the entry or shout in the yard is enough to make him raise his head and begin listening: whether they are coming for him, whether they are looking for him. And at such times his face expresses the utmost uneasiness and repulsion.

I like his broad face with its high cheek-bones, always pale and unhappy, and reflecting, as though in a mirror, a soul tormented by conflict and long-continued terror. His grimaces are strange and abnormal, but the delicate lines traced on his face by profound, genuine suffering show intelligence and sense, and there is a warm and healthy light in his eyes. I like the man himself, courteous, anxious to be of use, and extraordinarily gentle to everyone except Nikita. When anyone drops a button or a spoon, he jumps up from his bed quickly and picks it up; every day he says good-morning to his companions, and when he goes to bed he wishes them good-night.

Besides his continually overwrought condition and his grimaces, his madness shows itself in the following way also. Sometimes in the evenings he wraps himself in his dressing-gown, and, trembling all over, with his teeth chattering, begins walking rapidly from corner to corner and between the bedsteads. It seems as though he is in a violent fever. From the way he suddenly stops and glances at his companions, it can be seen that he is longing to say something very important, but, apparently reflecting that they would not listen, or would not understand him, he shakes his head impatiently and goes on pacing up and down. But soon the desire to speak gets the upper hand of every consideration, and he will let himself go and speak fervently and passionately. His talk is disordered and feverish like delirium, disconnected, and not always intelligible, but, on the other hand, something extremely fine may be felt in it, both in the words and the voice. When he talks you recognize in him the lunatic and the man. It is difficult to reproduce on paper his insane talk. He speaks of the baseness of mankind, of violence trampling on justice, of the glorious life which will one day be upon earth, of the window-gratings, which remind him every minute of the stupidity and cruelty of oppressors. It makes a disorderly, incoherent potpourri of themes old but not yet out of date.

2

SOME twelve or fifteen years ago an official called Gromov, a highly respectable and prosperous person, was living in his own house in the principal street of the town. He had two sons, Sergey and Ivan. When Sergey was a student in his fourth year he was taken ill with galloping consumption and died, and his death was, as it were, the first of a whole series of calamities which suddenly showered on the Gromov family. Within a week of Sergey's funeral the old father was put on his trial for fraud and misappropriation, and he died of typhoid in the prison hospital soon afterwards. The house, with all their belongings, was sold by auction, and Ivan Dmitritch and his mother were left entirely without means.

Hitherto in his father's lifetime, Ivan Dmitritch, who was studying in the University of Petersburg, had received an allowance of sixty or seventy roubles a month, and had had no conception of poverty; now he had to make an abrupt change in his life. He had to spend his time from morning to night giving lessons for next to nothing, to work at copying, and with all that to go hungry, as all his earnings were sent to keep his mother. Ivan Dmitritch could not stand such a life; he lost heart and strength, and, giving up the university, went home.

Here, through interest, he obtained the post of teacher in the district school, but could not get on with his colleagues, was not liked by the boys, and soon gave up the post. His mother died. He was for six months without work, living on nothing but bread and water; then he became a court usher. He kept this post until he was dismissed owing to his illness.

He had never even in his young student days given the impression of being perfectly healthy. He had always been pale, thin, and given to catching cold; he ate little and slept badly. A single glass of wine went to his head and made him hysterical. He always had a craving for society, but, owing to his irritable temperament and suspiciousness, he never became very intimate with anyone, and had no friends. He always spoke with contempt of his fellow-townsmen, saying that their coarse ignorance and sleepy animal existence seemed to him loathsome and horrible. He spoke in a loud tenor, with heat, and invariably either with scorn and indignation, or with wonder and enthusiasm, and always with perfect sincerity. Whatever one talked to him about he always brought it round to the same subject: that life was dull and stifling in the town; that the townspeople had no lofty interests, but lived a dingy, meaningless life, diversified by violence, coarse profligacy, and hypocrisy; that scoundrels were well fed and clothed, while honest men lived from hand to mouth; that they needed schools, a progressive local paper, a theatre, public lectures, the co-ordination of the intellectual elements; that society must see its failings and be horrified. In his criticisms of people he laid on the colors thick, using only black and white, and no fine shades; mankind was divided for him into honest men and scoundrels: there was nothing in between. He always spoke with passion and enthusiasm of women and of love, but he had never been in love.

In spite of the severity of his judgments and his nervousness, he was liked, and behind his back was spoken of affectionately as Vanya. His innate refinement and readiness to be of service, his good breeding, his moral purity, and his shabby coat, his frail appearance and family misfortunes, aroused a kind, warm, sorrowful feeling. Moreover, he was well educated and well read; according to the townspeople's notions, he knew everything, and was in their eyes something like a walking encyclopedia.

He had read a great deal. He would sit at the club, nervously pulling at his beard and looking through the magazines and books; and from his face one could see that he was not reading, but devouring the pages without giving himself time to digest what he read. It must be supposed that reading was one of his morbid habits, as he fell upon anything that came into his hands with equal avidity, even last year's newspapers and calendars. At home he always read lying down.

3

ONE autumn morning Ivan Dmitritch, turning up the collar of
his greatcoat and splashing through the mud, made his way by side-
streets and back lanes to see some artisan, and to collect some payment that was owing. He was in a gloomy mood, as he always was
in the morning. In one of the side-streets he was met by two
convicts in fetters and four soldiers with rifles in charge of them.
Ivan Dmitritch had very often met convicts before, and they had
always excited feelings of compassion and discomfort in him; but
now this meeting made a peculiar, strange impression on him.
It suddenly seemed to him for some reason that he, too, might
be put into fetters and led through the mud to prison like that.
After visiting the artisan, on the way home he met near the post
office a police superintendent of his acquaintance, who greeted
him and walked a few paces along the street with him, and for
some reason this seemed to him suspicious. At home he could not
get the convicts or the soldiers with their rifles out of his head
all day, and an unaccountable inward agitation prevented him
from reading or concentrating his mind. In the evening he did not
light his lamp, and at night he could not sleep, but kept thinking
that he might be arrested, put into fetters, and thrown into prison.
He did not know of any harm he had done, and could be certain
that he would never be guilty of murder, arson, or theft in the
future either; but was it not easy to commit a crime by accident,
unconsciously, and was not false witness always possible, and,
indeed, miscarriage of justice? It was not without good reason that
the agelong experience of the simple people teaches that beggary
and prison are ills none can be safe from. A judicial mistake is
very possible as legal proceedings are conducted nowadays, and
there is nothing to be wondered at in it. People who have an
official, professional relation to other men's sufferings—for instance, judges, police officers, doctors—in course of time, through

habit, grow so callous that they cannot, even if they wish it, take any but a formal attitude to their clients; in this respect they are not different from the peasant who slaughters sheep and calves in the back-yard, and does not notice the blood. With this formal, soulless attitude to human personality the judge needs but one thing—time—in order to deprive an innocent man of all rights of property, and to condemn him to penal servitude. Only the time spent on performing certain formalities for which the judge is paid his salary, and then—it is all over. Then you may look in vain for justice and protection in this dirty, wretched little town a hundred and fifty miles from a railway station! And, indeed, is it not absurd even to think of justice when every kind of violence is accepted by society as a rational and consistent necessity, and every act of mercy—for instance, a verdict of acquittal—calls forth a perfect outburst of dissatisfied and revengeful feeling?

In the morning Ivan Dmitritch got up from his bed in a state of horror, with cold perspiration on his forehead, completely convinced that he might be arrested any minute. Since his gloomy thoughts of yesterday had haunted him so long, he thought, it must be that there was some truth in them. They could not, indeed, have come into his mind without any grounds whatever.

A policeman walking slowly passed by the windows: that was not for nothing. Here were two men standing still and silent near the house. Why were they silent? And agonizing days and nights followed for Ivan Dmitritch. Everyone who passed by the windows or came into the yard seemed to him a spy or a detective. At midday the chief of the police usually drove down the street with a pair of horses; he was going from his estate near the town to the police department; but Ivan Dmitritch fancied every time that he was driving especially quickly, and that he had a peculiar expression: it was evident that he was in haste to announce that there was a very important criminal in the town. Ivan Dmitritch started at every ring at the bell and knock at the gate, and was agitated whenever he came upon anyone new at his landlady's; when he met police officers and gendarmes he smiled and began whistling so as to seem unconcerned. He could not sleep for whole nights in succession expecting to be arrested, but he snored loudly and sighed as though in deep sleep, that his landlady might think he was asleep; for if he could not sleep it meant that he was tormented by the stings of conscience—what a piece of evidence! Facts and common sense persuaded him that all these terrors were nonsense and morbidity, that if one looked at the matter more broadly there was nothing really terrible in arrest and imprisonment—so long as the conscience is at ease; but the more sensibly and logically he reasoned, the more acute and agonizing his mental distress became. It might be compared with the story of a hermit who tried to cut a dwelling-place for himself in a virgin forest; the more zealously he worked with his axe, the thicker the forest grew. In the end Ivan Dmitritch, seeing it was useless, gave up reasoning altogether, and abandoned himself entirely to despair and terror.

He began to avoid people and to seek solitude. His official work had been distasteful to him before: now it became unbearable to him. He was afraid they would somehow get him into trouble, would put a bribe in his pocket unnoticed and then denounce him, or that he would accidentally make a mistake in official papers that would appear to be fraudulent, or would lose other people's money. It is strange that his imagination had never at other times been so agile and inventive as now, when every day he thought of thousands of different reasons for being seriously anxious over his freedom and honor; but, on the other hand, his interest in the outer world, in books in particular, grew sensibly fainter, and his memory began to fail him.

In the spring when the snow melted there were found in the ravine near the cemetery two half-decomposed corpses—the bodies of an old woman and a boy bearing the traces of death by violence. Nothing was talked of but these bodies and their unknown murderers. That people might not think he had been guilty of the crime, Ivan Dmitritch walked about the streets, smiling, and when he met acquaintances he turned pale, flushed, and began declaring that there was no greater crime than the murder of the weak and defenceless. But this duplicity soon exhausted him, and after some reflection he decided that in his position the best thing to do was to hide in his landlady's cellar. He sat in the cellar all day and then all night, then another day, was fearfully cold, and waiting till dusk, stole secretly like a thief back to his room. He stood in the middle of the room till daybreak, listening without stirring. Very early in the morning, before sunrise, some workmen came into the house. Ivan Dmitritch knew perfectly well that they had come to mend the stove in the kitchen, but terror told him that they were police officers disguised as workmen. He slipped stealthily out of the flat, and, overcome by terror, ran along the street without his cap and coat. Dogs raced after him barking, a peasant shouted somewhere behind him, the wind whistled in his ears, and it seemed to Ivan Dmitritch that the force and violence of the whole world was massed together behind his back and was chasing after him.

He was stopped and brought home, and his landlady sent for a doctor. Doctor Andrey Yefimitch, of whom we shall have more to say hereafter, prescribed cold compresses on his head and laurel drops, shook his head, and went away, telling the landlady he should not come again, as one should not interfere with people who are going out of their minds. As he had not the means to live at home and be nursed, Ivan Dmitritch was soon sent to the hospital, and was there put into the ward for venereal patients. He could not sleep at night, was full of whims and fancies, and disturbed the patients, and was soon afterwards, by Andrey Yefimitch's orders, transferred to Ward No. 6.

Within a year Ivan Dmitritch was completely forgotten in the town, and his books, heaped up by his landlady in a sledge in the shed, were pulled to pieces by boys.

4

IVAN DMITRITCH's neighbor on the left hand is, as I have said already, the Jew Moiseika; his neighbor on the right hand is a peasant so rolling in fat that he is almost spherical, with a blankly stupid face, utterly devoid of thought. This is a motionless, gluttonous, unclean animal who has long ago lost all powers of thought or feeling. An acrid, stifling stench always comes from him.

Nikita, who has to clean up after him, beats him terribly with all his might, not sparing his fists; and what is dreadful is not his being beaten—that one can get used to—but the fact that this stupefied creature does not respond to the blows with a sound or a movement, nor by a look in the eyes, but only sways a little like a heavy barrel.

The fifth and last inhabitant of Ward No. 6 is a man of the artisan class who has once been a sorter in the post office, a thinnish, fair little man with a good-natured but rather sly face. To judge from the clear, cheerful look in his calm and intelligent eyes, he has some pleasant idea in his mind, and has some very important and agreeable secret. He has under his pillow and under his mattress something that he never shows anyone, not from fear of its being taken from him and stolen, but from modesty. Sometimes he goes to the window, and turning his back to his companions, puts something on his breast, and bending his head, looks at it; if you go up to him at such a moment, he is overcome with confusion and snatches something off his breast. But it is not difficult to guess his secret.

"Congratulate me," he often says to Ivan Dmitritch; "I have been presented with the Stanislav order of the second degree with the star. The second degree with the star is only given to foreigners, but for some reason they want to make an exception for me," he says with a smile, shrugging his shoulders in perplexity. "That I must confess I did not expect."

"I don't understand anything about that," Ivan Dmitritch replies morosely.

"But do you know what I shall attain to sooner or later?" the former sorter persists, screwing up his eyes slily. "I shall certainly get the Swedish 'Polar Star.' That's an order it is worth working for, a white cross with a black ribbon. It's very beautiful."

Probably in no other place is life so monotonous as in this ward. In the morning the patients, except the paralytic and the fat peasant, wash in the entry at a big tub and wipe themselves with the skirts of their dressing-gowns; after that they drink tea out of tin mugs which Nikita brings them out of the main building. Everyone is allowed one mugful. At midday they have soup made out of sour cabbage and boiled grain, in the evening their supper consists of grain left from dinner. In the intervals they lie down, sleep, look out of window, and walk from one corner to the other. And so every day. Even the former sorter aways talks of the same orders.

Fresh faces are rarely seen in Ward No. 6. The doctor has not taken in any new mental cases for a long time, and the people who are fond of visiting lunatic asylums are few in this world. Once every two months Semyon Lazaritch, the barber, appears in the ward. How he cuts the patients' hair, and how Nikita helps him to do it, and what a trepidation the lunatics are always thrown into by the arrival of the drunken, smiling barber, we will not describe.

No one even looks into the ward except the barber. The patients are condemned to see day after day no one but Nikita.

A rather strange rumor has, however, been circulating in the hospital of late.

It is rumored that the doctor has begun to visit Ward No. 6.

5

A STRANGE rumor!

Dr. Andrey Yefimitch Ragin is a strange man in his way. They say that when he was young he was very religious, and prepared himself for a clerical career, and that when he had finished his studies at the high school in 1863 he intended to enter a theological academy, but that his father, a surgeon and doctor of medicine, jeered at him and declared point-blank that he would disown him if he became a priest. How far this is true I don't know, but Andrey Yefimitch himself has more than once confessed that he has never had a natural bent for medicine or science in general.

However that may have been, when he finished his studies in the medical faculty he did not enter the priesthood. He showed no special devoutness, and was no more like a priest at the beginning of his medical career than he is now.

His exterior is heavy, coarse like a peasant's, his face, his beard, his flat hair, and his coarse, clumsy figure, suggest an overfed, intemperate, and harsh innkeeper on the highroad. His face is surly-looking and covered with blue veins, his eyes are little and his nose is red. With his height and broad shoulders he has huge hands and feet; one would think that a blow from his fist would knock the life out of anyone, but his step is soft, and his walk is cautious and insinuating; when he meets anyone in a narrow passage he is always the first to stop and make way, and to say, not in a bass, as one would expect, but in a high, soft tenor: "I beg your pardon!" He has a little swelling on his neck which prevents him from wearing stiff starched collars, and so he always goes about in soft linen or cotton shirts. Altogether he does not dress like a doctor. He wears the same suit for ten years, and the new clothes, which he usually buys at a Jewish shop, look as shabby and crumpled on him as his old ones; he sees patients and dines and pays visits all in the same coat; but this is not due to niggardliness, but to complete carelessness about his appearance.

When Andrey Yefimitch came to the town to take up his duties the "institution founded to the glory of God" was in a terrible condition. One could hardly breathe for the stench in the wards, in the passages, and in the courtyards of the hospital. The hospital servants, the nurses, and their children slept in the wards together with the patients. They complained that there was no living for beetles, bugs, and mice. The surgical wards were never free from erysipelas. There were only two scalpels and not one thermometer in the whole hospital; potatoes were kept in the baths. The superintendent, the housekeeper, and the medical assistant robbed the patients, and of the old doctor, Andrey Yefimitch's predecessor, people declared that he secretly sold the hospital alcohol, and that he kept a regular harem consisting of nurses and female patients. These disorderly proceedings were perfectly well known in the town, and were even exaggerated, but people took them calmly; some justified them on the ground that there were only peasants and working men in the hospital, who could not be dissatisfied, since they were much worse off at home than in the hospital—they couldn't be fed on woodcocks! Others said in excuse that the town alone, without help from the Zemstvo, was not equal to maintaining a good hospital; thank God for having one at all, even a poor one. And the newly formed Zemstvo did not open infirmaries either in the town or the neighborhood, relying on the fact that the town already had its hospital.

After looking over the hospital Andrey Yefimitch came to the conclusion that it was an immoral institution and extremely prejudicial to the health of the townspeople. In his opinion the most sensible thing that could be done was to let out the patients and close the hospital. But he reflected that his will alone was not enough to do this, and that it would be useless; if physical and moral impurity were driven out of one place, they would only move to another; one must wait for it to wither away of itself. Besides, if people open a hospital and put up with having it, it must be because they need it; superstition and all the nastiness and abominations of daily life were necessary, since in process of time they worked out to something sensible, just as manure turns into black earth. There was nothing on earth so good that it had not something nasty about its first origin.

When Andrey Yefimitch undertook his duties he was apparently not greatly concerned about the irregularities at the hospital. He only asked the attendants and nurses not to sleep in the wards, and had two cupboards of instruments put up; the superintendent, the housekeeper, the medical assistant, and the erysipelas remained unchanged.

Andrey Yefimitch loved intelligence and honesty intensely, but he had no strength of will nor belief in his right to organize an intelligent and honest life about him. He was absolutely unable to give orders, to forbid things, and to insist. It seemed as though he had taken a vow never to raise his voice and never to make use of the imperative. It was difficult for him to say "Fetch" or

"Bring"; when he wanted his meals he would cough hesitatingly and say to the cook: "How about tea? . . ." or "How about dinner? . . ." To dismiss the superintendent or to tell him to leave off stealing, or to abolish the unnecessary parasitic post altogether, was absolutely beyond his powers. When Andrey Yefimitch was deceived or flattered, or accounts he knew to be cooked were brought him to sign, he would turn as red as a crab and feel guilty, but yet he would sign the accounts. When the patients complained to him of being hungry or of the roughness of the nurses, he would be confused and mutter guiltily: "Very well, very well, I will go into it later. . . . Most likely there is some misunderstanding. . . ."

At first Andrey Yefimitch worked very zealously. He saw patients every day from morning till dinner-time, performed operations, and even attended confinements. The ladies said of him that he was attentive and clever at diagnosing diseases, especially those of women and children. But in process of time the work unmistakably wearied him by its monotony and obvious uselessness. To-day one sees thirty patients, and to-morrow they have increased to thirty-five, the next day forty, and so on from day to day, from year to year, while the mortality in the town did not decrease and the patients did not leave off coming. To be any real help to forty patients between morning and dinner was not physically possible, so it could but lead to deception. If twelve thousand patients were seen in a year it meant, if one looked at it simply, that twelve thousand men were deceived. To put those who were seriously ill into wards, and to treat them according to the principles of science, was impossible, too, because though there were principles there was no science; if he were to put aside philosophy and pedantically follow the rules as other doctors did, the things above all necessary were cleanliness and ventilation instead of dirt, wholesome nourishment instead of broth made of stinking, sour cabbage, and good assistants instead of thieves; and, indeed, why hinder people dying if death is the normal and legitimate end of everyone? What is gained if some shopkeeper or clerk lives an extra five or ten years? If the aim of medicine is by drugs to alleviate suffering, the question forces itself on one: why alleviate it? In the first place, they say that suffering leads man to perfection; and in the second, if mankind really learns to alleviate its sufferings with pills and drops, it will completely abandon religion and philosophy, in which it has hitherto found not merely protection from all sorts of trouble, but even happiness. Pushkin suffered terrible agonies before his death, poor Heine lay paralyzed for several years; why, then, should not some Andrey Yefimitch or Matryona Savishna be ill, since their lives had nothing of importance in them, and would have been entirely empty and like the life of an amœba except for suffering?

Oppressed by such reflections, Andrey Yefimitch relaxed his efforts and gave up visiting the hospital every day.

6

H<small>IS</small> life was passed like this. As a rule he got up at eight o'clock in the morning, dressed, and drank his tea. Then he sat down in his study to read, or went to the hospital. At the hospital the out-patients were sitting in the dark, narrow little corridor waiting to be seen by the doctor. The nurses and the attendants, tramping with their boots over the brick floors, ran by them; gaunt-looking patients in dressing-gowns passed; dead bodies and vessels full of filth were carried by; the children were crying, and there was a cold draught. Andrey Yefimitch knew that such surroundings were torture to feverish, consumptive, and impressionable patients; but what could be done? In the consulting-room he was met by his assistant, Sergey Sergeyitch—a fat little man with a plump, well-washed shaven face, with soft, smooth manners, wearing a new loosely cut suit, and looking more like a senator than a medical assistant. He had an immense practice in the town, wore a white tie, and considered himself more proficient than the doctor, who had no practice. In the corner of the consulting-room there stood a huge ikon in a shrine with a heavy lamp in front of it, and near it a candle-stand with a white cover on it. On the walls hung portraits of bishops, a view of the Svyatogorsky Monastery, and

wreaths of dried cornflowers. Sergey Sergeyitch was religious, and
liked solemnity and decorum. The ikon had been put up at his
expense; at his instructions some one of the patients read the
hymns of praise in the consulting-room on Sundays, and after the
reading Sergey Sergeyitch himself went through the wards with a
censer and burned incense.

There were a great many patients, but the time was short, and
so the work was confined to the asking of a few brief questions
and the administration of some drugs, such as castor-oil or volatile
ointment. Andrey Yefimitch would sit with his cheek resting in
his hand, lost in thought and asking questions mechanically.
Sergey Sergeyitch sat down too, rubbing his hands, and from time
to time putting in his word.

"We suffer pain and poverty," he would say, "because we do not
pray to the merciful God as we should. Yes!"

Andrey Yefimitch never performed any operations when he was
seeing patients; he had long ago given up doing so, and the sight
of blood upset him. When he had to open a child's mouth in order
to look at its throat, and the child cried and tried to defend itself
with its little hands, the noise in his ears made his head go round
and brought tears into his eyes. He would make haste to prescribe
a drug, and motion to the woman to take the child away.

He was soon wearied by the timidity of the patients and their
incoherence, by the proximity of the pious Sergey Sergeyitch, by
the portraits on the walls, and by his own questions which he had
asked over and over again for twenty years. And he would go away
after seeing five or six patients. The rest would be seen by his assistant in his absence.

With the agreeable thought that, thank God, he had no private
practice now, and that no one would interrupt him, Andrey
Yefimitch sat down to the table immediately on reaching home
and took up a book. He read a great deal and always with enjoyment. Half his salary went on buying books, and of the six rooms
that made up his abode three were heaped up with books and old
magazines. He liked best of all works on history and philosophy;
the only medical publication to which he subscribed was *The*

Doctor, of which he always read the last pages first. He would always go on reading for several hours without a break and without being weary. He did not read as rapidly and impulsively as Ivan Dmitritch had done in the past, but slowly and with concentration, often pausing over a passage which he liked or did not find intelligible. Near the books there always stood a decanter of vodka, and a salted cucumber or a pickled apple lay beside it, not on a plate, but on the baize table-cloth. Every half-hour he would pour himself out a glass of vodka and drink it without taking his eyes off the book. Then without looking at it he would feel for the cucumber and bite off a bit.

At three o'clock he would go cautiously to the kitchen door, cough, and say: "Daryushka, what about dinner? . . ."

After his dinner—a rather poor and untidily served one—Andrey Yefimitch would walk up and down his rooms with his arms folded, thinking. The clock would strike four, then five, and still he would be walking up and down thinking. Occasionally the kitchen door would creak, and the red and sleepy face of Daryushka would appear.

"Andrey Yefimitch, isn't it time for you to have your beer?" she would ask anxiously.

"No, it is not time yet . . ." he would answer. "I'll wait a little. . . . I'll wait a little. . . ."

Towards the evening the postmaster, Mihail Averyanitch, the only man in the town whose society did not bore Andrey Yefimitch, would come in. Mihail Averyanitch had once been a very rich land-owner, and had served in the cavalry, but had come to ruin, and was forced by poverty to take a job in the post office late in life. He had a hale and hearty appearance, luxuriant grey whiskers, the manners of a well-bred man, and a loud, pleasant voice. He was good-natured and emotional, but hot-tempered. When anyone in the post office made a protest, expressed disagreement, or even began to argue, Mihail Averyanitch would turn crimson, shake all over, and shout in a voice of thunder, "Hold your tongue!" so that the post office had long enjoyed the reputation of an institution which it was terrible to visit. Mihail Averyanitch

liked and respected Andrey Yefimitch for his culture and the lofti-
ness of his soul; he treated the other inhabitants of the town super-
ciliously, as though they were his subordinates.

"Here I am," he would say, going in to Andrey Yefimitch.
"Good-evening, my dear fellow! I'll be bound, you are getting sick
of me, aren't you?"

"On the contrary, I am delighted," said the doctor. "I am always
glad to see you."

The friends would sit down on the sofa in the study and for
some time would smoke in silence.

"Daryushka, what about the beer?" Andrey Yefimitch would
say.

They would drink their first bottle still in silence, the doctor
brooding and Mihail Averyanitch with a gay and animated face,
like a man who has something very interesting to tell. The doctor
was always the one to begin the conversation.

"What a pity," he would say quietly and slowly, not looking
his friend in the face (he never looked anyone in the face)—"what
a great pity it is that there are no people in our town who are
capable of carrying on intelligent and interesting conversation, or
care to do so. It is an immense privation for us. Even the educated
class do not rise above vulgarity; the level of their development, I
assure you, is not a bit higher than that of the lower orders."

"Perfectly true. I agree."

"You know, of course," the doctor went on quietly and deliberately, "that everything in this world is insignificant and uninteresting except the higher spiritual manifestations of the human
mind. Intellect draws a sharp line between the animals and man,
suggests the divinity of the latter, and to some extent even takes
the place of the immortality which does not exist. Consequently
the intellect is the only possible source of enjoyment. We see and
hear of no trace of intellect about us, so we are deprived of enjoyment. We have books, it is true, but that is not at all the same as
living talk and converse. If you will allow me to make a not quite
apt comparison: books are the printed score, while talk is the
singing."

"Perfectly true."

A silence would follow. Daryushka would come out of the kitchen and with an expression of blank dejection would stand in the doorway to listen, with her face propped on her fist.

"Eh!" Mihail Averyanitch would sigh. "To expect intelligence of this generation!"

And he would describe how wholesome, entertaining, and interesting life had been in the past. How intelligent the educated class in Russia used to be, and what lofty ideas it had of honor and friendship; how they used to lend money without an IOU, and it was thought a disgrace not to give a helping hand to a comrade in need; and what campaigns, what adventures, what skirmishes, what comrades, what women! And the Caucasus, what a marvellous country! The wife of a battalion commander, a queer woman, used to put on an officer's uniform and drive off into the mountains in the evening, alone, without a guide. It was said that she had a love affair with some princeling in the native village.

"Queen of Heaven, Holy Mother . . ." Daryushka would sigh.

"And how we drank! And how we ate! And what desperate liberals we were!"

Andrey Yefimitch would listen without hearing; he was musing as he sipped his beer.

"I often dream of intellectual people and conversation with them," he said suddenly, interrupting Mihail Averyanitch. "My father gave me an excellent education, but under the influence of the ideas of the sixties made me become a doctor. I believe if I had not obeyed him then, by now I should have been in the very centre of the intellectual movement. Most likely I should have become a member of some university. Of course, intellect, too, is transient and not eternal, but you know why I cherish a partiality for it. Life is a vexatious trap; when a thinking man reaches maturity and attains to full consciousness he cannot help feeling that he is in a trap from which there is no escape. Indeed, he is summoned without his choice by fortuitous circumstances from non-existence into life . . . what for? He tries to find out the meaning and object of his existence; he is told nothing, or he is told ab-

surdities; he knocks and it is not opened to him; death comes to
him—also without his choice. And so, just as in prison men held
together by common misfortune feel more at ease when they are
together, so one does not notice the trap in life when people with
a bent for analysis and generalization meet together and pass their
time in the interchange of proud and free ideas. In that sense the
intellect is the source of an enjoyment nothing can replace."

"Perfectly true."

Not looking his friend in the face, Andrey Yefimitch would
go on, quietly and with pauses, talking about intellectual people
and conversation with them, and Mihail Averyanitch would listen
attentively and agree: "Perfectly true."

"And you do not believe in the immortality of the soul?" he
would ask suddenly.

"No, honored Mihail Averyanitch; I do not believe it, and have
no grounds for believing it."

"I must own I doubt it too. And yet I have a feeling as though
I should never die. Oh, I think to myself: 'Old fogey, it is time
you were dead!' But there is a little voice in my soul says: 'Don't
believe it; you won't die.' "

Soon after nine o'clock Mihail Averyanitch would go away. As
he put on his fur coat in the entry he would say with a sigh:

"What a wilderness fate has carried us to, though, really! What's
most vexatious of all is to have to die here. Ech! . . ."

7

AFTER seeing his friend out Andrey Yefimitch would sit down
at the table and begin reading again. The stillness of the evening,
and afterwards of the night, was not broken by a single sound, and
it seemed as though time were standing still and brooding with
the doctor over the book, and as though there were nothing in
existence but the books and the lamp with the green shade. The
doctor's coarse peasant-like face was gradually lighted up by a

smile of delight and enthusiasm over the progress of the human intellect. Oh, why is not man immortal? he thought. What is the good of the brain centres and convolutions, what is the good of sight, speech, self-consciousness, genius, if it is all destined to depart into the soil, and in the end to grow cold together with the earth's crust, and then for millions of years to fly with the earth round the sun with no meaning and no object? To do that there was no need at all to draw man with his lofty, almost godlike intellect out of non-existence, and then, as though in mockery, to turn him into clay. The transmutation of substances! But what cowardice to comfort oneself with that cheap substitute for immortality! The unconscious processes that take place in nature are lower even than the stupidity of man, since in stupidity there is, anyway, consciousness and will, while in those processes there is absolutely nothing. Only the coward who has more fear of death than dignity can comfort himself with the fact that his body will in time live again in the grass, in the stones, in the toad. To find one's immortality in the transmutation of substances is as strange as to prophesy a brilliant future for the case after a precious violin has been broken and become useless.

When the clock struck, Andrey Yefimitch would sink back into his chair and close his eyes to think a little. And under the influence of the fine ideas of which he had been reading he would, unawares, recall his past and his present. The past was hateful—better not to think of it. And it was the same in the present as in the past. He knew that at the very time when his thoughts were floating together with the cooling earth round the sun, in the main building beside his abode people were suffering in sickness and physical impurity: someone perhaps could not sleep and was making war upon the insects, someone was being infected by erysipelas, or moaning over too tight a bandage; perhaps the patients were playing cards with the nurses and drinking vodka. According to the yearly return, twelve thousand people had been deceived; the whole hospital rested as it had done twenty years ago on thieving, filth, scandals, gossip, on gross quackery, and, as before, it was an immoral institution extremely injurious to the health of the in-

habitants. He knew that Nikita knocked the patients about behind the barred windows of Ward No. 6, and that Moiseika went
about the town every day begging alms.

On the other hand, he knew very well that a magical change
had taken place in medicine during the last twenty-five years.
When he was studying at the university he had fancied that medicine would soon be overtaken by the fate of alchemy and meta-
physics; but now when he was reading at night the science of
medicine touched him and excited his wonder, and even enthusiasm. What unexpected brilliance, what a revolution! Thanks to
the antiseptic system operations were performed such as the great
Pirogov had considered impossible even *in spe.* Ordinary Zemstvo
doctors were venturing to perform the resection of the kneecap; of
abdominal operations only one per cent. was fatal; while stone
was considered such a trifle that they did not even write about it.
A radical cure for syphilis had been discovered. And the theory of
heredity, hypnotism, the discoveries of Pasteur and of Koch,
hygiene based on statistics, and the work of our Zemstvo doctors!

Psychiatry with its modern classification of mental diseases,
methods of diagnosis, and treatment, was a perfect Elborus in comparison with what had been in the past. They no longer poured
cold water on the heads of lunatics nor put strait-waistcoats upon
them; they treated them with humanity, and even, so it was stated
in the papers, got up balls and entertainments for them. Andrey
Yefimitch knew that with modern tastes and views such an
abomination as Ward No. 6 was possible only a hundred and fifty
miles from a railway in a little town where the mayor and all the
town council were half-illiterate tradesmen who looked upon the
doctor as an oracle who must be believed without any criticism
even if he had poured molten lead into their mouths; in any other
place the public and the newspapers would long ago have torn this
little Bastille to pieces.

"But, after all, what of it?" Andrey Yefimitch would ask himself, opening his eyes. "There is the antiseptic system, there is
Koch, there is Pasteur, but the essential reality is not altered a bit;
ill-health and mortality are still the same. They get up balls and

entertainments for the mad, but still they don't let them go free; so it's all nonsense and vanity, and there is no difference in reality between the best Vienna clinic and my hospital." But depression and a feeling akin to envy prevented him from feeling indifferent; it must have been owing to exhaustion. His heavy head sank on to the book, he put his hands under his face to make it softer, and thought: "I serve in a pernicious institution and receive a salary from people whom I am deceiving. I am not honest, but then, I of myself am nothing, I am only part of an inevitable social evil: all local officials are pernicious and receive their salary for doing nothing. . . . And so for my dishonesty it is not I who am to blame, but the times. . . . If I had been born two hundred years later I should have been different. . . ."

When it struck three he would put out his lamp and go into his bedroom; he was not sleepy.

8

T w o years before, the Zemstvo in a liberal mood had decided to allow three hundred roubles a year to pay for additional medical service in the town till the Zemstvo hospital should be opened, and the district doctor, Yevgeny Fyodoritch Hobotov, was invited to the town to assist Andrey Yefimitch. He was a very young man —not yet thirty—tall and dark, with broad cheek-bones and little eyes; his forefathers had probably come from one of the many alien races of Russia. He arrived in the town without a farthing, with a small portmanteau, and a plain young woman whom he called his cook. This woman had a baby at the breast. Yevgeny Fyodoritch used to go about in a cap with a peak, and in high boots, and in the winter wore a sheepskin. He made great friends with Sergey Sergeyitch, the medical assistant, and with the treasurer, but held aloof from the other officials, and for some reason called them aristocrats. He had only one book in his lodgings, "The Latest Prescriptions of the Vienna Clinic for 1881." When he went to a patient he always took this book with him. He played billiards in the evening at the club: he did not like cards. He was very fond of using in conversation such expressions as "endless bobbery," "canting soft soap," "shut up with your finicking. . . ."

He visited the hospital twice a week, made the round of the wards, and saw out-patients. The complete absence of antiseptic treatment and the cupping roused his indignation, but he did not introduce any new system, being afraid of offending Andrey Yefimitch. He regarded his colleague as a sly old rascal, suspected him of being a man of large means, and secretly envied him. He would have been very glad to have his post.

9

ON A spring evening towards the end of March, when there was no snow left on the ground and the starlings were singing in the hospital garden, the doctor went out to see his friend the post-master as far as the gate. At that very moment the Jew Moiseika, returning with his booty, came into the yard. He had no cap on, and his bare feet were thrust into goloshes; in his hand he had a little bag of coppers.

"Give me a kopeck!" he said to the doctor, smiling, and shivering with cold. Andrey Yefimitch, who could never refuse anyone anything, gave him a ten-kopeck piece.

"How bad that is!" he thought, looking at the Jew's bare feet with their thin red ankles. "Why, it's wet."

And stirred by a feeling akin both to pity and disgust, he went into the lodge behind the Jew, looking now at his bald head, now at his ankles. As the doctor went in, Nikita jumped up from his heap of litter and stood at attention.

"Good-day, Nikita," Andrey Yefimitch said mildly. "That Jew should be provided with boots or something, he will catch cold."

"Certainly, your honor. I'll inform the superintendent."

"Please do; ask him in my name. Tell him that I asked."

The door into the ward was open. Ivan Dmitritch, lying propped on his elbow on the bed, listened in alarm to the unfamiliar voice, and suddenly recognized the doctor. He trembled all over with anger, jumped up, and with a red and wrathful face, with his eyes starting out of his head, ran out into the middle of the road.

"The doctor has come!" he shouted, and broke into a laugh. "At last! Gentlemen, I congratulate you. The doctor is honoring us with a visit! Cursed reptile!" he shrieked, and stamped in a frenzy such as had never been seen in the ward before. "Kill the reptile! No, killing's too good. Drown him in the midden-pit!"

Andrey Yefimitch, hearing this, looked into the ward from the entry and asked gently: "What for?"

"What for?" shouted Ivan Dmitritch, going up to him with a menacing air and convulsively wrapping himself in his dressing-gown. "What for? Thief!" he said with a look of repulsion, moving his lips as though he would spit at him. "Quack! hangman!"

"Calm yourself," said Andrey Yefimitch, smiling guiltily. "I assure you I have never stolen anything; and as to the rest, most likely you greatly exaggerate. I see you are angry with me. Calm yourself, I beg, if you can, and tell me coolly what are you angry for?"

"What are you keeping me here for?"

"Because you are ill."

"Yes, I am ill. But you know dozens, hundreds of madmen are walking about in freedom because your ignorance is incapable of distinguishing them from the sane. Why am I and these poor wretches to be shut up here like scapegoats for all the rest? You, your assistant, the superintendent, and all your hospital rabble, are immeasurably inferior to every one of us morally; why then are we shut up and you not? Where's the logic of it?"

"Morality and logic don't come in, it all depends on chance. If anyone is shut up he has to stay, and if anyone is not shut up he can walk about, that's all. There is neither morality nor logic in my being a doctor and your being a mental patient, there is nothing but idle chance."

"That twaddle I don't understand . . ." Ivan Dmitritch brought out in a hollow voice, and he sat down on his bed.

Moiseika, whom Nikita did not venture to search in the presence of the doctor, laid out on his bed pieces of bread, bits of paper, and little bones, and, still shivering with cold, began rapidly in a singsong voice saying something in Yiddish. He most likely imagined that he had opened a shop.

"Let me out," said Ivan Dmitritch, and his voice quivered.

"I cannot."

"But why, why?"

"Because it is not in my power. Think, what use will it be to you if I do let you out? Go. The townspeople or the police will detain you or bring you back."

"Yes, yes, that's true," said Ivan Dmitritch, and he rubbed his forehead. "It's awful! But what am I to do, what?"

Andrey Yefimitch liked Ivan Dmitritch's voice and his intelligent young face with its grimaces. He longed to be kind to the young man and soothe him; he sat down on the bed beside him, thought, and said:

"You ask me what to do. The very best thing in your position would be to run away. But, unhappily, that is useless. You would be taken up. When society protects itself from the criminal, mentally deranged, or otherwise inconvenient people, it is invincible. There is only one thing left for you: to resign yourself to the thought that your presence here is inevitable."

"It is no use to anyone."

"So long as prisons and madhouses exist someone must be shut up in them. If not you, I. If not I, some third person. Wait till in the distant future prisons and madhouses no longer exist, and there will be neither bars on the windows nor hospital gowns. Of course, that time will come sooner or later."

Ivan Dmitritch smiled ironically.

"You are jesting," he said, screwing up his eyes. "Such gentlemen as you and your assistant Nikita have nothing to do with the future, but you may be sure, sir, better days will come! I may express myself cheaply, you may laugh, but the dawn of a new life is at hand; truth and justice will triumph, and—our turn will come! I shall not live to see it, I shall perish, but some people's great-grandsons will see it. I greet them with all my heart and rejoice, rejoice with them! Onward! God be your help, friends!"

With shining eyes Ivan Dmitritch got up, and stretching his hands towards the window, went on with emotion in his voice:

"From behind these bars I bless you! Hurrah for truth and justice! I rejoice!"

"I see no particular reason to rejoice," said Andrey Yefimitch, who thought Ivan Dmitritch's movement theatrical, though he was delighted by it. "Prisons and madhouses there will not be, and truth, as you have just expressed it, will triumph; but the reality of things, you know, will not change, the laws of nature will still remain the same. People will suffer pain, grow old, and die just as they do now. However magnificent a dawn lighted up your life, you would yet in the end be nailed up in a coffin and thrown into a hole."

"And immortality?"

"Oh, come, now!"

"You don't believe in it, but I do. Somebody in Dostoevsky or Voltaire said that if there had not been a God men would have invented him. And I firmly believe that if there is no immortality the great intellect of man will sooner or later invent it."

"Well said," observed Andrey Yefimitch, smiling with pleasure; "it's a good thing you have faith. With such a belief one may live happily even shut up within walls. You have studied somewhere, I presume?"

"Yes, I have been at the university, but did not complete my studies."

"You are a reflecting and a thoughtful man. In any surroundings you can find tranquillity in yourself. Free and deep thinking which strives for the comprehension of life, and complete contempt for the foolish bustle of the world—those are two blessings beyond any that man has ever known. And you can possess them even though you lived behind threefold bars. Diogenes lived in a tub, yet he was happier than all the kings of the earth."

"Your Diogenes was a blockhead," said Ivan Dmitritch morosely. "Why do you talk to me about Diogenes and some foolish comprehension of life?" he cried, growing suddenly angry and leaping up. "I love life; I love it passionately. I have the mania of persecution, a continual agonizing terror; but I have moments when I am overwhelmed by the thirst for life, and then I am afraid of going mad. I want dreadfully to live, dreadfully!"

He walked up and down the ward in agitation, and said, dropping his voice:

"When I dream I am haunted by phantoms. People come to me, I hear voices and music, and I fancy I am walking through woods or by the seashore, and I long so passionately for movement, for interests. . . . Come, tell me, what news is there?" asked Ivan Dmitritch; "what's happening?"

"Do you wish to know about the town or in general?"

"Well, tell me first about the town, and then in general."

"Well, in the town it is appallingly dull. . . . There's no one to say a word to, no one to listen to. There are no new people. A young doctor called Hobotov has come here recently."

"He had come in my time. Well, he is a low cad, isn't he?"

"Yes, he is a man of no culture. It's strange, you know. . . . Judging by every sign, there is no intellectual stagnation in our capital cities; there is a movement—so there must be real people there too; but for some reason they always send us such men as I would rather not see. It's an unlucky town!"

"Yes, it is an unlucky town," sighed Ivan Dmitritch, and he laughed. "And how are things in general? What are they writing in the papers and reviews?"

It was by now dark in the ward. The doctor got up, and, standing, began to describe what was being written abroad and in Russia, and the tendency of thought that could be noticed now. Ivan Dmitritch listened attentively and put questions, but suddenly, as though recalling something terrible, clutched at his head and lay down on the bed with his back to the doctor.

"What's the matter?" asked Andrey Yefimitch.

"You will not hear another word from me," said Ivan Dmitritch rudely. "Leave me alone."

"Why so?"

"I tell you, leave me alone. Why the devil do you persist?"

Andrey Yefimitch shrugged his shoulders, heaved a sigh, and went out. As he crossed the entry he said: "You might clear up here, Nikita . . . there's an awfully stuffy smell."

"Certainly, your honor."

"What an agreeable young man!" thought Andrey Yefimitch, going back to his flat. "In all the years I have been living here I do believe he is the first I have met with whom one can talk. He is capable of reasoning and is interested in just the right things."

While he was reading, and afterwards, while he was going to bed, he kept thinking about Ivan Dmitritch, and when he woke next morning he remembered that he had the day before made the acquaintance of an intelligent and interesting man, and determined to visit him again as soon as possible.

10

IVAN DMITRITCH was lying in the same position as on the previous day, with his head clutched in both hands and his legs drawn up. His face was not visible.

"Good-day, my friend," said Andrey Yefimitch. "You are not asleep, are you?"

"In the first place, I am not your friend," Ivan Dmitritch articulated into the pillow; "and in the second, your efforts are useless; you will not get one word out of me."

"Strange," muttered Andrey Yefimitch in confusion. "Yesterday we talked peacefully, but suddenly for some reason you took offence and broke off all at once. . . . Probably I expressed myself awkwardly, or perhaps gave utterance to some idea which did not fit in with your convictions. . . ."

"Yes, a likely idea!" said Ivan Dmitritch, sitting up and looking at the doctor with irony and uneasiness. His eyes were red. "You can go and spy and probe somewhere else, it's no use your doing it here. I knew yesterday what you had come for."

"A strange fancy," laughed the doctor. "So you suppose me to be a spy?"

"Yes, I do. . . . A spy or a doctor who has been charged to test me—it's all the same——"

"Oh, excuse me, what a queer fellow you are really!"

The doctor sat down on the stool near the bed and shook his head reproachfully.

"But let us suppose you are right," he said, "let us suppose that I am treacherously trying to trap you into saying something so as to betray you to the police. You would be arrested and then tried. But would you be any worse off being tried and in prison than you are here? If you are banished to a settlement, or even sent to penal servitude, would it be worse than being shut up in this ward? I imagine it would be no worse. . . . What, then, are you afraid of?"

These words evidently had an effect on Ivan Dmitritch. He sat down quietly.

It was between four and five in the afternoon—the time when Andrey Yefimitch usually walked up and down his rooms, and Daryushka asked whether it was not time for his beer. It was a still, bright day.

"I came out for a walk after dinner, and here I have come, as you see," said the doctor. "It is quite spring."

"What month is it? March?" asked Ivan Dmitritch.

"Yes, the end of March."

"Is it very muddy?"

"No, not very. There are already paths in the garden."

"It would be nice now to drive in an open carriage somewhere into the country," said Ivan Dmitritch, rubbing his red eyes as though he were just awake, "then to come home to a warm, snug study, and . . . and to have a decent doctor to cure one's headache. . . . It's so long since I have lived like a human being. It's disgusting here! Insufferably disgusting!"

After his excitement of the previous day he was exhausted and listless, and spoke unwillingly. His fingers twitched, and from his face it could be seen that he had a splitting headache.

"There is no real difference between a warm, snug study and this ward," said Andrey Yefimitch. "A man's peace and contentment do not lie outside a man, but in himself."

"What do you mean?"

"The ordinary man looks for good and evil in external things—that is, in carriages, in studies—but a thinking man looks for it in himself."

"You should go and preach that philosophy in Greece, where it's warm and fragrant with the scent of pomegranates, but here it is not suited to the climate. With whom was it I was talking of Diogenes? Was it with you?"

"Yes, with me yesterday."

"Diogenes did not need a study or a warm habitation; it's hot there without. You can lie in your tub and eat oranges and olives. But bring him to Russia to live: he'd be begging to be let indoors in May, let alone December. He'd be doubled up with the cold."

"No. One can be insensible to cold as to every other pain. Marcus Aurelius says: 'A pain is a vivid idea of pain; make an effort of will to change that idea, dismiss it, cease to complain, and the pain will disappear.' That is true. The wise man, or simply the reflecting, thoughtful man, is distinguished precisely by his contempt for suffering; he is always contented and surprised at nothing."

"Then I am an idiot, since I suffer and am discontented and surprised at the baseness of mankind."

"You are wrong in that; if you will reflect more on the subject you will understand how insignificant is all that external world that agitates us. One must strive for the comprehension of life, and in that is true happiness."

"Comprehension . . ." repeated Ivan Dmitritch frowning. "External, internal. . . . Excuse me, but I don't understand it. I only know," he said, getting up and looking angrily at the doctor— "I only know that God has created me of warm blood and nerves, yes, indeed! If organic tissue is capable of life it must react to every stimulus. And I do! To pain I respond with tears and outcries, to baseness with indignation, to filth with loathing. To my mind, that is just what is called life. The lower the organism, the less sensitive it is, and the more feebly it reacts to stimulus; and the higher it is, the more responsively and vigorously it reacts to reality. How is it you don't know that? A doctor, and not know such trifles! To despise suffering, to be always contented, and to be surprised at nothing, one must reach this condition"—and Ivan Dmitritch pointed to the peasant who was a mass of fat—"or to harden oneself by suffering to such a point that one loses all sensibility to it—that is, in other words, to cease to live. You must excuse me, I am not a sage or a philosopher," Ivan Dmitritch continued with irritation, "and I don't understand anything about it. I am not capable of reasoning."

"On the contrary, your reasoning is excellent."

"The Stoics, whom you are parodying, were remarkable people, but their doctrine crystallized two thousand years ago and has not advanced, and will not advance, an inch forward, since it is not practical or living. It had a success only with the minority which spends its life in savoring all sort of theories and ruminating over them; the majority did not understand it. A doctrine which advocates indifference to wealth and to the comforts of life, and a contempt for suffering and death, is quite unintelligible to the vast majority of men, since that majority has never known wealth or the comforts of life; and to despise suffering would mean to it despising life itself, since the whole existence of man is made up of the sensations of hunger, cold, injury, loss, and a Hamlet-like dread of death. The whole of life lies in these sensations; one may be oppressed by it, one may hate it, but one cannot despise it. Yes, so, I repeat, the doctrine of the Stoics can never have a future; from the beginning of time up to to-day you see continually increasing the struggle, the sensibility to pain, the capacity of responding to stimulus."

Ivan Dmitritch suddenly lost the thread of his thoughts, stopped, and rubbed his forehead with vexation.

"I meant to say something important, but I have lost it," he said. "What was I saying? Oh, yes! This is what I mean: one of the Stoics sold himself into slavery to redeem his neighbor, so, you see, even a Stoic did react to stimulus, since, for such a generous act as the destruction of oneself for the sake of one's neighbor, he must have had a soul capable of pity and indignation. Here in prison I have forgotten everything I have learned, or else I could have recalled something else. Take Christ, for instance: Christ responded to reality by weeping, smiling, being sorrowful and moved to wrath, even overcome by misery. He did not go to meet His sufferings with a smile, He did not despise death, but prayed in the Garden of Gethsemane that this cup might pass Him by."

Ivan Dmitritch laughed and sat down.

"Granted that a man's peace and contentment lie not outside but in himself," he said, "granted that one must despise suffering and not be surprised at anything, yet on what ground do you preach the theory? Are you a sage? A philosopher?"

"No, I am not a philosopher, but everyone ought to preach it because it is reasonable."

"No, I want to know how it is that you consider yourself competent to judge of 'comprehension,' contempt for suffering, and so on. Have you ever suffered? Have you any idea of suffering? Allow me to ask you, were you ever thrashed in your childhood?"

"No, my parents had an aversion for corporal punishment."

"My father used to flog me cruelly; my father was a harsh, sickly Government clerk with a long nose and a yellow neck. But let us talk of you. No one has laid a finger on you all your life, no one has scared you nor beaten you; you are as strong as a bull. You grew up under your father's wing and studied at his expense, and then you dropped at once into a sinecure. For more than twenty years you have lived rent free with heating, lighting, and service all provided, and had the right to work how you pleased and as much as you pleased, even to do nothing. You were naturally a flabby, lazy man, and so you have tried to arrange your life so that nothing should disturb you or make you move. You have handed over your work to the assistant and the rest of the rabble while you sit in peace and warmth, save money, read, amuse yourself with reflections, with all sorts of lofty nonsense, and" (Ivan Dmitritch looked at the doctor's red nose) "with boozing; in fact, you have seen nothing of life, you know absolutely nothing of it, and are only theoretically acquainted with reality; you despise suffering and are surprised at nothing for a very simple reason: vanity of vanities, the external and the internal, contempt for life, for suffering and for death, comprehension, true happiness—that's the philosophy that suits the Russian sluggard best. You see a peasant beating his wife, for instance. Why interfere? Let him beat her, they will both die sooner or later, anyway; and, besides, he who beats injures by his blows, not the person he is beating, but himself. To get drunk is stupid and unseemly, but if you drink you die, and if you don't drink you die. A peasant woman comes with toothache . . . well, what of it? Pain is the idea of pain, and besides 'there is no living in this world without illness; we shall all die, and so, go away, woman, don't hinder me from thinking and drinking vodka.' A young man asks advice, what he is to do, how he is to live; anyone else would think before answering, but you have got the answer ready: strive for 'comprehension' or for true happiness. And what is that fantastic 'true happiness'? There's no answer, of course. We are kept here behind barred windows, tortured, left to rot; but that is very good and reasonable, because there is no difference at all between this ward and a warm, snug study. A convenient philosophy. You can do nothing, and your conscience is clear, and you feel you are wise. . . . No, sir, it is not philosophy, it's not thinking, it's not breadth of vision, but laziness, fakerism, drowsy stupefaction. Yes," cried Ivan Dmitritch, getting angry again, "you despise suffering, but I'll be bound if you pinch your finger in the door you will howl at the top of your voice."

"And perhaps I shouldn't howl," said Andrey Yefimitch, with a gentle smile.

"Oh, I dare say! Well, if you had a stroke of paralysis, or supposing some fool or bully took advantage of his position and rank to insult you in public, and if you knew he could do it with impunity, then you would understand what it means to put people off with comprehension and true happiness."

"That's original," said Andrey Yefimitch, laughing with pleasure and rubbing his hands. "I am agreeably struck by your inclination for drawing generalizations, and the sketch of my character you have just drawn is simply brilliant. I must confess that talking to you gives me great pleasure. Well, I've listened to you, and now you must graciously listen to me."

11

THE conversation went on for about an hour longer, and apparently made a deep impression on Andrey Yefimitch. He began going to the ward every day. He went there in the mornings and after dinner, and often the dusk of evening found him in conversation with Ivan Dmitritch. At first Ivan Dmitritch held aloof from him, suspected him of evil designs, and openly expressed his hostility. But afterwards he got used to him, and his abrupt manner changed to one of condescending irony.

Soon it was all over the hospital that the doctor, Andrey Yefimitch, had taken to visiting Ward No. 6. No one—neither Sergey Sergeyitch, nor Nikita, nor the nurses—could conceive why he went there, why he stayed there for hours together, what he was talking about, and why he did not write prescriptions. His actions seemed strange. Often Mihail Averyanitch did not find him at home, which had never happened in the past, and Daryushka was greatly perturbed, for the doctor drank his beer now at no definite time, and sometimes was even late for dinner.

One day—it was at the end of June—Dr. Hobotov went to see Andrey Yefimitch about something. Not finding him at home, he proceeded to look for him in the yard; there he was told that the old doctor had gone to see the mental patients. Going into the lodge and stopping in the entry, Hobotov heard the following conversation:

"We shall never agree, and you will not succeed in converting me to your faith," Ivan Dmitritch was saying irritably; "you are utterly ignorant of reality, and you have never known suffering, but have only like a leech fed beside the sufferings of others, while I have been in continual suffering from the day of my birth till to-day. For that reason, I tell you frankly, I consider myself superior to you and more competent in every respect. It's not for you to teach me."

"I have absolutely no ambition to convert you to my faith," said Andrey Yefimitch gently, and with regret that the other refused to understand him. "And that is not what matters, my friend; what matters is not that you have suffered and I have not. Joy and suffering are passing; let us leave them, never mind them. What matters is that you and I think; we see in each other people who are capable of thinking and reasoning, and that is a common bond between us however different our views. If you knew, my friend, how sick I am of the universal senselessness, ineptitude, stupidity, and with what delight I always talk with you! You are an intelligent man, and I enjoy your company."

Hobotov opened the door an inch and glanced into the ward; Ivan Dmitritch in his nightcap and the doctor Andrey Yefimitch were sitting side by side on the bed. The madman was grimacing, twitching, and convulsively wrapping himself in his gown, while the doctor sat motionless with bowed head, and his face was red and look helpless and sorrowful. Hobotov shrugged his shoulders, grinned, and glanced at Nikita. Nikita shrugged his shoulders too.

Next day Hobotov went to the lodge, accompanied by the assistant. Both stood in the entry and listened.

"I fancy our old man has gone clean off his chump!" said Hobotov as he came out of the lodge.

"Lord have mercy upon us sinners!" sighed the decorous Sergey Sergeyitch, scrupulously avoiding the puddles that he might not muddy his polished boots. "I must own, honored Yevgeny Fyodoritch, I have been expecting it for a long time."

12

AFTER this Andrey Yefimitch began to notice a mysterious air in all around him. The attendants, the nurses, and the patients looked at him inquisitively when they met him, and then whispered together. The superintendent's little daughter Masha, whom he liked to meet in the hospital garden, for some reason ran away from him now when he went up with a smile to stroke her on the head. The postmaster no longer said, "Perfectly true," as he listened to him, but in unaccountable confusion muttered, "Yes, yes, yes . . ." and looked at him with a grieved and thoughtful expression; for some reason he took to advising his friend to give up vodka and beer, but as a man of delicate feeling he did not say this directly, but hinted it, telling him first about the commanding officer of his battalion, an excellent man, and then about the priest of the regiment, a capital fellow, both of whom drank and fell ill, but on giving up drinking completely regained their health. On two or three occasions Andrey Yefimitch was visited by his colleague Hobotov, who also advised him to give up spirituous liquors, and for no apparent reason recommended him to take bromide.

In August Andrey Yefimitch got a letter from the mayor of the town asking him to come on very important business. On arriving at the town hall at the time fixed, Andrey Yefimitch found there the military commander, the superintendent of the district school, a member of the town council, Hobotov, and a plump, fair gentleman who was introduced to him as a doctor. This doctor, with a Polish surname difficult to pronounce, lived at a pedigree stud-farm twenty miles away, and was now on a visit to the town.

"There's something that concerns you," said the member of the town council, addressing Andrey Yefimitch after they had all greeted one another and sat down to the table. "Here Yevgeny Fyodoritch says that there is not room for the dispensary in the main building, and that it ought to be transferred to one of the lodges. That's of no consequence—of course it can be transferred, but the point is that the lodge wants doing up."

"Yes, it would have to be done up," said Andrey Yefimitch after a moment's thought. "If the corner lodge, for instance, were fitted up as a dispensary, I imagine it would cost at least five hundred roubles. An unproductive expenditure!"

Everyone was silent for a space.

"I had the honor of submitting to you ten years ago," Andrey Yefimitch went on in a low voice, "that the hospital in its present form is a luxury for the town beyond its means. It was built in the forties, but things were different then. The town spends too much on unnecessary buildings and superfluous staff. I believe with a different system two model hospitals might be maintained for the same money."

"Well, let us have a different system, then!" the member of the town council said briskly.

"I have already had the honor of submitting to you that the medical department should be transferred to the supervision of the Zemstvo."

"Yes, transfer the money to the Zemstvo and they will steal it," laughed the fair-haired doctor.

"That's what it always comes to," the member of the council assented, and he also laughed.

Andrey Yefimitch looked with apathetic, lusterless eyes at the fair-haired doctor and said: "One should be just."

Again there was silence. Tea was brought in. The military commander, for some reason much embarrassed, touched Andrey Yefimitch's hand across the table and said: "You have quite forgotten us, doctor. But of course you are a hermit: you don't play cards and don't like women. You would be dull with fellows like us."

They all began saying how boring it was for a decent person to live in such a town. No theater, no music, and at the last dance at the club there had been about twenty ladies and only two gentlemen. The young men did not dance, but spent all the time crowding round the refreshment bar or playing cards.

Not looking at anyone and speaking slowly in a low voice, Andrey Yefimitch began saying what a pity, what a terrible pity it was that the townspeople should waste their vital energy, their hearts, and their minds on cards and gossip, and should have neither the power nor the inclination to spend their time in interesting conversation and reading, and should refuse to take advantage of the enjoyments of the mind. The mind alone was interesting and worthy of attention, all the rest was low and petty. Hobotov listened to his colleague attentively and suddenly asked:

"Andrey Yefimitch, what day of the month is it?"

Having received an answer, the fair-haired doctor and he, in the tone of examiners conscious of their lack of skill, began asking Andrey Yefimitch what was the day of the week, how many days there were in the year, and whether it was true that there was a remarkable prophet living in Ward No. 6.

In response to the last question Andrey Yefimitch turned rather red and said: "Yes, he is mentally deranged, but he is an interesting young man."

They asked him no other questions.

When he was putting on his overcoat in the entry, the military commander laid a hand on his shoulder and said with a sigh:

"It's time for us old fellows to rest!"

As he came out of the hall, Andrey Yefimitch understood that it had been a committee appointed to enquire into his mental condition. He recalled the questions that had been asked him, flushed crimson, and for some reason, for the first time in his life, felt bitterly grieved for medical science.

"My God . . ." he thought, remembering how these doctors had just examined him; "why, they have only lately been hearing lectures on mental pathology; they had passed an examination—what's the explanation of this crass ignorance? They have not a conception of mental pathology!"

And for the first time in his life he felt insulted and moved to anger.

In the evening of the same day Mihail Averyanitch came to see him. The postmaster went up to him without waiting to greet him, took him by both hands, and said in an agitated voice:

"My dear fellow, my dear friend, show me that you believe in my genuine affection and look on me as your friend!" And preventing Andrey Yefimitch from speaking, he went on, growing excited: "I love you for your culture and nobility of soul. Listen to me, my dear fellow. The rules of their profession compel the doctors to conceal the truth from you, but I blurt out the plain truth like a soldier. You are not well! Excuse me, my dear fellow, but it is the truth; everyone about you has been noticing it for a long time. Dr. Yevgeny Fyodoritch has just told me that it is essential for you to rest and distract your mind for the sake of your health. Perfectly true! Excellent! In a day or two I am taking a holiday and am going away for a sniff of a different atmosphere. Show that you are a friend to me, let us go together! Let us go for a jaunt as in the good old days."

"I feel perfectly well," said Andrey Yefimitch after a moment's thought. "I can't go away. Allow me to show you my friendship in some other way."

To go off with no object, without his books, without his Daryushka, without his beer, to break abruptly through the routine of life, established for twenty years—the idea for the first minute struck him as wild and fantastic, but he remembered the conversation at the Zemstvo committee and the depressing feelings with which he had returned home, and the thought of a brief absence from the town in which stupid people looked on him as a madman was pleasant to him.

"And where precisely do you intend to go?" he asked.

"To Moscow, to Petersburg, to Warsaw. . . . I spent the five happiest years of my life in Warsaw. What a marvellous town! Let us go, my dear fellow!"

13

A week later it was suggested to Andrey Yefimitch that he should have a rest—that is, send in his resignation—a suggestion he received with indifference, and a week later still, Mihail Averyanitch and he were sitting in a posting carriage driving to the nearest railway station. The days were cool and bright, with a blue sky and a transparent distance. They were two days driving the hundred and fifty miles to the railway station, and stayed two nights on the way. When at the posting station the glasses given them for their tea had not been properly washed, or the drivers were slow in harnessing the horses, Mihail Averyanitch would turn crimson, and quivering all over would shout:

"Hold your tongue! Don't argue!"

And in the carriage he talked without ceasing for a moment, describing his campaigns in the Caucasus and in Poland. What adventures he had had, what meetings! He talked loudly and opened his eyes so wide with wonder that he might well be thought to be lying. Moreover, as he talked he breathed in Andrey Yefimitch's face and laughed into his ear. This bothered the doctor and prevented him from thinking or concentrating his mind.

In the train they travelled, from motives of economy, third-class in a non-smoking compartment. Half the passengers were decent people. Mihail Averyanitch soon made friends with everyone, and moving from one seat to another, kept saying loudly that they ought not to travel by these appalling lines. It was a regular swindle! A very different thing riding on a good horse: one could do over seventy miles a day and feel fresh and well after it. And our bad harvests were due to the draining of the Pinsk marshes; altogether, the way things were done was dreadful. He got excited, talked loudly, and would not let others speak. This endless chatter to the accompaniment of loud laughter and expressive gestures wearied Andrey Yefimitch.

"Which of us is the madman?" he thought with vexation. "I, who try not to disturb my fellow-passengers in any way, or this egoist who thinks that he is cleverer and more interesting than anyone here, and so will leave no one in peace?"

In Moscow Mihail Averyanitch put on a military coat without epaulettes and trousers with red braid on them. He wore a military cap and overcoat in the street, and soldiers saluted him. It seemed to Andrey Yefimitch, now, that his companion was a man who had flung away all that was good and kept only what was bad of all the characteristics of a country gentleman that he had once possessed. He liked to be waited on even when it was quite unnecessary. The matches would be lying before him on the table, and he would see them and shout to the waiter to give him the matches; he did not hesitate to appear before a maidservant in nothing but his underclothes; he used the familiar mode of address to all footmen indiscriminately, even old men, and when he was angry called them fools and blockheads. This, Andrey Yefimitch thought, was like a gentleman, but disgusting.

First of all Mihail Averyanitch led his friend to the Iversky Madonna. He prayed fervently, shedding tears and bowing down to the earth, and when he had finished, heaved a deep sigh and said:

"Even though one does not believe it makes one somehow easier when one prays a little. Kiss the ikon, my dear fellow."

Andrey Yefimitch was embarrassed and he kissed the image, while Mihail Averyanitch pursed up his lips and prayed in a whisper, and again tears came into his eyes. Then they went to the Kremlin and looked there at the Tsar-cannon and the Tsar-bell, and even touched them with their fingers, admired the view over the river, visited St. Saviour's and the Rumyantsev museum.

They dined at Tyestov's. Mihail Averyanitch looked a long time at the menu, stroking his whiskers, and said in the tone of a gourmand accustomed to dine in restaurants:

"We shall see what you give us to eat to-day, angel!"

14

THE doctor walked about, looked at things, ate and drank, but he had all the while one feeling: annoyance with Mihail Averyanitch. He longed to have a rest from his friend, to get away from him, to hide himself, while the friend thought it his duty not to let the doctor move a step away from him, and to provide him with as many distractions as possible. When there was nothing to look at he entertained him with conversation. For two days Andrey Yefimitch endured it, but on the third he announced to his friend that he was ill and wanted to stay at home for the whole day; his friend replied that in that case he would stay too—that really he needed rest, for he was run off his legs already. Andrey Yefimitch lay on the sofa, with his face to the back, and clenching his teeth, listened to his friend, who assured him with heat that sooner or later France would certainly thrash Germany, that there were a great many scoundrels in Moscow, and that it was impossible to judge of a horse's quality by its outward appearance. The doctor began to have a buzzing in his ears and palpitations of the heart, but out of delicacy could not bring himself to beg his friend to go away or hold his tongue. Fortunately Mihail Averyanitch grew weary of sitting in the hotel room, and after dinner he went out for a walk.

As soon as he was alone Andrey Yefimitch abandoned himself to a feeling of relief. How pleasant to lie motionless on the sofa and to know that one is alone in the room! Real happiness is impossible without solitude. The fallen angel betrayed God probably because he longed for solitude, of which the angels know nothing. Andrey Yefimitch wanted to think about what he had seen and heard during the last few days, but he could not get Mihail Averyanitch out of his head.

"Why, he has taken a holiday and come with me out of friendship, out of generosity," thought the doctor with vexation;

"nothing could be worse than this friendly supervision. I suppose he is good-natured and generous and a lively fellow, but he is a bore. An insufferable bore. In the same way there are people who never say anything but what is clever and good, yet one feels that they are dull-witted people."

For the following days Andrey Yefimitch declared himself ill and would not leave the hotel room; he lay with his face to the back of the sofa, and suffered agonies of weariness when his friend entertained him with conversation, or rested when his friend was absent. He was vexed with himself for having come, and with his friend, who grew every day more talkative and more free-and-easy; he could not succeed in attuning his thoughts to a serious and lofty level.

"This is what I get from the real life Ivan Dmitritch talked about," he thought, angry at his own pettiness. "It's of no consequence, though. . . . I shall go home, and everything will go on as before. . . ."

It was the same thing in Petersburg too; for whole days together he did not leave the hotel room, but lay on the sofa and only got up to drink beer.

Mihail Averyanitch was all haste to get to Warsaw.

"My dear man, what should I go there for?" said Andrey Yefimitch in an imploring voice. "You go alone and let me get home! I entreat you!"

"On no account," protested Mihail Averyanitch. "It's a marvellous town."

Andrey Yefimitch had not the strength of will to insist on his own way, and much against his inclination went to Warsaw. There he did not leave the hotel room, but lay on the sofa, furious with himself, with his friend, and with the waiters, who obstinately refused to understand Russian; while Mihail Averyanitch, healthy, hearty, and full of spirits as usual, went about the town from morning to night, looking for his old acquaintances. Several times he did not return home at night. After one night spent in some unknown haunt he returned home early in the morning, in a violently excited condition, with a red face and tousled hair. For a long time he walked up and down the rooms muttering something to himself, then stopped and said:

"Honor before everything."

After walking up and down a little longer he clutched his head in both hands and pronounced in a tragic voice: "Yes, honor before everything! Accursed be the moment when the idea first entered my head to visit this Babylon! My dear friend," he added, addressing the doctor, "you may despise me, I have played and lost; lend me five hundred roubles!"

Andrey Yefimitch counted out five hundred roubles and gave them to his friend without a word. The latter, still crimson with shame and anger, incoherently articulated some useless vow, put on his cap, and went out. Returning two hours later he flopped into an easy-chair, heaved a loud sigh, and said:

"My honor is saved. Let us go, my friend; I do not care to remain another hour in this accursed town. Scoundrels! Austrian spies!"

By the time the friends were back in their own town it was November, and deep snow was lying in the streets. Dr. Hobotov had Andrey Yefimitch's post; he was still living in his old lodgings, waiting for Andrey Yefimitch to arrive and clear out of the hospital apartments. The plain woman whom he called his cook was already established in one of the lodges.

Fresh scandals about the hospital were going the round of the town. It was said that the plain woman had quarrelled with the superintendent, and that the latter had crawled on his knees before her begging forgiveness. On the very first day he arrived Andrey Yefimitch had to look out for lodgings.

"My friend," the postmaster said to him timidly, "excuse an indiscreet question: what means have you at your disposal?"

Andrey Yefimitch, without a word, counted out his money and said: "Eighty-six roubles."

"I don't mean that," Mihail Averyanitch brought out in confusion, misunderstanding him; "I mean, what have you to live on?"

"I tell you, eighty-six roubles . . . I have nothing else."

Mihail Averyanitch looked upon the doctor as an honorable

man, yet he suspected that he had accumulated a fortune of at least twenty thousand. Now learning that Andrey Yefimitch was a beggar, that he had nothing to live on he was for some reason suddenly moved to tears and embraced his friend.

15

ANDREY YEFIMITCH now lodged in a little house with three windows. There were only three rooms besides the kitchen in the little house. The doctor lived in two of them which looked into the street, while Daryushka and the landlady with her three children lived in the third room and the kitchen. Sometimes the landlady's lover, a drunken peasant who was rowdy and reduced the children and Daryushka to terror, would come for the night. When he arrived and established himself in the kitchen and demanded vodka, they all felt very uncomfortable, and the doctor would be moved by pity to take the crying children into his room and let them lie on his floor, and this gave him great satisfaction.

He got up as before at eight o'clock, and after his morning tea sat down to read his old books and magazines: he had no money for new ones. Either because the books were old, or perhaps because of the change in his surroundings, reading exhausted him, and did not grip his attention as before. That he might not spend his time in idleness he made a detailed catalogue of his books and gummed little labels on their backs, and this mechanical, tedious work seemed to him more interesting than reading. The monotonous, tedious work lulled his thoughts to sleep in some unaccountable way, and the time passed quickly while he thought of nothing. Even sitting in the kitchen, peeling potatoes with Daryushka or picking over the buckwheat grain, seemed to him interesting. On Saturdays and Sundays he went to church. Standing near the wall and half closing his eyes, he listened to the singing and thought of his father, of his mother, of the university, of the religions of the world; he felt calm and melancholy, and as he went out of the church afterwards he regretted that the service was so soon over. He went twice to the hospital to talk to Ivan Dmitritch. But on both occasions Ivan Dmitritch was unusually excited and ill-humored; he bade the doctor leave him in peace, as he had long been sick of empty chatter, and declared, to make up for all his sufferings, he asked from the damned scoundrels only one favor—solitary confinement. Surely they would not refuse him even that? On both occasions when Andrey Yefimitch was taking leave of him and wishing him good-night, he answered rudely and said:

"Go to hell!"

And Andrey Yefimitch did not know now whether to go to him for the third time or not. He longed to go.

In old days Andrey Yefimitch used to walk about his rooms and think in the interval after dinner, but now from dinner-time till evening tea he lay on the sofa with his face to the back and gave himself up to trivial thoughts which he could not struggle against. He was mortified that after more than twenty years of service he had been given neither a pension nor any assistance. It is true he had not done his work honestly, but, then, all who are in the Service get a pension without distinction whether they are honest or not. Contemporary justice lies precisely in the bestowal of grades, orders, and pensions, not for moral qualities or capacities, but for service whatever it may have been like. Why was he alone to be an exception? He had no money at all. He was ashamed to pass by the shop and look at the woman who owned it. He owed thirty-two roubles for beer already. There was money owing to the landlady also. Daryushka sold old clothes and books on the sly, and told lies to the landlady, saying that the doctor was just going to receive a large sum of money.

He was angry with himself for having wasted on travelling the thousand roubles he had saved up. How useful that thousand roubles would have been now! He was vexed that people would not leave him in peace. Hobotov thought it his duty to look in on his sick colleague from time to time. Everything about him was revolting to Andrey Yefimitch—his well-fed face and vulgar, condescending tone, and his use of the word "colleague," and his high top-boots; the most revolting thing was that he thought it was his duty to treat Andrey Yefimitch, and thought that he really was treating him. On every visit he brought a bottle of bromide and rhubarb pills.

Mihail Averyanitch, too, thought it his duty to visit his friend and entertain him. Every time he went in to Andrey Yefimitch with an affectation of ease, laughed constrainedly, and began assuring him that he was looking very well to-day, and that, thank God, he was on the highroad to recovery, and from this it might be concluded that he looked on his friend's condition as hopeless. He had not yet repaid his Warsaw debt, and was overwhelmed by shame; he was constrained, and so tried to laugh louder and talk more amusingly. His anecdotes and descriptions seemed endless now, and were an agony both to Andrey Yefimitch and himself.

In his presence Andrey Yefimitch usually lay on the sofa with his face to the wall, and listened with his teeth clenched; his soul was oppressed with rankling disgust, and after every visit from his friend he felt as though this disgust had risen higher, and was mounting into his throat.

To stifle petty thoughts he made haste to reflect that he himself, and Hobotov, and Mihail Averyanitch, would all sooner or later perish without leaving any trace on the world. If one imagined some spirit flying by the earthly globe in space in a million years he would see nothing but clay and bare rocks. Everything—culture and the moral law—would pass away and not even a burdock would grow out of them. Of what consequence was shame in the presence of a shopkeeper, of what consequence was the insignificant Hobotov or the wearisome friendship of Mihail Averyanitch? It was all trivial and nonsensical.

But such reflections did not help him now. Scarcely had he imagined the earthly globe in a million years, when Hobotov in his high top-boots or Mihail Averyanitch with his forced laugh would appear from behind a bare rock, and he even heard the shamefaced whisper: "The Warsaw debt. . . . I will repay it in a day or two, my dear fellow, without fail. . . ."

16

ONE day Mihail Averyanitch came after dinner when Andrey
Yefimitch was lying on the sofa. It so happened that Hobotov
arrived at the same time with his bromide. Andrey Yefimitch got
up heavily and sat down, leaning both arms on the sofa.

"You have a much better color to-day than you had yesterday,
my dear man," began Mihail Averyanitch. "Yes, you look jolly.
Upon my soul, you do!"

"It's high time you were well, colleague," said Hobotov, yawning. "I'll be bound, you are sick of this bobbery."

"And we shall recover," said Mihail Averyanitch cheerfully.
"We shall live another hundred years! To be sure!"

"Not a hundred years, but another twenty," Hobotov said reassuringly. "It's all right, all right, colleague; don't lose heart. . . .
Don't go piling it on!"

"We'll show what we can do," laughed Mihail Averyanitch,
and he slapped his friend on the knee. "We'll show them yet!
Next summer, please God, we shall be off to the Caucasus, and
we will ride all over it on horseback—trot, trot, trot! And when
we are back from the Caucasus I shouldn't wonder if we will all
dance at the wedding." Mihail Averyanitch gave a sly wink. "We'll
marry you, my dear boy, we'll marry you. . . ."

Andrey Yefimitch felt suddenly that the rising disgust had
mounted to his throat, his heart began beating violently.

"That's vulgar," he said, getting up quickly and walking away
to the window. "Don't you understand that you are talking vulgar
nonsense?"

He meant to go on softly and politely, but against his will he
suddenly clenched his fists and raised them above his head.

"Leave me alone," he shouted in a voice unlike his own, flushing crimson and shaking all over. "Go away, both of you!"

Mihail Averyanitch and Hobotov got up and stared at him
first with amazement and then with alarm.

"Go away, both!" Andrey Yefimitch went on shouting. "Stupid people! Foolish people! I don't want either your friendship or your medicines, stupid man! Vulgar! Nasty!"

Hobotov and Mihail Averyanitch, looking at each other in bewilderment, staggered to the door and went out. Andrey Yefimitch snatched up the bottle of bromide and flung it after them; the bottle broke with a crash on the door-frame.

"Go to the devil!" he shouted in a tearful voice, running out into the passage. "To the devil!"

When his guests were gone Andrey Yefimitch lay down on the sofa, trembling as though in a fever, and went on for a long while repeating: "Stupid people! Foolish people!"

When he was calmer, what occurred to him first of all was the thought that poor Mihail Averyanitch must be feeling fearfully ashamed and depressed now, and that it was all dreadful. Nothing like this had ever happened to him before. Where was his intelligence and his tact? Where was his comprehension of things and his philosophical indifference?

The doctor could not sleep all night for shame and vexation with himself, and at ten o'clock next morning he went to the post office and apologized to the postmaster.

"We won't think again of what has happened," Mihail Averyanitch, greatly touched, said with a sigh, warmly pressing his hand. "Let bygones be bygones. Lyubavkin," he suddenly shouted so loud that all the postmen and other persons present started, "hand a chair; and you wait," he shouted to a peasant woman who was stretching out a registered letter to him through the grating. "Don't you see that I am busy? We will not remember the past," he went on, affectionately addressing Andrey Yefimitch; "sit down, I beg you, my dear fellow."

For a minute he stroked his knees in silence, and then said:

"I have never had a thought of taking offence. Illness is no joke, I understand. Your attack frightened the doctor and me yesterday, and we had a long talk about you afterwards. My dear friend, why won't you treat your illness seriously? You can't go on like this. . . . Excuse me speaking openly as a friend," whispered Mihail Averyanitch. "You live in the most unfavorable surroundings, in a crowd, in uncleanliness, no one to look after you, no money for proper treatment. . . . My dear friend, the doctor and I implore you with all our hearts, listen to our advice: go into the hospital! There you will have wholesome food and attendance and treatment. Though, between ourselves, Yevgeny Fyodoritch is *mauvais ton*, yet he does understand his work, you can fully rely upon him. He has promised me he will look after you."

Andrey Yefimitch was touched by the postmaster's genuine sympathy and the tears which suddenly glittered on his cheeks.

"My honored friend, don't believe it!" he whispered, laying his hand on his heart; "don't believe them. It's all a sham. My illness is only that in twenty years I have only found one intelligent man in the whole town, and he is mad. I am not ill at all, it's simply that I have got into an enchanted circle which there is no getting out of. I don't care; I am ready for anything."

"Go into the hospital, my dear fellow."

"I don't care if it were into the pit."

"Give me your word, my dear man, that you will obey Yevgeny Fyodoritch in everything."

"Certainly I will give you my word. But I repeat, my honored friend, I have got into an enchanted circle. Now everything, even the genuine sympathy of my friends, leads to the same thing—to my ruin. I am going to my ruin, and I have the manliness to recognize it."

"My dear fellow, you will recover."

"What's the use of saying that?" said Andrey Yefimitch, with irritation. "There are few men who at the end of their lives do not experience what I am experiencing now. When you are told that you have something such as diseased kidneys or enlarged heart, and you begin being treated for it, or are told you are mad or a criminal—that is, in fact, when people suddenly turn their attention to you—you may be sure you have got into an enchanted circle from which you will not escape. You will try to escape and make things worse. You had better give in, for no human efforts can save you. So it seems to me."

Meanwhile the public was crowding at the grating. That he might not be in their way, Andrey Yefimitch got up and began to take leave. Mihail Averyanitch made him promise on his honor once more, and escorted him to the outer door.

Towards evening on the same day Hobotov, in his sheepskin and his high top-boots, suddenly made his appearance, and said to Andrey Yefimitch in a tone as though nothing had happened the day before:

"I have come on business, colleague. I have come to ask you whether you would not join me in a consultation. Eh?"

Thinking that Hobotov wanted to distract his mind with an outing, or perhaps really to enable him to earn something, Andrey Yefimitch put on his coat and hat, and went out with him into the street. He was glad of the opportunity to smooth over his fault of the previous day and to be reconciled, and in his heart thanked Hobotov, who did not even allude to yesterday's scene and was evidently sparing him. One would never have expected such delicacy from this uncultured man.

"Where is your invalid?" asked Andrey Yefimitch.

"In the hospital. . . . I have long wanted to show him to you. A very interesting case."

They went into the hospital yard, and going round the main building, turned towards the lodge where the mental cases were kept, and all this, for some reason, in silence. When they went into the lodge Nikita as usual jumped up and stood at attention.

"One of the patients here has a lung complication," Hobotov said in an undertone, going into the ward with Andrey Yefimitch. "You wait here, I'll be back directly. I am going for a stethoscope."

And he went away.

17

IT WAS getting dusk. Ivan Dmitritch was lying on his bed with his face thrust into his pillow; the paralytic was sitting motionless, crying quietly and moving his lips. The fat peasant and the former sorter were asleep. It was quiet.

Andrey Yefimitch sat down on Ivan Dmitritch's bed and waited.

But half an hour passed, and instead of Hobotov, Nikita came into the ward with a dressing-gown, some underlinen, and a pair of slippers in a heap on his arm.

"Please change your things, your honor," he said softly. "Here is your bed; come this way," he added, pointing to an empty bed-stead which had obviously been recently brought into the ward. "It's all right; please God, you will recover."

Andrey Yefimitch understood it all. Without saying a word he crossed to the bed to which Nikita pointed and sat down; seeing that Nikita was standing waiting, he undressed entirely and he felt ashamed. Then he put on the hospital clothes; the drawers were very short, the shirt was long, and the dressing-gown smelt of smoked fish.

"Please God, you will recover," repeated Nikita, and he gathered up Andrey Yefimitch's clothes into his arms, went out, and shut the door after him.

"No matter . . ." thought Andrey Yefimitch, wrapping himself in his dressing-gown in a shame-faced way and feeling that he looked like a convict in his new costume. "It's no matter. . . . It does not matter whether it's a dress-coat or a uniform or this dressing-gown. . . ."

But how about his watch? And the notebook that was in the side-pocket? And his cigarettes? Where had Nikita taken his clothes? Now perhaps to the day of his death he would not put on trousers, a waistcoat, and high boots. It was all somehow strange and even incomprehensible at first. Andrey Yefimitch was even now convinced that there was no difference between his land-lady's house and Ward No. 6, that everything in this world was nonsense and vanity of vanities. And yet his hands were trembling, his feet were cold, and he was filled with dread at the thought that soon Ivan Dmitritch would get up and see that he was in a dressing-gown. He got up and walked across the room and sat down again.

Here he had been sitting already half an hour, an hour, and he was miserably sick of it: was it really possible to live here a day, a week, and even years like these people? Why, he had been sitting here, had walked about and sat down again; he could get up and look out of window and walk from corner to corner again, and then what? Sit so all the time, like a post, and think? No, that was scarcely possible.

Andrey Yefimitch lay down, but at once got up, wiped the cold sweat from his brow with his sleeve, and felt that his whole face smelt of smoked fish. He walked about again.

"It's some misunderstanding . . ." he said, turning out the palms of his hands in perplexity. "It must be cleared up. There is a misunderstanding. . . ."

Meanwhile Ivan Dmitritch woke up; he sat up and propped his cheeks on his fists. He spat. Then he glanced lazily at the doctor, and apparently for the first minute did not understand; but soon his sleepy face grew malicious and mocking.

"Aha! so they have put you in here, too, old fellow?" he said in a voice husky from sleepiness, screwing up one eye. "Very glad to see you. You sucked the blood of others, and now they will suck yours. Excellent!"

"It's a misunderstanding . . ." Andrey Yefimitch brought out, frightened by Ivan Dmitritch's words; he shrugged his shoulders and repeated: "It's some misunderstanding. . . ."

Ivan Dmitritch spat again and lay down.

"Cursed life," he grumbled, "and what's bitter and insulting, this life will not end in compensation for our sufferings, it will not end with apotheosis as it would in an opera, but with death; peasants will come and drag one's dead body by the arms and the legs to the cellar. Ugh! Well, it does not matter. . . . We shall have our good time in the other world. . . . I shall come here as a ghost from the other world and frighten these reptiles. I'll turn their hair grey."

Moiseika returned, and, seeing the doctor, held out his hand.

"Give me one little kopeck," he said.

18

ANDREY YEFIMITCH walked away to the window and looked out into the open country. It was getting dark, and on the horizon to the right a cold crimson moon was mounting upwards. Not far from the hospital fence, not much more than two hundred yards away, stood a tall white house shut in by a stone wall. This was the prison.

"So this is real life," thought Andrey Yefimitch, and he felt frightened.

The moon and the prison, and the nails on the fence, and the far-away flames at the bone-charring factory were all terrible. Behind him there was the sound of a sigh. Andrey Yefimitch looked round and saw a man with glittering stars and orders on his breast, who was smiling and slily winking. And this, too, seemed terrible.

Andrey Yefimitch assured himself that there was nothing special about the moon or the prison, that even sane persons wear orders, and that everything in time will decay and turn to earth, but he was suddenly overcome with despair; he clutched at the grating with both hands and shook it with all his might. The strong grating did not yield.

Then that it might not be so dreadful he went to Ivan Dmitritch's bed and sat down.

"I have lost heart, my dear fellow," he muttered, trembling and wiping away the cold sweat, "I have lost heart."

"You should be philosophical," said Ivan Dmitritch ironically.

"My God, my God. . . . Yes, yes. . . . You were pleased to say once that there was no philosophy in Russia, but that all people, even the paltriest, talk philosophy. But you know the philosophizing of the paltriest does not harm anyone," said Andrey Yefimitch in a tone as if he wanted to cry and complain. "Why, then, that malignant laugh, my friend, and how can these paltry creatures help philosophizing if they are not satisfied? For an intelligent, educated man, made in God's image, proud and loving freedom, to have no alternative but to be a doctor in a filthy, stupid, wretched little town, and to spend his whole life among bottles, leeches, mustard plasters! Quackery, narrowness, vulgarity! Oh, my God!"

"You are talking nonsense. If you don't like being a doctor you should have gone in for being a statesman."

"I could not, I could not do anything. We are weak, my dear friend. . . . I used to be indifferent. I reasoned boldly and soundly, but at the first coarse touch of life upon me I have lost heart. . . . Prostration. . . . We are weak, we are poor creatures . . . and you, too, my dear friend, you are intelligent, generous, you drew in good impulses with your mother's milk, but you had hardly entered upon life when you were exhausted and fell ill. . . . Weak, weak!"

Andrey Yefimitch was all the while at the approach of evening tormented by another persistent sensation besides terror and the feeling of resentment. At last he realized that he was longing for a smoke and for beer.

"I am going out, my friend," he said. "I will tell them to bring a light; I can't put up with this. . . . I am not equal to it. . . ."

Andrey Yefimitch went to the door and opened it, but at once Nikita jumped up and barred his way.

"Where are you going? You can't, you can't!" he said. "It's bedtime."

"But I'm only going out for a minute to walk about the yard," said Andrey Yefimitch.

"You can't, you can't; it's forbidden. You know that yourself."

"But what difference will it make to anyone if I do go out?" asked Andrey Yefimitch, shrugging his shoulders. "I don't understand. Nikita, I must go out!" he said in a trembling voice. "I must."

"Don't be disorderly, it's not right," Nikita said peremptorily.

"This is beyond everything," Ivan Dmitritch cried suddenly, and he jumped up. "What right has he not to let you out? How dare they keep us here? I believe it is clearly laid down in the law that no one can be deprived of freedom without trial! It's an outrage! It's tyranny!"

"Of course it's tyranny," said Andrey Yefimitch, encouraged by Ivan Dmitritch's outburst. "I must go out, I want to. He has no right! Open, I tell you."

"Do you hear, you dull-witted brute?" cried Ivan Dmitritch, and he banged on the door with his fist. "Open the door, or I will break it open! Torturer!"

"Open the door," cried Andrey Yefimitch, trembling all over; "I insist!"

"Talk away!" Nikita answered through the door, "talk away. . . ."

"Anyhow, go and call Yevgeny Fyodoritch! Say that I beg him to come for a minute!"

"His honor will come of himself to-morrow."

"They will never let us out," Ivan Dmitritch was going on meanwhile. "They will leave us to rot here! Oh, Lord, can there really be no hell in the next world, and will these wretches be forgiven? Where is justice? Open the door, you wretch! I am choking!" he cried in a hoarse voice, and flung himself upon the door. "I'll dash out my brains, murderers!"

Nikita opened the door quickly, and roughly with both his hands and his knee shoved Andrey Yefimitch back, then swung his arm and punched him in the face with his fist. It seemed to Andrey Yefimitch as though a huge salt wave enveloped him from his head downwards and dragged him to the bed; there really was a salt taste in his mouth: most likely the blood was running from his teeth. He waved his arms as though he were trying to swim out and clutched at a bedstead, and at the same moment felt Nikita hit him twice on the back.

Ivan Dmitritch gave a loud scream. He must have been beaten too.

Then all was still, the faint moonlight came through the grating, and a shadow like a net lay on the floor. It was terrible. Andrey Yefimitch lay and held his breath: he was expecting with horror to be struck again. He felt as though someone had taken a sickle, thrust it into him, and turned it round several times in his breast and bowels. He bit the pillow from pain and clenched his teeth, and all at once through the chaos in his brain there flashed the terrible unbearable thought that these people, who seemed now like black shadows in the moonlight, had to endure such pain day by day for years. How could it have happened that for more than twenty years he had not known it and had refused to know it? He knew nothing of pain, had no conception of it, so he was not to blame, but his conscience, as inexorable and as rough as Nikita, made him turn cold from the crown of his head to his heels. He leaped up, tried to cry out with all his might, and to run in haste to kill Nikita, and then Hobotov, the superintendent and the assistant, and then himself; but no sound came from his chest, and his legs would not obey him. Gasping for breath, he tore at the dressing-gown and the shirt on his breast, rent them, and fell senseless on the bed.

19

NEXT morning his head ached, there was a droning in his ears and a feeling of utter weakness all over. He was not ashamed at recalling his weakness the day before. He had been cowardly, had even been afraid of the moon, had openly expressed thoughts and feelings such as he had not expected in himself before; for instance, the thought that the paltry people who philosophized were really dissatisfied. But now nothing mattered to him.

He ate nothing, he drank nothing. He lay motionless and silent.

"It is all the same to me," he thought when they asked him questions. "I am not going to answer. . . . It's all the same to me."

After dinner Mihail Averyanitch brought him a quarter of a pound of tea and a pound of fruit pastilles. Daryushka came too and stood for a whole hour by the bed with an expression of dull grief on her face. Dr. Hobotov visited him. He brought a bottle of bromide and told Nikita to fumigate the ward with something.

Towards evening Andrey Yefimitch died of an apoplectic stroke.

At first he had a violent shivering fit and a feeling of sickness; something revolting as it seemed, penetrating through his whole body, even to his finger-tips, strained from his stomach to his head and flooded his eyes and ears. There was a greenness before his eyes. Andrey Yefimitch understood that his end had come, and remembered that Ivan Dmitritch, Mihail Averyanitch, and millions of people believed in immortality. And what if it really existed? But he did not want immortality, and he thought of it only for one instant. A herd of deer, extraordinarily beautiful and graceful, of which he had been reading the day before, ran by him; then a peasant woman stretched out her hand to him with a registered letter. . . . Mihail Averyanitch said something, then it all vanished, and Andrey Yefimitch sank into oblivion for ever.

The hospital porters came, took him by his arms and his legs, and carried him away to the chapel.

There he lay on the table, with open eyes, and the moon shed its light upon him at night. In the morning Sergey Sergeyitch came, prayed piously before the crucifix, and closed his former chief's eyes.

Next day Andrey Yefimitch was buried. Mihail Averyanitch and Daryushka were the only people at the funeral.

1892 A.D.

TOLSTOY *Hadji Murad*

A LIST OF TARTAR WORDS USED IN
"HADJI MURAD"

In the following story Tolstoy makes use of a number of Tartar words which he does not translate. As there are generally no one- or two-word equivalents for them in English, it would be difficult to avoid following his example and retaining these Tartar words. The reader, therefore, should refer to the following alphabetical list when he encounters one of them that needs explanation.

Aoul	A Tartar village.
Bar	Have.
Beshmet	A Tartar undergarment with sleeves.
Burka	A long round felt cape.
Dzhigit	The same as a *brave* among the Red Indians, but the word is inseparably connected with the idea of skilful horsemanship.
Gazavat	Holy War against the infidels.
Imam	The leader in the Holy War, uniting in himself supreme spiritual and temporal power.
Khansha	Khan's wife.
Kizyak	A fuel made of straw and manure.
Kunak	A sworn friend, an adopted brother.
Murid	A disciple or follower: "One who desires" to find the way in Muridism.
Muridism	Almost identical with Sufism.
Murshed	"One who shows" the way in Muridism.
Naib	A Tartar lieutenant or governor.
Pilau	An Oriental dish, prepared with rice and mutton or chicken.
Saklya	A Caucasian house, clay-plastered and often built of earth.
Shariat	The written Mohammedan law.
Tarikat	"The Path" leading to the higher life.
Yok	No, not.

422

Hadji Murad

I WAS returning home by the fields. It was mid-summer, the hay harvest was over and they were just beginning to reap the rye. At that season of the year there is a delightful variety of flowers—red, white, and pink scented tufty clover; milk-white ox-eye daisies with their bright yellow centres and pleasant spicy smell; yellow honey-scented rape blossoms; tall campanulas with white and lilac bells, tulip-shaped; creeping vetch; yellow, red, and pink scabious; faintly scented, neatly arranged purple plantains with blossoms slightly tinged with pink; cornflowers, the newly opened blossoms bright blue in the sunshine but growing paler and redder towards evening or when growing old; and delicate almond-scented dodder flowers that withered quickly. I gathered myself a large nosegay and was going home when I noticed in a ditch, in full bloom, a beautiful thistle plant of the crimson variety, which in our neighborhood they call "Tartar" and carefully avoid when mowing—or, if they do happen to cut it down, throw out from among the grass for fear of pricking their hands. Thinking to pick this thistle and put it in the centre of my nosegay, I climbed down into the ditch, and after driving away a velvety bumblebee that had penetrated deep into one of the flowers and had there fallen sweetly asleep, I set to work to pluck the flower. But this proved a very difficult task. Not only did the stalk prick on every side—even through the handkerchief I wrapped round my hand—

but it was so tough that I had to struggle with it for nearly five minutes, breaking the fibers one by one; and when I had at last plucked it, the stalk was all frayed and the flower itself no longer seemed so fresh and beautiful. Moreover, owing to its coarseness and stiffness, it did not seem in place among the delicate blossoms of my nosegay. I threw it away feeling sorry to have vainly destroyed a flower that looked beautiful in its proper place.

"But what energy and tenacity! With what determination it defended itself, and how dearly it sold its life!" thought I, remembering the effort it had cost me to pluck the flower. The way home led across black-earth fields that had just been ploughed up. I ascended the dusty path. The ploughed field belonged to a landed proprietor and was so large that on both sides and before me to the top of the hill nothing was visible but evenly furrowed and moist earth. The land was well tilled and nowhere was there a blade of grass or any kind of plant to be seen, it was all black. "Ah, what a destructive creature is man. . . . How many different plant-lives he destroys to support his own existence!" thought I, involuntarily looking around for some living thing in this lifeless black field. In front of me to the right of the road I saw some kind of little clump, and drawing nearer I found it was the same kind of thistle as that which I had vainly plucked and thrown away. This "Tartar" plant had three branches. One was broken and stuck out like the stump of a mutilated arm. Each of the other two bore a flower, once red but now blackened. One stalk was broken, and half of it hung down with a soiled flower at its tip. The other, though also soiled with black mud, still stood erect. Evidently a cartwheel had passed over the plant but it had risen again, and that was why, though erect, it stood twisted to one side, as if a piece of its body had been torn from it, its bowels drawn out, an arm torn off, and one of its eyes plucked out. Yet it stood firm and did not surrender to man who had destroyed all its brothers around it. . . .

"What vitality!" I thought. "Man has conquered everything and destroyed millions of plants, yet this one won't submit." And

I remembered a Caucasian episode of years ago, which I had partly seen myself, partly heard of from eye-witnesses, and in part imagined.

The episode, as it has taken shape in my memory and imagination, was as follows.

.   .   .   .

It happened towards the end of 1851.

On a cold November evening Hadji Murad rode into Makhmet, a hostile Chechen *aoul*[1] that lay some fifteen miles from Russian territory and was filled with the scented smoke of burning *kizyak*.[2] The strained chant of the muezzin had just ceased, and through the clear mountain air, impregnated with *kizyak* smoke, above the lowing of the cattle and the bleating of the sheep that were dispersing among the *saklyas*[3] (which were crowded together like the cells of a honeycomb), could be clearly heard the guttural voices of disputing men, and sounds of women's and children's voices rising from near the fountain below.

This Hadji Murad was Shamil's *naib*,[4] famous for his exploits, who used never to ride out without his banner and some dozens of *murids*, who caracoled and showed off before him. Now wrapped in hood and *burka*,[5] from under which protruded a rifle, he rode, a fugitive, with one *murid* only, trying to attract as little attention as possible and peering with his quick black eyes into the faces of those he met on his way.

When he entered the *aoul*, instead of riding up the road leading to the open square, he turned to the left into a narrow side street, and on reaching the second *saklya*, which was cut into the hillside, he stopped and looked round. There was no one under the penthouse in front, but on the roof of the *saklya* itself, behind the freshly plastered clay chimney, lay a man covered with a sheepskin. Hadji Murad touched him with the handle of his leather-

[1] *Aoul*, Tartar village.
[2] *Kizyak*, fuel made of straw and manure.
[3] *Saklya*, a Caucasian house, clay-plastered and often built of earth.
[4] *Naib*, lieutenant or governor.
[5] *Burka*, a long, round felt cape.

plaited whip and clicked his tongue, and an old man, wearing a greasy old *beshmet*[6] and a nightcap, rose from under the sheepskin. His moist red eyelids had no lashes, and he blinked to get them unstuck. Hadji Murad, repeating the customary *"Selaam aleikum!"* uncovered his face. *"Aleikum, selaam!"* said the old man, recognizing him, and smiling with his toothless mouth. And raising himself on his thin legs he began thrusting his feet into the wooden-heeled slippers that stood by the chimney. Then he leisurely slipped his arms into the sleeves of his crumpled sheepskin, and going to the ladder that leant against the roof he descended backwards. While he dressed and as he climbed down he kept shaking his head on its thin, shrivelled sunburnt neck and mumbling something with his toothless mouth. As soon as he reached the ground he hospitably seized Hadji Murad's bridle and right stirrup; but the strong active *murid* had quickly dismounted and, motioning the old man aside, took his place. Hadji Murad also dismounted, and walking with a slight limp, entered under the penthouse. A boy of fifteen, coming quickly out of the door, met him and wonderingly fixed his sparkling eyes, black as ripe sloes, on the new arrivals.

"Run to the mosque and call your father," ordered the old man as he hurried forward to open the thin, creaking door into the *saklya*.

As Hadji Murad entered the outer door, a slight, spare, middle-aged woman in a yellow smock, red *beshmet*, and wide blue trousers came through an inner door carrying cushions.

"May thy coming bring happiness!" said she, and bending nearly double began arranging the cushions along the front wall for the guest to sit on.

"May thy sons live!" answered Hadji Murad, taking off his *burka*, his rifle, and his sword, and handing them to the old man who carefully hung the rifle and sword on a nail beside the weapons of the master of the house, which were suspended between two large basins that glittered against the clean clay-plastered and carefully whitewashed wall.

[6] *Beshmet*, a Tartar undergarment with sleeves.

Hadji Murad adjusted the pistol at his back, came up to the cushions, and wrapping his Circassian coat closer round him, sat down. The old man squatted on his bare heels beside him, closed his eyes, and lifted his hands palms upwards. Hadji Murad did the same; then after repeating a prayer they both stroked their faces, passing their hands downwards till the palms joined at the end of their beards.

"*Ne habar?*" ("Is there anything new?") asked Hadji Murad, addressing the old man.

"*Habar yok*" ("Nothing new"), replied the old man, looking with his lifeless red eyes not at Hadji Murad's face but at his breast. "I live at the apiary and have only today come to see my son. . . . He knows."

Hadji Murad, understanding that the old man did not wish to say what he knew and what Hadji Murad wanted to know, slightly nodded his head and asked no more questions.

"There is no good news," said the old man. "The only news is that the hares keep discussing how to drive away the eagles, and the eagles tear first one and then another of them. The other day the Russian dogs burnt the hay in the Mitchit *aoul*. . . . May their faces be torn!" he added hoarsely and angrily.

Hadji Murad's *murid* entered the room, his strong legs striding softly over the earthen floor. Retaining only his dagger and pistol, he took off his *burka*, rifle, and sword as Hadji Murad had done, and hung them up on the same nails as his leader's weapons.

"Who is he?" asked the old man, pointing to the newcomer.

"My *murid*. Eldar is his name," said Hadji Murad.

"That is well," said the old man, and motioned Eldar to a place on a piece of felt beside Hadji Murad. Eldar sat down, crossing his legs and fixing his fine ram-like eyes on the old man who, having now started talking, was telling how their brave fellows had caught two Russian soldiers the week before and had killed one and sent the other to Shamil in Veden.

Hadji Murad heard him absently, looking at the door and listening to the sounds outside. Under the penthouse steps were heard, the door creaked, and Sado, the master of the house, came in. He was a man of about forty, with a small beard, long nose, and eyes as black, though not as glittering, as those of his fifteen-year-old son who had run to call him home and who now entered with his father and sat down by the door. The master of the house took off his wooden slippers at the door, and pushing his old and much-worn cap to the back of his head (which had remained unshaved so long that it was beginning to be overgrown with black hair), at once squatted down in front of Hadji Murad.

He too lifted his hands palms upwards, as the old man had done, repeated a prayer, and then stroked his face downwards. Only after that did he begin to speak. He told how an order had come from Shamil to seize Hadji Murad alive or dead, that Shamil's envoys had left only the day before, that the people were afraid to disobey Shamil's orders, and that therefore it was necessary to be careful.

"In my house," said Sado, "no one shall injure my *kunak*[7] while I live, but how will it be in the open fields? . . . We must think it over."

Hadji Murad listened with attention and nodded approvingly. When Sado had finished he said:

"Very well. Now we must send a man with a letter to the Russians. My *murid* will go but he will need a guide."

"I will send brother Bata," said Sado. "Go and call Bata," he added, turning to his son.

The boy instantly bounded to his nimble feet as if he were on springs, and swinging his arms, rapidly left the *saklya*. Some ten minutes later he returned with a sinewy, short-legged Chechen, burnt almost black by the sun, wearing a worn and tattered yellow Circassian coat with frayed sleeves, and crumpled black leggings.

Hadji Murad greeted the newcomer, and again without wasting a single word, immediately asked:

"Canst thou conduct my *murid* to the Russians?"

"I can," gaily replied Bata. "I can certainly do it. There is not another Chechen who would pass as I can. Another might agree

7 *Kunak*, sworn friend, brother by adoption.

to go and might promise anything, but would do nothing; but I can do it!"

"All right," said Hadji Murad. "Thou shalt receive three for thy trouble," and he held up three fingers.

Bata nodded to show that he understood, and added that it was not money he prized, but that he was ready to serve Hadji Murad for the honor alone. Every one in the mountains knew Hadji Murad, and how he slew the Russian swine.

"Very well. . . . A rope should be long but a speech short," said Hadji Murad.

"Well then I'll hold my tongue," said Bata.

"Where the river Argun bends by the cliff," said Hadji Murad, "there are two stacks in a glade in the forest—thou knowest?"

"I know."

"There my four horsemen are waiting for me," said Hadji Murad.

"Aye," answered Bata, nodding.

"Ask for Khan Mahoma. He knows what to do and what to say. Canst thou lead him to the Russian commander, Prince Voront-sov?"

"Yes, I'll take him."

"Canst thou take him and bring him back again?"

"I can."

"Then take him there and return to the wood. I shall be there too."

"I will do it all," said Bata, rising, and putting his hands on his heart he went out.

Hadji Murad turned to his host.

"A man must also be sent to Chekhi," he began, and took hold of one of the cartridge pouches of his Circassian coat, but let his hand drop immediately and became silent on seeing two women enter the *saklya*.

One was Sado's wife—the thin middle-aged woman who had arranged the cushions. The other was quite a young girl, wearing red trousers and a green *beshmet*. A necklace of silver coins covered the whole front of her dress, and at the end of the short but thick plait of hard black hair that hung between her thin shoulder-blades a silver ruble was suspended. Her eyes, as sloe-black as those of her father and brother, sparkled brightly in her young face which tried to be stern. She did not look at the visitors, but evidently felt their presence.

Sado's wife brought in a low round table on which stood tea, pancakes in butter, cheese, *churek* (that is, thinly rolled out bread), and honey. The girl carried a basin, a ewer, and a towel.

Sado and Hadji Murad kept silent as long as the women, with their coin ornaments tinkling, moved softly about in their red soft-soled slippers, setting out before the visitors the things they had brought. Eldar sat motionless as a statue, his ram-like eyes fixed on his crossed legs, all the time the women were in the *saklya*. Only after they had gone and their soft footsteps could no longer be heard behind the door, did he give a sigh of relief.

Hadji Murad having pulled out a bullet from one of the cartridge-pouches of his Circassian coat, and having taken out a rolled-up note that lay beneath it, held it out, saying:

"To be handed to my son."

"Where must the answer be sent?"

"To thee; and thou must forward it to me."

"It shall be done," said Sado, and placed the note in a cartridge-pocket of his own coat. Then he took up the metal ewer and moved the basin towards Hadji Murad.

Hadji Murad turned up the sleeves of his *beshmet* on his white muscular arms, held out his hands under the clear cold water which Sado poured from the ewer, and having wiped them on a clean unbleached towel, turned to the table. Eldar did the same. While the visitors ate, Sado sat opposite and thanked them several times for their visit. The boy sat by the door never taking his sparkling eyes off Hadji Murad's face, and smiled as if in confirmation of his father's words.

Though he had eaten nothing for more than twenty-four hours Hadji Murad ate only a little bread and cheese; then, drawing out a small knife from under his dagger, he spread some honey on a piece of bread.

"Our honey is good," said the old man, evidently pleased to see Hadji Murad eating his honey. "This year, above all other years, it is plentiful and good."

"I thank thee," said Hadji Murad and turned from the table. Eldar would have liked to go on eating but he followed his leader's example, and having moved away from the table, handed him the ewer and basin.

Sado knew that he was risking his life by receiving such a guest in his house, for after his quarrel with Shamil the latter had issued a proclamation to all the inhabitants of Chechnya forbidding them to receive Hadji Murad on pain of death. He knew that the inhabitants of the *aoul* might at any moment become aware of Hadji Murad's presence in his house and might demand his surrender. But this not only did not frighten Sado, it even gave him pleasure: he considered it his duty to protect his guest though it should cost him his life, and he was proud and pleased with himself because he was doing his duty.

"Whilst thou art in my house and my head is on my shoulders no one shall harm thee," he repeated to Hadji Murad.

Hadji Murad looked into his glittering eyes and understanding that this was true, said with some solemnity—

"Mayest thou receive joy and life!"

Sado silently laid his hand on his heart in token of thanks for these kind words.

Having closed the shutters of the *saklya* and laid some sticks in the fireplace, Sado, in an exceptionally bright and animated mood, left the room and went into that part of his *saklya* where his family all lived. The women had not yet gone to sleep, and were talking about the dangerous visitors who were spending the night in their guest-chamber.

AT VOZDVIZHENSK, the advanced fort situated some ten miles from the *aoul* in which Hadji Murad was spending the night, three solders and a non-commissioned officer left the fort and went beyond the Shahgirinsk Gate. The soldiers, dressed as Caucasian soldiers used to be in those days, wore sheepskin coats and caps, and boots that reached above their knees, and they carried their cloaks tightly rolled up and fastened across their shoulders. Shouldering arms, they first went some five hundred paces along the road and then turned off it and went some twenty paces to the right—the dead leaves rustling under their boots—till they reached the blackened trunk of a broken plane tree just visible through the darkness. There they stopped. It was at this plane tree that an ambush party was usually placed.

The bright stars, that had seemed to be running along the tree-tops while the soldiers were walking through the forest, now stood still, shining brightly between the bare branches of the trees.

"A good job it's dry," said the non-commissioned officer Panov, bringing down his long gun and bayonet with a clang from his shoulder and placing it against the plane tree.

The three soldiers did the same.

"Sure enough I've lost it!" muttered Panov crossly. "Must have left it behind or I've dropped it on the way."

"What are you looking for?" asked one of the soldiers in a bright, cheerful voice.

"The bowl of my pipe. Where the devil has it got to?"

"Have you got the stem?" asked the cheerful voice.

"Here it is."

"Then why not stick it straight into the ground?"

"Not worth bothering!"

"We'll manage that in a minute."

Smoking in ambush was forbidden, but this ambush hardly deserved the name. It was rather an outpost to prevent the mountaineers from bringing up a cannon unobserved and firing at the fort as they used to. Panov did not consider it necessary to forego the pleasure of smoking, and therefore accepted the cheerful soldier's offer. The latter took a knife from his pocket and made a small round hole in the ground. Having smoothed it, he adjusted the pipe-stem to it, then filled the hole with tobacco and pressed it down, and the pipe was ready. A sulphur match flared and for a moment lit up the broad-cheeked face of the soldier who lay on his stomach, the air whistled in the stem, and Panov smelt the pleasant odor of burning tobacco.

"Fixed it up?" said he, rising to his feet.

"Why, of course!"

"What a smart chap you are, Avdeev! . . . As wise as a judge! Now then, lad."

Avdeev rolled over on his side to make room for Panov, letting smoke escape from his mouth.

Panov lay down prone, and after wiping the mouthpiece with his sleeve, began to inhale.

When they had had their smoke the soldiers began to talk.

"They say the commander has had his fingers in the cash-box again," remarked one of them in a lazy voice. "He lost at cards, you see."

"He'll pay it back again," said Panov.

"Of course he will! He's a good officer," assented Avdeev.

"Good! good!" gloomily repeated the man who had started the conversation. "In my opinion the company ought to speak to him. 'If you've taken the money, tell us how much and when you'll repay it.'"

"That will be as the company decides," said Panov, tearing himself away from the pipe.

"Of course. 'The community is a strong man,'" assented Avdeev, quoting a proverb.

"There will be oats to buy and boots to get towards spring. The money will be wanted, and what shall we do if he's pocketed it?" insisted the dissatisfied one.

"I tell you it will be as the company wishes," repeated Panov. "It's not the first time: he takes it and gives it back."

In the Caucasus in those days each company chose men to manage its own commissariat. They received 6 rubles 50 kopeks a month per man from the treasury, and catered for the company. They planted cabbages, made hay, had their own carts, and prided themselves on their well-fed horses. The company's money was kept in a chest of which the commander had the key, and it often happened that he borrowed from the chest. This had just happened again, and the soldiers were talking about it. The morose soldier, Nikitin, wished to demand an account from the commander, while Panov and Avdeev considered that unnecessary.

After Panov, Nikitin had a smoke, and then spreading his cloak on the ground sat down on it leaning against the trunk of the plane tree. The soldiers were silent. Far above their heads the crowns of the trees rustled in the wind and suddenly, above this incessant low rustling, rose the howling, whining, weeping, and chuckling of jackals.

"Just listen to those accursed creatures—how they caterwaul!"

"They're laughing at you because your mouth's all on one side," remarked the high voice of the third soldier, a Ukrainian.

All was silent again, except for the wind that swayed the branches, now revealing and now hiding the stars.

"I say, Panov," suddenly asked the cheerful Avdeev, "do you ever feel dull?"

"Dull, why?" replied Panov reluctantly.

"Well, I do. . . . I feel so dull sometimes that I don't know what I might not be ready to do to myself."

"There now!" was all Panov replied.

"That time when I drank all the money it was from dullness. It took hold of me . . . took hold of me till I thought to myself, 'I'll just get blind drunk!' "

"But sometimes drinking makes it still worse."

"Yes, that's happened to me too. But what is a man to do with himself?"

"But what makes you feel so dull?"

"What, me? . . . Why, it's the longing for home."

"Is yours a wealthy home then?"

"No; we weren't wealthy, but things went properly—we lived well." And Avdeev began to relate what he had already told Panov many times.

"You see, I went as a soldier of my own free will, instead of my brother," he said. "He has children. They were five in family and I had only just married. Mother began begging me to go. So I thought, 'Well, maybe they will remember what I've done.' So I went to our proprietor . . . he was a good master and he said, 'You're a fine fellow, go!' So I went instead of my brother."

"Well, that was right," said Panov.

"And yet, will you believe me, Panov, it's chiefly because of that that I feel so dull now? 'Why did you go instead of your brother?' I say to myself. 'He's living like a king now over there, while you have to suffer here'; and the more I think of it the worse I feel. . . . It seems just a piece of ill-luck!"

Avdeev was silent.

"Perhaps we'd better have another smoke," said he after a pause.

"Well then, fix it up!"

But the soldiers were not to have their smoke. Hardly had Avdeev risen to fix the pipe-stem in its place when above the rustling of the trees they heard footsteps along the road. Panov took his gun and pushed Nikitin with his foot.

Nikitin rose and picked up his cloak.

The third soldier, Bondarenko, rose also, and said:

"And I have dreamt such a dream, mates. . . ."

"Sh!" said Avdeev, and the soldiers held their breath, listening. The footsteps of men in soft-soled boots were heard approaching. The fallen leaves and dry twigs could be heard rustling clearer and clearer through the darkness. Then came the peculiar guttural tones of Chechen voices. The soldiers could now not only hear men approaching, but could see two shadows passing through a clear space between the trees; one shadow taller than the other. When these shadows had come in line with the soldiers, Panov, gun in hand, stepped out on to the road, followed by his comrades.

"Who goes there?" cried he.

"Me, friendly Chechen," said the shorter one. This was Bata. "Gun, *yok!*[8] . . . sword, *yok!*" said he, pointing to himself. "Prince, want!"

The taller one stood silent beside his comrade. He too was unarmed.

[8] *Yok*, no, not.

"He means he's a scout, and wants the Colonel," explained Panov to his comrades.

"Prince Vorontsov . . . much want! Big business!" said Bata.

"All right, all right! We'll take you to him," said Panov. "I say, you'd better take them," said he to Avdeev, "you and Bondarenko; and when you've given them up to the officer on duty come back again. Mind," he added, "be careful to make them keep in front of you!"

"And what of this?" said Avdeev, moving his gun and bayonet as though stabbing someone. "I'd just give a dig, and let the steam out of him!"

"What'll he be worth when you've stuck him?" remarked Bondarenko.

"Now, march!"

When the steps of the two soldiers conducting the scouts could no longer be heard, Panov and Nikitin returned to their post.

"What the devil brings them here at night?" said Nikitin.

"Seems it's necessary," said Panov. "But it's getting chilly," he added, and unrolling his cloak he put it on and sat down by the tree.

About two hours later Avdeev and Bondarenko returned.

"Well, have you handed them over?"

"Yes. They weren't yet asleep at the Colonel's—they were taken straight in to him. And do you know, mates, those shaven-headed lads are fine!" continued Avdeev. "Yes, really. What a talk I had with them!"

"Of course you'd talk," remarked Nikitin disapprovingly.

"Really they're just like Russians. One of them is married. 'Molly,' says I, '*bar*?'[9] '*Bar*,' he says. Bondarenko, didn't I say '*bar*?' 'Many *bar*?' 'A couple,' says he. A couple! Such a good talk we had! Such nice fellows!"

"Nice, indeed!" said Nikitin. "If you met him alone he'd soon let the guts out of you."

"It will be getting light before long," said Panov.

"Yes, the stars are beginning to go out," said Avdeev, sitting down and making himself comfortable.

9 *Bar*, have.

And the soldiers were silent again.

The windows of the barracks and the soldiers' houses had long been dark in the fort; but there were still lights in the windows of the best house.

In it lived Prince Simon Mikhailovich Vorontsov, Commander of the Kurin Regiment, an Imperial Aide-de-Camp and son of the Commander-in-Chief. Vorontsov's wife, Marya Vasilevna, a famous Petersburg beauty, was with him and they lived in this little Caucasian fort more luxuriously than anyone had ever lived there before. To Vorontsov, and even more to his wife, it seemed that they were not only living a very modest life, but one full of privations, while to the inhabitants of the place their luxury was surprising and extraordinary.

Just now, at midnight, the host and hostess sat playing cards with their visitors, at a card-table lit by four candles, in the spacious drawing-room with its carpeted floor and rich curtains drawn across the windows. Vorontsov, who had a long face and wore the insignia and gold cords of an aide-de-camp, was partnered by a shaggy young man of gloomy appearance, a graduate of Petersburg University whom Princess Vorontsov had lately had sent to the Caucasus to be tutor to her little son (born of her first marriage). Against them played two officers: one a broad, red-faced man, Poltoratsky, a company commander who had exchanged out of the Guards; and the other the regimental adjutant, who sat very straight on his chair with a cold expression on his handsome face.

Princess Marya Vasilevna, a large-built, large-eyed, black-browed beauty, sat beside Poltoratsky—her crinoline touching his legs—and looked over his cards. In her words, her looks, her smile, her perfume, and in every movement of her body, there was something that reduced Poltoratsky to obliviousness of everything except the consciousness of her nearness, and he made blunder after blunder, trying his partner's temper more and more.

"No . . . that's too bad! You've wasted an ace again," said the regimental adjutant, flushing all over as Poltoratsky threw out an ace.

Poltoratsky turned his kindly, wide-set black eyes towards the dissatisfied adjutant uncomprehendingly, as though just aroused from sleep.

"Do forgive him!" said Marya Vasilevna, smiling. "There, you see! Didn't I tell you so?" she went on, turning to Poltoratsky.

"But that's not at all what you said," replied Poltoratsky, smiling.

"Wasn't it?" she queried, with an answering smile, which excited and delighted Poltoratsky to such a degree that he blushed crimson and seizing the cards began to shuffle.

"It isn't your turn to deal," said the adjutant sternly, and with his white ringed hand he began to deal himself, as though he wished to get rid of the cards as quickly as possible.

The prince's valet entered the drawing-room and announced that the officer on duty wanted to speak to him.

"Excuse me, gentlemen," said the prince, speaking Russian with an English accent. "Will you take my place, Marya?"

"Do you all agree?" asked the princess, rising quickly and lightly to her full height, rustling her silks, and smiling the radiant smile of a happy woman.

"I always agree to everything," replied the adjutant, very pleased that the princess—who could not play at all—was now going to play against him.

Poltoratsky only spread out his hands and smiled.

The rubber was nearly finished when the prince returned to the drawing-room, animated and obviously very pleased.

"Do you know what I propose?"

"What?"

"That we have some champagne."

"I am always ready for that," said Poltoratsky.

"Why not? We shall be delighted!" said the adjutant.

"Bring some, Vasili!" said the prince.

"What did they want you for?" asked Marya Vasilevna.

"It was the officer on duty and another man."

"Who? What about?" asked Marya Vasilevna quickly.

"I mustn't say," said Vorontsov, shrugging his shoulders.

"You mustn't say!" repeated Marya Vasilevna. "We'll see about that."

When the champagne was brought each of the visitors drank a glass, and having finished the game and settled the scores they began to take their leave.

"Is it your company that's ordered to the forest to-morrow?" the prince asked Poltoratsky as they said good-bye.

"Yes, mine . . . why?"

"Then we shall meet to-morrow," said the prince, smiling slightly.

"Very pleased," replied Poltoratsky, not quite understanding what Vorontsov was saying to him and preoccupied only by the thought that he would in a minute be pressing Marya Vasilevna's hand.

Marya Vasilevna, according to her wont, not only pressed his hand firmly but shook it vigorously, and again reminding him of his mistake in playing diamonds, she gave him what he took to be a delightful, affectionate, and meaning smile.

Poltoratsky went home in an ecstatic condition only to be understood by people like himself who, having grown up and been educated in society, meet a woman belonging to their own circle after months of isolated military life, and moreover a woman like Princess Vorontsov.

When he reached the little house in which he and his comrade lived he pushed the door, but it was locked. He knocked, with no result. He felt vexed, and began kicking the door and banging it with his sword. Then he heard a sound of footsteps and Vovilo—a domestic serf of his—undid the cabin-hook which fastened the door.

"What do you mean by locking yourself in, blockhead?"

"But how is it possible, sir . . . ?"

"You're tipsy again! I'll show you 'how it is possible'!" and Poltoratsky was about to strike Vovilo but changed his mind. "Oh, go to the devil! . . . Light a candle."

"In a minute."

Vovilo was really tipsy. He had been drinking at the name-day party of the ordnance-sergeant, Ivan Petrovich. On returning home he began comparing his life with that of the latter. Ivan

Petrovich had a salary, was married, and hoped in a year's time to get his discharge.

Vovilo had been taken "up" when a boy—that is, he had been taken into his owner's household service—and now although he was already over forty he was not married, but lived a campaigning life with his harum-scarum young master. He was a good master, who seldom struck him, but what kind of a life was it? "He promised to free me when we return from the Caucasus, but where am I to go with my freedom? . . . It's a dog's life!" thought Vovilo, and he felt so sleepy that, afraid lest someone should come in and steal something, he fastened the hook of the door and fell asleep.

.   .   .   .

Poltoratsky entered the bedroom which he shared with his comrade Tikhonov.

"Well, have you lost?" asked Tikhonov, waking up.

"No, as it happens, I haven't. I've won seventeen rubles, and we drank a bottle of Cliquot!"

"And you've looked at Marya Vasilevna?"

"Yes, and I've looked at Marya Vasilevna," repeated Poltoratsky.

"It will soon be time to get up," said Tikhonov. "We are to start at six."

"Vovilo!" shouted Poltoratsky, "see that you wake me up properly to-morrow at five!"

"How can I wake you if you fight?"

"I tell you you're to wake me! Do you hear?"

"All right." Vovilo went out, taking Poltoratsky's boots and clothes with him. Poltoratsky got into bed and smoked a cigarette and put out his candle, smiling the while. In the dark he saw before him the smiling face of Marya Vasilevna.

.   .   .   .

The Vorontsovs did not go to bed at once. When the visitors had left, Marya Vasilevna went up to her husband and standing in front of him, said severely—

"*Eh bien! Vous allez me dire ce que c'est.*"[10]

"*Mais, ma chère . . .*"

"*Pas de 'ma chère'! C'était un émissaire, n'est-ce pas?*"

"*Quand même, je ne puis pas vous le dire.*"

"*Vous ne pouvez pas? Alors, c'est moi qui vais vous le dire!*"

"*Vous?*"

"It was Hadji Murad, wasn't it?" said Marya Vasilevna, who had for some days past heard of the negotiations and thought that Hadji Murad himself had been to see her husband. Vorontsov could not altogether deny this, but disappointed her by saying that it was not Hadji Murad himself but only an emissary to announce that Hadji Murad would come to meet him next day at the spot where a wood-cutting expedition had been arranged.

In the monotonous life of the fortress the young Vorontsovs— both husband and wife—were glad of this occurrence, and it was already past two o'clock when, after speaking of the pleasure the news would give his father, they went to bed.

AFTER the three sleepless nights he had passed fleeing from the *murids* Shamil had sent to capture him, Hadji Murad fell asleep as soon as Sado, having bid him good-night, had gone out of the *saklya*. He slept fully dressed with his head on his hand, his elbow sinking deep into the red down-cushions his host had arranged for him.

At a little distance, by the wall, slept Eldar. He lay on his back, his strong young limbs stretched out so that his high chest, with the black cartridge-pouches sewn into the front of his white Circassian coat, was higher than his freshly shaven, blue-gleaming head, which had rolled off the pillow and was thrown back. His upper lip, on which a little soft down was just appearing, pouted

---

[10] "Well now! You're going to tell me what it is."

"But, my dear. . . ."

"Don't 'my dear' me! It was an emissary, wasn't it?"

"Supposing it was, still I must not tell you."

"You must not? Well then, I will tell you!"

"You?"

like a child's, now contracting and now expanding, as though he were sipping something. Like Hadji Murad he slept with pistol and dagger in his belt. The sticks in the grate burnt low, and a night-light in a niche in the wall gleamed faintly.

In the middle of the night the floor of the guest-chamber creaked, and Hadji Murad immediately rose, putting his hand to his pistol. Sado entered, treading softly on the earthen floor.

"What is it?" asked Hadji Murad, as if he had not been asleep at all.

"We must think," replied Sado, squatting down in front of him. "A woman from her roof saw you arrive and told her husband, and now the whole *aoul* knows. A neighbor has just been to tell my wife that the Elders have assembled in the mosque and want to detain you."

"I must be off!" said Hadji Murad.

"The horses are saddled," said Sado, quickly leaving the *saklya*.

"Eldar!" whispered Hadji Murad. And Eldar, hearing his name, and above all his master's voice, leapt to his feet, setting his cap straight as he did so.

Hadji Murad put on his weapons and then his *burka*. Eldar did the same, and they both went silently out of the *saklya* into the penthouse. The black-eyed boy brought their horses. Hearing the clatter of hoofs on the hard-beaten road, someone stuck his head out of the door of a neighboring *saklya*, and a man ran up the hill towards the mosque, clattering with his wooden shoes. There was no moon, but the stars shone brightly in the black sky so that the outlines of the *saklya* roofs could be seen in the darkness, the mosque with its minarets in the upper part of the village rising above the other buildings. From the mosque came a hum of voices.

Quickly seizing his gun, Hadji Murad placed his foot in the nar-row stirrup, and silently and easily throwing his body across, swung himself on to the high cushion of the saddle.

"May God reward you!" he said, addressing his host while his right foot felt instinctively for the stirrup, and with his whip he lightly touched the lad who held his horse, as a sign that he should let go. The boy stepped aside, and the horse, as if it knew what it had to do, started at a brisk pace down the lane towards the principal street. Eldar rode behind him. Sado in his sheepskin followed, almost running, swinging his arms and crossing now to one side and now to the other of the narrow side-street. At the place where the streets met, first one moving shadow and then another appeared in the road.

"Stop . . . who's that? Stop!" shouted a voice, and several men blocked the path.

Instead of stopping, Hadji Murad drew his pistol from his belt and increasing his speed rode straight at those who blocked the way. They separated, and without looking round he started down the road at a swift canter. Eldar followed him at a sharp trot. Two shots cracked behind them and two bullets whistled past without hitting either Hadji Murad or Eldar. Hadji Murad continued riding at the same pace, but having gone some three hundred yards he stopped his slightly panting horse and listened.

In front of him, lower down, gurgled rapidly running water. Behind him in the *aoul* cocks crowed, answering one another. Above these sounds he heard behind him the approaching tramp of horses and the voices of several men. Hadji Murad touched his horse and rode on at an even pace. Those behind him galloped and soon overtook him. They were some twenty mounted men, inhabitants of the *aoul*, who had decided to detain Hadji Murad or at least to make a show of detaining him in order to justify themselves in Shamil's eyes. When they came near enough to be seen in the darkness, Hadji Murad stopped, let go his bridle, and with an accustomed movement of his left hand unbuttoned the cover of his rifle, which he drew forth with his right. Eldar did the same.

"What do you want?" cried Hadji Murad. "Do you wish to take me? . . . Take me, then!" and he raised his rifle. The men from the *aoul* stopped, and Hadji Murad, rifle in hand, rode down into the ravine. The mounted men followed him but did not draw any nearer. When Hadji Murad had crossed to the other side of the ravine the men shouted to him that he should hear what they had to say. In reply he fired his rifle and put his horse to a gallop. When he reined it in his pursuers were no longer within hearing and the crowing of the cocks could also no longer be heard; only the murmur of the water in the forest sounded more distinctly and now and then came the cry of an owl. The black wall of the forest appeared quite close. It was in this forest that his *murids* awaited him.

On reaching it Hadji Murad paused, and drawing much air into his lungs he whistled and then listened silently. The next minute he was answered by a similar whistle from the forest. Hadji Murad turned from the road and entered it. When he had gone about a hundred paces he saw among the trunks of the trees a bonfire, the shadows of some men sitting round it, and, half lit-up by the firelight, a hobbled horse which was saddled. Four men were seated by the fire.

One of them rose quickly, and coming up to Hadji Murad took hold of his bridle and stirrup. This was Hadji Murad's sworn brother who managed his household affairs for him.

"Put out the fire," said Hadji Murad, dismounting.

The men began scattering the pile and trampling on the burning branches.

"Has Bata been here?" asked Hadji Murad, moving towards a *burka* that was spread on the ground.

"Yes, he went away long ago with Khan Mahoma."

"Which way did they go?"

"That way," answered Khanefi pointing in the opposite direction to that from which Hadji Murad had come.

"All right," said Hadji Murad, and unslinging his rifle he began to load it.

"We must take care—I have been pursued," he said to a man who was putting out the fire.

This was Gamzalo, a Chechen. Gamzalo approached the *burka*, took up a rifle that lay on it wrapped in its cover, and without a word went to that side of the glade from which Hadji Murad had come.

When Eldar had dismounted he took Hadji Murad's horse, and

having reined up both horses' heads high, tied them to two trees. Then he shouldered his rifle as Gamzalo had done and went to the other side of the glade. The bonfire was extinguished, the forest no longer looked as black as before, but in the sky the stars still shone, though faintly.

Lifting his eyes to the stars and seeing that the Pleiades had already risen half-way up the sky, Hadji Murad calculated that it must be long past midnight and that his nightly prayer was long overdue. He asked Khanefi for a ewer (they always carried one in their packs), and putting on his *burka* went to the water.

Having taken off his shoes and performed his ablutions, Hadji Murad stepped onto the *burka* with bare feet and then squatted down on his calves, and having first placed his fingers in his ears and closed his eyes, he turned to the south and recited the usual prayer.

When he had finished he returned to the place where the saddle-bags lay, and sitting down on the *burka* he leant his elbows on his knees and bowed his head and fell into deep thought.

Hadji Murad always had great faith in his own fortune. When planning anything he always felt in advance firmly convinced of success, and fate smiled on him. It had been so, with a few rare exceptions, during the whole course of his stormy military life; and so he hoped it would be now. He pictured to himself how— with the army Vorontsov would place at his disposal—he would march against Shamil and take him prisoner, and revenge himself on him; and how the Russian Tsar would reward him and how he would again rule not only over Avaria, but over the whole of Chechnya, which would submit to him. With these thoughts he unwittingly fell asleep.

He dreamt how he and his brave followers rushed at Shamil with songs and with the cry, "Hadji Murad is coming!" and how they seized him and his wives and how he heard the wives crying and sobbing. He woke up. The song, *Lya-il-allysha*, and the cry, "Hadji Murad is coming!" and the weeping of Shamil's wives, was the howling, weeping, and laughter of jackals that awoke him. Hadji Murad lifted his head, glanced at the sky which, seen between the trunks of the trees, was already growing light in the east, and inquired after Khan Mahoma of a *murid* who sat at some distance from him. On hearing that Khan Mahoma had not yet returned, Hadji Murad again bowed his head and at once fell asleep.

He was awakened by the merry voice of Khan Mahoma returning from his mission with Bata. Khan Mahoma at once sat down beside Hadji Murad and told him how the soldiers had met them and had led them to the prince himself, and how pleased the prince was and how he promised to meet them in the morning where the Russians would be felling trees beyond the Mitchik in the Shalin glade. Bata interrupted his fellow-envoy to add details of his own.

Hadji Murad asked particularly for the words with which Vorontsov had answered his offer to go over to the Russians, and Khan Mahoma and Bata replied with one voice that the prince promised to receive Hadji Murad as a guest, and to act so that it should be well for him.

Then Hadji Murad questioned them about the road, and when Khan Mahoma assured him that he knew the way well and would conduct him straight to the spot, Hadji Murad took out some money and gave Bata the promised three rubles. Then he ordered his men to take out of the saddle-bags his gold-ornamented weapons and his turban, and to clean themselves up so as to look well when they arrived among the Russians.

While they cleaned their weapons, harness, and horses, the stars faded away, it became quite light, and an early morning breeze sprang up.

EARLY in the morning, while it was still dark, two companies carrying axes and commanded by Poltoratsky marched six miles beyond the Shahgirinsk Gate, and having thrown out a line of sharpshooters set to work to fell trees as soon as the day broke. Towards eight o'clock the mist which had mingled with the perfumed smoke of the hissing and crackling damp green branches on the bonfires began to rise and the wood-fellers—who till then had not seen five paces off but had only heard one another—began to see both the bonfires and the road through the forest, blocked with fallen trees. The sun now appeared like a bright spot in the fog and now again was hidden.

In the glade, some way from the road, Poltoratsky, his sub-altern Tikhonov, two officers of the Third Company, and Baron Freze, an ex-officer of the Guards and a fellow-student of Poltoratsky's at the Cadet College, who had been reduced to the ranks for fighting a duel, were sitting on drums. Bits of paper that had contained food, cigarette stumps, and empty bottles, lay scattered around them. The officers had had some vodka and were now eating, and drinking porter. A drummer was uncorking their third bottle.

Poltoratsky, although he had not had enough sleep, was in that peculiar state of elation and kindly careless gaiety which he always felt when he found himself among his soldiers and with his comrades where there was a possibility of danger.

The officers were carrying on an animated conversation, the subject of which was the latest news: the death of General Sleptsov. None of them saw in this death that most important moment of a life, its termination and return to the source whence it sprang—they saw in it only the valor of a gallant officer who rushed at the mountaineers sword in hand and hacked them desperately.

Though all of them—and especially those who had been in action—knew and could not help knowing that in those days in the Caucasus, and in fact anywhere and at any time, such hand-to-hand hacking as is always imagined and described never occurs (or if hacking with swords and bayonets ever does occur, it is only those who are running away that get hacked), that fiction of hand-to-hand fighting endowed them with the calm pride and cheerfulness with which they sat on the drums—some with a jaunty air, others on the contrary in a very modest pose, and drank and joked without troubling about death, which might overtake them at any moment as it had overtaken Sleptsov. And in the midst of their talk, as if to confirm their expectations, they heard to the left of the road the pleasant stirring sound of a rifle-shot; and a bullet, merrily whistling somewhere in the misty air, flew past and crashed into a tree.

"Hullo!" exclaimed Poltoratsky in a merry voice; "why that's at our line. . . . There now, Kostya," and he turned to Freze, "now's your chance. Go back to the company. I will lead the whole company to support the cordon and we'll arrange a battle that will be simply delightful . . . and then we'll make a report."

Freze jumped to his feet and went at a quick pace towards the smoke-enveloped spot where he had left his company.

Poltoratsky's little Kabarda dapple-bay was brought to him, and he mounted and drew up his company and led it in the direction whence the shots were fired. The outposts stood on the skirts of the forest in front of the bare descending slope of a ravine. The wind was blowing in the direction of the forest, and not only was it possible to see the slope of the ravine, but the opposite side of it was also distinctly visible. When Poltoratsky rode up to the line the sun came out from behind the mist, and on the other side of the ravine, by the outskirts of a young forest, a few horsemen could be seen at a distance of a quarter of a mile. These were the Chechens who had pursued Hadji Murad and wanted to see him meet the Russians. One of them fired at the line. Several soldiers fired back. The Chechens retreated and the firing ceased.

But when Poltoratsky and his company came up he nevertheless gave orders to fire, and scarcely had the word been passed than along the whole line of sharpshooters the incessant, merry, stirring rattle of our rifles began, accompanied by pretty dissolving cloud-lets of smoke. The soldiers, pleased to have some distraction, hastened to load and fired shot after shot. The Chechens evidently caught the feeling of excitement, and leaping forward one after another fired a few shots at our men. One of these shots wounded a soldier. It was that same Avdeev who had lain in ambush the night before.

When his comrades approached him he was lying prone, holding his wounded stomach with both hands, and rocking himself with a rhythmic motion moaned softly. He belonged to Poltoratsky's company, and Poltoratsky, seeing a group of soldiers collected, rode up to them.

"What is it, lad? Been hit?" said Poltoratsky. "Where?"

Avdeev did not answer.

"I was just going to load, your honor, when I heard a click," said a soldier who had been with Avdeev; "and I look and see he's dropped his gun."

"Tut, tut, tut!" Poltoratsky clicked his tongue. "Does it hurt much, Avdeev?"

"It doesn't hurt but it stops me walking. A drop of vodka now, your honor!"

Some vodka (or rather the spirit drunk by the soldiers in the Caucasus) was found, and Panov, severely frowning, brought Avdeev a can-lid full. Avdeev tried to drink it but immediately handed back the lid.

"My soul turns against it," he said. "Drink it yourself."

Panov drank up the spirit.

Avdeev raised himself but sank back at once. They spread out a cloak and laid him on it.

"Your honor, the colonel is coming," said the sergeant-major to Poltoratsky.

"All right. Then will you see to him?" said Poltoratsky, and flourishing his whip he rode at a fast trot to meet Vorontsov.

Vorontsov was riding his thoroughbred English chestnut gelding, and was accompanied by the adjutant, a Cossack, and a Chechen interpreter.

"What's happening here," asked Vorontsov.

"Why, a skirmishing party attacked our advanced line," Poltoratsky answered.

"Come, come—you arranged the whole thing yourself!"

"Oh no, Prince, not I," said Poltoratsky with a smile; "they pushed forward of their own accord."

"I hear a soldier has been wounded?"

"Yes, it's a great pity. He's a good soldier."

"Seriously?"

"Seriously, I believe . . . in the stomach."

"And do you know where I am going?" Vorontsov asked.

"I don't."

"Can't you guess?"

"No."

"Hadji Murad has surrendered and we are now going to meet him."

"You don't mean to say so?"

"His envoy came to me yesterday," said Vorontsov, with difficulty repressing a smile of pleasure. "He will be waiting for me at the Shalin glade in a few minutes. Place sharpshooters as far as the glade, and then come and join me."

"I understand," said Poltoratsky, lifting his hand to his cap, and rode back to his company. He led the sharpshooters to the right himself, and ordered the sergeant-major to do the same on the left side.

The wounded Avdeev had meanwhile been taken back to the fort by some of the soldiers.

On his way back to rejoin Vorontsov, Poltoratsky noticed behind him several horsemen who were overtaking him. In front on a white-maned horse rode a man of imposing appearance. He wore a turban and carried weapons with gold ornaments. This man was Hadji Murad. He approached Poltoratsky and said something to him in Tartar. Raising his eyebrows, Poltoratsky made a gesture with his arms to show that he did not understand, and smiled. Hadji Murad gave him smile for smile, and that smile struck Poltoratsky by its childlike kindliness. Poltoratsky had never expected to see the terrible mountain chief look like that. He had expected to see a morose, hard-featured man, and here was a vivacious person whose smile was so kindly that Poltoratsky felt as if he were an old acquaintance. He had only one peculiarity: his eyes, set wide apart, which gazed from under their black brows calmly, attentively, and penetratingly into the eyes of others.

Hadji Murad's suite consisted of five men, among them was Khan Mahoma, who had been to see Prince Vorontsov that night. He was a rosy, round-faced fellow with black lashless eyes and a beaming expression, full of the joy of life. Then there was the Avar Khanefi, a thick-set, hairy man, whose eyebrows met. He was in charge of all Hadji Murad's property and led a stud-bred horse which carried tightly packed saddlebags. Two men of the suite were particularly striking. The first was a Lesghian: a youth, broad-shouldered but with a waist as slim as a woman's, beautiful ram-like eyes, and the beginnings of a brown beard. This was Eldar. The other, Gamzalo, was a Chechen with a short red beard and no eyebrows or eyelashes; he was blind in one eye and had a scar across his nose and face. Poltoratsky pointed out Vorontsov, who had just appeared on the road. Hadji Murad rode to meet him, and putting his right hand on his heart said something in Tartar and stopped. The Chechen interpreter translated.

"He says, 'I surrender myself to the will of the Russian Tsar. I wish to serve him,' he says. 'I wished to do so long ago but Shamil would not let me.'"

Having heard what the interpreter said, Vorontsov stretched out his hand in its wash-leather glove to Hadji Murad. Hadji Murad looked at it hesitatingly for a moment and then pressed it firmly, again saying something and looking first at the interpreter and then at Vorontsov.

"He says he did not wish to surrender to anyone but you, as you are the son of the Sirdar and he respects you much."

Vorontsov nodded to express his thanks. Hadji Murad again said something, pointing to his suite.

"He says that these men, his henchmen, will serve the Russians as well as he."

Vorontsov turned towards them and nodded to them too. The merry, black-eyed, lashless Chechen, Khan Mahoma, also nodded and said something which was probably amusing, for the hairy Avar drew his lips into a smile, showing his ivory-white teeth. But the red-haired Gamzalo's one red eye just glanced at Vorontsov and then was again fixed on the ears of his horse.

When Vorontsov and Hadji Murad with their retinues rode back to the fort, the soldiers released from the lines gathered in groups and made their own comments.

"What a lot of men that damned fellow has destroyed! And now see what a fuss they will make of him!"

"Naturally. He was Shamil's right hand, and now—no fear!"

"Still there's no denying it! he's a fine fellow—a regular *dzhigit!*"[11]

"And the red one! He squints at you like a beast!"

"Ugh! He must be a hound!"

They had all specially noticed the red one. Where the wood-felling was going on the soldiers nearest to the road ran out to look. Their officer shouted to them, but Vorontsov stopped him.

"Let them have a look at their old friend."

"You know who that is?" he added, turning to the nearest soldier, and speaking the words slowly with his English accent.

"No, your Excellency."

"Hadji Murad. . . . Heard of him?"

"How could we help it, your Excellency? We've beaten him many a time!"

"Yes, and we've had it hot from him too."

"Yes, that's true, your Excellency," answered the soldier, pleased to be talking with his chief.

Hadji Murad understood that they were speaking about him, and smiled brightly with his eyes.

Vorontsov returned to the fort in a very cheerful mood.

YOUNG Vorontsov was much pleased that it was he, and no one else, who had succeeded in winning over and receiving Hadji Murad—next to Shamil Russia's chief and most active enemy. There was only one unpleasant thing about it: General Meller-Zakomelsky was in command of the army at Vozdvizhensk, and the whole affair ought to have been carried out through him. As Vorontsov had done everything himself without reporting it there might be some unpleasantness, and this thought rather interfered with his satisfaction. On reaching his house he entrusted Hadji

[11] Among the Chechens, a *dzhigit* is the same as a *brave* among the Indians, but the word is inseparably connected with the idea of skilful horsemanship.

Murad's henchmen to the regimental adjutant and himself showed Hadji Murad into the house.

Princess Marya Vasilevna, elegantly dressed and smiling, and her little son, a handsome curly-headed child of six, met Hadji Murad in the drawing-room. The latter placed his hands on his heart, and through the interpreter—who had entered with him— said with solemnity that he regarded himself as the prince's *kunak*, since the prince had brought him into his own house; and that a *kunak's* whole family was as sacred as the *kunak* himself.

Hadji Murad's appearance and manners pleased Marya Vasilevna, and the fact that he flushed when she held out her large white hand to him inclined her still more in his favor. She invited him to sit down, and having asked him whether he drank coffee, had some served. He, however, declined it when it came. He understood a little Russian but could not speak it. When something was said which he could not understand he smiled, and his smile pleased Marya Vasilevna just as it had pleased Poltoratsky. The curly-haired, keen-eyed little boy (whom his mother called Bulka) standing beside her did not take his eyes off Hadji Murad, whom he had always heard spoken of as a great warrior.

Leaving Hadji Murad with his wife, Vorontsov went to his office to do what was necessary about reporting the fact of Hadji Murad's having come over to the Russians. When he had written a report to the general in command of the left flank—General Kozlovsky—at Grozny, and a letter to his father, Vorontsov hurried home, afraid that his wife might be vexed with him for forcing on her this terrible stranger, who had to be treated in such a way that he should not take offence, and yet not too kindly. But his fears were needless. Hadji Murad was sitting in an armchair with little Bulka, Vorontsov's stepson, on his knee, and with bent head was listening attentively to the interpreter who was translating to him the words of the laughing Marya Vasilevna. Marya Vasilevna was telling him that if every time a *kunak* admired anything of his he made him a present of it, he would soon have to go about like Adam. . . .

When the prince entered, Hadji Murad rose at once and, sur-

prising and offending Bulka by putting him off his knee, changing
the playful expression of his face to a stern and serious one. He
only sat down again when Vorontsov had himself taken a seat.

Continuing the conversation he answered Marya Vasilevna by
telling her that it was a law among his people that anything your
kunak admired must be presented to him.

"Thy son, *kunak!*" he said in Russian, patting the curly head of
the boy who had again climbed on his knee.

"He is delightful, your brigand!" said Marya Vasilevna to her
husband in French. "Bulka has been admiring his dagger, and he
has given it to him."

Bulka showed the dagger to his father. "*C'est un objet de
prix!*"[12] added she.

"*Il faudra trouver l'occasion de lui faire cadeau,*"[13] said
Vorontsov.

Hadji Murad, his eyes turned down, sat stroking the boy's
curly hair and saying: "*Dzhigit, dzhigit!*"

"A beautiful, beautiful dagger," said Vorontsov, half drawing
out the sharpened blade which had a ridge down the center. "I
thank thee!"

"Ask him what I can do for him," he said to the interpreter.

The interpreter translated, and Hadji Murad at once replied
that he wanted nothing but that he begged to be taken to a place
where he could say his prayers.

Vorontsov called his valet and told him to do what Hadji
Murad desired.

As soon as Hadji Murad was alone in the room allotted to him
his face altered. The pleased expression, now kindly and now
stately, vanished, and a look of anxiety showed itself. Vorontsov
had received him far better than Hadji Murad had expected. But
the better the reception the less did Hadji Murad trust Vorontsov
and his officers. He feared everything: that he might be seized,
chained, and sent to Siberia, or simply killed; and therefore he
was on his guard. He asked Eldar, when the latter entered his

[12] "It is a thing of value."
[13] "We must find an opportunity to make him a present."

room, where his *murids* had been put and whether their arms had been taken from them, and where the horses were. Eldar reported that the horses were in the prince's stables; that the men had been placed in a barn; that they retained their arms, and that the interpreter was giving them food and tea.

Hadji Murad shook his head in doubt, and after undressing said his prayers and told Eldar to bring him his silver dagger. He then dressed, and having fastened his belt sat down on the divan with his legs tucked under him, to await what might befall him.

At four in the afternoon the interpreter came to call him to dine with the prince.

At dinner he hardly ate anything except some *pilau*, to which he helped himself from the very part of the dish from which Marya Vasilevna had helped herself.

"He is afraid we shall poison him," Marya Vasilevna remarked to her husband. "He has helped himself from the place where I took my helping." Then instantly turning to Hadji Murad she asked him through the interpreter when he would pray again. Hadji Murad lifted five fingers and pointed to the sun. "Then it will soon be time," and Vorontsov drew out his watch and pressed a spring. The watch struck four and one quarter. This evidently surprised Hadji Murad, and he asked to hear it again and to be allowed to look at the watch.

"*Voilà l'occasion! Donnez-lui la montre,*"[14] said the Princess to her husband.

Vorontsov at once offered the watch to Hadji Murad.

The latter placed his hand on his breast and took the watch. He touched the spring several times, listened, and nodded his head approvingly.

After dinner, Meller-Zakomelsky's aide-de-camp was announced.

The aide-de-camp informed the prince that the general, having heard of Hadji Murad's arrival, was highly displeased that this had not been reported to him, and required Hadji Murad to be brought to him without delay. Vorontsov replied that the general's command should be obeyed, and through the interpreter informed

[14] "This is the opportunity! Give him the watch."

Hadji Murad of these orders and asked him to go to Meller with him.

When Marya Vasilevna heard what the aide-de-camp had come about, she at once understood that unpleasantness might arise between her husband and the general, and in spite of all her husband's attempts to dissuade her, decided to go with him and Hadji Murad.

"*Vous feriez bien mieux de rester—c'est mon affaire, non pas la vôtre. . . .*"

"*Vous ne pouvez pas m'empêcher d'aller voir madame la générale!*"[15]

"You could go some other time."

"But I wish to go now!"

There was no help for it, so Vorontsov agreed, and they all three went.

When they entered, Meller with somber politeness conducted Marya Vasilevna to his wife and told his aide-de-camp to show Hadji Murad into the waiting-room and not let him out till further orders.

"Please . . ." he said to Vorontsov, opening the door of his study and letting the prince enter before him.

Having entered the study he stopped in front of Vorontsov and, without offering him a seat, said:

"I am in command here and therefore all negotiations with the enemy have to be carried on through me! Why did you not report to me that Hadji Murad had come over?"

"An emissary came to me and announced his wish to capitulate only to me," replied Vorontsov growing pale with excitement, expecting some rude expression from the angry general and at the same time becoming infected with his anger.

"I ask you why I was not informed?"

"I intended to inform you, Baron, but . . ."

"You are not to address me as 'Baron,' but as 'Your Excel-

---

[15] "You would do much better to remain at home . . . this is my business, and not yours."
"You cannot prevent my going to see the general's wife!"

lency'!" And here the baron's pent-up irritation suddenly broke out and he uttered all that had long been boiling in his soul.

"I have not served my sovereign twenty-seven years in order that men who began their service yesterday, relying on family connections, should give orders under my very nose about matters that do not concern them!"

"Your Excellency, I request you not to say things that are incorrect!" interrupted Vorontsov.

"I am saying what is correct, and I won't allow . . ." said the general, still more irritably.

But at that moment Marya Vasilevna entered, rustling with her skirts and followed by a modest-looking little lady, Meller-Zakomelsky's wife.

"Come, come, Baron! Simon did not wish to displease you," began Marya Vasilevna.

"I am not speaking about that, Princess. . . ."

"Well, well, let's forget it all! . . . You know, 'A bad peace is better than a good quarrel!' . . . Oh dear, what am I saying?" and she laughed.

The angry general capitulated to the enchanting laugh of the beauty. A smile hovered under his moustache.

"I confess I was wrong," said Vorontsov, "but——"

"And I too got rather carried away," said Meller, and held out his hand to the prince.

Peace was re-established, and it was decided to leave Hadji Murad with the general for the present, and then to send him to the commander of the left flank.

Hadji Murad sat in the next room and though he did not understand what was said, he understood what it was necessary for him to understand—namely, that they were quarrelling about him, that his desertion of Shamil was a matter of immense importance to the Russians, and that therefore not only would they not exile or kill him, but that he would be able to demand much from them. He also understood that though Meller-Zakomelsky was the commanding-officer, he had not as much influence as his subordinate Vorontsov, and that Vorontsov was important and Meller-

Zakomelsky unimportant; and therefore when Meller-Zakomelsky sent for him and began to question him, Hadji Murad bore himself proudly and ceremoniously, saying that he had come from the mountains to serve the White Tsar and would give account only to his Sirdar, meaning the commander-in-chief, Prince Vorontsov senior, in Tiflis.

T H E wounded Avdeev was taken to the hospital—a small wooden building roofed with boards at the entrance of the fort—and was placed on one of the empty beds in the common ward. There were four patients in the ward: one ill with typhus and in high fever; another, pale, with dark shadows under his eyes, who had ague, was just expecting another attack and yawned continually; and two more who had been wounded in a raid three weeks before: one in the hand—he was up—and the other in the shoulder. The latter was sitting on a bed. All of them except the typhus patient surrounded and questioned the newcomer and those who had brought him.

'Sometimes they fire as if they were spilling peas over you, and nothing happens . . . and this time only about five shots were fired," related one of the bearers.

"Each man gets what fate sends!"

"Oh!" groaned Avdeev loudly, trying to master his pain when they began to place him on the bed; but he stopped groaning when he was on it, and only frowned and moved his feet continually. He held his hands over his wound and looked fixedly before him.

The doctor came, and gave orders to turn the wounded man over to see whether the bullet had passed out behind.

"What's this?" the doctor asked, pointing to the large white scars that crossed one another on the patient's back and loins.

"That was done long ago, your honor!" replied Avdeev with a groan.

They were scars left by the flogging Avdeev had received for the money he drank.

Avdeev was again turned over, and the doctor probed in his stomach for a long time and found the bullet, but failed to extract it. He put a dressing on the wound, and having stuck plaster over it went away. During the whole time the doctor was probing and bandaging the wound Avdeev lay with clenched teeth and closed eyes, but when the doctor had gone he opened them and looked around as though amazed. His eyes were turned on the other patients and on the surgeon's orderly, though he seemed to see not them but something else that surprised him.

His friends Panov and Serogin came in, but Avdeev continued to lie in the same position looking before him with surprise. It was long before he recognized his comrades, though his eyes gazed straight at them.

"I say, Peter, have you no message to send home?" said Panov.

Avdeev did not answer, though he was looking Panov in the face.

"I say, haven't you any orders to send home?" again repeated Panov, touching Avdeev's cold, large-boned hand.

Avdeev seemed to come to.

"Ah! . . . Panov!"

"Yes, I'm here. . . . I've come! Have you nothing for home? Serogin would write a letter."

"Serogin . . ." said Avdeev moving his eyes with difficulty towards Serogin, "will you write? . . . Well then, write so: 'Your son,' say, 'Peter, has given orders that you should live long.[16] He envied his brother' . . . I told you about that today . . . 'and now he is himself glad. Don't worry him. . . . Let him live. God grant it him. I am glad!' Write that."

Having said this he was silent for some time with his eyes fixed on Panov.

"And did you find your pipe?" he suddenly asked.

Panov did not reply.

"Your pipe . . . your pipe! I mean, have you found it?" Avdeev repeated.

---

[16] A popular expression, meaning that the sender of the message is already dead.

"It was in my bag."

"That's right! . . . Well, and now give me a candle to hold . . . I am going to die," said Avdeev.

Just then Poltoratsky came in to inquire after his soldier.

"How goes it, my lad! Badly?" said he.

Avdeev closed his eyes and shook his head negatively. His broad-cheeked face was pale and stern. He did not reply, but again said to Panov:

"Bring a candle. . . . I am going to die."

A wax taper was placed in his hand but his fingers would not bend, so it was placed between them and held up for him. Poltoratsky went away, and five minutes later the orderly put his ear to Avdeev's heart and said that all was over.

Avdeev's death was described in the following manner in the report sent to Tiflis:

"*23rd Nov.*—Two companies of the Kurin regiment advanced from the fort on a wood-felling expedition. At midday a considerable number of mountaineers suddenly attacked the wood-fellers. The sharpshooters began to retreat, but the 2nd Company charged with the bayonet and overthrew the mountaineers. In this affair two privates were slightly wounded and one killed. The mountaineers lost about a hundred men killed and wounded."

ON THE day Peter Avdeev died in the hospital at Vozdvizhensk, his old father with the wife of the brother in whose stead he had enlisted, and that brother's daughter—who was already approaching womanhood and almost of age to get married—were threshing oats on the hard-frozen threshing-floor.

There had been a heavy fall of snow the previous night, followed towards morning by a severe frost. The old man woke when the cocks were crowing for the third time, and seeing the bright moonlight through the frozen window-panes got down from the stove, put on his boots, his sheepskin coat and cap, and went out to the threshing-floor. Having worked there for a couple of hours he returned to the hut and awoke his son and the women. When the woman and the girl came to the threshing-floor they found it ready swept, with a wooden shovel sticking in the dry white snow, beside which were birch brooms with the twigs upwards and two rows of oat-sheaves laid ears to ears in a long line the whole length of the clean threshing-floor. They chose their flails and started threshing, keeping time with their triple blows. The old man struck powerfully with his heavy flail, breaking the straw, the girl struck the ears from above with measured blows, and the daughter-in-law turned the oats over with her flail.

The moon had set, dawn was breaking, and they were finishing the line of sheaves when Akim, the eldest son, in his sheepskin and cap, joined the threshers.

"What are you lazing about for?" shouted his father to him, pausing in his work and leaning on his flail.

"The horses had to be seen to."

" 'Horses seen to!' " the father repeated, mimicking him. "The old woman will look after them. . . . Take your flail! You're getting too fat, you drunkard!"

"Have you been standing me treat?" muttered the son.

"What?" said the old man, frowning sternly and missing a stroke.

The son silently took a flail and they began threshing with four flails.

"Trak, tapatam . . . trak, tapatam . . . trak . . ." came down the old man's heavy flail after the three others.

"Why, you've got a nape like a goodly gentleman! . . . Look here, my trousers have hardly anything to hang on!" said the old man, omitting his stroke and only swinging his flail in the air so as not to get out of time.

They had finished the row, and the women began removing the straw with rakes.

"Peter was a fool to go in your stead. They'd have knocked the nonsense out of you in the army, and he was worth five of such as you at home!"

"That's enough, father," said the daughter-in-law, as she threw aside the binders that had come off the sheaves.

"Yes, feed the six of you and get no work out of a single one! Peter used to work for two. He was not like . . ."

Along the trodden path from the house came the old man's wife, the frozen snow creaking under the new bark shoes she wore over her tightly wound woollen leg-bands. The men were shovelling the unwinnowed grain into heaps, the woman and the girl sweeping up what remained.

"The Elder has been and orders everybody to go and work for the master, carting bricks," said the old woman. "I've got breakfast ready. . . . Come along, won't you?"

"All right. . . . Harness the roan and go," said the old man to Akim, "and you'd better look out that you don't get me into trouble as you did the other day! . . . I can't help regretting Peter!"

"When he was at home you used to scold him," retorted Akim. "Now he's away you keep nagging at me."

"That shows you deserve it," said his mother in the same angry tones. "You'll never be Peter's equal."

"Oh, all right," said the son.

" 'All right,' indeed! You've drunk the meal, and now you say 'all right'!"

"Let bygones be bygones!" said the daughter-in-law.

The disagreements between father and son had begun long ago —almost from the time Peter went as a soldier. Even then the old man felt that he had parted with an eagle for a cuckoo. It is true that it was right—as the old man understood it—for a childless man to go in place of a family man. Akim had four children and Peter had none; but Peter was a worker like his father, skilful, observant, strong, enduring, and above all industrious. He was always at work. If he happened to pass by where people were working he lent a helping hand as his father would have done, and took a turn or two with the scythe, or loaded a cart, or felled a tree, or chopped some wood. The old man regretted his going away, but there was no help for it. Conscription in those days was like death. A soldier was a severed branch, and to think about him at home was to tear one's heart uselessly. Only occasionally, to prick his elder son, did the father mention him, as he had done that day. But his mother often thought of her younger son, and for a long time—more than a year now—she had been asking her husband to send Peter a little money, but the old man had made no response.

The Kurenkovs were a well-to-do family and the old man had some savings hidden away, but he would on no account have consented to touch what he had laid by. Now however the old woman having heard him mention their younger son, made up her mind to ask him again to send him at least a ruble after selling the oats. This she did. As soon as the young people had gone to work for the proprietor and the old folk were left alone together, she persuaded him to send Peter a ruble out of the oats-money.

So when ninety-six bushels of the winnowed oats had been packed onto three sledges lined with sacking carefully pinned together at the top with wooden skewers, she gave her husband a letter the church clerk had written at her dictation, and the old man promised when he got to town to enclose a ruble and send it off to the right address.

The old man, dressed in a new sheepskin with a homespun cloak over it, his legs wrapped round with warm white woollen leg-bands, took the letter, placed it in his wallet, said a prayer, got into the front sledge, and drove to town. His grandson drove in the last sledge. When he reached town the old man asked the innkeeper to read the letter to him, and listened to it attentively and approvingly.

In her letter Peter's mother first sent him her blessing, then greetings from everybody and the news of his godfather's death, and at the end she added that Aksinya (Peter's wife) had not wished to stay with them but had gone into service, where they heard she was living honestly and well. Then came a reference to the present of a ruble, and finally a message which the old woman, yielding to her sorrow, had dictated with tears in her eyes and the church clerk had taken down exactly, word for word:

"One thing more, my darling child, my sweet dove, my own Peterkin! I have wept my eyes out lamenting for thee, thou light of my eyes. To whom hast thou left me? . . ." At this point the old woman had sobbed and wept, and said: "That will do!" So the words stood in the letter; but it was not fated that Peter should receive the news of his wife's having left home, nor the present of the ruble, nor his mother's last words. The letter with the money in it came back with the announcement that Peter had been killed in the war, "defending his Tsar, his Fatherland, and the Orthodox Faith." That is how the army clerk expressed it.

The old woman, when this news reached her, wept for as long as she could spare time, and then set to work again. The very next Sunday she went to church and had a requiem chanted and Peter's name entered among those for whose souls prayers were to be said, and she distributed bits of holy bread to all the good people in memory of Peter, the servant of God.

Aksinya, his widow, also lamented loudly when she heard of the death of her beloved husband with whom she had lived but one short year. She regretted her husband and her own ruined life, and in her lamentations mentioned Peter's brown locks and his love, and the sadness of her life with her little orphaned Vanka, and bitterly reproached Peter for having had pity on his brother but none on her—obliged to wander among strangers!

But in the depth of her soul Aksinya was glad of her husband's death. She was pregnant a second time by the shopman with whom she was living, and no one would now have a right to scold her, and the shopman could marry her as he had said he would when he was persuading her to yield.

MICHAEL SEMENOVICH VORONTSOV, being the son of the Russian Ambassador, had been educated in England and possessed a European education quite exceptional among the higher Russian officials of his day. He was ambitious, gentle and kind in his manner with inferiors, and a finished courtier with superiors. He did not understand life without power and submission. He had obtained all the highest ranks and decorations and was looked upon as a clever commander, and even as the conqueror of Napoleon at Krasnoe.[17]

In 1852 he was over seventy, but young for his age, he moved briskly, and above all was in full possession of a facile, refined, and agreeable intellect which he used to maintain his power and strengthen and increase his popularity. He possessed large means—his own and his wife's (who had been a Countess Branitski)—and received an enormous salary as Viceroy, and he spent a great part of his means on building a palace and laying out a garden on the south coast of the Crimea.

On the evening of December the 4th, 1851, a courier's troyka drew up before his palace in Tiflis. An officer, tired and black with dust, sent by General Kozlovsky with the news of Hadji Murad's surrender to the Russians, entered the wide porch, stretching the stiffened muscles of his legs as he passed the sentinel. It was six o'clock, and Vorontsov was just going in to dinner when he was informed of the courier's arrival. He received him at once, and was therefore a few minutes late for dinner.

When he entered the drawing-room the thirty persons invited to dine, who were sitting beside Princess Elizabeth Ksaverevna Vorontsova, or standing in groups by the windows, turned their faces towards him. Vorontsov was dressed in his usual black military coat, with shoulder-straps but no epaulets, and wore the White Cross of the Order of St. George at his neck.

His clean-shaven, foxlike face wore a pleasant smile as, screwing up his eyes, he surveyed the assembly. Entering with quick soft steps he apologized to the ladies for being late, greeted the men, and approaching Princess Manana Orbelyani—a tall, fine, handsome woman of Oriental type about forty-five years of age—he offered her his arm to take her in to dinner. Princess Elizabeth Ksaverevna Vorontsova gave her arm to a red-haired general with bristly moustaches who was visiting Tiflis. A Georgian

[17] A town thirty miles south-west of Smolensk, at which, in November 1812, the rear-guard of Napoleon's army was defeated during the retreat from Moscow. It is mentioned in *War and Peace*.

prince offered his arm to Princess Vorontsova's friend, Countess Choiseuil. Doctor Andreevsky, the aide-de-camp, and others, with ladies or without, followed these first couples. Footmen in livery and knee-breeches drew back and replaced the guests' chairs when they sat down, while the major-domo ceremoniously ladled out steaming soup from a silver tureen.

Vorontsov took his place in the center of one side of the long table, and his wife sat opposite, with the general on her right. On the prince's right sat his lady, the beautiful Orbelyani; and on his left was a graceful, dark, red-cheeked Georgian woman, glittering with jewels and incessantly smiling.

"*Excellentes, chère amie!*"[18] replied Vorontsov to his wife's inquiry about what news the courier had brought him. "*Simon a eu de la chance!*"[19] And he began to tell aloud, so that everyone could hear, the striking news (for him alone not quite unexpected, because negotiations had long been going on) that Hadji Murad, the bravest and most famous of Shamil's officers, had come over to the Russians and would in a day or two be brought to Tiflis.

Everybody—even the young aides-de-camp and officials who sat at the far ends of the table and who had been quietly laughing at something among themselves—became silent and listened.

"And you, General, have you ever met this Hadji Murad?" asked the princess of her neighbor, the carroty general with the bristly moustaches, when the prince had finished speaking.

"More than once, Princess."

And the general went on to tell how Hadji Murad, after the mountaineers had captured Gergebel in 1843, had fallen upon General Pahlen's detachment and killed Colonel Zolotukhin almost before their very eyes.

Vorontsov listened to the general and smiled amiably, evidently pleased that the latter had joined in the conversation. But suddenly his face assumed an absent-minded and depressed expression.

The general, having started talking, had begun to tell of his second encounter with Hadji Murad.

[18] "Excellent, my dear!"
[19] "Simon has had good luck."

"Why, it was he, if your Excellency will please remember," said the general, "who arranged the ambush that attacked the rescue party in the 'Biscuit' expedition."

"Where?" asked Vorontsov, screwing up his eyes.

What the brave general spoke of as the "rescue" was the affair in the unfortunate Dargo campaign in which a whole detachment, including Prince Vorontsov who commanded it, would certainly have perished had it not been rescued by the arrival of fresh troops. Everyone knew that the whole Dargo campaign under Vorontsov's command—in which the Russians lost many killed and wounded and several cannon—had been a shameful affair, and therefore if anyone mentioned it in Vorontsov's presence they did so only in the aspect in which Vorontsov had reported it to the Tsar—as a brilliant achievement of the Russian army. But the word "rescue" plainly indicated that it was not a brilliant victory but a blunder costing many lives. Everybody understood this and some pretended not to notice the meaning of the general's words, others nervously waited to see what would follow, while a few exchanged glances and smiled. Only the carroty general with the bristly moustaches noticed nothing, and carried away by his narrative quietly replied:

"At the rescue, your Excellency."

Having started on his favorite theme, the general recounted circumstantially how Hadji Murad had so cleverly cut the detachment in two that if the rescue party had not arrived (he seemed to be particularly fond of repeating the word "rescue") not a man in the division would have escaped, because . . . He did not finish his story, for Manana Orbelyani having understood what was happening, interrupted him by asking if he had found comfortable quarters in Tiflis. The general, surprised, glanced at everybody all around and saw his aides-de-camp from the end of the table looking fixedly and significantly at him, and he suddenly understood! Without replying to the princess's question, he frowned, became silent, and began hurriedly swallowing the delicacy that lay on his plate, the appearance and taste of which both completely mystified him.

Everybody felt uncomfortable, but the awkwardness of the situation was relieved by the Georgian prince—a very stupid man but an extraordinarily refined and artful flatterer and courtier—who sat on the other side of Princess Vorontsova. Without seeming to have noticed anything he began to relate how Hadji Murad had carried off the widow of Akhmet Khan of Mekhtuli.

"He came into the village at night, seized what he wanted, and galloped off again with the whole party."

"Why did he want that particular woman?" asked the princess.

"Oh, he was her husband's enemy, and pursued him but could never once succeed in meeting him right up to the time of his death, so he revenged himself on the widow."

The princess translated this into French for her old friend Countess Choiseuil, who sat next to the Georgian prince.

"*Quelle horreur!*"[20] said the countess, closing her eyes and shaking her head.

"Oh no!" said Vorontsov, smiling. "I have been told that he treated his captive with chivalrous respect and afterwards released her."

"Yes, for a ransom!"

"Well, of course. But all the same he acted honorably."

These words of Vorontsov's set the tone for the further conversation. The courtiers understood that the more importance was attributed to Hadji Murad the better the prince would be pleased.

"The man's audacity is amazing. A remarkable man!"

"Why, in 1849 he dashed into Temir Khan Shura and plundered the shops in broad daylight."

An Armenian sitting at the end of the table, who had been in Temir Khan Shura at the time, related the particulars of that exploit of Hadji Murad's.

In fact, Hadji Murad was the sole topic of conversation during the whole dinner.

Everybody in succession praised his courage, his ability, and his magnanimity. Someone mentioned his having ordered twenty-six

[20] "How horrible!"

prisoners to be killed, but that too was met by the usual rejoinder, "What's to be done? À *la guerre, comme à la guerre!*"[21]

"He is a great man."

"Had he been born in Europe he might have been another Napoleon," said the stupid Georgian prince with a gift of flattery.

He knew that every mention of Napoleon was pleasant to Vorontsov, who wore the White Cross at his neck as a reward for having defeated him.

"Well, not Napoleon perhaps, but a gallant cavalry general if you like," said Vorontsov.

"If not Napoleon, then Murat."

"And his name is Hadji *Murad!*"

"Hadji Murad has surrendered and now there'll be an end to Shamil too," someone remarked.

"They feel that now" (this "now" meant under Vorontsov) "they can't hold out," remarked another.

"*Tout cela est grâce à vous!*"[22] said Manana Orbelyani.

Prince Vorontsov tried to moderate the waves of flattery which began to flow over him. Still, it was pleasant, and in the best of spirits he led his lady back into the drawing-room.

After dinner, when coffee was being served in the drawing-room, the prince was particularly amiably to everybody, and going up to the general with the red bristly moustaches he tried to appear not to have noticed his blunder.

Having made a round of the visitors he sat down to the card-table. He only played the old-fashioned game of ombre. His partners were the Georgian prince, an Armenian general (who had learnt the game of ombre from Prince Vorontsov's valet), and Doctor Andreevsky, a man remarkable for the great influence he exercised.

Placing beside him his gold snuff-box with a portrait of Alexander I on the lid, the prince tore open a pack of highly glazed cards and was going to spread them out, when his Italian valet, Giovanni, brought him a letter on a silver tray.

[21] "War is war."
[22] "All this is thanks to you!"

"Another courier, your Excellency."

Vorontsov laid down the cards, excused himself, opened the letter, and began to read.

The letter was from his son, who described Hadji Murad's surrender and his own encounter with Meller-Zakomelsky.

The princess came up and inquired what their son had written.

"It's all about the same matter. . . . *Il a eu quelques désagréments avec le commandant de la place. Simon a eu tort.*[23] . . . But 'All's well that ends well,'" he added in English, handing the letter to his wife; and turning to his respectfully waiting partners he asked them to draw cards.

When the first round had been dealt Vorontsov did what he was in the habit of doing when in a particularly pleasant mood: with his white, wrinkled old hand he took out a pinch of French snuff, carried it to his nose, and released it.

W HEN Hadji Murad appeared at the prince's palace next day, the waiting-room was already full of people. Yesterday's general with the bristly moustaches was there in full uniform with all his decorations, having come to take leave. There was the commander of a regiment who was in danger of being courtmartialled for misappropriating commissariat money, and there was a rich Armenian (patronized by Doctor Andreevsky) who wanted to obtain from the Government a renewal of his monopoly for the sale of vodka. There, dressed in black, was the widow of an officer who had been killed in action. She had come to ask for a pension, or for free education for her children. There was a ruined Georgian prince in a magnificent Georgian costume who was trying to obtain for himself some confiscated Church property. There was an official with a large roll of paper containing a new plan for subjugating the Caucasus. There was also a Khan who had come solely to be able to tell his people at home that he had called on the prince.

[23] "He has had some unpleasantness with the commandant of the place. Simon was in the wrong."

They all waited their turn and were one by one shown into the prince's cabinet and out again by the aide-de-camp, a handsome, fair-haired youth.

When Hadji Murad entered the waiting-room with his brisk though limping step all eyes were turned towards him and he heard his name whispered from various parts of the room.

He was dressed in a long white Circassian coat over a brown *beshmet* trimmed round the collar with fine silver lace. He wore black leggings and soft shoes of the same color which were stretched over his instep as tight as gloves. On his head he wore a high cap draped turban-fashion—that same turban for which, on the denunciation of Akhmet Khan, he had been arrested by General Klugenau and which had been the cause of his going over to Shamil.

He stepped briskly across the parquet floor of the waiting-room, his whole slender figure swaying slightly in consequence of his lameness in one leg which was shorter than the other. His eyes, set far apart, looked calmly before him and seemed to see no one.

The handsome aide-de-camp, having greeted him, asked him to take a seat while he went to announce him to the prince, but Hadji Murad declined to sit down and, putting his hand on his dagger, stood with one foot advanced, looking round contemptuously at all those present.

The prince's interpreter, Prince Tarkhanov, approached Hadji Murad and spoke to him. Hadji Murad answered abruptly and unwillingly. A Kumyk prince, who was there to lodge a complaint against a police official, came out of the prince's room, and then the aide-de-camp called Hadji Murad, led him to the door of the cabinet, and showed him in.

The Commander-in-Chief received Hadji Murad standing beside his table, and his old white face did not wear yesterday's smile but was rather stern and solemn.

On entering the large room with its enormous table and great windows with green venetian blinds, Hadji Murad placed his small sunburnt hands on his chest just where the front of his white coat overlapped, and lowering his eyes began, without hurrying, to speak distinctly and respectfully, using the Kumyk dialect which he spoke well.

"I place myself under the powerful protection of the great Tsar and of yourself," said he, "and promise to serve the White Tsar in faith and truth to the last drop of my blood, and I hope to be useful to you in the war with Shamil who is my enemy and yours."

Having heard the interpreter out, Vorontsov glanced at Hadji Murad and Hadji Murad glanced at Vorontsov.

The eyes of the two men met, and expressed to each other much that could not have been put into words and that was not at all what the interpreter said. Without words they told each other the whole truth. Vorontsov's eyes said that he did not believe a single word Hadji Murad was saying, and that he knew he was and always would be an enemy to everything Russian and had surrendered only because he was obliged to. Hadji Murad understood this and yet continued to give assurances of his fidelity. His eyes said, "That old man ought to be thinking of his death and not of war, but though he is old he is cunning, and I must be careful." Vorontsov understood this also, but nevertheless spoke to Hadji Murad in the way he considered necessary for the success of the war.

"Tell him," said Vorontsov, "that our sovereign is as merciful as he is mighty and will probably at my request pardon him and take him into his service. . . . Have you told him?" he asked, looking at Hadji Murad. . . . "Until I receive my master's gracious decision, tell him I take it on myself to receive him and make his sojourn among us pleasant."

Hadji Murad again pressed his hands to the center of his chest and began to say something with animation.

"He says," the interpreter translated, "that formerly, when he governed Avaria in 1839, he served the Russians faithfully and would never have deserted them had not his enemy, Akhmet Khan, wishing to ruin him, calumniated him to General Klugenau."

"I know, I know," said Vorontsov (though if he had ever known he had long forgotten it). "I know," he repeated, sitting down and motioning Hadji Murad to the divan that stood beside the wall. But Hadji Murad did not sit down. Shrugging his powerful shoulders as a sign that he could not bring himself to sit in the presence of so important a man, he went on, addressing the interpreter:

"Akhmet Khan and Shamil are both my enemies. Tell the prince that Akhmet Khan is dead and I cannot revenge myself on him, but Shamil lives and I will not die without taking vengeance on him," said he, knitting his brows and tightly closing his mouth.

"Yes, yes; but how does he want to revenge himself on Shamil?" said Vorontsov quietly to the interpreter. "And tell him he may sit down."

Hadji Murad again declined to sit down, and in answer to the question replied that his object in coming over to the Russians was to help them to destroy Shamil.

"Very well, very well," said Vorontsov; "but what exactly does he wish to do? . . . Sit down, sit down!"

Hadji Murad sat down, and said that if only they would send him to the Lesghian line and would give him an army, he would guarantee to raise the whole of Daghestan and Shamil would then be unable to hold out.

"That would be excellent. . . . I'll think it over," said Vorontsov.

The interpreter translated Vorontsov's words to Hadji Murad. Hadji Murad pondered.

"Tell the Sirdar one thing more," Hadji Murad began again, "that my family are in the hands of my enemy, and that as long as they are in the mountains I am bound and cannot serve him. Shamil would kill my wife and my mother and my children if I went openly against him. Let the prince first exchange my family for the prisoners he has, and then I will destroy Shamil or die!"

"All right, all right," said Vorontsov. "I will think it over. . . . Now let him go to the chief of staff and explain to him in detail his position, intentions, and wishes."

Thus ended the first interview between Hadji Murad and Vorontsov.

That evening an Italian opera was performed at the new theater, which was decorated in Oriental style. Vorontsov was in his box when the striking figure of the limping Hadji Murad wearing a turban appeared in the stalls. He came in with Loris-Melikov,[24] Vorontsov's aide-de-camp, in whose charge he was placed, and took a seat in the front row. Having sat through the first act with Oriental Mohammedan dignity, expressing no pleasure but only obvious indifference, he rose and looking calmly round at the audience went out, drawing to himself everybody's attention.

The next day was Monday and there was the usual evening party at the Vorontsovs'. In the large brightly lighted hall a band was playing, hidden among trees. Young women and women not very young wearing dresses that displayed their bare necks, arms, and breasts, turned round and round in the embrace of men in bright uniforms. At the buffet, footmen in red swallow-tail coats and wearing shoes and knee-breeches, poured out champagne and served sweetmeats to the ladies. The "Sirdar's" wife also, in spite of her age, went about half-dressed among the visitors smiling affably, and through the interpreter said a few amiable words to Hadji Murad who glanced at the visitors with the same indifference he had shown yesterday in the theater. After the hostess, other half-naked women came up to him and all of them stood shamelessly before him and smilingly asked him the same question: How he liked what he saw? Vorontsov himself, wearing gold epaulets and gold shoulder-knots with his white cross and ribbon at his neck, came up and asked him the same question, evidently feeling sure, like all the others, that Hadji Murad could not help being pleased at what he saw. Hadji Murad replied to Vorontsov as he had replied to them all, that among his people nothing of the kind was done, without expressing an opinion as to whether it was good or bad that it was so.

Here at the ball Hadji Murad tried to speak to Vorontsov about buying out his family, but Vorontsov, pretending that he had not heard him, walked away, and Loris-Melikov afterwards told Hadji Murad that this was not the place to talk about business.

---

[24] Count Michael Tarielovich Loris-Melikov, who afterwards became Minister of the Interior and framed the Liberal ukase which was signed by Alexander II the day that he was assassinated.

When it struck eleven Hadji Murad, having made sure of the time by the watch the Vorontsovs had given him, asked Loris-Melikov whether he might now leave. Loris-Melikov said he might, though it would be better to stay. In spite of this Hadji Murad did not stay, but drove in the phaeton placed at his disposal to the quarters that had been assigned to him.

ON THE fifth day of Hadji Murad's stay in Tiflis Loris-Melikov, the Viceroy's aide-de-camp, came to see him at the latter's command.

"My head and my hands are glad to serve the Sirdar," said Hadji Murad with his usual diplomatic expression, bowing his head and putting his hands to his chest. "Command me!" said he, looking amiably into Loris-Melikov's face.

Loris-Melikov sat down in an arm-chair placed by the table and Hadji Murad sank onto a low divan opposite and, resting his hands on his knees, bowed his head and listened attentively to what the other said to him.

Loris-Melikov, who spoke Tartar fluently, told him that though the prince knew about his past life, he yet wanted to hear the whole story for himself.

"Tell it me, and I will write it down and translate it into Russian and the prince will send it to the Emperor."

Hadji Murad remained silent for a while (he never interrupted anyone but always waited to see whether his collocutor had not something more to say), then he raised his head, shook back his cap, and smiled the peculiar childlike smile that had captivated Marya Vasilevna.

"I can do that," said he, evidently flattered by the thought that his story would be read by the Emperor.

"Thou must tell me" (in Tartar nobody is addressed as "you") "everything, deliberately from the beginning," said Loris-Melikov drawing a notebook from his pocket.

"I can do that, only there is much—very much—to tell! Many events have happened!" said Hadji Murad.

"If thou canst not do it all in one day thou wilt finish it another time," said Loris-Melikov.

"Shall I begin at the beginning?"

"Yes, at the very beginning . . . where thou wast born and where thou didst live."

Hadji Murad's head sank and he sat in that position for a long time. Then he took a stick that lay beside the divan, drew a little knife with an ivory gold-inlaid handle, sharp as a razor, from under his dagger, and started whittling the stick with it and speaking at the same time.

"Write: Born in Tselmess, a small *aoul*, 'the size of an ass's head,' as we in the mountains say," he began. "Not far from it, about two cannon-shots, lies Khunzakh where the Khans lived. Our family was closely connected with them.

"My mother, when my eldest brother Osman was born, nursed the eldest Khan, Abu Nutsal Khan. Then she nursed the second son of the Khan, Umma Khan, and reared him; but Akhmet my second brother died, and when I was born and the Khansha[25] bore Bulach Khan, my mother would not go as wet-nurse again. My father ordered her to, but she would not. She said: 'I should again kill my own son, and I will not go.' Then my father, who was passionate, struck her with a dagger and would have killed her had they not rescued her from him. So she did not give me up, and later on she composed a song . . . but I need not tell that."

"Yes, you must tell everything. It is necessary," said Loris-Melikov.

Hadji Murad grew thoughtful. He remembered how his mother had laid him to sleep beside her under a fur coat on the roof of the *saklya*, and he had asked her to show him the place in her side where the scar of her wound was still visible.

He repeated the song, which he remembered:

"*My white bosom was pierced by the blade of bright steel,*
But I laid my bright sun, my dear boy, close upon it
Till his body was bathed in the stream of my blood.

[25] *Khansha,* Khan's wife.

And the wound healed without aid of herbs or of grass.
As I feared not death, so my boy will ne'er fear it."

"My mother is now in Shamil's hands," he added, "and she must be rescued."

He remembered the fountain below the hill, when holding on to his mother's *sharovary* (loose Turkish trousers) he had gone with her for water. He remembered how she had shaved his head for the first time, and how the reflection of his round bluish head in the shining brass vessel that hung on the wall had astonished him. He remembered a lean dog that had licked his face. He remembered the strange smell of the *lepeshki* (a kind of flat cake) his mother had given him—a smell of smoke and of sour milk. He remembered how his mother had carried him in a basket on her back to visit his grandfather at the farmstead. He remembered his wrinkled grandfather with his grey hairs, and how he had hammered silver with his sinewy hands.

"Well, so my mother did not go as nurse," he said with a jerk of his head, "and the Khansha took another nurse but still remained fond of my mother, and my mother used to take us children to the Khansha's palace, and we played with her children and she was fond of us.

"There were three young Khans: Abu Nutsal Khan my brother Osman's foster-brother; Umma Khan my own sworn brother; and Bulach Khan the youngest—whom Shamil threw over the precipice. But that happened later.

"I was about sixteen when *murids* began to visit the *aouls*. They beat the stones with wooden scimitars and cried, 'Mussulmans, *Ghazavat!*' The Chechens all went over to Muridism and the Avars began to go over too. I was then living in the palace like a brother of the Khans. I could do as I liked, and I became rich. I had horses and weapons and money. I lived for pleasure and had no care, and went on like that till the time when Kazi-Mulla, the Imam, was killed and Hamzad succeeded him. Hamzad sent envoys to the Khans to say that if they did not join the *Ghazavat* he would destroy Khunzakh.

"This needed consideration. The Khans feared the Russians, but were also afraid to join in the Holy War. The old Khansha sent me with her second son, Umma Khan, to Tiflis to ask the Russian Commander-in-Chief for help against Hamzad. The Commander-in-Chief at Tiflis was Baron Rosen. He did not receive either me or Umma Khan. He sent word that he would help us, but did nothing. Only his officers came riding to us and played cards with Umma Khan. They made him drunk with wine and took him to bad places, and he lost all he had to them at cards. His body was as strong as a bull's and he was as brave as a lion, but his soul was weak as water. He would have gambled away his last horses and weapons if I had not made him come away.

"After visiting Tiflis my ideas changed and I advised the old Khansha and the Khans to join the *Ghazavat.* . . ."

"What made you change your mind?" asked Loris-Melikov. "Were you not pleased with the Russians?"

Hadji Murad paused.

"No, I was not pleased," he answered decidedly, closing his eyes. "And there was also another reason why I wished to join the *Ghazavat.*"

"What was that?"

"Why, near Tselmess the Khan and I encountered three *murids*, two of whom escaped but the third one I shot with my pistol.

"He was still alive when I approached to take his weapons. He looked up at me, and said, 'Thou hast killed me . . . I am happy; but thou art a Mussulman, young and strong. Join the *Ghazavat!* God wills it!' "

"And did you join it?"

"I did not, but it made me think," said Hadji Murad, and he went on with his tale.

"When Hamzad approached Khunzakh we sent our Elders to him to say that we would agree to join the *Ghazavat* if the Imam would send a learned man to explain it to us. Hamzad had our Elders' moustaches shaved off, their nostrils pierced, and cakes hung to their noses, and in that condition he sent them back to us.

"The Elders brought word that Hamzad was ready to send a sheik to teach us the *Ghazavat*, but only if the Khansha sent him her youngest son as a hostage. She took him at his word and sent her youngest son, Bulach Khan. Hamzad received him well and sent to invite the two elder brothers also. He sent word that he wished to serve the Khans as his father had served their father. . . . The Khansha was a weak, stupid, and conceited woman, as all women are when they are not under control. She was afraid to send away both sons and sent only Umma Khan. I went with him. We were met by *murids* about a mile before we arrived and they sang and shot and caracoled around us, and when we drew near, Hamzad came out of his tent and went up to Umma Khan's stirrup and received him as a Khan. He said, 'I have not done any harm to thy family and do not wish to do any. Only do not kill me and do not prevent my bringing the people over to the *Ghazavat*, and I will serve you with my whole army as my father served your father! Let me live in your house and I will help you with my advice, and you shall do as you like!'

"Umma Khan was slow of speech. He did not know how to reply and remained silent. Then I said that if this was so, let Hamzad come to Khunzakh and the Khansha and the Khans would receive him with honor. . . . But I was not allowed to finish —and here I first encountered Shamil, who was beside the Imam. He said to me, 'Thou hast not been asked. . . . It was the Khan!'

"I was silent, and Hamzad led Umma Khan into his tent. Afterwards Hamzad called me and ordered me to go to Khunzakh with his envoys. I went. The envoys began persuading the Khansha to send her eldest son also to Hamzad. I saw there was treachery and told her not to send him; but a woman has as much sense in her head as an egg has hair. She ordered her son to go. Abu Nutsal Khan did not wish to. Then she said, 'I see thou art afraid!' Like a bee she knew where to sting him most painfully. Abu Nutsal Khan flushed and did not speak to her any more, but ordered his horse to be saddled. I went with him.

"Hamzad met us with even greater honor than he had shown Umma Khan. He himself rode out two rifle-shot lengths down the hill to meet us. A large party of horsemen with their banners followed him, and they too sang, shot, and caracoled.

"When we reached the camp, Hamzad led the Khan into his tent and I remained with the horses. . . .

"I was some way down the hill when I heard shots fired in Hamzad's tent. I ran there and saw Umma Khan lying prone in a pool of blood, and Abu Nutsal was fighting the *murids*. One of his cheeks had been hacked off and hung down. He supported it with one hand and with the other stabbed with his dagger at all who came near him. I saw him strike down Hamzad's brother and aim a blow at another man, but then the *murids* fired at him and he fell."

Hadji Murad stopped and his sunburnt face flushed a dark red and his eyes became bloodshot.

"I was seized with fear and ran away."

"Really? . . . I thought thou never wast afraid," said Loris-Melikov.

"Never after that. . . . Since then I have always remembered that shame, and when I recalled it I feared nothing!"

"But enough! It is time for me to pray," said Hadji Murad drawing from an inner breast-pocket of his Circassian coat Vorontsov's repeater watch and carefully pressing the spring. The repeater struck twelve and a quarter. Hadji Murad listened with his head on one side, repressing a childlike smile.

"*Kunak* Vorontsov's present," he said, smiling.

"It is a good watch," said Loris-Melikov. "Well then, go thou and pray, and I will wait."

"*Yakshi*. Very well," said Hadji Murad and went to his bedroom.

Left by himself, Loris-Melikov wrote down in his notebook the chief things Hadji Murad had related, and then lighting a cigarette began to pace up and down the room. On reaching the door opposite the bedroom he heard animated voices speaking rapidly in Tartar. He guessed that the speakers were Hadji Murad's *murids*, and opening the door he went in to them.

The room was impregnated with that special leathery acid smell peculiar to the mountaineers. On a *burka* spread out on the floor sat the one-eyed, red-haired Gamzalo, in a tattered greasy *beshmet*, plaiting a bridle. He was saying something excitedly, speaking in a hoarse voice, but when Loris-Melikov entered he immediately became silent and continued his work without paying any attention to him.

In front of Gamzalo stood the merry Khan Mahoma showing his white teeth, his black lashless eyes glittering, and saying something over and over again. The handsome Eldar, his sleeves turned up on his strong arms, was polishing the girths of a saddle suspended from a nail. Khanefi, the principal worker and manager of the household, was not there, he was cooking their dinner in the kitchen.

"What were you disputing about?" asked Loris-Melikov after greeting them.

"Why, he keeps on praising Shamil," said Khan Mahoma giving his hand to Loris-Melikov. "He says Shamil is a great man, learned, holy, and a *dzhigit*."

"How is it that he has left him and still praises him?"

"He has left him and still praises him," repeated Khan Mahoma, his teeth showing and his eyes glittering.

"And does he really consider him a saint?" asked Loris-Melikov.

"If he were not a saint the people would not listen to him," said Gamzalo rapidly.

"Shamil is no saint, but Mansur was!" replied Khan Mahoma. "He was a real saint. When he was Imam the people were quite different. He used to ride through the *aouls* and the people used to come out and kiss the hem of his coat and confess their sins and vow to do no evil. Then all the people—so the old men say—lived like saints: not drinking, nor smoking, nor neglecting their prayers, and forgiving one another their sins even when blood had been spilt. If anyone then found money or anything, he tied it to a stake and set it up by the roadside. In those days God gave the people success in everything—not as now."

"In the mountains they don't smoke or drink now," said Gamzalo.

"Your Shamil is a *lamorey*," said Khan Mahoma, winking at Loris-Melikov. (*Lamorey* was a contemptuous term for a mountaineer.)

"Yes, *lamorey* means mountaineer," replied Gamzalo. "It is in the mountains that the eagles dwell."

"Smart fellow! Well hit!" said Khan Mahoma with a grin, pleased at his adversary's apt retort.

Seeing the silver cigarette-case in Loris-Melikov's hand, Khan Mahoma asked for a cigarette, and when Loris-Melikov remarked that they were forbidden to smoke, he winked with one eye and jerking his head in the direction of Hadji Murad's bedroom replied that they could do it as long as they were not seen. He at once began smoking—not inhaling—and pouting his red lips awkwardly as he blew out the smoke.

"That is wrong!" said Gamzalo severely, and left the room. Khan Mahoma winked in his direction, and while smoking asked Loris-Melikov where he could best buy a silk *beshmet* and a white cap.

"Why, hast thou so much money?"

"I have enough," replied Khan Mahoma with a wink.

"Ask him where he got the money," said Eldar, turning his handsome smiling face towards Loris-Melikov.

"Oh, I won it!" said Khan Mahoma quickly, and related how while walking in Tiflis the day before he had come upon a group of men—Russians and Armenians—playing at *orlyanka* (a kind of heads-and-tails). The stake was a large one: three gold pieces and much silver. Khan Mahoma at once saw what the game consisted in, and jingling the coppers he had in his pocket he went up to the players and said he would stake the whole amount.

"How couldst thou do it? Hadst thou so much?" asked Loris-Melikov.

"I had only twelve kopeks," said Khan Mahoma, grinning.

"But if thou hadst lost?"

"Why, this!" said Khan Mahoma pointing to his pistol.

"Wouldst thou have given that?"

"Give it indeed! I should have run away, and if anyone had tried to stop me I should have killed him—that's all!"

"Well, and didst thou win?"

"Aye, I won it all and went away!"

Loris-Melikov quite understood what sort of men Khan Mahoma and Eldar were. Khan Mahoma was a merry fellow, careless and ready for any spree. He did not know what to do with his superfluous vitality. He was always gay and reckless, and played with his own and other people's lives. For the sake of that sport with the life he had now come over to the Russians, and for the same sport he might go back to Shamil to-morrow.

Eldar was also quite easy to understand. He was a man entirely devoted to his *murshid*; calm, strong, and firm.

The red-haired Gamzalo was the only one Loris-Melikov did not understand. He saw that that man was not only loyal to Shamil but felt an insuperable aversion, contempt, repugnance, and hatred for all Russians, and Loris-Melikov could therefore not understand why he had come over to them. It occurred to him that, as some of the higher officials suspected, Hadji Murad's surrender and his tales of hatred of Shamil might be false, and that perhaps he had surrendered only to spy out the Russians' weak spots that, after escaping back to the mountains, he might be able to direct his forces accordingly. Gamzalo's whole person strengthened this suspicion.

"The others, and Hadji Murad himself, know how to hide their intentions, but this one betrays them by his open hatred," thought he.

Loris-Melikov tried to speak to him. He asked whether he did not feel dull. "No, I don't!" he growled hoarsely without stopping his work, and glancing at his questioner out of the corner of his one eye. He replied to all Loris-Melikov's other questions in a similar manner.

While Loris-Melikov was in the room Hadji Murad's fourth *murid* came in, the Avar Khanefi; a man with a hairy face and neck and an arched chest as rough as if it were overgrown with moss. He was strong and a hard worker, always engrossed in his duties, and like Eldar unquestioningly obedient to his master.

When he entered the room to fetch some rice, Loris-Melikov stopped him and asked where he came from and how long he had been with Hadji Murad.

"Five years," replied Khanefi. "I came from the same *aoul* as he. My father killed his uncle and they wished to kill me," he said calmly, looking from under his joined eyebrows straight into Loris-Melikov's face. "Then I asked them to adopt me as a brother."

"What do you mean by 'adopt as a brother'?"

"I did not shave my head nor cut my nails for two months, and then I came to them. They let me in to Patimat, his mother, and she gave me the breast and I became his brother."

Hadji Murad's voice could be heard from the next room and Eldar, immediately answering his call, promptly wiped his hands and went with large strides into the drawing-room.

"He asks thee to come," said he, coming back.

Loris-Melikov gave another cigarette to the merry Khan Mahoma and went into the drawing-room.

When Loris-Melikov entered the drawing-room Hadji Murad received him with a bright face.

"Well, shall I continue?" he asked, sitting down comfortably on the divan.

"Yes, certainly," said Loris-Melikov. "I have been in to have a talk with thy henchmen. . . . One is a jolly fellow!" he added.

"Yes, Khan Mahoma is a frivolous fellow," said Hadji Murad.

"I liked the young handsome one."

"Ah, that's Eldar. He's young but firm—made of iron!"

They were silent for a while.

"So I am to go on?"

"Yes, yes!"

"I told thee how the Khans were killed. . . . Well, having killed them Hamzad rode into Khunzakh and took up his quarters in their palace. The Khansha was the only one of the family left alive. Hamzad sent for her. She reproached him, so he winked to his *murid* Aseldar, who struck her from behind and killed her."

"Why did he kill her?" asked Loris-Melikov.

"What could he do? . . . Where the forelegs have gone the hind legs must follow! He killed off the whole family. Shamil killed the youngest son—threw him over a precipice. . . .

"Then the whole of Avaria surrendered to Hamzad. But my brother and I would not surrender. We wanted his blood for the blood of the Khans. We pretended to yield, but our only thought was how to get his blood. We consulted our grandfather and decided to await the time when he would come out of his palace, and then to kill him from an ambush. Someone overheard us and told Hamzad, who sent for grandfather and said, 'Mind, if it be true that thy grandsons are planning evil against me, thou and they shall hang from one rafter. I do God's work and cannot be hindered. . . . Go, and remember what I have said!'

"Our grandfather came home and told us.

"Then we decided not to wait but to do the deed on the first day of the feast in the mosque. Our comrades would not take part in it but my brother and I remained firm.

"We took two pistols each, put on our *burkas*, and went to the mosque. Hamzad entered the mosque with thirty *murids*. They all had drawn swords in their hands. Aseldar, his favorite *murid* (the one who had cut off Khansha's head), saw us, shouted to us to take off our *burkas*, and came towards me. I had my dagger in my hand and I killed him with it and rushed at Hamzad; but my brother Osman had already shot him. He was still alive and rushed at my brother dagger in hand, but I gave him a finishing blow on the head. There were thirty *murids* and we were only two. They killed my brother Osman, but I kept them at bay, leapt through the window, and escaped.

"When it was known that Hamzad had been killed all the people rose. The *murids* fled and those of them who did not flee were killed."

Hadji Murad paused, and breathed heavily.

"That was very good," he continued, "but afterwards everything was spoilt.

"Shamil succeeded Hamzad. He sent envoys to me to say that I should join him in attacking the Russians, and that if I refused he would destroy Khunzakh and kill me.

"I answered that I would not join him and would not let him come to me. . . ."

"Why didst thou not go with him?" asked Loris-Melikov.

Hadji Murad frowned and did not reply at once.

"I could not. The blood of my brother Osman and of Abu Nutsal Khan was on his hands. I did not go to him. General Rosen sent me an officer's commission and ordered me to govern Avaria. All this would have been well but that Rosen appointed as Khan of Kazi-Kumukh, first Mahomet-Murza, and afterwards Akhmet Khan, who hated me. He had been trying to get the Khansha's daughter, Sultanetta, in marriage for his son, but she would not give her to him, and he believed me to be the cause of this. . . . Yes, Akhmet Khan hated me and sent his henchmen to kill me, but I escaped from them. Then he spoke ill of me to General Klugenau. He said that I told the Avars not to supply wood to the Russian soldiers, and he also said that I had donned a turban —this one" (Hadji Murad touched his turban) "and that this meant that I had gone over to Shamil. The general did not believe him and gave orders that I should not be touched. But when the general went to Tiflis, Akhmet Khan did as he pleased. He sent a company of soldiers to seize me, put me in chains, and tied me to a cannon.

"So they kept me six days," he continued. "On the seventh day they untied me and started to take me to Temir-Khan-Shura. Forty soldiers with loaded guns had me in charge. My hands were tied and I knew that they had orders to kill me if I tried to escape.

"As we approached Mansokha the path became narrow, and on the right was an abyss about a hundred and twenty yards deep. I went to the right—to the very edge. A soldier wanted to stop me, but I jumped down and pulled him with me. He was killed outright but I, as you see, remained alive.

"Ribs, head, arms, and leg—all were broken! I tried to crawl but grew giddy and fell asleep. I awoke wet with blood. A shepherd saw me and called some people who carried me to an *aoul*. My ribs and head healed, and my leg too, only it has remained short," and Hadji Murad stretched out his crooked leg. "It still serves me, however, and that is well," said he.

"The people heard the news and began coming to me. I recovered and went to Tselmess. The Avars again called on me to rule over them," he went on, with tranquil, confident pride, "and I agreed."

He rose quickly and taking a portfolio out of a saddle-bag, drew out two discolored letters and handed one of them to Loris-Melikov. They were from General Klugenau, Loris-Melikov read the first letter, which was as follows:

"Lieutenant Hadji Murad, thou hast served under me and I was satisfied with thee and considered thee a good man.

"Recently Akhmet Khan informed me that thou art a traitor, that thou hast donned a turban and hast intercourse with Shamil, and that thou hast taught the people to disobey the Russian Government. I ordered thee to be arrested and brought before me but thou fledst. I do not know whether this is for thy good or not, as I do not know whether thou art guilty or not.

"Now hear me. If thy conscience is pure, if thou art not guilty in anything towards the great Tsar, come to me, fear no one. I am thy defender. The Khan can do nothing to thee, he is himself under my command, so thou hast nothing to fear."

Klugenau added that he always kept his word and was just, and he again exhorted Hadji Murad to appear before him.

When Loris-Melikov had read this letter Hadji Murad, before handing him the second one, told him what he had written in reply to the first.

"I wrote that I wore a turban not for Shamil's sake but for my soul's salvation; that I neither wished nor could go over to Shamil, because he had caused the death of my father, my brothers, and my relations; but that I could not join the Russians because I had been dishonored by them. (In Khunzakh, a scoundrel had spat on me while I was bound, and I could not join your people until that man was killed.) But above all I feared that liar, Akhmet Khan.

"Then the general sent me this letter," said Hadji Murad, handing Loris-Melikov the other discolored paper.

"Thou hast answered my first letter and I thank thee," read Loris-Melikov. "Thou writest that thou art not afraid to return but that the insult done thee by a certain giaour prevents it, but I assure thee that the Russian law is just and that thou shalt see him who dared to offend thee punished before thine eyes. I have already given orders to investigate the matter.

"Hear me, Hadji Murad! I have a right to be displeased with thee for not trusting me and my honor, but I forgive thee, for I know how suspicious mountaineers are in general. If thy conscience is pure, if thou hast put on a turban only for thy soul's salvation, then thou art right and mayst look me and the Russian Government boldly in the eye. He who dishonored thee shall, I assure thee, be punished and *thy property shall be restored to thee*, and thou shalt see and know what Russian law is. Moreover we Russians look at things differently, and thou hast not sunk in our eyes because some scoundrel has dishonored thee.

"I myself have consented to the Chimrints wearing turbans, and I regard their actions in the right light, and therefore I repeat that thou hast nothing to fear. Come to me with the man by whom I am sending thee this letter. He is faithful to me and is not the slave of thy enemies, but is the friend of a man who enjoys the special favor of the Government."

Further on Klugenau again tried to persuade Hadji Murad to come over to him.

"I did not believe him," said Hadji Murad when Loris-Melikov had finished reading, "and did not go to Klugenau. The chief thing for me was to revenge myself on Akhmet Khan, and that I could not do through the Russians. Then Akhmet Khan surrounded Tselmess and wanted to take me or kill me. I had too few men and could not drive him off, and just then came an envoy with a letter from Shamil promising to help me to defeat and kill Akhmet Khan and making me ruler over the whole of Avaria. I considered the matter for a long time and then went over to Shamil, and from that time I have fought the Russians continually."

Here Hadji Murad related all his military exploits, of which there were very many and some of which were already familiar to Loris-Melikov. All his campaigns and raids had been remarkable for the extraordinary rapidity of his movements and the boldness of his attacks, which were always crowned with success.

"There never was any friendship between me and Shamil," said Hadji Murad at the end of his story, "but he feared me and needed me. But it so happened that I was asked who should be Imam after Shamil, and I replied: 'He will be Imam whose sword is sharpest!'

"This was told to Shamil and he wanted to get rid of me. He sent me into Tabasaran. I went, and captured a thousand sheep and three hundred horses, but he said I had not done the right thing and dismissed me from being *Naib*, and ordered me to send him all the money. I sent him a thousand gold pieces. He sent his *murids* and they took from me all my property. He demanded that I should go to him, but I knew he wanted to kill me and I did not go. Then he sent to take me. I resisted and went over to Vorontsov. Only I did not take my family. My mother, my wives, and my son are in his hands. Tell the Sirdar that as long as my family is in Shamil's power I can do nothing."

"I will tell him," said Loris-Melikov.

"Take pains, try hard! . . . What is mine is thine, only help me with the Prince! I am tied up and the end of the rope is in Shamil's hands," said Hadji Murad concluding his story.

ON THE 20th of December Vorontsov wrote to Chernyshov, the Minister of War. The letter was in French:

"I did not write to you by the last post, dear Prince, as I wished first to decide what we should do with Hadji Murad, and for the last two or three days I have not been feeling quite well.

"In my last letter I informed you of Hadji Murad's arrival here.

He reached Tiflis on the 8th, and next day I made his acquaintance, and during the following seven or eight days have spoken to him and considered what use we can make of him in the future, and especially what we are to do with him at present, for he is much concerned about the fate of his family, and with every appearance of perfect frankness says that while they are in Shamil's hands he is paralyzed and cannot render us any service or show his gratitude for the friendly reception and forgiveness we have extended to him.

"His uncertainty about those dear to him makes him restless, and the persons I have appointed to live with him assure me that he does not sleep at night, eats hardly anything, prays continually, and asks only to be allowed to ride out accompanied by several Cossacks—the sole recreation and exercise possible for him and made necessary to him by life-long habit. Every day he comes to me to know whether I have any news of his family, and to ask me to have all the prisoners in our hands collected and offered to Shamil in exchange for them. He would also give a little money. There are people who would let him have some for the purpose. He keeps repeating to me: "Save my family and then give me a chance to serve thee" (preferably, in his opinion, on the Lesghian line), "and if within a month I do not render you great service, punish me as you think fit." I reply that to me all this appears very just, and that many among us would even not trust him so long as his family remain in the mountains and are not in our hands as hostages, and that I will do everything possible to collect the prisoners of our frontier, that I have no power under our laws to give money for the ransom of his family in addition to the sum he may himself be able to raise, but that I may perhaps find some other means of helping him. After that I told him frankly that in my opinion Shamil would not in any case give up the family, and that Shamil might tell him to straight out and promise him a full pardon and his former posts, and might threaten if Hadji Murad did not return, to kill his mother, his wives, and his six children. I asked him whether he could say frankly what he would do if he received such an announcement from Shamil. He lifted his eyes and arms to heaven, and said that everything is in God's hands, but that he would never surrender to his foe, for he is certain Shamil would not forgive him and he would therefore not have long to live. As to the destruction of his family, he did not think Shamil would act so rashly: firstly, to avoid making him a yet more desperate and dangerous foe, and secondly, because there were many people, and even very influential people, in Daghestan, who would dissuade Shamil from such a course. Finally, he repeated several times that whatever God might decree for him in the future, he was at present interested in nothing but his family's ransom, and he implored me in God's name to help him and allow him to return to the neighborhood of the Chechnya, where he could, with the help and consent of our commanders, have some intercourse with his family and regular news of their condition and of the best means to liberate them. He said that many people, and even some *Naibs* in that part of the enemy's territory, were more or less attached to him, and that among the whole of the population already subjugated by Russia or neutral it would be easy with our help to establish relations very useful for the attainment of the aim which gives him no peace day or night, and the attainment of which would set him at ease and would make it possible for him to act for our good and win our confidence.

"He asks to be sent back to Grozny with a convoy of twenty or thirty picked Cossacks who would serve him as a protection against foes and us as a guarantee of his good faith.

"You will understand, dear Prince, that I have been much perplexed by all this, for do what I will a great responsibility rests on me. It would be in the highest degree rash to trust him entirely, yet in order to deprive him of all means of escape we should have to lock him up, and in my opinion that would be both unjust and impolitic. A measure of that kind, the news of which would soon spread over the whole of Daghestan, would do us great harm by keeping back those who are now inclined more or less openly to oppose Shamil (and there are many such), and who are keenly watching to see how we treat the Imam's bravest and most adventurous officer now that he has found himself obliged to place himself in our hands. If we treat Hadji Murad as a prisoner all the good effect of the situation will be lost. Therefore I think that I could not act otherwise than as I have done, though at the same time I feel that I may be accused of having made a great mistake if Hadji Murad should take it into his head to escape again. In the service, and especially in a complicated situation such as this, it is difficult, not to say impossible, to follow any one straight path without risking mistakes and without accepting responsibility, but once a path seems to be the right one I must follow it, happen what may.

"I beg of you, dear Prince, to submit this to his Majesty the Emperor for his consideration; and I shall be happy if it pleases our most august monarch to approve my action.

"All that I have written above I have also written to Generals Zavodovsky and Kozlovsky, to guide the latter when communicating direct with Hadji Murad whom I have warned not to act or go anywhere without Kozlovsky's consent. I also told him that it would be all the better for us if he rode out with our convoy, as otherwise Shamil might spread a rumor that we were keeping him prisoner, but at the same time I made him promise never to go to Vozdvizhensk, because my son, to whom he first surrendered and whom he looks upon as his *kunak* (friend), is not the commander of that place and some unpleasant misunderstanding might easily arise. In any case Vozdvizhensk lies too near a thickly populated hostile settlement, while for the intercourse with his friends which he desires, Grozny is in all respects suitable.

"Besides the twenty chosen Cossacks who at his own request are to keep close to him, I am also sending Captain Loris-Melikov —a worthy, excellent, and highly intelligent officer who speaks Tartar, and knows Hadji Murad well and apparently enjoys his full confidence. During the ten days that Hadji Murad has spent here, he has, however, lived in the same house with Lieutenant-Colonel Prince Tarkhanov, who is in command of the Shoushin District and is here on business connected with the service. He is a truly worthy man whom I trust entirely. He also has won Hadji Murad's confidence, and through him alone—as he speaks Tartar perfectly

—we have discussed the most delicate and secret matters. I have consulted Tarkhanov about Hadji Murad, and he fully agrees with me that it was necessary either to act as I have done, or to put Hadji Murad in prison and guard him in the strictest manner (for if we once treat him badly he will not be easy to hold), or else to remove him from the country altogether. But these two last measures would not only destroy all the advantage accruing to us from Hadji Murad's quarrel with Shamil, but would inevitably check any growth of the present insubordination, and possible future revolt, of the people against Shamil's power. Prince Tarkhanov tells me he himself has no doubt of Hadji Murad's truthfulness, and that Hadji Murad is convinced that Shamil will never forgive him but would have him executed in spite of any promise of forgiveness. The only thing Tarkhanov has noticed in his intercourse with Hadji Murad that might cause any anxiety, is his attachment to his religion. Tarkhanov does not deny that Shamil might influence Hadji Murad from that side. But as I have already said, he will never persuade Hadji Murad that he will not take his life sooner or later should the latter return to him.

"This, dear Prince, is all I have to tell you about this episode in our affairs here."

THE report was dispatched from Tiflis on the 24th of December 1851, and on New Year's Eve a courier, having overdriven a dozen horses and beaten a dozen drivers till they bled, delivered it to Prince Chernyshov who at that time was Minister of War; and on the 1st of January 1852 Chernyshov took Vorontsov's report, among other papers, to the Emperor Nicholas.

Chernyshov disliked Vorontsov because of the general respect in which the latter was held and because of his immense wealth, and also because Vorontsov was a real artistocrat while Chernyshov, after all, was a *parvenu*, but especially because the Emperor was particularly well disposed towards Vorontsov. Therefore at every opportunity Chernyshov tried to injure Vorontsov.

When he had last presented a report about Caucasian affairs he had succeeded in arousing Nicholas's displeasure against Vorontsov because—through the carelessness of those in command—almost the whole of a small Caucasian detachment had been destroyed by the mountaineers. He now intended to present the steps taken by Vorontsov in relation to Hadji Murad in an unfavorable light. He wished to suggest to the Emperor that Vorontsov always protected and even indulged the natives to the detriment of the Russians, and that he had acted unwisely in allowing Hadji Murad to remain in the Caucasus for there was every reason to suspect that he had only come over to spy on our means of defence, and that it would therefore be better to transport him to Central Russia and make use of him only after his family had been rescued from the mountaineers and it had become possible to convince ourselves of his loyalty.

Chernyshov's plan did not succeed merely because on that New Year's Day Nicholas was in particularly bad spirits, and out of perversity would not have accepted any suggestion whatever from anyone, least of all from Chernyshov whom he only tolerated—regarding him as indispensable for the time being but looking upon him as a blackguard, for Nicholas knew of his endeavors at the trial of the Decembrists[26] to secure the conviction of Zachary Chernyshov, and of his attempt to obtain Zachary's property for himself. So thanks to Nicholas's ill temper Hadji Murad remained in the Caucasus, and his circumstances were not changed as they might have been had Cherynshov presented his report at another time.

It was half-past nine o'clock when through the mist of the cold morning (the thermometer showed 13 degrees below zero Fahrenheit) Chernyshov's fat, bearded coachman, sitting on the box of a small sledge (like the one Nicholas drove about in) with a sharp-angled, cushion-shaped azure velvet cap on his head, drew up at the entrance of the Winter Palace and gave a friendly nod to his chum, Prince Dolgoruky's coachman—who having brought his

---

[26] The military conspirators who tried to secure a Constitution for Russia in 1825, on the accession of Nicholas I.

master to the palace had himself long been waiting outside, in his big coat with the thickly wadded skirts, sitting on the reins and rubbing his numbed hands together. Chernyshov had on a long cloak with a large cape and a fluffy collar of silver beaver, and a regulation three-cornered hat with cocks' feathers. He threw back the bearskin apron of the sledge and carefully disengaged his chilled feet, on which he had no over-shoes (he prided himself on never wearing any). Clanking his spurs with an air of bravado he ascended the carpeted steps and passed through the hall door which was respectfully opened for him by the porter, and entered the hall. Having thrown off his cloak which an old Court lackey hurried forward to take, he went to a mirror and carefully removed the hat from his curled wig. Looking at himself in the mirror, he arranged the hair on his temples and the tuft above his forehead with an accustomed movement of his old hands, and adjusted his cross, the shoulder-knots of his uniform, and his large-initialled epaulets, and then went up the gently ascending carpeted stairs, his not very reliable old legs feebly mounting the shallow steps. Passing the Court lackeys in gala livery who stood obsequiously bowing, Chernyshov entered the waiting-room. He was respectfully met by a newly appointed aide-de-camp of the Emperor's in a shining new uniform with epaulets and shoulder-knots, whose face was still fresh and rosy and who had a small black moustache, and the hair on his temples brushed towards his eyes in the same way as the Emperor.

Prince Vasili Dolgoruky, Assistant-Minister of War, with an expression of *ennui* on his dull face—which was ornamented with similar whiskers, moustaches, and temple tufts brushed forward like Nicholas's—greeted him.

"*L'empereur?*" said Chernyshov, addressing the aide-de-camp and looking inquiringly towards the door leading to the cabinet.

"*Sa majesté vient de rentrer,*"[27] replied the aide-de-camp, evidently enjoying the sound of his own voice, and stepping so softly and steadily that had a tumbler of water been placed on his head none of it would have been spilt, he approached the door and dis-

[27] "His Majesty has just returned."

appeared, his whole body evincing reverence for the spot he was about to visit.

Dolgoruky meanwhile opened his portfolio to see that it contained the necessary papers, while Chernyshov, frowning, paced up and down to restore the circulation in his numbed feet, and thought over what he was about to report to the Emperor. He was near the door of the cabinet when it opened again and the aide-de-camp, even more radiant and respectful than before, came out and with a gesture invited the minister and his assistant to enter.

The Winter Palace had been rebuilt after a fire some considerable time before this, but Nicholas was still occupying rooms in the upper story. The cabinet in which he received the reports of his ministers and other high officials was a very lofty apartment with four large windows. A big portrait of the Emperor Alexander I hung on the front side of the room. Two bureaus stood between the windows, and several chairs were ranged along the walls. In the middle of the room was an enormous writing-table, with an arm-chair before it for Nicholas, and other chairs for those to whom he gave audience.

Nicholas sat at the table in a black coat with shoulder-straps but no epaulets, his enormous body—with his overgrown stomach tightly laced in—was thrown back, and he gazed at the newcomers with fixed, lifeless eyes. His long pale face, with its enormous receding forehead between the tufts of hair which were brushed forward and skilfully joined to the wig that covered his bald patch, was specially cold and stony that day. His eyes, always dim, looked duller than usual, the compressed lips under his upturned moustaches, the high collar which supported his chin, and his fat freshly shaven cheeks on which symmetrical sausage-shaped bits of whiskers had been left, gave his face a dissatisfied and even irate expression. His bad mood was caused by fatigue, due to the fact that he had been to a masquerade the night before, and while walking about as was his wont in his Horse Guards' uniform with a bird on the helmet, among the public which crowded round and timidly made way for his enormous, self-assured figure, he had again met the mask who at the previous masquerade had aroused his senile sensuality by her whiteness, her beautiful figure, and her tender voice. At that former masquerade she had disappeared after promising to meet him at the next one.

At yesterday's masquerade she had come up to him, and this time he had not let her go, but had led her to the box specially kept ready for that purpose, where he could be alone with her. Having arrived in silence at the door of the box Nicholas looked round to find the attendant, but he was not there. He frowned and pushed the door open himself, letting the lady enter first.

"*Il y a quelqu'un!*"[28] said the mask, stopping short.

And the box actually was occupied. On the small velvet-covered sofa, close together, sat an Uhlan officer and a pretty, fair curly-haired young woman in a domino, who had removed her mask. On catching sight of the angry figure of Nicholas drawn up to its full height, she quickly replaced her mask, but the Uhlan officer, rigid with fear, gazed at Nicholas with fixed eyes without rising from the sofa.

Used as he was to the terror he inspired in others, that terror always pleased Nicholas, and by way of contrast he sometimes liked to astound those plunged in terror by addressing kindly words to them. He did so on this occasion.

"Well, friend!" said he to the officer. "You are younger than I and might give up your place to me."

The officer jumped to his feet, and growing first pale and then red and bending almost double, he followed his partner silently out of the box, leaving Nicholas alone with his lady.

She proved to be a pretty, twenty-year-old virgin, the daughter of a Swedish governess. She told Nicholas how when quite a child she had fallen in love with him from his portraits; how she adored him and had made up her mind to attract his attention at any cost. Now she had succeeded and wanted nothing more—so she said.

The girl was taken to the place where Nicholas usually had rendezvous with women, and there he spent more than an hour with her.

When he returned to his room that night and lay on the hard

[28] "There's someone there!"

narrow bed about which he prided himself, and covered himself with the cloak which he considered to be (and spoke of as being) as famous as Napoleon's hat, it was a long time before he could fall asleep. He thought now of the frightened and elated expression on that girl's fair face, and now of the full, powerful shoulders of his established mistress, Nelidova, and he compared the two. That profligacy in a married man was a bad thing did not once enter his head, and he would have been greatly surprised had anyone censured him for it. Yet though convinced that he had acted rightly, some kind of unpleasant after-taste remained, and to stifle that feeling he dwelt on a thought that always tranquillized him—the thought of his own greatness.

Though he had fallen asleep so late, he rose before eight, and after attending to his toilet in the usual way—rubbing his big well-fed body all over with ice—and saying his prayers (repeating those he had been used to from childhood—the prayer to the Virgin, the Apostles' Creed, and the Lord's Prayer, without attaching any kind of meaning to the words he uttered), he went out through the smaller portico of the palace onto the embankment in his military cloak and cap.

On the embankment he met a student in the uniform of the School of Jurisprudence, who was as enormous as himself. On recognizing the uniform of that school, which he disliked for its freedom of thought, Nicholas frowned, but the stature of the student and the painstaking manner in which he drew himself up and saluted, ostentatiously sticking out his elbow, mollified his displeasure.

"Your name?" said he.

"Polosatov, your Imperial Majesty."

". . . fine fellow!"

The student continued to stand with his hand lifted to his hat. Nicholas stopped.

"Do you wish to enter the army?"

"Not at all, your Imperial Majesty."

"Blockhead!" And Nicholas turned away and continued his walk, and began uttering aloud the first words that came into his head.

"Kopervine . . . Kopervine——" he repeated several times (it was the name of yesterday's girl). "Horrid . . . horrid——" He did not think of what he was saying, but stifled his feelings by listening to the words.

"Yes, what would Russia be without me?" said he, feeling his former dissatisfaction returning. "What would—not Russia alone but Europe be, without me?" and calling to mind the weakness and stupidity of his brother-in-law the King of Prussia, he shook his head.

As he was returning to the small portico, he saw the carriage of Helena Pavlovna,[29] with a red-liveried footman, approaching the Saltykov entrance of the palace.

Helena Pavlovna was to him the personification of that futile class of people who discussed not merely science and poetry, but even the ways of governing men: imagining that they could govern themselves better than he, Nicholas, governed them! He knew that however much he crushed such people they reappeared again and again, and he recalled his brother, Michael Pavlovich, who had died not long before. A feeling of sadness and vexation came over him and with a dark frown he again began whispering the first words that came into his head, which he only ceased doing when he re-entered the palace.

On reaching his apartments he smoothed his whiskers and the hair on his temples and the wig on his bald patch, and twisted his moustaches upwards in front of the mirror, and then went straight to the cabinet in which he received reports.

He first received Chernyshov, who at once saw by his face, and especially by his eyes, that Nicholas was in a particularly bad humor that day, and knowing about the adventure of the night before he understood the cause. Having coldly greeted him and invited him to sit down, Nicholas fixed on him a lifeless gaze. The first matter Chernyshov reported upon was a case of embezzlement by commissariat officials which had just been discovered; the next was the movement of troops on the Prussian frontier; then came a list of rewards to be given at the New Year to some people omitted

[29] Widow of Nicholas's brother Michael: a clever, well-educated woman, interested in science, art, and public affairs.

from a former list; then Vorontsov's report about Hadji Murad; and lastly some unpleasant business concerning an attempt by a student of the Academy of Medicine on the life of a professor.

Nicholas heard the report of the embezzlement silently with compressed lips, his large white hand—with one ring on the fourth finger—stroking some sheets of paper, and his eyes steadily fixed on Chernyshov's forehead and on the tuft of hair above it.

Nicholas was convinced that everybody stole. He knew he would have to punish the commissariat officials now, and decided to send them all to serve in the ranks, but he also knew that this would not prevent those who succeeded them from acting in the same way. It was a characteristic of officials to steal, but it was his duty to punish them for doing so, and tired as he was of that duty he conscientiously performed it.

"It seems there is only one honest man in Russia!" said he.

Chernyshov at once understood that this one honest man was Nicholas himself, and smiled approvingly.

"It looks like it, your Imperial Majesty," said he.

"Leave it—I will give a decision," said Nicholas, taking the document and putting it on the left side of the table.

Then Chernyshov reported about the rewards to be given and about moving the army on the Prussian frontier.

Nicholas looked over the list and struck out some names, and then briefly and firmly gave orders to move two divisions to the Prussian frontier. He could not forgive the King of Prussia for granting a Constitution to his people after the events of 1848, and therefore while expressing most friendly feelings to his brother-in-law in letters and conversation, he considered it necessary to keep an army near the frontier in case of need. He might want to use these troops to defend his brother-in-law's throne if the people of Prussia rebelled (Nicholas saw a readiness for rebellion everywhere) as he had used troops to suppress the rising in Hungary a few years previously. They were also of use to give more weight and influence to such advice as he gave to the King of Prussia.

"Yes—what would Russia be like now if it were not for me?" he again thought.

"Well, what else is there?" said he.

"A courier from the Caucasus," said Chernyshov, and he reported what Vorontsov had written about Hadji Murad's surrender.

"Well, well!" said Nicholas. "It's a good beginning!"

"Evidently the plan devised by your Majesty begins to bear fruit," said Chernyshov.

This approval of his strategic talents was particularly pleasant to Nicholas because, though he prided himself upon them, at the bottom of his heart he knew that they did not really exist, and he now desired to hear more detailed praise of himself.

"How do you mean?" he asked.

"I mean that if your Majesty's plans had been adopted before, and we had moved forward slowly and steadily, cutting down forests and destroying the supplies of food, the Caucasus would have been subjugated long ago. I attribute Hadji Murad's surrender entirely to his having come to the conclusion that they can hold out no longer."

"True," said Nicholas.

Although the plan of a gradual advance into the enemy's territory by means of felling forests and destroying the food supplies was Ermolov's and Velyaminov's plan, and was quite contrary to Nicholas's own plan of seizing Shamil's place of residence and destroying that nest of robbers—which was the plan on which the Dargo expedition in 1845 (that cost so many lives) had been undertaken—Nicholas nevertheless attributed to himself also the plan of a slow advance and a systematic felling of forests and devastation of the country. It would seem that to believe the plan of a slow movement by felling forests and destroying food supplies to have been his own would have necessitated hiding the fact that he had insisted on quite contrary operations in 1845. But he did not hide it and was proud of the plan of the 1845 expedition as well as of the plan of a slow advance—though the two were obviously contrary to one another. Continual brazen flattery from everybody round him in the teeth of obvious facts had brought him to such a state that he no longer saw his own inconsistencies or measured his actions and words by reality, logic, or even simple common sense; but was quite convinced that all his orders, however senseless, unjust, and mutually contradictory they might be, became reasonable, just, and mutually accordant simply because he gave them. His decision in the case next reported to him—that of the student of the Academy of Medicine—was of that senseless kind.

The case was as follows: A young man who had twice failed in his examinations was being examined a third time, and when the examiner again would not pass him, the young man whose nerves were deranged, considering this to be an injustice, seized a penknife from the table in a paroxysm of fury, and rushing at the professor inflicted on him several trifling wounds.

"What's his name?" asked Nicholas.

"Bzhezovski."

"A Pole?"

"Of Polish descent and a Roman Catholic," answered Chernyshov.

Nicholas frowned. He had done much evil to the Poles. To justify that evil he had to feel certain that all Poles were rascals, and he considered them to be such and hated them in proportion to the evil he had done them.

"Wait a little," he said, closing his eyes and bowing his head.

Chernyshov, having more than once heard Nicholas say so, knew that when the Emperor had to take a decision it was only necessary for him to concentrate his attention for a few moments and the spirit moved him, and the best possible decision presented itself as though an inner voice had told him what to do. He was now thinking how most fully to satisfy the feeling of hatred against the Poles which this incident had stirred up within him, and the inner voice suggested the following decision. He took the report and in his large handwriting wrote on its margin with three orthographical mistakes:

"Diserves deth, but, thank God, we have no capitle punishment, and it is not for me to introduce it. Make him run the gauntlet of a thousand men twelve times.—Nicholas."

He signed, adding his unnaturally huge flourish.

Nicholas knew that twelve thousand strokes with the regulation rods were not only certain death with torture, but were a superfluous cruelty, for five thousand strokes were sufficient to kill the strongest man. But it pleased him to be ruthlessly cruel and it also pleased him to think that we have abolished capital punishment in Russia.

Having written his decision about the student, he pushed it across to Chernyshov.

"There," he said, "read it."

Chernyshov read it, and bowed his head as a sign of respectful amazement at the wisdom of the decision.

"Yes, and let all the students be present on the drill-ground at the punishment," added Nicholas.

"It will do them good! I will abolish this revolutionary spirit and will tear it up by the roots!" he thought.

"It shall be done," replied Chernyshov; and after a short pause he straightened the tuft on his forehead and returned to the Caucasian report.

"What do you command me to write in reply to Prince Vorontsov's dispatch?"

"To keep firmly to my system of destroying the dwellings and food supplies in Chechnya and to harass them by raids," answered Nicholas

"And what are your Majesty's commands with reference to Hadji Murad?" asked Chernyshov.

"Why, Vorontsov writes that he wants to make use of him in the Caucasus."

"Is it not dangerous?" said Chernyshov, avoiding Nicholas's gaze. "Prince Vorontsov is too confiding, I am afraid."

"And you—what do you think?" asked Nicholas sharply, detecting Chernyshov's intention of presenting Vorontsov's decision in an unfavorable light.

"Well, I should have thought it would be safer to deport him to Central Russia."

"You would have thought!" said Nicholas ironically. "But I

don't think so, and agree with Vorontsov. Write to him accordingly."

"It shall be done," said Chernyshov, rising and bowing himself out.

Dolgoruky also bowed himself out, having during the whole audience only uttered a few words (in reply to a question from Nicholas) about the movement of the army.

After Chernyshov, Nicholas received Bibikov, General-Governor of the Western Provinces. Having expressed his approval of the measures taken by Bibikov against the mutinous peasants who did not wish to accept the Orthodox Faith, he ordered him to have all those who did not submit tried by court-martial. That was equivalent to sentencing them to run the gauntlet. He also ordered the editor of a newspaper to be sent to serve in the ranks of the army for publishing information about the transfer of several thousand State peasants to the Imperial estates.

"I do this because I consider it necessary," said Nicholas, "and I will not allow it to be discussed."

Bibikov saw the cruelty of the order concerning the Uniate[30] peasants and the injustice of transferring State peasants (the only free peasants in Russia in those days) to the Crown, which meant making them serfs of the Imperial family. But it was impossible to express dissent. Not to agree with Nicholas's decisions would have meant the loss of that brilliant position which it had cost Bibikov forty years to attain and which he now enjoyed; and he therefore submissively bowed his dark head (already touched with grey) to indicate his submission and his readiness to fulfil the cruel, insensate, and dishonest supreme will.

Having dismissed Bibikov, Nicholas stretched himself, with a sense of duty well fulfilled, glanced at the clock, and went to get ready to go out. Having put on a uniform with epaulets, orders, and a ribbon, he went out into the reception hall where more than a hundred persons—men in uniforms and women in elegant

[30] The Uniates acknowledge the Pope of Rome, though in other respects they are in accord with the Orthodox Russo-Greek Church.

low-necked dresses, all standing in the places assigned to them—awaited his arrival with agitation.

He came out to them with a lifeless look in his eyes, his chest expanded, his stomach bulging out above and below its bandages, and feeling everybody's gaze tremulously and obsequiously fixed upon him he assumed an even more triumphant air. When his eyes met those of people he knew, remembering who was who, he stopped and addressed a few words to them sometimes in Russian and sometimes in French, and transfixing them with his cold glassy eye listened to what they said.

Having received all the New Year congratulations he passed on to church, where God, through His servants the priests, greeted and praised Nicholas just as worldly people did; and weary as he was of these greetings and praises Nicholas duly accepted them. All this was as it should be, because the welfare and happiness of the whole world depended on him, and wearied though he was he would still not refuse the universe his assistance.

When at the end of the service the magnificently arrayed deacon, his long hair crimped and carefully combed, began the chant *Many Years*, which was heartily caught up by the splendid choir, Nicholas looked round and noticed Nelidova, with her fine shoulders, standing by a window, and he decided the comparison with yesterday's girl in her favor.

After Mass he went to the Empress and spent a few minutes in the bosom of his family, joining with the children and his wife. Then passing through the Hermitage,[31] he visited the Minister of the Court, Volkonski, and among other things ordered him to pay out of a special fund a yearly pension to the mother of yesterday's girl. From there he went for his customary drive.

Dinner that day was served in the Pompeian Hall. Besides the younger sons of Nicholas and Michael there were also invited Baron Lieven, Count Rzhevski, Dolgoruky, the Prussian Ambassador, and the King of Prussia's aide-de-camp.

While waiting for the appearance of the Emperor and Empress

[31] A celebrated museum and picture gallery in St. Petersburg, adjoining the Winter Palace.

an interesting conversation took place between Baron Lieven and the Prussian Ambassador concerning the disquieting news from Poland.

"*La Pologne et le Caucase, ce sont les deux cautères de la Russie,*"[32] said Lieven. "*Il nous faut cent mille hommes à peu près, dans chacun de ces deux pays.*"

The Ambassador expressed a fictitious surprise that it should be so.

"*Vous dites la Pologne—*"[33] began the Ambassador.

"*Oh, oui, c'était un coup de maître de Metternich de nous en avoir laissé l'embarras. . . .*"

At this point the Empress, with her trembling head and fixed smile, entered followed by Nicholas.

At dinner Nicholas spoke of Hadji Murad's surrender and said that the war in the Caucasus must now soon come to an end in consequence of the measures he was taking to limit the scope of the mountaineers by felling their forests and by his system of erecting a series of small forts.

The Ambassador, having exchanged a rapid glance with the aide-de-camp—to whom he had only that morning spoken about Nicholas's unfortunate weakness for considering himself a great strategist—warmly praised this plan which once more demonstrated Nicholas's great strategic ability.

After dinner Nicholas drove to the ballet where hundreds of women marched around in tights and scanty clothing. One of them specially attracted him, and he had the German ballet-master sent for and gave orders that a diamond ring should be presented to him.

The next day, when Chernyshov came with his report, Nicholas again confirmed his order to Vorontsov—that now that Hadji Murad had surrendered, the Chechens should be more actively harassed than ever and the cordon round them tightened.

Chernyshov wrote in that sense to Vorontsov; and another

[32] "Poland and the Caucasus are Russia's two sores. We need about 100,000 men in each of those two countries."
[33] "You say that Poland—" "Oh yes, it was a masterstroke of Metternich's to leave us the bother of it. . . ."

courier, overdriving more horses and bruising the faces of more drivers, galloped to Tiflis.

IN OBEDIENCE to this command of Nicholas a raid was immediately made in Chechnya that same month, January 1852.

The detachment ordered for the raid consisted of four infantry battalions, two companies of Cossacks, and eight guns. The column marched along the road; and on both sides of it in a continuous line, now mounting, now descending, marched *Jagers* in high boots, sheepskin coats, and tall caps, with rifles on their shoulders and cartridges in their belts.

As usual when marching through hostile country, silence was observed as far as possible. Only occasionally the guns jingled jolting across a ditch, or an artillery horse snorted or neighed, not understanding that silence was ordered, or an angry commander shouted in a hoarse subdued voice to his subordinates that the line was spreading out too much or marching too near or too far from the column. Only once was the silence broken, when from a bramble patch between the line and the column a gazelle with a white breast and grey back jumped out followed by a buck of the same color with small backward-curving horns. Doubling up their forelegs at each big bound they took, the beautiful timid creatures came so close to the column that some of the soldiers rushed after them laughing and shouting, intending to bayonet them, but the gazelles turned back, slipped through the line of *Jägers*, and pursued by a few horsemen and the company's dogs, fled like birds to the mountains.

It was still winter, but towards noon, when the column (which had started early in the morning) had gone three miles, the sun had risen high enough and was powerful enough to make the men quite hot, and its rays were so bright that it was painful to look at the shining steel of the bayonets or at the reflections—like little suns—on the brass of the cannons.

The clear and rapid stream the detachment had just crossed lay behind, and in front were tilled fields and meadows in shallow valleys. Farther in front were the dark mysterious forest-clad hills with crags rising beyond them, and farther still on the lofty horizon were the ever-beautiful ever-changing snowy peaks that played with the light like diamonds.

At the head of the 5th Company, Butler, a tall handsome officer who had recently exchanged from the Guards, marched along in a black coat and tall cap, shouldering his sword. He was filled with a buoyant sense of the joy of living, the danger of death, a wish for action, and the consciousness of being part of an immense whole directed by a single will. This was his second time of going into action and he thought how in a moment they would be fired at, and he would not only not stoop when the shells flew overhead, or heed the whistle of the bullets, but would carry his head even more erect than before and would look round at his comrades and the soldiers with smiling eyes, and begin to talk in a perfectly calm voice about quite other matters.

The detachment turned off the good road onto a little-used one that crossed a stubbly maize field, and they were drawing near the forest when, with an ominous whistle, a shell flew past amid the baggage wagons—they could not see whence—and tore up the ground in the field by the roadside.

"It's beginning," said Butler with a bright smile to a comrade who was walking beside him.

And so it was. After the shell a thick crowd of mounted Chechens appeared with their banners from under the shelter of the forest. In the midst of the crowd could be seen a large green banner, and an old and very far-sighted sergeant-major informed the short-sighted Butler that Shamil himself must be there. The horsemen came down the hill and appeared to the right, at the highest part of the valley nearest the detachment, and began to descend. A little general in a thick black coat and tall cap rode up to Butler's company on his ambler, and ordered him to the right to encounter the descending horsemen. Butler quickly led his company in the direction indicated, but before he reached the valley he heard two cannon shots behind him. He looked round: two clouds of grey smoke had risen above two cannon and were spread-

ing along the valley. The mountaineers' horsemen—who had evidently not expected to meet artillery—retired. Butler's company
began firing at them and the whole ravine was filled with the
smoke of powder. Only higher up above the ravine could the
mountaineers be seen hurriedly retreating, though still firing back
at the Cossacks who pursued them. The company followed the
mountaineers farther, and on the slope of a second ravine came in
view of an *aoul*.

Following the Cossacks, Butler and his company entered the
aoul at a run, to find it deserted. The soldiers were ordered to
burn the corn and the hay as well as the *saklyas*, and the whole
aoul was soon filled with pungent smoke amid which the soldiers
rushed about dragging out of the *saklyas* what they could find,
and above all catching and shooting the fowls the mountaineers
had not been able to take away with them.

The officers sat down at some distance beyond the smoke, and
lunched and drank. The sergeant-major brought them some honey-
combs on a board. There was no sign of any Chechens and early
in the afternoon the order was given to retreat. The companies
formed into a column behind the *aoul* and Butler happened to be
in the rear-guard. As soon as they started Chechens appeared, following and firing at the detachment, but they ceased this pursuit
as soon as they came out into an open space.

Not one of Butler's company had been wounded, and he returned in a most happy and energetic mood. When after fording
the same stream it had crossed in the morning, the detachment
spread over the maize fields and the meadows, the singers[34] of
each company came forward and songs filled the air.

"Very diff'rent, very diff'rent, *Jägers* are, *Jägers* are!" sang Butler's singers, and his horse stepped merrily to the music. Trezorka,
the shaggy grey dog belonging to the company, ran in front, with
his tail curled up with an air of responsibility like a commander.
Butler felt buoyant, calm, and joyful. War presented itself to him
as consisting only in his exposing himself to danger and to possible
death, thereby gaining rewards and the respect of his comrades

[34] Each regiment had a choir of singers.

here, as well as of his friends in Russia. Strange to say, his imagination never pictured the other aspect of war: the death and wounds of the soldiers, officers, and mountaineers. To retain his poetic conception he even unconsciously avoided looking at the dead and wounded. So that day when we had three dead and twelve wounded, he passed by a corpse lying on its back and did not stop to look, seeing only with one eye the strange position of the waxen hand and a dark red spot on the head. The hillsmen appeared to him only as mounted *dzhigits* from whom he had to defend himself.

"You see, my dear sir," said his major in an interval between two songs, "it's not as it is with you in Petersburg—'Eyes right! Eyes left!' Here we have done our job, and now we go home and Masha will set a pie and some nice cabbage soup before us. That's life—don't you think so?—Now then! *As the Dawn Was Breaking!*" He called for his favorite song.

There was no wind, the air was fresh and clear and so transparent that the snow hills nearly a hundred miles away seemed quite near, and in the intervals between the songs the regular sound of the footsteps and the jingle of the guns was heard as a background on which each song began and ended. The song that was being sung in Butler's company was composed by a cadet in honor of the regiment, and went to a dance tune. The chorus was: "Very diff'rent, very diff'rent, *Jägers* are, *Jägers* are!"

Butler rode beside the officer next in rank above him, Major Petrov, with whom he lived, and he felt he could not be thankful enough to have exchanged from the Guards and come to the Caucasus. His chief reason for exchanging was that he had lost all he had at cards and was afraid that if he remained there he would be unable to resist playing though he had nothing more to lose. Now all that was over, his life was quite changed and was such a pleasant and brave one! He forgot that he was ruined, and forgot his unpaid debts. The Caucasus, the war, the soldiers, the officers—those tipsy, brave, good-natured fellows—and Major Petrov himself, all seemed so delightful that sometimes it appeared too good to be true that he was not in Petersburg—in a room filled with tobacco-smoke, turning down the corners of cards[35] and gambling, hating the holder of the bank and feeling a dull pain in his head—but was really here in this glorious region among these brave Caucasians.

The major and the daughter of a surgeon's orderly, formerly known as Masha, but now generally called by the more respectful name of Marya Dmitrievna, lived together as man and wife. Marya Dmitrievna was a handsome, fair-haired, very freckled, childless woman of thirty. Whatever her past may have been she was now the major's faithful companion and looked after him like a nurse—a very necessary matter, since he often drank himself into oblivion.

When they reached the fort everything happened as the major had foreseen. Marya Dmitrievna gave him and Butler, and two other officers of the detachment who had been invited, a nourishing and tasty dinner, and the major ate and drank till he was unable to speak, and then went off to his room to sleep.

Butler, having drunk rather more *chikhir* wine than was good for him, went to his bedroom, tired but contented, and hardly had time to undress before he fell into a sound, dreamless, and unbroken sleep with his hand under his handsome curly head.

THE *aoul* which had been destroyed was that in which Hadji Murad had spent the night before he went over to the Russians. Sado and his family had left the *aoul* on the approach of the Russian detachment, and when he returned he found his *saklya* in ruins—the roof fallen in, the door and the posts supporting the penthouse burned, and the interior filthy. His son, the handsome bright-eyed boy who had gazed with such ecstasy at Hadji Murad, was brought dead to the mosque on a horse covered with a *burka*: he had been stabbed in the back with a bayonet. The dignified woman who had served Hadji Murad when he was at the house now stood over her son's body, her smock torn in front, her withered old breasts exposed, her hair down, and she dug her nails

[35] A way of doubling one's stake at the game of *shtos*.

into her face till it bled, and wailed incessantly. Sado, taking a pick-axe and spade, had gone with his relatives to dig a grave for his son. The old grandfather sat by the wall of the ruined *saklya* cutting a stick and gazing stolidly in front of him. He had only just returned from the apiary. The two stacks of hay there had been burnt, the apricot and cherry trees he had planted and reared were broken and scorched, and worse still all the beehives and bees had been burnt. The wailing of the women and the little children, who cried with their mothers, mingled with the lowing of the hungry cattle for whom there was no food. The bigger children, instead of playing, followed their elders with frightened eyes. The fountain was polluted, evidently on purpose, so that the water could not be used. The mosque was polluted in the same way, and the Mullah and his assistants were cleaning it out. No one spoke of hatred of the Russians. The feeling experienced by all the Chechens, from the youngest to the oldest, was stronger than hate. It was not hatred, for they did not regard those Russian dogs as human beings, but it was such repulsion, disgust, and perplexity at the senseless cruelty of these creatures, that the desire to exterminate them—like the desire to exterminate rats, poisonous spiders, or wolves—was as natural an instinct as that of self-preservation.

The inhabitants of the *aoul* were confronted by the choice of remaining there and restoring with frightful effort what had been produced with such labor and had been so lightly and senselessly destroyed, facing every moment the possibility of a repetition of what had happened; or to submit to the Russians—contrary to their religion and despite the repulsion and contempt they felt for them. The old men prayed, and unanimously decided to send envoys to Shamil asking him for help. Then they immediately set to work to restore what had been destroyed.

On the morning after the raid, not very early, Butler left the house by the back porch meaning to take a stroll and a breath of fresh air before breakfast, which he usually had with Petrov.

The sun had already risen above the hills and it was painful to look at the brightly lit-up white walls of the houses on the right side of the street. But then as always it was cheerful and soothing to look to the left, at the dark receding and ascending forest-clad hills and at the dim line of snow peaks, which as usual pretended to be clouds. Butler looked at these mountains, inhaling deep breaths and rejoicing that he was alive, that it was just he that was alive, and that he lived in this beautiful place.

He was also rather pleased that he had behaved so well in yesterday's affair both during the advance and especially during the retreat when things were pretty hot; he was also pleased to remember how Masha (or Marya Dmitrievna), Petrov's mistress, had treated them at dinner on their return after the raid, and how she had been particularly nice and simple with everybody, but specially kind—as he thought—to him.

Marya Dmitrievna with her thick plait of hair, her broad shoulders, her high bosom, and the radiant smile on her kindly freckled face, involuntarily attracted Butler, who was a healthy young bachelor. It sometimes even seemed to him that she wanted him, but he considered that that would be doing his good-natured simple-hearted comrade a wrong, and he maintained a simple, respectful attitude towards her and was pleased with himself for doing so.

He was thinking of this when his meditations were disturbed by the tramp of many horses' hoofs along the dusty road in front of him, as if several men were riding that way. He looked up and saw at the end of the street a group of horsemen coming towards him at a walk. In front of a score of Cossacks rode two men: one in a white Circassian coat with a tall turban on his head, the other an officer in the Russian service, dark, with an aquiline nose, and much silver on his uniform and weapons. The man with the turban rode a fine chestnut horse with mane and tail of a lighter shade, a small head, and beautiful eyes. The officer's was a large, handsome Karabakh horse. Butler, a lover of horses, immediately recognized the great strength of the first horse and stopped to learn who these people were.

The officer addressed him. "This the house of commanding officer?" he asked, his foreign accent and his words betraying his foreign origin.

Butler replied that it was. "And who is that?" he added, coming nearer to the officer and indicating the man with the turban.

"That Hadji Murad. He come here to stay with the commander," said the officer.

Butler knew about Hadji Murad and about his having come over to the Russians, but he had not at all expected to see him here in this little fort. Hadji Murad gave him a friendly look.

"Good day, *kotkildy*," said Butler, repeating the Tartar greeting he had learnt.

"*Saubul!*" ("Be well!") replied Hadji Murad, nodding. He rode up to Butler and held out his hand, from two fingers of which hung his whip.

"Are you the chief?" he asked.

"No, the chief is in here. I will go and call him," said Butler addressing the officer, and he went up the steps and pushed the door. But the door of the visitors' entrance, as Marya Dmitrievna called it, was locked, and as it still remained closed after he had knocked, Butler went round to the back door. He called his orderly but received no reply, and finding neither of the two orderlies he went into the kitchen, where Marya Dmitrievna—flushed, with a kerchief tied round her head and her sleeves rolled up on her plump white arms—was rolling pastry, white as her hands, and cutting it into small pieces to make pies of.

"Where have the orderlies gone to?" asked Butler.

"Gone to drink," replied Marya Dmitrievna. "What do you want?"

"To have the front door opened. You have a whole horde of mountaineers in front of your house. Hadji Murad has come!"

"Invent something else!" said Marya Dmitrievna, smiling.

"I am not joking, he is really waiting by the porch!"

"Is it really true?" said she.

"Why should I wish to deceive you? Go and see, he's just at the porch!"

"Dear me, here's a go!" said Marya Dmitrievna pulling down her sleeves and putting up her hand to feel whether the hairpins in her thick plait were all in order. "Then I will go and wake Ivan Matveich."

"No, I'll go myself. And you Bondarenko, go and open the door," said he to Petrov's orderly who had just appeared.

"Well, so much the better!" said Marya Dmitrievna and returned to her work.

When he heard that Hadji Murad had come to his house, Ivan Matveich Petrov, the major, who had already heard that Hadji Murad was in Grozny, was not at all surprised. Sitting up in bed he rolled a cigarette, lit it, and began to dress, loudly clearing his throat and grumbling at the authorities who had sent "that devil" to him.

When he was ready he told his orderly to bring him some medicine. The orderly knew that "medicine" meant vodka, and brought some.

"There is nothing so bad as mixing," muttered the major when he had drunk the vodka and taken a bite of rye bread. "Yesterday I drank a little *chikhir* and now I have a headache. . . . Well, I'm ready," he added, and went to the parlor, into which Butler had already shown Hadji Murad and the officer who accompanied him.

The officer handed the major orders from the commander of the left flank to the effect that he should receive Hadji Murad and should allow him to have intercourse with the mountaineers through spies, but was on no account to allow him to leave the fort without a convoy of Cossacks.

Having read the order the major looked intently at Hadji Murad and again scrutinized the paper. After passing his eyes several times from one to the other in this manner, he at last fixed them on Hadji Murad and said:

"*Yakshi, Bek; yakshi!* ("Very well, sir, very well!") Let him stay here, and tell him I have orders not to let him out—and what is commanded is sacred! Well, Butler, where do you think we'd better lodge him? Shall we put him in the office?"

Butler had not time to answer before Marya Dmitrievna—who had come from the kitchen and was standing in the doorway—said to the major:

"Why? Keep him here! We will give him the guest-chamber and the storeroom. Then at any rate he will be within sight," said she, glancing at Hadji Murad; but meeting his eyes she turned quickly away.

"Do you know, I think Marya Dmitrievna is right," said Butler.

"Now then, now then, get away! Women have no business here," said the major frowning.

During the whole of this discussion Hadji Murad sat with his hand on the hilt of his dagger and a faint smile of contempt on his lips. He said it was all the same to him where he lodged, and that he wanted nothing but what the Sirdar had permitted—namely, to have communication with the mountaineers, and that he therefore wished they should be allowed to come to him.

The major said this should be done, and asked Butler to entertain the visitors till something could be got for them to eat and their rooms prepared. Meantime he himself would go across to the office to write what was necessary and to give some orders.

Hadji Murad's relations with his new acquaintances were at once very clearly defined. From the first he was repelled by and contemptuous of the major, to whom he always behaved very haughtily. Marya Dmitrievna, who prepared and served up his food, pleased him particularly. He liked her simplicity and especially the—to him—foreign type of her beauty, and he was influenced by the attraction she felt towards him and unconsciously conveyed. He tried not to look at her or speak to her, but his eyes involuntarily turned towards her and followed her movements. With Butler, from their first acquaintance, he immediately made friends and talked much and willingly with him, questioning him about his life, telling him of his own, communicating to him the news the spies brought him of his family's condition, and even consulting him as to how he ought to act.

The news he received through the spies was not good. During

the first four days of his stay in the fort they came to see him twice and both times brought bad news.

HADJI MURAD'S family had been removed to Vedeno soon after his desertion to the Russians, and were there kept under guard awaiting Shamil's decision. The women—his old mother Patimat and his two wives with their five little children—were kept under guard in the *saklya* of the officer Ibrahim Raschid, while Hadji Murad's son Yusuf, a youth of eighteen, was put in prison—that is, into a pit more than seven feet deep, together with seven criminals, who like himself were awaiting a decision as to their fate.

The decision was delayed because Shamil was away on a campaign against the Russians.

On January 6, 1852, he returned to Vedeno after a battle, in which according to the Russians he had been vanquished and had fled to Vedeno; but in which according to him and all the *murids* he had been victorious and had repulsed the Russians. In this battle he himself fired his rifle—a thing he seldom did—and drawing his sword would have charged straight at the Russians had not the *murids* who accompanied him held him back. Two of them were killed on the spot at his side.

It was noon when Shamil, surrounded by a party of *murids* who caracoled around him firing their rifles and pistols and continually singing *Lya illyah il Allah!* rode up to his place of residence.

All the inhabitants of the large *aoul* were in the street or on their roofs to meet their ruler, and as a sign of triumph they also fired off rifles and pistols. Shamil rode a white Arab steed which pulled at its bit as it approached the house. The horse had no gold or silver ornaments, its equipment was of the simplest—a delicately worked red leather bridle with a stripe down the middle, metal cup-shaped stirrups, and a red saddlecloth showing a little from under the saddle. The Imam wore a brown cloth cloak lined with black fur showing at the neck and sleeves, and was tightly girded round his long thin waist with a black strap which held a dagger. On his head he wore a tall cap with flat crown and black tassel, and round it was wound a white turban, one end of which hung down on his neck. He wore green slippers, and black leggings trimmed with plain braid.

He wore nothing bright—no gold or silver—and his tall, erect, powerful figure, clothed in garments without any ornaments, surrounded by *murids* with gold and silver on their clothes and weapons, produced on the people just the impression and influence he desired and knew how to produce. His pale face framed by a closely trimmed reddish beard, with his small eyes always screwed up, was as immovable as though hewn out of stone. As he rode through the *aoul* he felt the gaze of a thousand eyes turned eagerly on him, but he himself looked at no one.

Hadji Murad's wives had come out into the penthouse with the rest of the inmates of the *saklya* to see the Imam's entry. Only Patimat, Hadji Murad's old mother, did not go out but remained sitting on the floor of the *saklya* with her grey hair down, her long arms encircling her thin knees, blinking with her fiery black eyes as she watched the dying embers in the fireplace. Like her son she had always hated Shamil, and now she hated him more than ever and had no wish to see him. Neither did Hadji Murad's son see Shamil's triumphal entry. Sitting in the dark and fetid pit he heard the firing and singing, and endured tortures such as can only be felt by the young who are full of vitality and deprived of freedom. He only saw his unfortunate, dirty, and exhausted fellow-prisoners—embittered and for the most part filled with hatred of one another. He now passionately envied those who, enjoying fresh air and light and freedom, caracoled on fiery steeds around their chief, shooting and heartily singing: *Lya illyah il Allah!*

When he had crossed the *aoul* Shamil rode into the large courtyard adjoining the inner court where his seraglio was. Two armed Lesghians met him at the open gates of this outer court, which was crowded with people. Some had come from distant parts about their own affairs, some had come with petitions, and some had been summoned by Shamil to be tried and sentenced. As the Imam rode in, they all respectfully saluted him with their hands on their breasts, some of them kneeling down and remaining on their knees while he rode across the court from the outer to the inner gates. Though he recognized among the people who waited in the court many whom he disliked, and many tedious petitioners who wanted his attention, Shamil passed them all with the same immovable, stony expression on his face, and having entered the inner court dismounted at the penthouse in front of his apartment, to the left of the gate. He was worn out, mentally rather than physically, by the strain of the campaign, for in spite of the public declaration that he had been victorious he knew very well that his campaign had been unsuccessful, that many Chechen *aouls* had been burnt down and ruined, and that the unstable and fickle Chechens were wavering and those nearest the border line were ready to go over to the Russians.

All this had to be dealt with, and it oppressed him, for at that moment he did not wish to think at all. He only desired one thing: rest and the delights of family life, and the caresses of his favorite wife, the black-eyed quick-footed eighteen-year-old Aminal, who at that very moment was close at hand behind the fence that divided the inner court and separated the men's from the women's quarters (Shamil felt sure she was there with his other wives, looking through a chink in the fence while he dismounted). But not only was it impossible for him to go to her, he could not even lie down on his feather cushions and rest from his fatigues; he had first of all to perform the midday rites for which he had just then not the least inclination, but which as the religious leader of the people he could not omit, and which moreover were as necessary to him himself as his daily food. So he performed his ablutions and said his prayers and summoned those who were waiting for him.

The first to enter was Jemal Eddin, his father-in-law and teacher, a tall grey-haired good-looking old man with a beard white as snow and a rosy red face. He said a prayer and began questioning Shamil about the incidents of the campaign and telling him what had happened in the mountains during his absence.

Among events of many kinds—murders connected with blood-feuds, cattle-stealing, people accused of disobeying the Tarikat (smoking and drinking wine)—Jemal Eddin related how Hadji Murad had sent men to bring his family over to the Russians, but that this had been detected and the family had been brought to Vedeno where they were kept under guard and awaited the Imam's decision. In the next room, the guest-chamber, the Elders were assembled to discuss all these affairs, and Jemal Eddin advised Shamil to finish with them and let them go that same day, as they had already been waiting three days for him.

After eating his dinner—served to him in his room by Zeidat, a dark, sharp-nosed, disagreeable-looking woman whom he did not love but who was his eldest wife—Shamil passed into the guest-chamber.

The six old men who made up his council—white, grey, or red-bearded, with tall caps on their heads, some with turbans and some without, wearing new *beshmets* and Circassian coats girdled with straps on which their daggers were suspended—rose to greet him on his entrance. Shamil towered a head above them all. On entering the room he, as well as all the others, lifted his hands, palms upwards, closed his eyes and recited a prayer, and then stroked his face downwards with both hands, uniting them at the end of his beard. Having done this they all sat down, Shamil on a larger cushion than the others, and discussed the various cases before them.

In the case of the criminals the decisions were given according to the Shariat: two were sentenced to have a hand cut off for stealing, one man to be beheaded for murder, and three were pardoned. Then they came to the principal business: how to stop the Chechens from going over to the Russians. To counteract that tendency Jemal Eddin drew up the following proclamation:

"I wish you eternal peace with God the Almighty!

"I hear that the Russians flatter you and invite you to surrender to them. Do not believe what they say, and do not surrender but endure. If ye be not rewarded for it in this life ye shall receive your reward in the life to come. Remember what happened before when they took your arms from you! If God had not brought you to reason then, in 1840, ye would now be soldiers, and your wives would be dishonored and would no longer wear trousers.

"Judge of the future by the past. It is better to die in enmity with the Russians than to live with the Unbelievers. Endure for a little while and I will come with the Koran and the sword and will lead you against the enemy. But now I strictly command you not only to entertain no intention, but not even a thought, of submitting to the Russians!"

Shamil approved this proclamation, signed it, and had it sent out.

After this business they considered Hadji Murad's case. This was of the utmost importance to Shamil. Although he did not wish to admit it, he knew that if Hadji Murad with his agility, boldness, and courage, had been with him, what had now happened in Chechnya would not have occurred. It would therefore be well to make it up with Hadji Murad and have the benefit of his services again. But as this was not possible it would never do to allow him to help the Russians, and therefore he must be enticed back and killed. They might accomplish this either by sending a man to Tiflis who would kill him there, or by inducing him to come back and then killing him. The only means of doing the latter was by making use of his family and especially his son, whom Shamil knew he loved passionately. Therefore they must act through the son.

When the councillors had talked all this over, Shamil closed his eyes and sat silent.

The councillors knew that this meant that he was listening to the voice of the Prophet, who spoke to him and told him what to do.

After five minutes of solemn silence Shamil opened his eyes, and narrowing them more than usual, said:

"Bring Hadji Murad's son to me."

"He is here," replied Jemal Eddin, and in fact Yusuf, Hadji Murad's son, thin, pale, tattered, and evil-smelling, but still handsome in face and figure, with black eyes that burnt like his grandmother Patimat's, was already standing by the gate of the outside court waiting to be called in.

Yusuf did not share his father's feelings towards Shamil. He did not know all that had happened in the past, or if he knew it, not having lived through it he still did not understand why his father was so obstinately hostile to Shamil. To him who wanted only one thing—to continue living the easy, loose life that, as the *naib's* son, he had led in Khunzakh—it seemed quite unnecessary to be at enmity with Shamil. Out of defiance and a spirit of contradiction to his father he particularly admired Shamil, and shared the ecstatic adoration with which he was regarded in the mountains. With a peculiar feeling of tremulous veneration for the Imam he now entered the guest-chamber. As he stopped by the door he met the steady gaze of Shamil's half-closed eyes. He paused for a moment, and then approached Shamil and kissed his large, long-fingered hand.

"Thou art Hadji Murad's son?"

"I am, Imam."

"Thou knowest what he has done?"

"I know, Imam, and deplore it."

"Canst thou write?"

"I was preparing myself to be a Mullah——"

"Then write to thy father that if he will return to me now, before the Feast of Bairam, I will forgive him and everything shall be as it was before; but if not, and if he remains with the Russians"—and Shamil frowned sternly—"I will give thy grandmother, thy mother, and the rest to the different *aouls*, and thee I will behead!"

Not a muscle of Yusuf's face stirred, and he bowed his head to show that he understood Shamil's words.

"Write that and give it to my messenger."

Shamil ceased speaking, and looked at Yusuf for a long time in silence.

"Write that I have had pity on thee and will not kill thee, but will put out thine eyes as I do to all traitors! . . . Go!"

While in Shamil's presence Yusuf appeared calm, but when he

had been led out of the guest-chamber he rushed at his attendant, snatched the man's dagger from its sheath and tried to stab himself, but he was seized by the arms, bound, and led back to the pit.

That evening at dusk after he had finished his evening prayers, Shamil put on a white fur-lined cloak and passed out to the other side of the fence where his wives lived, and went straight to Aminal's room, but he did not find her there. She was with the older wives. Then Shamil, trying to remain unseen, hid behind the door and stood waiting for her. But Aminal was angry with him because he had given some silk stuff to Zeidat and not to her. She saw him come out and go into her room looking for her, and she purposely kept away. She stood a long time at the door of Zeidat's room, laughing softly at Shamil's white figure that kept going in and out of her room.

Having waited for her in vain, Shamil returned to his own apartments when it was already time for the midnight prayers.

HADJI MURAD had been a week in the major's house at the fort. Although Marya Dmitrievna quarrelled with the shaggy Khanefi (Hadji Murad had only brought two of his *murids*, Khanefi and Eldar, with him) and had turned him out of her kitchen—for which he nearly killed her—she evidently felt a particular respect and sympathy for Hadji Murad. She now no longer served him his dinner, having handed that duty over to Eldar, but she seized every opportunity of seeing him and rendering him service. She always took the liveliest interest in the negotiations about his family, knew how many wives and children he had, and their ages, and each time a spy came to see him she inquired as best she could into the results of the negotiations.

Butler during that week had become quite friendly with Hadji Murad. Sometimes the latter came to Butler's room, sometimes Butler went to Hadji Murad's: sometimes they conversed by the help of the interpreter, and sometimes they got on as best they could with signs and especially with smiles.

Hadji Murad had evidently taken a fancy to Butler, as could

be gathered from Eldar's relations with the latter. When Butler entered Hadji Murad's room Eldar met him with a pleased smile showing his glittering teeth, and hurried to put down a cushion for him to sit on and to relieve him of his sword if he was wearing one.

Butler also got to know, and became friendly with, the shaggy Khanefi, Hadji Murad's sworn brother. Khanefi knew many mountain songs and sang them well, and to please Butler, Hadji Murad often made Khanefi sing, choosing the songs he considered best. Khanefi had a high tenor voice and sang with extraordinary clearness and expression. One of the songs Hadji Murad specially liked impressed Butler by its solemnly mournful tone and he asked the interpreter to translate it.

The subject of the song was the very blood-feud that had existed between Khanefi and Hadji Murad. It ran as follows:

> "The earth will dry on my grave,
>   Mother, my Mother!
>   And thou wilt forget me!
> And over me rank grass will wave,
>   Father, my Father!
>   Nor wilt thou regret me
> When tears cease thy dark eyes to lave,
>   Sister, dear Sister!
>   No more will grief fret thee!

> "But thou, my Brother the elder, wilt never forget,
>   With vengeance denied me!
> And thou, my Brother the younger, wilt ever regret,
>   Till thou liest beside me!

> "Hotly thou camest, O death-bearing ball that I spurned,
>   For thou wast my slave!
> And thou, black earth, that battle-steed trampled and churned,
>   Wilt cover my grave!

*"Cold art Thou, O Death, yet I was thy Lord and thy Master!
My body sinks fast to the earth, my soul to Heaven flies faster."*

Hadji Murad always listened to this song with closed eyes and
when it ended on a long gradually dying note he always remarked
in Russian—

"Good song! Wise song!"

After Hadji Murad's arrival and his intimacy with him and his
murids, the poetry of the stirring mountain life took a still stronger
hold on Butler. He procured for himself a *beshmet* and a Circassian coat and leggings, and imagined himself a mountaineer living
the life those people lived.

On the day of Hadji Murad's departure the major invited
several officers to see him off. They were sitting, some at the table
where Marya Dmitrievna was pouring out tea, some at another
table on which stood vodka, *chikhir,* and light refreshments, when
Hadji Murad dressed for the journey came limping into the room
with soft, rapid footsteps.

They all rose and shook hands with him. The major offered him
a seat on the divan, but Hadji Murad thanked him and sat down
on a chair by the window.

The silence that followed his entrance did not at all abash him.
He looked attentively at all the faces and fixed an indifferent gaze
on the tea-table with the samovar and refreshments. Petrovsky, a
lively officer who now met Hadji Murad for the first time, asked
him through the interpreter whether he liked Tiflis.

"*Alya!*" he replied.

"He says 'Yes,' " translated the interpreter.

"What did he like there?"

Hadji Murad said something in reply.

"He liked the theater best of all."

"And how did he like the ball at the house of the commander-
in-chief?"

Hadji Murad frowned. "Every nation has its own customs!
Our women do not dress in such a way," said he, glancing at
Marya Dmitrievna.

"Well, didn't he like it?"

"We have a proverb," said Hadji Murad to the interpreter, "-'The dog gave meat to the ass and the ass gave hay to the dog, and both went hungry,' " and he smiled. "Its own customs seem good to each nation."

The conversation went no farther. Some of the officers took tea, some other refreshments, Hadji Murad accepted the tumbler of tea offered him and put it down before him.

"Won't you have cream and a bun?" asked Marya Dmitrievna, offering them to him.

Hadji Murad bowed his head.

"Well, I suppose it is good-bye!" said Butler, touching his knee. "When shall we meet again?"

"Good-bye, good-bye!" said Hadji Murad, in Russian, with a smile. "*Kunak bulug.* Strong *kunak* to thee! Time—*ayda*—go!" and he jerked his head in the direction in which he had to go.

Eldar appeared in the doorway carrying something large and white across his shoulder and a sword in his hand. Hadji Murad beckoned to him and he crossed the room with big strides and handed him a white *burka* and the sword. Hadji Murad rose, took the *burka*, threw it over his arm, and saying something to the interpreter handed it to Marya Dmitrievna.

"He says thou hast praised the *burka*, so accept it," said the interpreter.

"Oh, why?" said Marya Dmitrievna blushing.

"It is necessary. Like Adam," said Hadji Murad.

"Well, thank you," said Marya Dmitrievna, taking the *burka*. "God grant that you rescue your son," she added. "*Ulan yakshi.* Tell him that I wish him success in releasing his son."

Hadji Murad glanced at Marya Dmitrievna and nodded his head approvingly. Then he took the sword from Eldar and handed it to the major. The major took it and said to the interpreter, "Tell him to take my chestnut gelding. I have nothing else to give him."

Hadji Murad waved his hand in front of his face to show that he did not want anything and would not accept it. Then, pointing first to the mountains and then to his heart, he went out.

All the household followed him as far as the door, while the officers who remained inside the room drew the sword from its scabbard, examined its blade, and decided that it was a real Gurda.[36]

Butler accompanied Hadji Murad to the porch, and then came a very unexpected incident which might have ended fatally for Hadji Murad had it not been for his quick observation, determination, and agility.

The inhabitants of the Kumukh *aoul*, Tash-Kichu, which was friendly to the Russians, respected Hadji Murad greatly and had often come to the fort merely to look at the famous *naib*. They had sent messengers to him three days previously to ask him to visit their mosque on the Friday. But the Kumukh princes who lived in Tash-Kichu hated Hadji Murad because there was a blood-feud between them, and on hearing of this invitation they announced to the people that they would not allow him to enter the mosque. The people became excited and a fight occurred between them and the princes' supporters. The Russian authorities pacified the mountaineers and sent word to Hadji Murad not to go to the mosque.

Hadji Murad did not go and everyone supposed that the matter was settled.

But at the very moment of his departure, when he came out into the porch before which the horses stood waiting, Arslan Khan, one of the Kumukh princes and an acquaintance of Butler and the major, rode up to the house.

When he saw Hadji Murad he snatched a pistol from his belt and took aim, but before he could fire, Hadji Murad in spite of his lameness rushed down from the porch like a cat towards Arslan Khan who missed him.

Seizing Arslan Khan's horse by the bridle with one hand, Hadji Murad drew his dagger with the other and shouted something to him in Tartar.

Butler and Eldar both ran at once towards the enemies and

[36] A highly prized quality of blade.

caught them by the arms. The major, who had heard the shot, also came out.

"What do you mean by it, Arslan—starting such a nasty business on my premises?" said he, when he heard what had happened. "It's not right, friend! 'To the foe in the field you need not yield!'—but to start this kind of slaughter in front of my house——"

Arslan Khan, a little man with black moustaches, got off his horse pale and trembling, looked angrily at Hadji Murad, and went into the house with the major. Hadji. Murad, breathing heavily and smiling, returned to the horses.

"Why did he want to kill him?" Butler asked the interpreter.

"He says it is a law of theirs," the interpreter translated Hadji Murad's reply. "Arslan must avenge a relation's blood and so he tried to kill him."

"And supposing he overtakes him on the road?" asked Butler.

Hadji Murad smiled.

"Well, if he kills me it will prove that such is Allah's will. . . . Good-bye," he said again in Russian, taking his horse by the withers. Glancing round at everybody who had come out to see him off, his eyes rested kindly on Marya Dmitrievna.

"Good-bye, my lass," said he to her. "I thank you."

"God help you—God help you to rescue your family!" repeated Marya Dmitrievna.

He did not understand her words, but felt her sympathy for him and nodded to her.

"Mind, don't forget your *kunak*," said Butler.

"Tell him I am his true friend and will never forget him," answered Hadji Murad to the interpreter, and in spite of his short leg he swung himself lightly and quickly into the high saddle, barely touching the stirrup, and automatically feeling for his dagger and adjusting his sword. Then, with that peculiarly proud look with which only a Caucasian hill-man sits his horse—as though he were one with it—he rode away from the major's house. Khanefi and Eldar also mounted and having taken a friendly leave of their hosts and of the officers, rode off at a trot, following their *murshid*.

As usual after a departure, those who remained behind began to discuss those who had left.

"Plucky fellow! He rushed at Arslan like a wolf! His face quite changed!"

"But he'll be up to tricks—he's a terrible rogue, I should say," remarked Petrovsky.

"It's a pity there aren't more Russian rogues of such a kind!" suddenly put in Marya Dmitrievna with vexation. "He has lived a week with us and we have seen nothing but good from him. He is courteous, wise, and just," she added.

"How did you find that out?"

"No matter, I did find it out!"

"She's quite smitten, and that's a fact!" said the major, who had just entered the room.

"Well, and if I am smitten? What's that to you? Why run him down if he's a good man? Though he's a Tartar he's still a good man!"

"Quite true, Marya Dmitrievna," said Butler, "and you're quite right to take his part!"

LIFE in our advanced forts in the Chechen lines went on as usual. Since the events last narrated there had been two alarms when the companies were called out and militiamen galloped about; but both times the mountaineers who had caused the excitement got away, and once at Vozdvizhensk they killed a Cossack and succeeded in carrying off eight Cossack horses that were being watered. There had been no further raids since the one in which the *aoul* was destroyed, but an expedition on a large scale was expected in consequence of the appointment of a new commander of the left flank, Prince Baryatinsky. He was an old friend of the Viceroy's and had been in command of the Kabarda regiment. On his arrival at Grozny as commander of the whole left flank he at once mustered a detachment to continue to carry out the Tsar's commands as communicated by Chernyshov to Vorontsov. The detachment mustered at Vozdvizhensk left the fort and took up a position towards Kurin, where the troops were encamped and were felling the forest. Young Vorontsov lived in a splendid cloth tent, and his wife, Marya Vasilevna, often came to the camp and stayed the night. Baryatinsky's relations with Marya Vasilevna were no secret to anyone, and the officers who were not in the aristocratic set and the soldiers abused her in coarse terms— for her presence in camp caused them to be told off to lie in ambush at night. The mountaineers were in the habit of bringing guns within range and firing shells at the camp. The shells generally missed their aim and therefore at ordinary times no special measures were taken to prevent such firing, but now men were placed in ambush to hinder the mountaineers from injuring or frightening Marya Vasilevna with their cannon. To have to be always lying in ambush at night to save a lady from being frightened, offended and annoyed them, and therefore the soldiers, as well as the officers not admitted to the higher society, called Marya Vasilevna bad names.

Having obtained leave of absence from his fort, Butler came to the camp to visit some old mess-mates from the cadet corps and fellow officers of the Kurin regiment who were serving as adjutants and orderly officers. When he first arrived he had a very good time. He put up in Poltoratsky's tent and there met many acquaintances who gave him a hearty welcome. He also called on Vorontsov, whom he knew slightly, having once served in the same regiment with him. Vorontsov received him very kindly, introduced him to Prince Baryatinsky, and invited him to the farewell dinner he was giving in honor of General Kozlovsky, who until Baryatinsky's arrival had been in command of the left flank.

The dinner was magnificent. Special tents were erected in a line, and along the whole length of them a table was spread as for a dinner-party, with dinner-services and bottles. Everything recalled life in the Guards in Petersburg. Dinner was served at two o'clock. Kozlovsky sat in the middle on one side, Baryatinsky on the other. At Kozlovsky's right and left hand sat the Vorontsovs, husband and wife. All along the table on both sides sat the officers of the Kabarda and Kurin regiments. Butler sat next to Poltoratsky and they both chatted merrily and drank with the officers around them. When the roast was served and the orderlies had gone round and filled the champagne glasses, Poltoratsky said to Butler, with real anxiety:

"Our Kozlovsky will disgrace himself!"

"Why?"

"Why, he'll have to make a speech, and what good is he at that? . . . It's not as easy as capturing entrenchments under fire! And with a lady beside him too, and these aristocrats!"

"Really it's painful to look at him," said the officers to one another. And now the solemn moment had arrived. Baryatinsky rose and lifting his glass, addressed a short speech to Kozlovsky. When he had finished, Kozlovsky—who always had a trick of using the word "how" superfluously—rose and stammeringly began:

"In compliance with the august will of his Majesty I am leaving you—parting from you, gentlemen," said he. "But consider me as always remaining among you. The truth of the proverb, how 'One man in the field is no warrior,' is well known to you, gentlemen. . . . Therefore, how every reward I have received . . . how all the benefits showered on me by the great generosity of our sovereign the Emperor . . . how all my position—how my good name . . . how everything decidedly . . . how . . ." (here his voice trembled) ". . . how I am indebted to you for it, to you alone, my friends!" The wrinkled face puckered up still more, he gave a sob and tears came into his eyes. "How from my heart I offer you my sincerest, heartfelt gratitude!"

Kozlovsky could not go on but turned round and began to embrace the officers. The princess hid her face in her handkerchief. The prince blinked, with his mouth drawn awry. Many of the officers' eyes grew moist and Butler, who had hardly known Kozlovsky, could also not restrain his tears. He liked all this very much.

Then followed other toasts. Healths were drunk to Baryatinsky, Vorontsov, the officers, and the soldiers, and the visitors left the table intoxicated with wine and with the military elation to which they were always so prone. The weather was wonderful, sunny and calm, and the air fresh and bracing. Bonfires crackled and songs resounded on all sides. It might have been thought that everybody was celebrating some joyful event. Butler went to Poltoratsky's in the happiest, most emotional mood. Several officers had gathered there and a card-table was set. An adjutant started a bank with a hundred rubles. Two or three times Butler left the tent with his hand gripping the purse in his trousers-pocket, but at last he could resist the temptation no longer, and despite the promise he had given to his brother and to himself not to play, he began to do so. Before an hour was past, very red, perspiring, and soiled with chalk, he was sitting with both elbows on the table and writing on it—under cards bent for "corners" and "transports"[37]—the figures of his stakes. He had already lost so much that he was afraid to count up what was scored against him. But he knew without counting that all the pay he could draw in advance, added to the value of his horse, would not suffice to pay what the adjutant, a stranger to him, had written down against him. He would still have gone on playing, but the adjutant sternly laid down the cards he held in his large clean hands and added up the chalked figures of the score of Butler's losses. Butler, in confusion, began to make excuses for being unable to pay the whole of his debt at once, and said he would send it from home. When he said this he noticed that everybody pitied him and that they all—even Poltoratsky—avoided meeting his eye. That was his last evening there. He reflected that he need only have refrained from playing and have gone to the Vorontsovs who had invited him, and all would have been well, but now it was not only not well—it was terrible.

Having taken leave of his comrades and acquaintances he rode home and went to bed, and slept for eighteen hours as people usually sleep after losing heavily. From the fact that he asked her to lend him fifty kopeks to tip the Cossack who had escorted him, and from his sorrowful looks and short answers, Marya Dmitrievna guessed that he had lost at cards and she reproached the major for having given him leave of absence.

[37] These expressions relate to the game of *shtos*.

When he woke up at noon next day and remembered the situation he was in he longed again to plunge into the oblivion from which he had just emerged, but it was impossible. Steps had to be taken to repay the four hundred and seventy rubles he owed to the stranger. The first step he took was to write to his brother, confessing his sin and imploring him, for the last time, to lend him five hundred rubles on the security of the mill they still owned in common. Then he wrote to a stingy relative asking her to lend him five hundred rubles at whatever rate of interest she liked. Finally he went to the major, knowing that he—or rather Marya Dmitrievna—had some money, and asked him to lend him five hundred rubles.

"I'd let you have them at once," said the major, "but Masha won't! These women are so close-fisted—who the devil can understand them? . . . And yet you must get out of it somehow, devil take him! . . . Hasn't that brute the canteen-keeper got something?"

But it was no use trying to borrow from the canteen-keeper, so Butler's salvation could only come from his brother or his stingy relative.

Not having attained his aim in Chechnya, Hadji Murad returned to Tiflis and went every day to Vorontsov's, and whenever he could obtain audience he implored the Viceroy to gather together the mountaineer prisoners and exchange them for his family. He said that unless that were done his hands were tied and he could not serve the Russians and destroy Shamil as he desired to do. Vorontsov vaguely promised to do what he could, but put it off, saying that he would decide when General Argutinski reached Tiflis and he could talk the matter over with him.

Then Hadji Murad asked Vorontsov to allow him to go to live for a while in Nukha, a small town in Transcaucasia where he thought he could better carry on negotiations about his family with Shamil and with the people who were attached to himself. Moreover Nukha, being a Mohammedan town, had a mosque where he could more conveniently perform the rites of prayer demanded by the Mohammedan law. Vorontsov wrote to Petersburg about it but meanwhile gave Hadji Murad permission to go to Nukha.

For Vorontsov and the authorities in Petersburg, as well as for most Russians acquainted with Hadji Murad's history, the whole episode presented itself as a lucky turn in the Caucasian war, or simply as an interesting event. For Hadji Murad it was a terrible crisis in his life—especially latterly. He had escaped from the mountains partly to save himself and partly out of hatred of Shamil, and difficult as this flight had been he had attained his object, and for a time was glad of his success and really devised a plan to attack Shamil, but the rescue of his family—which he had thought would be easy to arrange—had proved more difficult than he expected.

Shamil had seized the family and kept them prisoners, threatening to hand the women over to the different *aouls* and to blind or kill the son. Now Hadji Murad had gone to Nukha intending to try by the aid of his adherents in Daghestan to rescue his family from Shamil by force or by cunning. The last spy who had come to see him in Nukha informed him that the Avars, who were devoted to him, were preparing to capture his family and themselves bring them over to the Russians, but that there were not enough of them and they could not risk making the attempt in Vedeno, where the family was at present imprisoned, but could do so only if the family were moved from Vedeno to some other place—in which case they promised to rescue them on the way.

Hadji Murad sent word to his friends that he would give three thousand rubles for the liberation of his family.

At Nukha a small house of five rooms was assigned to Hadji Murad near the mosque and the Khan's palace. The officers in charge of him, his interpreter, and his henchmen, stayed in the same house. Hadji Murad's life was spent in the expectation and reception of messengers from the mountains and in rides he was allowed to take in the neighborhood.

On 24th April, returning from one of these rides, Hadji Murad learnt that during his absence an official sent by Vorontsov had arrived from Tiflis. In spite of his longing to know what message the official had brought him he went to his bedroom and repeated his noonday prayer before going into the room where the officer in charge and the official were waiting. This room served him both as drawing- and reception-room. The official who had come from Tiflis, Councillor Kirillov, informed Hadji Murad of Vorontsov's wish that he should come to Tiflis on the 12th to meet General Argutinski.

"*Yakshi!*" said Hadji Murad angrily. The councillor did not please him. "Have you brought money?"

"I have," answered Kirillov.

"For two weeks now," said Hadji Murad, holding up first both hands and then four fingers. "Give here!"

"We'll give it you at once," said the official, getting his purse out of his travelling-bag. "What does he want with the money?" he went on in Russian, thinking that Hadji Murad would not understand. But Hadji Murad had understood, and glanced angrily at him. While getting out the money the councillor, wishing to begin a conversation with Hadji Murad in order to have something to tell Prince Vorontsov on his return, asked through the interpreter whether he was not feeling dull there. Hadji Murad glanced contemptuously out of the corner of his eye at the fat, unarmed little man dressed as a civilian, and did not reply. The interpreter repeated the question.

"Tell him that I cannot talk with him! Let him give me the money!" and having said this, Hadji Murad sat down at the table ready to count it.

Hadji Murad had an allowance of five gold pieces a day, and when Kirillov had got out the money and arranged it in seven piles of ten gold pieces each and pushed them towards Hadji Murad, the latter poured the gold into the sleeve of his Circassian coat, rose, quite unexpectedly smacked Councillor Kirillov on his bald pate, and turned to go.

The councillor jumped up and ordered the interpreter to tell Hadji Murad that he must not dare to behave like that to him who held a rank equal to that of colonel! The officer in charge confirmed this, but Hadji Murad only nodded to signify that he knew, and left the room.

"What is one to do with him?" said the officer in charge. "He'll stick his dagger into you, that's all! One cannot talk with those devils! I see that he is getting exasperated."

As soon as it began to grow dusk two spies with hoods covering their faces up to their eyes, came to him from the hills. The officer in charge led them to Hadji Murad's room. One of them was a fleshy, swarthy Tavlinian, the other a thin old man. The news they brought was not cheering. Hadji Murad's friends who had undertaken to rescue his family now definitely refused to do so, being afraid of Shamil, who threatened to punish with most terrible tortures anyone who helped Hadji Murad. Having heard the messengers he sat with his elbows on his crossed legs, and bowing his turbaned head remained silent a long time.

He was thinking and thinking resolutely. He knew that he was now considering the matter for the last time and that it was necessary to come to a decision. At last he raised his head, gave each of the messengers a gold piece, and said: "Go!"

"What answer will there be?"

"The answer will be as God pleases. . . . Go!"

The messengers rose and went away, and Hadji Murad continued to sit on the carpet leaning his elbows on his knees. He sat thus a long time and pondered.

"What am I to do? To take Shamil at his word and return to him?" he thought. "He is a fox and will deceive me. Even if he did not deceive me it would still be impossible to submit to that red liar. It is impossible . . . because now that I have been with the Russians he will not trust me," thought Hadji Murad; and he remembered a Tavlinian fable about a falcon who had been caught and lived among men and afterwards returned to his own kind in the hills. He returned, wearing jesses with bells, and the other falcons would not receive him. "Fly back to where they hung those silver bells on thee!" said they. "We have no bells and no jesses." The falcon did not want to leave his home and remained, but the other falcons did not wish to let him stay there and pecked him to death.

"And they would peck me to death in the same way," thought Hadji Murad. "Shall I remain here and conquer Caucasia for the Russian Tsar and earn renown, titles, riches?

"That could be done," thought he, recalling his interviews with Vorontsov and the flattering things the prince had said; "but I must decide at once, or Shamil will destroy my family."

That night he remained awake, thinking.

By MIDNIGHT his decision had been formed. He had decided that he must fly to the mountains, and break into Vedeno with the Avars still devoted to him, and either die or rescue his family. Whether after rescuing them he would return to the Russians or escape to Khunzakh and fight Shamil, he had not made up his mind. All he knew was that first of all he must escape from the Russians into the mountains, and he at once began to carry out his plan.

He drew his black wadded *beshmet* from under his pillow and went into his henchmen's room. They lived on the other side of the hall. As soon as he entered the hall, the outer door of which stood open, he was at once enveloped by the dewy freshness of the moonlit night and his ears were filled by the whistling and trilling of several nightingales in the garden by the house.

Having crossed the hall he opened the door of his henchmen's room. There was no light there, but the moon in its first quarter shone in at the window. A table and two chairs were standing on one side of the room, and four of his henchmen were lying on carpets or on *burkas* on the floor. Khanefi slept outside with the horses. Gamzalo heard the door creak, rose, turned round, and saw him. On recognizing him he lay down again, but Eldar, who lay beside him, jumped up and began putting on his *beshmet*, expecting his master's orders. Khan Mahoma and Bata slept on. Hadji Murad put down the *beshmet* he had brought on the table, which it hit with a dull sound, caused by the gold sewn up in it.

"Sew these in too," said Hadji Murad, handing Eldar the gold pieces he had received that day. Eldar took them and at once went into the moonlight, drew a small knife from under his dagger and started unstitching the lining of the *beshmet*. Gamzalo raised himself and sat up with his legs crossed.

"And you, Gamzalo, tell the men to examine the rifles and pistols and get the ammunition ready. Tomorrow we shall go far," said Hadji Murad.

"We have bullets and powder, everything shall be ready," replied Gamzalo, and roared out something incomprehensible. He understood why Hadji Murad had ordered the rifles to be loaded. From the first he had desired only one thing—to slay and stab as many Russians as possible and to escape to the hills—and this desire had increased day by day. Now at last he saw that Hadji Murad also wanted this and he was satisfied.

When Hadji Murad went away Gamzalo roused his comrades, and all four spent the rest of the night examining their rifles, pistols, flints, and accoutrements; replacing what was damaged, sprinkling fresh powder onto the pans, and stoppering with bullets wrapped in oiled rags packets filled with the right amount of powder for each charge, sharpening their swords and daggers and greasing the blades with tallow.

Before daybreak Hadji Murad again came out into the hall to get water for his ablutions. The songs of the nightingales that had burst into ecstasy at dawn were now even louder and more incessant, while from his henchmen's room, where the daggers were being sharpened, came the regular screech and rasp of iron against stone.

Hadji Murad got himself some water from a tub, and was already at his own door when above the sound of the grinding he heard from his *murids'* room the high tones of Khanefi's voice singing a familiar song. He stopped to listen. The song told of how a *dzhigit*, Hamzad, with his brave followers captured a herd of white horses from the Russians, and how a Russian prince followed him beyond the Terek and surrounded him with an army as large as a forest; and then the song went on to tell how Hamzad killed the horses, entrenched his men behind this gory bulwark, and fought the Russians as long as they had bullets in their rifles, daggers in their belts, and blood in their veins. But before he died Hamzad saw some birds flying in the sky and cried to them:

> *"Fly on, ye winged ones, fly to our homes!*
> *Tell ye our mothers, tell ye our sisters,*
> *Tell the white maidens, that fighting we died*
> *For Ghazavat! Tell them our bodies*
> *Never will lie and rest in a tomb!*
> *Wolves will devour and tear them to pieces,*
> *Ravens and vultures will pluck out our eyes."*

With that the song ended, and at the last words, sung to a mournful air, the merry Bata's vigorous voice joined in with a loud shout of *"Lya-il-lyakha-il Allakh!"* finishing with a shrill shriek. Then all was quiet again, except for the *tchuk, tchuk, tchuk, tchuk* and whistling of the nightingales from the garden and from behind the door the even grinding, and now and then the whiz, of iron sliding quickly along the whetstone.

Hadji Murad was so full of thought that he did not notice how he tilted his jug till the water began to pour out. He shook his head at himself and re-entered his room. After performing his morning ablutions he examined his weapons and sat down on his bed. There was nothing more for him to do. To be allowed to ride out he would have to get permission from the officer in charge, but it was not yet daylight and the officer was still asleep.

Khanefi's song reminded him of the song his mother had composed just after he was born—the song addressed to his father that Hadji Murad had repeated to Loris-Melikov.

And he seemed to see his mother before him—not wrinkled and grey-haired, with gaps between her teeth, as he had lately left her, but young and handsome, and strong enough to carry him in a basket on her back across the mountains to her father's when he was a heavy five-year-old boy.

And the recollection of himself as a little child reminded him of his beloved son, Yusuf, whose head he himself had shaved for the first time; and now this Yusuf was a handsome young *dzhigit*. He pictured him as he was when last he saw him on the day he left Tselmess. Yusuf brought him his horse and asked to be allowed to accompany him. He was ready dressed and armed, and led his own horse by the bridle, and his rosy handsome young face and the whole of his tall slender figure (he was taller than his father) breathed of daring, youth, and the joy of life. The breadth of his shoulders, though he was so young, the very wide youthful hips, the long slender waist, the strength of his long arms, and the power, flexibility, and agility of all his movements had always rejoiced Hadji Murad, who admired his son.

"Thou hadst better stay. Thou wilt be alone at home now. Take care of thy mother and thy grandmother," said Hadji Murad. And he remembered the spirited and proud look and the flush of pleasure with which Yusuf had replied that as long as he lived no one should injure his mother or grandmother. All the same, Yusuf had mounted and accompanied his father as far as the stream. There he turned back, and since then Hadji Murad had not seen his wife, his mother, or his son. And it was this son whose eyes Shamil threatened to put out! Of what would be done to his wife Hadji Murad did not wish to think.

These thoughts so excited him that he could not sit still any longer. He jumped up and went limping quickly to the door, opened it, and called Eldar. The sun had not yet risen, but it was already quite light. The nightingales were still singing.

"Go and tell the officer that I want to go out riding, and saddle the horses," said he.

BUTLER's only consolation all this time was the poetry of warfare, to which he gave himself up not only during his hours of service but also in private life. Dressed in his Circassian costume, he rode and swaggered about, and twice went into ambush with Bogdanovich, though neither time did they discover or kill anyone. This closeness to and friendship with Bogdanovich, famed for his courage, seemed pleasant and warlike to Butler. He had paid his debt, having borrowed the money of a Jew at an enormous rate of interest—that is to say, he had postponed his difficulties but had not solved them. He tried not to think of his position, and to find oblivion not only in the poetry of warfare but also in wine. He drank more and more every day, and day by day grew morally weaker. He was now no longer the chaste Joseph he had been towards Marya Dmitrievna, but on the contrary began courting her grossly, meeting to his surprise with a strong and de-cided repulse which put him to shame.

At the end of April there arrived at the fort a detachment with which Baryatinsky intended to effect an advance right through Chechnya, which had till then been considered impassable. In that detachment were two companies of the Kabarda regiment, and according to Caucasian custom these were treated as guests by the Kurin companies. The soldiers were lodged in the barracks, and were treated not only to supper, consisting of buckwheat-porridge and beef, but also to vodka. The officers shared the quarters of the Kurin officers, and as usual those in residence gave the new-comers a dinner at which the regimental singers performed and which ended up with a drinking-bout. Major Petrov, very drunk and no longer red but ashy pale, sat astride a chair and, drawing his sword, hacked at imaginary foes, alternately swearing and laughing, now embracing someone and now dancing to the tune of his favorite song.

> *"Shamil, he began to riot*
> *In the days gone by;*
> *Try, ry, rataty,*
> *In the years gone by!"*

Butler was there too. He tried to see the poetry of warfare in this also, but in the depth of his soul he was sorry for the major. To stop him, however, was quite impossible; and Butler, feeling that the fumes were mounting to his own head, quietly left the room and went home.

The moon lit up the white houses and the stone on the road. It was so light that every pebble, every straw, every little heap of dust was visible. As he approached the house he met Marya Dmitrievna with a shawl over her head and neck. After the rebuff she had given him Butler had avoided her, feeling rather ashamed, but now in the moonlight and after the wine he had drunk he was pleased to meet her and wished to make up to her again.

"Where are you off to?" he asked.

"Why, to see after my old man," she answered pleasantly. Her rejection of Butler's advances was quite sincere and decided, but she did not like his avoiding her as he had done lately.

"Why bother about him? He'll soon come back."

"But will he?"

"If he doesn't they'll bring him."

"Just so. . . . That's not right, you know! . . . But you think I'd better not go?"

"Yes, I do. We'd better go home."

Marya Dmitrievna turned back and walked beside him. The moon shone so brightly that a halo seemed to move along the road round the shadows of their heads. Butler was looking at this halo and making up his mind to tell her that he liked her as much as ever, but he did not know how to begin. She waited for him to speak, and they walked on in silence almost to the house, when some horsemen appeared from round the corner. These were an officer with an escort.

"Who's that coming now?" said Marya Dmitrievna, stepping aside. The moon was behind the rider so that she did not recognize him until he had almost come up to them. It was Peter Nikolaevich Kamenev, an officer who had formerly served with the major and whom Marya Dmitrievna therefore knew.

"Is that you, Peter Nikolaevich?" said she, addressing him.

"It's me," said Kamenev. "Ah, Butler, how d'you do? . . . Not asleep yet? Having a walk with Marya Dmitrievna! You'd better look out or the major will give it you. . . . Where is he?"

"Why, there. . . . Listen!" replied Marya Dmitrievna pointing in the direction whence came the sounds of a *tulumbas*[38] and songs. "They're on the spree."

[38] *Tulumbas*, a sort of kettledrum.

"Why? Are your people having a spree on their own?"

"No; some officers have come from Hasav-Yurt, and they are being entertained."

"Ah, that's good! I shall be in time. . . . I just want the major for a moment."

"On business?" asked Butler.

"Yes, just a little business matter."

"Good or bad?"

"It all depends. . . . Good for us but bad for some people," and Kamenev laughed.

By this time they had reached the major's house.

"Chikhirev," shouted Kamenev to one of his Cossacks, "come here!"

A Don Cossack rode up from among the others. He was dressed in the ordinary Don Cossack uniform with high boots and a mantle, and carried saddle-bags behind.

"Well, take the thing out," said Kamenev, dismounting.

The Cossack also dismounted, and took a sack out of his saddle-bag. Kamenev took the sack from him and inserted his hand.

"Well, shall I show you a novelty? You won't be frightened, Marya Dmitrievna?"

"Why should I be frightened?" she replied.

"Here it is!" said Kamenev taking out a man's head and holding it up in the light of the moon. "Do you recognize it?"

It was a shaven head with salient brows, black short-cut beard and moustaches, one eye open and the other half-closed. The shaven skull was cleft, but not right through, and there was congealed blood in the nose. The neck was wrapped in a blood-stained towel. Notwithstanding the many wounds on the head, the blue lips still bore a kindly childlike expression.

Marya Dmitrievna looked at it, and without a word turned away and went quickly into the house.

Butler could not tear his eye from the terrible head. It was the head of that very Hadji Murad with whom he had so recently spent his evenings in such friendly intercourse.

"What does this mean? Who has killed him?" he asked.

"He wanted to give us the slip, but was caught," said Kamenev, and he gave the head back to the Cossack and went into the house with Butler.

"He died like a hero," he added.

"But however did it all happen?"

"Just wait a bit. When the major comes I'll tell you all about it. That's what I am sent for. I take it round to all the forts and *aouls* and show it."

The major was sent for, and came back accompanied by two other officers as drunk as himself, and began embracing Kamenev.

"And I have brought you Hadji Murad's head," said Kamenev.

"No? . . . Killed?"

"Yes; wanted to escape."

"I always said he would bamboozle them! . . . And where is it? The head, I mean. . . . Let's see it."

The Cossack was called, and brought in the bag with the head. It was taken out and the major looked long at it with drunken eyes.

"All the same, he was a fine fellow," said he. "Let me kiss him!"

"Yes, it's true. It was a valiant head," said one of the officers.

When they had all looked at it, it was returned to the Cossack who put it in his bag, trying to let it bump against the floor as gently as possible.

"I say, Kamenev, what speech do you make when you show the head?" asked an officer.

"No! . . . Let me kiss him. He gave me a sword!" shouted the major.

Butler went out into the porch.

Marya Dmitrievna was sitting on the second step. She looked round at Butler and at once turned angrily away again.

"What's the matter, Marya Dmitrievna?" asked he.

"You're all cut-throats! . . . I hate it! You're cut-throats, really," and she got up.

"It might happen to anyone," remarked Butler, not knowing what to say. "That's war."

"War? War, indeed! . . . Cut-throats and nothing else. A dead body should be given back to the earth, and they're grinning at it there! . . . Cut-throats, really," she repeated, as she descended the steps and entered the house by the back door.

Butler returned to the room and asked Kamenev to tell them in detail how the thing had happened.

And Kamenev told them.

This is what had happened.

HADJI MURAD was allowed to go out riding in the neighborhood of the town, but never without a convoy of Cossacks. There was only half a troop of them altogether in Nukha, ten of whom were employed by the officers, so that if ten were sent out with Hadji Murad (according to the orders received) the same men would have had to go every other day. Therefore after ten had been sent out the first day, it was decided to send only five in future and Hadji Murad was asked not to take all his henchmen with him. But on April the 25th he rode out with all five. When he mounted, the commander, noticing that all five henchmen were going with him, told him that he was forbidden to take them all, but Hadji Murad pretended not to hear, touched his horse, and the commander did not insist.

With the Cossacks rode a non-commissioned officer, Nazarov, who had received the Cross of St. George for bravery. He was a young, healthy, brown-haired lad, as fresh as a rose. He was the eldest of a poor family belonging to the sect of Old Believers, had grown up without a father, and had maintained his old mother, three sisters, and two brothers.

"Mind, Nazarov, keep close to him!" shouted the commander.

"All right, your honor!" answered Nazarov, and rising in his stirrups and adjusting the rifle that hung at his back he started his fine large roan gelding at a trot. Four Cossacks followed him: Ferapontov, tall and thin, a regular thief and plunderer (it was he who had sold gunpowder to Gamzalo); Ignatov, a sturdy peasant who boasted of his strength, though he was no longer young and had nearly completed his service; Mishkin, a weakly lad at whom everybody laughed; and the young fair-haired Petrakov, his mother's only son, always amiable and jolly.

The morning had been misty, but it cleared up later on and the opening foliage, the young virgin grass, the sprouting corn, and the ripples of the rapid river just visible to the left of the road, all gathered in the sunshine.

Hadji Murad rode slowly along followed by the Cossacks and by his henchmen. They rode out along the road beyond the fort at a walk. They met women carrying baskets on their heads, soldiers driving carts, and creaking wagons drawn by buffaloes. When he had gone about a mile and a half Hadji Murad touched up his white Kabarda horse, which started at an amble that obliged the henchmen and Cossacks to ride at a quick trot to keep up with him.

"Ah, he's got a fine horse under him," said Ferapontov. "If only he were still an enemy I'd soon bring him down."

"Yes, mate. Three hundred rubles were offered for that horse in Tiflis."

"But I can get ahead of him on mine," said Nazarov.

"You get ahead? A likely thing!"

Hadji Murad kept increasing his pace.

"Hey, *kunak*, you mustn't do that. Steady!" cried Nazarov, starting to overtake Hadji Murad.

Hadji Murad looked round, said nothing, and continued to ride at the same pace.

"Mind, they're up to something, the devils!" said Ignatov. "See how they are tearing along."

So they rode for the best part of a mile in the direction of the mountains.

"I tell you it won't do!" shouted Nazarov.

Hadji Murad did not answer or look round, but only increased his pace to a gallop.

"Humbug! You won't get away!" shouted Nazarov, stung to the quick. He gave his big roan gelding a cut with his whip and, rising in his stirrups and bending forward, flew full speed in pursuit of Hadji Murad.

The sky was so bright, the air so clear, and life played so joyously in Nazarov's soul as, becoming one with his fine strong horse, he flew along the smooth road behind Hadji Murad, that the possibility of anything sad or dreadful happening never occurred to him. He rejoiced that with every step he was gaining on Hadji Murad.

Hadji Murad judged by the approaching tramp of the big horse behind him that he would soon be overtaken, and seizing his pistol with his right hand, with his left he began slightly to rein in his Kabarda horse which was excited by hearing the tramp of hoofs behind it.

"You mustn't, I tell you!" shouted Nazarov, almost level with Hadji Murad and stretching out his hand to seize the latter's bridle. But before he reached it a shot was fired. "What are you doing?" he screamed, clutching at his breast. "At them, lads!" and he reeled and fell forward on his saddle-bow.

But the mountaineers were beforehand in taking to their weapons, and fired their pistols at the Cossacks and hewed at them with their swords.

Nazarov hung on the neck of his horse, which careered round his comrades. The horse under Ignatov fell, crushing his leg, and two of the mountaineers, without dismounting, drew their swords and hacked at his head and arms. Petrakov was about to rush to his comrade's rescue when two shots—one in his back and the other in his side—stung him, and he fell from his horse like a sack.

Mishkin turned round and galloped off towards the fortress. Khanefi and Bata rushed after him, but he was already too far away and they could not catch him. When they saw that they could not overtake him they returned to the others.

Petrakov lay on his back, his stomach ripped open, his young face turned to the sky, and while dying he gasped for breath like a fish.

Gamzalo having finished off Ignatov with his sword, gave a cut to Nazarov too and threw him from his horse. Bata took their cartridge-pouches from the slain. Khanefi wished to take Nazarov's horse, but Hadji Murad called out to him to leave it, and dashed forward along the road. His *murids* galloped after him, driving away Nazarov's horse that tried to follow them. They were already among rice-fields more than six miles from Nukha when a shot was fired from the tower of that place to give the alarm.

"O GOOD Lord! O God! my God! What have they done?" cried the commander of the fort seizing his head with his hands when he heard of Hadji Murad's escape. "They've done for me! They've let him escape, the villains!" cried he, listening to Mishkin's account.

An alarm was raised everywhere and not only the Cossacks of the place were sent after the fugitives but also all the militia that could be mustered from the pro-Russian *aouls*. A thousand rubles reward was offered for the capture of Hadji Murad alive or dead, and two hours after he and his followers had escaped from the Cossacks more than two hundred mounted men were following the officer in charge at a gallop to find and capture the runaways.

After riding some miles along the high road Hadji Murad checked his panting horse, which, wet with sweat, had turned from white to grey.

To the right of the road could be seen the *saklyas* and minarets of the *aoul* Benerdzhik, on the left lay some fields, and beyond them the river. Although the way to the mountains lay to the right, Hadji Murad turned to the left, in the opposite direction, assuming that his pursuers would be sure to go to the right, while he, abandoning the road, would cross the Alazan and come out onto the high road on the other side where no one would expect him—ride along it to the forest, and then after recrossing the river make his way to the mountains.

Having come to this conclusion he turned to the left; but it proved impossible to reach the river. The rice-field which had to be crossed had just been flooded, as is always done in spring, and had become a bog in which the horses' legs sank above their pasterns. Hadji Murad and his henchmen turned now to the left, now to the right, hoping to find drier ground; but the field they were in had been equally flooded all over and was now saturated with water. The horses drew their feet out of the sticky mud into which they sank, with a pop like that of a cork drawn from a bottle, and stopped, panting, after every few steps. They struggled in this way so long that it began to grow dusk and they had still not reached the river. To their left lay a patch of higher ground overgrown with shrubs and Hadji Murad decided to ride in among these clumps and remain there till night to rest their exhausted horses and let them graze. The men themselves ate some bread and cheese they had brought with them. At last night came on and the moon that had been shining at first, hid behind the hill and it became dark. There were a great many nightingales in that neighborhood and there were two of them in these shrubs. As long as Hadji Murad and his men were making a noise among the bushes the nightingales had been silent, but when they became still the birds again began to call to one another and to sing.

Hadji Murad, awake to all the sounds of night, listened to them involuntarily, and their trills reminded him of the song about Hamzad which he had heard the night before when he went to get water. He might now at any moment find himself in the position in which Hamzad had been. He fancied that it would be so, and suddenly his soul became serious. He spread out his *burka* and performed his ablutions, and scarcely had he finished before a sound was heard approaching their shelter. It was the sound of many horses' feet plashing through the bog.

The keen-sighted Bata ran out to one edge of the clump, and peering through the darkness saw black shadows, which were men on foot and on horseback. Khanefi discerned a similar crowd on the other side. It was Karganov, the military commander of the district, with his militia.

"Well, then, we shall fight like Hamzad," thought Hadji Murad.

When the alarm was given, Karganov with a troop of militiamen and Cossacks had rushed off in pursuit of Hadji Murad, but had been unable to find any trace of him. He had already lost hope and was returning home when, towards evening, he met an old man and asked him if he had seen any horsemen about. The old man replied that he had. He had seen six horsemen floundering in the rice-field, and then had seen them enter the clump where he himself was getting wood. Karganov turned back, taking the old man with him, and seeing the hobbled horses he made sure that Hadji Murad was there. In the night he surrounded the clump and waited till morning to take Hadji Murad alive or dead.

Having understood that he was surrounded, and having discovered an old ditch among the shrubs, Hadji Murad decided to entrench himself in it and to resist as long as strength and ammunition lasted. He told his comrades this, and ordered them to throw up a bank in front of the ditch, and his henchmen at once set to work to cut down branches, dig up the earth with their daggers, and make an entrenchment. Hadji Murad himself worked with them.

As soon as it began to grow light the commander of the militia troop rode up to the clump and shouted:

"Hey! Hadji Murad, surrender! We are many and you are few!"

In reply came the report of a rifle, a cloudlet of smoke rose from the ditch and a bullet hit the militiaman's horse, which staggered under him and began to fall. The rifles of the militiamen who stood at the outskirt of the clump of shrubs began cracking in their turn, and their bullets whistled and hummed, cutting off leaves and twigs and striking the embankment, but not the men entrenched behind it. Only Gamzalo's horse, that had strayed from the others, was hit in the head by a bullet. It did not fall, but breaking its hobbles and rushing among the bushes it ran to the other horses, pressing close to them and watering the young grass with its blood. Hadji Murad and his men fired only when any of the militiamen came forward, and rarely missed their aim. Three militiamen were wounded, and the others, far from making up their minds to rush the entrenchment, retreated farther and farther back, only firing from a distance and at random.

So it continued for more than an hour. The sun had risen to about half the height of the trees, and Hadji Murad was already thinking of leaping on his horse and trying to make his way to the river, when the shouts were heard of many men who had just arrived. These were Hadji Aga of Mekhtuli with his followers. There were about two hundred of them. Hadji Aga had once been Hadji Murad's *kunak* and had lived with him in the mountains, but he had afterwards gone over to the Russians. With him was Akhmet Khan, the son of Hadji Murad's old enemy.

Like Karganov, Hadji Aga began by calling to Hadji Murad to surrender, and Hadji Murad answered as before with a shot.

"Swords out, my men!" cried Hadji Aga, drawing his own; and a hundred voices were raised by men who rushed shrieking in among the shrubs.

The militiamen ran in among the shrubs, but from behind the entrenchment came the crack of one shot after another. Some three men fell, and the attackers stopped at the outskirts of the clump and also began firing. As they fired they gradually approached the entrenchment, running across from behind one shrub to another. Some succeeded in getting across, others fell under the bullets of Hadji Murad or of his men. Hadji Murad fired without missing; Gamzalo too rarely wasted a shot, and shrieked with joy every time he saw that his bullet had hit its aim. Khan Mahoma sat at the edge of the ditch singing "*Il lyakha il Allah!*" and fired leisurely, but often missed. Eldar's whole body trembled with impatience to rush dagger in hand at the enemy, and he fired often and at random, constantly looking round at Hadji Murad and stretching out beyond the entrenchment. The shaggy Khanefi, with his sleeves rolled up, did the duty of a servant even here. He loaded the guns which Hadji Murad and Khan Mahoma passed to him, carefully driving home with a ramrod the bullets wrapped in greasy rags, and pouring dry powder out of the powder-flask onto the pans. Bata did not remain in the ditch as the others did, but kept running to the horses, driving them away to a safer place and, shrieking incessantly, fired without using a prop for his gun. He was the first to be wounded. A bullet entered his neck and he sat down splitting blood and swearing. Then Hadji Murad was wounded, the bullet piercing his shoulder. He tore some cotton wool from the lining of his *beshmet*, plugged the wound with it, and went on firing.

"Let us fly at them with our swords!" said Eldar for the third time, and he looked out from behind the bank of earth ready to rush at the enemy; but at that instant a bullet struck him and he reeled and fell backwards onto Hadji Murad's leg. Hadji Murad glanced at him. His eyes, beautiful like those of a ram, gazed intently and seriously at Hadji Murad. His mouth, the upper lip pouting like a child's, twitched without opening. Hadji Murad drew his leg away from under him and continued firing.

Khanefi bent over the dead Eldar and began taking the unused ammunition out of the cartridge-cases of his coat.

Khan Mahoma meanwhile continued to sing, loading leisurely and firing. The enemy ran from shrub to shrub, hallooing and shrieking and drawing ever nearer and nearer.

Another bullet hit Hadji Murad in the left side. He lay down in the ditch and again pulled some cotton wool out of his *beshmet* and plugged the wound. This wound in the side was fatal and he felt that he was dying. Memories and pictures succeeded one another with extraordinary rapidity in his imagination. Now he saw the powerful Abu Nutsal Khan, dagger in hand and holding up his severed cheek as he rushed at his foe; then he saw the weak, bloodless old Vorontsov with his cunning white face, and heard his soft voice; then he saw his son Yusuf, his wife Sofiat, and then the pale, red-bearded face of his enemy Shamil with its half-closed eyes. All these images passed through his mind without evoking any feeling within him—neither pity nor anger nor any kind of desire: everything seemed so insignificant in comparison with what was beginning, or had already begun, within him.

Yet his strong body continued the thing that he had commenced. Gathering together his last strength he rose from behind the bank, fired his pistol at a man who was just running towards him, and hit him. The man fell. Then Hadji Murad got quite out of the ditch, and limping heavily went dagger in hand straight at the foe.

Some shots cracked and he reeled and fell. Several militiamen with triumphant shrieks rushed towards the fallen body. But the body that seemed to be dead suddenly moved. First the uncovered, bleeding, shaven head rose; then the body with hands holding to the trunk of a tree. He seemed so terrible, that those who were running towards him stopped short. But suddenly a shudder passed through him, he staggered away from the tree and fell on his face, stretched out at full length like a thistle that had been mown down, and he moved no more.

He did not move, but still he felt.

When Hadji Aga, who was the first to reach him, struck him on the head with a large dagger, it seemed to Hadji Murad that someone was striking him with a hammer and he could not understand who was doing it or why. That was his last consciousness of any connection with his body. He felt nothing more and his enemies kicked and hacked at what had no longer anything in common with him.

Hadji Aga placed his foot on the back of the corpse and with two blows cut off the head, and carefully—not to soil his shoes with blood—rolled it away with his foot. Crimson blood spurted from the arteries of the neck, and black blood flowed from the head, soaking the grass.

Karganov and Hadji Aga and Akhmet Khan and all the militiamen gathered together—like sportsmen round a slaughtered animal—near the bodies of Hadji Murad and his men (Khanefi, Khan Mahoma, and Gamzalo they bound), and amid the powder-smoke which hung over the bushes they triumphed in their victory.

The nightingales, that had hushed their songs while the firing lasted, now started their trills once more: first one quite close, then others in the distance.

It was of this death that I was reminded by the crushed thistle in the midst of the ploughed field.

1896-1904 A.D.
(Published Posthumously)

BUNIN *Dry Valley*

WHAT had always struck us about Nathalia was her attachment to Dry Valley.

A foster-sister to our father, growing up in the same house with him, she had lived for all of eight years in our place at Lunevo, had lived there as one of our kin, and not as a former serf, a common servant. And for all of eight years, to use her own words, she had been resting up after Dry Valley, after that which the place had made her suffer. But it is not in vain people say that, no matter how you feed a wolf, he'll aye be eying the steppe. Having seen us through the toddling stage, having seen us grow up, she had gone back to Dry Valley anew.

I remember snatches of our childhood talks with her:

"Why, aren't you an orphan, Nathalia?"

"I am that. I take after my masters in everything. Anna Grigorievna, your grandmother, now, she folded her little hands in death when she was ever so young, just like my dear father and mother done!"

"What did they die from, then?"

"Why, their time to die come—and so they ups and dies."

"No, I mean what made them die so soon?"

"Such was God's will. The masters sent my father off for to be a soldier, on account of his misdoings; my mother didn't live to her full time on account of the masters' turkey-chicks. I, of course,

can't remember—how should I?—but here's how they told it in the
servants' quarters: she was the poultry-keeper, and you just couldn't
count the number of turkey-chicks she had charge of. They was
caught in a hail-storm whilst out on the common, and was all beat
to death, every single one on 'em.—She dashed off at a run toward
them, got there quick, gave one look—and the breath of life left
her."

"But how is it you never married?"

"Why, my bridegroom ain't growed up yet!"

"No, do tell us, without joking!"

"Well, they do be saying that the mistress, your auntie dear, was
set against me marrying. That's just why it was given out that I
was a high-born miss."

"Oh, now, what sort of a high-born miss are you!"

"I am that, to a *t*," Nathalia would answer with a sly little smile
which puckered up her lips into wrinkles, and then wiped her
mouth with her swarthy, crone's hand. "Why, I'm a sort of an
auntie to you, now. . . ."

As we were growing up, we listened ever more attentively to
what was being said in our house concerning Dry Valley: that
which had hitherto been incomprehensible was becoming ever
more comprehensible; the strange details of life in Dry Valley were
coming out ever more sharply. Who else but ourselves should
have felt that Nathalia, who had passed half her days leading
almost the same life as our father—who else should have felt that
she was truly of kin to us, the ancient and nobly sprung Khrushchevs! And now it turned out that this gentry had driven her
father into soldiering, and her mother into such fear and trembling
that her heart had burst at the sight of the perished turkey-chicks!

"And, to be sure," Nathalia used to say, "what else could a body
have done but drop dead from such a mishap? The masters would
have packed her off to God knows where!"

And later on we found out things still stranger concerning Dry
Valley: we found out that there were not, "in all Creation," folk
simpler, kindlier, than the masters of Dry Valley; but we also found
out that there were none "more hot-headed" than they. We found

out that the old house in Dry Valley was dark and sombre; that our mad grandfather, Petr Kyrillich, had been killed in this house by his own natural son, Gervasska, a friend of our father's and cousin to Nathalia. We found out that Aunt Tonia, too, had long ago gone mad from an unhappy love-affair: she lived in one of the old servants' huts near the run-down Dry Valley estate and ecstatically played French schottisches on a pianoforte that boomed and jangled from old age. We found out that Nathalia, likewise, had been going mad at cne time; that, while yet a slip of a girl, she had come to love, for all her life, our uncle Petr Petrovich, now dead, whereas he had sent her into exile to the farmstead at Little Ploughs. . . . Our absorbing dreams concerning Dry Valley could be easily understood. To us Dry Valley was only a poetical monument of the past. But what was it to Nathalia? For it was she who had said with great bitterness, as if in reply to some long-kept thought of her own:

"Why, at Dry Valley they used to sit down at table with bull-whips in their hands! It's dreadful even to think back on."

"What! With bull-whips? With dog-lashes, you mean?"

"Oh, they're all one!" said she.

"But what ever did they do that for?"

"Well, just in case of a quarrel."

"Were they always quarrelling at Dry Valley?"

"There weren't a day passed, God deliver us, but what there was a war! All hot-headed, they was—just plain gunpowder, you might say."

As for us, we simply swooned from delight at her words and exchanged enraptured looks. For a long time thereafter we pictured to ourselves the enormous garden, the enormous estate, the house with walls of oak logs, under a heavy and time-blackened roof of straw; and a dinner in the hall of this house: everybody is sitting at table, everybody is eating, throwing the bones on the floor, to the hunting-dogs; everyone is eying everyone else askance —and everyone has a dog-lash on his knees. . . . We dreamt of that golden time when we would grow up and would likewise dine with dog-lashes on *our* knees. Yet we well understood that it was not to Nathalia that these dog-lashes had afforded joy.

But, notwithstanding all this, she left Lunevo for Dry Valley, for the well-spring of her dark recollections. She had neither a nook of her own nor any near of kin there; and in Dry Valley she worked not for Aunt Tonia, who had long ago ceased to be her mistress, but for Claudia Markovna, the widow of the late Petr Petrovich. But then, Nathalia could not live without that very homestead.

"What can a body do? It's a matter of habit," she would say unassumingly. "Where the needle goes, now, the thread is bound to follow, I guess. The place of your birth is the place of your worth. . . ."

Nor was she the only one who was afflicted with an attachment for Dry Valley. And, besides, this was hardly an attachment, but rather something far deeper, far stronger. God, what passionate lovers of recollections, what ardent partisans of Dry Valley, were all the others of our servants as well! And that goes without saying for our Aunt Tonia, for our father.

Aunt Tonia passed her days in a hut, in utter poverty. Dry Valley had bereft her of happiness, and of reason, and of human semblance. Yet, despite all the persuasions of our father, she would never even entertain the idea of abandoning the nest she had been born in, of settling in Lunevo.

"Why, I'd rather break stones in the mountain quarries!" she was wont to say.

Our father was a man without a care in the world; for him, it seemed, there existed no attachments whatsoever. But a profound melancholy sounded in his stories of Dry Valley as well. It was already a long, long time ago that we had migrated from Dry Valley to Lunevo, which was a country-seat situated amid fields, and belonging to our great-aunt, Olga Kyrillovna. Yet he complained about his life almost to his very end:

"There's only one Khrushchev now left in the whole world— only one! And even that one is not at Dry Valley!"

True, it would not infrequently happen that right after such words he would fall into deep thought as he looked out of the window, out on a field, and would suddenly smile mockingly as he took his guitar down from the wall.

"Oh, Dry Valley is a fine place, too—may it perish from off the face of the earth!" he would add with the same sincerity with which he had been speaking just the minute before.

But his soul, as well, was a Dry Valley soul: a soul over which recollections had an inordinately great sway, the sway of the steppe, of its sluggish ways, of that ancient domesticity which blended into one the village, the domestics, and the manor-house of Dry Valley. True, we Khrushchevs are of a noble race, inscribed in the sixth Book of Heraldry, and there were among our legendary ancestors many renowned men of ancient Lithuanian blood, as well as many Tatar princelings, whose breed would more than once tell in us. But then, the blood of the Khrushchevs had been mingling with the blood of the serfs and of the village from time out of mind. Who had given life to Petr Kyrillich? Traditions speak with different tongues concerning this. Who was the sire of Gervasska, his slayer? From our earliest years we had heard that it was Petr Kyrillich himself. Whence was derived so sharp a dissimilarity in the characters of our father and our uncle? There is a speech of many tongues concerning this also. For was not Nathalia foster-sister to our father? Had he not exchanged crucifixes with Gervasska? It's long, long since time for the Khrushchevs to be reckoned as of kin to their domestics and their village!

My sister and I, too, lived for long in this yearning for Dry Valley, in its seductiveness. The domestics, the village, and the manor-house at Dry Valley made up one family. This family had been ruled even by our forebears. And a thing like that is long felt, even by posterity. The life of a family, of a line, of a clan, is deep, knotty, mysterious—quite often it is a fearsome thing. But in its dark depths, as well as in its traditions, its past, lies such a family's very strength. In written and other memorials Dry Valley is no richer than a Bashkir steppe. In Russia the place of these is taken by tradition. And tradition, as well as song, is a poisonous drug for the Slavic soul! Our former serfs, earnest sluggards and dreamers, all of them—where else could they ease their soul if not in our house?

Our father remained as the sole representative of the masters of

Dry Valley. And the first language in which we began to speak was that of Dry Valley. The first tales, the first songs that stirred us were also those of Dry Valley, told by Nathalia, by our father. Yes—and could anybody else have sung as did our father, who had been taught the art by the serfs, about his "mistress true and fair, with such a sprightly, queenly air"? Could anybody else have sung this song with such insouciant sadness, with such kindly reproachfulness, with such weak-willed soulfulness? Could anybody else have told a tale the way Nathalia did? And who was nearer and dearer to us than the mujiks of Dry Valley?

Dissensions, quarrels—there you have what the Khrushchevs have been famed for, time out of mind, like every family that has been long and closely living together. And at the time of our childhood there occurred such a quarrel between Dry Valley and Lunevo that for almost ten years Father would not set foot across the threshold of the house where he had been born. Thus it came about that we had not so much as a good look at Dry Valley during our childhood; we were there but once, and that in passing, on a journey to Zadonsk. But then, dreams are, at times, far more powerful than reality, and, dimly but ineradicably, there were impressed upon our memories a long summer day, certain undulating fields, and an abandoned high road, which had enchanted us with its vast vista and with the hollow-trunked willows which had survived here and there near it; we retained a memory of a beehive on one of these willows, growing far back from the road amid the fields of grain—a beehive left to the will of God amid fields flanking an abandoned road; we retained a memory of a wide turn by an upward-sloping field, of a few poverty-stricken, chimneyless huts overlooking an enormous, barren common, and of the yellowness of stony gullies beyond the huts, and of the whiteness of the shingle and the rubble at the bottom of these gullies. . . .

The first event which horrified us had likewise to do with Dry Valley: it was the murder of Grandfather by Gervasska. And, as we listened to the tale of this murder, we had an endless vision of these yellow gullies, retreating somewhere into the distance. It seemed to us all the time that it must have been through these very gullies that Gervasska had fled after having done his horrid deed, and then "plunged out of sight, like a stone to the bottom of the sea."

The mujiks of Dry Valley called at Lunevo not at all with the same ends in view as did the Dry Valley domestics, but about "gettin' a bit more ground, like"; but they, too, entered our house as if they had been born in it. They would bow from the waist before my father, would kiss his hand, and then, with a backward toss of their hair, would kiss him, as well as Nathalia and ourselves, on the lips, and each of us thrice. They would bring, by way of presents, honey, eggs, home-spun towels. And we, who had grown up amid fields, who were sensitive to smells, and no less avid for them than for songs and traditions—we retained forever in our memories that peculiar, pleasant odor, somehow reminiscent of flax, of which we became aware whenever we kissed the Dry Valley folk. We retained, as well, a memory of their presents, redolent of the old village amid the steppes: the honey smelt of blossoming buckwheat, and rotting hives of oak; the towels, of little outlying barns and huts innocent of chimneys, dating back to the times of our grandfather. . . .

The mujiks of Dry Valley did not tell any stories—and, besides, what tales had they to tell? There were even no traditions existing among them. Their graves are nameless, while their lives are so much alike, so meagre and so vestigeless! Inasmuch as the fruits of their labors and their cares were bread alone—the most realistic kind of bread, the kind you eat. They digged them ponds in the stony bed of the little Stone River, which had long since gone dry, and whose dry bed had come to be dignified by the name of Dry Valley. But ponds are, after all, nothing much to be relied upon: they *will* dry up. They builded them dwellings. But their dwellings are not long-enduring: the least bit of a spark, and they burn down to fine ashes. . . . What was it, then, that drew all of us (and Nathalia most of all) even to the barren common, to the huts and the gullies, to the ruined estate of Dry Valley? Was it aught else but this ancient domesticity, this our blood-kindred to the desolate lure of the steppe?

2

Nurses, old servants, are usually dignified by the use of their patronymics. She was always called only by her first name: at first by the familiar diminutive, Natashka, and later on, Nathalia. She did not look like a nurse—from her cradle to her grave she remained a true peasant woman. Yes, and Dry Valley, in its turn, had but little about it of that which is usually ascribed, in stories, to the nests of the landed gentry.

It was only in our late adolescence that it befell us to set foot in that homestead which had given birth to the soul of Nathalia, which had dominated her whole life—the homestead of which we had heard so much.

I remember the occasion just as though it were but yesterday. There had come a cloud-burst, with deafening peals of thunder and blindingly quick, fiery serpents of lightning, just toward evening, as we were driving up to Dry Valley. A dark-lilac cloud had careened heavily toward the northwest, majestically screening half the sky ahead of us. Flatly, sharply, and deathly white, the plain of grain-fields showed palely green below the enormous background of this cloud. The low, wet grass on the high-road was vivid and extraordinarily fresh; the horses, wet and somehow instantaneously grown gaunt, splashed along through the indigo-hued mire; the tarantass swished, moistly. And suddenly, just at the turn of the road into Dry Valley, amid the fields of tall, wet rye, we caught sight of a tall and exceedingly odd figure in dressing-gown and cowl; we could not determine whether this scarecrow was an old man or an old woman; it was beating a piebald muley-cow with an old, dry branch.

On our approach the branch began to work faster, and the cow, clumsily switching its tail, blundered out on the road, while the old scarecrow (we could by now see that it was a woman), shouting something, started walking toward the tarantass, and, having approached, drew her pale face toward us. Looking with fear into her dark, insane eyes, feeling her sharp, chill nose touching our noses, and becoming aware of her strong hut-odor, we exchanged kisses with her. Was this not Baba Yaga herself, that old hag, that old witch of the fairy-tale? However, there was a cowl, made out of some filthy rag, sticking up on the head of this Baba Yaga; her robe, torn, and wet to the waist, was put on right over her naked body, hardly concealing her gaunt breasts; she was shouting, just as if we were deaf, just as if it were her purpose to start a ferocious barrage of abuse; and by this shouting of hers, as well as all the other details, we gathered that this was Aunt Tonia.

Claudia Petrovna, too, began to shout—gaily, however, and as rapturously as a boarding-school miss. She was a fat little, short little woman, with a grey little tuft on her chin, with little eyes that were extraordinarily alive. Sitting by the open window of the big house with two great entrances, knitting away at a cotton sock, and with her spectacles raised to her forehead, she was watching the common, which had run over into the courtyard.

Nathalia, tiny, sunburned, in half-boots of felt, in a red woolen skirt and a grey blouse with a broad V at her dark, wrinkled neck —Nathalia bowed low, with a soft smile, as she stood near the entrance to the right. As I glimpsed this neck of hers, her thin collar-bone, her wearily sad eyes, I remember I reflected: "It was she who grew up together with our father; a long, long time ago, but precisely here, where of our grandfather's house of oaken timbers, a house that had burned several times, there has been left only this poor-looking habitation, while of the garden there are left only growths of shrubs and a few old birches and poplars, and of the offices and servants' quarters, only a hut, a granary, a barn, and an ice-house grown over with wormwood and bracken. . . ."

We smelt chips and charcoal burning under a samovar; there was a deluge of questions; there began to appear, from century-old what-nots, little crystal jam-dishes, gold tea-spoons worn down to the thinness of a maple-leaf, sugar cookies, saved against the arrival of guests. And while the conversation was coming to a glow (a conversation of intensified amicability, after the long quarrel), we went off rambling through the darkening chambers, seeking the balcony, which was also an exit into the garden.

Everything was blackened by time, plain, crude, in these empty, low-ceiled chambers, still adhering to the same arrangement as in Grandfather's day, although made over from what remained of those same rooms in which he had dwelt. In one corner of the butler's pantry a large image of St. Mercurius of Smolensk showed darkly—he whose iron sandals and helmet are preserved on a solea in the ancient cathedral at Smolensk. We had heard that Mercurius had been a doughty wight, who had been called to save the Smolensk region from the Tatars by the voice of an icon of the Mother of God, the icon of Œdigytria the Guider. Having overwhelmed the Tatars, the saint had fallen asleep and had been beheaded by his foes. Thereupon, having taken his head in his hands, he had come to the gates of the city, that he might make known what had befallen.—And one felt eerie when looking at the penny woodcut depiction of a headless man, holding in one hand a deathly-bluish head in a helmet, and in the other the icon of The Guider—when looking at this cherished image of Grandfather's, which had gone through several dreadful conflagrations and had split in the fire. It was thickly bound in silver, and on its reverse side guarded the genealogy of the Khrushchevs, inscribed with tildes.

As if in keeping with this image, heavy iron catches were fastened to the heavy leaves of the door, on both top and bottom. The floor-boards in the dining-room were inordinately wide, dark, and slippery; the windows were small, with frames that went up and down. Through this room, a diminished double of that same one where the Khrushchevs used to sit down at table with bull-whips in their hands, we passed into the parlor. Here, opposite the door of the balcony, had on a time stood the pianoforte on which Aunt Tonia had played when she had been enamored of Voitkevich, who was an officer in the army and a comrade of Petr Petrovich's. And farther on gaped doors leading into the lounging-room, and another, a corner room; in these, on a time, my grandfather had had his quarters.

The evening, as well as the day, was a murky one. Among the clouds, beyond the garden whose trees had almost all been chopped down, beyond the half-empty threshing-barn and the silvery poplars, heat-lightnings were flaring, momentarily revealing cloud-capped, rosily aureate mountains. The cloud-burst had probably missed the Troshin forest, which showed darkly far beyond the garden, on the slope of the hills beyond the gullies. From thence was borne to us the crisp, warm smell of oaks, which blended with the smell of verdure, with the moist, gentle breeze which occasionally ran through the tips of the birches (all that was left of a ruined garden-walk), through the high nettles, the quitch-grass, and the bushes around the balcony. And the deep quiet of evening, of the steppe, of the depths of Russia, reigned over everything.

"Come and have your tea," a low voice called us back.

It was Nathalia, participant in and witness of all this life, its chief narratrix; while behind her, watching attentively with her insane eyes, somewhat stooping, gliding decorously over the dark, smooth floor, moved her erstwhile mistress, Aunt Tonia. She had not taken off her cowl; but, instead of a robe, she now had on an old-fashioned dress of barège, and a silk shawl of a faded gold tint was thrown over her shoulders.

"*Où êtes-vous, mes enfants?*" she was shouting, with a genteel smile, and her voice, clear and cutting, like that of a parrot, rang out strangely in the empty, black chambers. . . .

3

EVEN as there was an enchantment about Nathalia, about her peasant simplicity, about all her lovely and pitiful soul, born of Dry Valley, so was there an enchantment about the ruined estate at Dry Valley itself.

There was a scent of jasmine in the old parlor with its warped floor-boards. The balcony, rotted and greyish blue from time (we had to leap down from it, owing to the absence of steps), was sunk in nettles, elder bushes, and priest's-cap. On hot days, when the

baking sun was right over the balcony, when its sagging French
window was open, and the joyous reflection of the panes was
transmitted to the tarnished oval mirror which hung on the wall
opposite the French window—on such days we were constantly recalling Aunt Tonia's pianoforte, which at one time had stood
under this mirror. At one time she had played on it, following the
yellowed pieces of music, with titles all in scrolls, the while *he*
had stood behind her, frowning, with his left hand firmly against
his hip, his jaws firmly clenched. Marvellous butterflies, in tiny
smocks of dazzlingly gay cotton prints, and in Japanese raiment,
and in shawls of black-and-lilac velvet, would flutter into the
parlor. And one evening, just before his departure, he had, in a fit
of vexation, slammed his palm down on one of them, as it was
quiveringly settling down to rest on the lid of the pianoforte. All
that was left of it was a little silvery dust. But when the wenches
who had been cleaning up wiped off this dust a few days later,
Aunt Tonia had hysterics.

From the parlor we would go out on the balcony, sit down on
its sun-warmed boards, and meditate, on and on.—The wind,
running through the garden, brought to us the silken rustling of
the birches with their satiny-white trunks, maculated with black,
and their wide-flung green branches; the wind, soughing and
rustling, came running from the fields, and a glaucous-golden oriole
would emit its raucous and joyous cry, darting like a wedge over
the white flowers, in pursuit of the chattering jackdaws that, with
their numerous kindred, used to inhabit the ruined chimneys and
dark garrets, where there was an odor of old bricks, and the golden
light fell in streaks through the skylights upon mounds of violet-
grey ashes. The window would die away; the bees crawled sleepily
over the flowers near the balcony, consummating their leisurely
task, and all one could hear amid the stillness was the even murmur, flowing like a ceaseless drizzle, of the silvery leafage of the
poplars. . . .

We rambled through the garden; we penetrated into the jungle
of the border hedges. There, amid these hedges, which blended
with the grain-fields, in the ancestral bath-house, with its ceiling

fallen through (the same bath-house where Nathalia had secreted a small mirror she had purloined from Petr Petrovich), lived white bunnies. How softly they hopped out on to the threshold, how oddly, wiggling their whiskers and split lips, they squinted their eyes, goggling and set far apart, at the tall cotton-thistles, at the bushes of henbane, and the thick growths of nettles that stifled the blackthorn and the small cherry orchard!

And in the half-open threshing-barn there lived a great horned owl. He perched on a cross-beam, choosing as dusky a place as possible, with his ears pricked up, with his yellow, unseeing pupils popping out, and he looked savage, fiendish. The sun was sinking far beyond the garden, into the sea of grain; evening was advancing, peaceful and clear; a cuckoo was cuckooing in the Troshin forest; somewhere over the meadows the pipes of old Stepa, the Shepherd, resounded plaintively. . . . The horned owl perched on, biding the coming of night. At night everything slept in the fields and the village and the manor-house. But the horned owl kept on hooting and weeping. On noiseless wings he would swoop around the threshing-barn and over the garden, fly up to Aunt Tonia's hut, sink gently to its roof, and then emit a painful cry. Aunt would wake up on her bench near the oven.

"Most sweet Jesus, have mercy upon me!" she would whisper, sighing.

The flies droned sleepily and discontentedly on the ceiling of the hot, dark hut. Not a night passed but something would turn up to disturb their slumbers. Now it would be a cow, scratching its side against the wall of the hut; now a rat would scamper over the jerkily jangling keys of the pianoforte, and, losing its footing, would tumble with a crash among the shards of crockery and other broken-up things which Aunt used to pile so carefully in a corner; now the old black tom-cat would come home late from traipsing around somewhere and would lazily beg to be let into the hut; or else this same horned owl would come a-flying, prophesying misfortune with its cries. And Aunt, overcoming her sleepiness, brushing away the flies which in the darkness crawled into her eyes, got up, groped along the benches, banged the door open, and, stepping out on the threshold, would, at a guess, send a rolling-pin whizzing at the starry sky. The horned owl, rustlingly catching his wings against the thatch, would dart off the roof and fall low somewhere into the darkness. He almost touched the ground, smoothly volplaned to the threshing-barn, and then, rocketing upward, would come to rest on its ridge. And his wail would again come floating to the manor-house. He perched there, as if recollecting something, and then would suddenly emit a scream of astonishment; would fall silent, and then unexpectedly launch into hysterical hoots, laughter, and squeals; again he would fall silent, and then break into moans, snivellings, and sobs. . . .

And the nights were dark, warm, with lilac-hued cloudlets, and calm,—calm. . . . The lisping of the drowsy poplars drowsily ran and streamed on. Heat-lightning would warily flicker over the dark Troshin woods, and there was ever the sun-warmed, crisp odor of oak-trees. Near the woods, above the plain of oats, against a sky-glade among the clouds, Scorpio, of a sepulchral mountain-blue, glowed as a silver triangle.

We returned to the manor-house late. Having breathed our fill of the dew, of the freshness of the steppe, of the field flowers and grasses, we carefully climbed up on the porch and stepped into the dark entry. And frequently we found Nathalia at prayer before the image of St. Mercurius. Barefooted, diminutive, with her arms crossed on her breast, she stood before him, whispering something, crossing herself, bowing low to him, who was invisible in the darkness. And she did all this as simply as though she were chatting with someone near and dear to her, and as simple, kindly, and benign as herself.

"Nathalia?" we could call to her softly.

"Yes, it's me," she would respond, softly and simply, interrupting her devotions.

"How is it you're not sleeping yet?"

"Why, I guess I'll catch up on my sleep in the grave. . . ."

We would sit down on the locker near the window-sill and would open the window; she remained standing, with her arms crossed on her breast. The heat-lightning flickered mysteriously, lighting up the dark chambers; a quail was drumming somewhere far off, out in the dewy steppe. With a warning uneasiness an awakened duck would quack on the pond. . . .

"Were you out for a stroll?"

"We were."

"Oh, well—you're young yet! Why, we used to stroll all night through, the same way. . . . One glow would drive us out; another would drive us in. . . ."

"You used to live well before, didn't you?"

"We did that."

And a long silence would ensue.

"Why does that horned owl cry so, nursie?" my sister would ask.

"There's nor rhyme nor reason to his crying. There's no getting rid of him! If only somebody would fire a gun to frighten him off! The way things are, a body gets to feeling downright eerie, always thinking mebbe its cries bode some ill. Why, that owl is forever frightening the young lady. And, mind you, she could easy be frightened to death!"

"Tell us, how did she begin to ail?"

"Why, you know how it is—tears, tears all the time, and longing. . . . Then she took to praying. . . . And, on top of that, she grew meaner and meaner to us maids, and ever more angry toward her brothers. . . ."

And, recalling the dog-lashes, we would ask:

"Then that means they weren't getting along well with one another?"

" 'Well' is hardly the word for it! And especially after she was took sick, now, and your grandfather died, and the young masters took a holt of the reins, and the late Petr Petrovich went and got married. All hot-headed, they was—just plain gunpowder, you might say!"

"And did they flog the servants often?"

"Why, there wasn't any such ways in our household. Just think of how I had misbehaved! And yet all that happened in the end was that Petr Petrovich ordered them to crop my hair real close with the sheep-shears, to put a threadbare shift of striped ticking on me, and to send me off to a far-off farm."

"And just what had been your fault?"

But the answer which followed was far from always direct and prompt. At times Nathalia would tell her story with amazing directness and thoroughness; but at others she would falter, pondering over something; then she would emit ever so slight a sigh, and, by her voice (since we could not see her face in the dark), we gathered that she was sadly smiling.

"Why, my fault lay in just that I—For I've already told you. . . . Young and foolish, that's what I was. 'Alack and alas, a sweet nightingale in a garden sang; 'tis an old, old tale. . . .' And, naturally, I being a girl at that time—"

My sister would ask her kindly:

"Come, nursie, say that poem to the very end—do!"

"This is no poem, but a song. . . . And, besides, I couldn't recall it now."

"That's not so—that's not so!"

"Oh, well, if you like—" And, in a patter, she would finish: "'Ah, woe—' I mean to say: 'Alack and alas, a sweet nightingale in a garden sang; 'tis an old, old tale! Dark the night; his song is a sweet heart-ache, and a silly lass tosses wide awake. . . .'"

Mustering up her courage, my sister would ask:

"And were you very much in love with uncle?"

And Nathalia would whisper, dully and briefly:

"Very much so."

"Do you always remember him in your prayers?"

"Always."

"Is it true what they say—that you fainted away when you were being carried off to Little Ploughs?"

"I fainted dead away. We girls working in the house was awful delicate. We was no end chicken-hearted and touchy when it come to being punished. . . . After all, you couldn't liken us to the commoner of our fellow-servants! When Evsenii Bodulya drove off with me, I became all dazed from grief and fear. . . .

As we was going through the town, I almost stifled, I was that unused to the air there. But as soon as we got out into the real steppe, why, I got to feeling so tender, and so sorry for myself! —There were an officer that looked like *him* dashing along toward us—and I just let a scream out of me and keeled over like I was dead! But when I come to myself, I just lay there in the cart and I thinks to myself: 'I feel fine, now; just like I were in the Kingdom of Heaven itself!' "

"Was our uncle stern?"

"God save us from such another!"

"But still, wasn't it Auntie who was the most self-willed of them all?"

"She were that,—she were just that! I'm telling you, now: they even brought her to a holy man. . . . We went through an awful lot with her! She ought to be living and enjoying herself, right proper; but no, she turned stubborn and proud, and so she got cracked. . . . How this Voitkevich gentleman used to love her, now! But there, it weren't no use!"

"Well, and what about Grandpa?"

"And what could I say about him? He were sort of feeble-minded, he were. And, of course, he had his crotchets as well. They was all hot-headed in them days. But then, the former masters, now, didn't look down on our sort. There was times when your papa dear would punish Gervasska at dinner-time—and Gervasska sure had it coming to him!—but, come evening, you'd see the two of them in the servants' quarters, raising Cain together and thrumming away on their balalaikas—"

"But tell us—was this Voitkevich good-looking?"

Nathalia would become thoughtful. Then:

"No, I wouldn't want to tell a lie," she would answer; "he were something like a Kalmuck. And yet he were serious and would get whatever he were after. He was forever reading poems to her—forever frightening her, now: 'I'm going to die, you'll see, and will come after you—' "

"Yes, but didn't Grandfather, too, go mad because of love?"

"It were on account of your grandmother. That's another

matter altogether, miss. And, besides, our house itself was gloomy; none too cheerful, God be with it! You just listen to my foolish speech, if it please you. . . ."

And, in an unhurried whisper, Nathalia would launch into a long, long narrative.

There were in this narrative jests, reservations, evasions; there were animation, pensiveness, unusual simplicity. But, side by side with all this, there were other things: a mysterious air, a stern and canorous half-whisper. But the prevalent element was a certain sadness of long standing. And everything was permeated with a feeling of an ancient faith in predestination, with a feeling of a never-voiced, vague, yet constant self-suggestion that every one —every one!—of us must take one role or another upon himself, in accordance with one dispensation of fate or another.

4

If one is to believe traditions, our great-grandsire, a man of means, had migrated from Kursk to Dry Valley only toward the end of his days; he had no liking for our localities, for their desolate spots, their forests. Why, there even came to be a proverb that "the forests were everywhere in the old days." People who had to make their way over our roads some two hundred years back had to make their way through thick forests. Stony River, as well as those uplands through which it ran, and the village and the estate, and the knolly fields all around—they all lost themselves in the forest.

However, things had no longer been so in Grandfather's time. In Grandfather's time the landscape was a different one: there was a spaciousness, half-pertaining to the steppe; there were denuded mountain-slopes; there were rye, oats, and buckwheat in the fields, and, by the high-road, infrequent hollow-trunked willows; while over the rise of Dry Valley there was only white flint to be seen. All that was left of the forests was but the single Troshin grove. But the garden had, of course, been a marvellous one. There had been a broad avenue of seventy spreading birches; clumps of cherry-trees, swamped in nettles; impassable thickets of raspberry bushes, acacias, lilacs; and, near where the borders of the garden verged with the grain-fields, well-nigh a whole grove of silvery poplars. The house was thatched with straw, but so thick, dark-hued, and impenetrable that no roof-iron could compare with it. And the house faced a courtyard, along the sides of which stretched the longest of offices and of servants' quarters, each building having several additions, while beyond the courtyard spread an endless green common, and the seigniorial village was scattered wide—a village large, poor, and care-free.

"It took entirely after its masters!" Nathalia used to say. "The masters, they was care-free, too: not at all good managers, nor greedy. Semion Kyrillich, that was brother to your grandpa, he divided up with us, taking for hisself what was bigger and better, which was their father's estate nigh the capital; as for us, all we got was Little Ploughs, Dry Valley, and four hundred souls thrown in. And of these four hundred, now, well-nigh half run off . . ."

Our grandfather, Petr Kyrillich, had died when he was about five-and-forty. Our father would often say that Grandfather had gone mad when a suddenly risen hurricane had sent a whole downpour of apples upon him as he lay asleep on a rug under an apple-tree in the garden. But in the servants' quarters, according to the words of Nathalia, Grandfather's feeble-mindedness was explained differently: they said that Petr Kyrillich had begun to fail through melancholy soon after the death of Grandmother, who had been a beauty; they said that a great storm had also swept over Dry Valley just before evening of the day she died, and that the hurricane which, together with a black cloud, had swooped down upon the sleeping Petr Kyrillich, had really staggered him with the idea that his own death was approaching. And so Petr Kyrillich—a stoop-shouldered, brown-haired man, with dark, solicitously kind eyes, who resembled Aunt Tonia a little—had finished his days in harmless lunacy. The Khrushchevs, according to Nathalia's words, had never known what to do with their money, and so now, in morocco half-boots and a gay Tatar kaftan (short, and fastened with hooks), he roamed all over the house, preoccupied and noiseless, and, looking over his shoulder, shoved gold pieces into the cracks of the oak timbers.

"I'm just putting that by for little Tonia's dowry," he would mutter whenever they caught him at it. "It's safer this way, my friends—much safer. But, after all, let it be as you wish; if you don't want me to do it, I won't. . . ."

And later he would do the same thing all over again. And if it were not that, he would take to shifting about the ponderous furniture in the dining-room or in the parlor; he was forever expecting someone to arrive, although his neighbors practically never visited Dry Valley. Or else he would complain that he was hungry and would concoct a cold mess for himself of bread, scallions, and bread-cider; he clumsily pounded and brayed the scallions in a wooden bowl, crumbled bread therein, poured in thick, foaming bread-cider, and sprinkled in so much salt that the mess would turn out to be bitter, and eating it would be too much for him.

But when, after dinner, life in the manor-house would become dormant, all having scattered to their favorite nooks and dozed off for long, long naps, the poor lonely fellow, who slept little even at night, was absolutely at a loss as to what to do with himself. And, having found the loneliness beyond his endurance, he would take to peeping into the bedrooms, into the entries, into the maids' rooms, and cautiously calling the sleepers:

"Are you asleep, Arcasha?—Are you asleep, Toniusha? . . ."

And, receiving an angry and loud response: "Do get away from me, Papa dear!"—he would offer a hasty reassurance:

"There, sleep, sleep, my soul—I'm not going to wake you!"

And he would again be on his way, avoiding only the butler's pantry, inasmuch as the flunkeys were an exceedingly rude race; but ten minutes later he would bob up on the same threshold anew, and, anew, with still greater caution, would call out, inventing the pretext that somebody had just driven through the village with jingle-bells that sounded like those of the stage-coach— "Could it possibly be Petie coming home on leave from his regiment?"—or else saying that a fearful cloud, full of hail-stones, was gathering.

"He, the darling old fellow, were very much afeard of a thunder-storm, now," Nathalia would tell us. "I was still a bare-headed slip of a girl then, but I remember it yet, for all that. Our house was all black, somehow. . . . None too cheerful, God be with it! And a day in summer is as long as a year. There was that many servants nobody knew what to do with 'em—of flunkeys alone there was five. . . . You know how things are: after dinner the young masters would retire for a rest, and, following their example, we their faithful louts would do the same. The wenches would go off to the maids' quarters; after dinner they would rattle their lace-bobbins and their spindles a bit for the looks of the thing, would scatter feathers and down all through the chambers (we was forever stuffing feather-beds), and then go off in a doze wherever they happened to be.

"As for the flunkeys, now—why, they was altogether too brazen; they just used to sit in their big room, braiding whips just to show off, weaving quail-nets, or thrumming away on their balalaikas, and a lot they had to care or grieve about! They'd stuff their guts with a lot of dried oat-meal and hasty pudding and then go to sleep. And at such a time Petr Kyrillich, he'd better not go near them—especially Gervasska. 'I say, my good fellows! Are you all asleep?' But Gervasska, he'd lift up his head from the bin he was lying on and ask: 'And how would you like for me to fill the seat of your breeches with nettles, right now?'—'Why, whom are you saying that to, loafer that you are?'—'I was talking to the hob-goblin, sir, in me sleep . . .'

"And so that's why Petr Kyrillich used to go to our rooms, for the most part: 'Arcasha, are you asleep?—Natka, are you asleep? . . .' And you'd jump up, all a-tremble. . . . But he'd say: 'There, sleep, sleep, my soul—I'm not going to wake you.' And again he'd take to pacing the dining-room, the parlor, and be look-ing out of the windows, out into the garden, all the time; mebbe there was a cloud to be seen. And thunder-storms, truth to tell, used to gather ever so often in the old days. Then, too, the thunder-storms was great ones. Just as soon as afternoon was come, the orioles would start in their screaming, and little clouds would start crawling up from beyant the garden. It would get all dark within the house; the witch-grass and the thick nettles would start in a'rustling; the turkey-hens and their chicks would hide theirselves under the balcony. . . . It were downright eerie and would put a body in the dumps!

"As for the old man, he'd sigh, cross hisself, and be all a-flutter to light a wax taper in front of the holy images and to hang up the sanctified towel he'd got from *his* late father—I was deathly afeard of that there towel. . . . Or else he'd chuck the scissors out of the window. That were first and foremost, them scissors; a very good thing, that, to ward off the lightning. You'd get burned right up to your waist when they made you clamber, after it was all over, after them scissors, right in amongst all them nettles, now, and they burning the very life out of you. We had a whole thick forest of 'em, a-growing and a-flourishing!"

Things had been jollier in the Dry Valley home when the French tutors were living there: at first a certain Louis Ivannovich, a fellow in the widest of pantaloons, which narrowed down at the ankles, with long moustaches and dreamy blue eyes, who combed his hair from one ear to the other to mask the bald patch on the crown of his head; and, later, an elderly, eternally chilled Mlle. Suzie. Yes, things were jollier when one could hear through all the rooms the thunderous voice of Louis Ivannovich yelling at Arcasha: "Go 'way and nevaire rrreturrrn!"—when one could hear in the class-room: "*Maître corbeau sur un arbre perché!*" and when Aunt Tonia, then a little girl, was doing her exercises on the pianoforte. For eight years these French people lived on at Dry Valley, remaining there so that Petr Kyrillich might not feel lonely or bored, remaining even after the children were taken to the capital city of the province; they left the house only just prior to the return of the youngsters for their third vacation. When this vacation was over, Petr Kyrillich no longer sent either Arcasha or little Tonia anywhere; it was enough, in his opinion, to send off only Petie. And the children were left for all time both without instruction and without supervision.—Nathalia used to say:

"I, now, was the youngest of them all. Well, Gervasska and your papa dear, now, was almost of the same years and therefore was the closest of friends and chums. Only it's the truth they say: A wolf is no kinsman to a steed. They got to be friends, now; they swore to be friends for all eternity; they even exchanged their crucifixes. But Gervasska in a short while ups and does something; he well-nigh drownded your papa dear in the pond! All scabby he were, this Gervasska, yet already a master hand at schemes that should have made him a convict. 'Well, now,' says he once to the young master, 'when you grow up, are you goin' to flog me?'—'I am that!'—'Oh, no, you ain't!'—'What d'you mean, I ain't?'—'Oh, nothin'!'—and this is what he thought up: we had a barrel standing above the ponds, just on the very slope of the hill; so what does he do but make a note of it and then sics on Arcad Petrovich to climb inside of it and dasts him to roll down the hill in it. 'You'll be the first, young master, to scoot down the hill, and then it'll be my turn. . . .' Well, now, the young master he just goes and listens to him: he climbs in, shoves off, and down the hill he goes thundering, right into the water! My, how he did go! Mother of God and Queen of Heaven! All you could see was the dust whirling along like a pillar! Thanks be, there turned out to be some shepherds near by. . . ."

As long as the French people lived on in the house at Dry Valley, the house had kept an inhabited appearance. In Grandmother's day there had yet been in it masters and managers, and such things as authority and submission, and reception-rooms and rooms for the family, and weekdays and holy days. An appearance of all this persisted even when the French people had lived there. But they went away, and the house was left entirely without managers. While the children had been small, the first place was seemingly occupied by Petr Kyrillich. But what could he do? Who was master over whom: he over the domestics, or the domestics over him? The pianoforte was closed down; the cloth vanished from the oak table—they dined without any table-cover, and whenever they could; there was no passing through the entries on account of the borzoi wolf-hounds. Things so fell out that there was never a soul to concern itself with keeping the place clean, and the dark, timbered walls, the dark, heavy doors and lintels, the old holy images, whose penny-woodcut countenances covered a whole corner in the dining-room—all these things turned black, speedily and altogether. Of nights—especially during a thunder-storm, when the garden rioted under the rain, and the visages of the painted saints in the dining-room were momently lit up, and the rosily golden, quivering sky would be revealed, would fling itself wide open over the garden, and then, amid the darkness, the peals of thunder split the air—of nights one felt afraid in the house. And in the daytime the house was drowsy, deserted, and filled with tedium.

With the years Petr Kyrillich grew weaker and weaker, was becoming ever more imperceptible; the decrepit Darya Ustinovna, Grandfather's foster-mother, was the official chatelaine. But her authority was almost on a par with his; while Demian, the overseer, did not interfere in the management of the household: all he knew was the husbandry of the field, occasionally saying with a lazy mockery: "Oh, well, I don't take any advantage of my masters. . . ." Our father, who was a youth at the time, had other things on his mind besides Dry Valley: his crazes were hunting, the balalaika, his love for Gervasska, who was numbered among the flunkeys, but who actually disappeared for days at a time with Father on certain swamps, or in the carriage-shed, studying the fine points of the balalaika and the shepherd's pipes.

"We all used to know," Nathalia would say, "that the house was for them only a place to sleep in. And if they wasn't sleeping in the house, then it meant they was either in the village or in the carriage-shed or else out hunting: in the winter it was hares; in the autumn, foxes; in the summer, quail, duck, or else bustard; they'd sit them down in a racing-cart, sling their light guns over their shoulders, call out for the bitch Dianka, and off they went, with God's blessing: now it would be Middle Hill; on the morrow it would be them Meshcherskia swamps; the day after it would be the steppes for them. And always with that there Gervasska. That lad were the head and front in everything, yet he made out like it were the young master who were dragging him on to every-thing. Arcad Petrovich loved him, who were his enemy, as if he was truly a brother to him, but he, this Gervasska, the further things went, the more he made sport of the young master, and that more and more cruelly. Arcad Petrovich might say: 'Well, now, Gervassii, let's have a go at the balalaikas! Teach me how to play *Beautiful the Sunset over the Dark Grove*, for God's sake!' But Gervasska, he'd just look at him, let the smoke out through his nose, and then say, with a sort of little sneering smile on him: 'You've got to kiss me hand first.' The young master, he'd turn all white, jump up from his place, and slap Gervasska's cheek for him, but the other would only toss his head and turn still blacker, frowning like he were a bandit or something. 'Stand up, you good-for-naught!' Gervasska would stand up, stretching hisself like he were a borzoi, the drugget breeches on him hanging all loose. He don't say a word. 'Ask my forgiveness!'—'My fault, sir.'—But the young master, he's like to choke, and he don't know what more to say. 'You'd better be saying "sir"!' he's shouting. 'I,' he says, 'am trying to be treating you like an equal, good-for-naught that you be; I,' he says, 'think at times I wouldn't begrudge giving up my soul for you. . . . But you—what are you up to? Are you angering me on purpose?'

"It's a curious thing," Nathalia would add, "it was Gervasska who used to make sport of the young master and your grandfather, and lord it over them, whereas the young lady used to do them very things to me. . . . The young master (and, truth to tell, your grandfather hisself, as well) thought the world and all of Gervasska, and I felt the same way about the young lady. . . . That is, as soon as I was come back from Little Ploughs and had come a little to my senses after my misbehavior. . . ."

5

IT WAS after Grandfather's death that they used to sit down at table armed with dog-lashes—after the flight of Gervasska and the marriage of Petr Petrovich; after Aunt Tonia, having become cracked, had consecrated herself as a bride of the Most Sweet

Jesus, and after Nathalia had come back from those same Little Ploughs. And the reason for Aunt Tonia's having become cracked, and for Nathalia's banishment to Little Ploughs, had been love.

The tedious, dull times of Grandfather were replaced by the times of the young master. Petr Petrovich (who had, unexpectedly to all, resigned from his regiment) returned to Dry Valley. And his coming proved the ruination both of Nathalia and of Aunt Tonia.

They both fell in love—and never noticed how they had come to do so.

It had seemed to them, at first, that life had simply become a blither affair. They had come to feel for the first time that they were young girls, and had given themselves up to the charm of this sensation.

Petr Petrovich had at first given a new turn to life in Dry Valley,—a turn festive and seigniorial. He arrived with his crony, Voitkevich; he brought a cook with him—a clean-shaven alcoholic, who eyed askance and with disdain the jelly-forms, nicked and turned green, and the crude knives and forks. Petr Petrovich wanted to show himself before his crony as hospitable, generous, rich—and went about it clumsily, boyishly. Yes, and he *was* almost a boy, very delicate and handsome in looks, but harsh and cruel by nature; a boy daring and self-assured, but easily confused, and that almost to tears, and then long harboring a secret malice against the one who had caused his confusion.

"I remember, Brother Arcadii," said he on the very first day of his stay in Dry Valley, "I remember we used to have some madeira in our cellar that was not at all bad. . . ."

Grandfather turned red and wanted to say something, but could not summon up enough courage and only started to tug at the bosom of his short Tatar kaftan. Arcadii Petrovich was astonished.

"What madeira?"

But Gervasska gave Petr Petrovich a brazen look and fleered.

"You've forgotten, sir, if you please," said he to Arcadii Petrovich, without even trying to conceal his mockery, "that, truth to tell, we had so much of that there madeira that we didn't know what to do with it. But us servants has managed to get rid of it.

'Tis a wine for the masters' table, but we, being fools, used to drink it in place of bread-cider."

"What's all this?" Petr Petrovich raised his voice, a dark flush, peculiarly his own, mantling his cheeks. "Keep still, you!"

Grandfather rapturously chimed in:

"That's right, that's right, Petie! Serve him out again!" he cried out joyously, in his piping voice, and almost burst into tears. "You simply can't imagine how he makes naught of me! I've already more than once thought of stealing up on him and bashing his head in with a brass pestle! Honest to God, that's what I've thought of doing! Some day I'll stick a dagger in his ribs!"

But Gervasska did not lose his presence of mind even at this point. "I've heard, sir, that there's a heavy penalty for that sort of thing," he retorted, frowning. "And then I, too, have an idea always popping into my head: it's high time for the old master to be going to the Kingdom of Heaven!"

Petr Petrovich used to say that after such an unexpectedly impertinent answer he had restrained himself only because a stranger was present. He said but one thing to Gervasska: "Get out of here this minute!" But afterwards he had become actually ashamed of his hot-headedness, and, hastily apologizing before Voitkevich, with a smile raised to him those charming eyes which all those who knew Petr Petrovich could not forget for a long while.

Nathalia, too, could not forget those eyes—for all too long a while.

Her happiness was unusually brief, and who could have thought that it would terminate in a journey to Little Ploughs—the most remarkable event in her whole life?

The farmstead of Little Ploughs has survived even to this day, although it has long since passed into the hands of a merchant from Tambov. It consists of an elongated hut, a storehouse, the long crane of a water-well, and a threshing-floor, surrounded by melon-patches. The farmstead had been like that even in Grandfather's day; however, even the town lying between it and Dry Valley has changed but little.

And Natashka's misdeed had consisted in her having stolen, altogether unexpectedly even to herself, a little folding silver-framed mirror belonging to Petr Petrovich.

She had caught a glimpse of this mirror and had been so taken by its beauty (as, however, she was by all things else that appertained to Petr Petrovich) that she had not been able to withstand the temptation. And for several days, until the mirror was missed, she lived in a stunned state, overwhelmed by her crime, under the witching spell of her dreadful secret and her treasure, as if she were the heroine of the fairy-tale concerning the Little Crimson Flower. Whenever she lay down to sleep she prayed to God that the night might pass as quickly as possible, and that, as quickly as possible, the morning might come. There was a gala mood in the house, which had taken on new life, had become filled with something new, something wondrous, upon the coming of the young master, as handsome as Adonis, dandified in dress, pomatumed, with a high red collar to the coat of his uniform, with a face swarthy, but as delicate as that of a miss.

There was a gala mood even in the entrance hall, where Natashka used to sleep, and where, at dawn, springing down from the coffer that was her bed, she at once recalled that there was joy in this world, because standing near the door and waiting to be cleaned was a pair of boots, so small and light that they were fit to be worn by any king's son. And the most frightening and festal thing of all lay beyond the garden, in the abandoned bath-house, where the small double mirror in its silver frame was hidden—beyond the garden, whither, while all were yet asleep, Natashka sped secretly through the dew-covered thickets, that she might gloat over the possession of her treasure, might bring it out on the threshold, open it in the hot morning sun, gaze at herself till her head swam, and then hide it, secrete it again, and again speed home, to wait all morning upon him whom she dared not even raise her eyes to and for whose sake, in an insane hope of proving to his liking, she used to look so long in the mirror.

But the fairy-tale of the Little Scarlet Flower had come to a speedy end—an exceedingly speedy end. It ended in such disgrace and shame as there was no name for, as Natashka thought, inasmuch as the most secretly cherished things she had borne within her soul became understood by all. It ended with none other than Petr Petrovich himself ordering her to have her hair cropped, so as to make her homely—her, who used to prim herself, used to blacken her eyebrows with stibium before the little mirror, having created some sort of a sweet secret, some unparalleled intimacy between herself and it.

He himself had discovered her crime and had transformed it into a simple theft, the silly prank of a little serving-wench, who, in a threadbare shift of striped ticking, with a face swollen from tears, was, in the presence of all the servants, put in a dung-cart and, disgraced, suddenly torn away from all that was near and dear to her, was driven off to some unknown, fearsome farmstead, into the distant prospects of the steppe. She already knew that there, on the farm, she would have to watch the chicks, the turkeys, and the melon-patches; there she would be baked brown by the sun, forgotten by the whole world; there, out on the steppe, the days would be as long as years, when the horizons sink in the shimmering mirage, and everything is so still, so sultry, that one feels like sleeping the sleep of the dead the livelong day, were one not compelled to listen to the subdued crackling of peas parched by the sun in their pods, to the housewifely fussing of the brood-hens in the hot earth, to the turkeys exchanging peacefully sad gobbles—were one not compelled to watch for the shadow, weirdly swooping downward, of a chicken-hawk and to leap up and scare him off with a high-pitched, long-drawn-out *shoo—oo!* . . .

There, on the farm, what would she not have to endure from the old peasant woman alone who had been given the power of life and death over her and who was probably already awaiting her victim with impatience! Natashka had but one advantage over those who are being carted off to the scaffold: the possibility of strangling herself. And that was the only thing that sustained her during her journey to the place of her banishment—of course a perpetual banishment, as she supposed.

En route, from one end of the district to the other, what had she not seen! However, her mind was taken up with other things.

She thought (or rather felt) but one thing: life was at an end. Her crime and disgrace were too great for her to hope for a return to life. As yet there remained near her a man she knew well—Evsei Bodulya. But what would happen when he would hand her over into the hands of that old peasant witch and, after sleeping over, would go off in the morning, abandoning her forever in a strange place?

After having wept her fill she had felt hungry, and Evsei, to her wonder, regarded this as a very simple matter and, as they had a bite, talked with her just as if nothing whatsoever had happened. And later on she had fallen asleep, and when she awoke, they were already in the town. And the town struck her only by its tedium, dry air, and sultriness, and also by a something vaguely frightening, depressing, like a dream which one could not relate.

All that remained in her memory of this day was that it was very hot in the steppe in the summertime, that there was nothing in the world as endless as a summer day or as long as a high-road. There also remained in her memory an impression that there were spots in the streets of the town paved with cobblestones over which the cart rattled most oddly; that, from afar, the town smelt of iron roofs, while in the middle of the square where they halted to rest and bait their horse, near the sheds of the slap-bang eating-places (which sheds were empty because it was toward evening), the smells were those of dust, of pitch, and of rotting hay, wisps of which, trodden into the horse-manure, always remain wherever the mujiks may have put up.

Evsei unharnessed the horse and let it feed from a bag that rested on the cart, shoved the cap, in which he had been sweltering, on the nape of his neck, wiped his sweat with his sleeve, and, all black from the baking sun, went off to a cook-shop. He gave exceedingly strict orders to Natashka to keep her eyes peeled, and, if anything happened, to yell so's the whole square might hear on 't. And Natashka sat there without stirring, without taking her eyes off the cupola of the cathedral (which at that time had just been built)—a cupola that glowed like an enormous silver star somewhere far beyond the houses. She sat there until Evsei, still chewing and by now grown cheerful, had returned and, holding a loaf of bread under his arm, began putting the horse back in the shafts.

"Me an' you, queenie, is a bit late!" he was muttering animatedly, but one could not tell whether he were addressing the horse or Natashka. "Oh, well, guess they won't kill us for it! Guess we ain't goin' to no fire—I ain't a-goin' to break me neck goin' back, neither; I thinks more of the master's hoss, brother, than I does of your damned mug," he was saying, this time apostrophizing the overseer at Dry Valley. "Look at him openin' his mug: 'I'll have you look sharp! In case anythin' goes wrong, I'll fix you so's you won't be able to sit down for a month of Sundays. . . .' 'Aaah,' thinks I, an' I got my bellyful of mistreatment right there an' then! You take the masters, now, an' even they ain't never took me breeches down yet. So where do you come in, you low-down, ornery houn'?—'Look sharp!' But why should I look sharp? Guess I ain't worse off for brains nor you be! If I feel like it, I won't come back at all, at all; I'll get the wench to where she's goin', an' then cross meself, an' that's the last they'll ever see of me. . . . Why, I do be wonderin' at this wench, now— what's the fool grievin' about? Ain't the world wide enough? Let some carters with oxen pass by the farm, or certain of the little ancients amongst the pilgrims, an' just say the word, an' in a minute you'll find yourself beyant Rostov, the father of all cities— Let 'em go an' look for you then!"

And the thought of "I'll strangle myself!" was replaced in the cropped head of Natashka by the thought of flight. The cart began to creak and sway. Evsei lapsed into silence and led the horse off to a well in the middle of the market-place. The sun was setting beyond a great monastery garden, in the direction they had come from, and the windows in the yellow jail which stood opposite the monastery, across the way, gleamed with gold. And the sight of the jail aroused the thought of flight still more. "There, escaped folk manage to get along too! Only, they do be saying that the holy little ancients scald with boiling milk the eyes of the wenches and lads they steal, and then palm them off as poor little unfortunates, to make kindly folk shell out; whilst the carters carry them off to the very sea and sell them to the Nogai Tatars. . . . Things so fall out, too, that the masters catch their runaways, forge leg-irons on to them, and put them in jail. . . . But I guess them prisons, as Gervasska says, is full of your own kind, and not of cattle!"

But the windows of the jail were dimming; her thoughts were becoming confused. No, running away was still more frightful than strangling oneself! Evsei, too, had fallen silent, had sobered up.

"We're a bit late, lassie," he was saying, by now uneasily, jumping up and perching sideways on the edge of the cart.

And the cart, getting out on the paved highway, again began to jolt, to jar, and to rattle sharply over the cobblestones.—"Ah, the best thing of all, now, would be to turn the cart back!" Natashka half-thought, half-felt. To turn it back, to gallop all the way to Dry Valley, and to fall down at the feet of her masters! But Evsei was urging his horse on. The cathedral no longer seemed a silver star beyond the houses. Ahead lay a white, barren street, the white, cobble-paved roadway, white houses; and all this terminated in the enormous white cathedral under its new cupola of white tin, and the sky over it had become a wan blue, and arid. . . . But there, at home, at this time the dew was already falling, the garden was fragrant with freshness, there was a pleasant odor issuing from the warm kitchen; far beyond the cultivated plains, beyond the silvery poplars on the boundaries of the garden, beyond the time-worn bath-house, so sacred to her, the evening glow was burning out, while the doors of the parlor were open on the balcony, the scarlet light of the glow mingling with the dusk in the corners of the room. . . .

And the young lady of the house, with a sallow-swarthy complexion and dark eyes, who resembled both Grandfather and Petr Petrovich, was every minute adjusting the sleeves of her light loose-fitting dress of orange silk, intently following the notes as she sat with her back to the evening glow, and, as she struck the yellowed keys, filling the parlor with the triumphantly canorous, delectably despairing strains of Oghinski's *Polonaise* and apparently paying no attention whatsoever to the military officer standing behind her: thickset, dark-visaged, with his left arm akimbo, and in grim concentration watching her agile hands. . . .

"She's got her man, and I have mine," Natashka used to half-think, half-feel on such evenings, and, the heart swooning within her, would run off into the chill, dewy garden, clambering deep into the wilderness of nettles and the acridly smelling damp burdocks, and then stand there, awaiting that which could never befall: that the young master, Petr Petrovich, might come down from the balcony, walk along the garden path, catch sight of her, and, suddenly turning aside, approach her with rapid strides, while she, from terror and happiness, let not a single sound escape her. . . .

But the cart rattled onward. All around her was the town, sultry and stinking—the same town she had hitherto pictured to herself as something enchanted. And Natashka, with a sickly wonder, gazed at the well-dressed populace pacing to and fro over the flagstones near the houses, near the gates and the shops with open doors—"And what ever made Evsei travel this way?" she was thinking. "How did he ever pluck up the courage to go rattling through here with his cart?"

But they passed the white cathedral, started going toward the shallow river down dusty hill-sides, rutted and pitted, past sooty smithies, past the tumbledown hovels of the local citizenry. . . . Again came the familiar odors of sun-warmed, fresh water, of slime, of the evening freshness of the fields. The first light glimmered in the distance on a hill, in a lonely little house near a turnpike.—And now they had come entirely out into the open, had crossed a bridge, and come up to the turnpike—and their eyes beheld the stone-paved, deserted road, showing dimly white and running away into the endless distance, into the indigo-blue of the fresh night over the steppe. The horse struck a jog-trot and, after passing the turnpike, fell into a steady walk. And again one could hear that at night all is quiet, exceedingly quiet, upon earth and in the sky—save for a jingle-bell sobbing somewhere far away.

It sobbed ever more audibly, ever more resoundingly, and finally blended with the well-timed beats of a troika, with the rhythmic rumble of wheels running and approaching over the paved high-road. The troika was driven by a young stage-driver (free, and not a serf); while in his half-covered carriage there was sitting an army officer, his chin buried in the collar of his hooded uniform over-coat. As he came up with the cart, he raised his head for an in-stant—and suddenly Natashka caught sight of his red collar, his black moustache, his youthful eyes, which were flashing under a casque that was somewhat like a bucket. She cried out and keeled over in a dead faint.

An insane thought had flared up in her head that this was Petr Petrovich, and, by that pain and tenderness which went like lightning through her susceptible, lowly heart, she had suddenly comprehended what she had been deprived of: of being near him.—Evsei made a dash for the travelling-jug and began dashing water over her cropped, lolling head.

Thereupon she was brought to by an attack of nausea and quickly put her head over the side of the cart. Evsei supported her clammy forehead with the palm of his hand.—And then, relieved, chilled, with the collar of her blouse sopping wet, she lay on her back and contemplated the stars. The thoroughly frightened Evsei kept silent, thinking that she had fallen asleep; he merely shook his head from time to time and occasionally (and hopefully) urged on his horse. The cart shook and ran on and on. But to the little wench it seemed that she was without a body, that now all she had left was her soul. And this soul felt "like it were in the Kingdom of Heaven itself."

A little scarlet flower, grown in faery gardens, was this love of hers. But into the steppe, into a wilderness still more primeval than the wilderness of Dry Valley, did she betake this her love, in order that there, in quietude and loneliness, she might over-come its first sweet and searing torments, and then for a long time, forever, till the headstone would be put over her grave, bury it deep within the depths of her Dry Valley soul. . . .

6

Love in Dry Valley was of an extraordinary nature. Extraordinary, too, was hatred.

Grandfather, who had perished just as ludicrously as his slayer, just as all those in Dry Valley were perishing, was killed in the same year that Nathalia was exiled. On the Feast of the Intercession of the Holy Virgin, which was a high holiday in Dry Valley, Petr Petrovich had invited a lot of guests and was very much excited: would the leader of the local nobility keep the promise he had given to attend? Grandfather, too, was joyously excited—no one knew over what.—The leader came, and the dinner was a glorious success. It was both noisy and jolly— Grandfather felt the gayest of all.

Early on the morning of the 2nd of October (the very next day) he was found on the floor of the parlor, dead.

In resigning from active service Petr Petrovich did not conceal the fact that he was sacrificing himself for the sake of saving the honor of the Khrushchevs, the ancestral nest and the ancestral estate. He did not conceal the fact that he would have to take the management of that estate, "willy-nilly," into his own hands. He would also have to form acquaintanceships, so that he might associate with the more enlightened and useful among the noblemen of the district, and simply to keep up his relations with the others.

And, in the beginning, he carried out all this punctiliously: he paid visits even to all the small landowners, even down to the small farm of his aunt, Olga Kyrillovna, a monstrously fat old woman who suffered from sleeping-sickness and who cleaned her teeth with snuff. . . . By fall no one any longer wondered that Petr Petrovich was managing the estate autocratically. And, too, by now his appearance was no longer merely that of a young Adonis of an officer who had come home on leave, but that of a proprietor, of a young landowner. Whenever he became confused now, the flush that mantled his cheeks was no longer as deep as on former occasions. He took good care of his person, had filled out, wore expensive Tatar jackets; he indulged himself in red Tatar slippers for his small feet; his small hands he adorned with turquoise rings. His lovely eyes proved to be, to the wonder of all, not black, but hazel, as befits a man with a dark complexion. Arcadii Petrovich, for some reason, felt embarrassed about looking into these eyes, was always at a loss about a topic of conversation with him, yielded to Petr Petrovich in everything at first, and, for days at a stretch, was away hunting.

On the Feast of the Intercession Petr Petrovich had wanted to charm every single one of his guests by his open-handed hospitality, and also to show that none other than he was the first personage in the house. But Grandfather was dreadfully in the way. Grandfather was blissfully happy, but tactless, garrulous, and pitiful, in his small velvet cap which had been blessed by contact with the bones of a saint, and in his new, inordinately wide, blue Cossack coat, made by the household tailor. Grandfather, too, had imagined himself an open-handedly hospitable host, and bustled about from early morning, contriving some silly ceremony out of the reception of the guests. One of the leaves of the door from the entrance hall into the dining-room was never opened. He himself moved back the metal catches at the top and bottom of this leaf, himself moving up a chair, and, all shaking, climbing up on it to reach the upper catch. And when he had thrown both leaves of the door open at last, he stationed himself on the threshold and, taking advantage of the silence of Petr Petrovich, who was almost fainting from humiliation and resentment, but who had determined to endure everything in patience, did not leave his place until the last guest had arrived. He did not take his eyes off the front entrance, and they had to open that door as well; this too, it appeared, was demanded by some old custom. In his excitement he shifted from foot to foot at his post; but whenever he caught sight of a guest entering, he would dash forward to meet him, hurriedly execute an old-fashioned scrape, hop upward a little, crossing his legs like a dancing master, deliver a low bow, and, spluttering in his agitation, say to each guest, even to those whom he did not know:

"Oh, how glad I am—how glad to see you! It's a long time since you've dropped in on me! Step in, do—step in!"

Petr Petrovich was also infuriated because Grandfather, for some reason, informed each and every guest of little Tonia's departure to Lunevo, to Olga Kyrillovna's: "Tonechka got sick from loneliness; she's gone off to her dear aunt for the whole autumn."

What were the guests to think after such unsolicited announcements? For the episode with Voitkevich was, of course, already known to all and sundry. Voitkevich may possibly have really had serious intentions, what with his enigmatic sighs whenever he was in Tonechka's vicinity, playing piano duets with her, reading Pushkin to her in a subterranean voice, or else reciting to her with morose pensiveness: "Thou art betrothed to one dead by holy words that thou hast said. . . ."

Yet Tonechka would flare up in fury at his every attempt, even the most innocent, to express his feelings—such as offering her a flower, for instance; and Voitkevich had suddenly gone away. But when he was gone, Tonechka took to having sleepless nights, to sitting by an open window in the dark, just as though awaiting a certain time, known only to herself, to break into loud sobbing and thus awaken Petr Petrovich. For a long time he would lie with clenched teeth, listening to her sobs, and to the broken, drowsy murmur of the poplars beyond the windows, in the dark garden: a murmur like the sound of a never-ceasing drizzle. Then he would go to calm her. The maids, too, with sleep-laden faces, went to calm her as well; occasionally Grandfather would also come running in alarm. Thereupon Tonechka would start in stamping her feet, shrieking as she did so:

"Get away from me—you're my bitter enemies, all of you!" And the thing would wind up with hideous vituperation—almost a brawl.

"But do understand—do understand," Petr Petrovich would hiss in fury, after driving the maids and Grandfather out of the room, slamming the door to, and grasping the hasp hard and fast, "do understand, you viper—what will people imagine?"

"Oh!" Tonechka would squeal out in a frenzy. "Papa dear, he's yelling all over the place that I have a big belly!"

And, clutching his head, Petr Petrovich would dash out of her room.

On the Feast of the Intercession, too, he had more than once felt like clutching his head. Gervasska, likewise, worried him: what if he should say something impertinent if Petr Petrovich were not careful of what *he* said?

Gervasska had shot up fearfully. Huge, ungainly, yet the most striking, the most intelligent among the servants, he, too, was togged out in a blue Cossack coat, loose, baggy trousers of the same color, and soft, heelless boots of goat-skin. A kerchief of lilac-colored woollen yarn was tied about his thin, dark neck. His black, dry, coarse hair he had combed back with a parting on one side, but had refused to have his hair clipped short in the back, and merely had it cut evenly all around. He had nothing to shave— there were only two or three scanty and coarse curls showing black on his chin and near the corners of his great mouth, of which it was said: "His mouth goes from ear to ear, an' it buttons in the rear." Lanky-legged, very broad in his bony, flat chest, with a small head and deep eye-sockets, with thin, ash-blue lips, and large, bluish teeth, he, this ancient Aryan, this Parsee of Dry Valley, had already received his nickname: The Borzoi. On seeing him bare his teeth, on hearing his occasional little coughs, many thought: "Oh, but you're going to croak soon, Borzoi!" But aloud they dignified this milksop by calling him by his full name and patronymic, Gervassii Aphanassievich—a dignity not extended to the other servants.

The masters, as well, feared him. The masters had the same quirks in their make-up as the servants did: they had either to command or to fear. To the wonder of the domestics, Gervasska had nothing whatsoever comin' to him for his impertinent answer to Grandfather on the day of Petr Petrovich's arrival. Arcadii Petrovich had said to Gervasska, succinctly: "You're absolutely an animal, brother!" To which he had received an answer that was likewise exceedingly succinct: "I can't stand him, sir!" But it had been Gervasska himself who had come to Petr Petrovich; he stopped on the threshold, and, as was his way, slouching back in a free and easy manner on his legs (which were disproportionately long as compared with his torso, and which were clad in the loosest of belled trousers), and with his left knee projecting angularly, made a request to be flogged.

"I'm entirely too rude and hot-headed a fellow, sir," he had said indifferently, his dark eyes sparkling.

And Petr Petrovich had sensed a hint in the word "hot-headed" and took water.

"There's plenty of time for that, my dear fellow—plenty of time!" he raised his voice with assumed sternness. "Get out of here! I can't bear the sight of anybody as impertinent as you. . . ."

Gervasska remained standing and kept silent. Then he said:

"Very well, if such be your will."

He stood yet awhile longer, twisting the coarse hair on his upper lip, moved his livid jaws like a dog, without his face expressing any emotion whatsoever, and then walked out. Since that time he had become firmly convinced of the advantage of this expedient: of expressing nothing on his face and being as succinct as possible in his answers. As for Petr Petrovich, he began avoiding not only having any conversation with him, but even looking him in the eyes.

Just as indifferently, just as enigmatically, did Gervasska conduct himself on the Feast of the Intercession. Everybody had run his or her feet off in getting ready for the holiday, giving and receiving instructions, scolding, arguing, scrubbing floors, cleaning the dark, heavy silver of the icons with chalk-paste that turned blue as one cleaned, kicking out the dogs that kept on creeping into the entries, worrying that the gelatine would not jellify, that there would be a shortage of forks, that the turnovers and faggots would be overdone. Gervasska alone fleered calmly and kept on saying to Casimir, the frantic alcoholic chef:

"Take it easy, father deacon, or else your under-cassock will bust."

"See that you don't get drunk," Petr Petrovich, stirred up over the uncertainty of the coming of the guest of honor, had absent-mindedly said to Gervasska.

"I ain't never drunk a drop in all me born days," Gervasska had let drop in answer, as if to an equal. "Drink don't interest me."

And later, in the presence of all the guests, Petr Petrovich had yelled all over the house, even ingratiatingly:

"Gervassii Aphanassievich! Don't you go and get lost now, please! Without you I'd be like a man without hands."

While Gervasska, in the politest manner possible, and with dignity, had responded:

"Don't put yourself out, sir, if you please. I wouldn't dast leave the room."

He waited on the guests as never before. He fully justified the words of Petr Petrovich, who said to the guests in his hearing:

"You can't even imagine to what an extent this dunder-head is impertinent! But he is positively a genius! He has hands of gold!"

How could Petr Petrovich have possibly even supposed that he was dropping into the cup the one drop that would make it overflow? Grandfather heard Petr Petrovich's words; the old man began to tug at the breast of his Cossack coat and suddenly called out to the leader of the nobility, across the whole table:

"Your Excellency! Extend your helping hand to us! I come to you as to a father with a complaint against this my servant! This one, this one—this Gervassii Aphanassievich Kulikov! He makes naught of me at every step! He, and none other—"

He was cut short, reasoned with, calmed down. Grandfather had been stirred to tears, but everybody had fallen to calming him down so unanimously, and with such respectfulness (somewhat mocking, of course), that he gave in and once more felt himself childishly happy. Gervasska stood at attention near the wall, with downcast eyes and with his head turned slightly to one side. Grandfather could see that this giant had too small a head, that it would be still smaller if it were to be clipped, that the nape of his neck was ridged, and that there was a particularly great amount of hair precisely at the back of his neck—coarse, black hair, roughly hacked, as if with a hatchet, and forming a protrusion over his thin neck. From sunburn, from the winds of the hunting-fields, Gervasska's dark face was scaling in spots, and bore pale-lilac blotches. And

Grandfather, in fear and alarm, cast occasional glances at Gervasska, but nevertheless shouted joyously to his guests:

"Very well, I forgive him! Only, because of that, I shan't let you go for three whole days, my dear guests! I shan't let you go, not for anything! But especially I beg of you not to go away before evening. When it gets on toward evening, I'm not myself; there's such a sadness falls upon me, and such eeriness!—There are little clouds rolling up. . . . Two more of Boney's mounseers were caught in the Troshin woods, they say. . . . I'm bound to die in the evening, sure as fate. . . . Remember my words! It was Martin Zadeka, the soothsayer, who foretold me that, himself. . . ."

But it was early in the morning that he died.

He had had his own way, after all; a great many people had remained, "for his sake," to sleep over. All evening they drank tea. There was an awesome quantity of jam, and that of all different sorts, so that one could always walk up and try a little of this and then walk up again and try a little of that. Then a great number of card-tables were placed about, and so many spermaceti candles were lit that they were reflected in all the mirrors, and there was an aureate glow, as if in a church, throughout the rooms, filled with the fumes of fragrant Zhukovski Latakia and with hubbub and conversation. But the main thing was that many did remain to stay overnight. And therefore there was not only a new day of merriment ahead, but there were also great cares and worries—for, had it not been for him, for Petr Kyrillich, the holiday would never have come off so well, there would never have been so animated and so rich a dinner!

"Yes, yes," Grandfather was thinking excitedly that night, after he had taken off his Cossack coat and was standing in his bedroom before a prie-dieu, before the waxen tapers burning on it, contemplating the blackened image of Mercurius, that holy man, "yes, yes—death is cruel to a sinner. . . . Let not the sun go down upon your wrath!"

But at this point he recalled that he had wanted to think upon something else. With his back hunched, and whispering the fiftieth Psalm, he paced through the room, snuffed the incense cone that looked something like a little nun (it was smoldering on his little night-table), picked up the Psalter, and, opening it, with a deep, happy sigh lifted up his eyes anew to the headless saint. And suddenly he struck upon that which he had wanted to think about, and a smile lit up his face:

"Yes, yes—'When the old man is alive, folks are fain to kill him off; when the old man is gone, they would fain buy him back!'"

Afraid of oversleeping, and of overlooking some instruction or other, he hardly slept at all. But early in the morning, when that peculiar quiet which follows only gala occasions still reigned throughout the rooms, still untidied and redolent of tobacco, he went cautiously, in his bare feet, into the parlor, solicitously picked up several bits of chalk which had been dropped near the unfolded tables with their green-cloth tops, and ah'd faintly as he caught a glimpse of the garden beyond the glass doors—of the bright sheen of a chill, azure sky—of the morning hoar-frost which covered with its silver the floor and the railing of the balcony—of the brown leaves among the denuded thickets under the balcony. He opened the door and sniffed the air: there was still an acrid and spirituous odor of autumnal corruption emanating from the bushes, but this odor was becoming lost amid a wintry freshness. The sun, which had barely appeared beyond the village, lit up the tree-tops of the picturesque garden-path—the tops of the half-denuded birches, white-trunked and spattered with fine, flaked gold—and there was a lovely, joyous tone of elusive lilac about these white-and-gold tree-tops, showing clearly against the azure of the sky. A dog ran past in the cold shadow of the balcony, crunching over the grass, which was frost-bitten and looked just as if it had been sprinkled with salt. This crunching reminded him that winter was not so far off, and, with an agreeable shudder of his shoulders, Grandfather stepped back into the room and, with bated breath, started to shift about and to place back the heavy furniture, which emitted a low growl as it was shoved over the floor. From time to time he glanced at the mirror, wherein the sky was reflected. Suddenly Gervasska entered, inaudibly and quickly:

without his Cossack coat, sleepy, and "as bad-tempered as the
Devil," as he himself happened to relate afterwards.

He entered and sternly called out in a whisper:

"Not so much noise, you! What are you shovin' your nose for
into work that ain't yourn?"

Grandfather lifted up his excited face and, with the same tenderness which had never forsaken him all day yesterday and all of last
night, answered, likewise in a whisper:

"There, you see what sort of a fellow you are, Gervassii! I forgave
you yesterday, but you, instead of being grateful to your master—"

"I'm sick an' tired of you, you old slobberin' fool!" Gervasska
cut him short. "Get out of me way!"

Grandfather looked with fright at the back of Gervasska's head,
now still more prominent above his thin neck, which was sticking
up out of the open collar of his white shirt. But he flared up and
blocked with his body the folding-table which he wanted to drag
into a corner.

"You get out of my way!" he cried out in a low voice, after an
instant's thought. "It's you who ought to be making way for the
master—you'll bring me to sticking a dagger in your ribs yet!"

"Ah!" said Gervasska in vexation, with a gleam of his teeth, and
struck him in the chest with the back of his hand.

Grandfather slipped on the smooth oaken floor, threw up his
arms—and struck one of his temples right against a sharp corner
of the table.

On catching sight of the blood, and of Grandfather's eyes, with
their pupils senselessly diverging, and of the gaping mouth, Gervasska, without himself knowing why he was doing it, tore off
Grandfather's still warm chest a little golden image and a
scapulary on a soiled, worn cord . . . looked over his shoulder, and
then tore Grandmother's wedding ring off the dead man's little
finger. . . . Then, inaudibly and quickly, he went out of the parlor
—and became a needle in a haystack.

The only living person among all the Dry Valley folk who saw
him after that was Nathalia.

7

W HIL E Nathalia was living in Little Ploughs, two more great events had taken place in Dry Valley. One was Petr Petrovich's marriage; the other, the departure of the two brothers as volunteers in the Crimean campaign.

She came back only after two years; everybody had forgotten all about her. And, having come back, she did not recognize Dry Valley, even as Dry Valley failed to recognize her.

On that summer evening when the cart, sent from the masters' manor-house, had come creaking up to the hut on the farm, and Natashka had jumped out on the threshold, Evsei Bodulya had cried out in wonder:

"Come, can it really be you, Natashka?"

"Why, and who else should it be?" Natashka had answered, with a barely perceptible smile. And Evsei had shaken his head.

"You sure has lost a great deal of your good looks!"

And yet she had merely become unlike her former self. From a cropped, round-faced, and clear-eyed slip of a girl she had become transformed into a short but graceful lass, rather thin, but not at all sickly, and reserved in asking or answering questions. She was barefooted, in a length of checked woollen material wrapped around her by way of a skirt, and in an embroidered blouse; although she had her head covered with a dark kerchief, after the way of the peasant women in our region, she was a trifle swarthy from the sun, and her face was covered with tiny freckles, the color of millet. But to Evsei, a true son of Dry Valley, the dark kerchief and the tan and the freckles all seemed ugly, of course. Yes, and she herself supposed that they were just that. However, anybody might have noticed, by that slight smile with which she had said: "Why, and who else should it be?" that she was proud of the changes which had taken place in her, and that she was apparently even pleased at being homely.

On the way to Dry Valley Evsei said:

"There, now, lass, you've become fit to be a bride. D'you want to get married, now?"

She merely tossed and shook her head.

"No, Uncle Evsei—I'll never marry."

"An' whatsomever may the reason for that be?" asked Evsei—and even took the pipe out of his mouth. And unhurriedly, half in jest and half in earnest, she explained that it weren't everybody, now, that could get married; she'd sure enough be put to waiting on the young mistress—whilst the young mistress had given herself to God, and therefore wouldn't let her get married; and, besides, she, Nathalia, had dreamt dreams that was all too plain, and that more nor once—

"Well, an' just what was it you dreamt?" asked Evsei.

"Why, just this and that—mere trifles," she answered him. "Gervasska, he frightened me no end at the time Petr Kyrillich come to die. He told me a lot of news, and I got to thinking— Well, and that's how I come to have the dreams."

"But is it really the truth, now, that this here Gervasska stopped over for a midday bite at your place?"

Natashka pondered awhile.

"He did that. He comes and he says: 'I'm come to you from the masters on important business; only let me have a little somethin' to eat first.' Well, we set out a meal for him, like we would for any wayfarer. Well, when he'd eaten his fill, he walks out of the hut and tips me a wink. I ran out—and, just round a corner of the hut, he made a clean breast of everything to me, and then went on his way."

"But how is it you didn't call out for the people in charge?"

"That's easier said nor done. He threatened to kill me. Ordered me not to say anything before dinner-time. But to the old man and woman he said: 'I'm goin' to get me some sleep under the store-house. . . .'"

All the domestics in Dry Valley regarded her with great curiosity; her friends and coevals in the maids' room pestered her with questions. But she answered her friends as briefly as ever, and just as though she were admiring from the side a certain role she had taken upon herself.

"I've had a good time," she kept on repeating.

While once, in the tone of a pilgrim woman, she had said:

"There's a plenty of all things at the Lord God's. I've had a good time."

And simply, without any shilly-shallyings, she stepped into the working, everyday life of Dry Valley, as though not at all surprised that there was no Grandfather, that the young masters had gone off to war as volunteers, that the young lady had become touched and was roaming all over the house, following in Grandfather's footsteps, that Dry Valley was being managed by a new mistress, who was a stranger to everybody,—small, plump, very lively, pregnant, who had come out of a Moscow finishing school and had at one time been governess with the masters of Chirkizovo, but who now used to speak of Petr Petrovich as Petrushka.

She had once called out at dinner: "Do call this—what d'you call her?—Natashka!"

And Natashka had entered, quickly and inaudibly, crossed herself, made a bow toward the corner where the holy images were, then to the lady and the young lady of the house, and stood waiting for interrogations and orders. Of course it was only the lady of the house who interrogated her; the young lady, who had shot up exceedingly and had become very thin and whose nose had grown still sharper, did not let even so much as a word drop as she fixedly and dully regarded Nathalia. And it was the mistress who had assigned Nathalia to attend the young lady. And Nathalia had made a curtsy and simply said:

"I'm at your service."

The young lady, regarding Nathalia just as attentively and indifferently as before, had suddenly pounced upon her on the evening of the same day, and, with her eyes crossed from fury, had cruelly and with delight yanked and torn Nathalia's hair because she had been clumsy in pulling off one of the young lady's stockings. Natashka began crying like a child, yet let everything pass without a word. But when she had gone into the maids' room and had sat down on a chest, she even smiled through the tears that hung on her eyelashes, as she picked the torn clusters out of her hair.

"My, but she's mean as mean!" said she. "I'm going to have a hard time with her."

The young lady, when she awoke the next morning, lay abed for a long time, while Natashka stood near the threshold and, with her head bowed, watched out of one corner of her eye the pale face of her mistress.

"Well, what did you see in your dreams?" the young mistress asked her at last, just as apathetically as if someone else were talking for her. Nathalia answered:

"Nothing, it seems."

And thereupon the young lady, just as precipitately as the day before, jumped out of bed, insanely let her cup fly at Nathalia, tea and all, and, falling on the bed and screaming, burst into bitter tears. Natashka managed to dodge the cup, and soon learned to dodge with extraordinary nimbleness. It turned out that the young lady would occasionally retort to those stupid serving-wenches who answered her question concerning their dreams with: "We ain't seen nothin'," by screaming: "Well, then, cook up some lie or other!" But since Natashka was not mistress of the art of lying, she had to develop another ability within her: that of dodging things.

Finally they brought a man of medicine for the young mistress. The man of medicine learnedly diagnosed her ailment as "pulmonary ossification," and prescribed a mountain of pills, a sea of black drops. Apprehensive of being poisoned, Tonia compelled Natashka to sample all these pills and drops, and, without demur, sample them all she did, one after the other. She had learned soon after her coming that the young lady had longed for her arrival as one benighted longs for the "light of day." It was none other than Tonia who had recalled her existence, had strained and strained her eyes watching for the cart to come from Little Ploughs, had ardently assured all and sundry that she would get entirely well, would be freed of every ache and yearning, just as soon at Natashka would return from banishment. Natashka had returned—and was met with utter indifference.

But: weren't the young lady's tears the tears of bitter disenchantment? Wasn't the cruel notion of compelling Nathalia to sample the medicines really a fierce avidity to get well? Natashka's heart gave a throb when she realized all this. She went out into the corridor, sat down on a coffer, and again began to weep. She wept softly, enjoying her tears; for long stretches at a time she stared fixedly through her tears at a point somewhere in the distance. She was doing just what other peasant women do on such occasions, yet her thoughts were of the little mirror, of her departure for Little Ploughs, of all she had lived through there—and once more her face would become distorted like a child's and she would fall to wailing, but barely audibly.

"Well, now, do you feel better?" the young mistress had asked her on one occasion as she had entered with swollen eyes.

"Better, miss," Natashka had said in a whisper, although, on account of the medicines, her heart would be stilled every now and then and her head was turning; and, walking up to the young lady, she had kissed her hand warmly.

And, for a long while thereafter, she walked about with drooping eyelashes, afraid to lift up her eyes at the young lady, touched by pity both for her mistress and for her own loneliness.

"Oo-ooh, you tuft-headed snake-in-the-grass!" Soloshka, one of her fellow-maids, had once yelled at her—Soloshka, who more often than anybody else had tried to become Nathalia's confidante in all her secrets and emotions, yet was forever running her head against Nathalia's brief, simple answers, precluding any of the charm of girlish friendship.

Natashka had smiled sadly.

"Oh, well," she had answered thoughtfully, "you're right, at that. Tell me who your friends are, and I'll tell you who you be.— There are times when I don't grieve as much after my father and my mother as I do after them tuft-head country folks of mine at Little Ploughs. . . ."

But she had hardly told the truth. She could not forget Little Ploughs; she could have told with rapture of many things concerning the place, had it not been for the role she had taken upon herself. Yet she had never really considered "them tuft-head country folks" as dear to her as her father and mother.

At Little Ploughs she had not at first considered as at all significant any of the new things surrounding her. She and Evsei had arrived toward morning, and on that morning the only things that had struck her as odd were that the hut was very long and very white, visible from afar among the surrounding plains; that the tuft-head woman who was stoking up the oven greeted them hospitably, while her tuft-head husband paid no attention to Evsei's talk. Evsei jabbered away with never a rest: about the masters, and about the Dry Valley overseer, and about the heat during their journey, and about what he had eaten in the town, and about Petr Petrovich—and, as a matter of course, about the affair of the little mirror, while Sharyi, the tuft-head mujik, or The Badger, as he was called in Dry Valley, had merely tossed his head from time to time, and, when Evsei had fallen quiet at last, suddenly glanced at him absent-mindedly, and most gaily began to sing *Blizzard Whirl, Blizzard Swirl* in a nasal whine. . . .

Then, little by little, she began coming to herself and to be wonderstruck by Little Ploughs, to find even more charm in the place and an ever-greater dissimilarity to Dry Valley. What was the hut of the tuft-heads alone worth, with its whiteness, its well-made, evenly cut thatch of reeds! How rich the orderliness of this hut's interior as compared with the slovenly poverty of the Dry Valley's dwellings! What costly tinsel images hung in one corner of this house—what wondrous paper flowers surrounded them—how beautifully the gaily broidered towels hung above them showed! And what about the flowered cloth on the table? And the dove-grey pots and pipkins, ranged row on row on the shelves near the oven?

But most amazing of all were her hosts. In just what way they were amazing she could not altogether understand, but she constantly felt that they were. Never yet had she seen any mujiks as neat, placid, and orderly as Sharyi. He was not tall; his head tapered to a wedge, and the thick, strong silver of its hair was clipped; he was clean-shaven, save for his moustaches, also silvery, and narrow, like a Tatar's; his face and neck were black from sunburn, and all

in deep wrinkles—but these, too, were somehow orderly, well defined, and, for some reason or other, called for. His walk was awkward, since he wore heavy boots; his breeches, of coarse white
linen, were stuck into these boots, and into his breeches he tucked
his shirt of the same material, roomy under the arm-pits, with a
turned-down collar. As he walked, he stooped over a little. But
neither this mannerism, nor his wrinkles, nor his grey hair, made
him look aged. There was none of our Dry Valley weariness, nor
of its sluggishness, about his face. His small eyes had a sharp and
slyly mocking look. He reminded Natashka of an old Serbian who
had once come wandering into Dry Valley with a boy who scraped
on a fiddle.

As for his tuft-head yoke-mate, Marina—she had been nicknamed
The Spear by the Dry Valley folk. Stately was this tall, fifty-year-
old woman. Her face, with its broad cheek-bones, was rather coarse,
yet almost good-looking because of its straightforwardness and the
austere liveliness of her eyes: one could not determine whether
they were agate or amber-grey, since they were as chatoyant as a
cat's. A yellowish tan covered evenly her smooth skin, so different
from the skin of the Dry Valley dwellers. A large black-and-gold,
red-dotted kerchief rested in a high turban on her head; by way of
a skirt she had a black, narrow length of woollen material closely
enveloping her elongated, almost maidenly contours and sharply
setting off the whiteness of her blouse. She shod her stockingless
feet in shoes with metal-tipped heels; her bare calves were thin,
but rounded out; from the sun they had become like polished yel-
low-brown wood. And when at times she would sing at her work,
contracting her eyebrows, in a strong, chesty voice, the song concerning the siege of Pochaev town by the unbelievers:

> *When the even-glow began*
> *And lit all Pochaev town—*

and of how the Mother of God had herself "come for to deliver"
the town's holy monastery—when she sang, there was in her voice
so much of hopelessness, of ululation, of something churchly, yet,

at the same time, so much of grandeur, of power, of menace, that Natashka, in eerie ecstasy, did not take her eyes off the singer.

This tuft-head couple had no children; Natashka was an orphan; and, had she been living in a Dry Valley household, she would have been called an adopted daughter and, at times, a thief; now they would have pitied her, now made her life miserable with recriminations. But these tuft-heads were almost cold to her, yet equable in their treatment of her, not at all inquisitive, and none too talkative.

In the autumn the country-wives and wenches of Kaluga were drafted for the reaping and the threshing; these women were dubbed "fly-aparts," because of their loose and motley sarafans. At such times the farm was a noisy place; there was a never-stilled din of talk. But Nathalia kept aloof from the fly-aparts; they had the repute of being loose, of having the pox; they were amply-bosomed, brazen, and saucy; they cursed atrociously and with gusto, bywords and pithy sayings simply pouring out of them; they mounted horses astride, like any mujik; they galloped along as if Old Nick himself were after them.

Had Nathalia's mode of life been an accustomed one, her grief would have become dissipated in frank confessions, in tears and songs. But then, her songs did not jibe with the songs of the others. The fly-aparts would lead off their songs in their coarse voices and then swell out in an inordinately close and stentorian chorus, with yells and whistling. All Sharyi would sing were things that were mocking and made you dance. While Marina in her songs—even the love-songs!—was austere, proud, and pensively sombre:

> *On the dam I willows planted,*
> *And they sway—*

she would narrate in a plaintive, drawling recitative, and then add, lowering her voice, decisively and hopelessly:

> *And the one I came to love—*
> *My own dear, my own love—*
> *Is gone away. . . .*

But what songs did Natashka know? What had remained in Dry Valley of Slavic song, which had degenerated there, had there become as shallow as a stream in dry weather? Only plaints against fate, against father and mother, because " 'gainst my will they are marryin' me, givin' me up to—" a cruel father-in-law, or a cruel mother-in-law, or cruel sisters-in-law. . . . Or else there were timorous reproaches to one who had whispered all sorts of sweet things into a fair one's ears and then had forsaken the owner thereof, up to them in trouble:

> *Weren't it only yesterday, before one an' all,*
> *That your own dear you did poor me call?*

And so in solitude, in the wilderness, she had drained, slowly, the first bitter-sweet venom of unrequited love, had overcome, through suffering, her shame, her jealousy, her fearful and endearing dreams, which had often come to her of nights, her unfulfillable reveries and expectations, which had long haunted her in the silent days of the steppe. Often a searing feeling of the wrong done her was replaced in her heart by tenderness—her passion and despair by resignation, by a desire for a life near *him* (though most unassuming, most unobtrusive), for a love forever hidden from all, and expecting nothing, demanding nothing.

The tidings, the news which reached her from Dry Valley, would sober her up. But if there were no tidings for a long time, if there were no feeling of the everyday life of Dry Valley, Dry Valley would begin to seem so lovely, so desired, that at times she had not strength enough to endure her loneliness and sorrow. . . . Suddenly Gervasska had appeared. Hurriedly, abruptly he had flung out to her all the news of Dry Valley; within half an hour he had told her what another could not have told in even a day—up to and including his "shoving" Grandfather to his death. And then he had said firmly:

"Well, and now good-bye forever!"

Burning her through and through with his huge eyes as she stood there overwhelmed, he called out as he set foot on the highway:

"And it's high time you knocked all that foolishness out of your head! He's like to marry any day, any minute now, whilst you ain't good enough to be his mistress, even.—Come to your senses!"

And come to her senses she did. She lived through the dreadful news, became her own self—and came to her senses.

After that the days began to drag one after the other, evenly, tediously, like those pilgrim women who kept on trudging over the paved road that ran past the farm, and, as they paused for a rest, held long conversations with her, teaching her patience and trustfulness in the Lord God, whose name was pronounced stolidly, piteously; but, above all, they taught her one rule: not to think.

"Whether we think or whether we don't, things ain't a-goin' to come out our way," the pilgrim women would say as they retied their bast slippers, puckering up their tortured faces and looking into the distance of the steppe with eyes of exhaustion. "There's a plenty of all things at the Lord God's. . . . Pluck a few scallions for us, lassie, when nobody's lookin'. . . ."

While others, as is their way, even sought to frighten her with her sins, with the other world; they held forth a promise of calamities and perils still worse than those of the present. And once Nathalia happened to dream two dreadful dreams, almost directly one after the other. She was forever thinking of Dry Valley—it was rather hard not to think of it at first! She thought of her young mistress, of Grandfather, of her own future; she was trying to foretell whether she would marry, and, if she did, when and whom. . . . On one occasion her thoughts so imperceptibly passed into a dream that, with perfect clearness, she saw that the time was just before the evening of a sultry, dusty, disquietingly windy day, and that she was hastening to a pond with buckets. . . . And suddenly she sees on a hillside a hideous, large-headed dwarf, a mujik in troddendown boots, hatless, with red elf-locks, all ruffled by the wind, in an unbelted shirt, fiery-red and fluttering. "Gaffer!" she called out in alarm and terror. "Why, is there a fire somewhere?"—"Everything's goin' to be blown down to the last stick right away!" the dwarf made answer, likewise in a shout that was muffled by the scorching wind. "There's a cloud comin' the like of which you never heard tell of! An' don't even dare think of gettin' married! . . ."

As for the other dream, it was still more frightful: she seemed to be standing, at noonday, in a hot, empty hut, which somebody had barred on the outside. She was well-nigh swooning, awaiting something to befall—and then, from behind the oven, there jumped out an enormous, grey he-goat. He got up on his hind legs and went straight for her—obscenely excited, with his eyes, which were burning like coals, joyously insane and imploring. "I'm your bridegroom!" he cried out in a human voice, running up to her quickly and awkwardly, with a quick patter of his small hind hoofs, and, at full speed, falling on her breast with his front ones. . . .

When, after such dreams, she would leap up on her bed in the entry, she all but died from the palpitation of her heart, from her fear of the dark, and from the thought that she had never a soul whom she might come running to.

"Lord Jesus!" she would whisper in a patter. "Mother of God, Queen of Heaven, and all ye sainted martyrs of God!" But, since all the sainted martyrs appeared to her brown-hued and headless, like St. Mercurius, she would feel still more terrified.

And when she came to thinking over her dreams, she'd start getting it into her head that her years as a young girl were at an end, that her destiny had already been determined (it was not for nothing that something extraordinary had befallen her: her love for the young master!), that some other trials were awaiting her, that she must emulate the self-restraint of the tuft-head couple, and the simplicity and resignation of the pilgrim women. And, since all natives of Dry Valley are aye fond of playing parts, of hypnotizing themselves with the ineluctability of that which apparently has to be, although they themselves invent the latter, Natashka consequently assumed a part as well.

8

S H E could hardly stand on her feet from joy when, on the eve of St. Peter's Day, having jumped out on the threshold, she understood that Bodulya had come to fetch her, as she caught sight of the dust-covered, ramshackle cart from Dry Valley; as she caught sight of the torn hat on Bodulya's shaggy head, of his tangled, sunfaded beard, his face, tired and excited, ill-favored and aged before its time, its features even somehow incomprehensively lowly and disproportionate. She caught sight, too, of a hound she knew well, likewise shaggy, bearing a certain resemblance not only to Bodulya but to all of Dry Valley; this hound was of a dull grey along his spine, while from the front his chest and thick-furred neck seemed just as if they had been smoked through and through by the smoke of a chimneyless hut.

But Bodulya had voiced his surprise—and she had become self-possessed, had felt an access of pride, and had entered into her part.

On the way home Bodulya had jabbered away about whatever happened to pop into his head. He spoke of the Crimean War, now seemingly rejoicing over it, now deploring it, and Natashka would say reasoningly:

"Well, now, it seems like them French mounseers has to be brought up short. . . ."

The entire long day *en route* to Dry Valley passed in an uncanny sensation of gazing with new eyes upon old, familiar things, of reliving, as she neared her native region, her former self, of noticing changes, of recognizing the people she met.

At the turn of the highway into Dry Valley, on the fallow lands grown over with goldilocks, a two-year-old colt was romping; an urchin, with one bare foot holding down a rope halter, was hugging the colt's neck and striving to throw his other foot over the colt's back; the animal would not submit, however, running about and jolting the urchin. And Natashka became joyously excited as she recognized the lad.

They came upon Nazarushka, the centenarian gaffer, who no longer sat in his empty cart like a mujik, squatting on his heels, but like a country-wife, with the legs stretched out; his shoulders were hunched up high, tensely and weakly, his eyes were colorless and pitifully mournful; "there weren't enough of him left to put in a coffin, even, he were that wasted away"; he had no head-covering, and was clad in a long, worn-out shirt, all leaden-hued from his constantly lying atop the oven. And again her heart gave a start: she recalled how, three years back, Arcadii Petrovich, the best-natured and lightest-hearted of men, had wanted to flog this same Nazarushka, who had been caught red-handed stealing a wisp of a radish out of the truck-garden, and how, almost dead with fright, he had wept in the midst of his fellow-servants, who had surrounded him and were laughing and shouting:

"'Tain't no use, Gran'pa—you sure will have to take your breeches down! There ain't no gettin' out of it!"

And how her heart had begun to thump when she caught sight of the common, of the string of huts, and the estate itself: the garden, the high roof of the house, the rear walls of the servants' quarters, of the storehouses, of the stables! A field of yellow rye, choked with corn-flowers, came up to these very walls, up to the quitch-grass and the cotton-thistles. Somebody's white, brown-spotted calf was deep among the oats, stripping and munching their clusters. All the surroundings were peaceful, simple, usual; it was only in her mind that everything was becoming even more unusual, ever more disquieting: in her mind, which had become altogether confused when the cart started rolling briskly through the yard, with borzois showing whitely here and there, as head-stones show in a country churchyard—when, after two years of living in a hut, she had first entered the cool house, so familiarly smelling of wax candles, of lime blossoms, of pantry odors, of Arcadii Petrovich's Cossack saddle, thrown down on a bench in the entry, of quail cages, now empty and hung over a window—and when she had timidly glanced up at St. Mercurius, who had been shifted out of Grandfather's bedroom into a corner of the entry. . . .

As of yore, the sombre dining-room was gaily lit by the sun, shining from the garden into the little windows. A chick, which for some unknown reason had got into the house, was emitting orphaned peeps as it wandered through the parlor. Lime blossoms were drying on the sun-warmed, brightly lit window-sills and giving forth a sweet fragrance. . . . It seemed as if all the things from of old which surrounded her now had taken on a new youth, as they always do in houses where there has been a recent death. In everything—everything!—and especially in the scent of the lime blossoms, she felt a part of her own soul, her childhood, her adolescence, her first love. And she felt pity for those who had grown up, who had died, who had changed. The lads and lasses of her own age had grown up. Many old men and women, whose heads nodded from decrepitude and who had occasionally looked out dully on God's world from the thresholds of the servants' quarters, had forever vanished out of that world. Daria Justinovna had vanished. Grandfather had vanished, who had feared death so, like a child, who had thought that death would overcome him slowly, preparing him for the final dreadful hour, and who had been mown down so unexpectedly, with such lightning speed, by its scythe.

And one could not believe that he no longer was, that it was precisely he who had crumbled to dust under the mound of a grave near the church in the Chirkizovo hamlet. One could not believe that this black, gaunt, sharp-nosed woman, now apathetic, now frenzied, now uneasily talkative and as frank with Nathalia as with an equal, and now pulling out handfuls of that same Nathalia's hair—one could not believe that this woman was the young lady Tonechka. One could not understand why the house was run by some Claudia Markovna or other—a little shrill-tongued woman with a tiny black moustache. . . . Once Natashka had timidly peeped into her bedroom, had caught a glimpse of the fateful little mirror—and had felt in her heart a sweet surging of all her former fears, joys, tenderness, expectation of shame and happiness, the odor of dew-covered burdocks under an evening glow. . . . But she drove deep within the secret places of her heart all her emotions, all her inclinations, and was ever taming, ever calming herself with the words of the pilgrim women, which words seemed to her the pinnacle of wisdom: "There's a plenty of all things at the Lord God's. . . ."

The old, old blood of Dry Valley was flowing in her veins! There was all too little flavor in the bread she ate, grown on the clayey soil surrounding Dry Valley. There was all too little savor in the water she drank, drawn from those ponds which her grand-sires had dug in the bed of the dried river. Neither of the basti-nado nor the rack was she afraid; the only thing she was afraid of was to be made a laughing-stock. Exhausting workdays did not frighten her; what frightened her was the unusual. Not even death held any terror for her; but she was thrown into trepidation by dreams, the darkness of night, storm, thunder—and fire. She bore within her, like a babe under the heart, a dim expectancy of some inevitable calamities or other. . . .

This expectancy aged her. Then, too, she was incessantly assur-ing herself that her youth had passed and was seeking confirmation of that belief in everything. And not even a year had gone by since her return to Dry Valley when there was not a trace left of that youthful feeling with which she had once more set foot across the threshold of its house.

Claudia Markovna was duly confined. Theodosia, the poultry-keeper, was elevated to nursedom. And Theodosia, who was still a young woman, donned the dark dress of an old woman and be-came filled with humility and the fear of God. The new Khrush-chev was as yet barely able to goggle his milk-sodden, meaningless little eyes; he dribbled saliva in bubbles; overcome by the weight of his head, he helplessly slumped forward, and bawled ferociously. And yet he was already styled the young master; ancient, ancient bits of baby talk were already heard issuing from the nursery:

"There he is, there he is, that old boogy-mans with hims big sack! Hey, there, boogy-mans—'tain't no use your comin' to us— we ain't a-goin' to let you have the young master! He ain't a-goin' to cry no more! . . ."

And Natashka followed Theodosia's example, considering herself a nurse also: the nurse and crony of her ailing young mistress.

Olga Kyrillovna died that winter, and Natashka managed to beg permission to go to the funeral with the old women who were rounding out their old days in the servants' quarters. At Lunevo, after the burial, she went through the ritual of eating shredded wheat and honey, which mess inspired her with aversion by its insipid and mawkish taste, and, upon returning to Dry Valley, told with touched emotion that the late mistress had "looked that natural, like she were alive," although even the old women could not pluck up enough courage to look at the coffin with that monstrous body.

And in the spring they imported a wizard from the Chermashnyi settlement for the young mistress: the celebrated Clim Erokhin, a comely, rich freeholder, with a hoary beard, with hoary, curly locks, parted in the middle; a very capable husbandman, usually very simple in his speech, but who became transformed into a magus by the bedside of the ailing. His clothing was remarkably sturdy and neat: an iron-drab coat, cut in at the waist and with long, belled skirts, a red sash, and strong, well-sewn boots. Crafty and keen were his small eyes; piously did they seek the holy images; carefully, with his well-built torso bent ever so slightly, would he enter the house; he started the conversation in a business-like manner. At first he spoke about the crops, about the rainfall and the drought; then he would drink tea,—leisurely, daintily; then he would again cross himself, and then (and only after all that) would inquire about the ailing person:

"It's sundown . . . gettin' dark . . . it's time," he would say with a mysterious air.

The young mistress was having the ague; she was on the verge of rolling off the bed to the floor in convulsions as, sitting in her bedroom at dusk, she waited for Clim to appear on the threshold. Nathalia, who was standing near her, was also enveloped in eerie fear from head to foot. The entire house was falling quiet; even the lady of the house herself was packing her room full of serving-wenches and talking in whispers. None durst light even a single candle; not a single voice durst raise itself. The merry Soloshka, who was doing sentry-go in the corridor near the young lady's door, in case Clim should call out or have some order to give—Soloshka felt things growing dark before her eyes, while her heart was thumping in her throat. And now he was going past her, untying, as he went, a small handkerchief with certain bits of shamanistic bones. Then, amid the graveyard silence, she heard his loud, odd voice resounding in the bedroom:

"Arise, bondswoman of God!"

Next his hoary head appeared out of the half-closed door.

"A board!" he let drop in a lifeless voice.

And the young lady, with her eyes popping out from terror, and her whole body grown as cold as a corpse, was made to stand upon this board, which was placed on the floor. It was so dark by now that Nathalia could barely distinguish Clim's face. And suddenly he was launching into his incantation, in a strange voice that somehow seemed to come from a distance:

"Philat shall arise . . . and shall the windows open . . . and throw the doors ajar . . . and call out and say: 'Come, pining—come, yearning! . . .'"

"Come, pining—come, yearning!" he was now calling out, with sudden power and awesome authority. "Pining, disappear—into woods dark, drear; thou art not wanted here! Out upon the ocean, where the sea-mew flies"—he had by now fallen to muttering, in a muffled, sinister patter—"out upon the wide sea Rowdy Isle doth rise. . . . There an old bitch lies, with grey fur and eyes. . . ."

And Nathalia felt that there were not, and that there could not be, any words more terrible than these, which at once carried all her soul somewhere to the marge of a wild, faery, primevally barbarous world. And one could not but believe in their potency, just as Clim himself could not but believe in it—Clim, who at times wrought downright miracles with those whom malady possessed; the same Clim who was saying, as he sat in the entry after his spell of witch-doctoring, mopping his sweating forehead with a handkerchief and again beginning on the tea:

"Well, now, there's still two more sundowns to go. . . . Mebbe, if God so wills, she'll get to feelin' summat easier. . . . Did you sow buckwheat this season, ma'am? They do be sayin' buckwheat's comin' up fine this year—fine as fine can be!"

They were expecting the masters to come back from Crimea that summer. But Arcadii Petrovich sent a registered letter with a new demand for money, and the news that they could not return before the beginning of autumn, by reason of Petr Petrovich's wound—a minor wound, but one that required rest. Danilovna, the Sibyl of Chirkizovo, had someone sent to her, to ask if this trouble would end well. Danilovna went off into a dance and fell to clicking her fingers, which, of course, signified: It would that. And the mistress was reassured.

As for the young lady and Nathalia, they had troubles of their own to think of. The young lady had felt eased-up at first. But toward the end of midsummer her trouble started all over again; again came the pining, and such a fear of thunder-storms, of conflagrations, and of something else, which she was keeping secret within her, that she had other things on her mind besides her brothers. And Nathalia got into the same frame of mind concerning them. Although she remembered to pray for Petr Petrovich's health in every prayer of hers (just as afterwards, throughout her life to her very grave, she used to pray for the repose of his soul), the young mistress was, nevertheless, the nearest of all to her by now. And her young mistress was infecting her ever more and more with her fears, expectations of calamities, and with that which she was keeping a secret.

And that summer was a sultry, dusty, windy one, with thunder-storms an everyday occurrence. Dark, disquieting rumors were circulating among the common folk: about some new war or other, about certain uprisings and conflagrations. Some were sayin' that, any minute now, all the mujiks would be allowed to go free, whilst others was sayin' just the opposite: startin' in with autumn, all the mujiks was goin' to be took an' made into clean-shaven recruities —every mother's son on 'em. And, as is ever the way in troublous times, vagabonds, fey folk, and monks sprang up in incomputable numbers. And the young mistress all but had fist-fights with the mistress, all on their account, furnishing them with bread and eggs.

One of these visitors was Dronya—lanky, red-haired, inordinately ragged. He was simply a drunkard, but played the little innocent. He'd walk through the yard toward the house in such deep thought that he knocked his head against walls and leapt away with a joyous face after every such collision.

"My little birdies!" he would cry out in a falsetto, hopping about, distorting his whole body, and especially his right arm, making something in the nature of a shield against the sun out of it. "My little birdies are off—they're off, flyin' through the heavens!"

And Nathalia, following the example of all peasant women, watched him as one is supposed to watch the lesser folk of God: stolidly and pityingly. As for the young lady, she would make a dash for the window, and, with tears, would shout in a piteous voice:

"Dronya, thou most worthy man of God, pray to God for me, sinner that I be!"

And at this shout Natashka's eyes would become staring from dread suppositions.

Another visitor was Timosha Klichinṣky, of the Klinchino settlement: small, womanishly fat, with big breasts, with the face of a squint-eyed baby that had grown daft and asthmatic from its corpulence, yellow of hair, in a blouse of white calico and short, small breeches. As he neared the front steps, he walked hastily, taking small steps and walking on the toes of his swollen feet, and his narrow little eyes had such a look as if he had just scrambled out of deep water or had just saved himself from almost inescapable peril.

"Troubbel!" he would mumble, gasping. "Troubbel. . . ."

They would calm him down, feed him, and await some word or exploit from him. But he said nothing, breathing hard through his nose and greedily smacking his lips. And having done with smacking his lips, he again tossed his sack over his shoulders and uneasily sought his staff.

"But when are you coming again?" the young mistress would

call after him. And he would answer also by calling out, in an incongruously high alto, for some reason confusing her patronymic:

"'Bout Holy Week—'bout Holy Week, Lukianovna!"

And the young mistress wailed piteously after him, by now in a tone that was near to confession:

"Holy man of God! Pray to God for me, sinner that I be!"

And the others present crossed themselves and sighed, inasmuch as there really were tidings of calamities coming from everywhere, almost every day—tidings of thunderstorms and conflagrations. And the ancient fear of fire was constantly growing in Dry Valley. Just as soon as the sandy-yellow sea of ripening grain would begin to dim under a cloud gathering at the back of the estate—just as soon as the first gust of wind swirled up over the common, and a distant thunder-peal rumbled by heavily—the country-wives rushed to bring the small, dark panels of the icons out on their thresholds, and to get ready pots of milk, which, as everybody knows, quenches a fire the fastest of all. And in the manor-house the scissors went flying out of the window into the nettles; the sanctified towel, of fearful potency, was taken out; the window-curtains were drawn; wax candles were lit with trembling hands. . . .

Even the lady of the house became infected with fear—and one could not tell whether this were a pretence or if she were in downright earnest. Formerly she used to say that a thunder-storm was "a phenomenon of nature." Now she, too, would make the sign of the cross and shut her eyes tight, crying out at every lightning-flash, and, in order to increase her own fright as well as the fright of those surrounding her, she was forever talking about a certain unusual thunder-storm which had broken out in the year 1771, in Tyrol, and which had killed one hundred and eleven people, all at one fell swoop. And those who heard her caught up the refrain and hastened to tell their own stories: now about the willow by the highway, burned to ashes by lightning; now about a peasant woman who had been stunned by thunder, just the other day, at Chirkizovo; now about a certain troika, so deafened by a thunder-peal while travelling that all the three horses had fallen on their knees.

Finally a certain Iushka attached himself to these vigils—"a monk who had transgressed," as he styled himself.

9

BY BIRTH Iushka was a mujik. However, he'd never done an honest day's work in all his life, but lived wherever God might send him, paying for the hospitality extended to him with stories about his utter idleness and about his "transgression." "I'm a mujik, brother, yet smart, an', to top it all off, I also look like a hunch-back," he used to say. "So why should I work?"

And, true enough, his gaze was like that of a hunch-back: caustic and clever. He had no hair growing on his face; his shoulders, because of rachitis of the thoracic cavity, he held raised; he gnawed his finger-nails; his fingers, with which he was every minute tossing back his long, bronze-red hair, were thin and strong. To till the soil had seemed to him "unseemly an' boresome." And so he'd gone to the abbey at Kiev, had "grown up a bit there," and had been expelled for his "transgression." Then, having reasoned out that to pretend to be a pilgrim to holy places, a man seeking salvation for his soul, was an old dodge and, on top of that, might turn out an unprofitable one, he tried to pretend something else: without taking off his cassock, he began to boast openly of his idleness and lewdness, to smoke and to drink as much as he could (he never grew drunk), to jeer and mock at the abbey, and to explain, with the aid of the most indecent gestures and bodily movements, for just what reason he had been driven out of that abbey.

"Well, you know how it is," he would tell the mujiks, winking, "you know—right off they took an' chucked this slave of God right out on his ear, for that same thing. An' so I ups an' starts rollin' home, to my own region. . . . I'll manage to get along, now!"

And he was right: get along he did. And White Russia, his home region, received him no less hospitably, shameless sinner that he was, than she did those who sought salvation for their souls:

it gave him food and drink, put him up for the night, listened to him with rapture.

"And so you just took a vow never to work?" the mujiks would ask him, their eyes glistening in anticipation of his caustic frank-nesses.

"The Devil alone could make me work now!" Iushka would respond. "I'm spoilt, brother, that's what! I'm more ruttish nor the goat we had in the abbey. You take these same wenches, now (I wouldn't want the grown women, not if you was to give 'em to me for nothin'); they fear me like death, an' yet they love me. Oh, well, I'm not so bad meself! I mayn't have no fancy feathers on me, but me bones is trim!"

Having bobbed up at the Dry Valley estate, he, like one who knew his way about, went straight into the house—into the entry, where Natashka was sitting on a bench, humming to herself: "I, a maiden young, as I swept the hut, found me something sweet." Catching sight of him, she jumped up in terror.

"Why, and who are you?" she cried out.

"A man," Iushka answered, quickly looking her over from head to foot. "Tell your missus I'm here."

"Who is it?" the mistress as well called out from the dining-room.

But Iushka reassured her in a moment; he told her he was an erstwhile monk and no desertin' soldier, as she had probably thought; that he was returnin' to his birthplace, an' that he begged that he be searched first an' then be allowed to stay overnight, to rest up a bit, like. And he so impressed the mistress with his straightforwardness that the very next day he was able to shift himself to the footmen's quarters and become absolutely one of the household. Thunder-storm followed thunder-storm, but he in-defatigably entertained his hostesses with stories; he struck upon the idea of boarding up the skylights in order to safeguard the roof from lightnings; he ran out on the steps during the most fearful thunder-claps, in order to demonstrate how little they were to be feared; he helped the serving-wenches to prepare and bring in the samovars.

The wenches eyed him askance, feeling his quick, lecherous

glances upon them, but they laughed at his jests, while Natashka, whom he had already more than once stopped in the dark corridor with a quick whisper: "I've fallen in love with you, wench!" durst not lift up her eyes to him. He was both repulsive to her because of the smell of atrocious tobacco which had permeated his whole cassock, and frightful . . . frightful.

She already knew to a certainty what would befall. She used to sleep alone in the corridor, near the door of her young lady's bedroom, and Iushka had already told her curtly: "I'll come. You may slit my throat, but I'll come. But if you start screamin', I'll burn the house down to the ground, an' all of you with it. . . ." But what deprived her of strength most of all was the consciousness that something *inevitable* was being consummated, that the realization of her fearful dream was at hand, that evidently it had been written down for her since birth that she was to perish with her young mistress.

By now all understood that the Devil himself came to dwell in the house of nights. All understood exactly what it was (outside of thunder-storms and conflagrations) that was driving the young mistress out of her mind, that compelled her to moan delectably and wildly in her sleep, only to leap up thereafter with such horrible screams that the most deafening peals of thunder were as nothing compared with them. She screamed:

"The Serpent of Eden, of Jerusalem, is strangling me!"

And who else should this Serpent be save the Fiend, save that grey he-goat that enters the rooms of women and maids of nights? And is there anything in the world more fearful than his visitations in the dark, on inclement nights with never-silenced peals of thunder, and with reflections of the lightnings upon the black icons? That passion, that lust with which the fly-by-night vagabond whispered to Natashka were also not human; how, then, could one offer resistance to them? Thinking of her fateful, her inevitable hour as she sat on her horse-blanket, spread on the floor in the corridor, and gazing intently into the darkness with a pounding heart, hearkening to every crackling and rustling in the sleeping house, even the least, she was already feeling the first attacks of that painful ailment which for a long time tortured her afterwards: her foot would suddenly begin to itch, a sharp, pricking spasm would pass through it, bending, twisting all the toes toward the sole—and then, excruciatingly, voluptuously twisting the sinews, ran over the legs, over the whole body, up to the very gullet, until there was a moment when she wanted to cry out, and that still more frenziedly, still more delectably and agonizingly, than the young mistress did. . . .

And the inevitable was consummated. Iushka came—precisely on that fearful night that marked the end of summer, on the night before the Day of Elijah the Dispenser, that ancient fire-darter. There was no thunder on that night, and there was no sleep for Natashka. She dozed off—and suddenly became wide awake, as if from a jolt. It was the very dead of night—she understood this with her insanely pounding heart. She leapt up and looked at one end of the corridor, then the other: on all sides the sky, silent, full of fire and mysteries, was flaring up, catching on flame, quivering, and blinding one with its golden and wan-blue heat-lightning. The entry was momently turning as light as day. She started running—and stopped as if she were rooted to the spot; the aspen timbers which had long been lying in the yard under the window showed blindingly white whenever the heat-lightning flared. She wanted to go into the dining-room. There one window was raised; one could hear the even noise of the garden. The room was still darker than the entry, but the fiery light flickered still more vividly outside all the panes; everything would be flooded with darkness, only, the next moment, to start quivering again, to burst into flame, now here, now there—and the whole garden, with its lace-work of tree-tops, its spectres of pale-green birches and poplars, would tremble, grow, and appear in silhouette against the enormous horizon, now golden, now pale violet.

" 'Out upon the wide sea Rowdy Isle doth rise . . .' " she fell to whispering. " 'There an old bitch lies, with grey fur and eyes. . . .' "

And no sooner had she uttered these primitively awesome words than, turning around, she caught sight of Iushka, who, with shoulders hunched up, was standing two paces away from her. A flash of heat-lightning lit up his face—pale, with the eyes like black rings. Inaudibly he ran up to her, quickly clasped her around the waist with his long arms—and, crushing her, with a single swing threw her first on her knees, then flat on her back, on the cold floor of the entry. . . .

Iushka came to her on the following night as well. He came also many other nights—and she, losing consciousness from horror and aversion, submissively gave herself up to him. She durst not even think of resisting him, nor of imploring protection from her mistresses or the domestics, just as her young lady durst not resist the devil who, of nights, took his delight in her, and just as (so they say) even Grandmother herself, an imperious belle, durst not resist her house-serf Tkach, a desperate good-for-naught and a thief, who was at long last sent off to Siberia, as a settler. . . . Finally Natashka palled upon Iushka; Dry Valley, too, palled upon him, and he vanished suddenly, even as he had suddenly appeared.

A month after his vanishing Nathalia felt that she was going to be a mother. And in September, on the day following the return of the young masters from the war, the manor-house at Dry Valley caught on fire and blazed long and fearfully: her other dream had been fulfilled as well. It caught on fire at dusk, during a downpour, from a bolt of lightning—from a golden ball, which, as Soloshka said, had leapt out of the stove in Grandfather's bedroom and had gone dashing, bouncing through all the rooms. As for Nathalia, who, upon catching sight of the smoke and fire, had started running with all her might from the bathhouse (the bathhouse, where she passed whole days and nights in tears)—Nathalia told afterwards that in the garden she had run up against someone clad in a red, close-fitting kaftan and a high Cossack cap with gold braid; he, too, was running with all *his* might through the wet bushes and burdocks. Whether all this had really happened or had been merely an illusory image, Nathalia could not vouch. The only well-authenticated thing is that the terror which had overwhelmed her had also freed her from the child she had been expecting.

And from that autumn she had faded. Her life entered that

everyday rut which she did not get out of until her very end. Aunt
Tonia was taken to the bones of a saint at Voronezh. After that
the Devil no longer dared approach her, and she calmed down, beginning to live like everybody else. The disorder of her mind and
soul told only in the glitter of her wild eyes, in her extreme sloven-
liness, in a furious irritability, and in a mood of depression whenever the weather was bad.

Nathalia, too, had been with her at the visit to the saint's bones,
and she, too, had attained during this journey to tranquillity, to a
solution of all that had already seemed inescapable. Into what
trembling she used to be thrown by the mere thought of her meeting with Petr Petrovich! No matter how she steeled herself in
preparation for it, it was beyond her power to imagine that meeting calmly. And what of Iushka—what of her disgrace, her ruin!
But the very uniqueness of this ruin, the unusual depth of her sufferings, that element of the fatal which was present in her misfortune (why, it was not in vain that the horror of the fire had well-
nigh coincided with it!), and the pilgrimage to the sainted martyr's
shrine—all these had given her the right to look simply and calmly
into the eyes not only of all those surrounding her, but even those
of Petr Petrovich. God himself had marked her and her young
mistress with His baleful finger; were *they* the ones to fear people?
As a black little nun, as a meek and simple servant, light and pure,
just as if she had already taken the viaticum—thus did she re-enter
the house at Dry Valley upon her return from Voronezh; unwaver-
ingly did she approach to kiss Petr Petrovich's hand. And for but
an instant did her heart quiver—youthfully, tenderly, like a young
girl's—when her lips touched his small, swarthy hand with its turquoise ring. . . .

Things dropped back to their everyday routine in Dry Valley.
Definite rumors concerning the emancipation of the serfs arrived,
and even evoked alarm among both the household servants and
the people in the village. What lay ahead of them—something
worse, perhaps? It's easy enough to say: Start living a new life!
The masters, too, were faced with living a new life, and yet they
hadn't known how to live even in the old way. . . . Grandfather's

death; then the war, and the comet, which latter threw the whole country into terror; next the burning of the manor-house, and after that the rumors concerning emancipation: all these had rapidly changed the faces and the souls of the masters, had deprived them of their youth, their insouciance, their former fits of flaring up and cooling down, but did give them ill nature, tedium, hard fault-finding with one another. "Squabbles," as our father used to put it, sprang up; things reached the dog-lashes-at-table stage. . . .

Need began to remind them of the insistent necessity of mending, somehow or other, their affairs, which had been thoroughly spoiled by the Crimean War, by the fire, by debts. And in the management of the estate the brothers only interfered with each other. One (Petr Petrovich) was absurdly greedy, stern, and suspicious; the other (Arcadii Petrovich) was absurdly generous, kind-hearted, and trustful. Having patched up an agreement, of sorts, between them, they decided upon an enterprise which was bound to bring in a big return. They mortgaged the estate and bought about three hundred underfed, gaunt horses; they collected them through almost the whole district, with the help of a certain gypsy by the name of Ilya Samsonov. Their intention was to feed the crow-baits up during the winter and to sell them at a profit in the spring. But, after having consumed an enormous quantity of flour and straw, the horses (almost all of them, one after the other) dropped dead toward the spring. . . .

And the discord between the brothers kept on growing and growing. At times things reached such a pass that they grabbed their knives and guns. And no one knows what the end of all this would have been had not a new calamity descended upon Dry Valley.

One winter day, in the fourth year after his return from the Crimea, Petr Petrovich went off to Lunevo, where he had a mistress. He lived for two days on the farm; all the time there he drank, and was tipsy even when he started for home. It was snowing very hard; the open sleigh, covered with a rug, was harnessed with two horses, but Petr Petrovich gave orders to unharness the off-horse, a young, hot-blooded animal that sank up to its belly in the porous snow, and to tie it behind the sleigh, while he himself lay down to sleep, with his head toward it. Dusk—misty, leaden-hued—was coming on. And, as he was falling off to sleep, Petr Petrovich called out to Evsei Bodulya (whom he frequently took with him instead of the regular coachman, Vasska the Cossack, being afraid that Vasska would do away with him, since all the domestics were incensed against him because of floggings)—Petr Petrovich called out: "Get along with you!" and kicked Evsei in the back. And the shaft-horse, a powerful bay, already wet, steaming, and with his milt clacking, dashed off with them over the snow-filled, "hard-sleddin'" road, into the dark turbidity of the desert plain, toward the ever-deepening, frowning winter night. . . .

But at midnight, when everybody at Dry Valley was already dead asleep, someone knocked in quick alarm at a window of the entry where Nathalia slept. She jumped down from her bench and, barefooted, ran out on the front steps. Near the steps, showing dimly and darkly, stood the open sleigh, the horses, and Evsei, who was holding a whip.

"Trouble, last—trouble!" he began to mumble, in a muffled voice—oddly, as if it were all a dream. "The master's been killed . . . by the off-horse. . . . It ran too fast, slipped up on its haunches, an' struck him with one of its fore hoofs as it were tryin' to get up. . . . Crushed his whole face in. . . . He's already beginnin' to get cold. . . . 'Tweren't me that done it—'tweren't me, s'help me Christ, 'tweren't me!"

Coming down the steps without a word, her bare feet sinking in the snow, Nathalia walked up to the open sleigh, crossed herself, sank to her knees, clasped the icy, bloodied head to her, and fell to kissing it and screaming, so that she could be heard all over the estate, in a wildly joyous scream, strangling from her sobs and her laughter.

10

WHENEVER it befell us to rest after cities in the quiet and poverty-stricken wilderness of Dry Valley, Nathalia would relate to us, anew and anew, the tale of her perished life. And at times her eyes would darken, would become fixed, her voice passing into a stern, measured half-whisper. And there was forever coming to my recollection the crude image of the saint which had hung in a corner of the entry in our old house. Beheaded, the saint had come to his fellow-townsmen, bringing his lifeless head in his hands as witness to his story. . . .

Even those few material traces of the past which we had on a time found in Dry Valley were vanishing by now. Our sires and grandsires had left us no portraits, no letters—not even the simple appurtenances of their daily existence. And whatever little there had been had all perished in the fire. For a long time there had been standing in the entry a certain trunk, bound with hair-seal-skin, worn bald in some spots and with tatters that had turned as hard as wood; it had been bound therewith a century ago, this trunk of Grandfather's, made of curly Karelian birch, and with drawers that could be pulled out. It had been stuffed chock-full of charred French vocabularies, and with churchly books that were unbelievably soiled and covered with wax-candle drippings. Subsequently this trunk, too, had vanished. The ponderous furniture that had stood in the dining-room and the parlor vanished as well or got broken. . . . The house was becoming ramshackle, settling more and more into the ground. All those long years which have passed over it since the time of the last events told of here had been for it the years of a lingering death. . . . And its past was becoming ever more legendary.

The Dry Valley folk grew amid a life that was dull, sombre, but still a life that was intricate, that had a semblance of a settled existence and of well-being. To judge by the inertia of this existence, to judge by the adherence of the Dry Valley folk to that existence, one might have thought that there would never be an end to it. But they, these descendants of the steppe nomads, were submissive, weak, "no end chicken-hearted and touchy when it come to being punished"! And, as under a plough furrowing a field the small hummocks over the underground passages and burrows of the hamsters disappear, one after the other, without leaving a trace, even so did the Dry Valley nests disappear before our eyes, rapidly and leaving never a trace. And the dwellers in those nests perished, scattered; as for those that had survived, somehow or other, they, also somehow or other, were dragging out the remnant of their days. And we had come not upon a social order, not upon life, but merely upon recollections of both, upon a half-wild simplicity of existence.

Ever more rarely with the years did we visit our steppe region. And ever more unkindred was it becoming to us, ever more faintly did we feel our tie with that mode of life and that class whence we had issued. Many of our clan are illustrious and of ancient lineage (even as our branch is). The chronicles cite our names; our ancestors were not only royal dapifers, and leaders in battle, and "men of high rank," but the nearest of fellow-champions, and even of kin, to the tsars. And, had they called themselves knights, had those of our branch been born a little more toward the west, how steadfastly we would speak of them, how long we would still maintain our position! A descendant of the knights could not say that within half a century a whole class had well-nigh vanished from off the face of the earth; that so many of us had degenerated, had gone out of our minds, had laid violent hands upon ourselves, had drunk ourselves to ruin, had sunk and simply become lost somewhere in the shuffle! Such a descendant could not confess, as I am confessing, that we have not even the least definite idea of the life not only of our remote ancestors, but actually of that of our great-grandsires; he could not confess that with every day it is becoming ever more difficult for us to imagine even that which occurred only half a century ago!

That place where the Lunevo estate had stood has long since been ploughed and sown, just as the ground has been ploughed and sown on the sites of many other estates as well. Dry Valley still held on, somehow or other. But, after having cut down the last birches in the garden, after having disposed, in parcels, of almost all the arable land, even its owner, the son of Petr Petrovich, forsook the old place; he went to work, becoming a conductor on a railroad. And the old women who dwelt in Dry Valley—Claudia Markovna, Aunt Tonia, Nathalia—were drearily dragging out their last years. Spring changed to summer, summer to autumn,

autumn to winter. . . . They had lost count of these changes. They lived by and in recollections, dreams, quarrels, cares for their daily bread. In the summer those places where the estate had of yore spread wide were sunk deep in fields of rye belonging to the mujiks. The house they surrounded had become visible from afar. The brushwood (all that was left of the garden) had become such a wilderness that the quail called near the very balcony. But summer wasn't so bad! "Summer is paradise for us!" the old women used to say. It was the rainy autumns and the snowy winters that were long and hard in Dry Valley. Cold and hunger reigned then in the empty, decaying house. It was drifted over by blizzards, penetrated through and through by the piercing, frosty Sarmatian wind. As for heating, the house was heated very rarely. Of evenings a small tin lamp shed its meager light through the windows of the mistress's chamber—the only habitable one. The mistress, with her eye-glasses on, wearing a short sheepskin coat and felt boots, knit away at a stocking, bending toward the little lamp. Nathalia dozed on the cold ledge of the oven. And the young mistress, looking like a Siberian shaman, sat in her hut and puffed on a pipe. When Aunt was not on the outs with Claudia Markovna, the latter would put her little lamp, not on the table, but on the windowsill. And Aunt Tonia sat in the strange, faint half-light which fell from the house into the interior of her icy hut, cluttered up with the broken pieces of old furniture, piled with shards of broken dishes, encumbered with the old pianoforte, which had slumped over on its side. So icy was this hut that the hens, toward the care of which all of Aunt Tonia's forces were directed, used to have their feet frozen as they passed the night on these shards and broken pieces of furniture. . . .

But now the Dry Valley estate is altogether empty. All those mentioned in this chronicle have died, and so have all their neighbors, all their coevals. And at times one thinks: "Come, now—*have* they ever really lived in this world?"

Only when visiting country churchyards does one feel that all this has actually happened; one feels even an eerie nearness to these people. But even to feel this one has to make an effort; one has to sit, to ponder, over the grave of a kinsman—that is, if one can but find it. It is a shameful thing to say, but it cannot be concealed: we do not know the graves of Grandfather, of Grandmother, of Petr Petrovich. All we know is that their place is near the altar of the little old church in the Chirkizovo hamlet. There is no getting through to this church in the winter-time: it is surrounded by waist-high snow-drifts, out of which a cross sticks up here and there, or the top of a bare bush, or even some single, scraggly twig.

On a summer day you drive through a hot, quiet, and empty village street, hitch your horse near the church enclosure, beyond which the fir-trees stand in a dark-green wall, baking in the heat of the sun. Beyond the wicket, open all the way, beyond the white church with its rusty cupola, is a whole grove of low, many-branched elms, ash-trees, osiers; shade and coolness are everywhere. One wanders for a long time along bushes, along hummocks and pits covered with thin churchyard grass, along stone plates, porous from the rains and snows, grown over with black, powdery moss, almost sunk into the ground. . . . Here are two or three monuments of iron. But whose are they? So greenish-aureate have they become that the inscriptions upon them can no longer be read.

Under what hummocks, then, are the bones of Grandmother, of Grandfather? Why, God alone knows! One is aware of but one thing: they are here somewhere, near at hand. And one sits and ponders, making an effort to picture these Khrushchevs, forgotten of all men. And their times begin to seem now infinitely distant, now ever so near. Thereupon, with joy, one says to oneself: "This isn't hard to imagine—it isn't! One must but remember that this gilded cross, leaning askew against the blue summer sky, was the same in their times as it is now. . . . That the rye was just as yellow, and ripening in just the same way in the fields, deserted and sultry, while here were shade, coolness, bushes . . . and amid the bushes, there had been ambling and grazing an old, white nag, just like the one I am seeing now, with shedding, age-green withers, and rosy, splitting hoofs. . . ."

1911 A.D.

OLYESHA *Envy*

PART ONE

IN THE lavatory in the morning he sings out aloud. He is more healthy, more brim-full of energy than anyone you could possibly imagine: he sings because there is nothing else he wants to do, because he has to. There are no words, no tunes, to the songs he sings, only "ta-ra-ra" in every imaginable tone of voice. What he sings can be transcribed somewhat as follows:

"I am enjoying my life, ta-ra! ta-ra! My intestines are functioning very well, ra-takta-ta-ra-ree! My gastric juices are behaving very nicely, ra-ta-ta-doo-ta-ta! Contract, O my bowels, contract! Tram-ba-ba-boom!"

When he leaves the bedroom he passes by my bed. I pretend to be still asleep. When he opens the door leading into the lavatory on the other side of the room, I follow him in my mind's eye. I hear him moving about in the lavatory—and in the lavatory there is hardly enough room to swing a cat. His back brushes against the door, his elbows dig into the walls, his feet are jammed to the floor. In the door there is a piece of plain glass. When he switches on the light the oval begins to glitter, an enchanting opal, an incredible poached egg. In my mind's eye the egg hovers in the dark depths of the corridor.

He weighs about fourteen stone. Not very long ago, when he was walking down the stairs, he noticed how his breasts were shaking.

At once he decided that he would have to begin still one more series of gymnastic exercises.

A perfect specimen of a man.

Usually he does his exercises, not in his bedroom, but in that rather vaguely defined portion of the room which has been given to me. There, there is more room, more air, more light, altogether more brilliance. A cool wind is wafted through the open doors of the balcony. Besides, in this part of the room there is a wash-basin. He gets a mat out of the bedroom. He stands naked to the waist, almost completely naked in a pair of woollen drawers held together by a single button over the middle of his stomach. The blue-and-pink world of the room moves round and round in the mother-of-pearl lens of the button. When he lies on his back on the mat and swings his legs one by one into the air, the button always gives way and then you can see the whole of the lower part of his stomach. An adorable tummy! Burnt to a tender shade of brown! The tummy of someone eminently capable of reproducing his species! Only once have I seen such a delightfully soft tummy —and then it was on an antelope. A single glance from a man with a tummy like that will make all his girl secretaries suffer torments of love for his sake.

He is exactly like a boy, washing. He whistles, jumps about on his feet, snorts, babbles monstrously through his teeth. Whenever he gathers the water in his hands and lifts it to his face he splashes it all over the straw surface of the mat, and the water scatters on the mat in perfect round bubbles. When he flicks the froth back into the basin, it boils up like a pancake on the stove. Sometimes his eyes are blinded with soap: he simply curses and rubs his eyes with his thumbs. He makes a terrible noise, gargling. Men passing beneath the balcony stop and turn their heads.

The mornings are always rose-colored and very quiet. Spring is in full swing here. Flowers stand in boxes on all the window-sills and through the chinks of the boxes filter the crimson flowers.

(Things don't like *me*. Furniture is always trying to play the most stupid tricks on me. Once a varnished angle literally bit me. My relations with the blankets are continually strained. The soup, when it comes to me, never cools. If some idiotic thing, such as a coin or a stud, falls off the table, it always rolls under a heavy piece of furniture and it is difficult to move the furniture. I crawl on the floor, and when I lift my head I see the sideboard laughing at me.)

His blue braces hang over his behind. He walks into the bedroom, takes his pince-nez off the chair, puts them on in front of the looking-glass and comes back again into my room. With one twist of his wrists—he stands in the attitude of someone who is just about to raise a heavy weight to his shoulders—the braces fall over his chest. He says nothing to me: and I pretend to be asleep. On the two metal squares of his braces the sun shines, a lustre of glowing lights. (Things adore *him.*)

He never has to brush his hair or trim his beard. His hair is short and his moustaches are small—little blobs right underneath his nose. Exactly like a rather fat little boy.

He places his hands on the bottle and pulls at the cork: and the cork screams. He pours a little eau-de-Cologne into the palm of his hand and then he smoothes it over his head, from his forehead to the back of his neck, and then back again.

He has two glasses of cold milk in the morning. He takes a jug from the sideboard, pours the milk into a glass, drinks it without troubling to sit down.

When I first saw him, I was utterly amazed. I could not imagine, could not possibly imagine—. There he stood, wearing a neat blue-grey suit, reeking of eau-de-Cologne. His lips tender, slightly protruding. A dandy of the first water.

Often at night I am roused by his snoring; and dazed and only half awake, I can never understand what he is saying. It is as though he were continually menacing me with his "krakatooooo . . . krra . . . ka . . . too-oooo."

They have given him a marvellous flat. Near the balcony windows there is a delicious vase on a lovely lacquered stand—a thin and delicate china vase, round and tall, of an exquisite transparent crimson—shaped exactly like a flamingo. The flat lies on the second floor. The balcony gently overhangs the street and the street is so wide that it is almost as wide as a main road. Below, a garden, heavily encumbered—there is a fine collection of trees scattered about in the garden—a garden on a piece of waste land and like an oven surrounded by walls on three sides.

He adores his food, but rarely dines at home. Yesterday evening he came home hungry, decided that he wanted something to eat. There was nothing on the sideboard. So he went out. There is a shop at the end of the street and he almost bought it up: half a pound of ham, a tin of sprats, herrings in a box, a hunking great loaf of bread, half a Dutch cheese, four apples, a dozen eggs, "Pea-pods of Persia" marmalade. Tea and scrambled eggs had to be prepared at once. (We have, I should add, a common kitchen and two cooks take it in turn to prepare the meals.)

"Tuck in, Kavalerov," he said. He was already eating, when he invited me to eat with him. He could not wait while the eggs were being taken out of the saucepan, and he peeled off the little white pieces which stuck to it like someone picking at enamel. His eyes were bloodshot. He spent his time taking off his pince-nez and putting them on again: and coughing and wheezing and waggling his ears.

I amused myself with a lesson in observation. Have you ever noticed how salt falls off the edge of a knife—without leaving any trace, so that the knife gleams as though it had never been touched with the salt? Or how pince-nez move over the bridge of a man's nose like bicycles? Or how men are surrounded all their lives with diminutive advertisements, scattered ant-heaps of verbiage—on forks and spoons and knives and on spectacles and on buttons and on pencils? Hardly anyone, of course, ever looks at them: but they too take part in the struggle for existence, from the smallest to the largest, from the almost invisible inscriptions on your knives and forks, to the gigantic, tremendous lettering on the hoardings. And they too take part in the class war: the letters on the street-signs wage continual war with the hoardings.

He ate as much as he could, then he stretched out his knife for the apples on the table. When he had stripped them of their yellow skins, he threw them away.

Once a Commissar overwhelmed him with high praise:

"Andrey Babichev, I may say, is one of the most remarkable figures in the state."

Andrey Petrovich Babichev occupies the position of managing director to the Food Trust. A fine sausage-maker, an excellent pastry-cook, a formidable *chef de cuisine*.

And I, I—Nikolay Kavalerov—I am his court fool!

2

HE IS the minister to men's gluttony.

He is at once avaricious and envious. He wants to have a hand in frying all the omelettes; he wants to make all the pies and all the cutlets; he wants to bake all the bread. From his own flesh he wants to produce everything men eat. This is the man who has given birth to the "Threepenny Bit."

His child grows. This "Threepenny Bit" of his is going to become a gigantic business house, the greatest restaurant in the world, the greatest kitchen imaginable. Here a two-course dinner is going to cost exactly threepence.

There is war on the kitchen front.

At least a thousand other kitchens can be considered totally vanquished.

He has finished with domesticity, that host of small bottles and demi-carafes. All mincing-machines, primus stoves, frying-pans, faucets—they are now assembled together: they have become one. If you like to think of it in that way, what has happened is the industrialization of the kitchen front.

He has even organized a series of Commissions to enquire into productivity. Machines for cleaning vegetables, manufactured in a soviet factory, have turned out to be excellent, beyond reproach. The kitchen itself was built by a German engineer. Please note that there are now a large number of business houses which are completing Babichev's orders.

From him I learnt the following story.

One day, this managing director of a great Trust actually

climbed up the steps of a house which was quite unknown to him, a house situated among the charms of a particularly disreputable thoroughfare. He carried a despatch-case under his arm and looked extraordinarily distinguished, just like a civil servant. He knocked at the first door he came across. Like Haroun al Raschid of old, he was paying a visit to the kitchen of a house in the suburbs—a house occupied by workmen! He saw the soot, the grime, the awful women wandering about in the dirt, the children who were crying. When he arrived, they immediately rushed at him. He was so huge that he took up all their space, blotted out all their light, left them with no room to breathe. They were angry. Besides, he was carrying a despatch-case and looked clean and smart. These awful women thereupon decided that he was one of the members of one of the Commissions: so they put their hands on their hips and played hell with him. Later, he walked out. They cried after him that the primus stove had gone out, that the window-panes had cracked, that the soup had far too much salt in it. He went out without being able to say what he wanted to say. He is a man utterly lacking in imagination.

This is what he ought to have said:

"Women! It is we who will clear up the soot, clean the smoke from your nostrils, snaffle the racket in your ears. It is we who will peel your potatoes for you by a magical process, in a split second of time! The hours you waste in the kitchen will be given back to you. We will give you back a half of your life! Look at that young woman making her husband's soup. Madam, you spend half your life making puddles of soup for your husband! We—we shall make it our business to transform those puddles you make for your husband into seas of gleaming splendor. For you, madam, we shall make whole oceans of cabbage soup, whole mountains of porridge, whole glaciers of jellies! Listen, O ye housewives, we promise you tiled floors that gleam in the sunshine, wine-vats of burnished copper, plates of lily-white purity, milk as weighty as mercury—and the odor of the soup you taste will bring a blush to the cheeks of the flowers on your table."

He is like a fakir—in ten places at once.

On his official notepaper he has a habit of introducing countless parentheses, he scrawls lines underneath countless words: he is terrified that he will be misunderstood, certain that everyone will make a mess of his least important instructions:

Here are some examples of the sort of letter he writes:

COMRADE PROKUDIN!

I want you to introduce cartons (12 different types) for sweets which have earned the approval of the public (chocolate, ginger-nuts), but I want the cartons to be quite distinct from anything that has gone before. I don't, *e.g.*, want a name like Rosa Luxemburg on the outside. (There appears to be a fruit bonbon called Rosa Luxemburg.) Better have something scientific (poetical? geographical? astronomical?)—something serious, a tantalizing sweet name like, *e.g.*, Esquimau? Telescope? Don't forget to ring me up at the head office tomorrow, Wednesday, between one and two. Mind you, if you forget . . .

COMRADE FOMINSKY!

I want you to arrange that everyone (*lunches from* 50 kopecks *to* 75 kopecks) should be served with a slice of meat (accurately and nicely cut as in the *better-class restaurants*). Please pay particular attention to this. Is it true that (1) meals taken with beer have been served without supplying the customer with plates? (2) peas are diminutive and have not been soaked in water long enough?

He distrusts everyone. He is as mean and meticulous as a house-keeper.

At ten o'clock in the morning he had an appointment at the cardboard-box factory. Eight men were waiting to be introduced to him. He met (1) the head of the Smoking Rooms; (2) the representative of the Far East Food Trust—while he was with the representative from the Far East he seized on a box of crabs and ran helter-skelter out of the room to show it to someone; when he came back, he put it aside, on a level with his elbows, and slowly recovered from his excitement: and all the time he could not keep his eyes off the blue box nor could he prevent himself from smiling continually and scratching his nose; (3) an engineer connected with the construction of one of his factories; (4) a German with whom he had a conference on the subject of motor-lorries—the conversation was carried on in German and came to an end, I think, with a proverb: I remember that their last words rhymed and that they both burst out laughing; (5) an artist who had brought along a sketch for an advertisement—Babichev said that he very much disliked the sketch: the blue, he said, ought to be darker, more scientifico-chemical, less romantic; (6) someone representing another restaurant proprietor, who wore cuff-links like milk-white bells; (7) a miserable little man with a curly beard who could talk about nothing but heads of cattle; and lastly, (8) that perfectly charming man up from the country. This last interview was altogether quite different from any of the others. Babichev lifted himself from his chair, moved towards him and almost embraced him. The man completely filled the room, timid, charming, charmingly awkward, sun-burnt, clear-eyed, the complete Levin of *Anna Karenina*. He smelt of new milk, the flowers of the field. And their conversation turned on the subject of a *Sovkhoz*. Everyone there assumed a gentle, dreaming expression, listening to them.

At twenty minutes past four Babichev adjourned the meeting to attend the Supreme Council of Soviet Economy.

3

IN THE evening he remains at home. He spends his time sitting under the green lamp-shade: the color of the lamp-shade is the color of palm leaves. He surrounds himself with files, notebooks, little slips of paper covered with interminable lists of figures. He tears a sheet off the calendar, jumps up, rushes to the bookcase, takes out a book, kneels on a chair, presses his stomach against the edge of the table, begins to read, his large heavy face buried in his hands. The green baize cloth over the table is covered with a thin sheet of glass. After all, I tell myself, there is nothing peculiar in all this. Here is a man who is simply working in the evening after he has left work. When he has found the page he wants, he jabs his pencil in his ear, tries to clear the wax away— nothing peculiar in that! But all the while he seems to be saying, "You're just a bourgeois, my dear Kavalerov, just a stupid little bourgeois." He does not say that aloud, of course: and it may be that he is thinking of something quite different, although there is no need for him to use words when he looks at me like that. There is a third person in the room telling me about what he is thinking, a third person who makes me almost wild with despair whenever I look up at Andrey Babichev.

"Threepenny Bit," he kept on muttering, in a shrill voice. "Threepenny Bit! Threepenny Bit!"

After that he broke out into wild laughter. He must have seen something which amused him in the columns of figures or in the book he was reading. He was still shaking with suppressed laughter when he beckoned to me. He marked a place on the page with his thumb and roared with laughter. I looked at what he was pointing to, but there was nothing there. What the devil are you laughing at? I thought. I knew nothing about his book or his work, I did not even know the elementary principles of what he was doing, but it was obvious that he had found something so contrary to all the established rules of procedure that he simply could not help himself from bursting out into laughter. He almost terrified me with that laughter of his; it was like the laughter of a priest. I listened to him laughing as I imagine a blind man listens to the sudden explosion of a rocket.

"You're just a bourgeois, my dear fellow. You understand nothing."

He did not say that, of course, but it was obvious that that was what he meant.

Sometimes he comes home very late. Then I have to take his orders on the telephone.

"Is that you, Kavalerov? Well, listen. They are going to ring me up from the Bread Trust. Tell them my phone number—2-73-05,

extension 62. Have you got that? Should I repeat it? Extension
62."

Later the Bread Trust telephone the house.

I say: "Bread Trust speaking? Comrade Babichev has gone along
to the headquarters. What? I said 'headquarters.' Telephone number 2–73–05, extension 62. Have you got that? Extension 62. Headquarters. Goodbye."

It was the Bread Trust ringing up for the managing director,
and Babichev, the managing director, had already gone along to
headquarters. What does all this mean to me? Nothing! I must
admit, however, that I derive enormous satisfaction in having a
part in Babichev's work at the Bread Trust. I find that I get an
extraordinary thrill in administrating things. I do nothing, really.
I'm just a toady. Why do I behave like this? Why do I do it?
Because I like him and respect him? Because I fear him? Certainly
not because I fear him—I don't fear him, I look on myself as his
equal, I am not a bourgeois, and one day I shall prove it to him.

I want to discover if he has any chinks in his armor. The first
time I saw him in the bathroom I felt certain that I had pierced
through his disguise.

As he came out of the bathroom he was still wiping himself with
his towel. He stood near the balcony, about five feet away from
me, rubbing himself down and cleaning his ears out all the time.
His back was turned towards me, and seeing him there, his whole
torso lit up in the sunlight, standing there with his back towards
me, I could have cried out at him with all the strength of my
lungs. His back spoke volumes. The fat was a curious delicate
yellow. Suddenly the Book of Judgement unfolded before my eyes
and I realized that Babichev's grandfather must have been an
athlete, must have had little rolls of fat in the proper places: it
was from his grandfather that the Commissar had inherited his
fine flesh, the peculiar clear tint of his body. What made me more
excited than anything else was the discovery of a little fold of
skin in the small of his back, an extraordinarily noble little fold
of skin, almost transparent, full of red blood, one of those birth-

marks which provide mothers with the essential clue for discovering stolen children.

"But you're a Grand Seigneur, Andrey Petrovich! You have been hiding it all the time." I almost shouted aloud.

He turned slowly towards me.

On his chest, just below the collar-bone, there was a deep scar, perfectly round, slightly uneven: it was as though a coin had been dropped on molten wax, as though a branch had been cut off from the stem, leaving the outline of its juncture with the bark, as though he had been to prison and had been shot trying to escape.

"Who was Jocasta?" he asked me once. Sometimes, and especially at night, he asks me the most unexpected questions. During the day he works at the office, and while he is working he sees the advertisements on the hoardings, and on his way back he peers into shop-windows, picks up stray, scattered words from other people's conversations: and all these form the raw material for our conversations at night. As I am the only person he knows who has no interest in the factory, he finds an extraordinary relief in talking to me when he comes home. He imagines that I am wholly incapable of discussing anything seriously. He thinks that after a day's work everybody falls into light-hearted chatter: in this way, talking with me, he pays his common debt to humanity. He asks me the most infantile questions—and using these infantile questions as a basis, we proceed with our conversations. Before him, I stand a fool: therefore he thinks I am always a fool.

"Do you like olives?" That is the sort of question he asks me.

"I do know who Jocasta was. I like olives. But I don't like and I can't bear your stupid questions. I am worth as much as you are. I am equal to you." That is how I ought to reply to him; but, honestly, I have not the courage. Always he towers above me.

4

F o r two weeks now I have been living under the same roof with
him. Two weeks ago he picked me up from the streets when I was
lying outside the doors of a pub, drunk.

They had thrown me out of the pub.

The quarrel started in a curious way. At first there was nothing
to suggest that we would end up in a rough-house. On the contrary, it looked as if we were all going to become fast friends—
drunkards are always companionable. There was a large party,
there was a girl with them, they invited me to join them. A perfectly charming girl, rather thin, wearing a blue silk blouse which
fell straight from her shoulders. It was she who made the pointed
remark about me. Of course, I refused to take it lying down. When
I had got half-way across the room, I turned back—I didn't want
to attack them. I was holding a glass of beer in my hand aloft, like
a lantern.

But when I turned back, there was a rain of caustic remarks
about me. Of course, I looked stupid. They had given me the bird,
the raspberry. Behind me there was a man who was actually laughing out loud. Someone threw a dried pea at my head, so I left my
table and strode right in front of them. At that moment the beer
would spill on to the table, I *would* catch my thumb in the handle
of the glass—and I couldn't get it out. Yes, I was drunk. I told
them what I thought of them. The deepest humiliation and the
most exalted pride went to swell the torrent of my words:

"You're just a lot of bloody fools—a lot of dirty tramps, running
away after you have had your pleasure with a girl." (They all
started to listen intently at that. I, who had got the raspberry,
spoke in a curiously distorted voice high above the clamor of the
mob.) "You—yes, you—sitting there under the palm-tree. Exhibit
number one. Stand up and show yourself. Gentlemen in the audience, I beg you to listen carefully to what I am going to say. Silence! Orchestra, play a waltz, something gentle, tuneful. As for
you, you old cart-horse—those wrinkles on your forehead, let me

tell you, they are not wrinkles, they are driving-reins. Your chin—
well, that's a cow. Your nose—let me explain, that's a coachman
sitting up on the box, a coachman suffering from one of the rarer
forms of leprosy. All the rest of you—you are all useless, worthless, hopeless! Sit down, all of you! Exhibit number two, the young
gentleman with a face like a thigh—charming! Gentlemen in the
audience, look carefully at these monsters. As for you—yes, you
over there—how did you manage to get through the doors, your
ears flapping out like that? You over there, clinging to the
wretched girl you have stolen from her mother's arms, ask her what
she thinks about your pimples. Gentlemen in the audience!" (I
gazed at each one in turn.) "They—they have actually had the
audacity to laugh in my face. That one over there laughed. Look
at him! He laughed and his laughter echoed like the squelch of a
stomach-pump. Young woman—

> "In the garden delighting in Spring, Princess,
>   There are no roses like yours.
> Ah! that someone should have plucked you, Princess,
>   Should have plucked your eighteen years.

"My dear, cry out for help! Oh, we shall save you! What is the
matter with you all? There—there is a man caressing you and all
you can do is to press him closer to your body. That's not the sort
of thing young women ought to do?" (I paused, then continued in
a solemn voice.) "Oh, I appeal to you. Come now and sit by me.
Why are you laughing at me? Stand up, and come to me! Here I
stand before you, O charming unknown, and all I ask of you is that
you should not leave my side. Stand up, thrust them away from
you, come and sit by my side! What do you imagine you will get
out of them? Do you think the god of love hides in their soiled
hands? Do you think they are intelligent? Or that they are charming? Or that they have any devotion for you? Come to me. When
I think of the comparison between those who are there and I who
stand here, I laugh out aloud. From me you will receive more,
infinitely more——"

I felt terribly afraid. I had a sudden vision of one of those dreams in which you know you are dreaming and you know that you can do anything you want to do, because soon you will awake again; but I knew then that I would never wake up again. The threads had been cut: there was no return.

Well, they threw me out.

I lay unconscious on the ground. Returning to consciousness, I said:

"I called to you, but you did not come. You are all bloody fools and I called to you, but you did not come." (By "fools" I meant all the women in the world.)

I lay over a grating; my face lay between the bars. I drunk in musty odors and down in the depths of the pit I saw things moving in the dust. As I crashed to the ground I had had time to notice the grating and the memory of its shape burdened my mind and gave color to my dreams. In my dreams, my terror, my fear of humiliation and inevitable retribution, in my uneasy mind accumulated and overflowed into a strange theory of persecution—I was being hounded down the streets, I was trying to shake myself free from all that overwhelming sense of terror. As I ran, I strained my heart: it was that which brought me out of my deep sleep.

I opened my eyes, trembled with joy at the thought of deliverance. Even then my awakening was incomplete and I saw myself standing on the border-line between two separate visions: the second of these visions assumed the shape of my unknown savior, the savior who was going to free my body from the menace of persecution. Thinking I was still dreaming, I covered his hands, his sleeves with kisses, I put my arm round his neck and wept bitter tears.

"Why am I so unhappy?" I asked. "The world is too much with me," I whispered.

"Raise your head," I heard him say. They took me into the motor-car. When I returned to consciousness again, I saw the pale, glittering sky stretching from my hands towards my head and even further. The vision of sky thundered in my ears. I trembled. Every time the vision came to an end I had a sudden fit of nausea, of sickness. In the morning when I woke up, I put my hands to my feet with a growing feeling of terror. I was still uncertain where I was or what had happened to me. All I could remember was that someone had been shaking me roughly. I thought they must have taken me back in an ambulance and that while I had been on the operating-table they had cut off my feet. I stretched out my hands, knowing that in a moment I would be touching the round core of the bandages; instead, I found myself lying on a divan in a large, clean, well-lit room with a balcony and low wide windows. It was still early. The rose-colored stones of the balcony were gently warming themselves in the rising sun.

When he came to see me later in the morning, I asked him what he was going to do with me.

"You looked so unhappy," he said. "I couldn't avoid feeling pity for you. Perhaps you dislike people interfering in your life? If you do, I can only say that I am sorry. If you want to, you can live here with me—live quietly here. Nothing would give me greater pleasure. There is room enough here for you, light and air enough here for you. And you can do some useful work for once in your life. You can correct proofs for me and arrange samples for me. What do you say?"

What was it that made a famous man lower himself to meet the gaze of this young unknown, the suspicious character lying there on the divan?

5

ONE evening two mysteries were solved.

"Andrey Petrovich," I said, "who is that fellow in the frame?"

On the table there stood the photograph of a young man, sunburnt.

"What? What?" He always has to say everything twice. His thoughts are gummed to the paper and he finds a great deal of difficulty in tearing them off.

"What? What?" He is still far away in the clouds.

"I said—who is this young man?"

"Oh—the young man. He's Volodya Makarov—most remarkable young man." (He never seems to speak in a normal manner. As if I could never ask him an intelligent question! Whenever I talk to him, he always replies with a proverb or a couplet from one of the poets—or else he just gurgles. Instead of saying in his usual voice, "a most remarkable young man," he scanned the words, almost as though he were reciting them: "a most re-mark-able young man.")

"What is he remarkable for?" I asked, trying to imitate his voice.

He took no notice of my imitation.

"N-no. Just an ordinary young man—a student. You have been sleeping in his bed," he said. "I ought to have told you that there is a sense in which it is true to say that he is my son. He has been living here with me for ten years. Volodya Makarov—he has now gone away—to his father's home—at Murom."

"Ah-a."

"Well, well . . ."

He rose from the table and walked round the room.

"He's eighteen and a really famous footballer." (Good God, a footballer of all things! I thought.)

"Good heavens!" I said. "If that isn't the cat's pyjamas! A famous footballer! Tell me, aren't you proud of him?" (What am I talking about?)

He was no longer listening to me, he was lost in the mist of his memories. From the threshold of the balcony he was staring into the distance towards the sky, thinking about that extraordinary footballer, Volodya Makarov.

"He's like no one else in the world," he said suddenly, turning towards me. (I began to feel that my presence there, at a time when he was trying to concentrate on Volodya Makarov, must have been particularly irritating.)

"In the first place, I owe my life to him. Ten years ago he saved me from the law. They were going to put my head on the block and beat me in the face with a hammer. He saved me." (He got an enormous amount of satisfaction in recalling these exploits and it was obvious that they often invaded his mind.) "But of course, that's not the main thing. The main thing is that he is like no one else on earth. Well, well . . ."

Thereupon he returned to the table.

"Tell me, why have you brought me here?"

"Ah," he said, crowing. He heard my question exactly a second after I had spoken.

"Why did I bring you here? You looked so sick in the mouth. I was touched to the heart. You were crying out so pitiably, I felt so terribly sorry for you."

"And the bed?"

"What bed . . . ?"

"I mean—when your friend comes home."

Then, without thinking what he was saying, simply, with an inflection of extraordinary gaiety in his voice, he said:

"You will have to give it up."

At that moment I ought to have rushed at him and struck his face. This man, this celebrity, had actually had the effrontery to have pity on me, he had actually felt sorrow over the lot of an unhappy mortal who had erred on his ways. But the feeling did not last long. I was biding my time. In a little while, I thought, he is going to throw me out of the house. Even now he speaks about me with the utmost cynicism.

"Andrey Petrovich," I said. "Do you realize what you are saying? You're a —— swine!"

"A—what?"

His thoughts slowly detached themselves from the paper, soon his ears will repeat what I have just said to him; trembling, I pray to the gods that his ears will deceive him. Has he really heard me? So much the worse if he has! What the sweet hell——

But a moment later something quite exterior to our conversation interrupted us. My stay in the house is going to be delayed a little longer.

Under the balcony, in the road, someone was calling out in a loud voice:

"Andrey!"

Andrey turned to the window.

"Andrey!"

He got up, suddenly, pushing the table away with his hands.

"Andrusha, my darling!"

He walked towards the window. I followed him. We both stared down into the street below. Darkness everywhere, the pavement lit only by the sparse light from the windows. In the centre of the road, a small, very broad little man.

"Good evening, Andrusha. How are you? How is the 'Three-penny Bit'?"

From my hiding-place I could see the balcony, and beyond it, an enormous Andrusha. From the revolting noises he made with his mouth, I thought he was drunk. The man in the roadway was still calling out, but less vociferously now.

"Why won't you talk to me? I have come to bring you some news. I have invented a machine. It's called 'Ophelia.' "

Andrey suddenly turned right round. In the road his shadow moved obliquely, producing a tempest in the gardens on the other side of the road. He sat on the edge of the table, beating a tattoo with his fingers on the plates.

"Be careful," shouted the squat little man in the road. "Don't get puffed up with pride, Andrey! I shall lose you, Andrey!"

Then Babichev leapt up. With clenched fists he hurled himself at the balcony. The trees were undoubtedly stirred to their depths. His shadow lay like a Buddha over the town.

"What's the matter with you, you little fool?" he said.

He struck the wobbling balustrade with his fists.

"What in hell do you want to come running here for?" he added. "Get out of here! If you don't, I'll have you arrested!"

"Goodbye," said a voice from below.

The little man in the street took off something which had been lying on his head, held it out at arm's-length, shook it up and down. (Was it a bowler? Yes, I am positive it was a bowler.) The man's courtesy was evidently an affectation. He walked away, far into the distance, keeping to the middle of the road, walking with curious little hopping strides.

"Good God!" said Andrey. "That—that was my brother Ivan. The—scum!"

He paced up and down the room, boiling with rage. Then he yelled at me again:

"Let me tell you what sort of a man he is! He's not worth the dirt on your shoes! He's not worth the dust in the lining of your coat pocket. He ought to be shot!"

In the photograph, the sunburnt figure of Volodya Makarov was smiling. His gleaming teeth, their extraordinary masculinity, the teeth of a Japanese.

6

IN THE evening he works. I sit on the divan. Between us there is a lamp-shade completely effacing the top half of his face. Below the lampshade, the lower hemisphere of his head hangs in mid-air, half the round top of a pillar-box.

"I was born on the day the new age was born," I say.

He is not listening to me. His silence wounds me terribly.

"I often think about the age we are living in—an age which will be famous in the annals of history. The truth is, of course, that those who were born then ought to combine with Youth. Together, they could work miracles. Isn't that so?"

Rhymes alone move him out of his solemnity. Extraordinary, that absurd rhymes should move such serious people.

"Youth—truth," he said, repeating the words over and over again. If I had told him that he had just that moment heard those words and that he was now repeating them like that, he would never have believed me.

"In Europe genius is rewarded. There they admire fame. If you show the least signs of genius, they will look after you, march you up the long avenue which leads to fame and glory. Here, no one can obtain an individual glory of his own. Isn't that so?"

I might just as well have been talking to myself. I almost shouted into his ears. I weighed my words carefully, ponderously;

whatever I did, he remained solemn, preoccupied with his thoughts.

"In our country you can't step over the barriers which lead along the road to fame. A genius might as well be dead unless he can lift up all those barriers, unless he can create a noise in the world. Look at me. I like having an argument. I like showing-off. I want to be famous. But in this country, no one pays any attention to men as individuals. I want people to listen carefully and attentively to what I have to tell them. Do you know, I wish I had been born in an obscure village somewhere in France, growing up full of my dreams of conquest, and then one day tramping out of the village and going off to Paris. There, I would put my heart into achieving my ambitions. Unfortunately, I wasn't born in the West. Nowadays, so I am told, I and everybody else, even those who are great in the world, are worth precisely nothing, as individuals. Slowly I have had to accustom myself to the hard truth. All the same it is a truth which I would like to quarrel with. I would like to have an argument with the truth. I say to myself: all you have got to do if you want to be famous is to become a musician or an author or a field-marshal, or walk across Niagara on a rope. Nowadays those are the only permissible way of achieving fame. Everyone with a grain of personality in him tries to achieve fame, tries to show himself . . . Just think! Here, at a time when the only subject of conversation is how a man can be useful to the state, at a time when men are taught to think realistically and sensibly about things and events generally—just think what would happen if someone suddenly took it into his head to do something entirely unexpected, something quite stupid and absurd, something which would make everyone stare at him. 'There!' he would say. 'That is what I am like and you are just like that, every one of you!' Go into the market-place and do something like that, something entirely without provocation, and then bow to your audience. 'I have lived,' you will say. 'I have done what I wanted to do.'"

He said nothing.

"For example. Go and kill yourself. Do it purposelessly, irrationally, out of sheer cussedness, just to show that you have the right to do what you like with yourself. Do it now! Hang yourself in your own doorway. Or better still, hang yourself in the old Varvarskaya, the new Nogeen. There's a terrific archway there. Have you seen it? It would have a tremendous effect if you hanged yourself there."

In the room where I lived before I came here, there was a terrible bed. I feared it as I fear ghosts. It was as hard as a beer-barrel and spectral bones spent their time clinking underneath the mattress. I had a blue blanket which I had bought at Kharkov in the Blagovesnchenskoy Bazaar, in the year of the famine. I met an old woman selling pies. The pies were covered with a blanket. Although they had been some time out of the oven, there was still some of the warmth of creation in them. Underneath the blanket they were palpitating and snuggling together like a lot of little puppies. In those days, like everyone else, I had a hard job making both ends meet, but I remember that that basket concealed so much domestic bliss, so much quiet warmth, that I resolved that one day I too would have a blanket like that. Later the dream was fulfilled. One night I slipped under a blue blanket, so warm that I simmered and boiled and twisted and turned and uncurled myself as I moved among the sheets. I was like a piece of gelatine. Going to sleep that night was like the memory of unattainable bliss. Only, as time passed, the patterns on the blanket swelled and swelled, and turned into little tea-cakes.

Now I sleep in the perfect divan.

If I move my body carefully enough, I can cause music to flow from the virginal springs. From the depths I summon a tinkling orchestra. To my mind's eye there rises the vision of bubbles floating gently to the surface of a lake. I sleep like a child. In this divan I return once more to the days of my childhood; like a child I measure the interval between the first sensation of overwhelming sleepiness and that last moment when the brain sinks into perfect rest. Just as I could then, I can now prolong those intervals, I can savor them, fill them with ordered images. Later, perfectly conscious, my eyes wide open, I can see those images taking on the color of dreams. The tinkle of the bubble as it rises from the depths of the lake suddenly changes and becomes a grape floating gently towards the surface, later a whole cluster of grapes, later a whole orchard of vines, a vineyard, where all the grapes and clusters are inextricably confused. Through the orchard there is a pathway lit up in the sun, warmth . . .

I am twenty-seven.

One day I was changing into a new shirt and looking at myself in the glass. I thought I could recognize my father in the reflection which was staring at me. There is, of course, no real similarity between us. I thought of him in the bedroom and how I had watched him when I was a boy as he changed his clothes, how sorry I was for him. He will never be famous or handsome, I thought. He is finished, completed, rounded-off. He will never be anything more than he is now. So I thought, feeling sorry for him and silently rejoicing over my victory. While I was in bed, I thought of the days when I had watched him dressing and undressing in the bedroom—then, at last, I recognized the resemblance. It was not a physical resemblance. It was a sexual resemblance. I felt that his seed lay within me. I felt as though at that moment someone had whispered into my ear, "Now you are complete, finished, rounded-off. There is nothing left for you to do. Go and give birth to a son, likewise."

I shall never be handsome or famous. I shall never walk from an unknown village to the capital. I shall never become a field-marshal or a Commissar or a professor or an athlete or an adventurer. All my life I have dreamed of an extraordinary, extraordinary love. Soon, very soon I shall return to my old room with its terrible bed—and my awful neighbor, the widow Procopovich. She is about forty, but in the yard they all call her "Anitchka." She it is who prepares the meals for the hairdressers' artels, and somewhere in the depths of the corridor she has a stove of her own. She feeds cats; silent, mangy-looking cats, which jump up to her hands every day, moving in curious galvanic leaps; and all day she strews giblets on the floor for them. The floor is always littered with a glistening, gleaming film of giblets. One day I slipped down the corridor on my back. I had trodden on the heart of some animal or other: it was small and tough and like the core of a chestnut. Wherever she goes she is treading over the cats and catching her feet in these coiling entrails of animals. Always she carries a knife in her hands and with the knife she slits through the surrounding coils, like the Princess cutting through the spider's web.

The widow Procopovich is old and fat and soft to touch. If you held her in your arms, you could quite easily squeeze all the stuffing out of her, and in this respect she resembles a sausage. One morning I found her at the wash-stand in the corridor. She was still wearing her nightdress. She smiled at me. It was the smile of a woman in the arms of her lover. Behind the door, on a little footstool, there was a basin. In the basin she had gathered all the hairs she had combed out of her head.

The widow Procopovich is the symbol of my male humiliation. Sometimes she seems to be saying, "I am ready. Come to me. I shall leave my door open tonight. Come in. I shall take you into my arms. Then we shall be together and, O my darling, how happy we shall be. Away with your dream of an unrealizable love-affair. Time casts her hoary hand on everyone. You are not what you used to be. You are too fat, your trousers are too short for you. What more do you desire? Do you still dream about the gawky girl, the one with the perfectly oval face, the one you want to take to bed with you. Away with your fine dreams! Already you have had children. Away with your dreams! Come to me. Come and sleep with me in the fine old bed which my husband won in the lottery. The counterpane is a beauty and you will fall in love with the embroidery as soon as you set eyes on it. Oh, I shall look after you, I shall share your sorrows!"

She makes me feel uncomfortable when she looks at me like that. Whenever she sees me she makes a little tittering noise at the back of her throat, a little bubble of sound and air which explodes in the violence of her passion for me.

"Go away, you dirty old bitch. It's not true that I am a father.

It's not true that I have had children! You're not the bedmate for me! Go away, you old bitch!"

I sleep on Babichev's divan.

In my dreams the most beautiful of women comes and slips into bed with me. At last my dreams are fulfilled. What shall I give her for the pleasure she has given me? When I think of the price I shall have to pay, I am filled with horror. No one has ever loved me for myself. Even prostitutes do their best to rook me. What will she want from me? As though she has read my thoughts, she whispers into my ear:

"Don't worry. All I want is a threepenny bit."

Some years ago, when I was still at school, they took me to the wax-works. In a glass case there was a handsome man in a frock-coat. I remember that there was a smoking hole in his chest and that someone was supporting him.

"It's President Carnot," said my father. "He was killed by the anarchists."

The President was dying. He was moaning and rolling his eyes. The life of the President was passing away to the slow tread of time. As I looked, I was amazed. He lay there, in someone's arms, his beard shooting up in the air in the green glass. He looked so extraordinarily handsome. Above my head I heard the whirring of the wings of time. I swallowed tears of inexpressible joy. It was then that I decided that one day I too would be famous, that there, in the glass case, I too would have a wax image, filled with the ineluctable roar of the wings of time, a roar which few people can hear but which awaits all those who pass by the green glass case. I decided that I would be just as handsome as the president.

Instead I write lyrics for the music-halls, monologues about Inspectors of Income Tax, about typists, about nepmen, about alimony.

> Oh, in the Government offices,
> People are tearing out their hair
> At the thought of Mollie
> Being given a dolly. . . .

But I still dream and hope that one day, in the large showcase, there will be the figure of a man with a large nose and a pale, rather ordinary face, dishevelled hair, cheeks puffed like a boy's, a coat with only one button, a card above the case with the following inscription in bold letters:

NICOLAY KAVALEROV

Just that, nothing more. And anyone seeing the inscription will shout out at the top of his voice, "Good heavens alive!" and perhaps he will remember certain stories and legends which were current in his youth. "So this is the man," they will say, "who darted hatred and envy at everyone alike, the man who was full of loud boasts and overweening pride, full of great plans, great projects. They say that in spite of all this he never accomplished anything, that he ended his life in misery, a criminal, a sneak-thief . . ."

7

FROM the Tverskaya I turn into a side street. I am on my way to the Nikitskaya. It is still early. The street bears a curious resemblance to the joints of a finger. I carry the most painful rheumatism from one joint to the next. Things don't like me. Because of me the street is ill.

An extraordinary little man in a bowler hat is walking along the road in front of me.

At first I thought he was in a hurry, but later I discovered that that peculiar manner of walking of his is something quite inseparable from him, so much a part of him.

He is carrying a pillow in a yellow pillowslip. He is holding it by one of the corners. Sometimes it bangs between his knees and then a dent appears. The dent disappears immediately afterwards.

Often in the centre of the town you will find a hedgerow flowering romantically in a deserted alley-way. We were walking beside one of those hedges.

A bird gleamed on the branch of a tree, shivering and whistling —the sound of shears closing, unclosing again. The man in front of me turns towards the bird: and walking behind him, all I can see is one side of his face, the first phase of the moon. He smiles.

"Good heavens," I almost say. "What an extraordinary resemblance!" I almost yell out loud, feeling that he too ought to know about that resemblance.

A bowler hat.

He takes it off and carries it in his hands. It is like an Easter cake. In the other hand he carries the pillow-case.

The windows are open. In one of the window-boxes on the first floor there are some flowers in a blue vase. The little man is attracted by the flowers. He leaves the pavement, crosses into the road, stands beneath the window, gazing at the blue vase. The bowler hat falls to the back of his head. He holds the pillow-case tightly in his hand and the swan's down scatters over his knees.

Standing behind a projecting wall I watch him.

He calls to the vase:

"Valya!"

Immediately afterwards, behind the window, a girl in a rose-red dress appears. She upsets the vase.

"Valya," he says. "I have come to take you away."

Silence. The water from the vase runs along the cornice.

"Look! I have brought you—can you see what I have brought you?"

(He lifts the pillow-case with both hands to the level of his stomach.)

"Do you recognize it? You have slept on it," he smiled. "Come back to me, Valya. You don't want to come back to me? If you come, I shall show you 'Ophelia.' Won't you come back, dear?"

Silence again. The girl leans out of the window, shaking her curly head. By her side the vase rolls along the sill. Then I remember that immediately she came to the window, almost before she had had time to see the man in the street, she fell against the sill with her elbows, making a little crackling sound.

In the sky the clouds are racing: in the window-pane their paths
are confused.

"Oh, please, Valya? Come down to me! Just—simply—come
down the stairs."

He waited for her.

A crowd accumulated in the road.

"You don't want to come with me? All right! Goodbye!"

He turns away, places his hat carefully on top of his head and
walks down the middle of the road in my direction.

"Wait a moment! Father! Father!"

He hurries on. He is right in front of me now. I can see him
plainly, a man who is no longer young, gasping for breath, pale
from too much walking. An extraordinary fat little man running
breathlessly with a pillow-case clenched firmly to his chest.

The window is deserted.

She runs after him. She reaches the corner where the little deserted alley-way comes to an end—but he has gone. I stand in front
of the hedge. I walk towards her and then she imagines that I may
be able to help her, that there is something I may be able to do
for her. The tears fall obliquely down her cheeks as on a vase. Her
whole body stiffens and now she is going to question me, passionately. I interrupted her. I say:

"You have swept past me like a branch full of flowers and
leaves."

In the evening I correct proofs.

"The blood collected from the slaughterhouse can therefore be
transformed into food and may be used either for the preparation
of sausages or for the manufacture of light and dark albumen,
sticking-paste, buttons, dyes, manure, cattle-feed or food for birds
and fishes. The crude oil obtained from the animals may be employed in the preparation of domestic fats, lard, margarine and artificial butter of all types, or for the production of fats used in industry, *e.g.* stearine, glycerine and machine-oil. Sheep's heads and
pig's trotters, after treatment in the electric spiral bore and the
automatic polishing machine, after being dried and heated in a
gas oven and cut to shape and steamed in the vat, may be trans-

formed into articles of an edible nature. Similarly, after treatment, the fat and hair as well as the bones . . ."

Someone calls for him on the telephone. At least twenty times every evening someone calls for him on the telephone. How can I tell the number of all the people he speaks to? Suddenly I hear him.

"I swear it's not cruelty."

I listen.

"No, of course there's nothing cruel about it. You ask me—and that is my answer to you. Once more—there is nothing cruel about it. Don't worry about it. Are you listening? He humiliated himself? How? By walking underneath your window? I don't believe it, that's all. It's one of his little tricks. He walks under my windows too. It's one of his hobbies, walking under windows. Yes, I know him quite well. What, you have been crying? All evening? What do you want to cry for? You should never let yourself cry. He is going dotty? Well, we'll have him taken to the asylum then. Ophelia? What Ophelia? Oh, I don't care! Ophelia—it's quite mad, all this talk about Ophelia! Do exactly as you like. I must say, you behaved splendidly. Yes, yes, of course! What! A pillow-case? No, no! Impossible!" (He roars with laughter.) "I can see that! The one you slept on? Goodness gracious! How? Each pillow-case has its own little secrets. Ha-ha! Of course. What I wanted to say was—no, don't worry. What? Yes, but of course!" (He stops speaking. For a long time he holds the ear-piece quietly to his ears. Then he roars with laughter all over again.) "He said—a branch? What? What sort of a branch? Full of flowers? Flowers and leaves? What? Yes, of course he must be mad."

8

T R Y to imagine a sausage. Just an ordinary sausage—full of tea. Imagine a piece of sausage which is perfectly round and imagine that at the closed end, where the skin is wrinkled and knotted, there is a piece of string hanging down, a little lamb's tail. Just an ordinary sausage. Imagine that it weighs about a pound and a half, and imagine the surface of the sausage suffused with a sort of sweat, and imagine that underneath the skin there are little yellow bubbles of fat. Where it has been cut, you will see the white speckles where the yellow bubbles ought to be.

Babichev was holding the sausage in the palm of his hand. While he was speaking, doors were opening and closing and men came in and surrounded him. The sausage lay vividly alive in his red hand. May I add that Babichev's hands concealed an enormous sense of the dignity of their functions.

"What do you think of my sausage?" he asked, turning from one to the other. "Look at it closely. It's a pity Shapiro isn't here. Someone must ring him up. Isn't it a darling? I said—ring up Shapiro! He can't come? Then get on the phone again."

Now the sausage lay on the table. With loving care Babichev constructed a little litter for it; then, still watching it closely, he moved away, caught his backside on the edge of the sofa and tumbled into the cushions. He rested his elbows on his thighs and roared with laughter. A moment later he peered at his fingertips, saw some grease lying on them and began to lick it.

"Kavalerov!" He stopped laughing. "Are you free now? Then go along and see Shapiro at the warehouse. You know where it is? Go right in and show him the sausage." He looked carefully at the sausage. "Yes—go along. Take it and show it to him. Then tell him to ring me up."

I took the sausage along to Shapiro at the warehouse. Babichev rang him up at once.

"Of course it is!" he yelled at the top of his voice. "It's the finest sausage in the world! We'll have it shown at the exhibition. Yes, at Milan. Of course! At the exhibition at Milan. Of course! Of course! Seventy per cent pure veal? Yes! No, you old fool, we won't be selling it at half a rouble. Good heavens, half a rouble! We shall put it on the market at thirty-five kopecks apiece. A fine sausage, don't you agree? A perfect beauty!"

He left me. His face was lit up with smiles, and I have never seen anyone with a face so much like a red cherry. I could see his head hanging suspended in the window of his car. As he tore down the stairs he threw his Tyrolean hat at the hall-porter. His eyes were popping out of his head. He was as heavy and noisy and abrupt as a wild boar.

At each of the offices he chortled: "It's my sausage! It's my sausage! Yes, that's the one I mean—it's my sausage! Didn't I tell you? Well, listen. Heavens alive!" At each office he telephoned Shapiro, and all that time I was hurrying through the street, carrying my parcel.

"I've sent it along this minute, my dear Solomon. Oh, you are going to have the surprise of your sweet life! You won't know what to think of it.

"You say it hasn't come yet. Never mind, Solomon, it's going to be the surprise of your sweet life when it comes."

His neck was sweating. He took a handkerchief and rubbed along his collar, used so much force that he almost tore it. Always he was making faces and it was evident that he was suffering deeply.

I went along to Shapiro. As soon as I reached the place, I had a sudden vision of myself bringing the sausage. On my arrival, everyone vanished. The streets were cleared as though by magic. The knowledge that I was the bearer of Babichev's famous sausage caused immense enthusiasm among them all. Shapiro was a melancholy little Jew with a nose like a figure six. His office consisted of a wooden shed tacked on to the larger building, and looking inside the door I saw a darkness full of the swirl of summer—the sort of darkness which rises before your eyes when you press your eyelids with tight fingers. On the window-sill there lay a telephone; by its side, on the wall, official documents hung on a nail.

Shapiro took the sausage in his hands, weighed it, caressed it —and all the while his head was bent curiously to one side. He lifted it to his nose. The smell entranced him. Later he left the shed, placed the sausage on a box and carefully cut off a small piece with a penknife. In perfect silence he chewed it, drew it towards the roof of his mouth, sucked it, slowly swallowed it.

The hand holding the penknife lifted a little, shaking with emotion. It was as though his hand were a messenger from the man, recording his sensations.

When he had swallowed the whole of it, he sighed deeply.

"Your Babichev is a genius—a genius," he said. "At last he has constructed the perfect sausage. He has attained perfection. You know, at thirty-five kopecks, no one has ever had such good value for their money."

The telephone bell rang. Slowly Shapiro raised himself from his chair, then he went to the door.

"So it is you, Comrade Babichev. My congratulations. Nothing would give me greater pleasure than to have the honor of kissing your cheeks, dear Comrade Babichev."

Babichev was shouting into the telephone so loudly that here, in this room, a long way from the telephone, I could hear his voice and I could hear the confused atmospheric distortions on the line. The whole apparatus was quivering under the weight of his speech—sometimes it even seemed to jump right outside Shapiro's puny grasp. When that happened, Shapiro would wag his fingers menacingly and make a face, imagining that he was threatening a wretched schoolboy who had forgotten to pay attention to him.

"What are you going to do with the sausage?" I asked. "Shall we leave it here?"

"He wants you to take it back home with you. He has kindly invited me to dinner with him tonight and we are going to eat the sausage."

That made me angry.

"Must I really drag the wretched thing home with me? Couldn't we buy another?"

"Of course we couldn't. It's not on the market yet. That one there is the first one we have ever made in the factory."

"Well—it will go bad."

Shapiro closed the penknife, ran his fingers along it, smiled slowly, almost imperceptibly, half closed his eyes and began to speak. He looked like an old Jewish prophet.

"I have already had the honor of complimenting Comrade

Babichev on the quality of his sausage. I would like you to know that it will have no smell at all for a day or two. If I thought it would smell, do you think I would have complimented Comrade Babichev? We are going to eat it this evening. Have no fear. Put it in the sun, anywhere—it will still smell like a rose."

He disappeared into the gloom of the shed. When he returned, he was carrying a piece of butter paper in his hands. A few seconds later he presented me with a parcel which he himself had wrapped up.

Almost since the day I met Babichev for the first time, I have heard people talking about that famous sausage of his. Everyone's ambition seemed to lie in the pursuit of a perfectly pure, perfectly nutritious, perfectly cheap sausage. From every conceivable source Andrey Babichev accumulated his knowledge. He asked questions here, gave advice there, always made little worried grunts as he moved among the workmen. Often when he left the telephone he seemed angry and disgruntled, but sometimes he showed a gentle delicacy and feeling for other people's opinions. But not always. In the end, of course, they managed to make the sausage he wanted them to make. In the end, out of those mysterious incubators there appeared a tremendously thick roly-poly of a sausage, a sausage literally *packed* with meat.

Babichev took a piece of the sausage in his hands and became suddenly quite purple. Terribly ashamed of himself, like a man introducing his wife to his friends for the first time, watching the expression on their faces to see what sort of an impression she had made on them. His face shone with happiness after that. He turned from one to the other and lifted up his hands in horror, as though he wanted to say: "No, no! Not at all like that! It's no good to me, absolutely no good to me! This is the sort of sausage which will be the death of men like me. Incomprehensible how human beings can fall so low as to produce things like this! A twirk of nature, a sport, something absolutely and finally incomprehensible. Take it away! I am ashamed of it."

I left them and walked vaguely away. In my hands I had a pound and a half of sausage.

I stood on the bridge.

The Palace of Work lay on my left, behind me the Kremlin. In the river, boats floated past and swimmers swam in the depths. A pinnace shot along the river, like a bird, exactly like a bird. From the height where I stood she looked like a tremendous almond which had been slit in two: later, she disappeared under the bridge. All I can remember now is the shape of the funnel, two people sitting on the deck, eating bortsh from a plate. A curl of transparent smoke moved towards me, then disappeared. As it melted in the air, it seemed to enter a fourth dimension, and there it hung, a mysterious, astral cloud, only barely visible.

I wanted to throw the sausage in the river.

Andrey Babichev is a very famous man, a member of the Society of Political Prisoners, an administrator—and for him today there had been a festival of rejoicing. Why? Simply because he had discovered a new genus of sausage? Can you imagine anyone rejoicing over a sausage? Can you imagine anyone achieving fame through sausages?

Today he shone with an exemplary lustre. Glory lay visible on his face. Therefore why should I be denied the expression of my love, my exaltation, my veneration in the sight of his glory? I am consumed with anger. He is an administrator, a communist, one of the founders of the new age: and this is the age when glory is fanned into a flame whenever the sausage-maker discovers a new genus of sausages. I don't understand this sort of glory. It is not the glory you read about in the old biographies, on the old monuments, in history books. Has the sense of glory made a *volte-face*? Has it changed everywhere on earth, or only here, here where a new world is being created before our eyes? Even if it is true that the sense of glory has only changed in this country, I am still capable of feeling the triumph, the immense importance of this new world which is growing up around me. I am not blind. I have got a head on my shoulders. There is no need for anyone to come and teach me, to explain things to me. I too know how to read and write. But I want fame! I want glory! I want to shine in the world, as Babichev shone today! But I don't want fame if I can get it for producing a new sort of sausage.

I wander aimlessly through the streets with the parcel under my arm. That wretched, mangy-looking sausage has become the master of my fate, it has taken the place of my will. I don't want it, I tell you!

Often I thought of throwing it over the parapet. Only the thought that the sausage would wrench itself free from the paper wrappings and suddenly shoot off on its own and disappear in the water like a torpedo, restrained me. There was another thought in my mind which filled me with terror. I could see Babichev walking towards me all the time, walking towards me like a terrible and unconquerable monument with staring eyes. I was afraid of him. I knew that he could do exactly what he wanted to do with me. He did not look at me, he saw through me. He did not see me at all. When his face turned towards mine, I saw that there was no light in his eyes: the only light came from the pince-nez where two perfectly round, perfectly empty metal discs shone in the sunlight. He was not in the least interested in looking at me, he had not the time and he had not the faintest desire to stare at me, but all the same I knew that he was looking right through me.

That night Solomon Shapiro came along with two friends. Babichev gave them all a dinner. The old Jew had brought a bottle of vodka. They nibbled at the sausage, they drank the wine. I refused to eat with them and instead I watched them from the gallery.

Artists have immortalized feasts before now. Their canvases have been crowded with generals feasting, dogs feasting, even quite ordinary gluttons feasting. A whole epoch stares at you from their canvases. Feathers stirring, clothes falling away, faces that glow and burn in a strange light.

I wish there had been a Tiepolo at that feast of ours. There they sit round the table in the light of a hundred candles, conversing so elegantly to each other. Draw them, paint them! Paint a portrait of a "Feast among Civil Servants."

Tiepolo, I can see your canvas now. I can see students staring at that canvas of yours: but those who are looking at it, their faces perched in the air, will never know the name of that fat giant over there, the one wearing blue braces, and they will never know what he was talking about and why he looked so pleased with himself. On the tip of his fork there lies a piece of nibbled sausage. Long ago it ought to have disappeared down his throat, but he has been so enthralled with the conversation that he has not yet had time to swallow it.

"Is there anyone here who knows anything about sausages?" asked the giant in the blue braces. "Is there anyone here who knows anything about sausages? Shut up, Solomon! You're a Jew and a Jew can't know anything about sausages—the only thing you know anything about is kosher meat. I tell you, there is no one here who knows anything about sausages. In this country sausages suffer from sclerosis. I want to explain. . . . It is my opinion that sausages ought to be *liquid*! One day—you just wait and see—I am going to make liquid sausages. Liquid sausages!"

9

WE MET at the aerodrome.

I say "we," but I should add that I was entirely neutral, something carried along with the tide. No one spoke to me, no one wanted to know what I thought of the place. I might just as well have stayed at home.

We were going to watch the first flight of a new type of soviet aeroplane. Babichev had been invited. We swept past the barriers. Even among such a distinguished gathering as this, Babichev was head and shoulders above everyone else. He had only to start a conversation with someone and immediately there would be a small circle of admirers listening with deferential attention. In his grey suit he looked extremely elegant. The curved shoulders towered over everyone else. His binoculars, hanging by leather straps, fell over his stomach. When he was talking to anyone he put his hands in his pockets and rocked silently backwards and forwards, from the tip of his heels to the tip of his toes and then back again, his legs straddled wide apart. Often he would scratch his nose, then look closely at his fingers, staring at them as though he might find some use for them as pincers. People who were listening to him aped him involuntarily: they even aped the play of his features. They found themselves scratching their noses—and that surprised them.

I was furious because he had deserted me. I went away and sat in the restaurant; feeling the wind brushing against my face, I thought of the countryside and drank my beer. I spent a long time over the beer, watching the delicate patterns the wind carved in the tablecloth.

There were untold miracles in the aerodrome. Near the barriers the field was covered with daisies, ordinary daisies with blazing yellow centers. And low on the horizon there were small puffs of curled cloud which looked as though they had been fired from a cannon. Wooden arrows, painted a brilliant red, were flying around me in all directions at once. High above our heads, now swelling, now contracting, hung the silken trunk of the wind indicator. Here, on the green grass, old battles had been fought and men had hunted wild deer—yes, here, among all the romantic legacies of the past, aeroplanes were flying. At the thought of these contrasts I began to experience an extraordinary pleasure. Perhaps, after all, it was only the rising and falling rhythm of the wind indicator which induced these meditations.

Ever since I was a child, the name of Lilienthal has been like a miracle in my eyes. It reminds me of the sound of the rustling of an insect's wing, or of something quivering between two bamboo poles. Since aviation began, the name has always had a place in my memory. Otto Lilienthal was killed. Because he was killed, aeroplanes no longer resemble birds and their wings are transparent and yellow. Before they rise in the air, aeroplanes seem to dig themselves in the ground, raising an enormous cloud of dust. They are like huge fishes. How true it is that aviation has become an industry in the twinkling of an eye.

Military music. The Commissar for War has arrived. He walks ahead of the others, passing quickly down the guard of honor. As he walks he scatters leaves in the air. The orchestra plays dance

music and the Commissar walks along to the beat of the elegant
rhythm of the orchestra.

I hurried to the barrier. They would not let me in. A soldier
said, "Get back there." Then he passed his hand across the top of
the barrier.

"Well," I said.

He turned away. His eyes were searching for more interesting
things in the field. The pilot was wearing a suit of red leather. His
shoulder-straps were drawn tightly over his thick, well-set shoulders. There he stood, in front of the Commissar, and neither of
them moved. The only movement came from the music. Babichev
stood bolt upright, his stomach sticking right out.

"Let me in!" I said, clutching the soldier by the arm.

"You'll be sent off the aerodrome if you are not careful," he
replied.

"But I tell you—I was inside. I only went out for a moment. I
was with Babichev."

He explained that you had to show your invitation card; I did
not have an invitation card. Babichev had simply taken me along
with him. I don't know why I was angry for not being allowed on
the field. Here, on the other side of the barrier, I could see just
as well. Only I was insistent. Something far more urgent than
a simple desire to get into the field prompted me to climb over
the wall. Suddenly I realized that here there was nothing that
really interested me, that all those important figures on the field
meant less than nothing to me, that my presence there would add
nothing to the general assembly. I stood apart from them, separate
and apart from all the men in the aerodrome, from everyone in
the world.

"I'm not a fool, comrade," I said. I was extraordinarily excited.
Even if I had searched longer for a better phrase to cool my excitement I don't think I would have succeeded. "What do you take
me for? I'm not a fool! I was with the people over there." I
pointed towards the group who were being introduced to the
Commissar for War.

"I don't believe a word of it," he said, smiling.

"Well, ask comrade Babichev." I made a megaphone with my hands and stood on tiptoe, shouting at the top of my voice.

"Andrey Petrovich!"

The music ceased. With the last rolling echo of the drum I thought I heard the rumbling of a subterranean earthquake.

"Comrade Babichev!"

He heard me. The Commissar for War heard me. Everyone turned in my direction, and the pilot lifted his hand to his cap, gracefully shielding the sun from his eyes.

I was petrified with fear. I crept behind the barrier and hid behind a fat little man who was wearing trousers which were far too short for him. I must have had an enormous amount of courage to have dared to attract their attention. They were hushed into silence. They stood at attention and none of them could see who it was who had shouted at them. They were waiting for something to happen. I did not have the courage to shout at them again.

But they knew who it was. They knew it was me. A moment later the silence came to an end. When they began to talk again I could have wept.

Then once more I raised myself on tiptoe and made a megaphone with my hands. When I shouted I almost deafened the soldier. I sent my words spinning into the far distance.

"You old sausage-maker!"

Then again:

"Old sausage-maker!"

Once more:

"Old sausage-maker! Old sausage-maker! Old sausage-maker!"

Babichev, wearing a Tyrolean hat, was still towering over all the others. I remember that I had a sudden desire to shut my eyes and lean over the barrier. I can no longer remember whether I did close my eyes, but I do remember that at that moment I saw Babichev turning towards me. For a tenth of a second he seemed to be gazing at me. He had no eyes, only the two little circles of his pince-nez which gleamed, like quicksilver, in the sunlight. I was overwhelmed with the thought of the inevitable retribution—

and somehow that overwhelming sense of the imminence of retribution brought me to a state like sleep; and in my sleep I seemed
to dream; and in my dream the most terrible thing of all was
Babichev's head, Babichev's head turning slowly towards me above
a body which remained perfectly motionless. His head seemed to
revolve round a pivot while the rest of his body remained perfectly
motionless.

10

I LEFT the aerodrome. But I could not tear myself away
from it at once—it still attracted me. I stood on a green mound,
leaning against a tree and covered with dust. All the ferns bowed
their heads before me, praying before a saint. I snipped off the
bone-like petals of a flower, sucked them and spat them out of my
mouth. As I stood there, I turned my pale face to the heavens.

An aeroplane left the hangars. It flew over my head, purring
strangely, flying across the line of my vision like a wooden lathe,
cropping the leaves of the trees. As it flew higher and higher I
followed it with my gaze towards the horizon. Sometimes it
blazed away like fire, then turned black. Distance lent it her enchantment—now it was like the barrel of a gun, now like a penknife, like the crunched petals of a lilac.

All this triumph had taken place without me. The first flight of
a new soviet aeroplane had taken place without me. So I declared
war on Babichev for insulting me.

Soon afterwards they came out of the gates. I saw Babichev's
dark-blue car. Alpers, the chauffeur, saw me, nodded; but I turned
my back on him, kicked up little earthworms with my feet.

I ought to go along and speak to Babichev, I thought. I ought
to go along and try to make him understand that it is not I, but
he, who is in the wrong. It was too late—he had passed out of
sight. He went first to the offices, they said, and later they told
me that he had gone along to the factory. Yes, he had gone along
to the "Threepenny Bit."

The devil he has! I thought of cursing everyone within sight, changed my mind and rushed after him, terribly afraid of missing him.

The factory was yellow in the sunlight. It hovered high in the air like a mirage, surrounded by forests and pasture-lands, a brilliant beehive floating in the air far in the distance.

I hurried on. Everywhere the noise was deafening, a Niagara of noise: and everywhere there was dust. I went round by the back way. A rope had been thrown across the entrance and at that moment a sparrow alighted on it, bending it a little, and then, for some reason, I remembered how I used to try and stand on my head when I was a child. As I went on I smiled, thinking of the enormous amount of sawdust I would gather on my shoulders when I fell over.

Where had he got to?

I can't get by. There is a lorry in my way. It won't move out of my way. It trembles, lurches forward and then springs back again, like a beetle walking along a horizontal plank, coming to the end and seeing the abyss which stares at its face.

Going down that road is like walking into the labyrinth of the ear.

"Could you please tell me where I could see Comrade Babichev?"

They tell me he is "over there."

"Over there?"

"Yes, over there."

I have to walk along a girder—below me a yawning chasm. It is difficult to keep one's balance walking over a girder over a yawning chasm. There is nothing to hold on to.

All around me there are those monstrous girders—black and cold. Like a shipyard. Terrible.

"Over there?"

"Yes, over there."

I shall never catch up with him. Suddenly I catch a glimpse of him walking over some baulks of timber. Immediately afterwards he disappears. I catch another glimpse of him a moment later, further away—and between us there is a gaping void. If I am not careful, he will go through one of the doors of the factory before I reach him.

He stood stock-still. There were other people with him: they were wearing caps and aprons. When I do get up to him, all I want to do is to say that I am sorry.

Then I saw a short cut. All I had to do was to climb a staircase. I could even hear his voice. Only a few more steps and I would be right on top of him! But it was not quite as easy as all that. I had to bend down on my hands and knees. Or else go back. While I was crawling up the steps, he flew past me, literally flew past me, flying on air.

I said I saw him flying on air. Actually all I saw was his nose, his two nostrils. Like looking up at the face of a statue.

Where had he got to?

He had disappeared out of sight. Flown away, borne along on a thin wafer of iron. As he flew impenetrable darkness followed him. Then I saw him standing on a small semicircular plate, making a tapping noise with his feet: he was standing on the platform of a crane constructed of girders, countless beams laid crosswise. When I saw his nose, I had been looking through long avenues between the girders.

I sat down on the stairs.

"Where is he?" I asked.

The workmen laughed at me. I laughed back. I was like the clown who trips over his heels as soon as he comes on the stage.

"It's not my fault," I said. "I am not sorry. It is he who ought to be sorry."

11

I DECIDED that I would not go back to him.

My own lodgings were now occupied by someone else. The lock hung on the door. The new occupier had gone away. I thought of the lock and the face of the widow Procopovich—they were exactly alike. Perhaps she will once more enter into my life.

Night descended over the boulevard. The morning flowered

above my head in beauty. There were other down-and-outs sleeping near me on the benches. They lay there, their bodies contorted, their hands deep in their pockets, pressed against their bellies, Chinamen strapped to a stake and beheaded. Dawn stroked them with her icy fingers. They snored and groaned and shook themselves, keeping very still, never opening their eyes, never moving their hands from their pockets.

The birds wake up. Suddenly they piped out in little thin tones —all the burden of their song—the voices of birds, the voices of grasses. Pigeons romped on the stones at my feet.

Trembling, I walked away. I yawned like a dog.

(Doors opened. Glasses were filled with milk. The judges announced their verdicts. The man who had been on his feet all night crept toward the window and stood there amazed, unable to recognize where he was in the overpowering glare of the light. The man who was ill asked if he could drink. The little boy ran into the kitchen to see if there were any mice in the mouse-trap. The morning had begun.)

That day I wrote a letter to Andrey Babichev.

I had lunch in the Palace of Labor on the Solyakaya. I drank a glass of beer and then I wrote:

DEAR ANDREY PETROVICH!

You have given me shelter. You have let me live with you under your roof, you have let me sleep in that wonderful bed of yours! You knew how miserable my life was before I met you. One heavenly night you took pity on me, you took a poor blind drunk to your heart.

You wrapped me in linen sheets. The sweetness, the loveliness of the sheets seems to have had no *raison-d'être* except to put my burning mind to rest, to lay quiet hands on my incurable insomnia.

Into my life there entered the bone buttons of your sheets. Staring at them it was sometimes possible to see the glowing iris swimming before my eyes. The memory of the glowing iris of the spectrum soared from my distant childhood.

You gave me a bed.

I want to tell you that the word "bed" seemed to come then from the distant, romantic past. It was a word which reminded me of all my childish toys.

You gave me a bed.

From the heights of your glory a bed came down to me, a rosy aureole which surrounded me with its enchanted warmth, with memories of childhood, with sweet regrets and with everlasting hopes. Then I began to hope that it would still be possible for me to recapture my long-lost youth.

You have loaded me with blessings, Andrey Petrovich.

Those moments when I thought of you as the famous man, when I thought of that great industrialist who had taken me into his house—I want to tell you what I thought of you in those moments.

Yes, I want to tell you the source of all my feeling for you— it was disgust!

Comrade Babichev, I simply loathe the sight of you.

I am writing this letter to you because I want you to feel humiliated.

From the first moment of my stay with you, you terrified me. You crushed me, you suppressed me.

I can see you standing in front of me now. All you are wearing is your trousers. You smell of sweat, a smell like the smell of beer. When I look at you closely, your face swells strangely, your chest heaves, you expand like the swollen clay of a statue. I feel as though I want to scream out aloud.

Who has given you the right to oppress me?

Precisely in what way am I worth less than you?

Are you more intelligent than I am?

Is your soul richer than mine?

More delicately poised?

Is it stronger than mine? Is it more significant than mine?

Is it greater, not because it was placed in you personally, but because it is intrinsically greater?

Why must I have to acknowledge your superiority over me?

Those are the questions I asked myself. Every day I found a

part of the answer. A month passed and now I know the truth and I have no longer any fear of you. You are a fat-headed bureaucrat—you are nothing more than that! It was not the overpowering significance of your personality that used to crush me—not a bit of it! Now, of course, I understand you perfectly. I can place you in the palm of my hand and study you to my satisfaction. My fear of you has passed away like a childish thing. I have thrown you to the earth and I have found that you are hollow.

Once I was tormented with doubts. I used to say, "Perhaps, after all, I am like a grain of miserable dust before you. Perhaps, after all, I, who am ambitious, do see you as someone towering above us all."

Now I know that you are just a fat-headed official, like all officials you are fat-headed, now and in the past and for everlasting. Like all officials, you are a tyrant to your inferiors. Nothing else will explain your ridiculous behavior over an ordinary piece of sausage, nothing else will explain why you deigned to pick up a strange young man from the streets. It was for the same reason, it was simply because you are a tyrant, that you took Volodya Makarov to your heart—although I know nothing about him except that he plays a game called football. You are a—Grand Seigneur! You want to surround yourself with court-fools and parasites. Yes, I am quite certain that Volodya Makarov will run away from you, he will not stand up to your insistent mockery. You have systematically made a fool of me. In the same way you have systematically made a fool of Volodya Makarov.

You told me that he was like a son to you and that he saved your life: all the time, while you were telling me these things, you were absorbed in your dreams. I remember now. It was all—all—lies! You felt uneasy, didn't you, when you realized that you had been acting the Grand Seigneur all your life? Ah, but I saw the birth-mark on your back.

In the first place, when you said that the bed belonged to someone else and that it would have to be given back when that "someone else" came back, you wounded me deeply. A moment after you had spoken, I realized that you were as cold and as insensitive towards him as you are towards me. *You* are the Grand Seigneur; *we* are the parasites.

Now, let me tell you that neither he nor I will ever come back to you. You have no respect for people. He won't come back to you unless he is a bigger fool than I am.

My destiny demands that I should neither be put in chains nor become a revolutionary. I shall never spend my life doing important things. I shall never spend my life making soda-water bottles or beehives.

But do you believe that that means that I am a child unworthy of his age? That therefore it is you who are worthy? Does it mean that you are everything, that I am nothing?

You found me by the wayside. . . .

What a fool you looked!

When you found me, you said to yourself, "Here's a worthless good-for-nothing. I'll make him do some work for a change. I shall be his teacher, his leader." You just didn't trouble to bring yourself down to the level of the man in the roadway. That's your pride, your self-conceit—not bringing yourself down to his level. A pretty-pretty official, Comrade Babichev.

Oh, what did you think of me, what did you think of that member of the proletariat who had strayed from the straight and narrow path? You decided to help me. Thank you! I am strong, strong—do you hear?—so strong that I can lose my way and find it again, and then lose it again, if it pleases me.

I often wonder what sort of emotions will be going through your mind when you read this letter. Perhaps you will try to get me expelled or sent to a lunatic asylum. You can do anything—you, the Grand Seigneur, member of the government. Once, do you remember, you said your brother ought to be shot? You said too, "Let's take him away to the hospital."

Your brother is extraordinary enough in all conscience. I can't understand him, but I know that his brain conceals unfathomable mysteries. The name "Ophelia" has a strangely moving sound and it seemed to me that you feared the sound of that name.

Anyhow, I have come to some significant conclusions. I can

see into the future. I am in your way. I know that I am worrying you. Yes, I am almost certain that I am worrying the life out of you. I won't let you—I won't let you elope with your brother's daughter. True, I only saw her once. It was I who spoke to her about the branch full of flowers and leaves. You have no imagination. You sneered at me. I heard you over the telephone. You have blackened my character in her eyes, just as you tried to smirch the honor of her father. It is simply not to your advantage that this girl, whom you want so much to seduce, should hang around him and love him—as you wanted us to love you. It is not to your advantage that she should have emotions. You want to make use of her, that's all: you want to make use of her in the same way that sheep's head and pigs' trotters can be used, "by treatment in an electric spiral bore . . ." (See your brochure.)

I won't let you. All you think of is that she is a dainty little morsel, don't you? You—you are a glutton and a belly-worshipper. How could you possibly refuse yourself anything that concerned your body? There is, of course, nothing on earth to prevent you from seducing her. What does it matter to you if she is your niece? What the hell do you care about family love? You want her for yourself! You want to tame her for your own selfish pleasures.

And that's why you got into a furious temper and hurled abuse at your brother. Anyone who met him would think he was a most remarkable, interesting man. Without knowing anything about him, I have come to the conclusion that he is a good fellow— although I haven't the faintest idea what he is good at. You rushed at him! I heard you shivering the balustrade with your hands. You have made the daughter leave her father's house!

You won't talk to me like that.

I stand here in defense of your brother and your brother's daughter. Listen, you old fool, you who laughed over the branch full of flowers and leaves, listen to what I am going to tell you. I said that, because that was the expression of my feelings for her. How did you express your feelings? . . . You said I was just a drunk because I addressed her in a language and in images that were totally unknown and foreign to you. Because they were unknown to you, they seemed to you to be amusing, perhaps even— terrible. Now you are smiling, but one day I shall make you laugh on the other side of your face. Don't for a moment think that I can only think in images. I can think just as well with real words. How? Well, I can talk about her, about Valya, using quite ordinary words. Therefore, my dear sausage-maker, I proceed to declaim a series of definitions. I hope they will worry the life out of you.

She stood before me . . . If you prefer my way, she was lighter even than the shadows, lighter than any shadow on the earth, than the shadow of the envious falling snow. I am afraid I have no alternative. I shall declaim the definitions in my own way. She did not hear me with her ears, only her forehead heard me, her head inclined a little. She was so sunburnt, her cheeks were so rounded, so delicately curved around her chin was her skin, that she was like a hazel-nut. Do you follow me? No! As she ran, her dress opened and I saw that she was not sunburnt all over and that a little blue vein . . .

Now I shall talk to you in your language, I am going to speak to you about the girl you wanted to seduce. Before me stood a girl aged about seventeen, almost a child, broad-shouldered, grey-eyed, short curly hair, an entirely charming adolescent as beautifully proportioned as a chessman—don't bluff yourself! That last little touch is entirely my own. You will add that she is not very tall.

I won't let you have her.

She is going to be *my* wife. I have dreamt about her all my life long.

Very well then. We shall fight it out. You are thirteen years older than I am. Those years which now lie behind you now lie in front of me. All you can do, the utmost limit of your powers, is to gain a partial sausage-success, or perhaps one day you will build up another of your rotten restaurants.

There is no limit to my dreams of conquest.

Not you—but I—shall have Valya. Together, our fame will resound throughout Europe, there where fame is still held in high honor.

I shall have Valya as the price I pay for my life, as the reward for all the humiliation I have been made to suffer, as the reward for a youth which was too short to enjoy, as the final, ultimate reward for my miserable existence.

Do you remember when I told you about the old cook who used to wash herself in the corridor? Well, there will be someone else soon. The room will be full of sunlight gleaming, in front of the window a blue basin, in the blue basin the windows will dance at their pleasure, and my Valya will wash herself in the blue basin, glistening, glittering like a salmon leaping, splashing and playing with her body, like an artist playing on a clavichord.

Whatever happens, I shall fulfil my desires. She will never be yours.

Goodbye, Comrade Babichev.

How could I have had the courage to spend a whole month playing such a humiliating part? I shall never come back to you. Wait a moment. It is just possible that the *first* man you fooled will come back to you. Give him my affectionate regards. However, there is nothing more delightful than the thought that I shall never have to return to you any more.

In future, whenever my pride is wounded, I know that by some peculiar association of ideas I shall remember the days I spent nailed to your desk. The thought of it terrifies me.

Evening. You are sitting at your desk. Your whole body is suffused in the rays of your self-conceit. The rays splutter and you say, "I am working. Keep quiet, Kavalerov. Don't interrupt me. Tch, tch. . . . Bourgeois!"

In the morning your praises ring from a thousand mouths.

"A great man, an extraordinary man—that Andrey Babichev."

As long as the toadies are singing hymns to you, as long as you remain puffed up in your pride, remember that there is a man who stands beside you—a man unknown to everybody, a man from whom no one ever asks advice—and this little fellow watches every move you make, watches you carefully, studies you, not from below, not servilely, but humanly, quietly; and inevitably he comes to the conclusion that you are a man who has been placed in a high position by the pressure of circumstance, not because you deserve your place in the world, for you are an ordinary fellow like the rest of us.

It is stupid of you to keep on making a fool of yourself.

That's all I wanted to tell you.

You wanted me to become your court-jester. Instead I have become your enemy.

"What do you want here, you little fool?" you screamed. I don't know what you think he wanted. Your body, your friends, your warehouses, your shops, the beehives in your garden? I can't imagine what you were talking about.

There is something I want to do. I want to frighten you. I want to fight you. I want to fight the most commonplace, the most egoistical, the most sensual, the most block-headed, the most conceited Grand Seigneur who has ever lived. I shall wage war upon you in the name of your brother, in the name of the girl you have seduced, in the name of all tenderness and pathos and singularity, in the name of those names which stir me to the depths of my soul, in the name of everything you trample underfoot—you, the greatest, the most remarkable man in the world.

My kind regards to Solomon Shapiro.

12

THE maid opened the door. Babichev had gone out. He had drunk his milk and now the thick glass lay on the table. Beside it, there was a plate full of biscuits shaped like characters in a Hebrew alphabet.

There is no purpose in human existence. The constant rumbling movement of the world is terrible and unbearable to me. When I first came here the sun used to fall on the lintel of the door at two o'clock in the afternoon. Now, thirty-six days later, at two o'clock it falls on another part of the house entirely. Watching the reflection of the sun on the walls is a childish game: but there is nothing else which reminds me so much of eternity.

I went on to the balcony.

At the end of the road there was a group of men listening to the church bells. It was impossible to see the church from the balcony. The church, they say, is famous for its bells. The men arched their heads, listening to them.

There was a time when I myself had stood at the corner of the street, for a good hour, listening to the bells. Through the curve of the little window in the tower, I could see inside. There, everything was dank and dark, like an attic, the joists covered with cobwebs. There, the bell-ringer played his maddening carillon, surrounded by his twenty bells: like a coachman, he throws his body violently forward, bends his head across his chest, whistles through his teeth. He hung at the center of a dark assemblage of ropes, now limp, now trembling on the weight of his outstretched hands, now lunging into the corner, now throwing all the ropes into vicious confusion—a strange musician, as full of dark deeds, as formless, as shapeless as Quasimodo.

Distance lent him a strange, almost terrifying appearance. Sometimes he seemed to be playing with nothing more important than kitchen crockery, beating the bells out of plates, and then there was not much in his music to distinguish it from the music you hear in a restaurant or at a music-hall.

From the balcony I listened attentively.

Tom-vir-lir-li! Tom-vir-lir-li! Tom-vir-lir-li!

Tomvirlirli! It was Tom Virlirli dancing there in the air.

> *Tom Virlirli,*
> *Tom with a knapsack on his back,*
> *Tom with the youthful eyes.*

I have spent many mornings listening to the music that dishevelled bell-ringer strikes from his bells. Tom—that was the ring of the largest of the saucepans, the greatest of the bells: and Virlirli was the ring of all the little saucers.

When I was living here, when I was living happily under this roof, Tom Virlirli became very real to me. The musical phrase became a word: later it became a man, a man who seemed strangely alive when he stood before me.

Who was he? A young man, staring over the town, an unknown young man who fed his eyes on the town as it lay before him asleep, a town which took no thought of his presence there. The early morning mist had just melted on the house-tops, the town itself lay in a valley of green and shimmering clouds. Tom Virlirli smiled. He placed his hand over his heart, stared intently at the town, tried to discover the images of his childhood in the sharp outlines of the houses.

He carried a knapsack on his back.

He had decided that whatever he set his heart on—he would have.

He had all youth's casual pride and indeed he was the personification of all men's youthful dreams.

Days pass—perhaps not more days than it takes for the sun's rays to move from the lintel of the door into another part of the house. Soon all the little boys who dream of walking through the town on a May morning, a knapsack on their backs, thinking only of fame and glory—soon they will all be singing the song of the man who accomplished what he set out to do:

> *Tom Virlirli,*
> *Tom with a knapsack on his back,*
> *Tom with the youthful eyes.*

Thus it was that, looking on a small church in Moscow, my dreams took on the color of western-European romanticism.

I shall leave the letter on the table, I thought. Then I shall collect my things—I shall put them in a knapsack?—and then I shall be ready to go. The letter, folded twice, lay on a glass plate beside the portrait of the only man I considered a companion of my misery.

There was a knock on the door.

I opened it.

There, in the doorway, smiling a broad Japanese smile, holding a knapsack in his hands—was Tom Virlirli. Only Tom Virlirli had a curious resemblance to Valya.

It was Volodya Makarov, sun-tanned Volodya Makarov. He looked at me with a surprised stare, then his eyes left me and roved about the room. Often he turned aside to gaze at the divan. Under the divan there were my shoes.

"How do?" I said.

He strode up to the divan, lingered there for a moment, turned towards the bedroom and, standing before the vase which was shaped like a flamingo, he said:

"Where is Andrey Petrovich? Has he gone to the office?"

"I really don't know," I said. "Even if he has, he will come back here tonight. Perhaps he has gone out and there is another idiot hanging on his arm. You were the first. I was the second. This other little idiot will be the third. Or perhaps there were others before you. Or perhaps he has gone out with a girl."

"What are you driving at?" said Tom Virlirli.

His brows twisted upwards as he tried to understand what I was saying.

He sat on the divan. The shoes were irritating him. It was obvious that he was taking extreme care not to touch them with the back of his boots.

"Why have you come back?" I asked. "What the hell made you come back here again? He has taken all he wants out of us! Now—don't you understand?—he is interested in other things, in other people. He wants a girl. He wants to get his hands on Valya —and Valya is his niece! What do you think of that, eh? Now— do you understand? Get out! No, listen to me!"

I threw myself at him, but he remained quite still. All my words fell on deaf ears.

"Listen! Do what I did! Tell him the truth!" I showed him the letter I had just written. "This is the letter I have just written to him."

He got up at last and left me. His knapsack lay in the corner of

the room, near the divan. He went to the telephone and spoke to
the operator.

I had to leave all my things behind.

I ran like hell.

13

I KEPT the letter. Later I decided to destroy it. The footballer was living under his roof as though he were his son. The
way he had thrown his knapsack into the corner, the way he had
lifted up the receiver and asked for the operator, the way he had
looked searchingly round the room—everything pointed to the
fact that he was behaving as though he were in his own home.
I had passed a wretched night. Perhaps this is why I never wrote
the things I wanted to say. Babichev will never understand now
why I was angry with him. He will think it was just envy and that
I resented Volodya's presence there.

Well, thank heaven I kept the letter.

If he had received it, it would be exactly like firing a blank
cartridge at him.

I was wrong about Volodya, of course. I thought he was just
a little doll Babichev was playing with. It follows that in my
letter I was wrong in trying to take him under my wing. Babichev
cultivates only his similars. Therefore they grow up as blind, as
full of overweening pride as himself.

When Volodya was staring at me, he seemed to be saying, "I
am sorry, but you are quite wrong. It is not I—the parasite. It is—
you. I stand on an equal footing with him. I—I am the son of the
Grand Seigneur."

I sat on the bench. Then I discovered something which filled
me with terror.

The piece of paper I was holding in my hands was not the letter
I wrote: it was bigger than mine. Mine was still there. In my hurry
to get away I had picked up the wrong letter. This is the letter I
picked up:

My dear Andrey Petrovich, how do you do? I hope you are quite well. Has your new lodger strangled you yet? Has Ivan Petrovich had the goodness to set Ophelia on you? Try to remember, if you can, that Ivan Petrovich and Kavalerov are both tarred with the same brush and that they are both after your blood. Be careful. You know how weak you are and how easily you can be imposed upon.

Why do you persist in having such faith in him? You are letting any little tramp into your house nowadays. Kick him out—to hell with him! The next morning, go up to him and say, "I sincerely hope you have spent a good night here. Now get to hell out of it!" You are so tender-hearted! When I read your letter, I thought of your pity for a poor drunk lying by the wayside and of how you thought it was the sort of thing that might easily have happened to me, and of how you had taken him home, thinking about me— and when I read all that, I burst out laughing. It was not like you to do that: it was like Ivan Petrovich.

Everything happened, of course, just as I thought it would. You took this little swine in and then you must have got worried; you didn't know what to do with him. Heaven knows, it is awkward, asking a man to get to hell out of your house. There, you see I am reading a lesson to you. It must be your work which makes you so tender-hearted, the herbs, the fruit, the bees and the calves. As for me, I am an engineer! Laugh, Andrey Petrovich! Laugh, till your guts slit! You always used to laugh at me. Now do you understand that I belong to the new generation?

What are my plans? I shall come back, of course. What are you going to do then with that monstrous animal you have brought into your house? What are you going to do if he suddenly bursts into tears and refuses to let me have my divan? Won't you have pity on him? Oh, I'm jealous all right. I shall, of course, throw him out of the house and bite a big piece out of his neck. You are unkind—you like hearing the sound of your own voice—you like banging your fists on the table—you like swaggering and blustering—but when it comes to doing things, my friend, you cry off. Without me, Valya would still be in the hands of Ivan Petrovich, she would still be being bullied by Ivan Petrovich. Is she still with you? She hasn't returned to Ivan, I hope. Won't you ever—ever—realize that Ivan Petrovich is no more than a ham actor and that he has admitted himself that he is a charlatan and that he is worth no more than twopence three farthings? Don't waste any more tears on him.

Try to have him taken to the hospital. That will make him run! Or suggest to Kavalerov that he should be taken to the hospital. That will make him smart.

Don't worry. You said yourself, "Volodya, teach me, and if you teach me, I shall teach you." Now at last, we are teaching each other.

I shall come back soon, very soon. Father sends you his blessing. Farewell, Murom! When I walk around it at night, it no longer seems like a homely town. Nothing but factories—no town anywhere. Everything here bows to the sovereignty of the factory. At night the town is plunged in Sinaitic darkness, but in the fields the factories are ablaze with lights. Like a pageant, a cavalcade.

One day in the town I saw a young calf running after the Inspector of Police—or rather, it was running after the portfolio he was carrying under his arm. It ran along, this young calf, smacking her lips, running after the Inspector of Police for all the world as though she wanted to get her teeth into the portfolio. Think of it! A hedgerow along the side of a road, pools of muddy water, the Inspector of Police walking along in a red hat and the young calf bounding after the portfolio. Nice contrast!

I don't, for example, like calves. I myself am a robot. You have never really appreciated my qualities. I have become a machine: or rather, if I am not yet a machine, I want to become a machine. Nowadays machines are wild animals, thoroughbreds, fierce, as proud as Lucifer. Not like your sausage-machines, or your primitive carving knives—they are only important because they can slit the throats of the more domestic animals. I tell you, I want to become a machine. And I want you to give me your advice about it. I want to be proud of my work—proud because I work! I want to be utterly indifferent to everything, except my work. Machines fill me with envy. Why is it that I am worth less than a machine? It is we who have invented them, we who have created them—

and now they have become even more fierce in their ways than we are. You turn the handle, and there they are, working away, accurate to the third or fourth decimal place. I want to be like that. Do you understand me, Andrey Petrovich? I want to be able to work to that degree of accuracy. I want to be precise, accurate, perfect. Oh, how I want to talk to you about these things.

In everything I do I imitate you. I even make a noise when I am eating, like you do.

How many times have I told myself how happy I ought to be! You have raised me up, Andrey Petrovich! There is no other Young Communist in the world who lives as I do. When I am with you, I am with the wisest of men, with the most remarkable and the most intelligent man on the earth. Anyone else would give everything he has to live as I do and many envy me. I want to thank you with all my heart, Andrey Petrovich. Don't laugh when I say that I love you. I do love you. You will say then that I am a machine who is making love to you, won't you? I do love you—and I do want to become a machine.

How are your plans working out? Has the "Threepenny Bit" been built yet? Is everything all right? And how is "Strength and Heat"? And how is "Kampfer"?

And is everything at home going on all right? I know about the strange, unknown young man lying there on my divan. He will bring fleas into the house. Do you remember that day when they brought me back from the football grounds? I always remember it. Do you remember? How frightened you were, Andrey Petrovich! You were frightened out of your wits, snivelling like a child. I lay stretched out on the divan like a bar of solid iron and I kept on looking at you while you were working, while you were writing by the light of the green lamp-shade: then suddenly you looked up and I gazed into your eyes, and suddenly I shut my eyes—like a child in the arms of his mother.

Football. I'm in the Moscow team. I shall be playing against the Germans, and probably, unless of course Chukhov plays, I shall be in the All-Russia team as well. What do you think about that?

Valya. Of course we are going to get married. In four years'
time. Smile, damn you! You think we won't be able to hold out all
that time. Please believe me when I say that we shall be married
in four years' time and not before. In four years' time I shall have
become the Edison of the new age. We shall exchange our first
kisses on the day you open the "Threepenny Bit." You don't
believe me? We have sworn a solemn oath that that is what we
shall do. On the day the "Threepenny Bit" is opened, we shall
embrace each other on the grandstand, to the music of the blaring
trumpets.

Don't ever forget me, Andrey Petrovich. When I come back, I
may find that Kavalerov has become your greatest friend, that you
have entirely forgotten about me and that he has taken my place
in your affections. I shall find him perhaps doing gymnastic exercises with you, helping you to build up the factory. How can I ever
tell what he is doing? Or perhaps I shall find that, after all, he has
turned out to be someone who is extraordinarily clever, someone
cleverer than I am, and that you will have sworn an oath of eternal
loyalty together, and I, the Edison of the new age, will find myself
without a home, thrown out, ejected. I can see you sitting down
between Valya and Ivan Petrovich—laughing at me. Are you
going to let that swine Kavalerov marry my Valya? Tell the truth.
If you do, I shall kill you, Andrey Petrovich—make no mistake
about that. If you do that, you will have shown yourself unfaithful
to all our plans and all our conversations together.

I've spent enough time now annoying you. You're too busy to
listen to me for an eternity. I want to be a machine, I want to be
accurate to an infinite number of places of decimals—and yet here
I am, talking too much. Perhaps because we are no longer together.
Goodbye, my dear, charming companion. Fare thee well!

14

AN ENORMOUS cloud, shaped like South America, hung above the city. It shone brilliantly, but its shadow lay like a menace on the ground. The shadow moved with astronomical slowness towards the road where Babichev lived.

All who came into the road felt as though they were swimming against the tide: and seeing the movement of the cloud, their eyes trembled in the darkness and the earth disappeared under their feet. They walked on the earth as though they were walking on the surface of a spinning globe.

I plunged among them.

A balcony hanging in the air. On the balustrade a waistcoat. The bells were no longer ringing from the churches. A young man appeared on the balcony. The advancing gloom puzzled him for a moment, then he raised his head, looked around, leant over the balustrade.

The staircase, then the door. I knock. My heart beats so loudly that the lapels of my coat shiver and tremble. I am spoiling for a fight.

They let me in. The man who opens the door for me pulls it towards his own body: and the first person I see is—Andrey Babichev. Andrey Babichev standing in the middle of the room, his feet set wide apart: between his feet, a whole army of Lilliputians could pass without difficulty.

His hands are thrust into his trouser pockets. His coat, unbuttoned, juts out behind, the two tails like festoons hiding behind his hands, enclosed in their pockets. The position of his body seems to say:

"Well, what do *you* want?"

I notice only Volodya Makarov, and Volodya Makarov is the only person I can hear.

I walk towards him. The rain begins to fall outside.

In another moment I shall fall on my knees before him.

"Don't send me away, Andrey Petrovich! Don't send me away! I understand everything now! Have faith in me, just as you have faith in Volodya Makarov! Trust me! I too am young! I too shall be the Edison of the new age. How I adore you! How could I ever have left you! How could I ever have been so blind! I will do anything if only you will love me again as you used to do. Forgive me! Take me again! Give me simply four years! . . ."

Instead of saying this, instead of falling on my knees, I said acidly:

"Why aren't you at work?"

"Get to hell out of here," was all they would say to me.

Their answer was perfectly timed: it was like a scene in a play. But it did not come to me at once: there was a definite interval before the sound had time to impinge on my ears.

Then something extraordinary happened.

It began to rain. So, I thought, there will be lightning as well.

I have no desire to talk in images. I like talking simply. I once read a book by Camille Flammarion called *Atmosphere*. (The name echoes in my ears like the sound of planets whirling. And surely Flammarion is the name of a star!) He describes, I remember, the mysteries of ball-lightning, the incredible disturbance it makes when it falls. A smooth round ball slides silently into a room—then blinding light! . . . Please understand at once that I have absolutely no intention of introducing commonplace comparisons into this book. But the clouds did really look suspicious; like clouds in a dream, they came steadily, ineluctably forward. It is raining now. The window in the bedroom is wide open. Windows should never be left open when there is a storm brewing. Besides, there is a hell of a draught from somewhere!

Amid the raindrops, as bitter as tears, amid the gusts of wind which set the flamingo vase alight and kindled flames among the curtains and even on the ceiling, Valya suddenly appeared from the bedroom.

No one else was frightened by her sudden apparition, but I—I was frightened. In truth, everything is simple; a friend arrives and all the others hurry forward to greet him.

It is possible of course that Babichev had gone out to fetch Valya, dreaming perhaps of just such an occasion as this. In the end, everything is simple. As for me, I ought to be taken to the hospital at once, treated by hypnotism—my thoughts are my symbols now and I spend my time attributing to ball-lightning the curious apparition of a woman.

I must break up that illusive sense of simplicity.

"Please go away," I hear someone saying.

"It's not so simple as all that," I say.

Another draught! The door has been open all the time. In the wind I have grown wings. It beats mercilessly across my shoulders, sometimes almost touching my eyelids: and half my face is anaesthetized by the wind.

"It's not so simple as all that," I said, pressing my body against the door, trying to squeeze the life out of this terrible wind.

"You went away, Volodya, didn't you? And while you were away, Babichev lived with Valya. Wait just four years; then you will see how Andrey Petrovich spends his time playing with little Valya on his knees. . . ."

I found myself on the other side of the door. Half of my face had been anaesthetized in the wind. Perhaps it was for this reason that I did not feel the blow when it came.

The door was bolted sharply. It was as though a branch had broken, as though I had fallen from a beautiful tree, lazy like ripe fruit, and like ripe fruit making hardly a sound as I fell.

"That is the limit," I said quietly, as I got up. "I am going to kill you, Andrey Babichev."

15

THE rain falls.

The rain hovers over the Tsvetnoy Boulevard, slithers across the circus, turns right towards the centre of the town, then, reaching the heights above Petrovskoy, suddenly turns dark and loses its vigorous strength.

I cross the Truba and half-way across the road my mind turns to that legendary fencing master who ran above the rain, parrying the raindrops with his sword. The sword glitters in the sunlight, the skirt of his coat flaps in the wind, and there he stands, hovering and revolving in the air, like the tenuous call of a flute. No rain has ever touched him. I have been told that this accomplishment of his he inherited from his father before him. For myself, I am drenched to the skin; I feel as though I have been slapped across the face.

Looking through the wrong end of a telescope, everything becomes brighter, clearer, and everything stands out in stereoscopic relief. The colors and the contours are more definite, and things, even the things you know well, are so absurdly small that it is like looking at the world through the eyes of a child, or in a dream. Have you noticed the smile that comes to the face of everyone when he looks through the wrong end of a telescope?

After the rain has fallen, the town seems brighter, clearer; it stands out in stereoscopic relief. You see the tram-cars for the first time covered in crimson paint. The pebbles on the causeway are not all the same color: if you look closely you will find some that are actually green. In the distance the artist comes out of the niche where he has been hiding from the rain and like a pigeon he patters along the stone paths. In the window there is a boy holding a piece of glass to the rays of the sun.

I bought an egg and a French loaf from a woman in the market.

I broke the egg against the mast of a tram-car in full view of all the passengers who were coming from the Petrovsky Gate.

I climbed the road. The benches reached up to my knees and here the paths were slightly convex. Here, mothers of children sat on the benches, or rather they sat on the handkerchiefs they had spread on the benches. Their faces were sunburnt, their eyes shone like fishes' scales. Above their necks they were sunburnt and all over their shoulders, but their swelling breasts were visible beneath their clothes and their breasts were white. Alone, a wanderer, conspiring with my melancholy, I drank from their white breasts, from pure mothers' milk, from the pride and purity of other marriages.

There was a nurse holding a doll in her hands and the doll was dressed in the manner of the Pope of Rome.

A sunflower seed hung obstinately on the lips of a girl who wore a red ribbon in her hair. Listening to the orchestra, she was unconscious of the fact that her feet were strolling through a puddle. The trumpets were like elephants' ears.

All—mothers, nurses, children, musicians, who had become one and inseparable with their instruments—they all thought of me as a fool. The musicians gazed only at me, and as they watched every movement I made their cheeks puffed and swelled out. The girl with the red ribbon in her hair began to laugh, then the petal dropped from her mouth. Then too she discovered that she was walking in a puddle and turned her back on me, as though she thought I were responsible for her feet.

I will show them that I am not a fool. In the whole world there is no one who understands me. Men think that everything they fail to understand is either terrible or ridiculous. Therefore shall I put terror into their hearts.

I walk up to a glass.

I like looking into shop-windows. Always they await you, trembling, on the other side of the road. As you walk round the town, doing the things you are accustomed to do, expecting nothing, neither miracles nor visions, suddenly you look up for a moment and there is the mirror gazing at you quietly. In that moment you realize that all the laws of the universe have suffered a sea-change.

All geometry, all optics, all physics, all the laws which govern your progress through the streets—they fall apart. You begin to think that you can see through the back of your head, and you smile nervously at the people who pass by, utterly astounded at your superiority.

"Aha," you say quietly, in a low voice.

That tram-car, which a moment ago seemed to be about to disappear for ever, suddenly returns to you, slicing through the road like a knife in butter. A straw hat, hanging by a blue ribbon on someone's arm—a moment before you had watched it and somehow it had attracted your attention, but you had no time to gaze after it. Now it appears to be following you, floating on air.

Distances are revealed before your eyes. You say, "Here is a house, a wall." And at the same time certainty nudges your elbow and you say, "No, it is not a house." Mysterious secrets are revealed to you. In the world which unfolds before your eyes there are no walls—and everything in the world becomes clear and simple, standing out in stereoscopic relief, like the world you see when you look through the wrong end of a telescope.

In this world everything is turned inside out. The laws of nature are broken and perspective no longer exists. Yet, as you spin round vertiginously in this world, in this extraordinary world, you can derive an enormous amount of pleasure in watching what is happening around you. Once the secret has been revealed to you, you hurry to the nearest window, you stare into the blue patterns of the glass where your face hangs suspended in the air, the only thing there is with a shape which is recognizable to you, the only pattern there is which conforms to the patterns of your everyday world. As you stare into the window, all the old patterns are lost and new shapes, new patterns, new projects, take their place. This is a world which it is impossible for a man to accustom himself to —though he stayed an hour. Here your features are a tropical garden, so green is the grass, so deeply blue the sky.

Unless you stand away from the window, you will never be able to tell from what direction that man is walking. If you want to discover these secrets, you must at least jump clear of your skin.

As I chewed the bread, I gazed at myself in the glass.

Then I turned away.

Someone came up to the window. Where he had come from it was impossible to tell. I prevented him from staring at the window, simply because I was there. When he saw me, the smile which lay in wait on his face ready to greet his face suddenly vanished. He reached to my shoulder. When he passed me he stood on tiptoe.

He hurried to the glass. All he found there was a caterpillar on the lapel of his coat. He flicked it away with his fingers, and as he flicked it he bent his arm, a violinist drawing on his bow.

I began to think about the optical illusions surrounding me, the sleight-of-hand performed so miraculously by the window-pane. The stranger came up to me.

"Where have you come from?" I asked. "What brought you here?"

"Where have I come from?" he said. (His clear, open eyes gazed into mine.) "I haven't come from anywhere. Just this moment I invented myself." He removed his bowler hat. By taking it off, he revealed a perfectly bald head.

He made an extravagant bow. It was the sort of bow by which a beggar replies to charity. Like all beggars, he had bags under his eyes, little vivid blue stockings. He was eating a sweet.

At that moment I recognized him: my friend, my teacher, my benefactor.

I seized him by the hand and drew myself close to him.

"There is just one thing I want to tell you."

He raised his eyebrows.

"What is it? Is it about Ophelia?"

I was just going to speak when I noticed that the sweet had melted in his mouth, was dribbling down the corner of his lips. Glowing with the amazing power of my love for him, I awaited his reply.

PART TWO

IVAN BABICHEV had no fear of old age. Occasionally he murmured a complaint about the way time passed him by or how the years were weighing on his shoulders, and he would complain sometimes about a mythical cancer on the stomach; but most of his complaints were light-hearted, probably untrue and certainly rhetorical.

Once he smiled, put his hand to his left breast and said:

"A curious sound—the sound of a broken heart."

And once he held his hands out and pointed to the veins swelling on the back of his hand. On this subject he spoke as follows:

This—this is the tree of life, a tree which tells me more than anything else about the secrets of life and death, more than the trees in the garden, which flower and turn to dust. I no longer remember the day when I first realized that in my hand I beheld the tree of life. I think now that it must have been quite early in life, in the heyday of my youth; for then, for the first time, I saw in the slow growth and final decay of the tree the true meaning of life and death: it was when I was a schoolboy, when time was measured by the length of the terms and by the length of the vacations. Later the tree assumed a darker blue and became more shapely; my blood no longer dark but apparelled in light, no longer a liquid, but rising like the dawn or the colors of a Japanese aquatint over the line of the bones.

Years passed. The tree grew old; and I too changed.

Those were happy years, those years I spent watching the tree growing. I would spend hours watching the leaves unfold. Soon they became brown and rugged, they seemed to conceal a hidden power, and in this hidden power I discovered my fortress against old age.

And now, my friends, look how weak they are! The branches have fallen away and there are large hollows in my hand. That's sclerosis, my friends. The skin has become transparent and all the tissues are like water—is not this the mist descending over the tree of my life, the mist which will one day envelop me entirely . . . ?

Once upon a time there were three Babichevs—all brothers. Ivan was the second. The eldest was called Roman. Roman was a revolutionary and he was executed for terrorism.

The youngest of the brothers, Andrey, emigrated. There was one day when Ivan wrote to his brother in Paris. "What do you think of it all? We've got a martyr in the family now," he wrote. "Won't grandmama be pleased?" To this letter his brother replied with his usual coarseness: "You're such a bloody fool!" And that was how the enmity between the brothers really began.

Ever since the days of his childhood Ivan had been a source of irritation to his family and his friends.

When he was twelve he experimented with an extraordinary invention he had made himself—a lamp-shade with bells hanging on the fringe. He showed it to the family. He was convinced that with the help of this invention anyone could go to sleep and dream about anything he wanted to dream.

"Good," said his father, who was the professor of Latin in the gymnasium. "I want to dream about Roman history."

"Be more precise, please," said Ivan promptly.

"Just Roman history—doesn't matter at all. Oh yes, I would like to dream about the battle of Pharsalia. Mind you, if I don't dream about it, there's something coming to you."

Later in the evening strange sounds came from the dining-room. In the study the professor lay stretched out on a chair, graven into a straight line by the power of his anger, as though in a grave. He had slammed the door to. The boy's mother paced up and down outside. While Vanya walked along the edge of the divan, a strange smile was playing upon his lips and he swung the lamp in the air, exactly like a Chinese rope-dancer waving a parasol. In the morning the professor jumped out of bed; he rushed at the wretched boy, who was sleeping the sleep of the just—the very lazy, very happy just. He was hauled out of bed by the skin of his neck. It was not yet daylight, and perhaps, if the professor had waited just a little longer, he might still have dreamt about the battle of Pharsalia. Instead he walked up to the window, tore the curtains apart and made a mock bow at the rising sun. The boy's mother did her best to prevent him from getting a thrashing. She held her arms out and screamed at the top of her voice:

"Don't hurt him! Don't hurt him! It's only a little mistake, really it is! Do you know why you didn't dream about the battle of Pharsalia? It was only because the sound of the bells didn't go in your direction, that's all it was! All this damp in the room. I—I—I saw the battle of Pharsalia! Oh, my darling, it was I who saw the battle of Pharsalia——"

"More lies," said the professor. "Tell me exactly what you saw. What were the Balearic slingers wearing? What were the Numidian archers wearing—tell me that?"

For a little while he kept his peace. "Then, quite suddenly, my mother burst into tears. After that I was whipped: I behaved like Galileo."

That same evening the maid was talking about how she had refused to marry Dobrodeev—that was the name of the man who had been proposing to her. "He's a liar," she said. "You can never believe what he tells you. Well, that same night, I dreamt about horses. They were trotting round a field and looked terrible—just as if they were wearing masks. And dreaming about a horse, let me tell you, means that someone is lying. . . ."

That day and the next Ivan's mother was being continually terrified out of her wits. Her lower jaw was continually trembling, and when she walked to the study door she walked like a somnambulist. They were all terrified. Even the cook, who spent her time standing over the oven, was terrified: and her lower jaw was continually trembling.

When his mother reached the study at last, she clutched her husband's shoulder. He was sitting at the table, trying to fasten the monogram which had fallen off his cigarette-holder. She spoke in a trembling, fearful voice.

"Please, Papa, go and talk to Frosia! It was Frosia who dreamt about the battle of—of Pharsalia."

No one knows what happened when the professor went to interview the maid, but everyone knows that two or three months after the adventure of the artificial dreams, Ivan was already working on another invention.

The story goes that he discovered a special sort of pipe and a special form of soap solution, and with those he had decided to make some enormous soap-bubbles, bubbles which would get larger and larger as they flew into the air. At first they were going to be about the size of the toys on a Christmas tree—and then about the size of a football—and then about the size of a rose-bush—and after that they would slowly go on accumulating air until they were the size of a small airship. At that point—when they had reached that point—they would burst and there would be a shower of golden rain all over the town.

His father was in the kitchen at the time. Like his forefathers before him, he was a man who took great pride in knowing the secrets of good cooking and he had a very high opinion of himself as a chef. For the soups—the recipe had been handed down from the dim past—the laurel leaves had to be just so; and he absolutely insisted on watching the egg in the saucepan until it reached the right temperature. It had to be cooked "to the skin" or it was no good to him.

He looked down from the kitchen window. There in the courtyard, near the wall, Ivan was happily dreaming. Stretching his yellow ears out of the window the professor began to listen and stare at the little boys who were surrounding his son. Ivan was talking about a special sort of soap solution and the bubbles he was going to make: they were going to be like airships, he said.

Once more the professor's bitterness began to rise in his throat. A year ago, Roman, his eldest son, had left him: he poured out all his spleen on his two younger sons. God has made a mistake in giving me sons, he thought bitterly.

He turned sharply from the window, still smiling angrily. When they were sitting down to supper he waited for Ivan to start talking about his plans, but Ivan absolutely refused to talk at all. Boiling over with anger, the professor thought, The boy despises me! He thinks I am just a fool—a fool! But later in the day, when the sun was setting, when he was drinking tea on the balcony, suddenly he saw a streak of glittering molten light, like a piece of glass far in the distance, over the flare of the setting sun—an enormous orange-colored ball of fire floating slowly and obliquely across the line of his vision.

The professor darted from the balcony, and through an open doorway leading into another part of the house he saw Ivan leaning out of a window and clapping his hands with extraordinary fervor.

"They gave me everything I asked for that day," said Ivan. "Father was frightened out of his skin. I kept on trying to look him in the face, but he was always turning away. Oh, I felt terribly sorry for him. His face got so black that I thought he was going to die. After that, I wasn't stuck up any more. That was an act of generosity on my part, not being stuck up any more. He was an old man and as hard as nails and he didn't have much intelligence, but he wasn't a man to worry over trifles. For instance, he didn't know that that same evening Ernest Vitollo was flying over the town in a balloon. There was terrific advertisements on all the hoardings, but he didn't notice them. Later on, I had to tell him it was a swindle, just had to. Those experiments were not much good, you know."

The truth is, of course, that Ivan was lying again. When he was twelve years old, flying had hardly advanced at all. It is difficult to believe that anyone actually flew over the provincial town he was living in. As for the invention and the experiments—that is another thing entirely. They were extremely brilliant.

Ivan Babichev continued to improvise. Everyone listened to him with delighted attention.

"We had a pretty terrible time that day," he said, referring to his experiments with dreams. "But I do think father dreamt about the battle of Pharsalia the next night. He didn't go to school. He spent the whole morning in his study with a bottle of Borjam which mother had brought him. But while he was dreaming, I don't think everything turned out well with history. I've got an idea that he couldn't stand the shock of seeing the battle come to an end with the arrival of the Balearic slingers in airships."

That was the end of Ivan Babichev's story about the bubbles and the soap solution.

There was another time when he entertained his friends with still more excerpts from his youth:

I remember there was a student called Chemiot who was madly in love with a girl. I can't remember her name. Let me see. Yes, it was Lili Kapitanski. She was called Kapitanski, I suppose, because she had a way of clicking her heels on the ground. We knew all about the student. He used to stand just below the balcony door, waiting for her to come out. There he would be, pining away, under the rails, trying to conjure his beloved out of the house. She was about sixteen—at that age, we used to think they were already old women. And poor Chemiot always looked so frightened, standing there under the window. He used to come up on a bicycle, wearing a blue forage cap, and his cheeks would be puffing and blowing and as red as a beetroot. At Easter, in May— it was one of those Easter days when the temperature never rose above ten degrees centigrade and the wind was as smooth and as soft as silk—you could tie a blue ribbon with it. Well, he rode up, full of despair and longing for his beloved, and there was Lili's aunt standing on the balcony, dressed in all the colors of the rainbow, like one of those chair-covers you used to see in country pubs, all frills and furbelows—and her hair was done up so that it looked like a snail. It was the girl's aunt. When she descended, as the saying goes, from the heights whereon she stood, she smiled sweetly, embraced him, opened out her arms and began to talk to him in a full-throated, dry voice.

"Lili is going to Cherson," she said. "She leaves this evening at seven forty. She is going away for the whole of the summer. But, my dear Sergey Sergeyevich, she has asked me to say goodbye to you. Goodbye, my dear Sergey."

With the insight of a lover the student understood everything, and he knew that somewhere in the golden shadows of the room poor Lili was crying her eyes out. He knew that she wanted nothing more than to come out on the balcony, and that she had seen him, without setting eyes on him, because he was wearing a white jacket—and white, according to all the laws of physics, contains all the colors of the spectrum and shines with a dazzling, almost Alpine brilliance. Yet, just because she lay entirely in the power of her aunt, she couldn't come out.

Well, I asked the student to lend me his bicycle. "I know how you can get your revenge," I said. "Please give me your bicycle. She is being packed off by force."

"How am I going to get my revenge?" he said. He was horribly frightened. Some days later I paid a visit to the aunt. I pretended that I had brought a cure for warts from my mother. On the curve of her lower lip there had always been an extremely large wart, and when I went along to see her, I made her kiss me, and used such force that my mouth charged into hers with the force of a catapult. My friends, believe me or not—with that kiss the student was avenged. Some time afterwards, flowers started to grow on her lip, little cornflowers which danced up and down to the tune of her breathing. The poor dear—she was overcome with shame. When she went out of doors, she would shriek to heaven in her agony— and then everyone ran away in panic.

Two things made me happy. One was that I was delighted with the success of my experiment—I was the first man to grow flowers on a wart! In the second place, I kept the bicycle. And let me tell you, bicycles weren't so common as they are now. In those days, if you had a bicycle, they had your portrait taken.

What happened to the aunt in the end?

Easy! The flowers grew until late in the autumn. She used to spend her time waiting hopefully for rainy days or days when there was a gale blowing. On those days she would set out through the side street, avoiding the busy parts of the town, until she came to the fields. The moral damage was enormous! She used to wrap her face in a scarf and then the flowers would caress her lips and whisper to her, the whisper of a bleak ill-spent youth, the ghost of a single kiss stamped out by angry feet. One day she sat on a hillside, took her scarf off and cried out, in a terrible voice:

"Oh, God in Heaven, grind him to powder; throw his ashes to the four corners of the earth! Send him, I pray thee, these accursed flowers!"

At that moment, as though hearing her words, the wind suddenly ceased. Immediately afterwards a raging bee took aim at the flower and began to trace buzzing figures of eight around the unhappy woman. She was pale with terror. She ran home as hard as her heels could carry her. She ordered the servant to say that she was not at home, and then she sat down in front of the glass and stared hard at her archaic face, adorned with archaic flowers. Where the bees had stung her, her face was monstrously swollen, like some huge tropical plant. She was petrified with fear. She began to think about nicking the flowers away, but even if she did, there was always the wart underneath. Besides, it was too risky. She might get blood-poisoning. . . .

Ivan Babichev was a jack-of-all-trades and master of none. He wrote poetry and music and painted extremely well: there were literally hundreds of things he could do. Once he even invented a dance, a dance specially contrived to show off his own particular particularities, his idiosyncrasies, his plumpness, his laziness, for like most men who achieve fame in their youth he was fat in the face and extremely sluggish. The dance was called "The Dance of the Waterlilies." Another time we find him selling paper snakes and whistles and Chinese lanterns: thenceforward, everyone admired him—partly for his high pressure salesmanship, partly for his attendant fame. In the road where he lived, he was called "the mechanic."

Afterwards, he studied engineering at the University of Petersburg. In the year his brother was executed, he got a job in the dockyard at Nikolaev, near Odessa, which lasted until the outbreak of the Great War.

But was he—was he really an engineer?

2

W A S he ever a real engineer?

In the year the "Threepenny Bit" was built, Ivan had a rather second-rate job. For a real engineer it was pretty low.

Just think of it! In the pubs he would spend his time drawing people's portraits or little sketches which they ordered from him, or he read people's character from the lines on their hands, or he showed his incredible powers of memory by repeating at least five hundred words immediately after they had been read aloud. Or else he would take a pack of cards from his waistcoat pocket and shuffle them, with the air of a card-sharper.

"Go on, go on!" they used to say. At that he would sit among them, and then the principal item on the program began at once. Ivan Babichev did the talking.

What did he talk about?

"We are the men who have reached the heights of our ambition," he would say, tapping the marble table-top with his beer-mug with a sound that reminded you of the scurry of horses' feet over hard asphalt. "We are the strong men! We are the men who have decided to live according to our visions! We are the men with strong will-power! We who are egoists—I am addressing myself to you, gentlemen, because you represent the quintessence of the intelligentsia in this benighted town of ours. We are the *avant-gardes*! Gentlemen—who stand in the forefront of civilization—I beg you to listen to me. Remember, a whole epoch has come to an end. A wave has broken on the shore, a wave seething with emotion, shining in the sunlight! Gentlemen, what is the greatest desire of your hearts? To disappear, leaving no trace behind you? No, my friends, it is not in this way that you should disappear! No! On the contrary! Come to me and I shall teach you the way of life."

His audience listened to him with a certain amount of respect, but without paying any attention to what he said. Occasionally they showed their approval by saying "Hear, hear!" and sometimes they even applauded him: and always, after the applause, his monologue would come to an abrupt end. At such moments it was his custom to bid them farewell by reciting a quatrain which went as follows:

> *I am not a German charlatan!*
> *I have never stolen a penny from the people!*
> *No, I am just a Soviet card-sharper,*
> *I, the miracle-worker of the age!*

Or else he said:

"The doors have been closed upon us! Can't you hear the sound of the doors as they close upon us? Don't run away! Don't try to get past the door! Stay where you are! By staying where you are, at least you will be in a position to demonstrate your pride. Stay and be proud! I am the leader you want. My name is the King of Platitudes. The man who drinks and weeps and drops his head on the table when he has drunk up all the beer and there is no more to be had—the place for such a man, I say, is by my side! Come to me all ye who are suffering or burdened with grief, all ye who are carried away on the shoulders of laughter and song! Those of you who have committed murder out of jealousy in your hearts and those of you who are going to tie a rope round your necks— I appeal to you all, children of a dying age, come to me! Philistines, dreamers, those of you who are fathers of families and love your daughters, those of you who are honest bourgeois, those of you who are faithful to your traditions, those of you who obey the codes of love and honor and duty, my dear soldiers and generals all—to arms! We who are fighting—it will be my special privilege to lead you to battle!"

He simply adored lobsters. He would tear them to pieces in his hands. And he was always untidy and his shirt was like one of those serviettes they give you in a public-house. He wore soiled cuffs, and if it were possible to imagine anyone combining the

extremes of filth and elegance, he succeeded admirably. For example, his bowler hat. For example, the flowers in his button-hole.
(The flowers used to remain in his button-hole until they had
almost blossomed forth into fruit.) For example, the fringe of his
trousers. For example, the little lambs'-tails which hung down
where his buttons ought to be.

"I simply adore crabs! Just look! I don't merely eat them—no, I
utterly ravish them, like the good little priest I am! Are you looking at me? Delicious crabs, aren't they? Look how they are crowned
with seaweed! Not seaweed? Very well then, herbs. I tell you, a
crab is an ocean liner dragged up from the ocean bed! Delicious
crabs! And have they come all the way from Kuma?"

He licked his hands carefully, then he looked inside his cuffs
and revealed further scattered fragments of the same lobster.

But was he ever an engineer? Did he ever, in his life, tell an un-
truth? Did he ever possess the soul of an engineer? It was impossible to imagine him working with machines and metals and
blueprints. Seeing him, you would have thought he was an actor
or an unfrocked priest. No one ever believed a word he said—and
he knew it. When he spoke there was always a twinkle in his eye.

Sometimes this fat little priest went to one pub, sometimes he
went to another. One day he even went so far as to permit himself
the honor of climbing on the table. He felt extremely awkward,
quite unprepared for a feat of such magnitude: and as he passed
among their raised heads he clutched grotesquely at the palm-
leaves. Suddenly bottles were being broken and the palm-tree
crashed to the ground. At that moment he stood up on the table,
brandished two beer-mugs, like dumb-bells, and started to ha-
rangue the mob:

"Here I stand upon the heights, looking down on my army of
warriors—an army which is crawling towards me. Oh, look upon
me! How noble an army it is! Oh, ye down-trodden actors, dreaming of glory, and ye who are unhappy in your love-affairs, and ye
who are old wives in disguise, and ye who are just looking—
office clerks, and ye who are consumed with ambition, and ye—

ye who are fools, look upon me, I beg you! Look at your king, at
your Ivan Babichev, who has come to you! The time is not yet ripe,
but soon—soon we shall set out on our journey. Oh, my army,
forward!"

He threw the mugs away and snatched an accordion out of
someone's hands and then placed it against his stomach. The
curious popping noise which came when he sat down nearly
caused a riot. Paper serviettes flew up to the ceiling. . . .

Men came forward from the counter. They were the men who
wear aprons and oilcloth cuffs.

"Beer! Beer!" he shouted. "More beer! A whole barrelful of
beer! Beer is a word pregnant with meaning! Let us drink to the
world!"

The proprietor of the pub refused to let him have any more
wine. Everyone, even the little priest Ivan, was hurried un-
ceremoniously outside. He was smaller than anyone else, but
he offered more resistance than anyone else when they tried to
push him. He was stubborn and angry, and when they tried to lift
him it seemed as though his stubbornness and anger had fallen
to his feet, they were so heavy. He was as unmovable as a corpse,
as heavy as an iron oil-cask.

Someone pulled his hat over his eyes.

In the street he tottered from one side of the road to the other,
as though he were being passed from hand to hand. Sometimes
he sang, sometimes he groaned aloud—and then he annoyed
everyone who passed by.

"Ophelia!" he sang out. "Oh, Ophelia, my darling!" He could
speak of nothing but Ophelia—a word which took wings and
flew above his head and carved figures of eight in the night air.

That same evening he paid a visit to his famous brother. Two
people were sitting at table facing each other, between them a
lamp hidden in a green shade. Volodya and his brother Andrey.
Volodya was asleep, his head lying over his book. Ivan was drunk.
He lurched towards the divan, trying to catch it with his feet, as
though it were a chair. He looked worried and haggard.

"You are—drunk," said his brother.

"How I hate the sight of you!" said Ivan. "You little tin-hat god, you——"

"Aren't you ashamed of yourself, Ivan? Lie down and go to sleep. I'll give you a pillow in a moment. Why on earth do you wear a bowler hat?"

"You don't believe a word I say, do you? You're just a bloody fool, Andrey! Don't interrupt! If you do, I'll smash that lamp-shade over Volodya's head! Keep quiet, blast you! Why won't you believe in my 'Ophelia'? Why do you persist in refusing to credit me with the invention of an epoch-making machine?"

"You haven't invented anything, Vanya! That's just a bee in your bonnet. Please understand that your jokes are in the worst of taste. You ought to be ashamed of yourself. You think I'm a fool, don't you? Well—just look at that damn-fool machine of yours! Just look at it! Do you really think a machine like that is going to work? And why on earth do you insist on calling it 'Ophelia'? And what the hell do you mean by keeping a bowler hat on your head when you are in here? What do you think you are—an old-clothes man or—a politician—or what?"

Ivan said nothing at first. Then, as though he had become sud denly sobered in a moment, he stood up and shook his fist at his brother. He walked menacingly towards him.

"You don't believe me? You refuse to believe me, don't you? Well, stand up! When the leader of an army of a million strong starts talking to you, you ought to know better than not to stand up. Get up! You—it's just that you haven't the courage to believe me. You talk about a machine like mine being a human impossibility. Well—let me tell you—I shall kill you with that machine of mine!"

"Don't shout so much," his brother replied. "You'll wake up Volodya."

"To hell with Volodya!" shouted Ivan at the top of his voice. "Oh, I know what you're thinking about. You want him to have my daughter. You want them to procreate together. Let me tell you, once and for all, my daughter is *not* an incubator! You shan't have her! I won't let you have her! I'll choke her with my own hands before——"

There was a momentary pause. A light shone in the corner of his eyes. He put his hands deep in his pockets, supporting his drooping belly; then he added, in a voice full of venom:

"You are making a mistake, little brother. You're making a fool of yourself. Ha-ha, my dearie, you think Volodya is nice because he belongs to the new generation. Well, let me tell you—you are making a fool of yourself, Andrey, my dearie. That's not the question at all. On the contrary, the question is quite different, quite different. . . ."

"What is the question?" said Andrey in a furious voice.

"It's just this. You're getting on in years, Andrey, my dearie. You want a son, that's all it is. In your heart, in the innermost recesses of your heart, you want to become a father. A family goes on for ever, doesn't it, Andrey? And for you, the symbol of the new generation is that utterly insignificant young man whose only claim to fame is his capacity to play football. Pah! You're mad!"

Volodya looked up.

"Praise the Edison of the new age," said Ivan in a loud voice. "Hurrah!" He bowed low in the direction of Volodya. "My dear Edison," he said, "you don't believe in this machine I have made, do you?"

"You, Ivan Petrovich," said Volodya, yawning, "ought to be sent to a lunatic asylum. They ought to have taken you long ago."

Andrey neighed like a horse.

The little priest hurled his hat on the floor.

"You——fools," he screamed. A little later, he said, "Andrey, you dare to let him talk like that to me! What do you mean by it, letting that little whipper-snapper talk to me in that tone of voice?"

Ivan did not notice his eyes, only his spectacles which shone in the light.

"Ivan!" said Andrey. "Don't ever come here again! Oh no, you're not a fool—you're the biggest swine on God's earth!"

3

EVERYWHERE there were rumors about the little priest.

From the public-houses the rumors crawled into the lodging-houses, and from there, by the backstairs, they reached the communal kitchens, just when everybody was washing or lighting the primus stove in the early morning, or when the boys who had been told to look after the milk were already decamping, when people were dancing naked under the hot shower-baths. Only, when they heard them, everyone added his own little detail to swell the harmony.

The rumors even reached the government offices, the rest-houses, the market squares.

According to one rumor, someone had appeared at the marriage of a cashier in the Yakimanka, although this "someone" was totally unknown to the family. The story goes that he was a little man in a bowler hat, a little man who was very nervous and looked very suspicious: and the story then goes on to relate that the little man was none other than Ivan Babichev. At the marriage-feast he made everyone look at him, forcibly attracted their attention, and delivered himself of a grave warning to all newly married couples generally. This is what they say he said:

"There is no reason for you to love one another, no reason at all why you should unite in the bonds of matrimony. Young man, leave your wife! Do you know what is going to be the fruit of your love-making together? You realize that you will be bringing into the world your most deadly enemy—an enemy who will gorge himself on your flesh!"

According to the rumor, the young husband was all for a fight. The bride, according to the rumor, fell in a dead faint on the floor. The uninvited guest thereupon departed in high anger. If you had been there, according to the rumor, you might have seen all the port wines in the bottles on the table suddenly turn into water.

There were other rumors about him. This is one of them:

They say that one day a motor-car was crossing that noisy road which some people call the Neglinnaya, by the Kuznetsky Bridge, and others the Tverskaya, by the Strastnoy Monastery. Well, in the car there was a fat, red-faced, important-looking gentleman with a portfolio under his arm.

Out of the crowd standing on the pavement someone suddenly ran out. Well, it was his brother, of course, that extremely famous and fortunate brother of his: and it was this brother who had seen him in the car and who had taken up his stand in the middle of the road and stood there holding his arms wide apart like a scarecrow, or like someone trying to stop a bolting horse, just by terrifying it and standing in the way. The chauffeur just managed to slow down in time. He sounded the hooter and went on slowly for a little while, while the scarecrow obstinately refused to budge even an inch.

"Stop!" the scarecrow shouted at the top of his voice. "Stop, Commissar! Stop, kidnapper!"

The chauffeur had no alternative. He stopped. The stream of traffic was suddenly immobilized. Some of the cars behind pressed forward irresponsibly on those in front, but the motor-buses, sounding their horns and quivering with suppressed excitement, stood quite still, ready to submit graciously, ready to lift their elephantine tires and withdraw in good order.

The arms of the man in the middle of the road were demanding immediate silence.

No one spoke.

"My brother . . ." he began. "Why is it that you are being carried in a motor-car while I have to walk on foot? Open the door and move up a little and let me in! It is not right that I should walk on foot. You are a prince among men, but I too—I am a prince among men!"

When he had finished talking, people rushed at him from every side; some jumped down from the motor-buses, others tore themselves away from the public-houses near by, still others came tearing down the boulevards. At that moment the man who was sitting in the motor-car, the man who was his brother, suddenly jumped up; and because the car stood so high above the ground, he towered over the assembly. In front of him there lay a seething barricade.

And standing there, he seemed so terrible that people imagined that he would walk over the car, stepping over the head of his chauffeur; they imagined he would walk right over them, over that barricade of seething humanity which surrounded him on all sides; they imagined him in the shape of a pillar crushing them all under his overpowering weight.

It was as though they had lifted him up high above the crowd of his partisans; sometimes he was propelled forward, sometimes backward. His bowler hat fell to the back of his neck and revealed a large white expanse of forehead, the forehead of a man pre-eminently tired of life.

Andrey forced him to get down by pulling at his trousers, by getting hold of his waistband and throwing him into the arms of a policeman.

"Take this man to the G.P.U.," he commanded.

One split second after he had spoken the whole visible universe awoke from its lethargy. Wheels shone in the sun, their hubs began to revolve, doors banged: everything that had been enclosed in lethargy before suddenly assumed once more its accustomed progress.

Ivan remained in prison for ten days.

When at last he came out of his prison his friends in the public-houses asked him whether it was true that he had been arrested through his brother handing him over to the police, in an extraordinary, sensational manner like that. He burst out laughing.

"All lies," he said. "A legend, no more than a legend. They arrested me in a pub. I was expecting them—they have been after me for a long time. That's just how legends begin. At the end of an epoch, in times of transition, the world cries out for a legend, for the legends of valor and heroism. Of course—I don't deny for a moment that I am pleased to be the subject of a legend. One day there will be a legend about that machine of mine as well— you know, that machine I have called 'Ophelia.' I am convinced that this civilization of ours will die with my name on its lips. To that end, indeed, all my efforts have been concentrated. I shall leave no stone unturned . . ."

When he was set free he was threatened with exile.

What was the incriminating evidence in the hands of the G.P.U.?

"Is it true that you called yourself a king?" asked the judge.

"Certainly. The King of Platitudes."

"Please explain yourself."

"You must understand that I have been the means of opening the eyes of a large and important section of the populace."

"You have opened their eyes. What have they been opened to?"

"I have opened their eyes to the fact that they are doomed to perish."

"You spoke just now about an important section of the populace. What do you mean by an 'important section of the populace'?"

"I mean—those who have lost their faith in the future of the revolution. May I explain myself?"

"Certainly."

"There exists a whole series of human sentiments which are doomed to perish."

"For example?"

"Pity, tenderness, pride, jealousy, love—almost the whole gamut of all the sensations experienced by mankind in this dying age. Under socialism we shall create new sensations, new sentiments to take their place."

"Go on."

"I can see that you understand me. Let me explain. The Communist who suffers the stings of jealousy is sat on by the powers that be. Even the Communist who is filled with sorrow for his fellow mortals is sat on. The tender flowers of pity, the shining lizards of vanity, the coiling serpents of jealousy—all these are to be banished from the heart of man under Communism.

"You must excuse me for speaking in this highly colored, highly technical manner. Perhaps it may seem to be too highly colored, too highly technical. You can follow me? Good! Thank you, no. I don't drink water. Ah, how I adore speaking in this highly colored way of mine.

"Now you know that the grave of a Komsomol who has committed suicide is treated in a very curious fashion. One moment someone places a wreath there, another moment someone hurls abuse and curses on the grave. In the new generation they say, 'Suicide is the expression of a pessimist ideology.' In the old days, they used to say, 'He had no alternative: he had to save his honor.' Look around you and you will see the new man under Communism accustoming himself to despise the sentiments of the past, those sentiments which were celebrated by the poets and by the muse of history. I want you to understand that it is my intention to organize the last, the final procession of just such sentiments as these."

"What do you mean by that? A conspiracy of the feelings?" said the judge.

"Yes, of course, a conspiracy of the feelings. With myself at the head."

"Continue."

"It is my intention to surround myself with a group—I hope you can follow me?

"Now, I imagine that you can, at a pinch, acknowledge that there is beauty in these old sentiments and affections. The love of women. Patriotism. There are many others, of course. Don't you believe that there are some memories which have the power to move us, even today, among all these sentiments and affections? Of course they do! As I was saying, it is my intention . . .

"You know that an electric-light bulb will sometimes go out quite suddenly. Burnt out, as they say. But you only have to shake it up and then it blazes away again and continues to shed its light for a considerable time. Inside the lamp, all is confusion. What has actually happened? By shaking it up, you have brought the tungsten filaments together again. The lamp once more returns to its accustomed ritual of existence, an existence at once short and illusive, doomed to perdition, feverish, far too bright. Then—a blaze of light! Then—darkness—darkness! The lamp will never come back to life again, and in the surrounding darkness you hear nothing except the hum of those dead, burnt-out filaments. Now, do you follow me? Let me tell you, there is an amazing beauty in that final blaze of light.

"It is my intention to shake up this civilization of ours.

"I want to shake up the heart of the burnt-out civilization we live in—so that the broken filaments will touch once more.

"I want to be the cause of an instantaneous explosion of beauty and——

"I want to discover the representatives of the world which is long past. Theirs are the sentiments which interest me most of all—jealousy, a man's love for a woman, soaring ambition. Somewhere I hope to find a madman whom I can present to you with the words, 'Here, my friend, is an exhibit of a particular sentiment, a particular type of consciousness which you characterize as madness.'

"Many are the characters who have played their part on the stage of the world which is past. The curtain falls. The actors hurry to the footlights and recite their last couplets. I want to be the intermediary between the actors and the audience. I want to be their musical accompanist and I want to be the last to leave the stage.

"I am conscious that on me there has fallen the honor of the leadership of the last parade of the sentiments.

"With gleaming eyes and through the slits of her mask, history is watching us. I want to be there, I want to be able to say to her, 'Here is your lover, your man filled with overweening pride; here your traitor, here your faithful friend, here your prodigal son —here are the standard-bearers of the passions, those passions which everyone now holds to be commonplace and vulgar. Before they disappear for ever, before they are exposed to the gaze of mockery and derision, let them come upon the stage for the last time, revealing themselves in one last effort of beauty.'

"I listen to people talking. I hear someone speaking about a razor-blade. About a madman who has cut his throat. The name of a woman flutters in the air around them. But the madman has not died. They stitched his throat up again, and then, like the damned fool he is, he goes and cuts himself in the same place all over again. Well, he is the sort of man I am looking for. And the woman too—I have been looking everywhere for her. The daemoniacal woman and the tragic lover—I have been looking for you all. Where can I find them? At the Slifasovsky Hospital? And where can I find the woman? Does she work in an office or shall I find her among the nepmen?

"I have spent hours and days searching for heroes.

"I look into unknown windows, I climb strange staircases. Sometimes I follow an unknown smile and I run after it, like a naturalist running after a butterfly. When I see them, I can hardly prevent myself from shouting out at the top of my voice, 'Stay a while. Tell me, you who are the flower of my heart, whose smile is a butterfly, where has thy butterfly gone? And what flowers are the flowers of my heart? Are they the wild roses of grief or the raspberries of vanity? Stay, stay a while, for I have need of you!'

"I want to surround myself with a multitude of men. Only then will I be able to choose among them, to discover the finest, the most singular specimens among them. I desire to form a shock-brigade of the sentiments which are passing out of the world . . .

"Yes, certainly, if you like, by all means call it a conspiracy of the sentiments. A peaceful revolution. A peaceful demonstration on the part of the sentiments which are passing out of the world.

"Suppose I discover somewhere a full-blooded hundred-per-cent example of pride. Well, I shall say to him, 'Show yourself! Show yourself to the people who are preventing you from satisfying your lust for power. Do something which will make them say, "How despicable he is! And how powerful he is!" ' Or else imagine I have the good fortune to find someone who is the quintessence of flippancy and lightmindedness. Then I shall say to him, 'Show yourself to the people, demonstrate the strength of your thought-lessness until they throw up their hands in fervent horror.'

"Let me recapitulate. The genius of passion empowers herself of the soul. One soul is ruled by the genius of pride, another by the genius of pity and sympathy. I want to be the means of collecting them all together; then I want to see them sport in the arena of the world."

THE JUDGE   Did you discover anyone like that?

IVAN   I searched for a long time. For a long while I spent my life searching for them. It was always very difficult. Perhaps, after all, no one understands me. In the end I found just one person.

JUDGE   Who was it?

IVAN   Do you want to know his name or do you want to know the name of the passion he suffered from?

JUDGE   Both.

IVAN   Nikolay Kavalerov. A man suffering from the passion of envy.

4

THEY left the looking-glass.

These two comic characters walked away together. One, smaller and fatter than the other, walked a little ahead: that was one of Ivan Babichev's little characteristics. Every time he wanted to speak to his companion, he had to turn his head right round. If he wanted to speak in long, involved sentences—and he never employed any other sort of sentence—he had to turn his head almost right round; nearly always, when he did this, he bumped into somebody. Then, after the jolt, he would bow and lift his hat and gather a nosegay of the most flattering excuses. He was the soul of honor and politeness. A gentle smile never left his face.

The day was closing down its shutters. A bearded gypsy, wearing a blue coat. His cheeks were richly painted and raised on his

shoulders he was carrying a polished brass basin. The day was
receding behind the gypsy's shoulders. The flat disk of the basin
was quite colorless and very bright. While the gypsy walked slowly
along the road the basin shook a little. All the daylight revolved
in the disk of the basin he was carrying.

Those who passed by watched him as he disappeared.

Like the sun, the disk of the basin fell in the west. The day had
come to a close.

The two men immediately turned into a public-house.

Kavalerov told Ivan that someone who was monstrously famous
had actually kicked him out of his house: but he gave no names.
Ivan told him exactly the same thing. He too had been kicked out
of his house by someone who was very famous.

"I'm perfectly sure you know who he is. Everyone knows him.
It's my brother, Andrey Petrovich Babichev. Have you ever heard
of him?"

Kavalerov looked down to the ground, blushing. He said nothing.

"We're in the same boat," said Ivan. "We ought to be friends,"
he added, beaming. "Kavalerov! That's the sort of name I like. It's
a high-flown, common or garden name, isn't it?"

Kavalerov thought: "That's true enough. I am high-flown and
common or garden myself."

"Pretty good beer," Ivan exclaimed. "In Poland they say 'Her
eyes are the color of beer.' Tell me, it's pretty good, isn't it?"

He paused for a moment.

"The important thing is that the famous person is my brother.
It is my brother who has stolen my daughter. Well, I shall have
my revenge on him. He stole my daughter from me. Not actually
stealing, of course. Don't stare at me like that. And do you know,
you have got a nose as long as the Equator. With a nose like that
you ought to be famous, you ought to be a hero. Wouldn't you
be happy if you were a hero? He took her, I was saying, by employing moral pressure. Could he be arrested for that? Could I
have him taken before a judge? She just left me. It's not his fault
so much as the fault of that dirty little swine who is living with
him."

He spoke a lot about Volodya.

Kavalerov's big toe was wriggling with embarrassment.

"It's that little swine who has spoilt my life for me. If only someone would give him a kick in the kidneys! When he is playing football, oh if only someone would kick him hard! If he asks for anything, Andrey gives it to him. That is the sort of man they call the 'representative of the new generation.' That is the sort of little swine who said Valya was miserable because I was mad and because I was systematically trying to make her mad too. The little swine! Between them they took her away from me and then Valya ran away and one of her friends had to take her in. . . . Oh, I've cursed that little devil! I've prayed that her mouth and her inside will change places! Just imagine it! The blockheads! . . . And she was the best and prettiest and purest ray of light in the world. I wanted someone entirely feminine, I wanted someone who had every feminine quality there was! Oh, how I wanted a pair of nice feminine ovaries. Womanhood—the greatness and glory of the past! We are all dying, Kavalerov! I wanted to hold the sacred name of womanhood above my head, like a flaming torch. I thought that womanhood would come to an end in this civilization of ours. I wanted to cultivate Woman. All these millions of aeons—they are nothing more than a cess-pool, a cess-pool full of machines and scrap-iron and tin and pieces of springs and loose screws. Dirty old cess-pool! Can't you see the pieces of rotten wood and the gleaming, phosphorescent fungi and the mold at the bottom? That is what our feelings, our sentiments are like. Instead of the flower of culture, a dirty old cess-pool! Nothing more! The representative of the new generation goes along to the cess-pool and goes down and brings up anything he wants. He brings up a bolt or a part of a machine, anything, and as for the piece of rotten wood, he just tramples on it, extinguishes it. Once I dreamt about a woman who would flower into glory in that cess-pool, whose emotions would be entirely new and utterly, inconceivably strange. A tremendous miracle of a flower! So wonderful that when the representative of the new generation came along to steal a piece of iron in the cess-pool he would be absolutely frightened out of his wits. He would draw his hands away and shut his eyes, blinded by the brilliant light of what had seemed to him to be just an ordinary piece of rotten wood.

"Once I found someone like that. Quite close to me. Valya. I thought she would cast a ray of light on this dying civilization and shine like a lamp above its long pilgrimage towards the great graveyard. But I was wrong. She has left me. She had abandoned the bedside of our old civilization. Once I used to think that women could be possessed by men, that their tenderness and their love would be ours for ever—I was wrong. I am the last dreamer on the surface of the world. By the side of the cess-pool I wander, like a wounded bat. . . ."

Kavalerov thought: "I shall take Valya away from them." For some reason he wanted to say that he had seen what had happened in the little side street with the flowering hedgerow. Instead he kept silent.

"We are in the same boat," Ivan continued. "I greet you! Young man, it gives me a great pleasure to know you. Drink up, man! So they threw you out too, Kavalerov? Tell me all about it. Of course—you have already told me all about it. You said it was a very famous man who kicked you out, wasn't it? You don't want to tell me who he was? Well, I suppose it is nothing to do with me. Do you hate him very, very much?"

Kavalerov nodded.

"That's very understandable, my dear fellow. As far as I can see, you have been spending your time calling him names. Don't interrupt! You have got a grudge against this famous man, haven't you? Obviously you think he has insulted you. Don't interrupt! Drink up!

"You are quite certain that it is this famous man who is preventing you from appearing in all your splendor? That he has usurped your rights? According to you, you are the one who ought to be the lord and master and all the time it is he who is the lord and master. And that has upset you, hasn't it?"

Among the cigarette-smoke the orchestra stirred. The pale face of the violinist lay over the violin.

"A violin and a violinist, they are just the same," said Ivan. "A violin is like a little violinist in a frock-coat—same shape, everything. Are you listening? You can hear the wood of the violin singing. Can you hear the voice of the wood singing in the orchestra, up the scale and then down the scale, all the scales. Have you ever heard such awful music in your life? Good God, have you ever heard such music in your life?"

He turned to the musicians.

"So you think that's a drum you've got there? You think it is playing with the orchestra, don't you? Let me tell you—it isn't! The fellow who is really the drum is the god of music hammering at your chests with his clenched fists. . . .

"My dear fellow, you are utterly eaten up with envy—that's what is the matter with you. We all envy the future. You can call it the envy of old men, if you like, the envy of a generation which has grown old for the first time. Let us talk about envy! Another bitter, miss!"

They were sitting by the broad window.

The rain began to fall again. Night came. The town shone as though hewn out of Cardiff coals. Men who passed looked into the window and pressed their noses against the pane.

"Yes, envy. We ought to play such a part in history that long after we have gone they will remember us with tears in their eyes, with illimitable enthusiasm—with despair and with anger. Without knowing it, you are the bearer of an historic mission. You belong to the center of things. In you there has been concentrated the envy of a race which is slowly perishing. A race which always envies whatever will take its place."

"What do you want me to do?" asked Kavalerov.

"My dear fellow, either you go under or else you must create a terrific scandal—there is no other alternative. Or else you must go out in a blaze of light. Bang the doors after you. But the most important thing is to go out in a terrific blaze of light! Then, Heaven help us, you'll leave such a mark on their silly faces that . . . Whatever else happens, they won't take to you. Don't give in without a fight. Now I am going to tell you about something that happened to me when I was a child.

"It was at a ball. We were acting in a play, dancing in a ballet which had been specially arranged for us in the ballroom. There was a girl there. Just try to imagine her. A typical beauty, about twelve years old, thin spindle legs, wearing a short satin frock, all frills and ribbons, like a snapdragon, beautiful, haughty, obviously spoilt. She kept on tossing her hair. She absolutely ruled over our lives, queened it over us. She did everything she wanted to do. Everyone had eyes for her and only for her. She was the center of all the attractions, the ultimate origin of everything that happened. She danced better than anyone else, flew up in the air better than anyone else, thought out new games we could play better than anyone else. She got all the best presents, all the best sweets, all the best flowers, all the best oranges—and finally, all the best compliments. I was thirteen then. Studying at the gymnasium. And she was actually queening it over me. She wasn't the only person in the world who had known the ecstasy of conquest; she was not the only one who had been spoilt by praise. I had! I, who was head of my class! I, who got all the prizes! I could not let her go on like that. Later on, I caught her up in the corridor and gave her the thrashing of her young life. I tore her ribbons, ruffled her hair, scratched her face—her beautiful face! I seized her by the scruff of the neck and banged her head against the columns. I adored her more than I adored anyone else in the world—and I hated her with all the passion of my soul! I ruffled her curls because I wanted to make her ashamed of herself; I wanted to smash up all her loveliness, all her glamor. I was the teacher! I assumed the responsibility of being the teacher who corrected the faults committed by the world. It was no good. I was disgraced. They kicked me out, of course, in the end. But, my dear fellow, remember this—that evening no one could think of anyone except me. It was I who had spoilt their party for them. Wherever the girl appeared everyone started to talk about me. That was the first time that I came face to face with the subject of envy. Oh, envy is a terrible thorn in man's flesh, weighs heavily on man's heart. Envy, once you are consumed with it, presses at your throat, throttles you, until your eyes pop out of their sockets. While I was tormenting her in the corridor, while she lay like a victim on the sacrificial altar, tears sprang in my eyes and I felt as though I were choking: and even then I began to tear at her clothes, trembling in the ecstasy of the touch of satin beneath my fingers. The satin set my teeth on edge and I found that my lips were trembling. You know how silk—how the touch of silk—will send a quiver up your spine, through your whole nervous system, making your face work into all sorts of grimaces. Everything seemed to be trying to stop me from doing what I wanted to do with this idiotic girl. Out of her body there flowed all the poison which you associate with plants and bees—from this child who had been so lovely, so innocent in the ballroom. The poison came running out of her dress, out of that soft pink silk she was wearing. I don't know whether I cried out aloud while I was beating her. If I did, this is what I think I said: 'Here's your place! Don't go thinking you are so high and mighty! Don't take things which don't belong to you! And don't take anything which belongs to me in my own right!'

"Listen carefully! I want to suggest an analogy to you. I'm thinking, of course, about the struggle of the centuries. Of course, when you hear it, it may occur to you that it's a bad analogy. Do you follow me? I want to talk about envy."

At that moment the music came to an end.

"Thank the Lord for that!" said Ivan gratefully. "I'm glad they have finished. Just look at the 'cello. Before he drew his bow over it, there wasn't much in it, was there? People have been torturing it for hours—and what does it look like? Now it shines like a wet thing—a 'cello which has been thoroughly refreshed. Think carefully over what I am telling you. I don't just talk: I hew my words from solid rock. Isn't that so, Kavalerov?

"My dear fellow, we have won our spurs, we have been honored and blessed in the sight of men—honor and blessedness are things which come naturally to us, there, where we have our place in the world. Here, in the dying civilization we live in. And how beautiful it is, this new world! In the world I am speaking about the finest talents will live side by side with the most sublime ecstasies: in her, everything will be concentrated and have its origin. This world, which is now marching forward to greet me, is a world which I love more than I can say, a world I adore and hate with every fibre of my being. I stifle! Tears roll down my cheeks! But grant that I may feel the new world under my hands, grant that I may tear her dress and pluck her eyes out! Don't leave me here in the cold! Don't take away from me the things which belong to me!

"We must have our revenge! All the thousands of people who are like us must have their revenge. Remember, Kavalerov, our enemies are not windmills; and remember that windmills sometimes hide warriors under their sails; remember that soldiers can be ruthless. Oh, your enemies are very real! Revenge yourself on them! Believe me, one day we shall go out in a blaze of light. Believe me, it is our heaven-sent duty to smash the cussedness of the rising generation. We are more powerful than they are. We also were the spoilt darlings of history.

"Make them talk about you, Kavalerov. Everyone knows that the world is coming to an end—everything is predetermined. Now, there is no other way. You, my dear fathead, must die! Every day, more and more humiliations will be piled upon your head; every day will add an inch to the stature of your enemy, that spoilt darling of an enemy of yours. We are doomed! Everyone knows that we are doomed. Seize destiny by the scruff of her neck; then, when the last moment comes, blaze like a rocket and hack at the clothes of the age which is taking your place! Say 'Farewell,' so that your words echo through all eternity!"

Kavalerov thought: "He can see into my mind."

"They have wronged you, haven't they? They even threw you out, didn't they?"

"Yes, they have wronged me," said Kavalerov bitterly. "All my life they have done their best to humiliate me."

"Who wronged you? Was it someone from the new world?"

Kavalerov wanted to say: "It was your brother who wronged me, your brother who has wronged us both." Instead, he said nothing.

"You're lucky. At least you can recognize your enemy. I too have an enemy like yours, someone I can recognize."

"What can I do?"

"I told you—you're lucky. When you have your revenge at last, you will be able to rejoice in the name of the old world which suckled you at her breast."

"What can I do?"

"Smash her! Leave an honorable memory of yourself as the hired assassin of the century! Smash your enemy on the threshold of two epochs! When she comes to you, she will be proud and haughty. She will imagine herself a genius, a cupid hovering with her train at the gates of the new world. Her nose is in the air and she no longer sees you. Bash her over the head by way of farewell! Now I give you my blessing." Here he raised his glass. "And I too will destroy the enemy at the gates! Let us drink to the fair name of Ophelia, for it *is* Ophelia who will be the sharp sword of my vengeance!"

Kavalerov opened his mouth. He wanted to say that he fully realized that they had a common enemy and that the common enemy was Ivan's brother. He wondered whether he ought to thank Ivan for suggesting that he should be the medium of Andrey's assassination; but he had no time to say what he wanted to say, for at that moment a gentleman approached Ivan, tapped him gently on the shoulder and told him to come quietly away. Ivan was being arrested. In a previous chapter we have explained why he was arrested.

"Farewell, dear fellow," said Ivan. "I walk the Stations of the Cross. Go and see my daughter, my dear fellow." He mentioned the road where she lived: its name had long burnt like a flame in Kavalerov's brain. "Go and see her, my dear fellow. Of course, you understand that when we are betrayed by someone like that, there is only one solution left to us. Revenge! Revenge!"

He finished his glass of beer and walked away, a little in front of the mysterious gentleman who had arrested him. As he moved to the door, he winked to the others, smiled all over his face and kept looking into the open end of his clarionet. At the door he

suddenly turned right round, held his bowler hat in his outstretched arms, and declaimed at the top of his voice:

> *I am not a German charlatan!*
> *I have not stolen a penny from the people!*
> *No, I am just a Soviet card-sharper,*
> *I, the miracle-worker of the age!*

5

"W HAT are you laughing at?" said Volodya. "Because you think
I am tired?"

"I am not laughing. I'm coughing."

Always, as soon as he reached his chair Volodya went to sleep.

He was easily tired. Andrey however had extraordinary powers
of endurance: he worked right through the day and half the night.
When he struck his fist on the table, the lamp-shade jumped up,
like the top of a kettle, but Volodya slept on. When he saw the
lamp-shade jumping in the air, Andrey began to think about
James Watt; he remembered a portrait of Watt staring at the lid
of the kettle as it hung suspended above the steam.

Everyone knows the story. Everyone has seen the portrait.

James Watt discovered the steam-engine.

What are you going to discover, Volodya? Are you too going
to discover a new machine? Are you going to reveal new secrets
from the earth, you who belong to the new age?

After that, Andrey Babichev began to hold a conversation with
himself. For a little while he left his work, and staring at Volodya,
who was sleeping quietly, he thought:

Perhaps, after all, Ivan is right. Perhaps I *am* just a bourgeois,
living an ordinary bourgeois existence. Why is Volodya so dear to
me? Because he has been living with me ever since he was a child,
because I have grown accustomed to his presence here? Because I
love him as a father always loves his son? Only that? As simple as

that? And would I still love him if he were a born fool. No, it is not that. It is because he has given a meaning to my life, because he has given it a sense of direction. I have been happy in my life. We are still far from living in the new age—but I believe that one day we shall all be living happily together, in that new age we dream about. I have been happy in my life. There he is, sleeping quite close to me: and the new age we dream about is sleeping there quite close to me. The new age is living here, under my own roof. I love him terribly. Why? Because he is, in a way, my son? Because he gives a meaning to my life? Because it will be he who will close my eyes when I am dead? No! I don't want that! I don't want to die in bed surrounded by cushions and pillows! In my heart I know that my last breath will be received, not by my family, but by the whole of humanity. Nonsense! I love him and adore him, in the same way that I cherish the new age. I love him and he is dear to me like a desire gratified. And if I am wrong, if he is not the standard-bearer of the new age, if he is not everything that I am not, well, I shall have him thrown out of the house, I who lie up to my neck in the old order of things, never able to escape from my own purgatory. I would have him thrown out of the house because there would no longer be any need of him; he would not be my son and together we would not be a family. I have had faith in him and I believe that he has justified my faith in him.

Together we are not simply a family: we are all humanity.

What does it all mean? Must a father's love for his son disappear from the world? Why does he love me, when he belongs wholly to the new age? In this age, is a father's love for his son still as common as it was in the past? I would leap for joy if I thought it was true! Will I be allowed to cherish him because he is my son and at the same time because he belongs to the new age? Ivan, that conspiracy of the sentiments of yours—horrible, worthless! Not all the sentiments are going to be destroyed! You're wrong, I can't tell you how wrong you are! There are still some which will remain with us."

Long, long ago, two people were running through the streets at night, in the dark night: sometimes they fell low among the gullies, sometimes they shot up and terrified the stars in their courses. One was a Commissar, the other a small boy: and it was the boy who had saved the life of the Commissar. The Commissar was an enormous man and the boy was unimaginably small. Anyone who had seen them as they ran through the streets that night would have imagined that there was only one man there, a giant who crouched low over the earth as he ran; and the little boy who ran by his side would have seemed to be nothing more than the hand of the giant.

They never parted.

The boy lived with the giant, grew up, became a Young Communist; later he became a student. He had been born in the house of a railway operative. He was the son of a rail-repairer.

His friends adored him. Even people who were older than he was adored him. Sometimes the fact that everyone liked him so much worried him; it seemed so undeserved. He was friendly with everyone; in him, as Ivan would say, the sentiment of friendship was extraordinarily developed. As if he wanted to acquire a sense of equilibrium and correct the errors which he had discovered in himself and as though he wanted to destroy some of the talents which had been granted to him at his birth, there were times when he did everything in his power, employed every imaginable artifice in order to destroy the impression of himself which lay in their minds. To them, he wanted to appear insignificant. He wanted to turn out the light which shone around him like a halo.

He wanted to help his unfortunate friends. He wanted to demonstrate to them his undying devotion, his readiness to make any sacrifice for them. He wanted to demonstrate the passionate strength of their friendship for them; so he searched among them, trying to find their outstanding qualities and talents. Wherever he appeared among them, they became rivals for his friendship.

"Why is it that people lose their tempers and get worried over trifles?" he said once. "There is no one who seems to understand the nature of time. No one seems to have any idea about practical things. Time—well, isn't time something quite practical? If everybody was practical, no one could afford to be angry or proud or to give way to their lower instincts. What are you laughing at? If you want to be rid of stupidities, you must have an understanding of time. You can have a grievance over something for an hour, or for a whole year. Shall we say that your recollection of what happened to offend you lasts another year. But even if you lived to be a thousand, you would never entirely forget what happened. It's all so silly! On the face of the clock, all you can see is three or perhaps four hours, and on the strength of those three or four hours you behave like a pack of poor blind mice. Well, then. No one will live to see the hands of the clock going right round the clock-face; and if you explain to people that they are living at a point on the clock-face, they will just laugh at you."

"But why only the lower instincts?" said someone. "The most elevated desires are just as short-lived. What about generosity, for example?"

"Obviously. . . . Listen to me. Generosity is something ordered, logical and practical. Don't laugh. It's true, isn't it? Look here, you're muddling me. You're purposely confusing me. Wait a moment. There was a revolution, wasn't there? A terrible revolution. Why was it so terrible? Wasn't it also extremely generous? In terms of the clock-face as a whole it was something fundamentally good. Very well. You have to think about these things in terms of the clock-face as a whole, not simply in terms of one or two of the divisions on the surface of the face. It follows therefore that there is no difference between generosity and cruelty. There is only one thing—Time. That's the iron law, the ineluctable logic of history. History and Time are one and the same thing. They are just like Siamese twins. Don't laugh, Andrey Petrovich. The most important thing in the world is undoubtedly and indisputably an understanding of the nature of time."

Or else he said:

"I want to smash the conceit of the bourgeois! There they are— all laughing at us. Old men saying: Where are your engineers, where are your surgeons, your professors, your inventors? Well, I am going to form a shock-brigade. There will be about a hundred people in it—and we shall be the ones who will smash the conceit of the bourgeois once and for all! You think I'm boasting? You never did understand anything! I am not letting my imagination run away with me at all. We're really going to get to work. We'll work like wild animals. Just you wait and see! One day people will come and bow to us in homage. And, by the way, I'm going to have Valya as one of our members."

Volodya woke up.

"I've just had a dream," he said, smiling. "I dreamt I was with Valya and we were standing on the roof and looking at the moon through a telescope."

"Good heavens! A telescope?"

"I remember I said, 'Over there, there is a sea of troubles.' What do you thing she said? She said, 'Is there really a sea of bubbles over there?'"

In the spring of that year Volodya spent a short holiday with his father at Murom, where his father worked in the locomotive engineering sheds. On the night of the third day after he had gone, Andrey was returning home when the chauffeur drove slowly past a bend in the road, and in the light of a lamp he saw someone lying on the roadside on an iron grating. Immediately he began to think of Volodya who had left him. He jumped up and touched the chauffeur on the shoulder. He wanted to say, "There isn't any resemblance, really," and he almost said these words. And it was quite true—there was no resemblance at all between Volodya and the man who was lying there. What happened was that, seeing the man, he immediately began to think of Volodya. He thought, "Perhaps Volodya is lying on the ground somewhere in the same pitiful attitude, just like that." He had been a fool; he had let his sentimentality run away with him. The car stopped dead.

Nikolay Kavalerov was lifted off the ground and they heard him talking drunkenly in his sleep. Andrey took him home, carried him up four flights of stairs, installed him in Volodya's divan and covered him with a rug. Nikolay Kavalerov lay face downwards, while the light from the window spread over his face in a curious

honeycomb pattern. When Andrey went to bed at last, he felt
happy and elated: the divan was no longer empty.

That night he dreamt that the young man he had brought home
had hanged himself on a telescope.

6

IN ANITCHKA'S bedroom there was an extraordinary bed. The
wood had been covered with an expensive, dark, cherry-colored
varnish and all round the inside of the bed there were mirrors.

Once, when there had been an unusual decrease in the number
of rows in the family, Anitchka's husband had gone to a fair.
There he stood on a raised platform, while all round him people
showered confetti on his head—he had won the prize in a lottery.
The showman gave him a printed form and immediately afterwards he entered into full possession of that extraordinary bed.
They had had to take it away on a cart. All the little boys whistled
after them as they hauled it through the streets.

The blue sky lay reflected in the burnished mirrors. The mirrors
were like blue eyes, opening and closing again, slowly, effortlessly.

The family lived on and went to pieces, but the bed survived all
Anitchka's misfortunes.

Kavalerov lives in a little corner behind the bed.

When he came to Anitchka, he said:

"If you let me have a part of the room, I'll pay you thirty roubles
a month."

Anitchka immediately agreed to keep him on these terms. She
smiled—a prolonged smile.

There was nowhere else he could go to. In his old lodgings there
was a new tenant: the new tenant absolutely refused to move out.
Kavalerov sold him his bed for four roubles. When he left at last,
the bed groaned aloud.

Anitchka's bed was like an organ.

It occupied half the room. The top of the curtains disappeared in the obscurity of the ceiling.

Kavalerov thought:

"If I were a child, if I were Anitchka's child, my childish mind would discover innumerable romantic designs in the shape of this amazing room of hers. Now that I am a grown man, I can see only the general outline, a few significant details here and there. . . . Once upon a time, when distance and length and weight and gravitation and time itself meant nothing to me, I would have climbed along those corridors which lie in the empty space between the frame of the spring mattress and the sides of the bed; I would have hidden myself in those columns which now seem no larger than a measuring rod; I would have hoisted imaginary catapults in the railings and shot stones at imaginary enemies—and the enemies would have taken to flight across the soft counterpane and they would have lost all their energy in its lovely softness: beneath the glass roof I would have organized audiences for the ambassadors, like the king in the novel I had just been reading: among the carvings I would have made fantastic travels—further and further—and then further; I would have crawled up the legs of the little cupids, along their little backsides; I would have crawled over them as men crawl over the face of the Buddha, being unable to comprehend it wholly with the eyes; then, at the last rainbow arch, there where the body feels an unrecognizable vertigo, there at the topmost peak, I would have rolled down the terrible avalanche of the pillows."

Ivan Babichev is taking Kavalerov for a walk. Dandelions ride high in the air, standing on tiptoe. They voyage abroad and their voyage is like a moving reflection of the surrounding heat. Babichev looks pale in the heat. His full moon-face shines in the sunlight, cast in stone.

"It's here," he said.

The roads were alight with flowers.

They traversed a waste land, then walked by the side of a hedgerow. In the garden behind the hedge, dogs were barking and rattling their chains. Kavalerov whistled. He wanted to tease them.

Everything is possible, and hearing his whistle one of the dogs might easily have escaped and jumped at them over the hedge; thinking of what might have happened, he felt a drop of terror congealing at the base of his stomach.

They walked on, into a green meadow, until they were on top of the red roofs of houses, on top of the high branches of trees. Kavalerov had no idea where he was. Even when he saw the towers of the Krestovskoy he could not imagine where he was. Somewhere in the distance they caught the sounds of steam-engines passing over rails, the peculiar murmur of the trams.

"I want to show you my machine," said Ivan, turning towards Kavalerov. "You'll have to pinch yourself hard if you're going to believe it. That's quite right. Now pinch yourself again—and again. Of course you're not dreaming. Tell yourself you are not dreaming. Just think. There we were, walking across a piece of waste land, and we saw a pool which never dries up shining in the sunlight, and we saw some old pots and pans hanging on the railings. Remember that many, many marvels have been found in rubbish-dumps on the roadside—all you have to do is to scrabble in the hedges and the gutters and you are bound to come across a miracle. Here is just what we want! A page from a book! Look carefully. It won't stay here very long—the wind will bear it away. It's an illustration from *Taras Bulba*. Do you recognize it? I think it must have been wrapped round some food and thrown out of the window over there. Now look at this! Here is an eternal monument to human despair—an old boot. It's not really worth looking at, is it? Old boots, after all, are too academic, too literary. Now—what's that? Upon my soul, a bottle of beer! Wait a moment. No, it's not empty; but tomorrow someone is bound to come along in a horse and cart and you will see it smashed under the wheels. Perhaps, after we have gone, someone will come walking along this selfsame road, deep in his dreams: he will get an enormous pleasure in contemplating the bottle and the broken glass. Who was it who said that broken bottles had achieved fame at last? Oh, how brilliantly it glitters in the dust! To the lonely traveller, staring at the pieces of broken glass, who knows how many adorable images rise to his eyes? Look! Look! Here's a button. Here's an iron hoop. Here's one of those towers of Babylon raised by human excrement. There—over there—can't you see that piece of bandage over there? Nothing extraordinary here, of course. Just the usual sort of piece of waste land. Now remember what we have been doing. It's really quite simple. I was bringing you along to see my machine, wasn't I? Pinch yourself again! Good! You're not dreaming, are you? Good. You see, I don't want you to say afterwards that you were not well, or that it was too hot, or that most of the things you saw were just mirages, things that came into your mind because you were so hot, or because you were so tired, or for some reason like that. No, my friend. I want to feel certain that you are feeling perfectly normal in every way. Because what I am about to show you is going to give you the surprise of your sweet life."

Kavalerov did his best to assure him that he was feeling perfectly normal.

They reach a small wooden fence.

"There she is," said Ivan. "Wait a moment. Let us sit down together by the running brook. I told you that I wanted to create the greatest machine in the world, a universal machine. I wanted to perfect a machine with literally thousands of separate functions —and I wanted it to be quite a small machine in spite of that. There she is, my friend. She is beautiful, with the beauty of aristocracy. I devoted all my energies to making her. I became a fanatic. It was my desire to subdue the hoary beast of mechanism. I wanted machinery to become simple and domesticated, I wanted a machine that would eat out of my hand. I wanted a machine which anyone could work by pulling a small lever—it would be just as easy as snapping the bolts of a door."

"I don't understand anything about engineering," moaned Kavalerov. "Machines frighten me."

"Well, I succeeded," continued Ivan. "Listen to me, Kavalerov. I invented that machine!"

Kavalerov had a horrible desire to go and look over the fence. He had a curious feeling that there was absolutely nothing on the other side of the fence.

"I tell you—she can lift mountains. She can fly in the air. She can carry things on her back, crush metals. She can be used either as a kitchen range or as a perambulator or as a long-range gun. In her there resides the genius of engineering!"

"But why are you laughing, Ivan Petrovich?" said Kavalerov. He had noticed the extraordinary light which was shining in Ivan's eyes.

"I am laughing because I have made a success of my life, because I can talk to you of these matters without my heart jumping and rearing in my breast like a scrambled egg in a saucepan. There are literally thousands of things she can do! I have invented a machine which can do everything. Now, do you understand? Well, you will see her in a minute."

He got up and placed his hand on Kavalerov's shoulder. In a solemn voice he continued:

"And now that I have invented it, I am not going to let it work. One day I discovered that the desire of my life had been granted to me. It was within my power to have my revenge on the age we live in. I debauched the machine. On purpose. As you might say, out of pure spite."

He laughed happily.

"Not quite like that, Kavalerov; but you know what I mean, don't you? On this machine, a machine of the highest conceivable technical accomplishment, I grafted all the most banal human sensations, the most banal human sensitivities. I have raped the machine. I have had my revenge on the world in the name of the age which gave me the intelligence to create a machine like that. Who could I leave it to? To the new world around me? To the new age which spends its time gorging on our souls, crushing the nineteenth century with the venom of a boa-constrictor crushing a poor little rabbit? Masticates it, chews it, then spits it out again. Assimilates all that is useful and spits out everything it doesn't want. Spits out the sensations that are most precious to us and swallows whole our mechanical knowledge. I have revenged myself on them in the name of our most precious possessions. I won't let them have my machine, I won't let them make use of it, I am not going to have them spewing the intelligence of my brain.

With this machine of mine I could have bequeathed everlasting happiness to the new age. On the day it was born I could have bequeathed to it the most perfect imaginable example of engineering science. But I won't let them have it! Instead, I shall give them a kick in the pants in the name of the age which is dying. When they see that machine of mine, you'll see their mouths watering. Just think. Here is a machine, a machine all ready for their fervent adoration, and then suddenly—quite suddenly—she reveals herself in the guise of a born liar, an ordinary sentimental good-for-nothing. Come here. I'm going to show it to you. This machine of mine, I tell you, it can do everything, absolutely everything—and yet now it is singing one of those sentimental songs of the age which is past, now she is gathering flowers in her garden. I laugh out loud when I think of the divinity of the machine, of the divinity of the rising generation. Therefore I gave it the name of a girl who went mad beecause she loved and because her love was not returned to her. I have named her 'Ophelia.' Very touching, very human—'Ophelia.' "

Ivan dragged Kavalerov along with him.

He bent over a little shutter in the fence and Kavalerov could not help noticing the amplitude of the two copper pendulums of his backside. His backside reflected the sun. Perhaps it was because it was too hot there, too much like being enclosed in a desert; perhaps it was because the scenery was strange to him, seemed totally unlike the scenery around Moscow; or perhaps it really was the effect of fatigue; whatever it was, Kavalerov found himself alone in the desert, far from the noisy crowds, and there, alone and solitary, he surrendered himself to the magic of the hallucination. He thought he could hear Ivan speaking to someone through the shutter. Latter he saw Ivan skipping backwards away from the shutter. Although there was a considerable distance between them, Kavalerov jumped back at the same time. It was as though fear lay hidden in the trees, holding them by the same traces, pulling them back at exactly the same moment.

"Who was that whistling?" Kavalerov cried out in a voice full of fear.

From the paling there came a piercing low whistle. Kavalerov turned his face away, covered it with his hands, like a man turning away from the wind. Ivan ran past him with little mincing steps and the whistle flew on, through him and past him. He appeared to be gliding along the invisible rays of whistling sound from the other side of the paling.

"I'm afraid! Oh, I'm afraid!" he said, muttering under his breath.

Holding hands, they ran down the slope, followed by the loud curses of the tramp they had disturbed. Looking down from the height of the paling, they had imagined at first that it was an old horse-cloth which someone had thrown negligently away. Instead . . .

The tramp was roused from his sleep. He sat on a little mound of earth, scrabbling among the grasses for a stone to throw at them. They disappeared down a lane.

"Oh, I'm so afraid," said Ivan. "She hates me—that's what it is! She is going to betray me. Oh, she is going to kill me."

Kavalerov pulled himself together. He was utterly ashamed of himself now. He remembered that when Ivan had jumped back, he had seen something that had excited his attention: only he had been too frightened to examine it carefully.

"Look here," he said. "It's no good going on like this. Do you know what it was? It was a little boy whistling through his fingers. Yes, I saw it. It was a little boy and the little boy popped up behind the fence and whistled at us. A little boy——"

"I told you so," said Ivan, smiling. "I told you you should come prepared for anything, didn't I? I told you to pinch yourself hard, didn't I?"

After that they had a row. Ivan found a public-house which was open. He had an enormous difficulty finding it. He refused to let Kavalerov come in with him. Kavalerov walked round the town in circles, had no idea where he was, tried to discover where he was by judging his approximate distance from the noisy murmur of the tramways. When he reached the main road, he stamped his feet angrily and turned back to the public-house. Ivan showed him to a chair, smiling all the time.

"I want to know," said Kavalerov, "I want to know why you are always tormenting me. Why are you always trying to make a fool of me? That's what I want to know. There simply wasn't any machine there at all, was there? There just couldn't be a machine like the one you were speaking about. All you like doing is lying. Why do you tell such lies?"

Tired out, he slumped into his chair.

"Now listen carefully, Kavalerov," said Ivan. "Order your beer and listen to the story I am going to tell you. Only listen carefully."

THE STORY OF THE MEETING OF THE TWO BROTHERS

Think of the "Threepenny Bit." Imagine the delicate tracery of the scaffolding.

Not unlike scaffolding everywhere else, of course, but think of the girders, the platforms, the staircases, all the entrances and exits. All very ordinary. The only thing that is not ordinary is the crowd. Everybody in the crowd saw a different building. They were all laughing, and they were all laughing for different reasons. Some admired it for its simplicity: those were the ones who said it was like a cross word puzzle. Someone said:

"It's absolutely no use having a wooden building so high. After a certain height, wooden planks lose their identity completely— they're not pleasing when they lose their identity. All this scaffolding spoils the essential grandeur of the building. The higher the mast, they say, the more danger of it coming to a sticky end. After all, there is something delicate and fragile in a building made of wood. Just the thing for a fire!"

Someone else said:

"Don't you think the girders are exactly like the strings of a violin? Did you hear me? I said 'a violin.'"

The man who had been speaking a moment before interrupted at this point.

"That's exactly what I said. I was admiring its delicacy. It is just like music, like a piece of musical notation."

Someone else taunted them:

"All right. So much for the violins. The only music I like is a wind-instrument, trumpets. What are you going to do about that?"

In the ordered arrangement of the girders a schoolboy discovered a strange mathematic: but even when he had made the discovery of this new science, he had no time to decipher the multiplication sign and the "equals" sign, for immediately after he had first noticed it the resemblance disappeared. The construction of the building was so delicate, so like a spider's web, that nothing seemed to remain in its place for long.

The poet thought the building resembled the siege of Troy. The raised towers . . .

He felt more sure of himself when the musicians appeared. They crawled across the wooden planks at the base of the building, almost obliterated in their instruments.

The evening was black, the lanterns white and globular; the bunting cast a deep red glow over everything. Looking down between the planks, the hollows wore a Sinaitic darkness like a robe, dark and remote. As the lanterns trembled in the air, their supporting wires whistled in the wind, and the shadows of the lanterns, moving along the ground, were like eyebrows, rising, falling, rising again. . . . Swarms of midges swarmed around the lanterns. In the distance windows twinkled, the shapes of houses suddenly revealed themselves and bent a little in the direction of the "Threepenny Bit." As long as the lanterns swung in the wind, the scaffolding appeared to be brilliantly alive, always in motion, floating on air, like a brigantine, sails flying, above the crowd.

Andrey Babichev crawled along the wooden planks at the base. There was a platform as large as life, stairs, hand-rails, a dark background, lights shining down on him. Even when they were a long way away the spectators could see the glint of the water in the glass on the table.

Babichev shone above the crowd, glittering like tin or as though he had been pricked out in electric lights. He was going to give a speech. Below, in a sort of tent formed by the platform, the actors were preparing for their appearance on the stage. From somewhere there came the sound of an oboe, rising sweetly. No one knew where it came from: for everyone it remained a mystery to the end. Equally mysterious was the top of a drum which flashed silver in the harsh light, flashed in their faces. In the canyon below, the actors were dressing. Anyone walking across the platform sent the boards tumbling on their heads showers of sawdust.

Babichev's appearance on the rostrum was the cause of immense enthusiasm among the audience. They took him for a compère, so neat he was, so deliberate, so entirely theatrical.

"There he is! There's the fat 'un!" they cried out in one voice.

"Bravo!" came the chorus from every part of the field.

Someone on the rostrum said, "Comrade Babichev is now going to speak to you." No one cheered. Everyone was keyed up with expectation. Many even stood on tiptoe. They all looked extraordinarily happy and there were exactly two sources to their enthusiasm. In the first place, Babichev was a famous man; and in the second place, he was extremely fat. For them his tremendous belly was something familiar, understandable. Babichev received an ovation: at least half the applause was due to the size of that belly of his. He began to speak.

He spoke about his plans for the "Threepenny Bit," its production levels, the surpassing excellence of the food he was going to sell there, the incredible benefits of communal kitchens.

He spoke about baby-food—there was going to be a special department in the "Threepenny Bit" for babies—he spoke about the preparation of milk slops, about children's growth, about spinal diseases, about anaemic complexions. Like all good speakers, he paid no attention at all to the people in the front rows and concentrated on those far away at the back. It was only when he had finished his speech that he was able to notice what had been happening immediately below him. In the front row no one was listening to Andrey Babichev. Instead, they were consumed with the most violent curiosity about a little man in a bowler hat. The man had detached himself from the audience; he had quietly slipped across the rope which served as a barrier dividing the platform from the audience, and there he stood, a little to one side.

Because he stood a little to one side, they all thought he must have had a perfectly good reason to be there. He stood with his back to the audience and leaned against the rope, and sometimes appeared to be actually sitting on it, obviously not worrying about the effect it would have on the audience if it broke. Swinging there on the rope he gave every indication of being perfectly at home.

Perhaps he was listening to the speaker, perhaps he was admiring the actresses. Peeping through the boards, he could see the skirt of a ballerina as it flashed past. Through the chinks he could see faces smiling up at him.

What was he carrying in his hands? What was it which distinguished him from everyone else? He was carrying a pillow which lay in a tremendous faded yellow pillow-slip, a pillow-slip on which many heads had lain in their time. When he had begun to swing on the rope, he had flung the pillow on the ground. It lay on the ground, like a little dachshund.

Andrey Babichev finished his speech. With one hand he wiped his mouth in a handkerchief, with the other he poured out a glass of water. The applause came to an end; the audience were already waiting expectantly for the actors to begin, when the little man in the bowler hat lifted his behind carefully away from the rope and stood bolt upright. In his outstretched hands he held the pillow. In a terrible voice, he shouted:

"Comrades, it is now *my* turn to speak!"

At that moment Andrey recognized that it was his brother. He clenched his fists at him. Ivan slowly climbed the steps to the rostrum. Someone ran along the platform, trying to stop him by threats and gestures. The man's hand hung in the air. With little jerking movements it seemed to be counting Ivan's steps as he proceeded slowly towards the rostrum.

One—two—four—si——

People whispered together in the audience. "They are trying to hypnotize him," they said.

Ivan held the pillow to his collar. At last he climbed on to the rostrum: he appeared clearly visible against the dark background, up this fine building of yours. All the nuts and bolts are going to fall apart, the concrete will fall to pieces and crumble like the body of a leper. Well, now . . . Every single girder will disobey your orders. Well, now, what am I telling you? All your grand ideas are going to be worth nothing, the sum-total of your achievement will be precisely zero, that useless flower i' the forest. That's what I am going to do."

"Poor Ivan, you're ill. You're delirious," said Andrey, speaking in a soft, gentle voice. Everyone expected him to shriek at the top of his voice: it surprised them that he should talk so gently. "What are you talking about? What do you mean by 'her'? I can't see 'her.' And what do you mean by saying that all my plans are useless flowers in the forest? All that has happened is that one of the lanterns smashed against a stanchion. Ivan, my poor Ivan . . ."

He walked up to Ivan, stretching out his hands. But Ivan turned away.

"Look!" he screamed, raising a solitary hand above his head. "Can't you see her? There she is—a little to the left—yes, there! Can't you see her? There she is sitting on one of your girders. Now, what you want is just a glass of water. Someone turn the hose on Andrey Babichev. There she is, sitting on her perch. Can't you see her? Aren't you frightened? Aren't you frightened?"

"It's only a shadow," said Andrey, "only a shadow. Come along now. I'll take you home. The concert can begin at once. You're keeping the actors waiting. The public wants to see the actors. Come along now."

"A shadow! It's not a shadow, Andrey. You think you are being funny. I'll make you laugh on the other side of your face. It is I, sitting on the perch, Andrey. I am the old world passing away and here I am, sitting on the perch. I am the accumulated intelligence of my age, the age which had the guts to invent formulae, to explore literature. I—I am the accumulated intelligence of dreams, the dreams you want to destroy . . ."

Ivan raised his other hand and shouted:

"Come, Ophelia! Come! The time is now ripe!"

The *thing*, which was sitting on its perch, glittered as it climbed

a background as dark as a child's slate, so dark that you could almost see the child's awful scribbling on the slate through the dazzling arc-lamps. When he reached the top of the rostrum, he paused.

A murmur ran through the crowd.

"He's carrying a pillow," they said.

Then he began to speak.

"Comrades," he said, "they want to take away from you the most precious thing you have—your domesticity. The horses of the revolution are forcing their way into your houses, they are going to put your children to the knife, they are going to kill your darling kittens. They are going to smash up your pots and pans, they are going to ravish your kitchenettes! Mothers, I appeal to you! I give you my last warning! The elephants of the revolution are going to ravish your kitchenettes!

"What was he talking about? He spat at our pots and pans! He ridiculed the quiet of family existence! He laughed at us for feeding our babies out of bottles! What did he want to deprive us of? What did he want to steal out of our heart's blood? He wanted to steal our homes, our more than precious homes! He wanted us to live as wanderers on the plains of history! Wives, he has spat at the soup you made for your husbands! Mothers, his one dream is to destroy the resemblance your children bear to you—O holy, precious resemblance! He wants to pry into your most secret parts; like a mouse, he wants to be able to slide into bed with you, peep into your night-gowns, snuggle in the hair under your armpits. To hell with him! Here is a pillow. I am the king of pillows. Tell him that we want to sleep on our own pillows! Tell him that our few remaining hairs of swan's down, our ruddy hairs—tell him that they have lain on these pillows! Tell him that at night, when we have loved each other, we have often kissed these pillows! Tell him that we shall die with our heads on our pillows; tell him that we shall kill anyone who tries to take our pillows away from us, and that they, too, shall die with their heads upon our pillows! Oh, tell him not to touch our pillows! Do not call upon us. Don't beckon to us. Don't tempt us. What can you offer us instead of our capacity to hate, to love, to cry, to hope, to pity, to forgive? Here is a pillow. Our coat of arms. Our banner. Against our pillows shall we receive the bullets you send among us. Oh, we shall stifle you under the weight of our pillows!"

He came to an abrupt end. He had said far too much. His last sentence came to an end with a sudden jerk, as though it had been twisted behind his back. He stopped suddenly, suddenly terrified. He was terrified because the man he was fulminating against absolutely refused to say a word, was listening to him attentively. It was exactly like something on the stage. Many people really did think it was all part of a turn. Actors often come out from the audience. Actors were now climbing out of their wooden penthouses—what more proof could you need? Like a butterfly the beautiful ballerina fluttered on to the stage. The clown wore a coat of monkey-skin. He crawled on to the platform, one hand grasping the planks, the other trailing an unusual type of musical instrument—a long trumpet with three funnels at the end. You can imagine that anything will happen when you see a clown in a red wig and a little coat of monkey-skin—so it was quite easy to imagine that climbing on to the stage and using his trumpet as a stick. Someone in a frock-coat darted on to the platform. He was trying to group the actors together and at the same time he was trying to get a better view of the stranger who had forcibly interrupted the normal progress of events. The actors themselves thought the man in the bowler hat was another actor, that he had been invited to amuse the audience, had invented this gag of his, had brought the pillow along—and had a row with Andrey Babichev. After that, they thought, he would go on with his real act. But no! With a sudden shriek of terror the clown fell right into his trumpet. Then a wave of fear began to envelop everyone who was there. Certainly, Ivan Babichev was not the cause of their fear. On the contrary, everyone thought his speech had been carefully prepared beforehand. In the silence which followed his speech, many people felt their hair rising on end.

"Why are you looking at me like that?" said Ivan, dropping his pillow on the ground.

Andrey gave a scream of terror which could be heard all over the field, in the houses, along the alley-ways, in bedrooms where old men, hearing it, raised themselves from their beds in mortal fear: and no one who was there knew that the giant Andrey and the little Ivan were brothers.

"What the blazes is the matter with you?" said the giant. "You're—you're a damned good-for-nothing!" he added.

His face swelled out. From his nostrils, his mouth, his ears, a dark fluid, like a sediment, suffused his face. Everyone turned away in horror. It was not Andrey who was speaking—the planks, the concrete, the joists, all the straight angles and all the formulas which had gone to make the building what it was—it was they who had assumed flesh. Their anger had overflowed and accumulated in Andrey's body.

Ivan did not move at all. Everyone expected him to move away, move backwards until he tripped over his pillow; instead, he squared his shoulders, marched up to the railing of the rostrum, shaded his eyes with his hand, shouted in a loud voice:

"Ophelia, where are you? I am waiting for you!"

Then the wind rose. Always the wind had been playing on the lanterns and everyone had become accustomed to the moving shapes of the shadows, to the squares changing into equilateral triangles, to the equilateral triangles changing into long conic loops. The wind rose. It was so strong that it forced against their shoulders, made them bend their heads low—even then they were so accustomed to it that they might have greeted it with a little noise of displeasure and afterwards forgotten all about it, if . . . if . . . But something rose behind their backs, flew above their heads. . . .

A brigantine, all sails flying, flew among them, her spars scream ing in the gale, the dark deck moving forward—like a rush of b protecting their young—then it collapsed with a crash agains of the girders, shivered, paused. One of the lanterns was sm against the keel.

"You're afraid, aren't you?" said Ivan. "Now I am goi you what I am going to do with you. I am going to le down, glittered as it turned back again, glittered and glistened as it hopped across the floor like a bird, exactly like a bird. Slowly it disappeared beneath the dark hollow between the girders.

They all ran away, panic-stricken, crying out aloud in their fear. The *thing* moved below the scaffolding with a curious clanging noise. Suddenly it reappeared, an orange-colored beam of light projecting from its shoulders. With a low whistle this shapeless void shot into the air like a spider, higher and higher it flew, to where the beams mingled in chaotic confusion, hung for a moment on the joists, then dropped gently to earth.

"Do as you have been told, Ophelia!" said Ivan, running up and down the platform. "Did you hear what they are going to do to our homes? I order you—now—to smash up the building."

While the people ran away, lowering clouds raced at their sides, storms gathered in their wake.

The "Threepenny Bit" crashed to the ground.

At this point Ivan paused for a second or two in his story.

"In the debris," he said, "I saw the drum lying on its side. I, I— Ivan Babichev—I put my feet through it. Ophelia hurried towards me. In her gaping jaws I recognized the body of Andrey Babichev. He had been badly mauled. He was dying."

"Give me the pillow, brother," he whispered. "I want to lie with my head on the pillow. I am dying, Ivan, dying . . ."

I placed the pillow on my knees. I placed his head on the pillow.

"We have conquered, Ophelia!" I said.

7

ONE Sunday morning Ivan Babichev went to see Kavalerov.

"Today I want you to meet Valya," he said, with an air of solemnity.

They left the house. It would be impossible to imagine a more charming walk. They marched through the empty streets and the streets were decked out in their Sunday best; later, they marched round the Theatre Square. There was no one else in the Square. The road to the Tverskaya was a deep blue. To see Moscow at its best during the summer you must go out on a Sunday morning. Only then, because the light is undisturbed by the traffic, does it appear to have that singular luminosity which suggests, all through the day, that the sun has only just risen. They walked across geometrical patterns of light and shade, or rather, across the solid shapes which formed themselves into stereoscopic patterns of light and shade in their eyes, for lights intersect in the air as well as on the ground. Just before they reached the Moscow Soviet they found themselves in complete darkness: but in the distance, between two huge buildings, there fell a shaft of massive sunlight, a shaft so thick and so dense that it was impossible to doubt its solidity. The dust, whirling within the shaft, had all the appearance of a wireless wave in motion.

At the corner of the Tverskaya and the Nikitskaya, they stopped to admire a hedgerow which was alight with flowers. Then, seeing a gate, they pushed it open and mounted a wooden staircase leading into an old disused gallery covered with a multitude of glass panels: through the panels they saw the sun shining over their heads.

The sky seemed to consist of a number of squares of varying shades of blue, becoming lighter and lighter as they receded in the direction of the roof. At least a quarter of the panels were cracked. Outside, near the floor, a number of threads of green ivy wound their way across the grass. Everything conspired together to suggest an atmosphere of childhood: it was the sort of gallery where you expected rabbits to pop up at any moment.

Ivan threw himself at the door. There were three doors, and he threw himself at the last of the three.

While walking across the room, Kavalerov had a sudden desire to pluck one of the green threads on the glass. He had hardly touched the ivy when he found himself dragging a whole forest of it across the floor, a forest which had lain invisible below. Somewhere in the forest there was a piece of jagged wire which had suddenly come to life: as though the scene of their behavior was not Moscow, but Italy, as though they were playing with marionettes and not with a forest. Standing on tiptoe, Kavalerov saw a courtyard surrounded by a stone wall. He noticed that the gallery lay somewhere between the first story and the second, and looking down, still shrouded in his visions of Italy, he saw a small bright-green courtyard.

Even before he had mounted the steps, he had heard voices and laughter coming from the courtyard: but he had had no time to discover their origin, and Ivan, knocking at the door, had distracted his attention. He knocked once, twice, three times. . . .

"There is no one here," he murmured. "She must be over there."

Kavalerov was still thinking about the broken glass and the lawn below. Why? There was nothing extraordinary in what he had seen. As Ivan knocked at the door, he made a sharp turn, turning so swiftly that his eyes perceived no more than a multi-colored streak of scenery, so swiftly that the time he took was no longer than the beat of a rhythm used in gymnastics. When he looked down at the green lawn, it seemed extraordinarily fresh and cool compared with the tasteless courtyard. At first he had hardly noticed it. It was only later that he became filled with a sense of wonder at its transparent freshness.

"She must be out," said Babichev. "Let me pass."

He looked through one of the glass panels. Kavalerov did the same a moment later.

He had thought it was a lawn, but really it was only the small courtyard covered with grass. He had seen clustered leaves on the trees surrounding the yard, and seeing them through the glass he had imagined a perfectly shapely lawn: all the beauty visible to the eye lay projected against the huge wall of the house next door, and Kavalerov, looking down from the height where he stood, suddenly realized that instead of a large park, all he could see was that narrow strip of grass. From their vantage point they could see everything around them towering above the grass, which lay on the earth like a carpet in a room full of furniture. Strange roofs re-

vealed their secrets. He saw weather-vanes in their natural grandeur, skylights invisible and unimaginable to people below; he
saw a child's balloon which had flown too high and now lay
irrecoverable among the gutters. Buildings, bearing aerials, tilted
towards the courtyard in graceful stages. The cupola of the church
which had recently been painted with red lead lay in an open
space of sky, seeming to float on air until Kavalerov suddenly
grasped it in his gaze. Far in the distance he saw the trolley of a
tram-car standing out like the mast of a ship, and he saw someone
leaning out of a distant window, someone who seemed to be
sniffing at the air or making a meal out of a cloud, someone who
seemed to be leaning on the moving mast.

The essential thing was—to get down into the courtyard.

They left the room. There was a gap in the stone wall which
separated that cold and dismal courtyard from the secret mysteries
of the lawn. Like bread withdrawn from the oven were those missing stones. Through the gap, a whole world was visible. The sun
shone on Kavalerov's uncovered head. A rope had been drawn
between two boys standing there below and a youngster jumped
out, throwing his body to one side and gliding over the rope, so
that it remained parallel with him. Instead of jumping over it, he
seemed to roll right round it, like a man rolling over the crest of a
wave; then he lifted his legs and thrust them apart, exactly as
though he were swimming. A moment later they saw him fly beneath it, his face turned upside-down, contorted, confused. When
the boy touched the ground again, Kavalerov heard a sound like a
sharp "ough!"—which might have been a little snort of excitement or only the echo of the scraping noise he made with his feet
when he touched the ground.

Ivan nudged Kavalerov's elbow.

"There she is! Look!" he whispered.

Everyone was crying out and clapping their hands. The young
athlete, who was almost naked, walked away, limping on one foot,
imitating perhaps the affectation which is common among sportsmen.

It was Volodya Makarov.

Kavalerov looked worried. Shame and fear had entered his soul. When Volodya smiled, he had revealed a row of white teeth which gleamed in the sun.

Above, in the gallery, someone was knocking at the door. Kavalerov turned back. To have been found spying over the wall— he would look so foolish if he was caught! Whoever it was, it was someone who was being perfectly dissected by the square panels of glass. Parts of the man's body appeared to possess an independent existence, and by an optical illusion the head appeared to move far in front of the rest of the body. Kavalerov recognized the head. It was Andrey Babichev walking across the gallery.

"Andrey Petrovich!" shouted Valya from the green meadow. "Andrey Petrovich! Come down!"

The strange guest departed. He disappeared from the gallery. There were too many obstacles in the way for Kavalerov to be able to see him as he came down. He had to run to catch up with him.

"Come along," shouted Valya.

Kavalerov saw Valya standing on the lawn, her feet set wide apart, her body firm and resilient. She was wearing a pair of small black bathing-drawers which revealed the whole length of her legs. On her feet there were no stockings, only a pair of white sports shoes which had no heels; it was this absence of heels which gave her her air of solidity and resilience. Standing there, she seemed to be entirely unfeminine: she had the figure of a man or of a boy. Her legs simmered in steam; they had been burnt brown by the sun and hardened by the falls and the blows she had received playing in the fields; all round them there were raw wounds covered with wax, where the scabs had been peeled off too early. Her knees were like orange skins. She had reached the age when children live in an unconscious delight in their physical perfection, at that age when they pay no heed to beauty, when they regret nothing and have no pride in their accomplishments. But above the black bathing-drawers there was more than a suspicion of the purity and loveliness of her body. When you saw her, you thought at once of how beautiful she would be when she had become a woman and had learnt the arts of chemistry in adorning herself, in adorning her beauty. Then there will no longer be scars on her legs and the scabs will have disappeared, and the sunburn will lie like a smooth vapor over the whole of her body.

He turned away and ran along by the side wall on the other side of the one which had been broken in two. As he ran his shoulders brushed against the stone.

"Where are you going?" Ivan shouted. "Where are you off to? Wait a moment!"

If he keeps on shouting like that, thought Kavalerov, terrified, they'll hear him: and then they'll see *me*.

And that was exactly what happened. On the other side of the wall everyone suddenly became very silent. They were all listening intently. Ivan caught up with Kavalerov.

"Listen, my dear fellow," he said. "Did you see him? It's my brother. They are all there, every one of them. Wait a moment! I am going to climb up the wall and give them a piece of my mind! What the blazes have you been doing to your shoulder? You're simply covered with dust!"

"Yes, I know your brother very well," said Kavalerov. He was almost whispering when he continued. "Yes, that was the brother of yours who ran after me. He's the famous man I was talking about. Our destinies have met at last. You told me I ought to have killed that brother of yours. What do you think I ought to do now?"

Valya was sitting on the stone wall.

"Papa!" she shouted, thunder-struck.

Ivan put his hands round his knees. His legs hung over the wall.

"Oh, Valya, my dear, gouge out my eyes!" he said, sighing and breathing hard. "I wish I was blind! I don't want to look at the world. I don't want to see your green meadows or your trees or your flowers, or the fools and the knights in armor who walk about in the world. Oh, Valya, I don't want to be able to see! I have made a mistake. Do you know, I thought all the sentiments and passions had vanished from the earth—but now I know that they a background as dark as a child's slate, so dark that you could almost see the child's awful scribbling on the slate through the dazzling arc-lamps. When he reached the top of the rostrum, he paused.

A murmur ran through the crowd.

"He's carrying a pillow," they said.

Then he began to speak.

"Comrades," he said, "they want to take away from you the most precious thing you have—your domesticity. The horses of the revolution are forcing their way into your houses, they are going to put your children to the knife, they are going to kill your darling kittens. They are going to smash up your pots and pans, they are going to ravish your kitchenettes! Mothers, I appeal to you! I give you my last warning! The elephants of the revolution are going to ravish your kitchenettes!

"What was he talking about? He spat at our pots and pans! He ridiculed the quiet of family existence! He laughed at us for feeding our babies out of bottles! What did he want to deprive us of? What did he want to steal out of our heart's blood? He wanted to steal our homes, our more than precious homes! He wanted us to live as wanderers on the plains of history! Wives, he has spat at the soup you made for your husbands! Mothers, his one dream is to destroy the resemblance your children bear to you—O holy, precious resemblance! He wants to pry into your most secret parts; like a mouse, he wants to be able to slide into bed with you, peep into your night-gowns, snuggle in the hair under your armpits. To hell with him! Here is a pillow. I am the king of pillows. Tell him that we want to sleep on our own pillows! Tell him that our few remaining hairs of swan's down, our ruddy hairs—tell him that they have lain on these pillows! Tell him that at night, when we have loved each other, we have often kissed these pillows! Tell him that we shall die with our heads on our pillows; tell him that we shall kill anyone who tries to take our pillows away from us, and that they, too, shall die with their heads upon our pillows! Oh, tell him not to touch our pillows! Do not call upon us. Don't beckon to us. Don't tempt us. What can you offer us instead of our

capacity to hate, to love, to cry, to hope, to pity, to forgive? Here
is a pillow. Our coat of arms. Our banner. Against our pillows
shall we receive the bullets you send among us. Oh, we shall stifle
you under the weight of our pillows!"

He came to an abrupt end. He had said far too much. His last
sentence came to an end with a sudden jerk, as though it had been
twisted behind his back. He stopped suddenly, suddenly terrified.
He was terrified because the man he was fulminating against
absolutely refused to say a word, was listening to him attentively.
It was exactly like something on the stage. Many people really did
think it was all part of a turn. Actors often come out from the
audience. Actors were now climbing out of their wooden penthouses—what more proof could you need? Like a butterfly the
beautiful ballerina fluttered on to the stage. The clown wore a
coat of monkey-skin. He crawled on to the platform, one hand
grasping the planks, the other trailing an unusual type of musical
instrument—a long trumpet with three funnels at the end. You
can imagine that anything will happen when you see a clown in a
red wig and a little coat of monkey-skin—so it was quite easy to
imagine that climbing on to the stage and using his trumpet as a
stick. Someone in a frock-coat darted on to the platform. He was
trying to group the actors together and at the same time he was
trying to get a better view of the stranger who had forcibly interrupted the normal progress of events. The actors themselves
thought the man in the bowler hat was another actor, that he had
been invited to amuse the audience, had invented this gag of his,
had brought the pillow along—and had a row with Andrey Babichev. After that, they thought, he would go on with his real
act. But no! With a sudden shriek of terror the clown fell right
into his trumpet. Then a wave of fear began to envelop everyone
who was there. Certainly, Ivan Babichev was not the cause of their
fear. On the contrary, everyone thought his speech had been carefully prepared beforehand. In the silence which followed his
speech, many people felt their hair rising on end.

"Why are you looking at me like that?" said Ivan, dropping his
pillow on the ground.

Andrey gave a scream of terror which could be heard all over the field, in the houses, along the alley-ways, in bedrooms where old men, hearing it, raised themselves from their beds in mortal fear: and no one who was there knew that the giant Andrey and the little Ivan were brothers.

"What the blazes is the matter with you?" said the giant. "You're—you're a damned good-for-nothing!" he added.

His face swelled out. From his nostrils, his mouth, his ears, a dark fluid, like a sediment, suffused his face. Everyone turned away in horror. It was not Andrey who was speaking—the planks, the concrete, the joists, all the straight angles and all the formulas which had gone to make the building what it was—it was they who had assumed flesh. Their anger had overflowed and accumulated in Andrey's body.

Ivan did not move at all. Everyone expected him to move away, move backwards until he tripped over his pillow; instead, he squared his shoulders, marched up to the railing of the rostrum, shaded his eyes with his hand, shouted in a loud voice:

"Ophelia, where are you? I am waiting for you!"

Then the wind rose. Always the wind had been playing on the lanterns and everyone had become accustomed to the moving shapes of the shadows, to the squares changing into equilateral triangles, to the equilateral triangles changing into long conic loops. The wind rose. It was so strong that it forced against their shoulders, made them bend their heads low—even then they were so accustomed to it that they might have greeted it with a little noise of displeasure and afterwards forgotten all about it, if . . . if . . . But something rose behind their backs, flew above their heads. . . .

A brigantine, all sails flying, flew among them, her spars screaming in the gale, the dark deck moving forward—like a rush of birds protecting their young—then it collapsed with a crash against one of the girders, shivered, paused. One of the lanterns was smashed against the keel.

"You're afraid, aren't you?" said Ivan. "Now I am going to tell you what I am going to do with you. I am going to let her break up this fine building of yours. All the nuts and bolts are going to fall apart, the concrete will fall to pieces and crumble like the body of a leper. Well, now . . . Every single girder will disobey your orders. Well, now, what am I telling you? All your grand ideas are going to be worth nothing, the sum-total of your achievement will be precisely zero, that useless flower i' the forest. That's what I am going to do."

"Poor Ivan, you're ill. You're delirious," said Andrey, speaking in a soft, gentle voice. Everyone expected him to shriek at the top of his voice: it surprised them that he should talk so gently. "What are you talking about? What do you mean by 'her'? I can't see 'her.' And what do you mean by saying that all my plans are useless flowers in the forest? All that has happened is that one of the lanterns smashed against a stanchion. Ivan, my poor Ivan . . ."

He walked up to Ivan, stretching out his hands. But Ivan turned away.

"Look!" he screamed, raising a solitary hand above his head. "Can't you see her? There she is—a little to the left—yes, there! Can't you see her? There she is sitting on one of your girders. Now, what you want is just a glass of water. Someone turn the hose on Andrey Babichev. There she is, sitting on her perch. Can't you see her? Aren't you frightened? Aren't you frightened?"

"It's only a shadow," said Andrey, "only a shadow. Come along now. I'll take you home. The concert can begin at once. You're keeping the actors waiting. The public wants to see the actors. Come along now."

"A shadow! It's not a shadow, Andrey. You think you are being funny. I'll make you laugh on the other side of your face. It is I, sitting on the perch, Andrey. I am the old world passing away and here I am, sitting on the perch. I am the accumulated intelligence of my age, the age which had the guts to invent formulae, to explore literature. I—I am the accumulated intelligence of dreams, the dreams you want to destroy . . ."

Ivan raised his other hand and shouted:

"Come, Ophelia! Come! The time is now ripe!"

The *thing*, which was sitting on its perch, glittered as it climbed down, glittered as it turned back again, glittered and glistened as it hopped across the floor like a bird, exactly like a bird. Slowly it disappeared beneath the dark hollow between the girders.

They all ran away, panic-stricken, crying out aloud in their fear. The *thing* moved below the scaffolding with a curious clanging noise. Suddenly it reappeared, an orange-colored beam of light projecting from its shoulders. With a low whistle this shapeless void shot into the air like a spider, higher and higher it flew, to where the beams mingled in chaotic confusion, hung for a moment on the joists, then dropped gently to earth.

"Do as you have been told, Ophelia!" said Ivan, running up and down the platform. "Did you hear what they are going to do to our homes? I order you—now—to smash up the building."

While the people ran away, lowering clouds raced at their sides, storms gathered in their wake.

The "Threepenny Bit" crashed to the ground.

At this point Ivan paused for a second or two in his story.

"In the debris," he said, "I saw the drum lying on its side. I, I— Ivan Babichev—I put my feet through it. Ophelia hurried towards me. In her gaping jaws I recognized the body of Andrey Babichev. He had been badly mauled. He was dying."

"Give me the pillow, brother," he whispered. "I want to lie with my head on the pillow. I am dying, Ivan, dying . . ."

I placed the pillow on my knees. I placed his head on the pillow.

"We have conquered, Ophelia!" I said.

7

ONE Sunday morning Ivan Babichev went to see Kavalerov.

"Today I want you to meet Valya," he said, with an air of solemnity.

They left the house. It would be impossible to imagine a more charming walk. They marched through the empty streets and the streets were decked out in their Sunday best; later, they marched round the Theatre Square. There was no one else in the Square. The road to the Tverskaya was a deep blue. To see Moscow at its best during the summer you must go out on a Sunday morning. Only then, because the light is undisturbed by the traffic, does it appear to have that singular luminosity which suggests, all through the day, that the sun has only just risen. They walked across geometrical patterns of light and shade, or rather, across the solid shapes which formed themselves into stereoscopic patterns of light and shade in their eyes, for lights intersect in the air as well as on the ground. Just before they reached the Moscow Soviet they found themselves in complete darkness: but in the distance, between two huge buildings, there fell a shaft of massive sunlight, a shaft so thick and so dense that it was impossible to doubt its solidity. The dust, whirling within the shaft, had all the appearance of a wireless wave in motion.

At the corner of the Tverskaya and the Nikitskaya, they stopped to admire a hedgerow which was alight with flowers. Then, seeing a gate, they pushed it open and mounted a wooden staircase leading into an old disused gallery covered with a multitude of glass panels: through the panels they saw the sun shining over their heads.

The sky seemed to consist of a number of squares of varying shades of blue, becoming lighter and lighter as they receded in the direction of the roof. At least a quarter of the panels were cracked. Outside, near the floor, a number of threads of green ivy wound their way across the grass. Everything conspired together to suggest an atmosphere of childhood: it was the sort of gallery where you expected rabbits to pop up at any moment.

Ivan threw himself at the door. There were three doors, and he threw himself at the last of the three.

While walking across the room, Kavalerov had a sudden desire to pluck one of the green threads on the glass. He had hardly touched the ivy when he found himself dragging a whole forest of it across the floor, a forest which had lain invisible below. Somewhere in the forest there was a piece of jagged wire which had suddenly come to life: as though the scene of their behavior was not Moscow, but Italy, as though they were playing with marionettes and not with a forest. Standing on tiptoe, Kavalerov saw a courtyard surrounded by a stone wall. He noticed that the gallery lay somewhere between the first story and the second, and looking down, still shrouded in his visions of Italy, he saw a small bright-green courtyard.

Even before he had mounted the steps, he had heard voices and laughter coming from the courtyard: but he had had no time to discover their origin, and Ivan, knocking at the door, had distracted his attention. He knocked once, twice, three times. . . .

"There is no one here," he murmured. "She must be over there."

Kavalerov was still thinking about the broken glass and the lawn below. Why? There was nothing extraordinary in what he had seen. As Ivan knocked at the door, he made a sharp turn, turning so swiftly that his eyes perceived no more than a multi-colored streak of scenery, so swiftly that the time he took was no longer than the beat of a rhythm used in gymnastics. When he looked down at the green lawn, it seemed extraordinarily fresh and cool compared with the tasteless courtyard. At first he had hardly noticed it. It was only later that he became filled with a sense of wonder at its transparent freshness.

"She must be out," said Babichev. "Let me pass."

He looked through one of the glass panels. Kavalerov did the same a moment later.

He had thought it was a lawn, but really it was only the small courtyard covered with grass. He had seen clustered leaves on the trees surrounding the yard, and seeing them through the glass he had imagined a perfectly shapely lawn: all the beauty visible to the eye lay projected against the huge wall of the house next door, and Kavalerov, looking down from the height where he stood, suddenly realized that instead of a large park, all he could see was that narrow strip of grass. From their vantage point they could see everything around them towering above the grass, which lay on the earth like a carpet in a room full of furniture. Strange roofs re-

vealed their secrets. He saw weather-vanes in their natural grandeur, skylights invisible and unimaginable to people below; he
saw a child's balloon which had flown too high and now lay
irrecoverable among the gutters. Buildings, bearing aerials, tilted
towards the courtyard in graceful stages. The cupola of the church
which had recently been painted with red lead lay in an open
space of sky, seeming to float on air until Kavalerov suddenly
grasped it in his gaze. Far in the distance he saw the trolley of a
tram-car standing out like the mast of a ship, and he saw someone
leaning out of a distant window, someone who seemed to be
sniffing at the air or making a meal out of a cloud, someone who
seemed to be leaning on the moving mast.

The essential thing was—to get down into the courtyard.

They left the room. There was a gap in the stone wall which
separated that cold and dismal courtyard from the secret mysteries
of the lawn. Like bread withdrawn from the oven were those missing stones. Through the gap, a whole world was visible. The sun
shone on Kavalerov's uncovered head. A rope had been drawn
between two boys standing there below and a youngster jumped
out, throwing his body to one side and gliding over the rope, so
that it remained parallel with him. Instead of jumping over it, he
seemed to roll right round it, like a man rolling over the crest of a
wave; then he lifted his legs and thrust them apart, exactly as
though he were swimming. A moment later they saw him fly beneath it, his face turned upside-down, contorted, confused. When
the boy touched the ground again, Kavalerov heard a sound like a
sharp "ough!"—which might have been a little snort of excitement or only the echo of the scraping noise he made with his feet
when he touched the ground.

Ivan nudged Kavalerov's elbow.

"There she is! Look!" he whispered.

Everyone was crying out and clapping their hands. The young
athlete, who was almost naked, walked away, limping on one foot,
imitating perhaps the affectation which is common among sportsmen.

It was Volodya Makarov.

Kavalerov looked worried. Shame and fear had entered his soul. When Volodya smiled, he had revealed a row of white teeth which gleamed in the sun.

Above, in the gallery, someone was knocking at the door. Kavalerov turned back. To have been found spying over the wall— he would look so foolish if he was caught! Whoever it was, it was someone who was being perfectly dissected by the square panels of glass. Parts of the man's body appeared to possess an independent existence, and by an optical illusion the head appeared to move far in front of the rest of the body. Kavalerov recognized the head. It was Andrey Babichev walking across the gallery.

"Andrey Petrovich!" shouted Valya from the green meadow. "Andrey Petrovich! Come down!"

The strange guest departed. He disappeared from the gallery. There were too many obstacles in the way for Kavalerov to be able to see him as he came down. He had to run to catch up with him.

"Come along," shouted Valya.

Kavalerov saw Valya standing on the lawn, her feet set wide apart, her body firm and resilient. She was wearing a pair of small black bathing-drawers which revealed the whole length of her legs. On her feet there were no stockings, only a pair of white sports shoes which had no heels; it was this absence of heels which gave her her air of solidity and resilience. Standing there, she seemed to be entirely unfeminine: she had the figure of a man or of a boy. Her legs simmered in steam; they had been burnt brown by the sun and hardened by the falls and the blows she had received playing in the fields; all round them there were raw wounds covered with wax, where the scabs had been peeled off too early. Her knees were like orange skins. She had reached the age when children live in an unconscious delight in their physical perfection, at that age when they pay no heed to beauty, when they regret nothing and have no pride in their accomplishments. But above the black bathing-drawers there was more than a suspicion of the purity and loveliness of her body. When you saw her, you thought at once of how beautiful she would be when she had become a woman and had learnt the arts of chemistry in adorning herself, in adorning her beauty. Then there will no longer be scars on her legs and the scabs will have disappeared, and the sunburn will lie like a smooth vapor over the whole of her body.

He turned away and ran along by the side wall on the other side of the one which had been broken in two. As he ran his shoulders brushed against the stone.

"Where are you going?" Ivan shouted. "Where are you off to? Wait a moment!"

If he keeps on shouting like that, thought Kavalerov, terrified, they'll hear him: and then they'll see *me*.

And that was exactly what happened. On the other side of the wall everyone suddenly became very silent. They were all listening intently. Ivan caught up with Kavalerov.

"Listen, my dear fellow," he said. "Did you see him? It's my brother. They are all there, every one of them. Wait a moment! I am going to climb up the wall and give them a piece of my mind! What the blazes have you been doing to your shoulder? You're simply covered with dust!"

"Yes, I know your brother very well," said Kavalerov. He was almost whispering when he continued. "Yes, that was the brother of yours who ran after me. He's the famous man I was talking about. Our destinies have met at last. You told me I ought to have killed that brother of yours. What do you think I ought to do now?"

Valya was sitting on the stone wall.

"Papa!" she shouted, thunder-struck.

Ivan put his hands round his knees. His legs hung over the wall.

"Oh, Valya, my dear, gouge out my eyes!" he said, sighing and breathing hard. "I wish I was blind! I don't want to look at the world. I don't want to see your green meadows or your trees or your flowers, or the fools and the knights in armor who walk about in the world. Oh, Valya, I don't want to be able to see! I have made a mistake. Do you know, I thought all the sentiments and passions had vanished from the earth—but now I know that they are still with us, Valya. For us, there is envy—more envy—still more envy. Oh, pluck out my eyes, Valya, my dear! I don't—I can't bear to see!"

He laid his hands, his head, his belly on her sweating knees. Immediately afterwards he fell heavily to the foot of the wall.

"Drink up, Kavalerov!" said Ivan. "Let us drink to our youth, which has passed away, to that conspiracy of the sentiments which has come to nothing, to that machine of mine which will never——"

"You're such an awful little fool, Ivan Petrovich." Kavalerov seized him by the collar. "Our youth has not passed away. On the contrary! Listen to me for a change! You say we are no longer as young as we were. I shall prove the opposite. Tomorrow—are you listening, Ivan?—tomorrow I'm going to kill your brother at football!"

8

NIKOLAY KAVALEROV had a seat in the grandstand. On his right there was a wooden cabin, and there, among a pile of handbills and hoardings and step-ladders and planks all huddled together, Valya sat surrounded by a large number of youngsters.

There was a light wind; the air clear and transparent. The wind ran in and out through the visible air. In front, an immense field of cropped grass which shone in the sun like lacquer.

Kavalerov kept on staring at the little cabin until his eyes almost popped from their sockets. When his eyes became tired, he gave full play to his imagination and began to envisage things that were too far away to hear or see. He was not alone in his admiration, and many of the people near him, in spite of their growing excitement about the extraordinary spectacle they were going to witness very soon, turned away from the field and gazed at the adorable girl in the pink dress—a girl who was almost a child, who seemed to be entirely indifferent to the palpitations in the hearts of those who were watching her movements. Everyone there seemed to be trying to hide an obvious desire to attract her attention, as though she were famous, or the daughter of someone famous.

Altogether, there were twenty thousand spectators. They were all waiting for the match to begin. They had been talking about it for months past. Nothing had excited them so much as the game which was about to be played between two teams representing Moscow and Germany.

In the grandstand there was terrific excitement, everyone shouting at the top of his voice. They were all being crushed into the boxes when somewhere a hand-rail snapped, making a sound like a duck quacking. While Kavalerov was searching for his place, and while his legs were mingled with the general confusion of all the legs around him, he saw a venerable old man in a cream-colored waistcoat walking along the gangway at the bottom, an old man who kept on moving his hands up and down to the rhythm of his breathing. No one took any notice of the old man. A gust of wind suddenly stirred them to greater heights of rustling and roaring: and above their heads flags waved in the air, flapping wildly, like lightning.

Kavalerov had to use all his strength to reach his seat. Valya was sitting above him, about thirty yards away to the right. Sometimes he thought his eyes were playing tricks with him. He would imagine that she had recognized him; then he would get up and make a bow. Or else he would imagine that the locket hanging round her throat had suddenly caught on fire. The wind played round her body. To keep her hat on her head, she had to hold it down with her hands, a hat which was shaped like a hood, made of soft raffia which glinted in the sun. The wind blew her sleeve up to her shoulders and revealed arms as well shaped as a vase. The programme in her hands flew away and disappeared among the crowd, beating its wings.

A month before the match, the great topic of discussion had been whether Hetzke would be playing and whether he would play centre forward. Hetzke was already on the field. He was recognized as soon as the Germans came on the field, to the sound of a military march. The spectators always recognize famous men like that —even when there is nothing to distinguish them from the rest of the crowd.

"Hetzke! Hetzke!" they roared, experiencing an extraordinary pleasure in the sight of a famous player and experiencing an even greater pleasure in the sound of their own voices.

Hetzke was a small round-shouldered little man. He walked away from the team and stood apart from them, standing bolt upright and raising his hands above his head and joining them together and shaking them at the spectators. This form of greeting was unknown in Moscow and the spectators were consequently moved to still further applause.

In the sunlit air, all the eleven men of the German team were outlined against the grass: their light yellow togs in vivid contrast with the lush green of the fields. Their jerseys were orange, almost gold; on the right breast they wore a pale-green monogram. Their black shorts flapped gaily in the wind.

Volodya Makarov put on his jersey. Against his skin, it felt unbelievably cool and fresh. He stared out of the window of the dressing-room. The German team were already standing about in the centre of the field.

"Do we go along now?" he asked.

"Go along," said the captain.

The Soviet team ran out on to the field. They wore red jerseys and white shorts. The moment they came in sight all the spectators lolled against the railings and shuffled loudly on the bare boards. A roar of voices drowned the music.

During the first half the Germans decided to play with the wind behind them, and as the wind was extremely strong, most of the game was played on our side of the field. When one of our backs gave a tremendous flying kick at the ball, sending it spinning in the sky in a tremendous parabolic arc, the ball had to travel against the wind; it stopped dead on its path, as though it had struck a wall, and turned back, yellow in the sun, and came down finally at the point where the back had kicked it. The Germans attacked furiously. Hetzke, the famous Hetzke, was terrible! Everyone stared at him and no one had eyes for anybody else.

Whenever he got the ball at his feet, Valya, sitting high up in the stand, screamed at the top of her voice, as though she had just seen a terrible accident. Hetzke would thrust his way through our backs and leave them cowering after his fierce onslaught: then, when he was right in front of the goal-posts, he would give the ball a tremendous kick. At moments like these Valya would lean against her neighbor, hide her face in his shoulder and hold him by the hands, thinking only of how she could avoid looking at the terrible misfortune which was about to happen. But all the time she would be looking round, peering below her eyelashes at that terrible man who had become as black as sin through running in the heat.

Volodya Makarov was the goalkeeper of the Soviet team. Once, he caught the ball in his hands. Hetzke, powerless to carry through the shot he had just begun, cunningly altered direction left and had time to run back. As he ran, Valya saw his bent shoulders, the sweat gleaming through the tight black jersey, and seeing him there, running, she sat up again and began to laugh, first because she was pleased with the success of our team, and secondly because she remembered, with a feeling of shame, that she had just been shouting at the top of her voice and had even been holding on to her neighbor's hands.

"Makarov! Makarov! Bravo!" she shouted. Everyone else shouted the same thing.

The ball was always flying towards our goal-posts. It would bounce against them and you could see them groaning under its weight, and then there would be a little shower of white paint; and seeing that, Volodya would spring up in the air and catch it at heights which were mathematically absurd and demonstrably impossible. As he sprang up in the air, the sloping wall of the spectators would spin up vertically as everyone came to their feet to watch the relentless fate which was waiting for them in the arena, stirred to the depths of their hearts at the thought that the other side might score a goal. Even the umpire would become excited: you could see him running the whole length of the field, blowing his whistle for all he was worth. Once Volodya missed the ball. He caught up with it, hurled himself at it as it flew above his head: he seemed to be breaking all the laws of nature at once, for he seemed to be borne along on nothing except a wave of indignation. On this wave he flew above the grass with the ball in his arms, spinning round and round, exactly as though someone had stuck him to it with a nail. Wrapping himself round the ball, he pressed his stomach, his knees, his chin with all his power into the sides of the ball, like a cloth thrown on a fire to put it out. The force of the ball hurled him ten feet away from where he was standing. When at last he crashed to the ground he was like a bomb wrapped in tinsel. The German forwards rushed at him, but he just managed to kick the ball clear. Then it appeared once more high above the battlefield.

Volodya remained at the goal-posts. He refused to keep still and spent his time walking from one post to the other, slowly recovering the energy he had lost in the previous encounter. His whole body was tingling. He stretched his arms and clapped his sides and kicked up little pellets of earth with the point of his boots. Before the game he had looked really elegant, but now he resembled nothing more than an incongruous mass composed of a pair of enormous gloves, a few tattered rags and patches of blackened flesh. He had not long to wait. Once more the German attack veered in the direction of our goal-posts.

Volodya had a passionate desire for victory, yet he watched all the men on our side with fear in his heart. He thought that he alone knew how to play against Hetzke, that he alone knew Hetzke's weaknesses, that he alone knew how to defend the team against the German attack. At the same time he had an extraordinary desire to know what Hetzke was thinking of his team, and every time he yelled out "Hurrah!" because one of our backs' had been playing particularly well, he wanted to shout out at Hetzke:

"What do you think of our game, eh? Don't you agree that we are playing well?"

Hetzke was the exact opposite of Volodya. Volodya was just a professional, while Hetzke was an artist at the game. While Volodya spent all his time thinking about how the game was going and whether his team would win, Hetzke strove to demonstrate his artistry. He was an old hand, too experienced in cunning to care very much about the honor of his side. The only thing that really interested him was his own personal success or failure. Because he had got into hot water for accepting a bribe, he belonged to no association and was debarred from playing in League games: the only games he was allowed to play in were friendlies or matches against foreign teams, played in a foreign country. In him luck and artistry had joined hands and any team he joined became at once something to be reckoned with. Whatever team it was, he despised it and he despised the men he was playing against. He knew that he could send the ball anywhere he liked, absolutely anywhere. Anything that occurred when he was not on the ball left him entirely unconcerned. A poisonous little devil.

At half-time they thought the Soviet team was up to the mark of the Germans. The Germans were not maintaining the attack and Hetzke was actually hindering them from winning: he broke up their formations, played too much alone, never helped anyone else, relied entirely on himself. Once he had the ball at his feet he concentrated every movement of the game on himself, as though weaving and unweaving a continual thread along a continual shuttle. He ran from one end of the field to the other and then back again—all this according to a plan of attack which no one else could understand. He was relying solely on himself, on his own powers of endurance, on the swiftness of his legs, on his curious power of overcoming all adversaries. The spectators, of course, imagined that the second half would end in a smashing defeat for their opponents: they thought Hetzke would be played out by then, and besides, the wind was behind us. They thought that all our men had to do was to hold on and keep the ball as far away from our own goal-posts as possible.

Hetzke, however, succeeded once more in doing what he wanted to do. Ten minutes before half-time, he ran back from the far end of the field, took the ball on his stomach, stood stock-still for a moment, keeping the others, who had run up, right off the ball. Then he turned towards the centre-line. Avoiding the only Soviet back who could reach him, he dribbled the ball towards our goal-posts. In front of him there was a clear field. He kept his eyes now on the ball, now on the line of the posts, exactly as though he were measuring its potential speed, the direction it would take when it left his feet, as though he were calculating the precise moment when it would leave the ground.

A long- drawn "o-o-o-o" came from the people in the grand-stand.

Volodya stood with his arms wide apart, ready for anything that might happen. He seemed to be holding on to an invisible cask of beer. Hetzke was still dribbling the ball towards the goal-posts when Volodya threw himself at Hetzke's feet: in the confusion the ball bounced from one to the other, whirled round inside an invisible vat. There was so much shouting that it was impossible to see what happened after that. A little later the ball lifted uncer-tainly in the air. Hetzke caught it on his head, nodded—as though he were greeting someone—and the ball fell at his feet again.

So the Soviet team lost the first goal.

In the grandstand there was a terrific hubbub. Binoculars sud-denly swerved towards the Soviet goal-posts; and Hetzke, looking down at his feet all the time, ran towards the centre-line again. He gave the impression of affected indifference.

Someone lifted Volodya to his feet.

9

LIKE all the others, Valya turned round. Kavalerov saw her look-ing towards him. He felt certain that she was looking at him and at him alone: and therefore he became restless and irritated. All round him people seemed to be laughing at him—at his strange refusal to keep still, even for a moment.

He looked round at his neighbors and he was astounded when

he saw Andrey Babichev sitting in the same row as himself, only a few paces away. Seeing those white hands turning the screws of the binoculars, seeing the huge body, the grey coat, the clipped moustaches, he felt suddenly sick. The binoculars were like explosive shells, and the leather straps, which hung round Babichev's neck, had a curious resemblance to the halters round a horse.

The Germans were playing near our goalposts again.

Suddenly the ball swerved in the air—someone had kicked it with terrific force. It flew high above the field and then turned in the direction of the grandstand. Kavalerov heard it whistling above the heads of the spectators. For a moment it remained poised in the air, silently revolving, carefully showing every part of the leather in turn: then it crashed down on the boards at their feet. The players grouped themselves together. They were utterly dumbfounded. The dappled green field, which had been in continual movement, suddenly paused petrified, like a film on the screen when the celluloid has been torn. The lights have been turned on in the room, but the mechanic has not yet had time to switch off the current and so the screen remains strangely brilliant and the hero stands out against the screen completely motionless, although he had been driving like wind through the air when the film came to an end. Kavalerov became even more bitter. Absolutely everyone was laughing at him. It was as if at that moment they had all realized how ridiculous it was for grown men to gaze at the movements of a leather ball for an hour and a half on end, watching a game none of them could understand and watching it with an extraordinary, almost passionate devotion, knowing all the time that it was futile and pointless.

Thousands of people turned to gaze at him, smiling and laughing uproariously.

Perhaps even Valya was laughing at him, laughing at him simply because he was there with the ball at his feet, or because she felt a pang of triumph at the thought of her enemy looking so ridiculous. He smiled grimly, moved his foot away from the ball, which then lost what support it had, bounced against his heel, curled under his feet with the fidelity and affection of a kitten.

"Good! Good!" Babichev yelled, a little spitefully and rather surprised at himself for shouting so loud.

Kavalerov refused to have anything to do with the ball. Two large white hands groped their way towards it. Someone picked it up and passed it to Babichev, who drew himself up to his full height, threw out his stomach, and holding the ball between his fingers raised it above his head. He was swinging his body slowly from side to side so that he could fling it far on to the field. When this sort of thing happened to him he always wanted to burst out laughing; but he realized the overwhelming necessity for an expression of ponderous gravity and improved on his natural solemnity by frowning and pursing his fresh red lips.

He swung his body forward and hurled the ball into the field. Immediately, as though by the stroke of a magician's wand, the field came to life again.

He doesn't even want to recognize me, thought Kavalerov, becoming more and more bitter.

At half-time the score was 1-0 in favor of the Germans. Already the faces of the players were covered with dark patches of mud and there was grass clinging all over their bodies. As they ran to the dressing-rooms, their bare legs moved up and down with immense force, as though they were treading water. The Germans were recognizable only by the redness which extended downwards from their faces—when they mingled with the Russians, they produced a curiously variegated pattern. As they ran to the dressing-rooms they gazed intently at the spectators, sitting in their enclosures, but as they peered into the faces of the spectators they saw not one of them individually. Their smiles, their eyes were directed towards the crowd, but their eyes were blind, almost transparent against their dark faces. Men who had seen them only as little colored dolls running backwards and forwards across the field, saw them at last face to face. The peculiar murmur of the game pursued them even into the dressing-rooms. Hetzke, who looked exactly like a gypsy, followed them while he sucked at a wound in his elbow.

Those who knew all about the measurements of the players

were shocked when they saw their deep wounds, when they saw their sorry breathing, their tattered rags. From a distance they had the charming aspect of people seen on a fair-ground.

Kavalerov found himself being crushed on all sides. When at last he did manage to slip under the railings, he sighed with relief. There, in the shadow, he ran along with the others to the back of the stand. The restaurant lay on the lawn under the trees; it was invaded by force of arms. The little man in the cream-colored waistcoat was eating an ice and staring malevolently and with fear at the people around him. There was still another crowd surging round the dressing-room door.

"Hurrah for Makarov! Hurrah!" they shouted, with extraordinary enthusiasm. Those who were particularly enthusiastic hammered on the walls and on the barbed wire gratings, like men demented, like men escaping from a swarm of bees. Some of them climbed among the dark trees. There like sylphs in the wind, they held their balance by cunning.

Above the group the body of a man floated in the air, half naked. It was Volodya Makarov.

Kavalerov felt that he lacked the courage to go among them, in their triumphal round. He looked through the gaps, shifting from one leg to the other at the back of the crowd.

At last Volodya was allowed to stand on his feet. One of his socks had slipped down to his ankle, forming a green ring round his pear-shaped, hairless calves. His tattered jersey had fallen to pieces, and with an expression of pious modesty he was folding his arms across his naked breast.

Valya and Andrey Babichev came on the scene.

The enthusiasts took it into their heads to applaud all three.

Babichev looked at Volodya with an expression of deep affection.

Then the wind rose. A stick, colored like a barber's pole, suddenly fell on the ground and all the leaves of all the trees faced the west. The triumphal round was broken up, the portrait had fallen to the ground and lay there, smashed into little pieces— everyone ran away out of reach of the clouds of dust. Valya suffered more than any of the others. Her pink dress flew above her knees, so light it was—as light as the skin of a berry. Kavalerov saw how transparent was her dress. The wind brushed it against her face and Kavalerov saw her profile against the brilliant transparence of the cloth spread out like a fan. As she tried to beat it down, he saw her across a cloud of dust, turning round and round and becoming more and more entangled in the folds, almost tripping over her feet. She tried hard to keep the hem of her skirt round her knees, but she had no success. For decency's sake she began to employ half-measures; she covered her bare legs with her hands and hid her knees behind them, folding herself into three separate and distinctive parcels, like a girl who has been bathing, like a girl who has been caught naked unawares.

The umpire blew his whistle. The military march began all over again. So ended all their happy confusion. The second half began a moment later. Volodya disappeared from view.

"The Germans will get at least two more goals," said a little boy as he ran past them.

Valya was still fighting the wind. When she tried to grab the hem of her skirt she had to move her position at least ten times. In the end he found herself near Kavalerov. She could hear his little whispered taunts.

She stood there with her feet planted wide apart. In her hands she held the hat which had been blown away by the wind; she had caught it on its flight. But she had not yet recovered from her escapade with the skirt, and she looked at Kavalerov without seeing him, inclining her head to one side, so that her auburn hair fell softly against her cheek.

The sun gleamed on her shoulders, and as she swayed her collar-bone flashed like a knife. Kavalerov saw her like this for less than a tenth of a second. In that moment of time he realized the strength of the irremediable anguish which lay in wait for him for the rest of his life, because he had seen her standing there, because she had seemed so strange to him, like a visitant from a new world. In that moment of time while he was watching her, he saw her staggering purity, the sweetness of her charm, knew that she was in love with Volodya, felt the mystery of her loveliness.

Babichev was waiting for her, his arms outstretched.

"Oh, Valya!" said Kavalerov. "All my life I have desired you. Have pity on me . . ."

She did not hear him. As she ran away, she rode on the wind.

10

THAT night Kavalerov returned home drunk.

He wanted a drink. He went along the corridor and turned the faucet as high as he could. He got horribly drenched and the faucet stayed where it was, flooding everything and making a sound like a trumpet blowing. Going into Anitchka's room, he stopped at the door; the electric light was still burning and he could see the widow arrayed in luminous cotton-wool. She was lying on the gigantic bed, her bare legs hanging over the edge. She looked as if she had just got ready for sleep.

Kavalerov stepped in. She said nothing. She was like someone under a spell; and it seemed to Kavalerov that she made a sign to him and smiled, wanting him to come in.

He went right in.

She did not try to resist him, even opened her arms wide apart for his embraces.

"Oh, so it's you, you little idiot," she whispered. "My dear woolly lamb . . ."

During the night he kept on waking up in a drunken torture of thirst. He was the centre of an invasion of violent, recurring dreams of water. When he woke up, there was silence in the room. A second before he awoke, he suddenly remembered the tap which was still squirting water all over the corridor—or so he thought. He was so struck with the peculiar vision of the water in the corridor that he jumped out of bed. But there was no water in the corridor. He went to bed again. While he had been asleep, the widow had turned off the tap, undressed him, mended his braces for him. When he woke up again in the morning, he felt

extraordinarily ill at ease. He lay back in bed utterly astounded at
all the unaccustomed luxury which surrounded him: he was like
the drunken beggar in the comedy picked up by the rich merchant
and taken to his palace. In the mirror he saw the unusual spectacle
of his own reflection prefaced by the soles of his feet, which had
gone clean through the bedclothes. He found that he was lying
in an extraordinarily desirable attitude, one arm folded above his
head, one side of his body brilliantly illuminated in the rays of
the sun. He saw himself floating on spacious bands of aerial light,
he saw himself floating upon the cupola of a church. Bunches of
grapes hung above his head, cupids danced fandangos, apples rolled
out of a cornucopia, and beyond and within everything he saw he
heard the solemn drone of an organ. He was lying, of course, in
Anitchka's bed.

"Oh, how you remind me of *him*," she whispered ardently,
bending over his body.

Above the bed there hung a photograph, the portrait of a man
who looked as though he had become a grandfather at a ridi-
culously early age, a man dresed in the grim and shabby frock-
coat of an age which had passed. His neck was very strong, very
tubular: he seemed to be about fifty years of age.

"You are just like my poor, dear husband," said Anitchka,
throwing her arms round him. His head disappeared in her arm-
pit and became enshrouded in the tent of her arms. Then the gates
of the tent drew apart and shame and something like ecstasy
overflowed in the widow's soul.

"He used to take me just like that—quietly—without saying
a single word—never saying anything at all——then, then . . . Oh,
my sweet and saucy one!"

Kavalerov struck out at her with his fists.

At first she seemed only puzzled. Kavalerov jumped out of
bed, churning up the layers of bedclothes, dragging the sheets
after him as he walked away. She threw herself against the door,
her hands crying out for help: then she ran about the room,
pursued by her goods and chattels, like a girl in Pompeii. The
laundry basket crashed to the floor. The chair fell on its side.

He struck her three or four times in the back: a moment later he gave her a rabbit punch. She was like a tyre, covered in grease.

The chair was balancing itself on one leg.

"Oh, he used to beat me just like you!" she said, crying out through her tears.

Kavalerov got into bed again. He sunk once more among the sheets. He felt ill. He lay unconscious on the bed all day and in the evening the widow lay by his side. She snored. Kavalerov began to imagine that his throat was shaped like a tunnel, leading into the outer darkness of the world: in the vaults of the tunnel he hid in secret. Earth trembled and shook under his feet. Under the pressure of the air flowing from the depths of the tunnel, Kavalerov tumbled and fell. The widow was whimpering in her sleep. When she stopped whimpering, she swallowed a mouthful of saliva with an extraordinarily loud gurgling sound. Her snoring consisted of a series of explosions, the explosions of a soda-water siphon.

Kavalerov rolled in the bed, weeping. She got up and put a wet towel on his forehead. The wet towel made him so excited that he shot out of bed. At first he began to search for it blindly with his hands, and then, when he had found it, he crumpled it up, placed it against his cheeks, kissed it, whispering:

"They have taken you away from me. It is so difficult to live— so difficult . . ."

The widow fell asleep the moment she got into bed. She lay with her head lying on the looking-glass. In sleep she appeared to be coated with a soft film of sickly sweetness. She slept with her mouth wide open and from time to time she made awful noises with her throat, the noises old women make when they go to bed.

But the bugs were very much awake. They rustled and their song was like the sudden crash of fabric being ripped across. Their secret hiding-places, invisible during the day, were suddenly revealed. The wooden posters of the bed started to grow and swell to an enormous size.

Slowly the window turned pink in the sunlight.

The bed remained wreathed in impenetrable darkness. The

mysterious progenies of the night scuttled from their hiding-
places, crawled along the walls, flowed around the bodies of people
sleeping, crept into the bed.

Kavalerov shot up suddenly. His eyes were wide open.
Ivan was standing in front of him.

11

KAVALEROV began to dress at once.

Anitchka seemed to be sleeping in a kneeling position, one arm
round her stomach. Very carefully, so that he should not disturb
her, he lifted the counterpane, threw it round his shoulders, stood
bolt upright in front of Ivan.

"Beautiful," said Ivan. "Like a lizard in the sunshine. Now you
can show yourself to the people. Come on! We're in the devil of a
hurry!"

"Hell, I'm feeling sick!" said Kavalerov. He smiled gently: his
smile excused him from the necessity for searching for trousers,
coat, shoes. "Does it matter—not having any shoes on my feet?"

Ivan had already disappeared down the corridor. Kavalerov
rushed after him.

"I have suffered indignities too long," he thought. "Now the
day of atonement is at hand."

They were dragged along in a human current. At the first
corner they came to a shining highway opened to their gaze.

"Here we are," said Ivan, taking him by the hand. "Here we
are at the Threepenny Bit."

Kavalerov saw the gardens, the circular cupolas of leaves, the
arches of transparent stone, the balloon flying above all the green
grass.

"Come along in!" said Ivan. There was a note of command in
his voice.

They ran along the ivy-covered wall, then jumped down. It
was easier for Kavalerov. The blue counterpane opened like a

parachute: he floated in the air above the crowd. At the foot of
a large stone staircase he came to earth. Terrified, ashamed of
his nakedness, he started to crawl beneath the counterpane. He
was like an insect folding her wings. He hid behind a plinth.

At the top of the staircase he saw Andrey Babichev surrounded
by a thronging crowd. Andrey Babichev it was who summoned
Volodya into the presence: and when Volodya came up to him
he put his arms round his shoulders.

"They are bringing it along immediately," said Andrey Babichev,
smiling.

This is what Kavalerov saw: on the path to the staircase an
orchestra marched towards them and Valya was floating in the
air above the orchestra, supported by the music. She rose and
fell in an extraordinary sympathy with the waves of sound, her
ribbons flew high above her head, her dress arching and swelling
at her side, her hair standing on end.

When the last bars of the music had melted in the air, she was
hurled to the head of the staircase, straight into Volodya's arms.
The rest ran away, terrified. The lovers were alone, surrounded
by a wide circle of Andrey's visitors.

Kavalerov saw nothing more. He was suddenly seized with icy
terror. A strange shadow trembled before his eyes. He turned to
move away, and in the movement of turning he recognized it—it
was Ophelia, Ophelia sitting contentedly on the grass only a few
feet away.

"Aha-a-a-a!" he yelled at the top of his voice. He began to run.

Ophelia, tinkling softly, caught hold of the edge of the counterpane. He slipped away. As he ran he realized that he was quite
naked; he realized that he was tripping over his feet, and falling
on to the sharpest stones. He ran up the staircase. They were
watching him from the landing. Even Valya was leaning over
the bannisters, gazing at him.

"Ophelia! Go back, Ophelia!" Ivan was shouting. "She can't
hear me! Ophelia . . . stop!"

"Hold her!"

"She'll kill him!"

"Oh—o!"

"Look out! Look out! Look out!"

Half-way up the staircase Kavalerov paused for a moment. Ivan was trying to climb up the wall. The ivy gave way. The crowd disappeared. Ivan hung on the wall, his arms stretched wide apart. An extraordinary *thing* of iron was slowly advancing across the lawn. A needle, glittering in the sun, moved from the region of its head. Ivan was crying out as loud as he could. His hands lost their hold on the wall. He fell to the ground. His bowler hat rolled into a plot of dandelions. He sat there with his back to the wall, his hands folded in front of his face. As the machine came towards him, it lopped off the heads of the dandelions in its path.

Kavalerov shouted in a terrible voice:

"Save him! Are you going to let a machine kill a man?"

There was no reply.

"My place is with you!" Kavalerov roared. "Master, let me die by your side!"

It was already too late. Ivan screamed. It was the scream of a shot rabbit. Hearing it, Kavalerov fell to the ground. As he was falling, he had a clear picture of Ivan being slowly pinned against the wall by Ophelia's needle.

Ivan fell forward. His body revolved around the terrible needle.

Kavalerov put his hands to his face. There was nothing he wanted to see, nothing he wanted to hear. The gentle tinkle of the machine still rung in his ears as it climbed the stairs.

"No! No! No!" he cried. He used up all the force of his lungs. "She'll kill me! Have mercy on me! Oh, have mercy on me! I never said anything impolite to the machine! It's not my fault! Valya—Valya, save me!"

12

KAVALEROV was ill for three days. When he got well again, he fled.

Staring at a point in the corner of the room, he got up. He dressed like an automaton. Immediately he noticed that there was a new leather button-strap on his braces, so the widow must have taken the safety-pin away. Where did she get it from? From an old pair belonging to her husband? Kavalerov felt acutely conscious of the horror of his position and rushed away, leaving his coat behind. On the way, he slipped out of the red braces and threw them on the road.

At the entrance to the passage he remained quite still for a moment. Then, hearing nothing, he stepped out boldly and he found his thoughts racing in his brain to the sound of a strange orchestration. The sweetest sensations of joy and melancholy entered his heart. The morning was alight with beauty and there was a soft wind, the brush of air when you turn over the pages of a book. The sky became a deeper blue. He found himself standing in front of something extraordinarily foul and horrible. A terrified kitten jumped out of a dustbin and the dirt followed in its wake. He searched for poetry in the foul siege of his curses— found none. But he still stood there, his head held high, his arms stretched apart.

Then, for the first time, he realized that there was a barrier between his past and his future. Catastrophe enmeshed him in her claws. Turn yourself away from the past! Now! Immediately! in the space of a heart-beat must I traverse the barriers! I must slough my savage skin, full of strange errors and accumulated horrors.

He stood up straight, his eyes wide open. The field of his vision pulsated around him, curiously pink in color. By running he had weakened his strength. He felt sick.

He understood at last the gravity of his error. It was bound to have happened; and there was no escape now. He had been too frivolous, too proud. All his life he had held too high an opinion of himself. After all, was he not lazy? Was he not foul-mouthed and lecherous?

As he looked across that filthy courtyard, everything became instantaneously clear to him.

He turned back, picked up his braces, dressed properly. A spoon rattled and the widow turned to embrace him, but without going into her room again he left the house. Once more he slept in the boulevards. Once more he returned to her. This time he had come armed with resolution.

"I shall have to put the widow in her place," he thought. "I won't let her talk about the past. I am drunk and I can't live in the streets any longer!"

The widow was lighting spills in front of the fire. She looked up at him, squinting, smirking. He went right in. Ivan's bowler hat hung on the cupboard rail.

Ivan was sitting on the edge of the bed. He looked exactly like a smaller edition of his famous brother. The counterpane he had wrapt around him, like a cloud. On the table stood a bottle of wine. Ivan was sipping the red wine out of a glass. It was obvious that he had only that moment got up, his face still heavy with sleep, his fingers still scratched ambiguously beneath the blankets.

"What in hell is all this?" This was Kavalerov's famous reply to the existence of the visible universe.

Ivan smiled tenderly.

"It means, my dear fellow, that there is nothing like a glass of port wine. Anitchka! Bring me another glass!"

Anitchka came in. She unlocked the cupboard.

"Don't be jealous, Kolya," she said, throwing her arms around Kavalerov. "Poor boy—all alone in the world. I am so sorry for you all!"

"What in hell is all this?" Kavalerov repeated in a lower voice.

"Shut up saying the same thing over and over again," said Ivan angrily. "It doesn't mean anything—particularly."

He climbed out of bed, clutching at his pyjama trousers with one hand and pouring out a glass of port for Kavalerov with the other.

"Drink up, Kavalerov! We have spoken about our sensations long enough! We have forgotten the only one that really matters —indifference! Don't you believe me? It is my profound belief that indifference is the only faculty of the human soul which is worth anything at all. Let us be indifferent! Kavalerov, look at your glass! There, there, peace at last! Hurrah! Hurrah for Anitchka! And by the way, I have some important news for you. Tonight it is your turn to sleep with Anitchka!"

1927 A.D.

PERMANENT LIBRARY BOOKS

The Permanent Library makes available to the general reader those works of the world's great writers which have long been out of print, or which are not readily obtainable. They give a better understanding of the wide range of the talents of these masters of literature. The volumes are carefully edited, durably bound and tastefully designed. The average length is in excess of 700 pages.

GREAT FRENCH SHORT NOVELS
edited by F. W. DUPEE *$5.00*

GREAT ADVENTURES AND EXPLORATIONS
edited by VILHJALMUR STEFANSSON *$5.00*

SHORT NOVELS OF COLETTE
with an introduction by GLENWAY WESCOTT *$5.00*

GREAT RUSSIAN SHORT NOVELS
edited by PHILIP RAHV *$5.00*

THE GREAT SHORT NOVELS OF HENRY JAMES
edited by PHILIP RAHV *$5.00*

THE SHORT NOVELS OF DOSTOEVSKY
with an introduction by THOMAS MANN *$5.00*

GREEK PLAYS IN MODERN TRANSLATION
edited by DUDLEY FITTS *$5.00*

GREAT AMERICAN SHORT NOVELS
edited by WILLIAM PHILLIPS *$4.00*

THE PERMANENT GOETHE
edited by THOMAS MANN *$5.00*

THE SHORT NOVELS OF BALZAC
with an introduction by JULES ROMAINS *$4.00*

THE SHORT NOVELS OF TOLSTOY
edited by PHILIP RAHV *$4.00*

THE SHORT STORIES OF DOSTOEVSKY
with an introduction by WILLIAM PHILLIPS *$4.00*

THE BOSTONIANS
by HENRY JAMES *$3.00*